EVERYMAN'S LIBRARY

EVERYMAN,
I WILL GO WITH THEE,
AND BE THY GUIDE,
IN THY MOST NEED
TO GO BY THY SIDE

ANGELA CARTER

THE BLOODY CHAMBER

AND OTHER STORIES

WISE CHILDREN

FIREWORKS

WITH AN INTRODUCTION BY
JOAN ACOCELLA

EVERYMAN'S LIBRARY
Alfred A. Knopf New York London Toronto

383

THIS IS A BORZOI BOOK
PUBLISHED BY ALFRED A. KNOPF

First included in Everyman's Library, 2018

Typography by Peter B. Willberg

The Bloody Chamber and Other Stories first published in Great Britain by Victor Gollancz, London, in 1979, and in the United States as *The Bloody Chamber and Other Adult Tales* by Harper and Row, New York, in 1979. *Wise Children* first published in Great Britain by Chatto and Windus, London, in 1991, and in the United States by Farrar, Straus and Giroux, New York, in 1991. This edition published in the United States by arrangement with Farrar, Straus and Giroux. All rights reserved. *Fireworks* first published in Great Britain as *Fireworks: Nine Profane Pieces* by Quartet, London, in 1974, and in the United States as *Fireworks: Nine Stories in Various Disguises* by Harper and Row, New York, in 1981. Revised edition published as *Fireworks* by Chatto and Windus, London, in 1987.

Further copyright information may be found in the Acknowledgments at the back of this volume.

www.randomhouse/everymans
www.everymanslibrary.co.uk

ISBN 978-1-101-90799-3 (US)
978-1-84159-383-8 (UK)

A CIP catalogue reference for this book is available from the British Library

Book design by Barbara de Wilde and Carol Devine Carson

Typeset in the UK by Input Data Services Ltd, Somerset.

Printed and bound in Germany by GGP Media GmbH, Pössneck

CONTENTS

FIREWORKS

INTRODUCTION

The English novelist Angela Carter is best known for her 1979 book *The Bloody Chamber*, which is a kind of modernization of the classic European fairy tales. This does not mean that Carter's Little Red Riding Hood chews gum or rides a motorcycle but that the strange things in those tales – the werewolves and snow maidens, the spider-hung caves and liquefying mirrors – are made to live again by means of a prose informed by the wonders of cinema and psychoanalysis and Symbolist poetry. In Carter's 'Beauty and the Beast', retitled 'The Tiger's Bride', the beast doesn't change into a beauty. The beauty is changed into a beast, a beautiful one, by means of one of the more memorable sex acts in twentieth-century fiction. At the end of the tale, the heroine is ushered, naked, into the beast's chamber. He paces back and forth:

> I squatted on the wet straw and stretched out my hand. I was now within the field of force of his golden eyes. He growled at the back of his throat, lowered his head, sank on to his forepaws, snarled, showed me his red gullet, his yellow teeth. I never moved. He snuffed the air, as if to smell my fear; he could not.
>
> Slowly, slowly he began to drag his heavy, gleaming weight across the floor towards me.
>
> A tremendous throbbing, as of the engine that makes the earth turn, filled the little room; he had begun to purr. . . .
>
> He dragged himself closer and closer to me, until I felt the harsh velvet of his head against my hand, then a tongue, abrasive as sand-paper. 'He will lick the skin off me!'
>
> And each stroke of his tongue ripped off skin after successive skin, all the skins of a life in the world, and left behind a nascent patina of shiny hairs. My earrings turned back to water and trickled down my shoulders; I shrugged the drops off my beautiful fur.

Imagine that: a great, warm, wet, abrasive tongue licking off skin after skin, down to the bottommost skin, which then sprouts shiny little hairs.

Because Carter took on fairy tales, and also because she

favored an *outré* look – she liked long, flowing skirts and in her late years sported a great, disorderly mane of grey hair (Andrew Motion said she looked like 'someone who'd been left out in a hurricane') – she was sometimes slotted as a 'white witch', the sort of person who reads Tarot cards and believes that the trees speak to her. Therefore it was good to see Edmund Gordon, in his *The Invention of Angela Carter* (2016), the first full-scale biography of the writer, reclaim her from the fairy kingdom and place her within what sounds like a real life. Unsurprisingly, we find out that the white witch cared about her advances and sales and reviews.

Carter was born in 1940 and grew up in a quiet, middle-class suburb of London, the second child of a strait-laced mother, Olive – she turned off the TV if a divorced actor came on the screen – and a father, Hugh, who was the night editor of London's Press Association. Both parents spoiled Angela outrageously. She was crammed with treats, bombarded with kittens and story books. Her mother never put her to bed until after midnight, when Hugh got back from work – she wanted her company – and even then, the child was often allowed to stay up. Hugh brought home long rolls of white paper from the office for her, and as her parents chatted, she wrote stories in crayon.

She grew to be a tall, pudgy child, with a stammer. Between those disadvantages and extreme shyness, which she covered with a frosty manner, she had few friends. Olive redoubled her attentions. Angela was not allowed to dress herself, or to go to the bathroom alone. Finally, she rebelled, went on a diet, and changed from a fat, obliging girl to skinny, rude girl. She slouched around in short skirts and fishnet stockings, smoking and saying offensive things to her mother.

She was a good student, though. The 1944 Butler Act, riding the same democratic wave as the American G. I. Bill, provided free secondary education for all in the state sector and also established a system of 'direct grants' to a number of independent schools which would then offer free places to gifted children from regular backgrounds. Carter, as an adult, had a theory that the Butler Act created Britain's first real intelligentsia, a group of people who had no interest in using education to maintain the class system but who simply wanted to operate in a world of ideas. If so, she was one of them. She went to a demanding independent school, Streatham Hill & Clapham High, and did well in the subjects she cared about, above all English and French. (Her French teacher loaned her a record of a Comédie Française actor reading Baudelaire and Rimbaud, and thereby made her a linguistic high-flyer for life.) Her teachers urged her to apply to Oxford. Olive, hearing that, pronounced it an excellent idea and said that she and Hugh would take an apartment in Oxford to be close to her. Angela thereupon dropped all thought of going to university. Marriage, she realized, would be her only way of escaping her parents.

Through her father's connections, she got a job as a reporter, and soon, while working on a story about the new folk music movement – this was now the late fifties – she met a serious-minded young man, Paul Carter, an industrial chemist who moonlighted as a producer and seller of English folk-song records. Paul was apparently the first man to take a romantic interest in Angela. Or, as she put it, 'I finally bumped into somebody who would ... have sexual intercourse with me.' But Paul insisted that they be engaged first, and so Angela found herself, at twenty, a married woman.

They seem to have been happy at the beginning. Paul taught Angela to love English folk music and thereby gave her a great gift. The folk iconography, in time, would offer her an escape hatch from the rather grey realism dominant in the fiction of that period. Folklore also presented her with a set of emotions that, while releasing her, eventually, from sixties truculence, nevertheless felt *true*, not genteel. 'Few nations have spent quite as long as England in creating an official mask,' she wrote in 1962:

> What are we like? Oh, you know. Reserved. Imperturbable. Anti-romantic. Practical. . . . But study our folk heritage, our great and still living heritage of rough and ready poetry, and there is the authentic face. The man who emerges from English folk song is as merry as a cricket, as lecherous as a goat, a Gargantua in appetites and mirth, with a pulsing vein of lyric poetry in his body.

This is somewhat cheerier than she would ever be, or than English folk song was. Still, it pointed her in a hopeful direction.

But soon the marriage was failing. Paul was subject to engulfing depressions. Sometimes he and Angela barely spoke for days. She felt swollen with unexpressed emotion. 'I want to touch him all the time, with my hands & my mouth,' she wrote in her diary. '(Poor luv, it annoys him.)' The note of sarcasm here is interesting. Through some miracle, Angela, who had little sexual self-confidence – she once described herself as 'a great, lumpy, butch cow . . . titless and broadbeamed' – did not allow Paul's withdrawal to demoralize her. She wanted to save herself. On her twenty-second birthday, her Uncle Cecil, knowing that she was unhappy, invited her to lunch at an Italian restaurant and told her to apply to university. As she recalled, he said to her, 'If you've got a degree, you can always get a job. You can leave your husband any time you want.'

She took his advice. The couple had recently moved to Bristol, for Paul's work, and she enrolled in the university there, studying English. The Bristol department was not an ideal situation for her, because, like many English departments in mid-twentieth century Britain, it was dominated by the principles of F. R. Leavis, who was intent on rescuing English fiction's 'great tradition' from the showy, the sentimental, and the bizarre. Carter, who called Leavis's followers the 'eat up your broccoli' school of criticism, managed to hide out in medieval studies, which she loved. She also encountered Freud, whose writings gave her a quasi-scientific support for the world of shock, dream, and eros that she now saw as the realm of art. Within a few years, too, she became enamored of the Surrealists and learned to feel, like them, that the goal of art was not truth, as the Leavisites would have it, but the marvellous, or that the marvelous *was* the truth.

All of this fed into her developing feminism. She was to become an ardent feminist, but not an orthodox one. Her main concern was not with women's being granted justice; she hated the idea of put-upon, suffering women and implied that they had it coming, by being such weaklings. What she wanted for women was that they should seize what they needed – power, freedom, sex – and she saw no fundamental difference between men and women that should prevent women from having those things. To use the current language, gender, to her, was a social construction. As she wrote to a friend,

> Somebody asked me who my favourite women writers were the other day, meaning, I guess, some kind of writers who expressed a specifically feminine sensibility – I said Emily Brontë, who's pure butch, and cursed myself afterwards because the greatest feminine writer who's ever lived is Dostoevsky, followed closely by Herman Melville. . . . And D. H. Lawrence is infinitely more feminine than Jane Austen, if one is talking about these qualities of sensitivity, vulnerability and perception traditionally ascribed by male critics to female novelists. . . . D. H. Lawrence's tragedy is that he thought he was a man.

I don't know what she means about Dostoevsky, but her general statement should sound familiar in our day of fluid gender definitions.

Energized by her discoveries, she became a bustling presence in her department and the co-editor of its literary magazine. In this stapled-together publication the best items were the poems of one Rankin Crowe, which turned out to be a *nom de plume* of Angela Carter. (It is a misspelled version of the name of a cowboy whose self-published 1970 memoir, *Rankin Crow and the Oregon County*, she must have read. She liked cowboys. She went to see Sergio Leone westerns.) Especially striking is a poem called 'Unicorn'. In the Middle Ages there was a belief that the only way to catch a unicorn was to send a virgin, alone, into the woods. The unicorn, spying the girl, would come and lay his head in her lap. Such a virgin is the speaker in Carter's poem, but she is not a tender little thing. She is naked, with breasts 'like carrier bags' and 'curious plantations of pubic hair'. The unicorn is drawn to her by 'the fragrance of her moist / garden plot'. He will be sorry. '"I have sharp teeth inside my mouth,' she says. 'Inside my dark red lips.'

At the same time, Carter was producing the first novels that she would be willing to publish. She wrote at a furious speed, turning out narratives of violence that were sometimes layered with comedy, sometimes not. In *Shadow Dance* (1966), her first novel, a man named Honeybuzzard carves up the face of an annoyingly virtuous girl, Ghislaine. (After she gets out of the hospital he finishes the job, strangling her and leaving her naked corpse in an attic.) A year after that came *The Magic Toyshop*, in which the orphaned heroine is sent to live with her uncle, a sadistic puppeteer. In one scene he forces her to play Leda to a mechanical swan. Her next two efforts were in a similar vein. There are excellent things in all these books, but there is also a strong suggestion that Carter is still trying to drive her mother crazy. Even when the material is not shocking, the treatment is often self-indulgent. An editor once forwarded to her a reader's report describing a novel of hers as 'a queer little book'. Carter, always lovably forthright, replied that the person who wrote that 'put her finger on my weakest spot, which is a tendency to a batty kind of whimsicality'. She said she was sure she would work out some satisfactory solution.

She did. In 1969, Carter received a Somerset Maugham Award, worth five hundred pounds, to be used for foreign travel. She decided that she would grant herself an old wish, to go to Japan. Paul stayed home. 'I arrived by air, in the dark,' she wrote. 'When night descended over the ocean, many unfamiliar stars sprang out in the sky; as we approached land, there began to blossom below me such an irregular confusion of small lights it was difficult to be certain if the starry sky lay above or below me. So the aeroplane ascended or descended into an electric city where nothing was what it seemed at first and I was absolutely confused.' I see her there, dizzy, suspended between two blankets of light. It is like a conversion experience, and, writing two years after the event, she surely knew that.

*

Soon, at a Tokyo coffee house, a Japanese man, Sozo Araki, twenty-four years old – that is, six years younger than she – stopped at her table. She described the scene in a later, unpublished story: ' "Where are you from?" he asked her. "England," she said. "That must be terribly boring," he said & gave her the great international seducer's smile.' They ended up, that evening, in a 'love hotel', the kind of hotel that rents rooms by the hour. When they woke up in the morning, she went back to where she was staying, to take a shower, while he played *pachinko*, a Japanese version of pinball. Then they met again, had breakfast, and went to another hotel. It is hard to say what Carter and Araki talked about when they weren't having sex. Araki had recently dropped out of a university program in political science, intending to write a novel. Meanwhile he was working as a private tutor. He and Angela apparently did discuss fiction. He liked Faulkner and Dostoevsky. It seems, though, that he liked Elvis Presley and *pachinko* better.

But literary companionship was not what she was looking for. Nor, it appears, were her interests primarily sexual. Sex was certainly part of the picture, but Carter seems to have been seeking a sort of rapture, a sensation of being carried to a new place, or to an old, ideal one. 'His face did not, when I first met him, seem to me the face of a stranger,' she later wrote of Araki. 'It seemed a face long known & well remembered . . . His image was already present somewhere in my head, & I was seeking to discover him in reality, searching every face for the right face – that is, the face that corresponded to my notions of the imagined face of the one I should love.' At the end of her two years' stay in Japan, she wrote that she had taken certain notions '(like living for love) as far as they will go'. The experience may not have been love, exactly, but something *like* love – an idea, like a Platonic idea.

As for the husband who was waiting for her in England, 'I can't live with him any more,' she wrote to a friend, 'or I'll kill myself & that's that.' Two weeks after she met Araki she had to go to Hong Kong briefly. In the airport's departure lounge, she took off her wedding ring and left it in an ashtray. (She wrote to Paul soon after, asking for a divorce. He took it badly. More than forty years later, he refused to speak to Edmund Gordon for the biography.) That was one jailer disposed of. The other did the job herself. While Angela was back in England that winter, renewing her visa, Olive suffered a pulmonary embolism. Angela went to the hospital, but Olive, upon seeing her, turned her face to the wall. (She had always disliked Paul, but she disliked divorce more.) She died a few days later.

Angela returned to Tokyo, moved in with Araki, and soon found that she had to acquire an additional sort of freedom. Araki liked to go out with his friends at night, and Angela's joining them was not convenient. For one thing, she had never learned to speak more than a few words of Japanese. Furthermore, as she soon realized, he was seeing other women – lots of them. (She came to describe him as an 'ambulant penis'.) One night, as they were undressing, Carter saw a smear of lipstick on Araki's underpants. She didn't wear lipstick. Describing the episode to a friend, she wrote that she burst out laughing: 'I wait with baited breath for what surprises next week may bring. I shall probably discover ... a Mars bar in his anus.' Carter always said that Japan was what turned her into a thoroughgoing feminist. The young women of Tokyo, she wrote, acted as though they had 'become their own dolls'. Her rejection of that position, and of the enforced gender identity that lay behind it, meant, to her, that she could put up with Araki's infidelities. Indeed, it seems that she began to enjoy having the night to herself, so that she could work in quiet and then go to bed with Araki when he came home at five in the morning, once the trains started running again. But if she could tolerate this routine, he couldn't. While he was out tom-catting, she was earning their daily bread, and as he later said, 'I didn't want to be a gigolo any more.' He left her.

She was broken-hearted, and furious. She had panic attacks. She couldn't eat. Finally she comforted herself with a young Korean, Mansu Kō. She relieved him of his virginity. In gratitude, he brought her a can of pineapple. He moved in with her almost immediately, and did all the cooking and cleaning. He was two inches shorter than she, and nineteen years old, though, she wrote, he looked fourteen: 'Every time I pull down his underpants I feel more & more like Humbert Humbert.' (She was thirty-one.) Kō spoke less English than Araki had, and didn't have much to say, anyway. 'Apart from the sheer delight, he *does* bore me,' she wrote. The boredom didn't cancel out delight: 'the childlike delicacy and precision with which he stirs sugar into his coffee; his small sigh of content ... the way he carries his head, like a bird'. But after five months with him, she went back to England.

'Apart from the sheer delight, he *does* bore me.' That was what Carter discovered in Japan: the mixed, middle states of the heart, which, now that she had thrown pretty much everything else away, she had time to pay attention to and, with the clarity she had gained, to present in stark imagery. While she was in Japan, she wrote a novel, but her best work went into short fiction – tales, she called them – which, with some post-Japan pieces, she later published as *Fireworks* (1974). The collection's best piece, 'Souvenir of Japan', is her tribute to Araki. Here is the 'pleasure hotel' they went to on their first night:

> We were shown into a room like a paper box. It contained nothing but a mattress spread on the floor. We lay down immediately and began to kiss one another. Then a maid soundlessly opened the sliding door and, stepping out of her slippers, crept in on stockinged feet, breathing apologies. She carried a tray which contained two cups of tea and a plate of candies. She put the tray down on the matted floor beside us and backed, bowing and apologizing, from the room whilst our uninterrupted kiss continued. He started to unfasten my shirt and then she came back again. This time, she carried an armful of towels. I was stripped stark naked when she returned for a third time to bring the receipt for his money.

There, love is mixed with comedy. Three paragraphs later it is mixed with death, a beautiful death: 'I should have liked to have had him embalmed and been able to keep him beside me in a glass coffin, so that I could watch him all the time and he would not have been able to get away from me.' Glass coffin – it's like 'Snow White'. And that's where she was headed: to fairy tales.

In 1976, she accepted a commission to translate Perrault's fairy tales. She had been back in England for four years, but she was still living off the psychological tank-dive of her Japanese period. After the Perrault volume was published, she embarked on *The Bloody Chamber*, with her own, rewritten versions of Perrault and the Grimms. This is her great book, the one that only she could have written, the one in which everything that was good in her came to the fore and everything that had been bad became good. She was always best in the short form, as her friend Salman Rushdie observed. In her novels, he wrote, her voice, 'that moonstone-and-rhinestone mix of opulence and flim-flam, can be exhausting. In her stories, she can dazzle and swoop, and quit while she's ahead.' The truth is that she never cared much about character development or plot, which are the meat of the novel. In a tale, she could disperse with them, and just go for emotion and image. We get Bluebeard smoking a cigar 'fat as a baby's arm', and the Erl-King gathering his dinner in the woods: 'He knows which of the frilled, blotched, rotten fungi are fit to eat; he understands their eldritch ways, how they spring up overnight in lightless places and thrive on dead things.' In 'The Company of Wolves', Carter's famous version of 'Little Red Riding Hood', the heroine doesn't struggle with the wolf. She goes to bed with him. Her grandmother's bones rattle beneath the bed. She doesn't hear them.

That was her peak, *Fireworks* and *The Bloody Chamber*. Strange to say, she wrote most of those unsettling stories in a period of relative contentment. Maybe, in order to get past the showy aggressiveness of her early work – the red hot lips and the like – she needed some contentment. In any case, she told an interviewer that she had a rather nice time in her thirties: 'I started doing things like foreign travel and having a house, and you know, watching television and things like that.' Soon she had someone steady to do these things with. One day, when she had been back from Japan for two years – she was now thirty-four – one of her water taps burst. She had seen a construction worker in the house across the street; she ran to get him. His name was Mark Pearce, another nineteen-year-old. 'He came in,' Carter said, 'and never left.'

Pearce was strikingly handsome – she claimed, significantly, that he looked like a werewolf (others said he looked like Jesus) – and he was very, very silent, but she didn't mind that. She liked to do the talking, as she liked being older. He went on doing construction work, she went on writing, and that was their life, except for one big change, in 1983: Carter, age forty-three, had a son, Alexander. This made her very happy – she had long wanted a child and had had several phantom pregnancies – but Pearce was really the one who raised Alex.

It was a bohemian household, with dirty dishes always stacked in the sink, and a welcoming atmosphere. Carter was a good cook. Salman Rushdie reported that during the fatwa imposed on him by the Ayatollah Khomeini, his bodyguards always liked it when he went to visit Carter, because she invariably had a nice meal for them to eat, and a TV for them to watch.

As the years passed, Carter came to need the feminist pride she had developed when young. In the 1980s, there was a much-trumpeted new spurt of energy in English fiction, with the entry of a number of talented young men, notably Rushdie, Ian McEwan, Martin Amis, and Julian Barnes. In 1981, Rushdie's second novel, *Midnight's Children*, won the Booker Prize. McEwan's second novel, *The Comfort of Strangers*, was shortlisted for the prize that year. Julian Barnes's *Flaubert's Parrot* was shortlisted in 1984. Carter was never shortlisted, let alone awarded, and she did feel that this was, in part, because she was a woman. In 1984 she told an interviewer:

> I've never had any problem getting published. It would be whingeing to say that men who are no better than I are very much more famous and very much richer and also regarded as . . . the right stuff. It would ill become me. But it's amazing what the Old Boys' club does for itself. They list the 'important British contemporary writers', and they'll list Malcolm Bradbury and Kingsley Amis, and they'll leave out Doris Lessing, who's the only one with a really huge international reputation.

There was a generational aspect, too. Carter was most of a decade older than the others, born a few months into the Second World War rather than after it, and her Freudian-influenced, 'mythic' subject matter – dark woods, bloody chambers – was out of step with their more postmodern concerns, their explorations of language, narrative, and representation. Still, there is no question that being female was a part of the reason she received less attention. Rushdie says that though Carter did wish for greater recognition, 'she was not ever envious of other people's success'. That must have been a comfort to them.

Soon after her son was born, Carter started to age quickly,

as she recorded in her diary. ('I catch myself in the mirror looking like my father.') She resented this, and reacted defiantly, adopting, according to one friend, a madwoman-in-the-attic look. At the same time she seems to have become happier as she got older. This is certainly suggested by her final novel, *Wise Children*, in which a seventy-five-year-old woman, Dora Chance, tells of the life she and her identical twin sister, Nora, had as music-hall artists. In a sense, the book is about what happens to women when they're no longer saleable, but it contains so much life and fun – so many nice dresses and memorable fornications and wild parties and just theater, theater, just the smell of the place ('we were *wet* for it,' says Dora) – that one has trouble locating a note of regret. Nora and Dora now live in a basement apartment with an ex-wife of their father's, drinking endless cups of tea from breakfast until six in the evening, at which point they switch to gin. The whole thing is as loveable and comfortable as an old shoe. This is Carter's most popular book after *The Bloody Chamber*.

Early in 1991, just before *Wise Children* was published, Carter went to the doctor with a pain in her chest and was told that she had a cancerous tumor on her right lung that had spread to her lymph nodes, making it inoperable. Strong-minded woman that she was, she laid aside her plans for a new novel – *Adela*, about Jane Eyre's pupil, Mr Rochester's daughter – and went to work, fast, with an assistant, on a collection of her non-fiction. (Over the years she had written many, many magazine articles. She needed the money.) She and Mark got married, as they had neglected to do previously, and, week after week, she got dressed and sat up straight to have goodbye teas with her friends. Finally, after a year's illness, she died at home, aged fifty-one. She was young, and she had had only a few years of absolutely first-rank work, but that is true of many writers, including some of the greatest. She had had her time, and it was wonderful.

Joan Acocella

JOAN ACOCELLA is a staff writer for *The New Yorker*.

SELECT BIBLIOGRAPHY

EDMUND GORDON, *The Invention of Angela Carter: A Biography*, Chatto & Windus, London, 2016 / Oxford Unversity Press, New York, 2017.

LORNA SAGE, *Angela Carter (Writers and Their Work)*, 2nd edition, Northcote House Publishers, Tavistock, 2007.

LORNA SAGE, ed., *Flesh and the Mirror: Essays on the Art of Angela Carter*, 2nd edition, Virago Press, London, 2007.

Introduction by SALMAN RUSHDIE in *Burning Your Boats: The Collected Stories,* Angela Carter, Chatto & Windus, London, 1995 / Penguin USA, New York, 1997.

CHRONOLOGY

DATE	AUTHOR'S LIFE	LITERARY CONTEXT
1940	Born Angela Olive Stalker, 7 May, Eastbourne, Sussex. Parents Hugh (a journalist) and Olive live in London, but have rented a flat in Eastbourne to be near Angela's eleven-year-old brother, Hughie, who has been evacuated there. By the end of the year Olive and the two children move to Wath-upon-Dearne, Yorkshire, to live with grandmother, Jane Farthing.	Greene: *The Power and the Glory.* Hemingway: *For Whom the Bell Tolls.* Stead: *The Man Who Loved Children.*
1941–4	Lives with tough, folksy grandmother (model for many later characters in novels and stories).	Coward: *Blithe Spirit* (1941). Du Maurier: *Frenchman's Creek* (1942). De Beauvoir: *She Came to Stay* (1943). Borges: *Ficciones* (1944). Colette: *Gigi* (1944).
1945	Family moves back to Balham, south London, to a house full of books. Angela begins attending Hearnville Road School.	Waugh: *Brideshead Revisited.* Orwell: *Animal Farm.* Mitford: *The Pursuit of Love.*
1946	Writes novel *Bill and Tom Go to Pussy Market* (precursor of much writing about cats).	Peake: *Titus Groan.* Taylor: *Palladian.*
1947		Compton-Burnett: *Manservant and Maidservant.* Camus: *The Plague.* Mann: *Doctor Faustus.*
1948		Bowen: *The Heat of the Day.* Greene: *The Heart of the Matter.*
1949		Smith: *I Capture the Castle.* Orwell: *Nineteen Eighty-Four.*
1950–1	Comes first in London Essay Competition (for 'Man's Duty to Animals'), passes eleven-plus, gains place at Streatham Hill & Clapham High School (1951).	Highsmith: *Strangers on a Train.* Lessing: *The Grass is Singing* (1950). Beckett: *Molloy.* Powell: *A Question of Upbringing.*

HISTORICAL EVENTS

Chamberlain resigns. Wartime coalition government formed under Churchill. France falls to Germans; evacuation of Dunkirk. Battle of Britain, the Blitz, formation of Home Guard, introduction of rationing. Italy joins war, allied with Germany.

USSR changes sides in WW2; Germans invade. Surprise attack by Japanese on Pearl Harbor brings US into war (1941).
Singapore falls to Japanese (1942).
Russian victory at Stalingrad, Germans repulsed in North Africa, Allies invade Italy (1943).
Allies land in Normandy, Red Army takes Belgrade, Budapest. UK: Butler's Education Act (1944).
Death of Roosevelt; Truman becomes US President. Hitler, Mussolini die, Germany surrenders. Atomic bombing of Hiroshima and Nagasaki brings WW2 to an end. Foundation of United Nations. UK: Labour government formed under Clement Attlee.
Leading Nazis tried at Nuremberg for war crimes. Churchill marks beginning of Cold War with 'Iron Curtain' speech. Programme of nationalization of industry and public utilities in UK begins.
India and Pakistan independence. Europe receives aid for post-war recovery from Marshall Plan.

State of Israel established. Soviet blockade of Berlin; Allied airlift. South Africa adopts apartheid policy. Gandhi assassinated in India. UK: foundation of National Health Service. *Empire Windrush* docks in Tilbury, 22 June, beginning Afro-Caribbean immigration.
Foundation of NATO. China: Communist revolution. Germany divided into East and West. Ireland becomes republic, withdraws from Commonwealth.
Outbreak of Korean War (1950). UK: Churchill returns to power; Burgess and Maclean (Soviet spies) defect to USSR (1951).

DATE	AUTHOR'S LIFE	LITERARY CONTEXT
1950–1 *cont.*		Taylor: *A Game of Hide and Seek* (1951). Yourcenar: *Memoirs of Hadrian.*
1952		Allingham: *The Tiger in the Smoke.* Beckett: *Waiting for Godot.* Lessing: *Martha Quest.* Pym: *Excellent Women.*
1953		Hartley: *The Go-Between.* Lehmann: *The Echoing Grove.* Pym: *Jane and Prudence.*
1954		K. Amis: *Lucky Jim.* Golding: *Lord of the Flies.* Réage: *The Story of O.* Murdoch: *Under the Net.* Sagan: *Bonjour Tristesse.* Tolkien: *The Lord of the Rings* (to 1955).
1955	Mother has heart attack.	Highsmith: *The Talented Mr Ripley.* Nabokov: *Lolita.*
1956		Baldwin: *Giovanni's Room.* Beckett: *Malone Dies.* Macaulay: *The Towers of Trebizond.* Metalious: *Peyton Place.*
1957		Durrell: *Justine.* Pasternak: *Doctor Zhivago.*
1958	Goes on rigorous diet, becomes 'pencil-thin' (her brother's description). Leaves school and begins to work for *Croydon Advertiser.*	Achebe: *Things Fall Apart.* Lampedusa: *The Leopard.* Murdoch: *The Bell.*
1959	Becomes anorexic.	Comyns: *The Vet's Daughter.* Jackson: *The Haunting of Hill House.* Spark: *Memento Mori.*
1960	Marries Paul Carter, 10 September.	Banks: *The L-Shaped Room.* Lee: *To Kill a Mockingbird.* O'Brien: *The Country Girls.* Updike: *Rabbit, Run.*
1961	Moves to Bristol when Paul gets job at Bristol Technical College. Writing poetry and fiction.	Dawson: *The Ha-Ha.* Heller: *Catch-22.* Highsmith: *This Sweet Sickness.* Murdoch: *A Severed Head.*

CHRONOLOGY

HISTORICAL EVENTS

Eisenhower becomes US President. UK: Elizabeth II becomes Queen, first atomic bomb produced, London smog kills 12,000.

End of Korean War. Stalin dies, Tito President of Yugoslavia. European Court of Human Rights set up. Everest climbed for first time, by Edmund Hillary and Sherpa Tenzing. DNA's structure identified by James Watson and Francis Crick.

Outbreak of Vietnam War. Nasser comes to power in Egypt. UK: commercial TV begins.

Warsaw Pact formed. UK: Anthony Eden becomes Prime Minister.

Denunciation of Stalin by Khrushchev. USSR invades Hungary. Suez Crisis. UK: first nuclear power station.

EEC founded (Treaty of Rome). Sputnik launched. Ghana gains independence. UK: Macmillan Prime Minister.

Egypt and Syria form United Arab Republic (to 1961). UK: CND (Campaign for Nuclear Disarmament) founded.

Fidel Castro takes power in Cuba. De Gaulle French President (until 1969). UK: Harold Macmillan makes 'never had it so good' speech about British economy.

Sharpeville Massacre, South Africa, African National Congress (ANC) outlawed. J. F. Kennedy US President. UK: Macmillan makes 'Wind of Change' speech about end of British Empire.

Yuri Gagarin first man in space. Berlin Wall divides East Berlin from West. Cuba: Bay of Pigs invasion. UK: application to join EEC (UK membership blocked by De Gaulle throughout the 1960s). Contraceptive pill widely available for first time.

DATE	AUTHOR'S LIFE	LITERARY CONTEXT
1961 *cont.*		Spark: *The Prime of Miss Jean Brodie.*
1962	Writes fiction about bohemian life and sexual mores, contributes articles about folk music to *Western Daily Press.* Starts English course at Bristol University.	Lessing: *The Golden Notebook.* Nabokov: *Pale Fire.* Yates: *Eleven Kinds of Loneliness.*
1963		Macarthy: *The Group.* Plath: *The Bell Jar.* Spark: *The Girls of Slender Means.* Vonnegut: *Cat's Cradle.*
1964	Begins writing novel about Clifton demi-monde, later published as *Shadow Dance.* Writes dissertation: 'Some Speculations on Possible Relationships between the Medieval Period and 20th Century Folk Song Poetry'.	Bellow: *Herzog.* Murdoch: *The Italian Girl.*
1965	Sends MS of *Shadow Dance* to Heinemann, revises it under instruction from Janice Robertson. Graduates and embarks on MA.	Cabrera Infante: *Three Trapped Tigers.* Drabble: *The Millstone.* Forster: *Georgy Girl.*
1966	Writes *The Magic Toyshop.* Abandons MA. Writes articles on Bob Dylan and the Who for *London Magazine. Shadow Dance* published. Starts *A Bunch of Joys* (non-fiction, about provincial nightlife).	Endo: *Silence.* Rhys: *Wide Sargasso Sea.* Scott: *The Jewel in the Crown.* West: *The Birds Fall Down.*
1967	Heinemann reject *A Bunch of Joys*, but selections published by *Guardian, Daily Telegraph, New Society.* Teaches liberal studies to economists at University of Bath. Writes *Several Perceptions.*	Kavan: *Ice.* Kundera: *The Joke.* Márquez: *One Hundred Years of Solitude.* Stoppard: *Rosencrantz and Guildenstern are Dead.*
1968	Writes several fairy tales, begins evening classes at West of England College of Art. Writes *Heroes and Villains.*	Bowen: *Eva Trout.* Drabble: *Jerusalem the Golden.* Le Guin: *A Wizard of Earthsea.* Updike: *Couples.* Yourcenar: *The Abyss.*

CHRONOLOGY

HISTORICAL EVENTS

Cuban Missile Crisis. UK: agreement with French to build Concorde, supersonic airliner.

President Kennedy assassinated in Dallas. Civil Rights March, Washington. UK: Profumo affair, Alec Douglas-Home Prime Minister. Beatles release *Please Please Me*, first LP.

President Johnson re-elected, declares 'war on poverty'. Race riots in US cities. Warren Commission (investigating Kennedy assassination) decides 'Oswald acted alone'. UK: Labour wins election with small majority (five seats), Harold Wilson becomes Prime Minister.

UK: Wilson government introduces comprehensive education. Winston Churchill dies.

China: Mao's Cultural Revolution launched. UK: Wilson increases Labour majority to ninety-six seats.

Arab–Israeli Six-Day War. First heart-transplant operation. UK: homosexuality and abortion legalized.

Soviet invasion of Czechoslovakia. Student protests throughout Europe, anti-Vietnam War activism in US. Martin Luther king assassinated. UK: Enoch Powell opposes Commonwealth immigration with 'rivers of blood' speech.

DATE	AUTHOR'S LIFE	LITERARY CONTEXT
1969	Begins writing *Love*, inspired by Constant's *Adolphe*. Wins Somerset Maugham Award, uses money to visit US with Paul and to visit Japan alone. Meets Sozo Araki. Separation from Paul. Mother dies.	Nobel Prize: Beckett. K. Amis: *The Green Man.* Atwood: *The Edible Woman.* Le Guin: *The Left Hand of Darkness.* Roth: *Portnoy's Complaint.* Vonnegut: *Slaughterhouse-Five.*
1970	Living in Tokyo. Writes 'The Executioner's Beautiful Daughter', 'A Souvenir of Japan' and 'The Loves of Lady Purple' (*Fireworks*). Does translating work.	Farrell: *Troubles.* Morrison: *The Bluest Eye.* Spark: *The Driver's Seat.*
1971	Writes *The Infernal Desire Machines of Dr Hoffman*, inspired by Borges and Márquez. *Love* published. Returns to Japan via USSR.	Doctorow: *The Book of Daniel.* Selby: *The Room.*
1972	Moves to north London. Receives Arts Council grant, commissioned to translate Xavière Gauthier's *Surréalisme et sexualité.*	Calvino: *Invisible Cities.* Thompson: *Fear and Loathing in Las Vegas.*
1973	Writes for *Spare Rib*. Commissioned to write *The Sadeian Woman* by Carmen Callil, beginning her relationship with Virago. Deborah Rogers becomes her agent. Moves to Bath. Begins writing *The Passion of New Eve.*	Murdoch: *The Black Prince.* Pynchon: *Gravity's Rainbow.*
1974	Travels to Japan for launch of *Love*, returns via USSR. Quartet publish *Fireworks*, admired by Lorna Sage, Olivia Manning, Ian McEwan and Robert Coover. Meets Mark Pearce.	Bainbridge: *The Bottle Factory Outing.* Gordimer: *The Conservationist.* Le Guin: *The Dispossessed.*
1975	Writes radio play *Vampirella* and the short story 'The Erl-King'. Becomes involved with performance artists Shirley Cameron and Roland Miller.	Bradbury: *The History Man.* Márquez: *The Autumn of the Patriarch.* Saadawi: *Woman at Point Zero.*
1976	Befriends Salman Rushdie. Moves to Clapham, south London. Translates Perrault fairy tales for Gollancz. Begins work at University of Sheffield.	Carver: *Will You Please Be Quiet, Please?* Ford: *A Piece of My Heart.*

CHRONOLOGY

HISTORICAL EVENTS

Neil Armstrong first man on moon. UK: 'Troubles' reignite in Northern Ireland, North Sea oil discovered, capital punishment abolished, voting age lowered to eighteen

UK: Edward Heath Prime Minister. Beatles break up.

Aswan Dam opened, Egypt. United Nations General Assembly admits People's Republic of China and expels the Republic of China (Taiwan). UK: decimal currency introduced.

Strategic Arms Limitation Treaty (SALT) signed by USSR and US. UK: miners' strike. Direct rule imposed on Northern Ireland after Bloody Sunday.

Arab–Israeli war, Middle East oil embargo. UK: three-day week to save energy, IRA extend bombing campaign to London. UK joins EEC.

Nixon resigns as US President after Watergate scandal. UK: Social Contract with unions drawn up by Harold Wilson.

End of Vietnam War. UK: Voters opt to stay in EEC in referendum.

Soweto massacre in South Africa. Jimmy Carter becomes US President. UK: James Callaghan replaces Wilson as Prime Minister. National Theatre opens in London.

DATE	AUTHOR'S LIFE	LITERARY CONTEXT
1977	Submits 'The Company of Wolves' to Emma Tennant's magazine *Bananas*. *The Passion of New Eve* published by Gollancz.	Bainbridge: *Injury Time*. Coover: *The Public Burning*. Morrison: *Song of Solomon*. Murdoch: *The Sea, the Sea*. Thomas Ellis: *The Sin Eater*.
1978	Teaches on two writing courses, in Ambleside and Hebden Bridge. Also takes over from Angus Wilson on University of East Anglia's Creative Writing Course.	K. Amis: *Jake's Thing*. Byatt: *The Virgin in the Garden*. Lessing: *Collected Stories*. Munro: *Who Do You Think You Are?*
1979	*The Sadeian Woman* (Virago). *The Bloody Chamber* (Chatto & Windus) published, receiving glowing reviews.	Calvino: *If on a winter's night a traveller*. Fitzgerald: *Offshore*.
1980	Embarks on a year's teaching at Brown University, Providence, RI. Writes 'The Cabinet of Edgar Allan Poe' and two short stories inspired by Lizzie Borden.	Burgess: *Earthly Powers*. Drabble: *The Middle Ground*. Golding: *Rites of Passage*. Robinson: *Housekeeping*.
1981	Collection of journalism (*Nothing Sacred*) commissioned by Virago. Writing *Nights at the Circus*.	Keane: *Good Behaviour*. Márquez: *Chronicle of a Death Foretold*. McEwan: *The Comfort of Strangers*. Rushdie: *Midnight's Children*.
1982	In Dublin to celebrate Joyce's centenary, meets film-maker Neil Jordan and her hero Borges.	Allende: *The House of the Spirits*. Fitzgerald: *At Freddie's*. Walker: *The Color Purple*.
1983	Judges Booker Prize. Finishes *Nights at the Circus*. Reviews non-fiction for *Guardian* and *New Society*. Works with Neil Jordan on *Company of Wolves* script. Son (Alexander Robert Pearce) born 7 November.	Bradbury: *Rates of Exchange*. Bradley: *The Mists of Avalon*. Hill: *The Woman in Black*. Koetzee: *Life and Times of Michael K*. Weldon: *The Life and Loves of a She-Devil*.
1984	Writer-in-Residence, University of Adelaide. Returns to UK May, *Company of Wolves* released September. *Nights at the Circus* published. Contracted by Virago to edit *Wayward Girls and Wicked Women* (short stories about women).	M. Amis: *Money*. Barnes: *Flaubert's Parrot*. Bernhard: *Cutting Timber*. Brookner: *Hotel du Lac*. Duras: *The Lover*. Wesley: *The Camomile Lawn*.

CHRONOLOGY

HISTORICAL EVENTS

Egyptian leader Sadat visits Jerusalem. Pakistan hold first elections. UK: Queen Elizabeth II's Silver Jubilee.

US, Israel, Egypt sign Camp David Agreement. P. W. Botha comes to power in South Africa. UK: birth of first 'test-tube baby', Louise Brown.

Islamic revolution in Iran: Ayatollah Khomeini takes power. US and USSR sign SALT-2. Soviet forces invade Afghanistan. UK: 'Winter of Discontent' public-sector strikes. Margaret Thatcher Prime Minister.

Solidarity movement begins at Gdansk, Poland, under Lech Walesa. UK: Republican prisoners in Maze, Belfast, go on hunger strike.

Ronald Reagan US President. UK: Social Democratic Party founded. First AIDS cases detected. Race riots in Toxteth and London.

Israel invades Lebanon, expels Palestinians from country. Lech Walesa released from imprisonment. UK: Falklands War with Argentina.

Strategic Defence Initiative ('Star Wars') announced by Reagan. Microsoft launches Word. UK becomes net importer of machinery.

India: Indira Gandhi assassinated. UK: miners' strike, British Telecom privatized, first of wave of privatization of public utilities under Thatcherism.

DATE	AUTHOR'S LIFE	LITERARY CONTEXT
1985	Takes up post teaching creative writing, University of Texas at Austin. Third volume of short stories, *Black Venus*, published October.	Atwood: *The Handmaid's Tale.* Márquez: *Love in the Time of Cholera.* Lessing: *The Good Terrorist.* Tyler: *The Accidental Tourist.*
1986	Writes screenplay for *The Magic Toyshop.* Takes up post at University of Iowa Writers' Workshop.	Brookner: *A Misalliance.* Munro: *The Progress of Love.*
1987	Chatto & Windus reissue *Fireworks* and *Love.* Begins writing *Wise Children.* Publicity tour of Australia and New Zealand.	Ackroyd: *Chatterton.* Duras: *Practicalities.* Lively: *Moon Tiger.* Morrison: *Beloved.* Vonnegut: *Bluebeard.*
1988	Father dies, 23 May. Takes part in 20 June Group with Antonia Fraser and Harold Pinter. Takes position at Writers' Institute, State University of New York at Albany.	Atwood: *Cat's Eye.* Carey: *Oscar and Lucinda.* Lessing: *The Fifth Child.* Rushdie: *The Satanic Verses.*
1989	Travelling in Florence with family, is horrified to learn of the fatwa on close friend Salman Rushdie. Gives Borges memorial lecture at the Royal Society of Arts. Buys barge, *Crowfoot.*	Barnes: *A History of the World in 10 1/2 Chapters.* Clarke: *The Chymical Wedding.* Eco: *Foucault's Pendulum.* Tan: *The Joy Luck Club.* Winterson: *Sexing the Cherry.*
1990	Works on *The Virago Book of Fairy Tales.*	Byatt: *Possession.* Howard: *The Light Years.* Pynchon: *Vineland.*
1991	Diagnosed with cancer. Marries Mark Pearce. *Wise Children* published.	M. Amis: *Time's Arrow.* Barker: *Regeneration.* Smiley: *A Thousand Acres.* Trevor: *Two Lives.*
1992	Dies 16 February.	Byatt: *Angels and Insects.*

HISTORICAL EVENTS

Famine in Ethiopia. Cruise liner *Achille Lauro* hijacked by Palestinian terrorists. UK: miners' strike ends.

State of Emergency declared in South Africa. Mir space station launched. UK: Britain and France agree to build Channel tunnel.

President Reagan admits culpability in Iran–Contra affair. EC passes Single European Act. Palestinians launch First Intifada. UK: Church of England Synod votes to allow ordination of women, hurricane kills twenty-three in south east.

Hungary allows limited travel to West, beginning loosening of USSR's grip on Eastern Europe. Worldwide Web first discussed. UK: SDP and Liberals merge to form Liberal Democrats.

Collapse of Communism in Eastern Europe, Berlin Wall dismantled. Tiananmen Square massacre in China. Tim Berners-Lee instigates the Worldwide Web. UK: Hillsborough disaster, Guildford Four verdicts quashed.

Germany reunified, Yugoslavia begins to disintegrate. Nelson Mandela released from prison. UK: Thatcher resigns. Britain joins Exchange Rate Mechanism (ERM).

USSR collapses into fifteen sovereign republics. Gulf War begins. UK: Birmingham Six freed.

War in Nagorno-Karabakh. Maastrict Treaty on European Union signed. UK leaves ERM on 'Black Wednesday'.

THE BLOODY CHAMBER

AND OTHER STORIES

THE BLOODY CHAMBER

I REMEMBER HOW, that night, I lay awake in the wagon-lit in a tender, delicious ecstasy of excitement, my burning cheek pressed against the impeccable linen of the pillow and the pounding of my heart mimicking that of the great pistons ceaselessly thrusting the train that bore me through the night, away from Paris, away from girlhood, away from the white, enclosed quietude of my mother's apartment, into the unguessable country of marriage.

And I remember I tenderly imagined how, at this very moment, my mother would be moving slowly about the narrow bedroom I had left behind for ever, folding up and putting away all my little relics, the tumbled garments I would not need any more, the scores for which there had been no room in my trunks, the concert programmes I'd abandoned; she would linger over this torn ribbon and that faded photograph with all the half-joyous, half-sorrowful emotions of a woman on her daughter's wedding day. And, in the midst of my bridal triumph, I felt a pang of loss as if, when he put the gold band on my finger, I had, in some way, ceased to be her child in becoming his wife.

Are you sure, she'd said when they delivered the gigantic box that held the wedding dress he'd bought me, wrapped up in tissue paper and red ribbon like a Christmas gift of crystallized fruit. Are you sure you love him? There was a dress for her, too; black silk, with the dull, prismatic sheen of oil on water, finer than anything she'd worn since that adventurous girlhood in Indo-China, daughter of a rich tea planter. My eagle-featured, indomitable mother; what other student at the Conservatoire could boast that her mother had outfaced a junkful of Chinese pirates, nursed a village through a visitation of the plague, shot a man-eating tiger with her own hand and all before she was as old as I?

'Are you sure you love him?'

'I'm sure I want to marry him,' I said.

And would say no more. She sighed, as if it was with

reluctance that she might at last banish the spectre of poverty from its habitual place at our meagre table. For my mother herself had gladly, scandalously, defiantly beggared herself for love; and, one fine day, her gallant soldier never returned from the wars, leaving his wife and child a legacy of tears that never quite dried, a cigar box full of medals and the antique service revolver that my mother, grown magnificently eccentric in hardship, kept always in her reticule, in case – how I teased her – she was surprised by footpads on her way home from the grocer's shop.

Now and then a starburst of lights spattered the drawn blinds as if the railway company had lit up all the stations through which we passed in celebration of the bride. My satin nightdress had just been shaken from its wrappings; it had slipped over my young girl's pointed breasts and shoulders, supple as a garment of heavy water, and now teasingly caressed me, egregious, insinuating, nudging between my thighs as I shifted restlessly in my narrow berth. His kiss, his kiss with tongue and teeth in it and a rasp of beard, had hinted to me, though with the same exquisite tact as this nightdress he'd given me, of the wedding night, which would be voluptuously deferred until we lay in his great ancestral bed in the sea-girt, pinnacled domain that lay, still, beyond the grasp of my imagination . . . that magic place, the fairy castle whose walls were made of foam, that legendary habitation in which he had been born. To which, one day, I might bear an heir. Our destination, my destiny.

Above the syncopated roar of the train, I could hear his even, steady breathing. Only the communicating door kept me from my husband and it stood open. If I rose up on my elbow, I could see the dark, leonine shape of his head and my nostrils caught a whiff of the opulent male scent of leather and spices that always accompanied him and sometimes, during his courtship, had been the only hint he gave me that he had come into my mother's sitting room, for, though he was a big man, he moved as softly as if all his shoes had soles of velvet, as if his footfall turned the carpet into snow.

He had loved to surprise me in my abstracted solitude at the piano. He would tell them not to announce him, then soundlessly open the door and softly creep up behind me with his bouquet of hot-house flowers or his box of marrons glacés, lay his offering upon the keys and clasp his hands over my eyes as I was lost in a Debussy prelude. But that perfume of spiced leather always betrayed him; after my first shock, I was forced always to mimic surprise, so that he would not be disappointed.

He was older than I. He was much older than I; there were streaks of pure silver in his dark mane. But his strange, heavy, almost waxen face was not lined by experience. Rather, experience seemed to have washed it perfectly smooth, like a stone on a beach whose fissures have been eroded by successive tides. And sometimes that face, in stillness when he listened to me playing, with the heavy eyelids folded over eyes that always disturbed me by their absolute absence of light, seemed to me like a mask, as if his real face, the face that truly reflected all the life he had led in the world before he met me, before, even, I was born, as though that face lay underneath this mask. Or else, elsewhere. As though he had laid by the face in which he had lived for so long in order to offer my youth a face unsigned by the years.

And, elsewhere, I might see him plain. Elsewhere. But, where?

In, perhaps, that castle to which the train now took us, that marvellous castle in which he had been born.

Even when he asked me to marry him, and I said: 'Yes,' still he did not lose that heavy, fleshy composure of his. I know it must seem a curious analogy, a man with a flower, but sometimes he seemed to me like a lily. Yes. A lily. Possessed of that strange, ominous calm of a sentient vegetable, like one of those cobra-headed, funereal lilies whose white sheaths are curled out of a flesh as thick and tensely yielding to the touch as vellum. When I said that I would marry him, not one muscle in his face stirred, but he let out a long, extinguished sigh. I thought: Oh! how he must want me! And it was as though the imponderable weight of his desire was a force I might not withstand, not by virtue of its violence but because of its very gravity.

He had the ring ready in a leather box lined with crimson velvet, a fire opal the size of a pigeon's egg set in a complicated circle of dark antique gold. My old nurse, who still lived with my mother and me, squinted at the ring askance; opals are bad luck, she said. But this opal had been his own mother's ring, and his grandmother's, and her mother's before that, given to an ancestor by Catherine de Medici . . . every bride that came to the castle wore it, time out of mind. And did he give it to his other wives and have it back from them? asked the old woman rudely; yet she was a snob. She hid her incredulous joy at my marital coup – her little Marquise – behind a façade of fault-finding. But, here, she touched me. I shrugged and turned my back pettishly on her. I did not want to remember how he had loved other women before me, but the knowledge often teased me in the threadbare self-confidence of the small hours.

I was seventeen and knew nothing of the world; my Marquis had been married before, more than once, and I remained a little bemused that, after those others, he should now have chosen me. Indeed, was he not still in mourning for his last wife? Tsk, tsk, went my old nurse. And even my mother had been reluctant to see her girl whisked off by a man so recently bereaved. A Romanian countess, a lady of high fashion. Dead just three short months before I met him, a boating accident, at his home, in Brittany. They never found her body but I rummaged through the back copies of the society magazines my old nanny kept in a trunk under her bed and tracked down her photograph. The sharp muzzle of a pretty, witty, naughty monkey; such potent and bizarre charm, of a dark, bright, wild yet worldly thing whose natural habitat must have been some luxurious interior decorator's jungle filled with potted palms and tame, squawking parakeets.

Before that? *Her* face is common property; everyone painted her but the Redon engraving I liked best, *The Evening Star Walking on the Rim of Night.* To see her skeletal, enigmatic grace, you would never think she had been a barmaid in a café in Montmartre until Puvis de Chavannes saw her and had her expose her flat breasts and elongated thighs to his brush. And yet it was the absinthe doomed her, or so they said.

The first of all his ladies? That sumptuous diva; I had heard her sing Isolde, precociously musical child that I was, taken to the opera for a birthday treat. My first opera; I had heard her sing Isolde. With what white-hot passion had she burned from the stage! So that you could tell she would die young. We sat high up, halfway to heaven in the gods, yet she half-blinded me. And my father, still alive (oh, so long ago), took hold of my sticky little hand, to comfort me, in the last act, yet all I heard was the glory of her voice.

Married three times within my own brief lifetime to three

different graces, now, as if to demonstrate the eclecticism of his taste, he had invited me to join this gallery of beautiful women, I, the poor widow's child with my mouse-coloured hair that still bore the kinks of the plaits from which it had so recently been freed, my bony hips, my nervous, pianist's fingers.

He was rich as Croesus. The night before our wedding – a simple affair, at the Mairie, because his countess was so recently gone – he took my mother and me, curious coincidence, to see *Tristan*. And, do you know, my heart swelled and ached so during the Liebestod that I thought I must truly love him. Yes. I did. On his arm, all eyes were upon me. The whispering crowd in the foyer parted like the Red Sea to let us through. My skin crisped at his touch.

How my circumstances had changed since the first time I heard those voluptuous chords that carry such a charge of deathly passion in them! Now, we sat in a loge, in red velvet armchairs, and a braided, bewigged flunkey brought us a silver bucket of iced champagne in the interval. The froth spilled over the rim of my glass and drenched my hands, I thought: My cup runneth over. And I had on a Poiret dress. He had prevailed upon my reluctant mother to let him buy my trousseau; what would I have gone to him in, otherwise? Twice-darned underwear, faded gingham, serge skirts, hand-me-downs. So, for the opera, I wore a sinuous shift of white muslin tied with a silk string under the breasts. And everyone stared at me. And at his wedding gift.

His wedding gift, clasped round my throat. A choker of rubies, two inches wide, like an extraordinarily precious slit throat.

After the Terror, in the early days of the Directory, the aristos who'd escaped the guillotine had an ironic fad of tying a red ribbon round their necks at just the point where the blade would have sliced it through, a red ribbon like the memory of a wound. And his grandmother, taken with the notion, had her ribbon made up in rubies; such a gesture of luxurious defiance! That night at the opera comes back to me even now . . . the white dress; the frail child within it; and the flashing crimson jewels round her throat, bright as arterial blood.

I saw him watching me in the gilded mirrors with the assessing eye of a connoisseur inspecting horseflesh, or even of a housewife in the market, inspecting cuts on the slab. I'd never seen, or else had never acknowledged, that regard of his before, the sheer carnal avarice of it; and it was strangely magnified by the monocle lodged in his left eye. When I saw him look at me with lust, I dropped my eyes but, in glancing away from him, I caught sight of myself in the mirror. And I saw myself, suddenly, as he saw me, my pale face, the way the muscles in my neck stuck out like thin wire. I saw how much that cruel necklace became me. And, for the first time in my innocent and confined life, I sensed in myself a potentiality for corruption that took my breath away.

The next day, we were married.

The train slowed, shuddered to a halt. Lights; clank of metal; a voice declaring the name of an unknown, never-to-be-visited station; silence of the night; the rhythm of his breathing, that I should sleep with, now, for the rest of my life. And I could not sleep. I stealthily sat up, raised the blind a little and huddled against the cold window that misted over with the warmth of my breathing, gazing out at the dark platform towards those rectangles of domestic lamplight that promised warmth, company, a supper of sausages hissing in a pan on the stove for the station master, his children tucked up in bed asleep in the brick house with the painted shutters . . . all the paraphernalia of the everyday world from which I, with my stunning marriage, had exiled myself.

Into marriage, into exile; I sensed it, I knew it – that, henceforth, I would always be lonely. Yet that was part of the already familiar weight of the fire opal that glimmered like a gypsy's magic ball, so that I could not take my eyes off it when I played the piano. This ring, the bloody bandage of rubies, the wardrobe of clothes from Poiret and Worth, his scent of Russian leather – all had conspired to seduce me so utterly that I could not say I felt one single twinge of regret for the world of tartines and maman that now receded from me as if drawn away on a string, like a child's toy, as the train began to throb again as if in delighted anticipation of the distance it would take me.

The first grey streamers of the dawn now flew in the sky and an eldritch half-light seeped into the railway carriage. I heard no change in his breathing but my heightened, excited senses told me he was awake and gazing at me. A huge man, an enormous man, and his eyes, dark and motionless as those eyes the ancient

Egyptians painted upon their sarcophagi, fixed upon me. I felt a certain tension in the pit of my stomach, to be so watched, in such silence. A match struck. He was igniting a Romeo y Julieta fat as a baby's arm.

'Soon,' he said in his resonant voice that was like the tolling of a bell and I felt, all at once, a sharp premonition of dread that lasted only as long as the match flared and I could see his white, broad face as if it were hovering, disembodied, above the sheets, illuminated from below like a grotesque carnival head. Then the flame died, the cigar glowed and filled the compartment with a remembered fragrance that made me think of my father, how he would hug me in a warm fug of Havana, when I was a little girl, before he kissed me and left me and died.

As soon as my husband handed me down from the high step of the train, I smelled the amniotic salinity of the ocean. It was November; the trees, stunted by the Atlantic gales, were bare and the lonely halt was deserted but for his leather-gaitered chauffeur waiting meekly beside the sleek black motor car. It was cold; I drew my furs about me, a wrap of white and black, broad stripes of ermine and sable, with a collar from which my head rose like the calyx of a wildflower. (I swear to you, I had never been vain until I met him.) The bell clanged; the straining train leapt its leash and left us at that lonely wayside halt where only he and I had descended. Oh, the wonder of it; how all that might of iron and steam had paused only to suit his convenience. The richest man in France.

'Madame.'

The chauffeur eyed me; was he comparing me, invidiously, to the countess, the artist's model, the opera singer? I hid behind my furs as if they were a system of soft shields. My husband liked me to wear my opal over my kid glove, a showy, theatrical trick – but the moment the ironic chauffeur glimpsed its simmering flash he smiled, as though it was proof positive I was his master's wife. And we drove towards the widening dawn, that now streaked half the sky with a wintry bouquet of pink of roses, orange of tiger-lilies, as if my husband had ordered me a sky from a florist. The day broke around me like a cool dream.

Sea; sand; a sky that melts into the sea – a landscape of misty pastels with a look about it of being continuously on the point of melting. A landscape with all the deliquescent harmonies of

Debussy, of the études I played for him, the reverie I'd been playing that afternoon in the salon of the princess where I'd first met him, among the teacups and the little cakes, I, the orphan, hired out of charity to give them their digestive of music.

And, ah! his castle. The faery solitude of the place; with its turrets of misty blue, its courtyard, its spiked gate, his castle that lay on the very bosom of the sea with seabirds mewing about its attics, the casements opening on to the green and purple, evanescent departures of the ocean, cut off by the tide from land for half a day . . . that castle, at home neither on the land nor on the water, a mysterious, amphibious place, contravening the materiality of both earth and the waves, with the melancholy of a mermaiden who perches on her rock and waits, endlessly, for a lover who had drowned far away, long ago. That lovely, sad, sea-siren of a place!

The tide was low; at this hour, so early in the morning, the causeway rose up out of the sea. As the car turned on to the wet cobbles between the slow margins of water, he reached out for my hand that had his sultry, witchy ring on it, pressed my fingers, kissed my palm with extraordinary tenderness. His face was as still as ever I'd seen it, still as a pond iced thickly over, yet his lips, that always looked so strangely red and naked between the black fringes of his beard, now curved a little. He smiled; he welcomed his bride home.

No room, no corridor that did not rustle with the sound of the sea and all the ceilings, the walls on which his ancestors in the stern regalia of rank lined up with their dark eyes and white faces, were stippled with refracted light from the waves which were always in motion; that luminous, murmurous castle of which I was the châtelaine, I, the little music student whose mother had sold all her jewellery, even her wedding ring, to pay the fees at the Conservatoire.

First of all, there was the small ordeal of my initial interview with the housekeeper, who kept this extraordinary machine, this anchored, castellated ocean liner, in smooth running order no matter who stood on the bridge; how tenuous, I thought, might be my authority here! She had a bland, pale, impassive, dislikeable face beneath the impeccably starched white linen head-dress of the region. Her greeting, correct but lifeless, chilled me; daydreaming, I dared presume too much on my status . . . briefly wondered how I might install my old nurse, so much loved, however cosily incompetent, in her place. Ill-considered schemings! He told me this one had been his foster mother; was bound to his family in the utmost feudal complicity, 'as much part of the house as I am, my dear'. Now her thin lips offered me a proud little smile. She would be my ally as long as I was his. And with that, I must be content.

But, here, it would be easy to be content. In the turret suite he had given me for my very own, I could gaze out over the tumultuous Atlantic and imagine myself the Queen of the Sea. There was a Bechstein for me in the music room and, on the wall, another wedding present – an early Flemish primitive of Saint Cecilia at her celestial organ. In the prim charm of this saint, with her plump, sallow cheeks and crinkled brown hair, I saw myself as I could have wished to be. I warmed to a loving sensitivity I had not hitherto suspected in him. Then he led me up a delicate spiral staircase to my bedroom; before she discreetly vanished, the housekeeper set him chuckling with some, I dare say, lewd blessing for newlyweds in her native Breton. That I did not understand. That he, smiling, refused to interpret.

And there lay the grand, hereditary matrimonial bed, itself the size, almost, of my little room at home, with the gargoyles carved on its surfaces of ebony, vermilion lacquer, gold leaf; and its white gauze curtains, billowing in the sea breeze. Our bed. And surrounded by so many mirrors! Mirrors on all the walls, in stately frames of contorted gold, that reflected more white lilies than I'd ever seen in my life before. He'd filled the room with them, to greet the bride, the young bride. The young bride, who had become that multitude of girls I saw in the mirrors, identical in their chic navy blue tailor-mades, for travelling, madame, or walking. A maid had dealt with the furs. Henceforth, a maid would deal with everything.

'See,' he said, gesturing towards those elegant girls. 'I have acquired a whole harem for myself!'

I found that I was trembling. My breath came thickly. I could not meet his eye and turned my head away, out of pride, out of shyness, and watched a dozen husbands approach me in a dozen mirrors and slowly, methodically, teasingly, unfasten the buttons of my jacket and slip it from my shoulders. Enough! No; more! Off comes the skirt; and, next, the blouse of apricot linen that cost more than the dress I had for first communion. The play of the waves outside in the cold sun glittered on his monocle; his movements seemed to me deliberately coarse, vulgar. The blood rushed to my face again, and stayed there.

And yet, you see, I guessed it might be so – that we should have a formal disrobing of the bride, a ritual from the brothel. Sheltered as my life had been, how could I have failed, even in the world of prim bohemia in which I lived, to have heard hints of *his* world?

He stripped me, gourmand that he was, as if he were stripping the leaves off an artichoke – but do not imagine much finesse about it; this artichoke was no particular treat for the diner nor was he yet in any greedy haste. He approached his familiar treat with a weary appetite. And when nothing but my scarlet, palpitating core remained, I saw, in the mirror, the living image of an etching by Rops from the collection he had shown me when our engagement permitted us to be alone together . . . the child with her sticklike limbs, naked but for her button boots, her gloves, shielding her face with her hand as though her face were the last repository of her modesty; and the old, monocled lecher who examined her, limb by limb. He in his London tailoring; she, bare as a lamb chop. Most pornographic of all confrontations. And so my purchaser unwrapped his bargain. And, as at the opera, when I had first seen my flesh in his eyes, I was aghast to feel myself stirring.

At once he closed my legs like a book and I saw again the rare movement of his lips that meant he smiled.

Not yet. Later. Anticipation is the greater part of pleasure, my little love.

And I began to shudder, like a racehorse before a race, yet also with a kind of fear, for I felt both a strange, impersonal arousal at the thought of love and at the same time a repugnance I could not stifle for his white, heavy flesh that had too much in common with the armfuls of arum lilies that filled my bedroom in great glass jars, those undertakers' lilies with the heavy pollen that powders your fingers as if you had dipped them in turmeric. The lilies I always associate with him; that are white. And stain you.

This scene from a voluptuary's life was now abruptly terminated. It turns out he has business to attend to; his estates, his companies – even on your honeymoon? Even then, said the red lips that kissed me before he left me alone with my bewildered senses – a wet, silken brush from his beard; a hint of the pointed tip of the tongue. Disgruntled, I wrapped a négligé of antique lace around me to sip the little breakfast of hot chocolate the maid brought me; after that, since it was second nature to me, there was nowhere to go but the music room and soon I settled down at my piano.

Yet only a series of subtle discords flowed from beneath my fingers: out of tune ... only a little out of tune; but I'd been blessed with perfect pitch and could not bear to play any more. Sea breezes are bad for pianos; we shall need a resident piano-tuner on the premises if I'm to continue with my studies! I flung down the lid in a little fury of disappointment; what should I do now, how shall I pass the long, sea-lit hours until my husband beds me?

I shivered to think of *that*.

His library seemed the source of his habitual odour of Russian leather. Row upon row of calf-bound volumes, brown and olive, with gilt lettering on their spines, the octavo in brilliant scarlet morocco. A deep-buttoned leather sofa to recline on. A lectern, carved like a spread eagle, that held open upon it an edition of Huysmans's *Là-bas*, from some over-exquisite private press; it had been bound like a missal, in brass, with gems of coloured glass. The rugs on the floor, deep, pulsing blues of heaven and red of the heart's dearest blood, came from Isfahan and Bokhara; the dark panelling gleamed; there was the lulling music of the sea and a fire of apple logs. The flames flickered along the spines inside a glass-fronted case that held books still crisp and new. Eliphas Levy; the name meant nothing to me. I squinted at a title or two: *The Initiation*, *The Key of Mysteries*, *The Secret of Pandora's Box*, and yawned. Nothing, here, to detain a seventeen-year-old girl waiting for her first embrace. I should have liked, best of all, a novel in yellow paper; I wanted to curl up on the rug before the blazing fire, lose myself in a cheap novel, munch sticky liqueur chocolates. If I rang for them, a maid would bring me chocolates.

Nevertheless, I opened the doors of that bookcase idly to browse. And I think I knew, I knew by some tingling of the fingertips, even before I opened that slim volume with no title at all on the spine, what I should find inside it. When he showed me the Rops, newly bought, dearly prized, had he not hinted that he was a connoisseur of such things? Yet I had not bargained for this, the girl with tears hanging on her cheeks like stuck pearls, her cunt a split fig below the great globes of her buttocks on which the knotted tails of the cat were about to descend, while a man in a black mask fingered with his free hand his prick, that curved upwards like the scimitar he held. The picture had a caption: 'Reproof of curiosity'. My mother, with all the precision of her eccentricity, had told me what it was that lovers did; I was innocent but not naïve. *The Adventures of Eulalie at the Harem of the Grand Turk* had been printed, according to the flyleaf, in Amsterdam in 1748, a rare collector's piece. Had some ancestor brought it back himself from that northern city? Or had my husband bought it for himself, from one of those dusty little bookshops on the Left Bank where an old man peers at you through spectacles an inch thick, daring you to inspect his wares . . . I turned the pages in the anticipation of fear; the print was rusty. Here was another steel engraving: 'Immolation of the wives of the Sultan'. I knew enough for what I saw in that book to make me gasp.

There was a pungent intensification of the odour of leather that suffused his library; his shadow fell across the massacre.

'My little nun has found the prayerbooks, has she?' he demanded, with a curious mixture of mockery and relish; then, seeing my painful, furious bewilderment, he laughed at me aloud, snatched the book from my hands and put it down on the sofa.

'Have the nasty pictures scared Baby? Baby mustn't play with grownups' toys until she's learned how to handle them, must she?'

Then he kissed me. And with, this time, no reticence. He kissed me and laid his hand imperatively upon my breast, beneath the sheath of ancient lace. I stumbled on the winding stair that led to the bedroom, to the carved, gilded bed on which he had been conceived. I stammered foolishly: We've not taken luncheon yet; and, besides, it is broad daylight . . .

All the better to see you.

He made me put on my choker, the family heirloom of one woman who had escaped the blade. With trembling fingers, I fastened the thing about my neck. It was cold as ice and chilled me. He twined my hair into a rope and lifted it off my shoulders so that he could the better kiss the downy furrows below my ears;

that made me shudder. And he kissed those blazing rubies, too. He kissed them before he kissed my mouth. Rapt, he intoned: 'Of her apparel she retains/Only her sonorous jewellery.'

A dozen husbands impaled a dozen brides while the mewing gulls swung on invisible trapezes in the empty air outside.

I was brought to my senses by the insistent shrilling of the telephone. He lay beside me, felled like an oak, breathing stertorously, as if he had been fighting with me. In the course of that one-sided struggle, I had seen his deathly composure shatter like a porcelain vase flung against a wall; I had heard him shriek and blaspheme at the orgasm; I had bled. And perhaps I had seen his face without its mask; and perhaps I had not. Yet I had been infinitely dishevelled by the loss of my virginity.

I gathered myself together, reached into the cloisonné cupboard beside the bed that concealed the telephone and addressed the mouthpiece. His agent in New York. Urgent.

I shook him awake and rolled over on my side, cradling my spent body in my arms. His voice buzzed like a hive of distant bees. My husband. My husband, who, with so much love, filled my bedroom with lilies until it looked like an embalming parlour. Those somnolent lilies, that wave their heavy heads, distributing their lush, insolent incense reminiscent of pampered flesh.

When he'd finished with the agent, he turned to me and stroked the ruby necklace that bit into my neck, but with such tenderness now, that I ceased flinching and he caressed my breasts. My dear one, my little love, my child, did it hurt her? He's so sorry for it, such impetuousness, he could not help himself; you see, he loves her so . . . and this lover's recitative of his brought my tears in a flood. I clung to him as though only the one who had inflicted the pain could comfort me for suffering it. For a while, he murmured to me in a voice I'd never heard before, a voice like the soft consolations of the sea. But then he unwound the tendrils of my hair from the buttons of his smoking jacket, kissed my cheek briskly and told me the agent from New York had called with such urgent business that he must leave as soon as the tide was low enough. Leave the castle? Leave France! And would be away for at least six weeks.

'But it is our honeymoon!'

A deal, an enterprise of hazard and chance involving several millions, lay in the balance, he said. He drew away from me into that wax-works stillness of his; I was only a little girl, I did not understand. And, he said unspoken to my wounded vanity, I have had too many honeymoons to find them in the least pressing commitments. I know quite well that this child I've bought with a handful of coloured stones and the pelts of dead beasts won't run away. But, after he'd called his Paris agent to book a passage for the States next day – just one tiny call, my little one – we should have time for dinner together.

And I had to be content with that.

A Mexican dish of pheasant with hazelnuts and chocolate; salad; white, voluptuous cheese; a sorbet of muscat grapes and Asti spumante. A celebration of Krug exploded festively. And then acrid black coffee in precious little cups so fine it shadowed the birds with which they were painted. I had Cointreau, he had cognac in the library, with the purple velvet curtains drawn against the night, where he took me to perch on his knee in a leather armchair beside the flickering log fire. He had made me change into that chaste little Poiret shift of white muslin; he seemed especially fond of it, my breasts showed through the flimsy stuff, he said, like little soft white doves that sleep, each one, with a pink eye open. But he would not let me take off my ruby choker, although it was growing very uncomfortable, nor fasten up my descending hair, the sign of a virginity so recently ruptured that still remained a wounded presence between us. He twined his fingers in my hair until I winced; I said, I remember, very little.

'The maid will have changed our sheets already,' he said. 'We do not hang the bloody sheets out of the window to prove to the whole of Brittany you are a virgin, not in these civilized times. But I should tell you it would have been the first time in all my married lives I could have shown my interested tenants such a flag.'

Then I realized, with a shock of surprise, how it must have been my innocence that captivated him – the silent music, he said, of my unknowingness, like *La Terrasse des audiences au clair de lune* played upon a piano with keys of ether. You must remember how ill at ease I was in that luxurious place, how unease had been my constant companion during the whole length of my courtship by this grave satyr who now gently martyrized my hair. To know that my naïvety gave him some pleasure made me take heart. Courage! I shall act the fine lady to the manner born one day, if only by virtue of default.

Then, slowly yet teasingly, as if he were giving a child a great, mysterious treat, he took out a bunch of keys from some interior hidey-hole in his jacket – key after key, a key, he said, for every lock in the house. Keys of all kinds – huge, ancient things of black iron; others slender, delicate, almost baroque; wafer-thin Yale keys for safes and boxes. And, during his absence, it was I who must take care of them all.

I eyed the heavy bunch with circumspection. Until that moment, I had not given a single thought to the practical aspects of marriage with a great house, great wealth, a great man, whose key ring was as crowded as that of a prison warder. Here were the clumsy and archaic keys for the dungeons, for dungeons we had in plenty although they had been converted to cellars for his wines; the dusty bottles inhabited in racks all those deep holes of pain in the rock on which the castle was built. These are the keys to the kitchens, this is the key to the picture gallery, a treasure house filled by five centuries of avid collectors – oh! he foresaw I would spend hours there.

He had amply indulged his taste for the Symbolists, he told me with a glint of greed. There was Moreau's great portrait of his first wife, the famous *Sacrificial Victim* with the imprint of the lacelike chains on her pellucid skin. Did I know the story of the painting of that picture? How, when she took off her clothes for him for the first time, she fresh from her bar in Montmartre, she had robed herself involuntarily in a blush that reddened her breasts, her shoulders, her arms, her whole body? He had thought of that story, of that dear girl, when first he had undressed me . . . Ensor, the great Ensor, his monolithic canvas: *The Foolish Virgins*. Two or three late Gauguins, his special favourite the one of the tranced brown girl in the deserted house which was called: *Out of the Night We Come, Into the Night We Go*. And, besides the additions he had made himself, his marvellous inheritance of Watteaus, Poussins and a pair of very special Fragonards, commissioned for a licentious ancestor who, it was said, had posed for the master's brush himself with his own two daughters . . . He broke off his catalogue of treasures abruptly.

Your thin white face, chérie; he said, as if he saw it for the first time. Your thin white face, with its promise of debauchery only a connoisseur could detect.

A log fell in the fire, instigating a shower of sparks; the opal on my finger spurted green flame. I felt as giddy as if I were on the edge of a precipice; I was afraid, not so much of him, of his monstrous presence, heavy as if he had been gifted at birth with more specific *gravity* than the rest of us, the presence that, even when I thought myself most in love with him, always subtly oppressed me ... No. I was not afraid of him; but of myself. I seemed reborn in his unreflective eyes, reborn in unfamiliar shapes. I hardly recognized myself from his descriptions of me and yet, and yet – might there not be a grain of beastly truth in them? And, in the red firelight, I blushed again, unnoticed, to think he might have chosen me because, in my innocence, he sensed a rare talent for corruption.

Here is the key to the china cabinet – don't laugh, my darling; there's a king's ransom in Sèvres in that closet, and a queen's ransom in Limoges. And a key to the locked, barred room where five generations of plate were kept.

Keys, keys, keys. He would trust me with the keys to his office, although I was only a baby; and the keys to his safes, where he kept the jewels I should wear, he promised me, when we returned to Paris. Such jewels! Why, I would be able to change my earrings and necklaces three times a day, just as the Empress Josephine used to change her underwear. He doubted, he said, with that hollow, knocking sound that served him for a chuckle, I would be quite so interested in his share certificates although they, of course, were worth infinitely more.

Outside our firelit privacy, I could hear the sound of the tide drawing back from the pebbles of the foreshore; it was nearly time for him to leave me. One single key remained unaccounted for on the ring and he hesitated over it; for a moment, I thought he was going to unfasten it from its brothers, slip it back into his pocket and take it away with him.

'What is *that* key?' I demanded, for his chaffing had made me bold. 'The key to your heart? Give it me!'

He dangled the key tantalizingly above my head, out of reach of my straining fingers; those bare red lips of his cracked sidelong in a smile.

'Ah, no,' he said. 'Not the key to my heart. Rather, the key to my enfer.'

He left it on the ring, fastened the ring together, shook it musically, like a carillon. Then threw the keys in a jingling heap in my lap. I could feel the cold metal chilling my thighs through my thin muslin frock. He bent over me to drop a beard-masked kiss on my forehead.

'Every man must have one secret, even if only one, from his wife,' he said. 'Promise me this, my whey-faced piano-player; promise me you'll use all the keys on the ring except that last little one I showed you. Play with anything you find, jewels, silver plate; make toy boats of my share certificates, if it pleases you, and send them sailing off to America after me. All is yours, everywhere is open to you – except the lock that this single key fits. Yet all it is is the key to a little room at the foot of the west tower, behind the still-room, at the end of a dark little corridor full of horrid cobwebs that would get into your hair and frighten you if you ventured there. Oh, and you'd find it such a dull little room! But you must promise me, if you love me, to leave it well alone. It is only a private study, a hideaway, a "den", as the English say, where I can go, sometimes, on those infrequent yet inevitable occasions when the yoke of marriage seems to weigh too heavily on my shoulders. There I can go, you understand, to savour the rare pleasure of imagining myself wifeless.'

There was a little thin starlight in the courtyard as, wrapped in my furs, I saw him to his car. His last words were, that he had telephoned the mainland and taken a piano-tuner on to the staff; this man would arrive to take up his duties the next day. He pressed me to his vicuña breast, once, and then drove away.

I had drowsed away that afternoon and now I could not sleep. I lay tossing and turning in his ancestral bed until another daybreak discoloured the dozen mirrors that were iridescent with the reflections of the sea. The perfume of the lilies weighed on my senses; when I thought that, henceforth, I would always share these sheets with a man whose skin, as theirs did, contained that toad-like, clammy hint of moisture, I felt a vague desolation that within me, now my female wound had healed, there had awoken a certain queasy craving like the cravings of pregnant women for the taste of coal or chalk or tainted food, for the renewal of his caresses. Had he not hinted to me, in his flesh as in his speech and looks, of the thousand, thousand baroque intersections of flesh upon flesh? I lay in our wide bed accompanied by, a sleepless companion, my dark newborn curiosity.

I lay in bed alone. And I longed for him. And he disgusted me.

Were there jewels enough in all his safes to recompense me for this predicament? Did all that castle hold enough riches to recompense me for the company of the libertine with whom I must share it? And what, precisely, was the nature of my desirous dread for this mysterious being who, to show his mastery over me, had abandoned me on my wedding night?

Then I sat straight up in bed, under the sardonic masks of the gargoyles carved above me, riven by a wild surmise. Might he have left me, not for Wall Street but for an importunate mistress tucked away God knows where who knew how to pleasure him far better than a girl whose fingers had been exercised, hitherto, only by the practice of scales and arpeggios? And, slowly, soothed, I sank back on to the heaping pillows; I acknowledged that the jealous scare I'd just given myself was not unmixed with a little tincture of relief.

At last I drifted into slumber, as daylight filled the room and chased bad dreams away. But the last thing I remembered, before I slept, was the tall jar of lilies beside the bed, how the thick glass distorted their fat stems so they looked like arms, dismembered arms, drifting drowned in greenish water.

Coffee and croissants to console this bridal, solitary waking. Delicious. Honey, too, in a section of comb on a glass saucer. The maid squeezed the aromatic juice from an orange into a chilled goblet while I watched her as I lay in the lazy, midday bed of the rich. Yet nothing, this morning, gave me more than a fleeting pleasure except to hear that the piano-tuner had been at work already. When the maid told me that, I sprang out of bed and pulled on my old serge skirt and flannel blouse, costume of a student, in which I felt far more at ease with myself than in any of my fine new clothes.

After my three hours of practice, I called the piano-tuner in, to thank him. He was blind, of course; but young, with a gentle mouth and grey eyes that fixed upon me although they could not see me. He was a blacksmith's son from the village across the causeway; a chorister in the church whom the good priest had taught a trade so that he could make a living. All most satisfactory. Yes. He thought he would be happy here. And if, he added shyly, he might sometimes be allowed to hear me play . . . for, you see, he loved music. Yes. Of course, I said. Certainly. He seemed to know that I had smiled.

After I dismissed him, even though I'd woken so late, it was still barely time for my 'five o'clock'. The housekeeper, who, thoughtfully forewarned by my husband, had restrained herself from interrupting my music, now made me a solemn visitation with a lengthy menu for a late luncheon. When I told her I did not need it, she looked at me obliquely, along her nose. I understood at once that one of my principal functions as châtelaine was to provide work for the staff. But, all the same, I asserted myself and said I would wait until dinner-time, although I looked forward nervously to the solitary meal. Then I found I had to tell her what I would like to have prepared for me; my imagination, still that of a schoolgirl, ran riot. A fowl in cream – or should I anticipate Christmas with a varnished turkey? No; I have decided. Avocado and shrimp, lots of it, followed by no entrée at all. But surprise me for dessert with every ice-cream in the ice box. She noted all down but sniffed; I'd shocked her. Such tastes! Child that I was, I giggled when she left me.

But, now . . . what shall I do, now?

I could have spent a happy hour unpacking the trunks that contained my trousseau but the maid had done that already, the dresses, the tailor-mades hung in the wardrobe in my dressing room, the hats on wooden heads to keep their shape, the shoes on wooden feet as if all these inanimate objects were imitating the appearance of life, to mock me. I did not like to linger in my overcrowded dressing room, nor in my lugubriously lily-scented bedroom. How shall I pass the time?

I shall take a bath in my own bathroom! And found the taps were little dolphins made of gold, with chips of turquoise for eyes. And there was a tank of goldfish, who swam in and out of moving fronds of weeds, as bored, I thought, as I was. How I wished he had not left me. How I wished it were possible to chat with, say, a maid; or, the piano-tuner . . . but I knew already my new rank forbade overtures of friendship to the staff.

I had been hoping to defer the call as long as I could, so that I should have something to look forward to in the dead waste of time I foresaw before me, after my dinner was done with, but, at a quarter before seven, when darkness already surrounded the castle, I could contain myself no longer. I telephoned my mother. And astonished myself by bursting into tears when I heard her voice.

No, nothing was the matter. Mother, I have gold bath taps.

I said, gold bath taps!

No; I suppose that's nothing to cry about, Mother.

The line was bad, I could hardly make out her congratulations, her questions, her concern, but I was a little comforted when I put the receiver down.

Yet there still remained one whole hour to dinner and the whole, unimaginable desert of the rest of the evening.

The bunch of keys lay, where he had left them, on the rug before the library fire which had warmed their metal so that they no longer felt cold to the touch but warm, almost, as my own skin. How careless I was; a maid, tending the logs, eyed me reproachfully as if I'd set a trap for her as I picked up the clinking bundle of keys, the keys to the interior doors of this lovely prison of which I was both the inmate and the mistress and had scarcely seen. When I remembered that, I felt the exhilaration of the explorer.

Lights! More lights!

At the touch of a switch, the dreaming library was brilliantly illuminated. I ran crazily about the castle, switching on every light I could find – I ordered the servants to light up all their quarters, too, so the castle would shine like a seaborne birthday cake lit with a thousand candles, one for every year of its life, and everybody on shore would wonder at it. When everything was lit as brightly as the café in the Gare du Nord, the significance of the possessions implied by that bunch of keys no longer intimidated me, for I was determined, now, to search through them all for evidence of my husband's true nature.

His office first, evidently.

A mahogany desk half a mile wide, with an impeccable blotter and a bank of telephones. I allowed myself the luxury of opening the safe that contained the jewellery and delved sufficiently among the leather boxes to find out how my marriage had given me access to a jinn's treasury – parures, bracelets, rings . . . While I was thus surrounded by diamonds, a maid knocked on the door and entered before I spoke; a subtle discourtesy. I would speak to my husband about it. She eyed my serge skirt superciliously; did madame plan to dress for dinner?

She made a moue of disdain when I laughed to hear that, she was far more the lady than I. But, imagine – to dress up in one of my Poiret extravaganzas, with the jewelled turban and aigrette on my head, roped with pearl to the navel, to sit down all alone in the baronial dining hall at the head of that massive board at which King Mark was reputed to have fed his knights . . . I grew calmer under the cold eye of her disapproval. I adopted the crisp inflections of an officer's daughter. No, I would not dress for dinner. Furthermore, I was not hungry enough for dinner itself. She must tell the housekeeper to cancel the dormitory feast I'd ordered. Could they leave me sandwiches and a flask of coffee in my music room? And would they all dismiss for the night?

Mais oui, madame.

I knew by her bereft intonation I had let them down again but I did not care; I was armed against them by the brilliance of his hoard. But I would not find his heart amongst the glittering stones; as soon as she had gone, I began a systematic search of the drawers of his desk.

All was in order, so I found nothing. Not a random doodle on an old envelope, nor the faded photograph of a woman. Only the files of business correspondence, the bills from the home farms, the invoices from tailors, the billets-doux from international financiers. Nothing. And this absence of the evidence of his real life began to impress me strangely; there must, I thought, be a great deal to conceal if he takes such pains to hide it.

His office was a singularly impersonal room, facing inwards, on to the courtyard, as though he wanted to turn his back on the siren sea in order to keep a clear head while he bankrupted a small businessman in Amsterdam or – I noticed with a thrill of distaste – engaged in some business in Laos that must, from certain cryptic references to his amateur botanist's enthusiasm for rare poppies, be to do with opium. Was he not rich enough to do without crime? Or was the crime itself his profit? And yet I saw enough to appreciate his zeal for secrecy.

Now I had ransacked his desk, I must spend a cool-headed quarter of an hour putting every last letter back where I had found it, and, as I covered the traces of my visit, by some chance, as I reached inside a little drawer that had stuck fast, I must have touched a hidden spring, for a secret drawer flew open within that drawer itself; and this secret drawer contained – at last! – a file marked: *Personal.*

I was alone, but for my reflection in the uncurtained window.

I had the brief notion that his heart, pressed flat as a flower, crimson and thin as tissue paper, lay in this file. It was a very thin one.

I could have wished, perhaps, I had not found that touching, ill-spelt note, on a paper napkin marked *La Coupole,* that began: 'My darling, I cannot wait for the moment when you may make me yours completely.' The diva had sent him a page of the score of *Tristan*, the Liebestod, with the single, cryptic word: 'Until . . .' scrawled across it. But the strangest of all these love letters was a postcard with a view of a village graveyard, among mountains, where some black-coated ghoul enthusiastically dug at a grave; this little scene, executed with the lurid exuberance of Grand Guignol, was captioned: 'Typical Transylvanian Scene – Midnight, All Hallows.' And, on the other side, the message: 'On the occasion of this marriage to the descendant of Dracula – always remember, "the supreme and unique pleasure of love is the certainty that one is doing evil". Toutes amitiés, C.'

A joke. A joke in the worst possible taste; for had he not been married to a Romanian countess? And then I remembered her pretty, witty face, and her name – Carmilla. My most recent predecessor in this castle had been, it would seem, the most sophisticated.

I put away the file, sobered. Nothing in my life of family love and music had prepared me for these grown-up games and yet these were clues to his self that showed me, at least, how much he had been loved, even if they did not reveal any good reason for it. But I wanted to know still more; and, as I closed the office door and locked it, the means to discover more fell in my way.

Fell, indeed; and with the clatter of a dropped canteen of cutlery, for, as I turned the slick Yale lock, I contrived, somehow, to open up the key ring itself, so that all the keys tumbled loose on the floor. And the very first key I picked out of that pile was, as luck or ill fortune had it, the key to the room he had forbidden me, the room he would keep for his own so that he could go there when he wished to feel himself once more a bachelor.

I made my decision to explore it before I felt a faint resurgence of my ill-defined fear of his waxen stillness. Perhaps I half-imagined, then, that I might find his real self in his den, waiting there to see if indeed I had obeyed him; that he had sent a moving figure of himself to New York, the enigmatic, self-sustaining carapace of his public person, while the real man, whose face I had glimpsed in the storm of orgasm, occupied himself with pressing private business in the study at the foot of the west tower, behind the still-room. Yet, if that were so, it was imperative that I should find him, should know him; and I was too deluded by his apparent taste for me to think my disobedience might truly offend him.

I took the forbidden key from the heap and left the others lying there.

It was now very late and the castle was adrift, as far as it could go from the land, in the middle of the silent ocean where, at my orders, it floated, like a garland of light. And all silent, all still, but for the murmuring of the waves.

I felt no fear, no intimation of dread. Now I walked as firmly as I had done in my mother's house.

Not a narrow, dusty little passage at all; why had he lied to me? But an ill-lit one, certainly; the electricity, for some reason, did not extend here, so I retreated to the still-room and found a bundle of waxed tapers in a cupboard, stored there with matches to light the oak board at grand dinners. I put a match to my little taper and advanced with it in my hand, like a penitent, along the corridor hung with heavy, I think Venetian, tapestries. The flame picked out, here, the head of a man, there, the rich breast of a woman spilling through a rent in her dress – the Rape of the Sabines, perhaps? The naked swords and immolated horses suggested some grisly mythological subject. The corridor wound downwards; there was an almost imperceptible ramp to the thickly carpeted floor. The heavy hangings on the wall muffled my footsteps, even my breathing. For some reason, it grew very warm; the sweat sprang out in beads on my brow. I could no longer hear the sound of the sea.

A long, a winding corridor, as if I were in the viscera of the castle; and this corridor led to a door of worm-eaten oak, low, round-topped, barred with black iron.

And still I felt no fear, no raising of the hairs on the back of the neck, no pricking of the thumbs.

The key slid into the new lock as easily as a hot knife into butter.

No fear; but a hesitation, a holding of the spiritual breath.

If I had found some traces of his heart in a file marked: *Personal*, perhaps, here, in his subterranean privacy, I might find a little of his soul. It was the consciousness of the possibility of such a discovery, of its possible strangeness, that kept me for a moment motionless, before, in the foolhardiness of my already subtly tainted innocence, I turned the key and the door creaked slowly back.

'There is a striking resemblance between the act of love and the ministrations of a torturer,' opined my husband's favourite poet; I had learned something of the nature of that similarity on my marriage bed. And now my taper showed me the outlines of a rack. There was also a great wheel, like the ones I had seen in woodcuts of the martyrdoms of the saints, in my old nurse's little store of holy books. And – just one glimpse of it before my little flame caved in and I was left in absolute darkness – a metal figure, hinged at the side, which I knew to be spiked on the inside and to have the name: the Iron Maiden.

Absolute darkness. And, about me, the instruments of mutilation.

Until that moment, this spoiled child did not know she had inherited nerves and a will from the mother who had defied the yellow outlaws of Indo-China. My mother's spirit drove me on, into that dreadful place, in a cold ecstasy to know the very worst. I fumbled for the matches in my pocket; what a dim, lugubrious light they gave! And yet, enough, oh, more than enough, to see a room designed for desecration and some dark night of unimaginable lovers whose embraces were annihilation.

The walls of this stark torture chamber were the naked rock; they gleamed as if they were sweating with fright. At the four corners of the room were funerary urns, of great antiquity, Etruscan, perhaps, and, on three-legged ebony stands, the bowls of incense he had left burning which filled the room with a sacerdotal reek. Wheel, rack and Iron Maiden were, I saw, displayed as grandly as if they were items of statuary and I was almost consoled, then, and almost persuaded myself that I might have stumbled only upon a little museum of his perversity, that he had installed these monstrous items here only for contemplation.

Yet at the centre of the room lay a catafalque, a doomed, ominous bier of Renaissance workmanship, surrounded by long white candles and, at its foot, an armful of the same lilies with which he had filled my bedroom, stowed in a four-foot-high jar glazed with a sombre Chinese red. I scarcely dared examine this catafalque and its occupant more closely; yet I knew I must.

Each time I struck a match to light those candles round her bed, it seemed a garment of that innocence of mine for which he had lusted fell away from me.

The opera singer lay, quite naked, under a thin sheet of very rare and precious linen, such as the princes of Italy used to shroud those whom they had poisoned. I touched her, very gently, on the white breast; she was cool, he had embalmed her. On her throat I could see the blue imprint of his strangler's fingers. The cool, sad flame of the candles flickered on her white, closed eyelids. The worst thing was, the dead lips smiled.

Beyond the catafalque, in the middle of the shadows, a white, nacreous glimmer; as my eyes accustomed themselves to the gathering darkness, I at last – oh, horrors! – made out a skull; yes, a skull, so utterly denuded, now, of flesh, that it scarcely seemed possible the stark bone had once been richly upholstered with life. And this skull was strung up by a system of unseen cords, so that it appeared to hang, disembodied, in the still, heavy air, and it had been crowned with a wreath of white roses, and a veil of lace, the final image of his bride.

Yet the skull was still so beautiful, had shaped with its sheer planes so imperiously the face that had once existed above it, that I recognized her the moment I saw her; face of the evening star walking on the rim of night. One false step, oh, my poor, dear girl, next in the fated sisterhood of his wives; one false step and into the abyss of the dark you stumbled.

And where was she, the latest dead, the Romanian countess who might have thought her blood would survive his depredations? I knew she must be here, in the place that had wound me through the castle towards it on a spool of inexorability. But, at first, I could see no sign of her. Then, for some reason – perhaps some change of atmosphere wrought by my presence – the metal shell of the Iron Maiden emitted a ghostly twang; my feverish imagination might have guessed its occupant was trying to clamber out, though, even in the midst of my rising hysteria, I knew she must be dead to find a home there.

With trembling fingers, I prised open the front of the upright coffin, with its sculpted face caught in a rictus of pain. Then, overcome, I dropped the key I still held in my other hand. It dropped into the forming pool of her blood.

She was pierced, not by one but by a hundred spikes, this child of the land of the vampires who seemed so newly dead, so full of blood . . . oh God! how recently had he become a widower? How long had he kept her in this obscene cell? Had it been all the time he had courted me, in the clear light of Paris?

I closed the lid of her coffin very gently and burst into a tumult of sobbing that contained both pity for his other victims and also a dreadful anguish to know I, too, was one of them.

The candles flared, as if in a draught from a door to elsewhere. The light caught the fire opal on my hand so that it flashed, once, with a baleful light, as if to tell me the eye of God – his eye – was upon me. My first thought, when I saw the ring for which I had sold myself to this fate, was, how to escape it.

I retained sufficient presence of mind to snuff out the candles round the bier with my fingers, to gather up my taper, to look around, although shuddering, to ensure I had left behind me no traces of my visit.

I retrieved the key from the pool of blood, wrapped it in my handkerchief to keep my hands clean, and fled the room, slamming the door behind me.

It crashed to with a juddering reverberation, like the door of hell.

I could not take refuge in my bedroom, for that retained the memory of his presence trapped in the fathomless silvering of his mirrors. My music room seemed the safest place, although I looked at the picture of Saint Cecilia with a faint dread; what had been the nature of her martyrdom? My mind was in a tumult; schemes for flight jostled with one another . . . as soon as the tide receded from the causeway, I would make for the mainland – on foot, running, stumbling; I did not trust that leather-clad chauffeur, nor the well-behaved housekeeper, and I dared not take any of the pale, ghostly maids into my confidence, either, since they were his creatures, all. Once at the village, I would fling myself directly on the mercy of the gendarmerie.

But – could I trust them, either? His forefathers had ruled this coast for eight centuries, from this castle whose moat was the Atlantic. Might not the police, the advocates, even the judge, all be in his service, turning a common blind eye to his vices since he was milord whose word must be obeyed? Who, on this distant coast, would believe the white-faced girl from Paris who came running to them with a shuddering tale of blood, of fear, of the ogre murmuring in the shadows? Or, rather, they would immediately know it to be true. But were all honour-bound to let me carry it no further.

Assistance. My mother. I ran to the telephone; and the line, of course, was dead.

Dead as his wives.

A thick darkness, unlit by any star, still glazed the windows. Every lamp in my room burned, to keep the dark outside, yet it seemed still to encroach on me, to be present beside me but as if masked by my lights, the night like a permeable substance that could seep into my skin. I looked at the precious little clock made from hypocritically innocent flowers long ago, in Dresden; the hands had scarcely moved one single hour forward from when I first descended to that private slaughterhouse of his. Time was his servant, too; it would trap me, here, in a night that would last until he came back to me, like a black sun on a hopeless morning.

And yet the time might still be my friend; at that hour, that very hour, he set sail for New York.

To know that, in a few moments, my husband would have left France calmed my agitation a little. My reason told me I had nothing to fear; the tide that would take him away to the New World would let me out of the imprisonment of the castle. Surely I could easily evade the servants. Anybody can buy a ticket at a railway station. Yet I was still filled with unease. I opened the lid of the piano; perhaps I thought my own particular magic might help me, now, that I could create a pentacle out of music that would keep me from harm for, if my music had first ensnared him, then might it not also give me the power to free myself from him?

Mechanically, I began to play but my fingers were stiff and

shaking. At first, I could manage nothing better than the exercises of Czerny but simply the act of playing soothed me and, for solace, for the sake of the harmonious rationality of its sublime mathematics, I searched among his scores until I found *The Well-Tempered Clavier.* I set myself the therapeutic task of playing all Bach's equations, every one, and, I told myself, if I played them all through without a single mistake – then the morning would find me once more a virgin.

Crash of a dropped stick.

His silver-headed cane! What else? Sly, cunning, he had returned; he was waiting for me outside the door!

I rose to my feet; fear gave me strength. I flung back my head defiantly.

'Come in!' My voice astonished me by its firmness, its clarity.

The door slowly, nervously opened and I saw, not the massive, irredeemable bulk of my husband but the slight, stooping figure of the piano-tuner, and he looked far more terrified of me than my mother's daughter would have been of the Devil himself. In the torture chamber, it seemed to me that I would never laugh again; now, helplessly, laugh I did, with relief, and, after a moment's hesitation, the boy's face softened and he smiled a little, almost in shame. Though they were blind, his eyes were singularly sweet.

'Forgive me,' said Jean-Yves. 'I know I've given you grounds for dismissing me, that I should be crouching outside your door at midnight . . . but I heard you walking about, up and down – I sleep in a room at the foot of the west tower – and some intuition told me you could not sleep and might, perhaps, pass the insomniac hours at your piano. And I could not resist that. Besides, I stumbled over these – '

And he displayed the ring of keys I'd dropped outside my husband's office door, the ring from which one key was missing. I took them from him, looked round for a place to stow them, fixed on the piano stool as if to hide them would protect me. Still he stood smiling at me. How hard it was to make everyday conversation.

'It's perfect,' I said. 'The piano. Perfectly in tune.'

But he was full of the loquacity of embarrassment, as though I would only forgive him for his impudence if he explained the cause of it thoroughly.

'When I heard you play this afternoon, I thought I'd never heard such a touch. Such technique. A treat for me, to hear a virtuoso! So I crept up to your door now, humbly as a little dog might, madame, and put my ear to the keyhole and listened, and listened until my stick fell to the floor through a momentary clumsiness of mine, and I was discovered.'

He had the most touchingly ingenuous smile.

'Perfectly in tune,' I repeated. To my surprise, now I had said it, I found I could not say anything else. I could only repeat: 'In tune . . . perfect . . . in tune,' over and over again. I saw a dawning surprise in his face. My head throbbed. To see him, in his lovely, blind humanity, seemed to hurt me very piercingly, somewhere inside my breast; his figure blurred, the room swayed about me. After the dreadful revelation of that bloody chamber, it was his tender look that made me faint.

When I recovered consciousness, I found I was lying in the piano-tuner's arms and he was tucking the satin cushion from the piano-stool under my head.

'You are in some great distress,' he said. 'No bride should suffer so much, so early in her marriage.'

His speech had the rhythms of the countryside, the rhythms of the tides.

'Any bride brought to this castle should come ready dressed in mourning, should bring a priest and a coffin with her,' I said.

'What's this?'

It was too late to keep silent; and if he, too, were one of my husband's creatures, then at least he had been kind to me. So I told him everything, the keys, the interdiction, my disobedience, the room, the rack, the skull, the corpses, the blood.

'I can scarcely believe it,' he said, wondering. 'That man . . . so rich; so well-born.'

'Here's proof,' I said and tumbled the fatal key out of my handkerchief on to the silken rug.

'Oh God,' he said. 'I can smell the blood.'

He took my hand; he pressed his arms about me. Although he was scarcely more than a boy, I felt a great strength flow into me from his touch.

'We whisper all manner of strange tales up and down the coast,' he said. 'There was a Marquis, once, who used to hunt young girls on the mainland; he hunted them with dogs, as though they were foxes. My grandfather had it from his grandfather, how the Marquis pulled a head out of his saddle bag and showed it to the blacksmith while the man was shoeing his horse. "A fine specimen of the genus, brunette, eh, Guillaume?" And it was the head of the blacksmith's wife.'

But, in these more democratic times, my husband must travel as far as Paris to do his hunting in the salons. Jean-Yves knew the moment I shuddered.

'Oh, madame! I thought all these were old wives' tales, chattering of fools, spooks to scare bad children into good behaviour! Yet how could you know, a stranger, that the old name for this place is the Castle of Murder?'

How could I know, indeed? Except that, in my heart, I'd always known its lord would be the death of me.

'Hark!' said my friend suddenly. 'The sea has changed key; it must be near morning, the tide is going down.'

He helped me up. I looked from the window, towards the mainland, along the causeway where the stones gleamed wetly in the thin light of the end of the night and, with an almost unimaginable horror, a horror the intensity of which I cannot transmit to you, I saw, in the distance, still far away yet drawing moment by moment inexorably nearer, the twin headlamps of his great black car, gouging tunnels through the shifting mist.

My husband had indeed returned; this time, it was no fancy.

'The key!' said Jean-Yves. 'It must go back on the ring, with the others. As though nothing had happened.'

But the key was still caked with wet blood and I ran to my bathroom and held it under the hot tap. Crimson water swirled down the basin but, as if the key itself were hurt, the bloody token stuck. The turquoise eyes of the dolphin taps winked at me derisively; they knew my husband had been too clever for me! I scrubbed the stain with my nail brush but still it would not budge. I thought how the car would be rolling silently towards the closed courtyard gate; the more I scrubbed the key, the more vivid grew the stain.

The bell in the gatehouse would jangle. The porter's drowsy son would push back the patchwork quilt, yawning, pull the shirt over his head, thrust his feet into his sabots ... slowly, slowly; open the door for your master as slowly as you can.

And still the bloodstain mocked the fresh water that spilled from the mouth of the leering dolphin.

'You have no more time,' said Jean-Yves. 'He is here. I know it. I must stay with you.'

'You shall not!' I said. 'Go back to your room, now. Please.'

He hesitated. I put an edge of steel in my voice, for I knew I must meet my lord alone.

'Leave me!'

As soon as he had gone, I dealt with the keys and went to my bedroom. The causeway was empty; Jean-Yves was correct, my husband had already entered the castle. I pulled the curtains close, stripped off my clothes and pulled the bedcurtain around me as a pungent aroma of Russian leather assured me my husband was once again beside me.

'Dearest!'

With the most treacherous, lascivious tenderness, he kissed my eyes, and, mimicking the new bride newly wakened, I flung my arms around him, for on my seeming acquiescence depended my salvation.

'Da Silva of Rio outwitted me,' he said wryly. 'My New York agent telegraphed Le Havre and saved me a wasted journey. So we may resume our interrupted pleasures, my love.'

I did not believe one word of it. I knew I had behaved exactly according to his desires; had he not bought me so that I should do so? I had been tricked into my own betrayal to that illimitable darkness whose source I had been compelled to seek in his absence and, now that I had met that shadowed reality of his that came to life only in the presence of its own atrocities, I must pay the price of my new knowledge. The secret of Pandora's box; but he had given me the box, himself, knowing I must learn the secret. I had played a game in which every move was governed by a destiny as oppressive and omnipotent as himself, since that destiny was himself; and I had lost. Lost at that charade of innocence and vice in which he had engaged me. Lost, as the victim loses to the executioner.

His hand brushed my breast, beneath the sheet. I strained my nerves yet could not help but flinch from the intimate touch, for it made me think of the piercing embrace of the Iron Maiden and of his lost lovers in the vault. When he saw my reluctance, his eyes veiled over and yet his appetite did not diminish. His tongue ran over red lips already wet. Silent, mysterious, he moved away from me to draw off his jacket. He took the gold watch from his waistcoat and laid it on the dressing table, like a good bourgeois; scooped out his rattling loose change and now – oh God! – makes a great play of patting his pockets officiously, puzzled lips pursed, searching for something that has been mislaid. Then turns to me with a ghastly, a triumphant smile.

'But of course! I gave the keys to you!'

'Your keys? Why, of course. Here, they're under the pillow; wait a moment – what – Ah! No . . . now, where can I have left them? I was whiling away the evening without you at the piano, I remember. Of course! The music room!'

Brusquely he flung my négligé of antique lace on the bed.

'Go and get them.'

'Now? This moment? Can't it wait until morning, my darling?'

I forced myself to be seductive. I saw myself, pale, pliant as a plant that begs to be trampled underfoot, a dozen vulnerable, appealing girls reflected in as many mirrors, and I saw how he almost failed to resist me. If he had come to me in bed, I would have strangled him, then.

But he half-snarled: 'No. It won't wait. Now.'

The unearthly light of dawn filled the room; had only one previous dawn broken upon me in that vile place? And there was nothing for it but to go and fetch the keys from the music stool and pray he would not examine them too closely, pray to God his eyes would fail him, that he might be struck blind.

When I came back into the bedroom carrying the bunch of keys that jangled at every step like a curious musical instrument, he was sitting on the bed in his immaculate shirtsleeves, his head sunk in his hands.

And it seemed to me he was in despair.

Strange. In spite of my fear of him, that made me whiter than my wrap, I felt there emanate from him, at that moment, a stench of absolute despair, rank and ghastly, as if the lilies that surrounded him had all at once begun to fester, or the Russian leather of his scent were reverting to the elements of flayed hide and excrement of which it was composed. The chthonic gravity of his presence exerted a tremendous pressure on the room, so that the blood pounded in my ears as if we had been precipitated to the bottom of the sea, beneath the waves that pounded against the shore.

I held my life in my hands amongst those keys and, in a moment, would place it between his well-manicured fingers. The evidence of that bloody chamber had showed me I could expect no mercy. Yet, when he raised his head and stared at me with his blind, shuttered eyes as though he did not recognize me, I felt a terrified pity for him, for this man who lived in such strange, secret places that, if I loved him enough to follow him, I should have to die.

The atrocious loneliness of that monster!

The monocle had fallen from his face. His curling mane was disordered, as if he had run his hands through it in his distraction. I saw how he had lost his impassivity and was now filled with suppressed excitement. The hand he stretched out for those counters in his game of love and death shook a little; the face that turned towards me contained a sombre delirium that seemed to me compounded of a ghastly, yes, shame but also of a terrible, guilty joy as he slowly ascertained how I had sinned.

That tell-tale stain had resolved itself into a mark the shape and brilliance of the heart on a playing card. He disengaged the key from the ring and looked at it for a while, solitary, brooding.

'It is the key that leads to the kingdom of the unimaginable,' he said. His voice was low and had in it the timbre of certain great cathedral organs that seem, when they are played, to be conversing with God.

I could not restrain a sob.

'Oh, my love, my little love who brought me a white gift of music,' he said, almost as if grieving. 'My little love, you'll never know how much I hate daylight!'

Then he sharply ordered: 'Kneel!'

I knelt before him and he pressed the key lightly to my forehead, held it there for a moment. I felt a faint tingling of the skin and, when I involuntarily glanced at myself in the mirror, I saw the heart-shaped stain had transferred itself to my forehead, to the space between the eyebrows, like the caste mark of a brahmin woman. Or the mark of Cain. And now the key gleamed as freshly as if it had just been cut. He clipped it back on the ring, emitting that same, heavy sigh as he had done when I said that I would marry him.

'My virgin of the arpeggios, prepare yourself for martyrdom.'

'What form shall it take?' I said.

'Decapitation,' he whispered, almost voluptuously. 'Go and bathe yourself; put on that white dress you wore to hear *Tristan* and the necklace that prefigures your end. And I shall take myself off to the armoury, my dear, to sharpen my great-grandfather's ceremonial sword.'

'The servants?'

'We shall have absolute privacy for our last rites; I have already dismissed them. If you look out of the window you can see them going to the mainland.'

It was now the full, pale light of morning; the weather was grey, indeterminate, the sea had an oily, sinister look, a gloomy day on which to die. Along the causeway I could see trooping every maid and scullion, every pot-boy and pan-scourer, valet, laundress and vassal who worked in that great house, most on foot, a few on bicycles. The faceless housekeeper trudged along with a great basket in which, I guessed, she'd stowed as much as she could ransack from the larder. The Marquis must have given the chauffeur leave to borrow the motor for the day, for it went last of all, at a stately pace, as though the procession were a cortège and the car already bore my coffin to the mainland for burial.

But I knew no good Breton earth would cover me, like a last, faithful lover; I had another fate.

'I have given them all a day's holiday, to celebrate our wedding,' he said. And smiled.

However hard I stared at the receding company, I could see no sign of Jean-Yves, our latest servant, hired but the preceding morning.

'Go, now. Bathe yourself; dress yourself. The lustratory ritual and the ceremonial robing; after that, the sacrifice. Wait in the music room until I telephone for you. No, my dear!' And he smiled, as I started, recalling the line was dead. 'One may call inside the castle just as much as one pleases; but, outside – never.'

I scrubbed my forehead with the nail brush as I had scrubbed the key but this red mark would not go away, either, no matter what I did, and I knew I should wear it until I died, though that would not be long. Then I went to my dressing room and put on that white muslin shift, costume of a victim of an auto-da-fé, he had bought me to listen to the Liebestod in. Twelve young women combed out twelve listless sheaves of brown hair in the mirrors; soon, there would be none. The mass of lilies that surrounded me exhaled, now, the odour of their withering. They looked like the trumpets of the angels of death.

On the dressing table, coiled like a snake about to strike, lay the ruby choker.

Already almost lifeless, cold at heart, I descended the spiral staircase to the music room but there I found I had not been abandoned.

'I can be of some comfort to you,' the boy said. 'Though not much use.'

We pushed the piano stool in front of the open window so that, for as long as I could, I would be able to smell the ancient, reconciling smell of the sea that, in time, will cleanse everything, scour the old bones white, wash away all the stains. The last little chambermaid had trotted along the causeway long ago and now the tide, fated as I, came tumbling in, the crisp wavelets splashing on the old stones.

'You do not deserve this,' he said.

'Who can say what I deserve or no?' I said. 'I've done nothing; but that may be sufficient reason for condemning me.'

'You disobeyed him,' he said. 'That is sufficient reason for him to punish you.'

'I only did what he knew I would.'

'Like Eve,' he said.

The telephone rang a shrill imperative. Let it ring. But my lover lifted me up and set me on my feet; I knew I must answer it. The receiver felt heavy as earth.

'The courtyard. Immediately.'

My lover kissed me, he took my hand. He would come with me if I would lead him. Courage. When I thought of courage, I thought of my mother. Then I saw a muscle in my lover's face quiver.

'Hoofbeats!' he said.

I cast one last, desperate glance from the window and, like a miracle, I saw a horse and rider galloping at a vertiginous speed along the causeway, though the waves crashed, now, high as the horse's fetlocks. A rider, her black skirts tucked up around her waist so she could ride hard and fast, a crazy, magnificent horsewoman in widow's weeds.

As the telephone rang again.

'Am I to wait all morning?'

Every moment, my mother drew nearer.

'She will be too late,' Jean-Yves said and yet he could not restrain a note of hope that, though it must be so, yet it might not be so.

The third, intransigent call.

'Shall I come up to heaven to fetch you down, Saint Cecilia? You wicked woman, do you wish me to compound my crimes by desecrating the marriage bed?'

So I must go to the courtyard where my husband waited in his London-tailored trousers and the shirt from Turnbull and Asser, beside the mounting block, with, in his hand, the sword which his great-grandfather had presented to the little corporal, in token of surrender to the Republic, before he shot himself. The heavy sword, unsheathed, grey as that November morning, sharp as childbirth, mortal.

When my husband saw my companion, he observed: 'Let the blind lead the blind, eh? But does even a youth as besotted as you are think she was truly blind to her own desires when she took my ring? Give it me back, whore.'

The fires in the opal had all died down. I gladly slipped it from my finger and, even in that dolorous place, my heart was lighter for the lack of it. My husband took it lovingly and lodged it on the tip of his little finger; it would go no further.

'It will serve me for a dozen more fiancées,' he said. 'To the block, woman. No – leave the boy; I shall deal with him later, utilizing a less exalted instrument than the one with which I do my wife the honour of her immolation, for do not fear that in death you will be divided.'

Slowly, slowly, one foot before the other, I crossed the cobbles. The longer I dawdled over my execution, the more time it gave the avenging angel to descend . . .

'Don't loiter, girl! Do you think I shall lose appetite for the meal if you are so long about serving it? No; I shall grow hungrier, more ravenous with each moment, more cruel . . . Run to me, run! I have a place prepared for your exquisite corpse in my display of flesh!'

He raised the sword and cut bright segments from the air with it, but still I lingered although my hopes, so recently raised, now began to flag. If she is not here by now, her horse must have stumbled on the causeway, have plunged into the sea . . . One thing only made me glad; that my lover would not see me die.

My husband laid my branded forehead on the stone and, as he had done once before, twisted my hair into a rope and drew it away from my neck.

'Such a pretty neck,' he said with what seemed to be a genuine, retrospective tenderness. 'A neck like the stem of a young plant.'

I felt the silken bristle of his beard and the wet touch of his lips as he kissed my nape. And, once again, of my apparel I must retain only my gems; the sharp blade ripped my dress in two and it fell from me. A little green moss, growing in the crevices of the mounting block, would be the last thing I should see in all the world.

The whizz of that heavy sword.

And – a great battering and pounding at the gate, the jangling of the bell, the frenzied neighing of a horse! The unholy silence of the place shattered in an instant. The blade did *not* descend, the necklace did *not* sever, my head did *not* roll. For, for an instant, the beast wavered in his stroke, a sufficient split second of astonished indecision to let me spring upright and dart to the assistance of my lover as he struggled sightlessly with the great bolts that kept her out.

The Marquis stood transfixed, utterly dazed, at a loss. It must have been as if he had been watching his beloved *Tristan* for the twelfth, the thirteenth time and Tristan stirred, then leapt from his bier in the last act, announced in a jaunty aria interposed from Verdi that bygones were bygones, crying over spilt milk did nobody any good and, as for himself, he proposed to live happily ever after. The puppet master, open-mouthed, wide-eyed, impotent at the last, saw his dolls break free of their strings, abandon the rituals he had ordained for them since time began and start to live for themselves; the king, aghast, witnesses the revolt of his pawns.

You never saw such a wild thing as my mother, her hat seized by the winds and blown out to sea so that her hair was her white mane, her black lisle legs exposed to the thigh, her skirts tucked round her waist, one hand on the reins of the rearing horse while the other clasped my father's service revolver and, behind her, the breakers of the savage, indifferent sea, like the witnesses of a furious justice. And my husband stood stock-still, as if she had been Medusa, the sword still raised over his head as in those clockwork tableaux of Bluebeard that you see in glass cases at fairs.

And then it was as though a curious child pushed his centime into the slot and set all in motion. The heavy, bearded figure roared out aloud, braying with fury, and, wielding the honourable sword as if it were a matter of death or glory, charged us, all three.

On her eighteenth birthday, my mother had disposed of a man-eating tiger that had ravaged the villages in the hills north of Hanoi. Now, without a moment's hesitation, she raised my father's gun, took aim and put a single, irreproachable bullet through my husband's head.

We lead a quiet life, the three of us. I inherited, of course, enormous wealth but we have given most of it away to various charities. The castle is now a school for the blind, though I pray that the children who live there are not haunted by any sad ghosts looking for, crying for, the husband who will never return to the bloody chamber, the contents of which are buried or burned, the door sealed.

I felt I had a right to retain sufficient funds to start a little music school here, on the outskirts of Paris, and we do well enough. Sometimes we can even afford to go to the Opera, though never to sit in a box, of course. We know we are the source of many whisperings and much gossip but the three of us know the truth of it and mere chatter can never harm us. I can only bless the – what shall I call it? – the *maternal telepathy* that sent my mother running headlong from the telephone to the station after I had called her, that night. I never heard you cry before, she said, by way of explanation. Not when you were happy. And who ever cried because of gold bath taps?

The night train, the one I had taken; she lay in her berth, sleepless as I had been. When she could not find a taxi at that lonely halt, she borrowed old Dobbin from a bemused farmer, for some internal urgency told her that she must reach me before the incoming tide sealed me away from her for ever. My poor old nurse, left scandalized at home – what? interrupt milord on his honeymoon? – she died soon after. She had taken so much secret pleasure in the fact that her little girl had become a marquise; and now here I was, scarcely a penny the richer, widowed at seventeen in the most dubious circumstances and busily engaged in setting up house with a piano-tuner. Poor thing, she passed away in a sorry state of disillusion! But I do believe my mother loves him as much as I do.

No paint nor powder, no matter how thick or white, can mask that red mark on my forehead; I am glad he cannot see it – not for fear of his revulsion, since I know he sees me clearly with his heart – but, because it spares my shame.

THE COURTSHIP OF MR LYON

OUTSIDE HER KITCHEN window, the hedgerow glistened as if the snow possessed a light of its own; when the sky darkened towards evening, an unearthly, reflected pallor remained behind upon the winter's landscape, while still the soft flakes floated down. This lovely girl, whose skin possesses that same, inner light so you would have thought she, too, was made all of snow, pauses in her chores in the mean kitchen to look out at the country road. Nothing has passed that way all day; the road is white and unmarked as a spilled bolt of bridal satin.

Father said he would be home before nightfall.

The snow brought down all the telephone wires; he couldn't have called, even with the best of news.

The roads are bad. I hope he'll be safe.

But the old car stuck fast in a rut, wouldn't budge an inch; the engine whirred, coughed and died and he was far from home. Ruined, once; then ruined again, as he had learnt from his lawyers that very morning; at the conclusion of the lengthy, slow attempt to restore his fortunes, he had turned out his pockets to find the cash for petrol to take him home. And not even enough money left over to buy his Beauty, his girl-child, his pet, the one white rose she said she wanted; the only gift she wanted, no matter how the case went, how rich he might once again be. She had asked for so little and he had not been able to give it to her. He cursed the useless car, the last straw that broke his spirit; then, nothing for it but to fasten his old sheepskin coat around him, abandon the heap of metal and set off down the snow-filled lane to look for help.

Behind wrought iron gates, a short, snowy drive performed a reticent flourish before a miniature, perfect, Palladian house that seemed to hide itself shyly behind snow-laden skirts of an antique cypress. It was almost night; that house, with its sweet, retiring melancholy grace, would have seemed deserted but for a light that flickered in an upstairs window, so vague it might have been the reflection of a star, if any stars could have penetrated the snow that whirled yet more thickly. Chilled through, he pressed the latch of the gate and saw, with a pang, how, on the withered ghost of a tangle of thorns, there clung, still, the faded rag of a white rose.

The gate clanged loudly shut behind him; too loudly. For an instant, that reverberating clang seemed final, emphatic, ominous as if the gate, now closed, barred all within it from the world outside the walled, wintry garden. And, from a distance, though from what distance he could not tell, he heard the most singular sound in the world: a great roaring, as of a beast of prey.

In too much need to allow himself to be intimidated, he squared up to the mahogany door. This door was equipped with a knocker in the shape of a lion's head, with a ring through the nose; as he raised his hand towards it, it came to him this lion's head was not, as he had thought at first, made of brass, but, instead, of solid gold. Before, however, he could announce his presence, the door swung silently inward on well-oiled hinges and he saw a white hall where the candles of a great chandelier cast their benign light upon so many, many flowers in great, free-standing jars of crystal that it seemed the whole of spring drew him into its warmth with a profound intake of perfumed breath. Yet there was no living person in the hall.

The door behind him closed as silently as it had opened, yet, this time, he felt no fear although he knew by the pervasive atmosphere of a suspension of reality that he had entered a place of privilege where all the laws of the world he knew need not necessarily apply, for the very rich are often very eccentric and the house was plainly that of an exceedingly wealthy man. As it was, when nobody came to help him with his coat, he took it off himself. At that, the crystals of the chandelier tinkled a little, as if emitting a pleased chuckle, and the door of a cloakroom opened of its own accord. There were, however, no clothes at all in this cloakroom, not even the statutory country-house garden mackintosh to greet his own squirearchal sheepskin, but, when he emerged again into the hall, he found a greeting waiting for him at last – there was, of all things, a liver and white King Charles spaniel crouched, with head intelligently cocked, on the Kelim runner. It gave him further, comforting proof of his unseen host's wealth and eccentricity to see the dog wore, in place of a collar, a diamond necklace.

The dog sprang to its feet in welcome and busily shepherded him (how amusing!) to a snug little leather-panelled study on the first floor, where a low table was drawn up to a roaring log fire. On the table, a silver tray; round the neck of the whisky decanter, a silver tag with the legend: *Drink me*, while the cover of the silver dish was engraved with the exhortation: *Eat me*, in a flowing hand. This dish contained sandwiches of thick-cut roast beef, still bloody. He drank the one with soda and ate the other with some excellent mustard thoughtfully provided in a stoneware pot, and, when the spaniel saw to it he had served himself, she trotted off about her own business.

All that remained to make Beauty's father entirely comfortable was to find, in a curtained recess, not only a telephone but the card of a garage that advertised a twenty-four-hour rescue service; a couple of calls later and he had confirmed, thank God, there was no serious trouble, only the car's age and the cold weather . . . could he pick it up from the village in an hour? And directions to the village, but half a mile away, were supplied, in a new tone of deference, as soon as he described the house from where he was calling.

And he was disconcerted but, in his impecunious circumstances, relieved to hear the bill would go on his hospitable if absent host's account; no question, assured the mechanic. It was the master's custom.

Time for another whisky as he tried, unsuccessfully, to call Beauty and tell her he would be late; but the lines were still down, although, miraculously, the storm had cleared as the moon rose and now a glance between the velvet curtains revealed a landscape as of ivory with an inlay of silver. Then the spaniel appeared again, with his hat in her careful mouth, prettily wagging her tail, as if to tell him it was time to be gone, that this magical hospitality was over.

As the door swung to behind him, he saw the lion's eyes were made of agate.

Great wreaths of snow now precariously curded the rose trees and, when he brushed against a stem on his way to the gate, a chill armful softly thudded to the ground to reveal, as if miraculously preserved beneath it, one last, single, perfect rose that might have been the last rose left living in all the white winter, and of so intense and yet delicate a fragrance it seemed to ring like a dulcimer on the frozen air.

How could his host, so mysterious, so kind, deny Beauty her present?

Not now distant but close at hand, close as that mahogany front door, rose a mighty, furious roaring; the garden seemed to hold its breath in apprehension. But still, because he loved his daughter, Beauty's father stole the rose.

At that, every window of the house blazed with furious light and a fugal baying, as of a pride of lions, introduced his host.

There is always a dignity about great bulk, an assertiveness, a quality of being more *there* than most of us are. The being who now confronted Beauty's father seemed to him, in his confusion, vaster than the house he owned, ponderous yet swift, and the moonlight glittered on his great, mazy head of hair, on the eyes green as agate, on the golden hairs of the great paws that grasped his shoulders so that their claws pierced the sheepskin as he shook him like an angry child shakes a doll.

This leonine apparition shook Beauty's father until his teeth rattled and then dropped him sprawling on his knees while the spaniel, darting from the open door, danced round them, yapping distractedly, like a lady at whose dinner party blows have been exchanged.

'My good fellow – ' stammered Beauty's father; but the only response was a renewed roar.

'Good fellow? I am no good fellow! I am the Beast, and you must call me Beast, while I call you, Thief!'

'Forgive me for robbing your garden, Beast!'

Head of a lion; mane and mighty paws of a lion; he reared on his hind legs like an angry lion yet wore a smoking jacket of dull red brocade and was the owner of that lovely house and the low hills that cupped it.

'It was for my daughter,' said Beauty's father. 'All she wanted, in the whole world, was one white, perfect rose.'

The Beast rudely snatched the photograph her father drew from his wallet and inspected it, first brusquely, then with a strange kind of wonder, almost the dawning of surmise. The camera had captured a certain look she had, sometimes, of absolute sweetness and absolute gravity, as if her eyes might pierce appearances and see your soul. When he handed the picture back, the Beast took good care not to scratch the surface with his claws.

'Take her the rose, then, but bring her to dinner,' he growled; and what else was there to be done?

Although her father had told her of the nature of the one who waited for her, she could not control an instinctual shudder of fear when she saw him, for a lion is a lion and a man is a man and, though lions are more beautiful by far than we are, yet they belong to a different order of beauty and, besides, they have no respect for us: why should they? Yet wild things have a far more rational fear of us than is ours of them, and some kind of sadness in his agate eyes, that looked almost blind, as if sick of sight, moved her heart.

He sat, impassive as a figurehead, at the top of the table; the dining room was Queen Anne, tapestried, a gem. Apart from an aromatic soup kept hot over a spirit lamp, the food, though exquisite, was cold – a cold bird, a cold soufflé, cheese. He asked her father to serve them from a buffet and, himself, ate nothing. He grudgingly admitted what she had already guessed, that he disliked the presence of servants because, she thought, a constant human presence would remind him too bitterly of his otherness, but the spaniel sat at his feet throughout the meal, jumping up from time to time to see that everything was in order.

How strange he was. She found his bewildering difference from herself almost intolerable; its presence choked her. There seemed a heavy, soundless pressure upon her in his house, as if it lay under water, and when she saw the great paws lying on the arm of his chair, she thought: they are the death of any tender herbivore. And such a one she felt herself to be, Miss Lamb, spotless, sacrificial.

Yet she stayed, and smiled, because her father wanted her to do so; and when the Beast told her how he would aid her father's appeal against the judgment, she smiled with both her mouth and her eyes. But when, as they sipped their brandy, the Beast, in the diffuse, rumbling purr with which he conversed, suggested, with a hint of shyness, of fear of refusal, that she should stay here, with him, in comfort, while her father returned to London to take up the legal cudgels again, she forced a smile. For she knew with a pang of dread, as soon as he spoke, that it would be so and her visit to the Beast must be, on some magically reciprocal scale, the price of her father's good fortune.

Do not think she had no will of her own; only, she was possessed by a sense of obligation to an unusual degree and, besides, she would gladly have gone to the ends of the earth for her father, whom she loved dearly.

Her bedroom contained a marvellous glass bed; she had a bathroom, with towels thick as fleece and vials of suave unguents; and a little parlour of her own, the walls of which were covered with an antique paper of birds of paradise and Chinamen, where there were precious books and pictures and the flowers grown by invisible gardeners in the Beast's hothouses. Next morning, her father kissed her and drove away with a renewed hope about him that made her glad, but, all the same, she longed for the shabby home of their poverty. The unaccustomed luxury about her she found poignant, because it gave no pleasure to its possessor and himself she did not see all day as if, curious reversal, she frightened him, although the spaniel came and sat with her, to keep her company. Today, the spaniel wore a neat choker of turquoises.

Who prepared her meals? Loneliness of the Beast; all the time she stayed there, she saw no evidence of another human presence but the trays of food that arrived on a dumb waiter inside a mahogany cupboard in her parlour. Dinner was eggs Benedict and grilled veal; she ate it as she browsed in a book she had found in the rosewood revolving bookcase, a collection of courtly and elegant French fairy tales about white cats who were transformed princesses and fairies who were birds. Then she pulled a sprig of muscat grapes from a fat bunch for her dessert and found herself yawning; she discovered she was bored. At that, the spaniel took hold of her skirt with its velvet mouth and gave it a firm but gentle tug. She allowed the dog to trot before her to the study in which her father had been entertained and there, to her well-disguised dismay, she found her host, seated beside the fire with a tray of coffee at his elbow from which she must pour.

The voice that seemed to issue from a cave full of echoes, his dark, soft rumbling growl; after her day of pastel-coloured idleness, how could she converse with the possessor of a voice that seemed an instrument created to inspire the terror that the chords of great organs bring? Fascinated, almost awed, she watched the firelight play on the gold fringes of his mane; he was irradiated, as if with a kind of halo, and she thought of the first great beast of the Apocalypse, the winged lion with his paw upon the Gospel, Saint Mark. Small talk turned to dust in her mouth; small talk had never, at the best of times, been Beauty's forte, and she had little practice at it.

But he, hesitantly, as if he himself were in awe of a young girl who looked as if she had been carved out of a single pearl, asked after her father's law case; and her dead mother; and how they, who had been so rich, had come to be so poor. He forced himself to master his shyness, which was that of a wild creature, and so she contrived to master her own – to such effect that soon she was chattering away to him as if she had known him all her life. When the little cupid in the gilt clock on the mantelpiece struck its miniature tambourine, she was astonished to discover it did so twelve times.

'So late! You will want to sleep,' he said.

At that, they both fell silent, as if these strange companions were suddenly overcome with embarrassment to find themselves together, alone, in that room in the depths of the winter's night. As she was about to rise, he flung himself at her feet and buried his head in her lap. She stayed stock-still, transfixed; she felt his hot breath on her fingers, the stiff bristles of his muzzle grazing her skin, the rough lapping of his tongue and then, with a flood of compassion, understood: all he is doing is kissing my hands.

He drew back his head and gazed at her with his green, inscrutable eyes, in which she saw her face repeated twice, as small as if it were in bud. Then, without another word, he sprang from the room and she saw, with an indescribable shock, he went on all fours.

Next day, all day, the hills on which the snow still settled echoed with the Beast's rumbling roar: has master gone a-hunting? Beauty asked the spaniel. But the spaniel growled, almost bad-temperedly, as if to say, that she would not have answered, even if she could have.

Beauty would pass the day in her suite reading or, perhaps, doing a little embroidery; a box of coloured silks and a frame had been provided for her. Or, well wrapped up, she wandered in the walled garden, among the leafless roses, with the spaniel at her heels, and did a little raking and rearranging. An idle, restful time; a holiday. The enchantment of that bright, sad, pretty place enveloped her and she found that, against all her expectations, she was happy there. She no longer felt the slightest apprehension at her nightly interviews with the Beast. All the natural laws of the world were held in suspension, here, where an army of invisibles tenderly waited on her, and she would talk with the lion, under the patient chaperonage of the brown-eyed dog, on the nature of the moon and its borrowed light, about the stars and the substances of which they were made, about the variable transformations of the weather. Yet still his strangeness made her shiver; and when he helplessly fell before her to kiss her hands, as he did every night when they parted, she would retreat nervously into her skin, flinching at his touch.

The telephone shrilled; for her. Her father. Such news!

The Beast sunk his great head on to his paws. You will come back to me? It will be lonely here, without you.

She was moved almost to tears that he should care for her so. It was in her heart to drop a kiss upon his shaggy mane but, though she stretched out her hand towards him, she could not bring herself to touch him of her own free will, he was so different from herself. But, yes, she said; I will come back. Soon, before the winter is over. Then the taxi came and took her away.

You are never at the mercy of the elements in London, where the huddled warmth of humanity melts the snow before it has time to settle; and her father was as good as rich again, since his hirsute friend's lawyers had the business so well in hand that his credit brought them nothing but the best. A resplendent hotel; the opera, theatres; a whole new wardrobe for his darling, so she could step out on his arm to parties, to receptions, to restaurants, and life was as she had never known it, for her father had ruined himself before her birth killed her mother.

Although the Beast was the source of this new-found prosperity and they talked of him often, now that they were so far away from the timeless spell of his house it seemed to possess the radiant and finite quality of dream and the Beast himself, so monstrous, so benign, some kind of spirit of good fortune who had smiled on them and let them go. She sent him flowers, white roses in return for the ones he had given her; and when she left the florist, she experienced a sudden sense of perfect freedom, as if she had just escaped from an unknown danger, had been grazed by the possibility of some change but, finally, left intact. Yet, with this exhilaration, a desolating emptiness. But her father was waiting for her at the hotel; they had planned a delicious expedition to buy her furs and she was as eager for the treat as any girl might be.

Since the flowers in the shop were the same all the year round, nothing in the window could tell her that winter had almost gone.

Returning late from supper after the theatre, she took off her earrings in front of the mirror; Beauty. She smiled at herself with satisfaction. She was learning, at the end of her adolescence, how to be a spoiled child and that pearly skin of hers was plumping out, a little, with high living and compliments. A certain inwardness was beginning to transform the lines around her mouth, those signatures of the personality, and her sweetness and her gravity could sometimes turn a mite petulant when things went not quite as she wanted them to go. You could not have said that her freshness was fading but she smiled at herself in mirrors a little too often, these days, and the face that smiled back was not quite the one she had seen contained in the Beast's agate eyes. Her face was acquiring, instead of beauty, a lacquer of the invincible prettiness that characterizes certain pampered, exquisite, expensive cats.

The soft wind of spring breathed in from the near-by park through the open windows; she did not know why it made her want to cry.

There was a sudden, urgent, scrabbling sound, as of claws, at her door.

Her trance before the mirror broke; all at once, she remembered everything perfectly. Spring was here and she had broken her promise. Now the Beast himself had come in pursuit of her! First, she was frightened of his anger; then, mysteriously joyful, she ran to open the door. But it was his liver and white spotted spaniel who hurled herself into the girl's arms in a flurry of little barks and gruff murmurings, of whimpering and relief.

Yet where was the well-brushed, jewelled dog who had sat beside her embroidery frame in the parlour with birds of paradise nodding on the walls? This one's fringed ears were matted with mud, her coat was dusty and snarled, she was thin as a dog that has walked a long way and, if she had not been a dog, she would have been in tears.

After that first, rapturous greeting, she did not wait for Beauty to order her food and water; she seized the chiffon hem of her evening dress, whimpered and tugged. Threw back her head, howled, then tugged and whimpered again.

There was a slow, late train that would take her to the station where she had left for London three months ago. Beauty scribbled a note for her father, threw a coat round her shoulders. Quickly, quickly, urged the spaniel soundlessly; and Beauty knew the Beast was dying.

In the thick dark before dawn, the station master roused a sleepy driver for her. Fast as you can.

It seemed December still possessed his garden. The ground was hard as iron, the skirts of the dark cypress moved on the chill wind with a mournful rustle and there were no green shoots on the roses as if, this year, they would not bloom. And not one light in any of the windows, only, in the topmost attic, the faintest smear of radiance on a pane, the thin ghost of a light on the verge of extinction.

The spaniel had slept a little, in her arms, for the poor thing was exhausted. But now her grieving agitation fed Beauty's urgency and, as the girl pushed open the front door, she saw, with a thrust of conscience, how the golden door knocker was thickly muffled in black crêpe.

The door did not open silently, as before, but with a doleful groaning of the hinges and, this time, on to perfect darkness. Beauty clicked her gold cigarette lighter; the tapers in the chandelier had drowned in their own wax and the prisms were wreathed with drifting arabesques of cobwebs. The flowers in the glass jars were dead, as if nobody had had the heart to replace them after she was gone. Dust, everywhere; and it was cold. There was an air of exhaustion, of despair in the house and, worse, a kind of physical disillusion, as if its glamour had been sustained by a cheap conjuring trick and now the conjurer, having failed to pull the crowds, had departed to try his luck elsewhere.

Beauty found a candle to light her way and followed the faithful spaniel up the staircase, past the study, past her suite, through a house echoing with desertion up a little back staircase dedicated to mice and spiders, stumbling, ripping the hem of her dress in her haste.

What a modest bedroom! An attic, with a sloping roof, they might have given the chambermaid if the Beast had employed staff. A night light on the mantelpiece, no curtains at the windows, no carpet on the floor and a narrow, iron bedstead on which he lay, sadly diminished, his bulk scarcely disturbing the faded patchwork quilt, his mane a greyish rat's nest and his eyes closed. On the stick-backed chair where his clothes had been thrown, the roses she had sent him were thrust into the jug from the washstand but they were all dead.

The spaniel jumped up on the bed and burrowed her way under the scanty covers, softly keening.

'Oh, Beast,' said Beauty. 'I have come home.'

His eyelids flickered. How was it she had never noticed before that his agate eyes were equipped with lids, like those of a man? Was it because she had only looked at her own face, reflected there?

'I'm dying, Beauty,' he said in a cracked whisper of his former purr. 'Since you left me, I have been sick. I could not go hunting, I found I had not the stomach to kill the gentle beasts, I could not eat. I am sick and I must die; but I shall die happy because you have come to say good-bye to me.'

She flung herself upon him, so that the iron bedstead groaned, and covered his poor paws with her kisses.

'Don't die, Beast! If you'll have me, I'll never leave you.'

When her lips touched the meat-hook claws, they drew back into their pads and she saw how he had always kept his fists clenched but now, painfully, tentatively, at last began to stretch his fingers. Her tears fell on his face like snow and, under their soft transformation, the bones showed through the pelt, the flesh through the wide, tawny brow. And then it was no longer a lion in her arms but a man, a man with an unkempt mane of hair and, how strange, a broken nose, such as the noses of retired boxers, that gave him a distant, heroic resemblance to the handsomest of all the beasts.

'Do you know,' said Mr Lyon, 'I think I might be able to

manage a little breakfast today, Beauty, if you would eat something with me.'

Mr and Mrs Lyon walk in the garden; the old spaniel drowses on the grass, in a drift of fallen petals.

THE TIGER'S BRIDE

MY FATHER LOST me to The Beast at cards.

There's a special madness strikes travellers from the North when they reach the lovely land where the lemon trees grow. We come from countries of cold weather; at home, we are at war with nature but here, oh! you think you've come to the blessed plot where the lion lies down with the lamb. Everything flowers; no harsh wind stirs the voluptuous air. The sun spills fruit for you. And the deathly, sensual lethargy of the sweet South infects the starved brain; it gasps: 'Luxury! more luxury!' But then the snow comes, you cannot escape it, it followed us from Russia as if it ran behind our carriage, and in this dark, bitter city has caught up with us at last, flocking against the windowpanes to mock my father's expectations of perpetual pleasure as the veins in his forehead stand out and throb, his hands shake as he deals the Devil's picture books.

The candles dropped hot, acrid gouts of wax on my bare shoulders. I watched with the furious cynicism peculiar to women whom circumstances force mutely to witness folly, while my father, fired in his desperation by more and yet more draughts of the firewater they call 'grappa', rids himself of the last scraps of my inheritance. When we left Russia, we owned black earth, blue forest with bear and wild boar, serfs, cornfields, farmyards, my beloved horses, white nights of cool summer, the fireworks of the northern lights. What a burden all those possessions must have been to him, because he laughs as if with glee as he beggars himself; he is in such a passion to donate all to The Beast.

Everyone who comes to this city must play a hand with the *grand seigneur*; few come. They did not warn us at Milan, or, if they did, we did not understand them – my limping Italian, the bewildering dialect of the region. Indeed, I myself spoke up in favour of this remote, provincial place, out of fashion two hundred years, because, oh irony, it boasted no casino. I did not know that the price of a stay in its Decembral solitude was a game with Milord.

The hour was late. The chill damp of this place creeps into the stones, into your bones, into the spongy pith of the lungs; it insinuated itself with a shiver into our parlour, where Milord came to play in the privacy essential to him. Who could refuse the invitation his valet brought to our lodging? Not my profligate father, certainly; the mirror above the table gave me back his frenzy, my impassivity, the withering candles, the emptying bottles, the coloured tide of the cards as they rose and fell, the still mask that concealed all the features of The Beast but for the yellow eyes that strayed, now and then, from his unfurled hand towards myself.

'La Bestia!' said our landlady, gingerly fingering an envelope with his huge crest of a tiger rampant on it, something of fear, something of wonder in her face. And I could not ask her why they called the master of the place, 'La Bestia' – was it to do with that heraldic signature? – because her tongue was so thickened by the phlegmy, bronchitic speech of the region I scarcely managed to make out a thing she said except, when she saw me: 'Che bella!'

Since I could toddle, always the pretty one, with my glossy, nut-brown curls, my rosy cheeks. And born on Christmas Day – her 'Christmas rose', my English nurse called me. The peasants said: 'The living image of her mother,' crossing themselves out of respect for the dead. My mother did not blossom long; bartered for her dowry to such a feckless sprig of the Russian nobility that she soon died of his gaming, his whoring, his agonizing repentances. And The Beast gave me the rose from his own impeccable if outmoded buttonhole when he arrived, the valet brushing the snow off his black cloak. This white rose, unnatural, out of season, that now my nervous fingers ripped, petal by petal, apart as my father magnificently concluded the career he had made of catastrophe.

This is a melancholy, introspective region; a sunless, featureless landscape, the sullen river sweating fog, the shorn, hunkering willows. And a cruel city; the sombre piazza, a place uniquely suited to public executions, under the beetling shadow of that malign barn of a church. They used to hang condemned men in cages from the city walls; unkindness comes naturally to them, their eyes are set too close together, they have thin lips. Poor food, pasta soaked in oil, boiled beef with sauce of bitter herbs. A funereal hush about the place, the inhabitants huddled up against the cold so you can hardly see their faces. And they lie to you and cheat you, innkeepers, coachmen, everybody. God, how they fleeced us!

The treacherous South, where you think there is no winter but forget you take it with you.

My senses were increasingly troubled by the fuddling perfume of Milord, far too potent a reek of purplish civet at such close quarters in so small a room. He must bathe himself in scent, soak his shirts and underlinen in it; what can he smell of, that needs so much camouflage?

I never saw a man so big look so two-dimensional, in spite of the quaint elegance of The Beast, in the old-fashioned tailcoat that might, from its looks, have been bought in those distant years before he imposed seclusion on himself; he does not feel he need keep up with the times. There is a crude clumsiness about his outlines, that are on the ungainly, giant side; and he has an odd air of self-imposed restraint, as if fighting a battle with himself to remain upright when he would far rather drop down on all fours. He throws our human aspirations to the godlike sadly awry, poor fellow; only from a distance would you think The Beast not much different from any other man, although he wears a mask with a man's face painted most beautifully on it. Oh, yes, a beautiful face; but one with too much formal symmetry of feature to be entirely human: one profile of his mask is the mirror image of the other, too perfect, uncanny. He wears a wig, too, false hair tied at the nape with a bow, a wig of the kind you see in old-fashioned portraits. A chaste silk stock stuck with a pearl hides his throat. And gloves of blond kid that are yet so huge and clumsy they do not seem to cover hands.

He is a carnival figure made of papier mâché and crêpe hair; and yet he has the Devil's knack at cards.

His masked voice echoes as from a great distance as he stoops over his hand and he has such a growling impediment in his speech that only his valet, who understands him, can interpret for him, as if his master were the clumsy doll and he the ventriloquist.

The wick slumped in the eroded wax, the candles guttered.

By the time my rose had lost all its petals, my father, too, was left with nothing.

'Except the girl.'

Gambling is a sickness. My father said he loved me yet he staked his daughter on a hand of cards. He fanned them out; in the mirror, I saw wild hope light up his eyes. His collar was unfastened, his rumpled hair stood up on end, he had the anguish of a man in the last stages of debauchery. The draughts came out of the old walls and bit me, I was colder than I'd ever been in Russia, when nights are coldest there.

A queen, a king, an ace. I saw them in the mirror. Oh, I know he thought he could not lose me; besides, back with me would come all he had lost, the unravelled fortunes of our family at one blow restored. And would he not win, as well, The Beast's hereditary palazzo outside the city; his immense revenues; his lands around the river; his rents, his treasure chest, his Mantegnas, his Giulio Romanos, his Cellini salt-cellars, his titles . . . the very city itself.

You must not think my father valued me at less than a king's ransom; but, at *no more* than a king's ransom.

It was cold as hell in the parlour. And it seemed to me, child of the severe North, that it was not my flesh but, truly, my father's soul that was in peril.

My father, of course, believed in miracles; what gambler does not? In pursuit of just such a miracle as this, had we not travelled from the land of bears and shooting stars?

So we teetered on the brink.

The Beast bayed; laid down all three remaining aces.

The indifferent servants now glided smoothly forward as on wheels to douse the candles one by one. To look at them you would think that nothing of any moment had occurred. They yawned a little resentfully; it was almost morning, we had kept them out of bed. The Beast's man brought his cloak. My father sat amongst these preparations for departure, staring on at the betrayal of his cards upon the table.

The Beast's man informed me crisply that he, the valet, would call for me and my bags tomorrow, at ten, and conduct me forthwith to The Beast's palazzo. Capisco? So shocked was I that I scarcely did 'capisco'; he repeated my orders patiently, he was a strange, thin, quick little man who walked with an irregular, jolting rhythm upon splayed feet in curious, wedge-shaped shoes.

Where my father had been red as fire, now he was white as the snow that caked the windowpane. His eyes swam; soon he would cry.

'"Like the base Indian,"' he said; he loved rhetoric. '"One whose hand,/Like the base Indian, threw a pearl away/Richer than all his tribe . . ." I have lost my pearl, my pearl beyond price.'

At that, The Beast made a sudden, dreadful noise, halfway between a growl and a roar; the candles flared. The quick valet, the prim hypocrite, interpreted unblinking: 'My master says: If you are so careless of your treasures, you should expect them to be taken from you.'

He gave us the bow and smile his master could not offer us and they departed.

I watched the snow until, just before dawn, it stopped falling; a hard frost settled, next morning there was a light like iron.

The Beast's carriage, of an elegant if antique design, was black as a hearse and it was drawn by a dashing black gelding who blew smoke from his nostrils and stamped upon the packed snow with enough sprightly appearance of life to give me some hope that not all the world was locked in ice, as I was. I had always held a little towards Gulliver's opinion, that horses are better than we are, and, that day, I would have been glad to depart with him to the kingdom of horses, if I'd been given the chance.

The valet sat up on the box in a natty black and gold livery, clasping, of all things, a bunch of his master's damned white roses as if a gift of flowers would reconcile a woman to any humiliation. He sprang down with preternatural agility to place them ceremoniously in my reluctant hand. My tear-beslobbered father wants a rose to show that I forgive him. When I break off a stem, I prick my finger and so he gets his rose all smeared with blood.

The valet crouched at my feet to tuck the rugs about me with a strange kind of unflattering obsequiousness yet he forgot his station sufficiently to scratch busily beneath his white periwig with an over-supple index finger as he offered me what my old nurse would have called an 'old-fashioned look', ironic, sly, a smidgen of disdain in it. And pity? No pity. His eyes were moist and brown, his face seamed with the innocent cunning of an ancient baby. He had an irritating habit of chattering to himself under his breath all the time as he packed up his master's winnings. I drew the curtains to conceal the sight of my father's farewell; my spite was sharp as broken glass

Lost to The Beast! And what, I wondered, might be the exact nature of his 'beastliness'? My English nurse once told me about a tiger-man she saw in London, when she was a little girl, to scare me into good behaviour, for I was a wild wee thing and she could not tame me into submission with a frown or the bribe of a spoonful of jam. If you don't stop plaguing the nursemaids, my beauty, the tiger-man will come and take you away. They'd brought him from Sumatra, in the Indies, she said; his hinder parts were all hairy and only from the head downwards did he resemble a man.

And yet The Beast goes always masked; it cannot be his face that looks like mine.

But the tiger-man, in spite of his hairiness, could take a glass of ale in his hand like a good Christian and drink it down. Had she not seen him do so, at the sign of The George, by the steps of Upper Moor Fields when she was just as high as me and lisped and toddled, too. Then she would sigh for London, across the North Sea of the lapse of years. But, if this young lady was not a good little girl and did not eat her boiled beetroot, then the tiger-man would put on his big black travelling cloak lined with fur, just like your daddy's, and hire the Erl-King's galloper of wind and ride through the night straight to the nursery and –

Yes, my beauty! GOBBLE YOU UP!

How I'd squeal in delighted terror, half believing her, half knowing that she teased me. And there were things I knew that I must not tell her. In our lost farmyard, where the giggling nursemaids initiated me into the mysteries of what the bull did to the cows, I heard about the waggoner's daughter. Hush, hush, don't let on to your nursie we said so; the waggoner's lass, hare-lipped, squint-eyed, ugly as sin, who would have taken her? Yet, to her shame, her belly swelled amid the cruel mockery of the ostlers and her son was born of a bear, they whispered. Born with a full pelt and teeth; that proved it. But, when he grew up, he was a good shepherd, although he never married, lived in a hut outside the village and could make the wind blow any way he wanted to besides being able to tell which eggs would become cocks, which hens.

The wondering peasants once brought my father a skull with horns four inches long on either side of it and would not go back to the field where their poor plough disturbed it until the priest went with them; for this skull had the jaw-bone of a *man*, had it not?

Old wives' tales, nursery fears! I knew well enough the reason for the trepidation I cosily titillated with superstitious marvels of my childhood on the day my childhood ended. For now my own skin was my sole capital in the world and today I'd make my first investment.

We had left the city far behind us and were now traversing a wide, flat dish of snow where the mutilated stumps of the willows flourished their ciliate heads athwart frozen ditches; mist diminished the horizon, brought down the sky until it seemed no more than a few inches above us. As far as eye could see, not one thing living. How starveling, how bereft the dead season of this spurious Eden in which all the fruit was blighted by cold! And my frail roses, already faded. I opened the carriage door and tossed the defunct bouquet into the rucked, frost-stiff mud of the road. Suddenly a sharp, freezing wind arose and pelted my face with a dry rice of powdered snow. The mist lifted sufficiently to reveal before me an acreage of half-derelict façades of sheer red brick, the vast man-trap, the megalomaniac citadel of his palazzo.

It was a world in itself but a dead one, a burned-out planet. I saw The Beast bought solitude, not luxury, with his money.

The little black horse trotted smartly through the figured bronze doors that stood open to the weather like those of a barn and the valet handed me out of the carriage on to the scarred tiles of the great hall itself, into the odorous warmth of a stable, sweet with hay, acrid with horse dung. An equine chorus of neighings and soft drummings of hooves broke out beneath the tall roof, where the beams were scabbed with last summer's swallows' nests; a dozen gracile muzzles lifted from their mangers and turned towards us, ears erect. The Beast had given his horses the use of the dining room. The walls were painted, aptly enough, with a fresco of horses, dogs and men in a wood where fruit and blossom grew on the bough together.

The valet tweaked politely at my sleeve. Milord is waiting.

Gaping doors and broken windows let the wind in everywhere. We mounted one staircase after another, our feet clopping on the marble. Through archways and open doors, I glimpsed suites of vaulted chambers opening one out of another like systems of Chinese boxes into the infinite complexity of the innards of the place. He and I and the wind were the only things stirring; and all the furniture was under dust sheets, the chandeliers bundled up in cloth, pictures taken from their hooks and propped with their faces to the walls as if their master could not bear to look at them. The palace was dismantled, as if its owner were about to move house or had never properly moved in; The Beast had chosen to live in an uninhabited place.

The valet darted me a reassuring glance from his brown, eloquent eyes, yet a glance with so much queer superciliousness in it that it did not comfort me, and went bounding ahead of me on his bandy legs, softly chattering to himself. I held my head high and followed him; but, for all my pride, my heart was heavy.

Milord has his eyrie high above the house, a small, stifling, darkened room; he keeps his shutters locked at noon. I was out of breath by the time we reached it and returned to him the silence with which he greeted me. I will not smile. He cannot smile.

In his rarely disturbed privacy, The Beast wears a garment of Ottoman design, a loose, dull purple gown with gold embroidery round the neck that falls from his shoulders to conceal his feet. The feet of the chair he sits in are handsomely clawed. He hides his hands in his ample sleeves. The artificial masterpiece of his face appals me. A small fire in a small grate. A rushing wind rattles the shutters.

The valet coughed. To him fell the delicate task of transmitting to me his master's wishes.

'My master – '

A stick fell in the grate. It made a mighty clatter in that dreadful silence; the valet started; lost his place in his speech, began again.

'My master has but one desire.'

The thick, rich, wild scent with which Milord had soaked himself the previous evening hangs all about us, ascends in cursive blue from the smoke of a precious Chinese pot.

'He wishes only – '

Now, in the face of my impassivity, the valet twittered, his ironic composure gone, for the desire of a master, however trivial, may yet sound unbearably insolent in the mouth of a servant and his role of go-between clearly caused him a good deal of embarrassment. He gulped; he swallowed, at last contrived to unleash an unpunctuated flood.

'My master's sole desire is to see the pretty young lady unclothed nude without her dress and that only for the one time after which she will be returned to her father undamaged with bankers' orders for the sum which he lost to my master at cards and also a number of fine presents such as furs, jewels and horses – '

I remained standing. During this interview, my eyes were level with those inside the mask that now evaded mine as if, to his credit, he was ashamed of his own request even as his mouthpiece made it for him. Agitato, molto agitato, the valet wrung his white-gloved hands.

'Desnuda – '

I could scarcely believe my ears. I let out a raucous guffaw; no young lady laughs like that! my old nurse used to remonstrate. But I did. And do. At the clamour of my heartless mirth, the valet danced backwards with perturbation, palpitating his fingers as if attempting to wrench them off, expostulating, wordlessly pleading. I felt that I owed it to him to make my reply in as exquisite a Tuscan as I could master.

'You may put me in a windowless room, sir, and I promise you I will pull my skirt up to my waist, ready for you. But there must be a sheet over my face, to hide it; though the sheet must be laid over me so lightly that it will not choke me. So I shall be covered completely from the waist upwards, and no lights. There you can visit me once, sir, and only the once. After that I must be driven directly to the city and deposited in the public square, in front of the church. If you wish to give me money, then I should be pleased to receive it. But I must stress that you should give me only the same amount of money that you would give to any other woman in such circumstances. However, if you choose not to give me a present, then that is your right.'

How pleased I was to see I struck The Beast to the heart! For, after a baker's dozen heartbeats, one single tear swelled, glittering, at the corner of the masked eye. A tear! A tear, I hoped, of shame. The tear trembled for a moment on an edge of painted bone, then tumbled down the painted cheek to fall, with an abrupt tinkle, on the tiled floor.

The valet, ticking and clucking to himself, hastily ushered me out of the room. A mauve cloud of his master's perfume billowed out into the chill corridor with us and dissipated itself on the spinning winds.

A cell had been prepared for me, a veritable cell, windowless, airless, lightless, in the viscera of the palace. The valet lit a lamp for me; a narrow bed, a dark cupboard with fruit and flowers carved on it bulked out of the gloom.

'I shall twist a noose out of my bed linen and hang myself with it,' I said.

'Oh, no,' said the valet, fixing upon me wide and suddenly melancholy eyes. 'Oh, no, you will not. You are a woman of honour.'

And what was *he* doing in my bedroom, this jigging caricature of a man? Was he to be my warder until I submitted to The Beast's whim or he to mine? Am I in such reduced circumstances that I may not have a lady's maid? As if in reply to my unspoken demand, the valet clapped his hands.

'To assuage your loneliness, madame ...'

A knocking and clattering behind the door of the cupboard; the door swings open and out glides a soubrette from an operetta, with glossy, nut-brown curls, rosy cheeks, blue, rolling eyes; it takes me a moment to recognize her, in her little cap, her white stockings, her frilled petticoats. She carries a looking glass in one hand and a powder puff in the other and there is a musical box where her heart should be; she tinkles as she rolls towards me on her tiny wheels.

'Nothing human lives here,' said the valet.

My maid halted, bowed; from a split seam at the side of her bodice protrudes the handle of a key. She is a marvellous machine, the most delicately balanced system of cords and pulleys in the world.

'We have dispensed with servants,' the valet said. 'We surround ourselves, instead, for utility and pleasure, with simulacra and find it no less convenient than do most gentlemen.'

This clockwork twin of mine halted before me, her bowels

churning out a settecento minuet, and offered me the bold carnation of her smile. Click, click – she raises her arm and busily dusts my cheeks with pink, powdered chalk that makes me cough; then thrusts towards me her little mirror.

I saw within it not my own face but that of my father, as if I had put on his face when I arrived at The Beast's palace as the discharge of his debt. What, you self-deluding fool, are you crying still? And drunk, too. He tossed back his grappa and hurled the tumbler away.

Seeing my astonished fright, the valet took the mirror away from me, breathed on it, polished it with the ham of his gloved fist, handed it back to me. Now all I saw was myself, haggard from a sleepless night, pale enough to need my maid's supply of rouge.

I heard the key turn in the heavy door and the valet's footsteps patter down the stone passage. Meanwhile, my double continued to powder the air, emitting her jangling tune but, as it turned out, she was not inexhaustible; soon she was powdering more and yet more languorously, her metal heart slowed in imitation of fatigue, her musical box ran down until the notes separated themselves out of the tune and plopped like single raindrops and, as if sleep had overtaken her, at last she moved no longer. As she succumbed to sleep, I had no option but to do so, too. I dropped on that narrow bed as if felled.

Time passed but I do not know how much; then the valet woke me with rolls and honey. I gestured the tray away but he set it down firmly beside the lamp and took from it a little shagreen box, which he offered to me.

I turned away my head.

'Oh, my lady!' Such hurt cracked his high-pitched voice! He dextrously unfastened the gold clasp; on a bed of crimson velvet lay a single diamond earring, perfect as a tear.

I snapped the box shut and tossed it into a corner. This sudden, sharp movement must have disturbed the mechanism of the doll; she jerked her arm almost as if to reprimand me, letting out a rippling fart of gavotte. Then was still again.

'Very well,' said the valet, put out. And indicated it was time for me to visit my host again. He did not let me wash or comb my hair. There was so little natural light in the interior of the palace that I could not tell whether it was day or night.

You would not think The Beast had budged an inch since I last saw him; he sat in his huge chair, with his hands in his sleeves, and the heavy air never moved. I might have slept an hour, a night, or a month, but his sculptured calm, the stifling air remained just as it had been. The incense rose from the pot, still traced the same signature on the air. The same fire burned.

Take off my clothes for you, like a ballet girl? Is that all you want of me?

'The sight of a young lady's skin that no man has seen before – ' stammered the valet.

I wished I'd rolled in the hay with every lad on my father's farm, to disqualify myself from this humiliating bargain. That he should want so little was the reason why I could not give it; I did not need to speak for The Beast to understand me.

A tear came from his other eye. And then he moved; he buried his cardboard carnival head with its ribboned weight of false hair in, I would say, his arms; he withdrew his, I might say, hands from his sleeves and I saw his furred pads, his excoriating claws.

The dropped tear caught upon his fur and shone. And in my room for hours I hear those paws pad back and forth outside my door.

When the valet arrived again with his silver salver, I had a pair of diamond earrings of the finest water in the world; I threw the other into the corner where the first one lay. The valet twittered with aggrieved regret but did not offer to lead me to The Beast again. Instead, he smiled ingratiatingly and confided: 'My master, he say: invite the young lady to go riding.'

'What's this?'

He briskly mimicked the action of a gallop and, to my amazement, tunelessly croaked: 'Tantivy! tantivy! a-hunting we will go!'

'I'll run away, I'll ride to the city.'

'Oh, no,' he said. 'Are you not a woman of honour?'

He clapped his hands and my maidservant clicked and jangled into the imitation of life. She rolled towards the cupboard where she had come from and reached inside it to fetch out over her synthetic arm my riding habit. Of all things. My very own riding habit, that I'd left behind me in a trunk in a loft in that country house outside Petersburg that we'd lost long ago, before, even, we set out on this wild pilgrimage to the cruel South. Either the very riding habit my old nurse had sewn for me or else a copy of it perfect to the lost button on the right sleeve, the ripped hem held up with a pin. I turned the worn cloth about in my hands, looking for a clue. The wind that sprinted through the palace made the door tremble in its frame; had the north wind blown my garments across Europe to me? At home, the bear's son directed the winds at his pleasure; what democracy of magic held this palace and the fir forest in common? Or, should I be prepared to accept it as proof of the axiom my father had drummed into me: that, if you have enough money, anything is possible?

'Tantivy,' suggested the now twinkling valet, evidently charmed at the pleasure mixed with my bewilderment. The clockwork maid held my jacket out to me and I allowed myself to shrug into it as if reluctantly, although I was half mad to get out into the open air, away from this deathly palace, even in such company.

The doors of the hall let the bright day in; I saw that it was morning. Our horses, saddled and bridled, beasts in bondage, were waiting for us, striking sparks from the tiles with their impatient hooves while their stablemates lolled at ease among the straw, conversing with one another in the mute speech of horses. A pigeon or two, feathers puffed to keep out the cold, strutted about, pecking at ears of corn. The little black gelding who had brought me here greeted me with a ringing neigh that resonated inside the misty roof as in a sounding box and I knew he was meant for me to ride.

I always adored horses, noblest of creatures, such wounded sensitivity in their wise eyes, such rational restraint of energy at their high-strung hindquarters. I lirruped and hurrumphed to my shining black companion and he acknowledged my greeting with a kiss on the forehead from his soft lips. There was a little shaggy pony nuzzling away at the *trompe l'œil* foliage beneath the hooves of the painted horses on the wall, into whose saddle the valet sprang with a flourish as of the circus. Then The Beast, wrapped in a black fur-lined cloak, came to heave himself aloft a grave grey mare. No natural horseman he; he clung to her mane like a shipwrecked sailor to a spar.

Cold, that morning, yet dazzling with the sharp winter sunlight that wounds the retina. There was a scurrying wind about that seemed to go with us, as if the masked, immense one who did not speak carried it inside his cloak and let it out at his pleasure, for it stirred the horses' manes but did not lift the lowland mists.

A bereft landscape in the sad browns and sepias of winter lay all about us, the marshland drearily protracting itself towards the wide river. Those decapitated willows. Now and then, the swoop of a bird, its irreconcilable cry.

A profound sense of strangeness slowly began to possess me. I knew my two companions were not, in any way, as other men, the simian retainer and the master for whom he spoke, the one with clawed fore-paws who was in a plot with the witches who let the winds out of their knotted handkerchiefs up towards the Finnish border. I knew they lived according to a different logic than I had done until my father abandoned me to the wild beasts by his human carelessness. This knowledge gave me a certain fearfulness still; but, I would say, not much . . . I was a young girl, a virgin, and therefore men denied me rationality just as they denied it to all those who were not exactly like themselves, in all their unreason. If I could see not one single soul in that wilderness of desolation all around me, then the six of us – mounts and riders, both – could boast amongst us not one soul, either, since all the best religions in the world state categorically that not beasts nor women were equipped with the flimsy, insubstantial things when the good Lord opened the gates of Eden and let Eve and her familiars tumble out. Understand, then, that though I would not say I privately engaged in metaphysical speculation as we rode through the reedy approaches to the river, I certainly meditated on the nature of my own state, how I had been bought and sold, passed from hand to hand. That clockwork girl who powdered my cheeks for me; had I not been allotted only the same kind of imitative life amongst men that the doll-maker had given her?

Yet, as to the true nature of the being of this clawed magus who rode his pale horse in a style that made me recall how Kublai Khan's leopards went out hunting on horseback, of that I had no notion.

We came to the bank of the river that was so wide we could not see across it, so still with winter that it scarcely seemed to flow. The horses lowered their heads to drink. The valet cleared his throat, about to speak; we were in a place of perfect privacy, beyond a brake of winter-bare rushes, a hedge of reeds.

'If you will not let him see you without your clothes – '

I involuntarily shook my head –

'– you must, then, prepare yourself for the sight of my master, naked.'

The river broke on the pebbles with a diminishing sigh. My composure deserted me; all at once I was on the brink of panic. I did not think that I could bear the sight of him, whatever he was. The mare raised her dripping muzzle and looked at me keenly, as if urging me. This river broke again at my feet. I was far from home.

'You,' said the valet, 'must.'

When I saw how scared he was I might refuse, I nodded.

The reed bowed down in a sudden snarl of wind that brought with it a gust of the heavy odour of his disguise. The valet held out his master's cloak to screen him from me as he removed the mask. The horses stirred.

The tiger will never lie down with the lamb; he acknowledges no pact that is not reciprocal. The lamb must learn to run with the tigers.

A great, feline, tawny shape whose pelt was barred with a savage geometry of bars the colour of burned wood. His domed, heavy head, so terrible he must hide it. How subtle the muscles, how profound the tread. The annihilating vehemence of his eyes, like twin suns.

I felt my breast ripped apart as if I suffered a marvellous wound.

The valet moved forward as if to cover up his master now the girl had acknowledged him, but I said: 'No.' The tiger sat still as a heraldic beast, in the pact he had made with his own ferocity to do me no harm. He was far larger than I could have imagined, from the poor, shabby things I'd seen once, in the Czar's menagerie at Petersburg, the golden fruit of their eyes dimming, withering in the far North of captivity. Nothing about him reminded me of humanity.

I therefore, shivering, now unfastened my jacket, to show him I would do him no harm. Yet I was clumsy and blushed a little, for no man had seen me naked and I was a proud girl. Pride it was, not shame, that thwarted my fingers so; and a certain trepidation lest this frail little article of human upholstery before him might not be, in itself, grand enough to satisfy his expectations of us, since those, for all I knew, might have grown infinite during the endless time he had been waiting. The wind clattered in the rushes, purled and eddied in the river.

I showed his grave silence my white skin, my red nipples, and the horses turned their heads to watch me, also, as if they, too, were courteously curious as to the fleshly nature of women. Then The Beast lowered his massive head; Enough! said the valet with a gesture. The wind died down, all was still again.

Then they went off together, the valet on his pony, the tiger running before him like a hound, and I walked along the river bank for a while. I felt I was at liberty for the first time in my life. Then the winter sun began to tarnish, a few flakes of snow drifted from the darkening sky and, when I returned to the horses, I found The Beast mounted again on his grey mare, cloaked and masked and once more, to all appearances, a man, while the valet had a fine catch of waterfowl dangling from his hand and the corpse of a young roebuck slung behind his saddle. I climbed up on the black gelding in silence and so we returned to the palace as the snow fell more and more heavily, obscuring the tracks that we had left behind us.

The valet did not return me to my cell but, instead, to an elegant, if old-fashioned boudoir with sofas of faded pink brocade, a jinn's treasury of Oriental carpets, tintinnabulation of cut-glass chandeliers. Candles in antlered holders struck rainbows from the prismatic hearts of my diamond earrings, that lay on my new dressing table at which my attentive maid stood ready with her powder puff and mirror. Intending to fix the ornaments in my ears, I took the looking glass from her hand, but it was in the midst of one of its magic fits again and I did not see my own face in it but that of my father; at first I thought he smiled at me. Then I saw he was smiling with pure gratification.

He sat, I saw, in the parlour of our lodgings, at the very table where he had lost me, but now he was busily engaged in counting out a tremendous pile of banknotes. My father's circumstances had changed already; well-shaven, neatly barbered, smart new clothes. A frosted glass of sparkling wine sat convenient to his hand beside an ice bucket. The Beast had clearly paid cash on the nail for his glimpse of my bosom, and paid up promptly, as if it had not been a sight I might have died of showing. Then I saw my father's trunks were packed, ready for departure. Could he so easily leave me here?

There was a note on the table with the money, in a fine hand. I could read it quite clearly. 'The young lady will arrive immediately.' Some harlot with whom he'd briskly negotiated a liaison on the strength of his spoils? Not at all. For, at that moment, the valet knocked at my door to announce that I might leave the palace at any time hereafter, and he bore over his arm a handsome sable cloak, my very own little gratuity, The Beast's morning gift, in which he proposed to pack me up and send me off.

When I looked at the mirror again, my father had disappeared and all I saw was a pale, hollow-eyed girl whom I scarcely recognized. The valet asked politely when he should prepare the carriage, as if he did not doubt that I would leave with my booty at the first opportunity while my maid, whose face was no longer the spit of my own, continued bonnily to beam. I will dress her in my own clothes, wind her up, send her back to perform the part of my father's daughter.

'Leave me alone,' I said to the valet.

He did not need to lock the door, now. I fixed the earrings in my ears. They were very heavy. Then I took off my riding habit, left it where it lay on the floor. But, when I got down to my shift, my arms dropped to my sides. I was unaccustomed to nakedness. I was so unused to my own skin that to take off all my clothes involved a kind of flaying. I thought The Beast had wanted a little thing compared with what I was prepared to give him; but it is not natural for humankind to go naked, not since first we hid our loins with fig leaves. He had demanded the abominable. I felt as much atrocious pain as if I was stripping off my own underpelt and the smiling girl stood poised in the oblivion of her balked simulation of life, watching me peel down to the cold, white meat of contract and, if she did not see me, then so much more like the market place, where the eyes that watch you take no account of your existence.

And it seemed my entire life, since I had left the North, had passed under the indifferent gaze of eyes like hers.

Then I was flinching stark, except for his irreproachable tears.

I huddled in the furs I must return to him, to keep me from the lacerating winds that raced along the corridors. I knew the way to his den without the valet to guide me.

No response to my tentative rap on his door.

Then the wind blew the valet whirling along the passage. He must have decided that, if one should go naked, then all should go naked; without his livery, he revealed himself, as I had suspected, a delicate creature, covered with silken moth-grey fur, brown fingers supple as leather, chocolate muzzle, the gentlest creature in the world. He gibbered a little to see my fine furs and jewels as if I were dressed up for the opera and, with a great deal of tender ceremony, removed the sables from my shoulders. The sables thereupon resolved themselves into a pack of black, squeaking rats that rattled immediately down the stairs on their hard little feet and were lost to sight.

The valet bowed me inside The Beast's room.

The purple dressing gown, the mask, the wig, were laid out on his chair; a glove was planted on each arm. The empty house of his appearance was ready for him but he had abandoned it. There was a reek of fur and piss; the incense pot lay broken in pieces on the floor. Half-burned sticks were scattered from the extinguished fire. A candle stuck by its own grease to the mantelpiece lit two narrow flames in the pupils of the tiger's eyes.

He was pacing backwards and forwards, backwards and forwards, the tip of his heavy tail twitching as he paced out the length and breadth of his imprisonment between the gnawed and bloody bones.

He will gobble you up.

Nursery fears made flesh and sinew; earliest and most archaic of fears, fear of devourment. The beast and his carnivorous bed of bone and I, white, shaking, raw, approaching him as if offering, in myself, the key to a peaceable kingdom in which his appetite need not be my extinction.

He went still as stone. He was far more frightened of me than I was of him.

I squatted on the wet straw and stretched out my hand. I was now within the field of force of his golden eyes. He growled at the back of his throat, lowered his head, sank on to his forepaws, snarled, showed me his red gullet, his yellow teeth. I never moved. He snuffed the air, as if to smell my fear; he could not.

Slowly, slowly he began to drag his heavy, gleaming weight across the floor towards me.

A tremendous throbbing, as of the engine that makes the earth turn, filled the little room; he had begun to purr.

The sweet thunder of this purr shook the old walls, made the shutters batter the windows until they burst apart and let in the white light of the snowy moon. Tiles came crashing down from the roof; I heard them fall into the courtyard far below. The reverberations of his purring rocked the foundations of the house, the walls began to dance. I thought: 'It will all fall, everything will disintegrate.'

He dragged himself closer and closer to me, until I felt the harsh velvet of his head against my hand, then a tongue, abrasive as sandpaper. 'He will lick the skin off me!'

And each stroke of his tongue ripped off skin after successive skin, all the skins of a life in the world, and left behind a nascent patina of shining hairs. My earrings turned back to water and trickled down my shoulders; I shrugged the drops off my beautiful fur.

PUSS-IN-BOOTS

FIGARO HERE; FIGARO, there, I tell you! Figaro upstairs, Figaro downstairs and – oh, my goodness me, this little Figaro can slip into my lady's chamber smart as you like at any time whatsoever that he takes the fancy for, don't you know, he's a cat of the world, cosmopolitan, sophisticated; he can tell when a furry friend is the Missus' best company. For what lady in all the world could say 'no' to the passionate yet toujours discret advances of a fine marmalade cat? (Unless it be her eyes incontinently overflow at the slightest whiff of fur, which happened once, as you shall hear.)

A tom, sirs, a ginger tom and proud of it. Proud of his fine, white shirtfront that dazzles harmoniously against his orange and tangerine tessellations (oh! what a fiery suit of lights have I); proud of his bird-entrancing eye and more than military whiskers; proud, to a fault, some say, of his fine, musical voice. All the windows in the square fly open when I break into impromptu song at the spectacle of the moon above Bergamo. If the poor players in the square, the sullen rout of ragged trash that haunts the provinces, are rewarded with a hail of pennies when they set up their makeshift stage and start their raucous choruses, then how much more liberally do the citizens deluge me with pails of the freshest water, vegetables hardly spoiled and, occasionally, slippers, shoes and boots.

Do you see these fine, high, shining leather boots of mine? A young cavalry officer made me the tribute of, first, one; then, after I celebrate his generosity with a fresh obbligato, the moon no fuller than my heart – whoops! I nimbly spring aside – down comes the other. Their high heels will click like castanets when Puss takes his promenade upon the tiles, for my song recalls flamenco, all cats have a Spanish tinge although Puss himself elegantly lubricates his virile, muscular, native Bergamasque with French, since that is the only language in which you can purr.

'Merrrrrrrrrci!'

Instanter I draw my new boots on over the natty white

stockings that terminate my hinder legs. That young man, observing with curiosity by moonlight the use to which I put his footwear, calls out: 'Hey, Puss! Puss, there!'

'At your service, sir!'

'Up to my balcony, young Puss!'

He leans out, in his nightshirt, offering encouragement as I swing succinctly up the façade, forepaws on a curly cherub's pate, hindpaws on a stucco wreath, bring them up to meet your forepaws while, first paw forward, hup! on to the stone nymph's tit; left paw down a bit, the satyr's bum should do the trick. Nothing to it, once you know how, rococo's no problem. Acrobatics? Born to them; Puss can perform a back somersault whilst holding aloft a glass of vino in his right paw and *never spill a drop.*

But, to my shame, the famous death-defying triple somersault en plein air, that is, in middle air, that is, unsupported and without a safety net, I, Puss, have never yet attempted though often I have dashingly brought off the double tour, to the applause of all.

'You strike me as a cat of parts,' says this young man when I'm arrived at his window-sill. I made him a handsome genuflection, rump out, tail up, head down, to facilitate his friendly chuck under my chin; and, as involuntary free gift, my natural, my habitual smile.

For all cats have this particularity, each and every one, from the meanest alley sneaker to the proudest, whitest she that ever graced a pontiff's pillow – we have our smiles, as it were, painted on. Those small, cool, quiet Mona Lisa smiles that smile we must, no matter whether it's been fun or it's been not. So all cats have a politician's air; we smile and smile and so they think we're villains. But, I note, this young man is something of a smiler hisself.

'A sandwich,' he offers. 'And, perhaps, a snifter of brandy.'

His lodgings are poor, though he's handsome enough and even en déshabillé, nightcap and all, there's a neat, smart, dandified air about him. Here is one who knows what's what, thinks I; a man who keeps up appearances in the bedchamber can never embarrass you out of it. And excellent beef sandwiches; I relish a lean slice of roast beef and early learned a taste for spirits, since I started life as a wine-shop cat, hunting cellar rats for my keep, before the world sharpened my wits enough to let me live by them.

And the upshot of this midnight interview? I'm engaged, on the spot, as Sir's valet: valet de chambre and, from time to time, his body servant, for, when funds are running low, as they must do for every gallant officer when the pickings fall off, he pawns the quilt, doesn't he. Then faithful Puss curls up on his chest to keep him warm at nights. And if he don't like me to knead his nipples, which, out of the purest affection and the desire – ouch! he says – to test the retractability of my claws, I do in moments of absence of mind, then what other valet could slip into a young girl's sacred privacy and deliver her a billet-doux at the very moment when she's reading her prayerbook with her sainted mother? A task I once or twice perform for him, to his infinite gratitude.

And, as you will hear, brought him at last to the best of fortunes for us all.

So Puss got his post at the same time as his boots and I dare say the Master and I have much in common for he's proud as the devil, touchy as tin-tacks, lecherous as liquorice and, though I say it as loves him, as quick-witted a rascal as ever put on clean linen.

When times were hard, I'd pilfer the market for breakfast – a herring, an orange, a loaf; we never went hungry. Puss served him well in the gaming salons, too, for a cat may move from lap to lap with impunity and cast his eye over any hand of cards. A cat can jump on the dice – he can't resist to see it roll! poor thing, mistook it for a bird; and, after I've been, limp-spined, stiff-legged, playing the silly buggers, scooped up to be chastised, who can remember how the dice fell in the first place?

And we had, besides, less . . . gentlemanly means of maintenance when they closed the tables to us, as, churlishly, they sometimes did. I'd perform my little Spanish dance while he went round with his hat: *olé!* But he only put my loyalty and affection to the test of this humiliation when the cupboard was as bare as his backside; after, in fact, he'd sunk so low as to pawn his drawers.

So all went right as ninepence and you never saw such boon companions as Puss and his master; until the man must needs go fall in love.

'Head over heels, Puss.'

I went about my ablutions, tonguing my arsehole with the impeccable hygienic integrity of cats, one leg stuck in the air like a ham bone; I choose to remain silent. Love? What has my rakish master, for whom I've jumped through the window of every brothel in the city, besides haunting the virginal back garden of the convent and god knows what other goatish errands, to do with the tender passion?

'And she. A princess in a tower. Remote and shining as Aldebaran. Chained to a dolt and dragon-guarded.'

I withdrew my head from my privates and fixed him with my most satiric smile; I dare him warble on in *that* strain.

'All cats are cynics,' he opines, quailing beneath my yellow glare.

It is the hazard of it draws him, see.

There is a lady sits in a window for one hour and one hour only, at the tenderest time of dusk. You can scarcely see her features, the curtains almost hide her; shrouded like a holy image, she looks out at the piazza as the shops shut up, the stalls go down, the night comes on. And that is all the world she ever sees. Never a girl in all Bergamo so secluded except, on Sundays, they let her go to Mass, bundled up in black, with a veil on. And then she is in the company of an aged hag, her keeper, who grumps along grim as a prison dinner.

How did he see that secret face? Who else but Puss revealed it?

Back we come from the tables so late, so very late at night we found, to our emergent surprise, that all at once it was early in the morning. His pockets were heavy with silver and both our guts sweetly a-gurgle with champagne; Lady Luck had sat with us, what fine spirits were we in! Winter and cold weather. The pious trot to church already with little lanterns through the chill fog as we go ungodly rolling home.

See, a black barque, like a state funeral; and Puss takes it into his bubbly-addled brain to board her. Tacking obliquely to her side, I rub my marmalade pate against her shin; how could any duenna, be she never so stern, take offence at such attentions to her chargeling from a little cat? (As it turns out, this one: *attishoo!* does.) A white hand fragrant as Arabia descends from the black cloak and reciprocally rubs behind his ears at just the ecstatic spot. Puss lets rip a roaring purr, rears briefly on his high-heeled boots; jig with joy and pirouette with glee – she laughs to see and draws her veil aside. Puss glimpses high above, as it were, an alabaster lamp lit behind by dawn's first flush: her face.

And she smiling.

For a moment, just that moment, you would have thought it was May morning.

'Come along! Come! Don't dawdle over the nasty beast!' snaps the old hag, with the one tooth in her mouth, and warts; she sneezes.

The veil comes down; so cold it is, and dark, again.

It was not I alone who saw her; with that smile he swears she stole his heart.

Love.

I've sat inscrutably by and washed my face and sparkling dicky with my clever paw while he made the beast with two backs with every harlot in the city, besides a number of good wives, dutiful daughters, rosy country girls come to sell celery and endive on the corner, and the chambermaid who strips the bed, what's more. The Mayor's wife, even, shed her diamond earrings for him and the wife of the notary unshuffled her petticoats and, if I could, I would blush to remember how her daughter shook out her flaxen plaits and jumped in bed between them and she not sixteen years old. But never the word, 'love', has fallen from his lips, nor in nor out of any of these transports, until my master saw the wife of Signor Panteleone as she went walking out to Mass, and she lifted up her veil though not for him.

And now he is half sick with it and will go to the tables no more for lack of heart and never even pats the bustling rump of the chambermaid in his new-found, maudlin celibacy, so we get our slops left festering for days and the sheets filthy and the wench goes banging about bad-temperedly with her broom enough to fetch the plaster off the walls.

I'll swear he lives for Sunday morning, though never before was he a religious man. Saturday nights, he bathes himself punctiliously, even, I'm glad to see, washes behind his ears, perfumes himself, presses his uniform so you'd think he had a right to wear it. So much in love he very rarely panders to the pleasures, even of Onan, as he lies tossing on his couch, for he cannot sleep for fear he miss the summoning bell. Then out into the cold morning, harking after that black, vague shape, hapless fisherman for this sealed oyster with such a pearl in it. He creeps behind her across the square; how can so amorous bear to be so inconspicuous? And yet, he must; though, sometimes, the old hag sneezes and says she swears there is a cat about.

He will insinuate himself into the pew behind milady and sometimes contrive to touch the hem of her garment, when they all kneel, and never a thought to his orisons; she is the divinity he's come to worship. Then sits silent, in a dream, till bed-time; what pleasure is his company for me?

He won't eat, either. I brought him a fine pigeon from the inn kitchen, fresh off the spit, parfumé avec tarragon, but he wouldn't touch it so I crunched it up, bones and all. Performing, as ever after meals, my meditative toilette, I pondered, thus: one, he is in a fair way to ruining us both by neglecting his business; two, love is desire sustained by unfulfilment. If I lead him to her bed-chamber and there he takes his fill of her lily-white, he'll be right as rain in two shakes and next day tricks as usual.

Then Master and his Puss will soon be solvent once again.

Which, at the moment, very much not, sir.

This Signor Panteleone employs, his only servant but the hag, a kitchen cat, a sleek, spry tabby whom I accost. Grasping the slack of her neck firmly between my teeth, I gave her the customary tribute of a few firm thrusts of my striped loins and, when she got her breath back, she assured me in the friendliest fashion the old man was a fool and a miser who kept herself on short commons for the sake of the mousing and the young lady a soft-hearted creature who smuggled breast of chicken and sometimes, when the hag-dragon-governess napped at midday, snatched this pretty kitty out of the hearth and into her bedroom to play with reels of silk and run after trailed handkerchiefs, when she and she had as much fun together as two Cinderellas at an all-girls' ball.

Poor, lonely lady, married so young to an old dodderer with his bald pate and his goggle eyes and his limp, his avarice, his gore belly, his rheumaticks, and his flag hangs all the time at half-mast indeed; and jealous as he is impotent, tabby declares – he'd put a stop to all the rutting in the world, if he had his way, just to certify his young wife don't get from another what she can't get from him.

'Then shall we hatch a plot to antler him, my precious?'

Nothing loath, she tells me the best time for this accomplishment should be the one day in all the week he forsakes his wife and his counting-house to ride off into the country to extort most grasping rents from starveling tenant farmers. And she's left all alone, then, behind so many bolts and bars you wouldn't believe; all alone – but for the hag!

Aha! This hag turns out to be the biggest snag; an iron- plated, copper-bottomed, sworn man-hater of some sixty bitter winters who – as ill luck would have it – shatters, clatters, erupts into paroxysms of the *sneeze* at the very glimpse of a cat's whisker. No chance of Puss worming his winsome way into *that* one's affections, nor for my tabby, neither! But, oh my dear, I say; see how my ingenuity rises to this challenge . . . So we resume the sweetest part of our conversation in the dusty convenience of the coalhole and she promises me, least she can do, to see the fair, hitherto-inaccessible one gets a letter safe if I slip it to her and slip it to her forthwith I do, though somewhat discommoded by my boots.

He spent three hours over his letter, did my master, as long as it takes me to lick the coaldust off my dicky. He tears up half a quire of paper, splays five pen-nibs with the force of his adoration: 'Look not for any peace, my heart; having become a slave to this beauty's tyranny, dazzled am I by this sun's rays and my torments cannot be assuaged.' *That's* not the high road to the rumpling of the bedcovers; she's got *one* ninny between them already!

'Speak from the heart,' I finally exhort. 'And all good women have a missionary streak, sir; convince her her orifice will be your salvation and she's yours.'

'When I want your advice, Puss, I'll ask for it,' he says, all at once hoity-toity. But at last he manages to pen ten pages; a rake, a profligate, a card-sharper, a cashiered officer well on the way to rack and ruin when first he saw, as if it were a glimpse of grace, her face . . . his angel, his good angel, who will lead him from perdition.

Oh, what a masterpiece he penned!

'Such tears she wept at his addresses!' says my tabby friend. 'Oh, Tabs, she sobs – for she calls me "Tabs" – I never meant to wreak such havoc with a pure heart when I smiled to see a booted cat! And put his paper next to her heart and swore, it was a good soul that sent her his vows and she was too much in love with virtue to withstand him. If, she adds, for she's a sensible girl, he's neither old as the hills nor ugly as sin, that is.'

An admirable little note the lady's sent him in return, per

Figaro here and there; she adopts a responsive yet uncompromising tone. For, says she, how can she usefully discuss his passion further without a glimpse of his person?

He kisses her letter once, twice, a thousand times; she must and will see me! I shall serenade her this very evening!

So, when dusk falls, off we trot to the piazza, he with an old guitar he pawned his sword to buy and most, if I may say so, outlandishly rigged out in some kind of vagabond mountebank's outfit he bartered his gold-braided waistcoat with poor Pierrot braying in the square for, moonstruck zany, lovelorn loon he was himself and even plastered his face with flour to make it white, poor fool, and so ram home his heartsick state.

There she is, the evening star with the clouds around her; but such a creaking of carts in the square, such a clatter and crash as they dismantle the stalls, such an ululation of ballad-singers and oration of nostrum-peddlers and perturbation of errand boys that though he wails out his heart to her: 'Oh, my beloved!', why she, all in a dream, sits with her gaze in the middle distance, where there's a crescent moon stuck on the sky behind the cathedral pretty as a painted stage, and so is she.

Does she hear him?

Not a grace-note.

Does she see him?

Never a glance.

'Up you go, Puss; tell her to look my way!'

If rococo's a piece of cake, that chaste, tasteful, early Palladian stumped many a better cat than I in its time. Agility's not in it, when it comes to Palladian; daring alone will carry the day and, though the first storey's graced with a hefty caryatid whose bulbous loincloth and tremendous pects facilitate the first ascent, the Doric column on her head proves a horse of a different colour, I can tell you. Had I not seen my precious Tabby crouched in the gutter above me keening encouragement, I, even I, might never have braved that flying, upward leap that brought me, as if Harlequin himself on wires, in one bound to her window-sill.

'Dear god!' the lady says, and jumps. I see she, too, ah, sentimental thing! clutches a well-thumbed letter. 'Puss in boots!'

I bow to her with a courtly flourish. What luck to hear no sniff or sneeze; where's hag? A sudden flux sped her to the privy – not a moment to lose.

'Cast your eye below,' I hiss. 'Him you know of lurks below, in white with the big hat, ready to sing you an evening ditty.'

The bedroom door creaks open, then, and: whee! through the air Puss goes, discretion is the better part. And, for both their sweet sakes I did it, the sight of both their bright eyes inspired me to the never-before-attempted, by me or any other cat, in boots or out of them – the death-defying triple somersault!

And a three-storey drop to ground, what's more; a grand descent.

Only the merest trifle winded, I'm proud to say, I neatly land on all my fours and Tabs goes wild, huzzah! But has my master witnessed my triumph? Has he, my arse. He's tuning up that old mandolin and breaks, as down I come, again into his song.

I would never have said, in the normal course of things, his voice would charm the birds out of the trees, like mine; and yet the bustle died for him, the homeward-turning costers paused in their tracks to hearken, the preening street girls forgot their hard-edged smiles as they turned to him and some of the old ones wept, they did.

Tabs, up on the roof there, prick up your ears! For by its power I know my heart is in his voice.

And now the lady lowers her eyes to him and smiles, as once she smiled at me.

Then, bang! a stern hand pulls the shutters to. And it was as if all the violets in all the baskets of all the flower-sellers drooped and faded at once; and spring stopped dead in its tracks and might, this time, not come at all; and the bustle and the business of the square, that had so magically quieted for his song, now rose up again with the harsh clamour of the loss of love.

And we trudge drearily off to dirty sheets and a mean supper of bread and cheese, all I can steal him, but at least the poor soul manifests a hearty appetite now she knows he's in the world and not the ugliest of mortals; for the first time since that fateful morning, sleeps sound. But sleep comes hard to Puss tonight. He takes a midnight stroll across the square, soon comfortably discusses a choice morsel of salt cod his tabby friend found among the ashes on the hearth before our converse turns to other matters.

'Rats!' she says. 'And take your boots off, you uncouth bugger;

those three-inch heels wreak havoc with the soft flesh of my underbelly!'

When we'd recovered ourselves a little, I ask her what she means by those 'rats' of hers and she proposes her scheme to me. How my master must pose as a *rat-catcher* and I, his ambulant marmalade rat-trap. How we will then go kill the rats that ravage milady's bedchamber, the day the old fool goes to fetch his rents, and she can have her will of the lad at leisure for, if there is one thing the hag fears more than a cat, it is a rat and she'll cower in a cupboard till the last rat is off the premises before she comes out. Oh, this tabby one, sharp as a tack is she! I congratulate her ingenuity with a few affectionate cuffs round the head and home again, for breakfast, ubiquitous Puss, here, there and everywhere, who's your Figaro?

Master applauds the rat ploy; but, as to the rats themselves, how are they to arrive in the house in the first place? he queries.

'Nothing easier, sir; my accomplice, a witty soubrette who lives among the cinders, dedicated as she is to the young lady's happiness, will personally strew a large number of dead and dying rats she has herself collected about the bedroom of the said ingénue's duenna, and, most particularly, that of the said ingénue herself. This to be done tomorrow morning, as soon as Sir Pantaloon rides out to fetch his rents. By good fortune, down in the square, plying for hire, a rat-catcher! Since our hag cannot abide either a rat or a cat, it falls to milady to escort the rat-catcher, none other than yourself, sir, and his intrepid hunter, myself, to the site of the infestation.

'Once you're in her bedroom, sir, if *you* don't know what to do, then I can't help you.'

'Keep your foul thoughts to yourself, Puss.'

Some things, I see, are sacrosanct from humour.

Sure enough, prompt at five in the bleak next morning, I observe with my own eyes the lovely lady's lubbery husband hump off on his horse like a sack of potatoes to rake in his dues. We're ready with our sign: SIGNOR FURIOSO, THE LIVING DEATH OF RATS; and in the leathers he's borrowed from the porter, I hardly recognize him myself, not with the false moustache. He coaxes the chambermaid with a few kisses – poor, deceived girl! love knows no shame – and so we install ourselves under a certain shuttered window with the great pile of traps she's lent us, the sign of our profession, Puss perched atop them bearing the humble yet determined look of a sworn enemy of vermin.

We've not waited more than fifteen minutes – and just as well, so many rat-plagued Bergamots approach us already and are not easily dissuaded from employing us – when the front door flies open on a lusty scream. The hag, aghast, flings her arms round flinching Furioso; how fortuitous to find him! But, at the whiff of me, she's sneezing so valiantly, her eyes awash, the vertical gutters of her nostrils aswill with snot, she barely can depict the scenes inside, rattus domesticus dead in her bed and all; and worse! in the Missus' room.

So Signor Furioso and his questing Puss are ushered into the very sanctuary of the goddess, our presence announced by a fanfare from her keeper on the noseharp. *Attishhoooo!!!*

Sweet and pleasant in a morning gown of loose linen, our ingénue jumps at the tattoo of my boot heels but recovers instantly and the wheezing, hawking hag is in no state to sniffle more than: 'Ain't I seen that cat before?'

'Not a chance,' says my master. 'Why, he's come but yesterday with me from Milano.'

So she has to make do with that.

My Tabs has lined the very stairs with rats; she's made a morgue of the hag's room but something more lively of the lady's. For some of her prey she's very cleverly not killed but crippled; a big black beastie weaves its way towards us over the turkey carpet, Puss, pounce! Between screaming and sneezing, the hag's in a fine state, I can tell you, though milady exhibits a most praiseworthy and collected presence of mind, being, I guess, a young woman of no small grasp so, perhaps, she has a sniff of the plot, already.

My master goes down hands and knees under the bed.

'My god!' he cries. 'There's the biggest hole, here in the wainscoting, I ever saw in all my professional career! And there's an army of black rats gathering behind it, ready to storm through! To arms!'

But, for all her terror, the hag's loath to leave the Master and me alone to deal with the rats; she casts her eye on a silver-backed hair-brush, a coral rosary, twitters, hovers, screeches, mutters until milady assures her, amidst scenes of rising pandemonium:

'I shall stay here myself and see that Signor Furioso doesn't make off with my trinkets. You go and recover yourself with an infusion of friar's balsam and don't come back until I call.'

The hag departs; quick as a flash, la belle turns the key in the door on her and softly laughs, the naughty one.

Dusting the slut-fluff from his knees, Signor Furioso now stands slowly upright; swiftly, he removes his false moustache, for no element of the farcical must mar this first, delirious encounter of these lovers, must it. (Poor soul, how his hands tremble!)

Accustomed as I am to the splendid, feline nakedness of my kind, that offers no concealment of that soul made manifest in the flesh of lovers, I am always a little moved by the poignant reticence with which humanity shyly hesitates to divest itself of its clutter of concealing rags in the presence of desire. So, first, these two smile, a little, as if to say: 'How strange to meet you here!', uncertain of a loving welcome, still. And do I deceive myself, or do I see a tear a-twinkle in the corner of his eye? But who is it steps towards the other first? Why, she; women, I think, are, of the two sexes, the more keenly tuned to the sweet music of their bodies. (A penny for my foul thoughts, indeed! Does she, that wise, grave personage in the négligé, think you've staged this grand charade merely in order to kiss her hand?) But, then – oh, what a pretty blush! steps back; now it's his turn to take two steps forward in the saraband of Eros.

I could wish, though, they'd dance a little faster; the hag will soon recover from her spasms and shall she find them in flagrante?

His hand, then, trembling, upon her bosom; hers, initially more hesitant, sequentially more purposeful, upon his breeches. Then their strange trance breaks; that sentimental havering done, I never saw two fall to it with such appetite. As if the whirlwind got into their fingers, they strip each other bare in a twinkling and she falls back on the bed, shows him the target, he displays the dart, scores an instant bullseye. Bravo! Never can that old bed have shook with such a storm before. And their sweet, choked mutterings, poor things: 'I never . . .' 'My darling . . .' 'More . . .' And etc. etc. Enough to melt the thorniest heart.

He rises up on his elbows once and gasps at me: 'Mimic the murder of the rats, Puss! Mask the music of Venus with the clamour of Diana!'

A-hunting we shall go! Loyal to the last, I play catch as catch can with Tab's dead rats, giving the dying the coup de grâce and baying with resonant vigour to drown the extravagant screeches that break forth from that (who would have suspected?) more passionate young woman as she comes off in fine style. (Full marks, Master.)

At that, the old hag comes battering at the door. What's going on? Whyfor the racket? And the door rattles on its hinges.

'Peace!' cries Signor Furioso. 'Haven't I just now blocked the great hole?'

But milady's in no hurry to don her smock again, she takes her lovely time about it; so full of pleasure gratified her languorous limbs you'd think her very navel smiled. She pecks my master prettily thank-you on the cheek, wets the gum on his false moustache with the tip of her strawberry tongue and sticks it back on his upper lip for him, then lets her wardress into the scene of the faux carnage with the most modest and irreproachable air in the world.

'See! Puss has slaughtered all the rats.'

I rush, purring proud, to greet the hag; instantly, her eyes o'erflow.

'Why the bedclothes so disordered?' she squeaks, not quite blinded, yet, by phlegm and chosen for her post from all the other applicants on account of her suspicious mind, even (oh, dutiful) when in grande peur des rats.

'Puss had a mighty battle with the biggest beast you ever saw upon this very bed; can't you see the bloodstains on the sheets? And now, what do we owe you, Signor Furioso, for this singular service?'

'A hundred ducats,' says I, quick as a flash, for I know my master, left to himself, would, like an honourable fool, take nothing.

'That's the entire household expenses for a month!' wails avarice's well-chosen accomplice.

'And worth every penny! For those rats would have eaten us out of house and home.' I see the glimmerings of sturdy backbone in this little lady. 'Go, pay them from your private savings that I know of, that you've skimmed off the housekeeping.'

Muttering and moaning but nothing for it except do as she is bid; and the furious Sir and I take off a laundry basket full of dead rats as souvenir – we drop it, plop! in the nearest sewer. And sit down to one dinner honestly paid for, for a wonder.

But the young fool is off his feed, again. Pushes his plate aside, laughs, weeps, buries his head in his hands and, time and time again, goes to the window to stare at the shutters behind which his sweetheart scrubs the blood away and my dear Tabs rests from her supreme exertions. He sits, for a while, and scribbles; rips the page in four, hurls it aside. I spear a falling fragment with a claw. Dear God, he's took to writing poetry.

'I must and will have her for ever,' he exclaims.

I see my plan has come to nothing. Satisfaction has not satisfied him; that soul they both saw in one another's bodies has such insatiable hunger no single meal could ever appease it. I fall to the toilette of my hinder parts, my favourite stance when contemplating the ways of the world.

'How can I live without her?'

You did so for twenty-seven years, sir, and never missed her for a moment.

'I'm burning with the fever of love!'

Then we're spared the expense of fires.

'I shall steal her away from her husband to live with me.'

'What do you propose to live on, sir?'

'Kisses,' he said distractedly. 'Embraces.'

'Well, you won't grow fat on that, sir; though *she* will. And then, more mouths to feed.'

'I'm sick and tired of your foul-mouthed barbs, Puss,' he snaps. And yet my heart is moved, for now he speaks the plain, clear, foolish rhetoric of love and who is there cunning enough to help him to happiness but I? Scheme, loyal Puss, scheme!

My wash completed, I step out across the square to visit that charming she who's wormed her way directly into my own hitherto-untrammelled heart with her sharp wits and her pretty ways. She exhibits warm emotion to see me; and, oh! what news she has to tell me! News of a rapt and personal nature, that turns my mind to thoughts of the future, and, yes, domestic plans of most familial nature. She's saved me a pig's trotter, a whole, entire pig's trotter the Missus smuggled to her with a wink. A feast! Masticating, I muse.

'Recapitulate,' I suggest, 'the daily motions of Sir Pantaloon when he's at home.'

They set the cathedral clock by him, so rigid and so regular his habits. Up at the crack, he meagrely breakfasts off yesterday's crusts and a cup of cold water, to spare the expense of heating it up. Down to his counting-house, counting out his money, until a bowl of well-watered gruel at midday. The afternoon he devotes to usury, bankrupting, here, a small tradesman, there, a weeping widow, for fun and profit. Dinner's luxurious, at four; soup, with a bit of rancid beef or a tough bird in it – he's an arrangement with the butcher, takes unsold stock off his hands in return for a shut mouth about a pie that had a finger in it. From four-thirty until five-thirty, he unlocks the shutters and lets his wife look out, oh, don't I know! while hag sits beside her to make sure she doesn't smile. (Oh, that blessed flux, those precious loose minutes that set the game in motion!)

And while she breathes the air of evening, why, he checks up on his chest of gems, his bales of silk, all those treasures he loves too much to share with daylight and if he wastes a candle when he so indulges himself, why, any man is entitled to one little extravagance. Another draught of Adam's ale healthfully concludes the day; up he tucks besides Missus and, since she is his prize possession, consents to finger her a little. He palpitates her hide and slaps her flanks: 'What a good bargain!' Alack, can do no more, not wishing to profligate his natural essence. And so drifts off to sinless slumber amid the prospects of tomorrow's gold.

'How rich is he?'

'Croesus.'

'Enough to keep two loving couples?'

'Sumptuous.'

Early in the uncandled morning, groping to the privy bleared with sleep, were the old man to place his foot upon the subfusc yet volatile fur of a shadow-camouflaged young tabby cat –

'You read my thoughts, my love.'

I say to my master: 'Now, you get yourself a doctor's gown, impedimenta all complete or I'm done with you.'

'What's this, Puss?'

'Do as I say and never mind the reason! The less you know of why, the better.'

So he expends a few of the hag's ducats on a black gown with a white collar and his skull cap and his black bag and, under my direction, makes himself another sign that announces, with all due pomposity, how he is Il Famed Dottore: *Aches cured*, *pains prevented, bones set, graduate of Bologna, physician extraordinary.* He demands to know, is she to play the invalid to give him further access to her bedroom?

'I'll clasp her in my arms and jump out of the window; we too shall both perform the triple somersault of love.'

'You just mind your own business, sir, and let me mind it for you after my own fashion.'

Another raw and misty morning! Here in the hills, will the weather ever change? So bleak it is, and dreary; but there he stands, grave as a sermon in his black gown and half the market people come with coughs and boils and broken heads and I dispense the plasters and the vials of coloured water I'd fore-thoughtfully stowed in his bag, he too agitato to sell for himself. (And, who knows, might we not have stumbled on a profitable profession for future pursuit, if my present plans miscarry?)

Until dawn shoots his little yet how flaming arrow past the cathedral on which the clock strikes six. At the last stroke, that famous door flies open once again and – *eeeeeeeeeeeeech!* the hag lets rip.

'Oh, Doctor, oh, Doctor, come quick as you can; our good man's taken a sorry tumble!'

And weeping fit to float a smack, she is, so doesn't see the doctor's apprentice is most colourfully and completely furred and whiskered.

The old booby's flat out at the foot of the stair, his head at an acute angle that might turn chronic and a big bunch of keys, still, gripped in his right hand as if they were the keys to heaven marked: *Wanted on voyage.* And Missus, in her wrap, bends over him with a pretty air of concern.

'A fall – ' she begins when she sees the doctor but stops short when she sees your servant, Puss, looking as suitably down-in-the-mouth as his chronic smile will let him, humping his master's stock-in-trade and hawing like a sawbones. 'You, again,' she says, and can't forbear to giggle. But the dragon's too blubbered to hear.

My master puts his ear to the old man's chest and shakes his head dolefully; then takes the mirror from his pocket and puts it to the old man's mouth. Not a breath clouds it. Oh, sad! Oh, sorrowful!

'Dead, is he?' sobs the hag. 'Broke his neck, has he?'

And she slyly makes a little grab for the keys, in spite of her well-orchestrated distress; but Missus slaps her hand and she gives over.

'Let's get him to a softer bed,' says Master.

He ups the corpse, carries it aloft to the room we know full well, bumps Pantaloon down, twitches an eyelid, taps a kneecap, feels a pulse.

'Dead as a doornail,' he pronounces. 'It's not a doctor you want, it's an undertaker.'

Missus has a handkerchief very dutifully and correctly to her eyes.

'You just run along and get one,' she says to hag. 'And then I'll read the will. Because don't think he's forgotten you, thou faithful servant. Oh, my goodness, no.'

So off goes hag; you never saw a woman of her accumulated Christmases sprint so fast. As soon as they are left alone, no trifling, this time; they're at it, hammer and tongs, down on the carpet since the bed is occupé. Up and down, up and down his arse; in and out, in and out her legs. Then she heaves him up and throws him on his back, her turn at the grind, now, and you'd think she'll never stop.

Toujours discret, Puss occupies himself in unfastening the shutters and throwing the windows open to the beautiful beginnings of morning in whose lively yet fragrant air his sensitive nostrils catch the first and vernal hint of spring. In a few moments, my dear friend joins me. I notice already – or is it only my fond imagination? – a charming new *portliness* in her gait, hitherto so elastic, so spring-heeled. And there we sit upon the window-sill, like the two genii and protectors of the house; ah, Puss, your rambling days are over. I shall become a hearthrug cat, a fat and cosy cushion cat, sing to the moon no more, settle at last amid the sedentary joys of a domesticity we two, she and I, have so richly earned.

Their cries of rapture rouse me from this pleasant revery.

The hag chooses, naturellement, this tender if outrageous moment to return with the undertaker in his chiffoned topper, plus a brace of mutes black as beetles, glum as bailiffs, bearing the elm box between them to take the corpse away in. But they cheer up something wonderful at the unexpected spectacle before them and he and she conclude their amorous interlude amidst roars of approbation and torrents of applause.

But what a racket the hag makes! Police, murder, thieves! Until the Master chucks her purseful of gold back again, for a gratuity. (Meanwhile, I note that sensible young woman, mother-naked as she is, has yet the presence of mind to catch hold of her husband's keyring and sharply tug it from his sere, cold grip. Once she's got the keys secure, she's in charge of all.)

'Now, no more of your nonsense!' she snaps to hag. 'If I hereby give you the sack, you'll get a handsome gift to go along with you for now' – flourishing the keys – 'I am a rich widow and here' – indicating to all my bare yet blissful master – 'is the young man who'll be my second husband.'

When the governess found Signor Panteleone had indeed remembered her in his will, left her a keepsake of the cup he drank his morning water from, she made not a squeak more, pocketed a fat sum with thanks and, sneezing, took herself off with no more cries of 'murder', neither. The old buffoon briskly bundled in his coffin and buried; Master comes into a great fortune and Missus rounding out already and they as happy as pigs in plunk.

But my Tabs beat her to it, since cats don't take much time about engendering; three fine, new-minted ginger kittens, all complete with snowy socks and shirtfronts, tumble in the cream and tangle Missus' knitting and put a smile on every face, not just their mother's and proud father's for Tabs and I smile all day long and, these days, we put our hearts in it.

So may all your wives, if you need them, be rich and pretty; and all your husbands, if you want them, be young and virile; and all your cats as wily, perspicacious and resourceful as:

PUSS-IN-BOOTS.

THE ERL-KING

THE LUCIDITY, THE clarity of the light that afternoon was sufficient to itself; perfect transparency must be impenetrable, these vertical bars of a brass-coloured distillation of light coming down from sulphur-yellow interstices in a sky hunkered with grey clouds that bulge with more rain. It struck the wood with nicotine-stained fingers, the leaves glittered. A cold day of late October, when the withered blackberries dangled like their own dour spooks on the discoloured brambles. There were crisp husks of beechmast and cast acorn cups underfoot in the russet slime of dead bracken where the rains of the equinox had so soaked the earth that the cold oozed up through the soles of the shoes, lancinating cold of the approach of winter that grips hold of your belly and squeezes it tight. Now the stark elders have an anorexic look; there is not much in the autumn wood to make you smile but it is not yet, not quite yet, the saddest time of the year. Only, there is a haunting sense of the imminent cessation of being; the year, in turning, turns in on itself. Introspective weather, a sickroom hush.

The woods enclose. You step between the first trees and then you are no longer in the open air; the wood swallows you up. There is no way through the wood any more, this wood has reverted to its original privacy. Once you are inside it, you must stay there until it lets you out again for there is no clue to guide you through in perfect safety; grass grew over the track years ago and now the rabbits and the foxes make their own runs in the subtle labyrinth and nobody comes. The trees stir with a noise like taffeta skirts of women who have lost themselves in the woods and hunt round hopelessly for the way out. Tumbling crows play tig in the branches of the elms they clotted with their nests, now and then raucously cawing. A little stream with soft margins of marsh runs through the wood but it has grown sullen with the time of the year; the silent, blackish water thickens, now, to ice. All will fall still, all lapse.

A young girl would go into the wood as trustingly as Red Riding Hood to her granny's house but this light admits of no ambiguities and, here, she will be trapped in her own illusion because everything in the wood is exactly as it seems.

The woods enclose and then enclose again, like a system of Chinese boxes opening one into another; the intimate perspectives of the wood changed endlessly around the interloper, the imaginary traveller walking towards an invented distance that perpetually receded before me. It is easy to lose yourself in these woods.

The two notes of the song of a bird rose on the still air, as if my girlish and delicious loneliness had been made into a sound. There was a little tangled mist in the thickets, mimicking the tufts of old man's beard that flossed the lower branches of the trees and bushes; heavy bunches of red berries as ripe and delicious as goblin or enchanted fruit hung on the hawthorns but the old grass withers, retreats. One by one, the ferns have curled up their hundred eyes and curled back into the earth. The trees threaded a cat's cradle of half-stripped branches over me so that I felt I was in a house of nets and though the cold wind that always heralds your presence, had I but known it then, blew gentle around me, I thought that nobody was in the wood but me.

Erl-King will do you grievous harm.

Piercingly, now, there came again the call of the bird, as desolate as if it came from the throat of the last bird left alive. That call, with all the melancholy of the failing year in it, went directly to my heart.

I walked through the wood until all its perspectives converged upon a darkening clearing; as soon as I saw them, I knew at once that all its occupants had been waiting for me from the moment I first stepped into the wood, with the endless patience of wild things, who have all the time in the world.

It was a garden where all the flowers were birds and beasts; ash-soft doves, diminutive wrens, freckled thrushes, robins in their tawny bibs, huge, helmeted crows that shone like patent leather, a blackbird with a yellow bill, voles, shrews, fieldfares, little brown bunnies with their ears laid together along their backs like spoons, crouching at his feet. A lean, tall, reddish hare, up on its great hind legs, nose a-twitch. The rusty fox, its muzzle sharpened to a point, laid its head upon his knee. On the trunk of a scarlet rowan a squirrel clung, to watch him; a cock pheasant delicately stretched his shimmering neck from a brake of thorn to peer at him. There was a goat of uncanny whiteness, gleaming like a goat of snow, who turned her mild eyes towards me and bleated softly, so that he knew I had arrived.

He smiles. He lays down his pipe, his elder bird-call. He lays upon me his irrevocable hand.

His eyes are quite green, as if from too much looking at the wood.

There are some eyes can eat you.

The Erl-King lives by himself all alone in the heart of the wood in a house which has only the one room. His house is made of sticks and stones and has grown a pelt of yellow lichen. Grass and weeds grow in the mossy roof. He chops fallen branches for his fire and draws his water from the stream in a tin pail.

What does he eat? Why, the bounty of the woodland! Stewed nettles; savoury messes of chickweed sprinkled with nutmeg; he cooks the foliage of shepherd's purse as if it were cabbage. He knows which of the frilled, blotched, rotted fungi are fit to eat; he understands their eldritch ways, how they spring up overnight in lightless places and thrive on dead things. Even the homely wood blewits, that you cook like tripe, with milk and onions, and the egg-yolk yellow chanterelle with its fan-vaulting and faint scent of apricots, all spring up overnight like bubbles of earth, unsustained by nature, existing in a void. And I could believe that it has been the same with him; he came alive from the desire of the woods.

He goes out in the morning to gather his unnatural treasures, he handles them as delicately as he does pigeons' eggs, he lays them in one of the baskets he weaves from osiers. He makes salads of the dandelion that he calls rude names, 'bum-pipes' or 'piss-the-beds', and flavours them with a few leaves of wild strawberry but he will not touch the brambles, he says the Devil spits on them at Michaelmas.

His nanny goat, the colour of whey, gives him her abundant milk and he can make soft cheese that has a unique, rank, amniotic taste. Sometimes he traps a rabbit in a snare of string and makes a soup or stew, seasoned with wild garlic. He knows all about the wood and the creatures in it. He told me about the grass snakes, how the old ones open their mouths wide when they smell danger and the thin little ones disappear down the old ones' throats until the fright is over and out they come again, to run around as usual. He told me how the wise toad who squats among the kingcups by the stream in summer has a very precious jewel in his head. He said the owl was a baker's daughter; then he smiled at me. He showed me how to thread mats from reeds and weave osier twigs into baskets and into the little cages in which he keeps his singing birds.

His kitchen shakes and shivers with birdsong from cage upon cage of singing birds, larks and linnets, which he piles up one on another against the wall, a wall of trapped birds. How cruel it is, to keep wild birds in cages! But he laughs at me when I say that; laughs, and shows his white, pointed teeth with the spittle gleaming on them.

He is an excellent housewife. His rustic home is spick and span. He puts his well-scoured saucepan and skillet neatly on the hearth side by side, like a pair of polished shoes. Over the hearth hang bunches of drying mushrooms, the thin, curling kind they call jew's-ears, which have grown on the elder trees since Judas hanged himself on one; this is the kind of lore he tells me, tempting my half-belief. He hangs up herbs in bunches to dry, too – thyme, marjoram, sage, vervain, southernwood, yarrow. The room is musical and aromatic and there is always a wood fire crackling in the grate, a sweet, acrid smoke, a bright, glancing flame. But you cannot get a tune out of the old fiddle hanging on the wall beside the birds because all its strings are broken.

Now, when I go for walks, sometimes in the mornings when the frost has put its shiny thumbprint on the undergrowth or sometimes, though less frequently, yet more enticingly, in the evenings when the cold darkness settles down, I always go to the Erl-King and he lays me down on his bed of rustling straw where I lie at the mercy of his huge hands.

He is the tender butcher who showed me how the price of flesh is love; skin the rabbit, he says! Off come all my clothes.

When he combs his hair that is the colour of dead leaves, dead leaves fall out of it; they rustle and drift to the ground as though he were a tree and he can stand as still as a tree, when he wants the doves to flutter softly, crooning as they come, down upon his shoulders, those silly, fat, trusting woodies with the pretty wedding rings round their necks. He makes his whistles out of an elder twig and that is what he uses to call the birds out of the air – all the birds come; and the sweetest singers he will keep in cages.

The wind stirs the dark wood; it blows through the bushes. A little of the cold air that blows over graveyards always goes with him, it crisps the hairs on the back of my neck but I am not afraid of him; only, afraid of vertigo, of the vertigo with which he seizes me. Afraid of falling down.

Falling as a bird would fall through the air if the Erl-King tied up the winds in his handkerchief and knotted the ends together so they could not get out. Then the moving currents of the air would no longer sustain them and all the birds would fall at the imperative of gravity, as I fall down for him, and I know it is only because he is kind to me that I do not fall still further. The earth with its fragile fleece of last summer's dying leaves and grasses supports me only out of complicity with him, because his flesh is of the same substance as those leaves that are slowly turning into earth.

He could thrust me into the seed-bed of next year's generation and I would have to wait until he whistled me up from my darkness before I could come back again.

Yet, when he shakes out those two clear notes from his bird call, I come, like any other trusting thing that perches on the crook of his wrist.

I found the Erl-King sitting on an ivy-covered stump winding all the birds in the wood to him on a diatonic spool of sound, one rising note, one falling note; such a sweet piercing call that down there came a soft, chirruping jostle of birds. The clearing was cluttered with dead leaves, some the colour of honey, some the colour of cinders, some the colour of earth. He seemed so much the spirit of the place I saw without surprise how the fox laid its muzzle fearlessly upon his knee. The brown light of the end of the day drained into the moist, heavy earth; all silent, all still and the cool smell of night coming. The first drops of rain fell. In the wood, no shelter but his cottage.

That was the way I walked into the bird-haunted solitude of the Erl-King, who keeps his feathered things in little cages he has woven out of osier twigs and there they sit and sing for him.

Goat's milk to drink, from a chipped tin mug; we shall eat the oatcakes he has baked on the hearthstone. Rattle of the rain on the roof. The latch clanks on the door; we are shut up inside with one another, in the brown room crisp with the scent of burning logs that shiver with tiny flame, and I lie down on the Erl-King's creaking palliasse of straw. His skin is the tint and texture of sour cream, he has stiff, russet nipples ripe as berries. Like a tree that bears bloom and fruit on the same bough together, how pleasing, how lovely.

And now – ach! I feel your sharp teeth in the subaqueous depths of your kisses. The equinoctial gales seize the bare elms and make them whizz and whirl like dervishes; you sink your teeth into my throat and make me scream.

The white moon above the clearing coldly illuminates the still tableaux of our embracements. How sweet I roamed, or, rather, used to roam; once I was the perfect child of the meadows of summer, but then the year turned, the light clarified and I saw the gaunt Erl-King, tall as a tree with birds in its branches, and he drew me towards him on his magic lasso of inhuman music.

If I strung that old fiddle with your hair, we could waltz together to the music as the exhausted daylight founders among the trees; we should have better music than the shrill prothalamions of the larks stacked in their pretty cages as the roof creaks with the freight of birds you've lured to it while we engage in your profane mysteries under the leaves.

He strips me to my last nakedness, that underskin of mauve, pearlized satin, like a skinned rabbit; then dresses me again in an embrace so lucid and encompassing it might be made of water. And shakes over me dead leaves as if into the stream I have become.

Sometimes the birds, at random, all singing, strike a chord.

His skin covers me entirely; we are like two halves of a seed, enclosed in the same integument. I should like to grow enormously small, so that you could swallow me, like those queens in fairy tales who conceive when they swallow a grain of corn or a sesame seed. Then I could lodge inside your body and you would bear me.

The candle flutters and goes out. His touch both consoles and devastates me; I feel my heart pulse, then wither, naked as a stone on the roaring mattress while the lovely, moony night slides through the window to dapple the flanks of this innocent who makes cages to keep the sweet birds in. Eat me, drink me; thirsty, cankered, goblin-ridden, I go back and back to him to have his fingers strip the tattered skin away and clothe me in his dress of water, this garment that drenches me, its slithering odour, its capacity for drowning.

Now the crows drop winter from their wings, invoke the harshest season with their cry.

It is growing colder. Scarcely a leaf left on the trees and the birds come to him in even greater numbers because, in this hard weather, it is lean pickings. The blackbirds and thrushes must hunt the snails from hedge bottoms and crack the shells on stones. But the Erl-King gives them corn and when he whistles to them, a moment later you cannot see him for the birds that have covered him like a soft fall of feathered snow. He spreads out a goblin feast of fruit for me, such appalling succulence; I lie above him and see the light from the fire sucked into the black vortex of his eye, the omission of light at the centre, there, that exerts on me such a tremendous pressure, it draws me inwards.

Eyes green as apples. Green as dead sea fruit.

A wind rises; it makes a singular, wild, low, rushing sound.

What big eyes you have. Eyes of an incomparable luminosity, the numinous phosphorescence of the eyes of lycanthropes. The gelid green of your eyes fixes my reflective face. It is a preservative, like a green liquid amber; it catches me. I am afraid I will be trapped in it for ever like the poor little ants and flies that stuck their feet in resin before the sea covered the Baltic. He winds me into the circle of his eye on a reel of birdsong. There is a black hole in the middle of both your eyes; it is their still centre, looking there makes me giddy, as if I might fall into it.

Your green eye is a reducing chamber. If I look into it long enough, I will become as small as my own reflection, I will diminish to a point and vanish. I will be drawn down into that black whirlpool and be consumed by you. I shall become so small you can keep me in one of your osier cages and mock my loss of liberty. I have seen the cage you are weaving for me; it is a very pretty one and I shall sit, hereafter, in my cage among the other singing birds but I – I shall be dumb, from spite.

When I realized what the Erl-King meant to do to me, I was shaken with a terrible fear and I did not know what to do for I loved him with all my heart and yet I had no wish to join the whistling congregation he kept in his cages although he looked after them very affectionately, gave them fresh water every day and fed them well. His embraces were his enticements and yet, oh yet! they were the branches of which the trap itself was woven. But in his innocence he never knew he might be the death of me, although I knew from the first moment I saw him how Erl-King would do me grievous harm.

Although the bow hangs beside the old fiddle on the wall, all the strings are broken so you cannot play it. I don't know what kind of tunes you might play on it, if it were strung again; lullabies for foolish virgins, perhaps, and now I know the birds don't sing, they only cry because they can't find their way out of the wood, have lost their flesh when they were dipped in the corrosive pools of his regard and now must live in cages.

Sometimes he lays his head on my lap and lets me comb his lovely hair for him; his combings are leaves of every tree in the wood and dryly susurrate around my feet. His hair falls down over my knees. Silence like a dream in front of the spitting fire while he lies at my feet and I comb the dead leaves out of his languorous hair. The robin has built his nest in the thatch again, this year; he perches on an unburnt log, cleans his beak, ruffles his plumage. There is a plaintive sweetness in his song and a certain melancholy, because the year is over – the robin, the friend of man, in spite of the wound in his breast from which Erl-King tore out his heart.

Lay your head on my knee so that I can't see the greenish inward-turning suns of your eyes any more.

My hands shake.

I shall take two huge handfuls of his rustling hair as he lies half dreaming, half waking, and wind them into ropes, very softly, so he will not wake up, and, softly, with hands as gentle as rain, I shall strangle him with them.

Then she will open all the cages and let the birds free; they will change back into young girls, every one, each with the crimson imprint of his love-bite on their throats.

She will carve off his great mane with the knife he uses to skin the rabbits; she will string the old fiddle with five single strings of ash-brown hair.

Then it will play discordant music without a hand touching it. The bow will dance over the new strings of its own accord and they will cry out: 'Mother, mother, you have murdered me!'

THE SNOW CHILD

MIDWINTER – INVINCIBLE, IMMACULATE. The Count and his wife go riding, he on a grey mare and she on a black one, she wrapped in the glittering pelts of black foxes; and she wore high, black, shining boots with scarlet heels, and spurs. Fresh snow fell on snow already fallen; when it ceased, the whole world was white. 'I wish I had a girl as white as snow,' says the Count. They ride on. They come to a hole in the snow; this hole is filled with blood. He says: 'I wish I had a girl as red as blood.' So they ride on again; here is a raven, perched on a bare bough. 'I wish I had a girl as black as that bird's feather.'

As soon as he completed her description, there she stood, beside the road, white skin, red mouth, black hair and stark naked; she was the child of his desire and the Countess hated her. The Count lifted her up and sat her in front of him on his saddle but the Countess had only one thought: how shall I be rid of her?

The Countess dropped her glove in the snow and told the girl to get down to look for it; she meant to gallop off and leave her there but the Count said: 'I'll buy you new gloves.' At that, the furs sprang off the Countess's shoulders and twined round the naked girl. Then the Countess threw her diamond brooch through the ice of a frozen pond: 'Dive in and fetch it for me,' she said; she thought the girl would drown. But the Count said: 'Is she a fish, to swim in such cold weather?' Then her boots leapt off the Countess's feet and on to the girl's legs. Now the Countess was bare as a bone and the girl furred and booted; the Count felt sorry for his wife. They came to a bush of roses, all in flower. 'Pick me one,' said the Countess to the girl. 'I can't deny you that,' said the Count.

So the girl picks a rose; pricks her finger on the thorn; bleeds; screams; falls.

Weeping, the Count got off his horse, unfastened his breeches and thrust his virile member into the dead girl. The Countess reined in her stamping mare and watched him narrowly; he was soon finished.

Then the girl began to melt. Soon there was nothing left of her but a feather a bird might have dropped; a bloodstain, like the trace of a fox's kill on the snow; and the rose she had pulled off the bush. Now the Countess had all her clothes on again. With her long hand, she stroked her furs. The Count picked up the rose, bowed and handed it to his wife; when she touched it, she dropped it.

'It bites!' she said.

THE LADY OF THE HOUSE OF LOVE

AT LAST THE revenants became so troublesome the peasants abandoned the village and it fell solely into the possession of subtle and vindictive inhabitants who manifest their presences by shadows that fall almost imperceptibly awry, too many shadows, even at midday, shadows that have no source in anything visible; by the sound, sometimes, of sobbing in a derelict bedroom where a cracked mirror suspended from a wall does not reflect a presence; by a sense of unease that will afflict the traveller unwise enough to pause to drink from the fountain in the square that still gushes spring water from a faucet stuck in a stone lion's mouth. A cat prowls in a weedy garden; he grins and spits, arches his back, bounces away from an intangible on four fear-stiffened legs. Now all shun the village below the château in which the beautiful somnambulist helplessly perpetuates her ancestral crimes.

Wearing an antique bridal gown, the beautiful queen of the vampires sits all alone in her dark, high house under the eyes of the portraits of her demented and atrocious ancestors, each one of whom, through her, projects a baleful posthumous existence; she counts out the Tarot cards, ceaselessly construing a constellation of possibilities as if the random fall of the cards on the red plush tablecloth before her could precipitate her from her chill, shuttered room into a country of perpetual summer and obliterate the perennial sadness of a girl who is both death and the maiden.

Her voice is filled with distant sonorities, like reverberations in a cave: now you are at the place of annihilation, now you are at the place of annihilation. And she is herself a cave full of echoes, she is a system of repetitions, she is a closed circuit. 'Can a bird sing only the song it knows or can it learn a new song?' She draws her long, sharp fingernail across the bars of the cage in which her pet lark sings, striking a plangent twang like that of the plucked heartstrings of a woman of metal. Her hair falls down like tears.

The castle is mostly given over to ghostly occupants but she herself has her own suite of drawing room and bedroom. Closely barred shutters and heavy velvet curtains keep out every leak of natural light. There is a round table on a single leg covered with a red plush cloth on which she lays out her inevitable Tarot; this room is never more than faintly illuminated by a heavily shaded lamp on the mantelpiece and the dark red figured wallpaper is obscurely, distressingly patterned by the rain that drives in through the neglected roof and leaves behind it random areas of staining, ominous marks like those left on the sheets by dead lovers. Depredations of rot and fungus everywhere. The unlit chandelier is so heavy with dust the individual prisms no longer show any shapes; industrious spiders have woven canopies in the corners of this ornate and rotting place, have trapped the porcelain vases on the mantelpiece in soft grey nets. But the mistress of all this disintegration notices nothing.

She sits in a chair covered in moth-ravaged burgundy velvet at the low, round table and distributes the cards; sometimes the lark sings, but more often remains a sullen mound of drab feathers. Sometimes the Countess will wake it for a brief cadenza by strumming the bars of its cage; she likes to hear it announce how it cannot escape.

She rises when the sun sets and goes immediately to her table where she plays her game of patience until she grows hungry, until she becomes ravenous. She is so beautiful she is unnatural; her beauty is an abnormality, a deformity, for none of her features exhibit any of those touching imperfections that reconcile us to the imperfection of the human condition. Her beauty is a symptom of her disorder, of her soullessness.

The white hands of the tenebrous belle deal the hand of destiny. Her fingernails are longer than those of the mandarins of ancient China and each is pared to a fine point. These and teeth as fine and white as spikes of spun sugar are the visible signs of the destiny she wistfully attempts to evade via the arcana; her claws and teeth have been sharpened on centuries of corpses, she is the last bud of the poison tree that sprang from the loins of Vlad the Impaler who picnicked on corpses in the forests of Transylvania.

The walls of her bedroom are hung with black satin, embroidered with tears of pearl. At the room's four corners are funerary urns and bowls which emit slumbrous, pungent fumes of incense.

In the centre is an elaborate catafalque, in ebony, surrounded by long candles in enormous silver candlesticks. In a white lace négligé stained a little with blood, the Countess climbs up on her catafalque at dawn each morning and lies down in an open coffin.

A chignoned priest of the Orthodox faith staked out her wicked father at a Carpathian crossroad before her milk teeth grew. Just as they staked him out, the fatal Count cried: 'Nosferatu is dead; long live Nosferatu!' Now she possesses all the haunted forests and mysterious habitations of his vast domain; she is the hereditary commandant of the army of shadows who camp in the village below her château, who penetrate the woods in the form of owls, bats and foxes, who make the milk curdle and the butter refuse to come, who ride the horses all night on a wild hunt so they are sacks of skin and bone in the morning, who milk the cows dry and, especially, torment pubescent girls with fainting fits, disorders of the blood, diseases of the imagination.

But the Countess herself is indifferent to her own weird authority, as if she were dreaming it. In her dream, she would like to be human; but she does not know if that is possible. The Tarot always shows the same configuration: always she turns up La Papesse, La Mort, La Tour Abolie, wisdom, death, dissolution.

On moonless nights, her keeper lets her out into the garden. This garden, an exceedingly sombre place, bears a strong resemblance to a burial ground and all the roses her dead mother planted have grown up into a huge, spiked wall that incarcerates her in the castle of her inheritance. When the back door opens, the Countess will sniff the air and howl. She drops, now, on all fours. Crouching, quivering, she catches the scent of her prey. Delicious crunch of the fragile bones of rabbits and small, furry things she pursues with fleet, four-footed speed; she will creep home, whimpering, with blood smeared on her cheeks. She pours water from the ewer in her bedroom into the bowl, she washes her face with the wincing, fastidious gestures of a cat.

The voracious margin of huntress's nights in the gloomy garden, crouch and pounce, surrounds her habitual tormented somnambulism, her life or imitation of life. The eyes of this nocturnal creature enlarge and glow. All claws and teeth, she strikes, she gorges; but nothing can console her for the ghastliness of her condition, nothing. She resorts to the magic comfort of the Tarot pack and shuffles the cards, lays them out, reads them, gathers them up with a sigh, shuffles them again, constantly constructing hypotheses about a future which is irreversible.

An old mute looks after her, to make sure she never sees the sun, that all day she stays in her coffin, to keep mirrors and all reflective surfaces away from her – in short, to perform all the functions of the servants of vampires. Everything about this beautiful and ghastly lady is as it should be, queen of night, queen of terror – except her horrible reluctance for the role.

Nevertheless, if an unwise adventurer pauses in the square of the deserted village to refresh himself at the fountain, a crone in a black dress and white apron presently emerges from a house. She will invite you with smiles and gestures; you will follow her. The Countess wants fresh meat. When she was a little girl, she was like a fox and contented herself entirely with baby rabbits that squeaked piteously as she bit into their necks with a nauseated voluptuousness, with voles and field-mice that palpitated for a bare moment between her embroidress's fingers. But now she is a woman, she must have men. If you stop too long beside the giggling fountain, you will be led by the hand to the Countess's larder.

All day, she lies in her coffin in her négligé of blood-stained lace. When the sun drops behind the mountain, she yawns and stirs and puts on the only dress she has, her mother's wedding dress, to sit and read her cards until she grows hungry. She loathes the food she eats; she would have liked to take the rabbits home with her, feed them on lettuce, pet them and make them a nest in her red-and-black chinoiserie escritoire, but hunger always overcomes her. She sinks her teeth into the neck where an artery throbs with fear; she will drop the deflated skin from which she has extracted all the nourishment with a small cry of both pain and disgust. And it is the same with the shepherd boys and gipsy lads who, ignorant or foolhardy, come to wash the dust from their feet in the water of the fountain; the Countess's governess brings them into the drawing room where the cards on the table always show the Grim Reaper. The Countess herself will serve them coffee in tiny cracked, precious cups, and little sugar cakes. The hobbledehoys sit with a spilling cup in one hand and a biscuit in the other, gaping at the Countess in her satin finery as she pours from a silver pot and chatters distractedly to put them at their fatal ease. A certain desolate stillness of her eyes indicates she is inconsolable. She would like to caress their lean brown cheeks and stroke their ragged hair. When she takes them by the hand and leads them to her bedroom, they can scarcely believe their luck.

Afterwards, her governess will tidy the remains into a neat pile and wrap it in its own discarded clothes. This mortal parcel she then discreetly buries in the garden. The blood on the Countess's cheeks will be mixed with tears; her keeper probes her fingernails for her with a little silver toothpick, to get rid of the fragments of skin and bone that have lodged there.

Fee fie fo fum
I smell the blood of an Englishman.

One hot, ripe summer in the pubescent years of the present century, a young officer in the British army, blond, blue-eyed, heavy-muscled, visiting friends in Vienna, decided to spend the remainder of his furlough exploring the little-known uplands of Romania. When he quixotically decided to travel the rutted cart-tracks by bicycle, he saw all the humour of it: 'on two wheels in the land of the vampires'. So, laughing, he sets out on his adventure.

He has the special quality of virginity, most and least ambiguous of states: ignorance, yet at the same time, power in potentia, and, furthermore, unknowingness, which is not the same as ignorance. He is more than he knows – and has about him, besides, the special glamour of that generation for whom history has already prepared a special, exemplary fate in the trenches of France. This being, rooted in change and time, is about to collide with the timeless Gothic eternity of the vampires, for whom all is as it has always been and will be, whose cards always fall in the same pattern.

Although so young, he is also rational. He has chosen the most rational mode of transport in the world for his trip round the Carpathians. To ride a bicycle is in itself some protection against superstitious fears, since the bicycle is the product of pure reason applied to motion. Geometry at the service of man! Give me two spheres and a straight line and I will show you how far I can take them. Voltaire himself might have invented the bicycle, since it contributes so much to man's welfare and nothing at all to his bane. Beneficial to the health, it emits no harmful fumes and permits only the most decorous speeds. How can a bicycle ever be an implement of harm?

A single kiss woke up the Sleeping Beauty in the Wood.

The waxen fingers of the Countess, fingers of a holy image, turn up the card called Les Amoureux. Never, never before . . . never before has the Countess cast herself a fate involving love. She shakes, she trembles, her great eyes close beneath her finely veined, nervously fluttering eyelids; the lovely cartomancer has, this time, the first time, dealt herself a hand of love and death.

> Be he alive or be he dead
> I'll grind his bones to make my bread.

At the mauvish beginnings of evening, the English m'sieu toils up the hill to the village he glimpsed from a great way off; he must dismount and push his bicycle before him, the path too steep to ride. He hopes to find a friendly inn to rest the night; he's hot, hungry, thirsty, weary, dusty . . . At first, such disappointment, to discover the roofs of all the cottages caved in and tall weeds thrusting through the piles of fallen tiles, shutters hanging disconsolately from their hinges, an entirely uninhabited place. And the rank vegetation whispers, as if foul secrets, here, where, if one were sufficiently imaginative, one could almost imagine twisted faces appearing momentarily beneath the crumbling eaves . . . but the adventure of it all, and the consolation of the poignant brightness of the hollyhocks still bravely blooming in the shaggy gardens, and the beauty of the flaming sunset, all these considerations soon overcame his disappointment, even assuaged the faint unease he'd felt. And the fountain where the village women used to wash their clothes still gushed out bright, clear water; he gratefully washed his feet and hands, applied his mouth to the faucet, then let the icy stream run over his face.

When he raised his dripping, gratified head from the lion's mouth, he saw, silently arrived beside him in the square, an old woman who smiled eagerly, almost conciliatorily at him. She wore a black dress and a white apron, with a housekeeper's key ring at the waist; her grey hair was neatly coiled in a chignon beneath the white linen headdress worn by elderly women of that region. She bobbed a curtsy at the young man and beckoned him to follow her. When he hesitated, she pointed towards the great bulk of the mansion above them, whose façade loured over the village, rubbed her stomach, pointed to her mouth, rubbed her stomach again, clearly miming an invitation to supper. Then she beckoned him again, this time turning determinedly upon her heel as though she would brook no opposition.

A great, intoxicated surge of the heavy scent of red roses blew into his face as soon as they left the village, inducing a sensuous vertigo; a blast of rich, faintly corrupt sweetness strong enough, almost, to fell him. Too many roses. Too many roses bloomed on enormous thickets that lined the path, thickets bristling with thorns, and the flowers themselves were almost too luxuriant, their huge congregations of plush petals somehow obscene in their excess, their whorled, tightly budded cores outrageous in their implications. The mansion emerged grudgingly out of this jungle.

In the subtle and haunting light of the setting sun, that golden light rich with nostalgia for the day that is just past, the sombre visage of the place, part manor house, part fortified farmhouse, immense, rambling, a dilapidated eagle's nest atop the crag down which its attendant village meandered, reminded him of childhood tales on winter evenings, when he and his brothers and sisters scared themselves half out of their wits with ghost stories set in just such places and then had to have candles to light them up newly terrifying stairs to bed. He could almost have regretted accepting the crone's unspoken invitation; but now, standing before the door of time-eroded oak while she selected a huge iron key from the clanking ringful at her waist, he knew it was too late to turn back and brusquely reminded himself he was no child, now, to be frightened of his own fancies.

The old lady unlocked the door, which swung back on melodramatically creaking hinges, and fussily took charge of his bicycle, in spite of his protests. He felt a certain involuntary sinking of the heart to see his beautiful two-wheeled symbol of rationality vanish into the dark entrails of the mansion, to, no doubt, some damp outhouse where they would not oil it or check its tyres. But, in for a penny, in for a pound – in his youth and strength and blond beauty, in the invisible, even unacknowledged pentacle of his virginity, the young man stepped over the threshold of Nosferatu's castle and did not shiver in the blast of cold air, as from the mouth of a grave, that emanated from the lightless, cavernous interior.

The crone took him to a little chamber where there was a black oak table spread with a clean white cloth and this cloth was carefully laid with heavy silverware, a little tarnished, as if someone with foul breath had breathed on it, but laid with one place only. Curiouser and curiouser; invited to the castle for dinner, now he must dine alone. All the same, he sat down as she had bid him. Although it was not yet dark outside, the curtains were closely drawn and only the sparing light trickling from a single oil lamp showed him how dismal his surroundings were. The crone bustled about to get him a bottle of wine and a glass from an ancient cabinet of wormy oak; while he bemusedly drank his wine, she disappeared but soon returned bearing a steaming platter of the local spiced meat stew with dumplings, and a shank of black bread. He was hungry after his long day's ride, he ate heartily and polished his plate with the crust, but this coarse food was hardly the entertainment he'd expected from the gentry and he was puzzled by the assessing glint in the dumb woman's eyes as she watched him eating.

But she darted off to get him a second helping as soon as he'd finished the first one and she seemed so friendly and helpful, besides, that he knew he could count on a bed for the night in the castle, as well as his supper, so he sharply reprimanded himself for his own childish lack of enthusiasm for the eerie silence, the clammy chill of the place.

When he'd put away the second plateful, the old woman came and gestured he should leave the table and follow her once again. She made a pantomime of drinking; he deduced he was now invited to take after-dinner coffee in another room with some more elevated member of the household who had not wished to dine with him but, all the same, wanted to make his acquaintance. An honour, no doubt; in deference to his host's opinion of himself, he straightened his tie, brushed the crumbs from his tweed jacket.

He was surprised to find how ruinous the interior of the house was – cobwebs, worm-eaten beams, crumbling plaster; but the mute crone resolutely wound him on the reel of her lantern down endless corridors, up winding staircases, through the galleries where the painted eyes of family portraits briefly flickered as they passed, eyes that belonged, he noticed, to faces, one and all, of a quite memorable beastliness. At last she paused and, behind the door where they'd halted, he heard a faint, metallic twang as of, perhaps, a chord struck on a harpsichord. And then, wonderfully, the liquid cascade of the song of a lark, bringing to him, in the heart – had he but known it – of Juliet's tomb, all the freshness of morning.

The crone rapped with her knuckles on the panels; the most seductively caressing voice he had ever heard in his life softly called out, in heavily accented French, the adopted language of the Romanian aristocracy: 'Entrez.'

First of all, he saw only a shape, a shape imbued with a faint luminosity since it caught and reflected in its yellowed surfaces what little light there was in the room; this shape resolved itself into that of, of all things, a hoop-skirted dress of white satin draped here and there with lace, a dress fifty or sixty years out of fashion but once, obviously, intended for a wedding. And then he saw the girl who wore the dress, a girl with the fragility of the skeleton of a moth, so thin, so frail that her dress seemed to him to hang suspended, as if untenanted in the dank air, a fabulous lending, a self-articulated garment in which she lived like a ghost in a machine. All the light in the room came from a low-burning lamp with a thick greenish shade on a distant mantelpiece; the crone who accompanied him shielded her lantern with her hand, as if to protect her mistress from too suddenly seeing, or their guest from too suddenly seeing her.

So that it was little by little, as his eyes grew accustomed to the half-dark, that he saw how beautiful and how very young the bedizened scarecrow was, and he thought of a child dressing up in her mother's clothes, perhaps a child putting on the clothes of a dead mother in order to bring her, however briefly, to life again.

The Countess stood behind a low table, beside a pretty, silly, gilt-and-wire birdcage, hands outstretched in a distracted attitude that was almost one of flight; she looked as startled by their entry as if she had not requested it. With her stark white face, her lovely death's head surrounded by long dark hair that fell down as straight as if it were soaking wet, she looked like a shipwrecked bride. Her huge dark eyes almost broke his heart with their waiflike, lost look; yet he was disturbed, almost repelled, by her extraordinarily fleshy mouth, a mouth with wide, full, prominent lips of a vibrant purplish-crimson, a morbid mouth. Even – but he put the thought away from him immediately – a whore's mouth. She shivered all the time, a starveling chill, a malarial agitation of the bones. He thought she must be only sixteen or seventeen years old, no more, with the hectic, unhealthy beauty of a consumptive. She was the châtelaine of all this decay.

With many tender precautions, the crone now raised the light she held to show his hostess her guest's face. At that, the Countess let out a faint, mewing cry and made a blind, appalled gesture with her hands, as if pushing him away, so that she knocked against the table and a butterfly dazzle of painted cards fell to the floor. Her mouth formed a round 'o' of woe, she swayed a little and then sank into her chair, where she lay as if now scarcely capable of moving. A bewildering reception. Tsk'ing under her breath, the crone busily poked about on the table until she found an enormous pair of dark green glasses, such as blind beggars wear, and perched them on the Countess's nose.

He went forward to pick up her cards for her from a carpet that, he saw to his surprise, was part rotted away, partly encroached upon by all kinds of virulent-looking fungi. He retrieved the cards and shuffled them carelessly together, for they meant nothing to him, though they seemed strange playthings for a young girl. What a grisly picture of a capering skeleton! He covered it up with a happier one – of two young lovers, smiling at one another, and put her toys back into a hand so slender you could almost see the frail net of bone beneath the translucent skin, a hand with fingernails as long, as finely pointed, as banjo picks.

At his touch, she seemed to revive a little and almost smiled, raising herself upright.

'Coffee,' she said. 'You must have coffee.' And scooped up her cards into a pile so that the crone could set before her a silver spirit kettle, a silver coffee pot, cream jug, sugar basin, cups ready on a silver tray, a strange touch of elegance, even if discoloured, in this devastated interior whose mistress ethereally shone as if with her own blighted, submarine radiance.

The crone found him a chair and, tittering noiselessly, departed, leaving the room a little darker.

While the young lady attended to the coffee-making, he had time to contemplate with some distaste a further series of family portraits which decorated the stained and peeling walls of the room; these livid faces all seemed contorted with a febrile madness and the blubber lips, the huge, demented eyes that all had in common bore a disquieting resemblance to those of the hapless victim of inbreeding now patiently filtering her fragrant brew, even if some rare grace has so finely transformed those features when it came to her case. The lark, its chorus done, had long ago fallen silent; no sound but the chink of silver on china. Soon, she held out to him a tiny cup of rose-painted china.

'Welcome,' she said in her voice with the rushing sonorities of the ocean in it, a voice that seemed to come elsewhere than from her white, still throat. 'Welcome to my château. I rarely receive visitors and that's a misfortune since nothing animates me half as much as the presence of a stranger . . . This place is so lonely, now the village is deserted, and my one companion, alas, she cannot speak. Often I am so silent that I think I, too, will soon forget how to do so and nobody here will ever talk any more.'

She offered him a sugar biscuit from a Limoges plate; her fingernails struck carillons from the antique china. Her voice, issuing from those red lips like the obese roses in her garden, lips that do not move – her voice is curiously disembodied; she is like a doll, he thought, a ventriloquist's doll, or, more, like a great, ingenious piece of clockwork. For she seemed inadequately powered by some slow energy of which she was not in control; as if she had been wound up years ago, when she was born, and now the mechanism was inexorably running down and would leave her lifeless. This idea that she might be an automaton, made of white velvet and black fur, that could not move of its own accord, never quite deserted him; indeed, it deeply moved his heart. The carnival air of her white dress emphasized her unreality, like a sad Columbine who lost her way in the wood a long time ago and never reached the fair.

'And the light. I must apologize for the lack of light . . . a hereditary affliction of the eyes . . .'

Her blind spectacles gave him his handsome face back to himself twice over; if he presented himself to her naked face, he would dazzle her like the sun she is forbidden to look at because it would shrivel her up at once, poor night bird, poor butcher bird.

Vous serez ma proie.

You have such a fine throat, m'sieu, like a column of marble. When you came through the door retaining about you all the golden light of the summer's day of which I know nothing, nothing, the card called 'Les Amoureux' had just emerged from the tumbling chaos of imagery before me; it seemed to me you had stepped off the card into my darkness and, for a moment, I thought, perhaps, you might irradiate it.

I do not mean to hurt you. I shall wait for you in my bride's dress in the dark.

The bridegroom is come, he will go into the chamber which has been prepared for him.

I am condemned to solitude and dark; I do not mean to hurt you.

I will be very gentle.

(And could love free me from the shadows? Can a bird sing only the song it knows, or can it learn a new song?)

See, how I'm ready for you. I've always been ready for you; I've been waiting for you in my wedding dress, why have you delayed for so long . . . it will all be over very quickly.

You will feel no pain, my darling.

She herself is a haunted house. She does not possess herself; her ancestors sometimes come and peer out of the windows of her eyes and that is very frightening. She has the mysterious solitude of ambiguous states; she hovers in a no-man's land between life and death, sleeping and waking, behind the hedge of spiked flowers, Nosferatu's sanguinary rosebud. The beastly forebears on the walls condemn her to a perpetual repetition of their passions.

(One kiss, however, and only one, woke up the Sleeping Beauty in the Wood.)

Nervously, to conceal her inner voices, she keeps up a front of inconsequential chatter in French while her ancestors leer and grimace on the walls; however hard she tries to think of any other, she only knows of one kind of consummation.

He was struck, once again, by the birdlike, predatory claws which tipped her marvellous hands; the sense of strangeness that had been growing on him since he buried his head under the streaming water in the village, since he entered the dark portals of the fatal castle, now fully overcame him. Had he been a cat, he would have bounced backwards from her hands on four fear-stiffened legs, but he is not a cat: he is a hero.

A fundamental disbelief in what he sees before him sustains him, even in the boudoir of Countess Nosferatu herself; he would have said, perhaps, that there are some things which, even if they *are* true, we should not believe possible. He might have said: it is folly to believe one's eyes. Not so much that he does not believe in her; he can see her, she is real. If she takes off her dark glasses, from her eyes will stream all the images that populate this vampire-haunted land, but, since he himself is immune to shadow, due to his virginity – he does not yet know what there is to be afraid of – and due to his heroism, which makes him like the sun, he sees before him, first and foremost, an inbred, highly strung girl child, fatherless, motherless, kept in the dark too long and pale as a plant that never sees the light, half-blinded by some hereditary condition of the eyes. And though he feels unease, he cannot feel terror; so he is like the boy in the fairy tale, who does not know how to shudder, and not spooks, ghouls, beasties, the Devil himself and all his retinue could do the trick.

This lack of imagination gives his heroism to the hero.

He will learn to shudder in the trenches. But this girl cannot make him shudder.

Now it is dark. Bats swoop and squeak outside the tightly shuttered windows. The coffee is all drunk, the sugar biscuits eaten. Her chatter comes trickling and diminishing to a stop; she twists her fingers together, picks at the lace of her dress, shifts nervously in her chair. Owls shriek; the impedimenta of her condition squeak and gibber all around us. Now you are at the place of annihilation, now you are at the place of annihilation. She turns her head away from the blue beams of his eyes; she knows no other consummation than the only one she can offer him. She has not eaten for three days. It is dinner-time. It is bed-time.

Suivez-moi.
Je vous attendais.
Vous serez ma proie.

The raven caws on the accursed roof. 'Dinner-time, dinner-time,' clang the portraits on the walls. A ghastly hunger gnaws her entrails; she has waited for him all her life without knowing it.

The handsome bicyclist, scarcely believing his luck, will follow her into her bedroom; the candles around her sacrificial altar burn with a low, clear flame, light catches on the silver tears stitched to the wall. She will assure him, in the very voice of temptation: 'My clothes have but to fall and you will see before you a succession of mysteries.'

She has no mouth with which to kiss, no hands with which to caress, only the fangs and talons of a beast of prey. To touch the mineral sheen of the flesh revealed in the cool candle gleam is to invite her fatal embrace; in her low, sweet voice, she will croon the lullaby of the House of Nosferatu.

Embraces, kisses; your golden head, of a lion, although I have never seen a lion, only imagined one, of the sun, even if I've only seen the picture of the sun on the Tarot card, your golden head of the lover whom I dreamed would one day free me, this head will fall back, its eyes roll upwards in a spasm you will mistake for that of love and not of death. The bridegroom bleeds on my inverted marriage bed. Stark and dead, poor bicyclist; he has paid the price of a night with the Countess and some think it too high a fee while some do not.

Tomorrow, her keeper will bury his bones under her roses. The food her roses feed on gives them their rich colour, their swooning odour, that breathes lasciviously of forbidden pleasures.

Suivez-moi.

'Suivez-moi!'

The handsome bicyclist, fearful for his hostess's health, her sanity, gingerly follows her hysterical imperiousness into the other room; he would like to take her into his arms and protect her from the ancestors who leer down from the walls.

What a macabre bedroom!

His colonel, an old goat with jaded appetites, had given him the visiting card of a brothel in Paris where, the satyr assured him, ten louis would buy just such a lugubrious bedroom, with a naked girl upon a coffin; offstage, the brothel pianist played the *Dies Irae* on a harmonium and, amidst all the perfumes of the embalming parlour, the customer took his necrophiliac pleasure of a pretended corpse. He had good-naturedly refused the old man's offer of such an initiation; how can he now take criminal advantage of the disordered girl with fever-hot, bone-dry, taloned hands and eyes that deny all the erotic promises of her body with their terror, their sadness, their dreadful, balked tenderness?

So delicate and damned, poor thing. Quite damned.

Yet I do believe she scarcely knows what she is doing.

She is shaking as if her limbs were not efficiently joined together, as if she might shake into pieces. She raises her hands to unfasten the neck of her dress and her eyes well with tears, they trickle down beneath the rim of her dark glasses. She can't take off her mother's wedding dress unless she takes off her dark glasses; she has fumbled the ritual, it is no longer inexorable. The mechanism within her fails her, now, when she needs it most. When she takes off the dark glasses, they slip from her fingers and smash to pieces on the tiled floor. There is no room in her drama for improvisation; and this unexpected, mundane noise of breaking glass breaks the wicked spell in the room, entirely. She gapes blindly down at the splinters and ineffectively smears the tears across her face with her fist. What is she to do now?

When she kneels to try to gather the fragments of glass together, a sharp sliver pierces deeply into the pad of her thumb; she cries out, sharp, real. She kneels among the broken glass and watches the bright bead of blood form a drop. She has never seen her own blood before, not her *own* blood. It exercises upon her an awed fascination.

Into this vile and murderous room, the handsome bicyclist brings the innocent remedies of the nursery; in himself, by his presence, he is an exorcism. He gently takes her hand away from her and dabs the blood with his own handkerchief, but still it spurts out. And so he puts his mouth to the wound. He will kiss it better for her, as her mother, had she lived, would have done.

All the silver tears fall from the wall with a flimsy tinkle. Her painted ancestors turn away their eyes and grind their fangs.

How can she bear the pain of becoming human?

The end of exile is the end of being.

He was awakened by larksong. The shutters, the curtains, even the long-sealed windows of the horrid bedroom were all opened up and light and air streamed in; now you could see how tawdry it all was, how thin and cheap the satin, the catafalque not ebony at all but black-painted paper stretched on struts of wood, as in the theatre. The wind had blown droves of petals from the roses outside into the room and this crimson residue swirled fragrantly about the floor. The candles had burnt out and she must have set her pet lark free because it perched on the edge of the silly coffin to sing him its ecstatic morning song. His bones were stiff and aching, he'd slept on the floor with his bundled-up jacket for a pillow, after he'd put her to bed.

But now there was no trace of her to be seen, except, lightly tossed across the crumpled black satin bedcover, a lace négligé lightly soiled with blood, as it might be from a woman's menses, and a rose that must have come from the fierce bushes nodding through the window. The air was heavy with incense and roses and made him cough. The Countess must have got up early to enjoy the sunshine, slipped outside to gather him a rose. He got to his feet, coaxed the lark on to his wrist and took it to the window. At first, it exhibited the reluctance for the sky of a long-caged thing, but, when he tossed it up on to the currents of the air, it spread its wings and was up and away into the clear blue bowl of the heavens; he watched its trajectory with a lift of joy in his heart.

Then he padded into the boudoir, his mind busy with plans. We shall take her to Zurich, to a clinic; she will be treated for nervous hysteria. Then to an eye specialist, for her photophobia, and to a dentist to put her teeth into better shape. Any competent manicurist will deal with her claws. We shall turn her into the lovely girl she is; I shall cure her of all these nightmares.

The heavy curtains are pulled back, to let in brilliant fusillades of early morning light; in the desolation of the boudoir, she sits at her round table in her white dress, with the cards laid out before her. She has dropped off to sleep over the cards of destiny that are so fingered, so soiled, so worn by constant shuffling that you can no longer make the image out on any single one of them.

She is not sleeping.

In death, she looked far older, less beautiful and so, for the first time, fully human.

I will vanish in the morning light; I was only an invention of darkness.

And I leave you as a souvenir the dark, fanged rose I plucked from between my thighs, like a flower laid on a grave. On a grave.

My keeper will attend to everything.

Nosferatu always attends his own obsequies; she will not go

to the graveyard unattended. And now the crone materialized, weeping, and roughly gestured him to be gone. After a search in some foul-smelling outhouses, he discovered his bicycle and, abandoning his holiday, rode directly to Bucharest where, at the poste restante, he found a telegram summoning him to rejoin his regiment at once. Much later, when he changed back into uniform in his quarters, he discovered he still had the Countess's rose, he must have tucked it into the breast pocket of his cycling jacket after he had found her body. Curiously enough, although he had brought it so far away from Romania, the flower did not seem to be quite dead and, on impulse, because the girl had been so lovely and her death so unexpected and pathetic, he decided to try and resurrect her rose. He filled his tooth glass with water from the carafe on his locker and popped the rose into it, so that its withered head floated on the surface.

When he returned from the mess that evening, the heavy fragrance of Count Nosferatu's roses drifted down the stone corridor of the barracks to greet him, and his spartan quarters brimmed with the reeling odour of a glowing, velvet, monstrous flower whose petals had regained all their former bloom and elasticity, their corrupt, brilliant, baleful splendour.

Next day, his regiment embarked for France.

THE WEREWOLF

IT IS A northern country; they have cold weather, they have cold hearts.

Cold; tempest; wild beasts in the forest. It is a hard life. Their houses are built of logs, dark and smoky within. There will be a crude icon of the virgin behind a guttering candle, the leg of a pig hung up to cure, a string of drying mushrooms. A bed, a stool, a table. Harsh, brief, poor lives.

To these upland woodsmen, the Devil is as real as you or I. More so; they have not seen us nor even know that we exist, but the Devil they glimpse often in the graveyards, those bleak and touching townships of the dead where the graves are marked with portraits of the deceased in the naïf style and there are no flowers to put in front of them, no flowers grow there, so they put out small, votive offerings, little loaves, sometimes a cake that the bears come lumbering from the margins of the forest to snatch away. At midnight, especially on Walpurgisnacht, the Devil holds picnics in the graveyards and invites the witches; then they dig up fresh corpses, and eat them. Anyone will tell you that.

Wreaths of garlic on the doors keep out the vampires. A blue-eyed child born feet first on the night of St John's Eve will have second sight. When they discover a witch – some old woman whose cheeses ripen when her neighbours' do not, another old woman whose black cat, oh, sinister! *follows her about all the time*, they strip the crone, search for her marks, for the supernumerary nipple her familiar sucks. They soon find it. Then they stone her to death.

Winter and cold weather.

Go and visit grandmother, who has been sick. Take her the oatcakes I've baked for her on the hearthstone and a little pot of butter.

The good child does as her mother bids – five miles' trudge through the forest; do not leave the path because of the bears, the wild boar, the starving wolves. Here, take your father's hunting knife; you know how to use it.

The child had a scabby coat of sheepskin to keep out the cold, she knew the forest too well to fear it but she must always be on her guard. When she heard that freezing howl of a wolf, she dropped her gifts, seized her knife and turned on the beast.

It was a huge one, with red eyes and running, grizzled chops; any but a mountaineer's child would have died of fright at the sight of it. It went for her throat, as wolves do, but she made a great swipe at it with her father's knife and slashed off its right forepaw.

The wolf let out a gulp, almost a sob, when it saw what had happened to it; wolves are less brave than they seem. It went lolloping off disconsolately between the trees as well as it could on three legs, leaving a trail of blood behind it. The child wiped the blade of her knife clean on her apron, wrapped up the wolf's paw in the cloth in which her mother had packed the oatcakes and went on towards her grandmother's house. Soon it came on to snow so thickly that the path and any footsteps, track or spoor that might have been upon it were obscured.

She found her grandmother was so sick she had taken to her bed and fallen into a fretful sleep, moaning and shaking so that the child guessed she had a fever. She felt the forehead, it burned. She shook out the cloth from her basket, to use it to make the old woman a cold compress, and the wolf's paw fell to the floor.

But it was no longer a wolf's paw. It was a hand, chopped off at the wrist, a hand toughened with work and freckled with old age. There was a wedding ring on the third finger and a wart on the index finger. By the wart, she knew it for her grandmother's hand.

She pulled back the sheet but the old woman woke up, at that, and began to struggle, squawking and shrieking like a thing possessed. But the child was strong, and armed with her father's hunting knife; she managed to hold her grandmother down long enough to see the cause of her fever. There was a bloody stump where her right hand should have been, festering already.

The child crossed herself and cried out so loud the neighbours heard her and came rushing in. They knew the wart on the hand at once for a witch's nipple; they drove the old woman, in her shift as she was, out into the snow with sticks, beating her old carcass as far as the edge of the forest, and pelted her with stones until she fell down dead.

Now the child lived in her grandmother's house; she prospered.

THE COMPANY OF WOLVES

ONE BEAST AND only one howls in the woods by night.

The wolf is carnivore incarnate and he's as cunning as he is ferocious; once he's had a taste of flesh then nothing else will do.

At night, the eyes of wolves shine like candle flames, yellowish, reddish, but that is because the pupils of their eyes fatten on darkness and catch the light from your lantern to flash it back to you – red for danger; if a wolf's eyes reflect only moonlight, then they gleam a cold and unnatural green, a mineral, a piercing colour. If the benighted traveller spies those luminous, terrible sequins stitched suddenly on the black thickets, then he knows he must run, if fear has not struck him stock-still.

But those eyes are all you will be able to glimpse of the forest assassins as they cluster invisibly round your smell of meat as you go through the wood unwisely late. They will be like shadows, they will be like wraiths, grey members of a congregation of nightmare; hark! his long, wavering howl . . . an aria of fear made audible.

The wolfsong is the sound of the rending you will suffer, in itself a murdering.

It is winter and cold weather. In this region of mountain and forest, there is now nothing for the wolves to eat. Goats and sheep are locked up in the byre, the deer departed for the remaining pasturage on the southern slopes – wolves grow lean and famished. There is so little flesh on them that you could count the starveling ribs through their pelts, if they gave you time before they pounced. Those slavering jaws; the lolling tongue; the rime of saliva on the grizzled chops – of all the teeming perils of the night and the forest, ghosts, hobgoblins, ogres that grill babies upon gridirons, witches that fatten their captives in cages for cannibal tables, the wolf is worst for he cannot listen to reason.

You are always in danger in the forest, where no people are. Step between the portals of the great pines where the shaggy branches tangle about you, trapping the unwary traveller in nets as if the vegetation itself were in a plot with the wolves who live there, as though the wicked trees go fishing on behalf of their friends – step between the gateposts of the forest with the greatest trepidation and infinite precautions; for if you stray from the path for one instant, the wolves will eat you. They are grey as famine, they are as unkind as plague.

The grave-eyed children of the sparse villages always carry knives with them when they go out to tend the little flocks of goats that provide the homesteads with acrid milk and rank, maggoty cheeses. Their knives are half as big as they are, the blades are sharpened daily.

But the wolves have ways of arriving at your own hearth-side. We try and try but sometimes we cannot keep them out. There is no winter's night the cottager does not fear to see a lean, grey, famished snout questing under the door, and there was a woman once bitten in her own kitchen as she was straining the macaroni.

Fear and flee the wolf; for, worst of all, the wolf may be more than he seems.

There was a hunter once, near here, that trapped a wolf in a pit. This wolf had massacred the sheep and goats; eaten up a mad old man who used to live by himself in a hut halfway up the mountain and sing to Jesus all day; pounced on a girl looking after the sheep, but she made such a commotion that men came with rifles and scared him away and tried to track him into the forest but he was cunning and easily gave them the slip. So this hunter dug a pit and put a duck in it, for bait, all alive-oh; and he covered the pit with straw smeared with wolf dung. Quack, quack! went the duck and a wolf came slinking out of the forest, a big one, a heavy one, he weighed as much as a grown man and the straw gave way beneath him – into the pit he tumbled. The hunter jumped down after him, slit his throat, cut off all his paws for a trophy.

And then no wolf at all lay in front of the hunter but the bloody trunk of a man, headless, footless, dying, dead.

A witch from up the valley once turned an entire wedding party into wolves because the groom had settled on another girl. She used to order them to visit her, at night, from spite, and they would sit and howl around her cottage for her, serenading her with their misery.

Not so very long ago, a young woman in our village married

a man who vanished clean away on her wedding night. The bed was made with new sheets and the bride lay down in it; the groom said, he was going out to relieve himself, insisted on it, for the sake of decency, and she drew the coverlet up to her chin and she lay there. And she waited and she waited and then she waited again – surely he's been gone a long time? Until she jumps up in bed and shrieks to hear a howling, coming on the wind from the forest.

That long-drawn, wavering howl has, for all its fearful resonance, some inherent sadness in it, as if the beasts would love to be less beastly if only they knew how and never cease to mourn their own condition. There is a vast melancholy in the canticles of the wolves, melancholy infinite as the forest, endless as these long nights of winter and yet that ghastly sadness, that mourning for their own, irremediable appetites, can never move the heart for not one phrase in it hints at the possibility of redemption; grace could not come to the wolf from its own despair, only through some external mediator, so that, sometimes, the beast will look as if he half welcomes the knife that despatches him.

The young woman's brothers searched the outhouses and the hay-stacks but never found any remains so the sensible girl dried her eyes and found herself another husband not too shy to piss into a pot who spent the nights indoors. She gave him a pair of bonny babies and all went right as a trivet until, one freezing night, the night of the solstice, the hinge of the year when things do not fit together as well as they should, the longest night, her first good man came home again.

A great thump on the door announced him as she was stirring the soup for the father of her children and she knew him the moment she lifted the latch to him although it was years since she'd worn black for him and now he was in rags and his hair hung down his back and never saw a comb, alive with lice.

'Here I am again, missus,' he said. 'Get me my bowl of cabbage and be quick about it.'

Then her second husband came in with wood for the fire and when the first one saw she'd slept with another man and, worse, clapped his red eyes on her little children who'd crept into the kitchen to see what all the din was about, he shouted: 'I wish I were a wolf again, to teach this whore a lesson!' So a wolf he instantly became and tore off the eldest boy's left foot before he was chopped up with the hatchet they used for chopping logs. But when the wolf lay bleeding and gasping its last, the pelt peeled off again and he was just as he had been, years ago, when he ran away from his marriage bed, so that she wept and her second husband beat her.

They say there's an ointment the Devil gives you that turns you into a wolf the minute you rub it on. Or, that he was born feet first and had a wolf for his father and his torso is a man's but his legs and genitals are a wolf's. And he has a wolf's heart.

Seven years is a werewolf's natural span but if you burn his human clothing you condemn him to wolfishness for the rest of his life, so old wives hereabouts think it some protection to throw a hat or an apron at the werewolf, as if clothes made the man. Yet by the eyes, those phosphorescent eyes, you know him in all his shapes; the eyes alone unchanged by metamorphosis.

Before he can become a wolf, the lycanthrope strips stark naked. If you spy a naked man among the pines, you must run as if the Devil were after you.

It is midwinter and the robin, the friend of man, sits on the handle of the gardener's spade and sings. It is the worst time in all the year for wolves but this strong-minded child insists she will go off through the wood. She is quite sure the wild beasts cannot harm her although, well-warned, she lays a carving knife in the basket her mother has packed with cheeses. There is a bottle of harsh liquor distilled from brambles; a batch of flat oatcakes baked on the hearthstone; a pot or two of jam. The flaxen-haired girl will take these delicious gifts to a reclusive grandmother so old the burden of her years is crushing her to death. Granny lives two hours' trudge through the winter woods; the child wraps herself up in her thick shawl, draws it over her head. She steps into her stout wooden shoes; she is dressed and ready and it is Christmas Eve. The malign door of the solstice still swings upon its hinges but she has been too much loved ever to feel scared.

Children do not stay young for long in this savage country. There are no toys for them to play with so they work hard and grow wise but this one, so pretty and the youngest of her family, a little late-comer, had been indulged by her mother and the grandmother who'd knitted her the red shawl that, today, has the ominous if brilliant look of blood on snow. Her breasts have just begun to swell; her hair is like lint, so fair it hardly makes a shadow on her pale forehead; her cheeks are an emblematic scarlet and white and she has just started her woman's bleeding, the clock inside her that will strike, henceforward, once a month.

She stands and moves within the invisible pentacle of her own virginity. She is an unbroken egg; she is a sealed vessel; she has inside her a magic space the entrance to which is shut tight with a plug of membrane; she is a closed system; she does not know how to shiver. She has her knife and she is afraid of nothing.

Her father might forbid her, if he were home, but he is away in the forest, gathering wood, and her mother cannot deny her.

The forest closed upon her like a pair of jaws.

There is always something to look at in the forest, even in the middle of winter – the huddled mounds of birds, succumbed to the lethargy of the season, heaped on the creaking boughs and too forlorn to sing; the bright frills of the winter fungi on the blotched trunks of the trees; the cuneiform slots of rabbits and deer, the herringbone tracks of the birds, a hare as lean as a rasher of bacon streaking across the path where the thin sunlight dapples the russet brakes of last year's bracken.

When she heard the freezing howl of a distant wolf, her practised hand sprang to the handle of her knife, but she saw no sign of a wolf at all, nor of a naked man, neither, but then she heard a clattering among the brushwood and there sprang on to the path a fully clothed one, a very handsome young one, in the green coat and wideawake hat of a hunter, laden with carcasses of game birds. She had her hand on her knife at the first rustle of twigs but he laughed with a flash of white teeth when he saw her and made her a comic yet flattering little bow; she'd never seen such a fine fellow before, not among the rustic clowns of her native village. So on they went together, through the thickening light of the afternoon.

Soon they were laughing and joking like old friends. When he offered to carry her basket, she gave it to him although her knife was in it because he told her his rifle would protect them. As the day darkened, it began to snow again; she felt the first flakes settle on her eyelashes but now there was only half a mile to go and there would be a fire, and hot tea, and a welcome, a warm one, surely, for the dashing huntsman as well as for herself.

This young man had a remarkable object in his pocket. It was a compass. She looked at the little round glass face in the palm of his hand and watched the wavering needle with a vague wonder. He assured her this compass had taken him safely through the wood on his hunting trip because the needle always told him with perfect accuracy where the north was. She did not believe it; she knew she should never leave the path on the way through the wood or else she would be lost instantly. He laughed at her again; gleaming trails of spittle clung to his teeth. He said, if he plunged off the path into the forest that surrounded them, he could guarantee to arrive at her grandmother's house a good quarter of an hour before she did, plotting his way through the undergrowth with his compass, while she trudged the long way, along the winding path.

I don't believe you. Besides, aren't you afraid of the wolves?

He only tapped the gleaming butt of his rifle and grinned.

Is it a bet? he asked her. Shall we make a game of it? What will you give me if I get to your grandmother's house before you?

What would you like? she asked disingenuously.

A kiss.

Commonplaces of a rustic seduction; she lowered her eyes and blushed.

He went through the undergrowth and took her basket with him but she forgot to be afraid of the beasts, although now the moon was rising, for she wanted to dawdle on her way to make sure the handsome gentleman would win his wager.

Grandmother's house stood by itself a little way out of the village. The freshly falling snow blew in eddies about the kitchen garden and the young man stepped delicately up the snowy path to the door as if he were reluctant to get his feet wet, swinging his bundle of game and the girl's basket and humming a little tune to himself.

There is a faint trace of blood on his chin; he has been snacking on his catch.

He rapped upon the panels with his knuckles.

Aged and frail, granny is three-quarters succumbed to the mortality the ache in her bones promises her and almost ready to give in entirely. A boy came out from the village to build up her hearth for the night an hour ago and the kitchen crackles with busy firelight. She has her Bible for company, she is a pious old woman. She is propped up on several pillows in the bed set into the wall peasant-fashion, wrapped up in the patchwork quilt she made before she was married, more years ago than she cares to remember. Two china spaniels with liver-coloured blotches on their coats and black noses sit on either side of the fireplace. There is a bright rug of woven rags on the pantiles. The grandfather clock ticks away her eroding time.

We keep the wolves outside by living well.

He rapped upon the panels with his hairy knuckles.

It is your granddaughter, he mimicked in a high soprano.

Lift up the latch and walk in, my darling.

You can tell them by their eyes, eyes of a beast of prey, nocturnal, devastating eyes as red as a wound; you can hurl your Bible at him and your apron after, granny, you thought that was a sure prophylactic against these infernal vermin . . . now call on Christ and his mother and all the angels in heaven to protect you but it won't do you any good.

His feral muzzle is sharp as a knife; he drops his golden burden of gnawed pheasant on the table and puts down your dear girl's basket, too. Oh, my God, what have you done with her?

Off with his disguise, that coat of forest-coloured cloth, the hat with the feather tucked into the ribbon; his matted hair streams down his white shirt and she can see the lice moving in it. The sticks in the hearth shift and hiss; night and the forest has come into the kitchen with darkness tangled in its hair.

He strips off his shirt. His skin is the colour and texture of vellum. A crisp stripe of hair runs down his belly, his nipples are ripe and dark as poison fruit but he's so thin you could count the ribs under his skin if only he gave you the time. He strips off his trousers and she can see how hairy his legs are. His genitals, huge. Ah! huge.

The last thing the old lady saw in all this world was a young man, eyes like cinders, naked as a stone, approaching her bed.

The wolf is carnivore incarnate.

When he had finished with her, he licked his chops and quickly dressed himself again, until he was just as he had been when he came through her door. He burned the inedible hair in the fireplace and wrapped the bones up in a napkin that he hid away under the bed in the wooden chest in which he found a clean pair of sheets. These he carefully put on the bed instead of the tell-tale stained ones he stowed away in the laundry basket.

He plumped up the pillows and shook out the patchwork quilt, he picked up the Bible from the floor, closed it and laid it on the table. All was as it had been before except that grandmother was gone. The sticks twitched in the grate, the clock ticked and the young man sat patiently, deceitfully beside the bed in granny's nightcap.

Rat-a-tap-tap.

Who's there, he quavers in granny's antique falsetto.

Only your granddaughter.

So she came in, bringing with her a flurry of snow that melted in tears on the tiles, and perhaps she was a little disappointed to see only her grandmother sitting beside the fire. But then he flung off the blanket and sprang to the door, pressing his back against it so that she could not get out again.

The girl looked round the room and saw there was not even the indentation of a head on the smooth cheek of the pillow and how, for the first time she'd seen it so, the Bible lay closed on the table. The tick of the clock cracked like a whip. She wanted her knife from her basket but she did not dare reach for it because his eyes were fixed upon her – huge eyes that now seemed to shine with a unique, interior light, eyes the size of saucers, saucers full of Greek fire, diabolic phosphorescence.

What big eyes you have.

All the better to see you with.

No trace at all of the old woman except for a tuft of white hair that had caught in the bark of an unburned log. When the girl saw that, she knew she was in danger of death.

Where is my grandmother?

There's nobody here but we two, my darling.

Now a great howling rose up all around them, near, very near, as close as the kitchen garden, the howling of a multitude of wolves; she knew the worst wolves are hairy on the inside and she shivered, in spite of the scarlet shawl she pulled more closely round herself as if it could protect her although it was as red as the blood she must spill.

Who has come to sing us carols, she said.

Those are the voices of my brothers, darling; I love the company of wolves. Look out of the window and you'll see them.

Snow half-caked the lattice and she opened it to look into the garden. It was a white night of moon and snow; the blizzard whirled round the gaunt, grey beasts who squatted on their haunches among the rows of winter cabbage, pointing their sharp snouts to the moon and howling as if their hearts would break. Ten wolves; twenty wolves – so many wolves she could not count them, howling in concert as if demented or deranged. Their eyes reflected the light from the kitchen and shone like a hundred candles.

It is very cold, poor things, she said; no wonder they howl so.

She closed the window on the wolves' threnody and took off her scarlet shawl, the colour of poppies, the colour of sacrifices, the colour of her menses, and, since her fear did her no good, she ceased to be afraid.

What shall I do with my shawl?

Throw it on the fire, dear one. You won't need it again.

She bundled up her shawl and threw it on the blaze, which instantly consumed it. Then she drew her blouse over her head; her small breasts gleamed as if the snow had invaded the room.

What shall I do with my blouse?

Into the fire with it, too, my pet.

The thin muslin went flaring up the chimney like a magic bird and now off came her skirt, her woollen stockings, her shoes, and on to the fire they went, too, and were gone for good. The firelight shone through the edges of her skin; now she was clothed only in her untouched integument of flesh. This dazzling, naked she combed out her hair with her fingers; her hair looked white as the snow outside. Then went directly to the man with red eyes in whose unkempt mane the lice moved; she stood up on tiptoe and unbuttoned the collar of his shirt.

What big arms you have.

All the better to hug you with.

Every wolf in the world now howled a prothalamion outside the window as she freely gave the kiss she owed him.

What big teeth you have!

She saw how his jaw began to slaver and the room was full of the clamour of the forest's Liebestod but the wise child never flinched, even when he answered:

All the better to eat you with.

The girl burst out laughing; she knew she was nobody's meat. She laughed at him full in the face, she ripped off his shirt for him and flung it into the fire, in the fiery wake of her own discarded clothing. The flames danced like dead souls on Walpurgisnacht and the old bones under the bed set up a terrible clattering but she did not pay them any heed.

Carnivore incarnate, only immaculate flesh appeases him.

She will lay his fearful head on her lap and she will pick out the lice from his pelt and perhaps she will put the lice into her mouth and eat them, as he will bid her, as she would do in a savage marriage ceremony.

The blizzard will die down.

The blizzard died down, leaving the mountains as randomly covered with snow as if a blind woman had thrown a sheet over them, the upper branches of the forest pines limed, creaking, swollen with the fall.

Snowlight, moonlight, a confusion of paw-prints.

All silent, all still.

Midnight; and the clock strikes. It is Christmas Day, the werewolves' birthday, the door of the solstice stands wide open; let them all sink through.

See! sweet and sound she sleeps in granny's bed, between the paws of the tender wolf.

WOLF-ALICE

COULD THIS RAGGED girl with brindled lugs have spoken like we do she would have called herself a wolf, but she cannot speak, although she howls because she is lonely – yet 'howl' is not the right word for it, since she is young enough to make the noise that pups do, bubbling, delicious, like that of a panful of fat on the fire. Sometimes the sharp ears of her foster kindred hear her across the irreparable gulf of absence; they answer her from faraway pine forest and the bald mountain rim. Their counterpoint crosses and criss-crosses the night sky; they are trying to talk to her but they cannot do so because she does not understand their language even if she knows how to use it for she is not a wolf herself, although suckled by wolves.

Her panting tongue hangs out; her red lips are thick and fresh. Her legs are long, lean and muscular. Her elbows, hands and knees are thickly callused because she always runs on all fours. She never walks; she trots or gallops. Her pace is not our pace.

Two-legs looks, four-legs sniffs. Her long nose is always a-quiver, sifting every scent it meets. With this useful tool, she lengthily investigates everything she glimpses. She can net so much more of the world than we can through the fine, hairy, sensitive filters of her nostrils that her poor eyesight does not trouble her. Her nose is sharper by night than our eyes are by day so it is the night she prefers, when the cool reflected light of the moon does not make her eyes smart and draws out the various fragrances from the woodland where she wanders when she can. But the wolves keep well away from the peasants' shotguns, now, and she will no longer find them there.

Wide shoulders, long arms and she sleeps succinctly curled into a ball as if she were cradling her spine in her tail. Nothing about her is human except that she is *not* a wolf; it is as if the fur she thought she wore had melted into her skin and become part of it, although it does not exist. Like the wild beasts, she lives without a future. She inhabits only the present tense, a fugue of the continuous, a world of sensual immediacy as without hope as it is without despair.

When they found her in the wolf's den beside the bullet-riddled corpse of her foster mother, she was no more than a little brown scrap so snarled in her own brown hair they did not, at first, think she was a child but a cub; she snapped at her would-be saviours with her spiky canines until they tied her up by force. She spent her first days amongst us crouched stock-still, staring at the whitewashed wall of her cell in the convent to which they took her. The nuns poured water over her, poked her with sticks to rouse her. Then she might snatch bread from their hands and race with it into a corner to mumble it with her back towards them; it was a great day among the novices when she learned to sit up on her hind legs and beg for a crust.

They found that, if she were treated with a little kindness, she was not intractable. She learned to recognize her own dish; then, to drink from a cup. They found that she could quite easily be taught a few, simple tricks but she did not feel the cold and it took a long time to wheedle a shift over her head to cover up her bold nakedness. Yet she always seemed wild, impatient of restraint, capricious in temper; when the Mother Superior tried to teach her to give thanks for her recovery from the wolves, she arched her back, pawed the floor, retreated to a far corner of the chapel, crouched, trembled, urinated, defecated – reverted entirely, it would seem, to her natural state. Therefore, without a qualm, this nine days' wonder and continuing embarrassment of a child was delivered over to the bereft and unsanctified household of the Duke.

Deposited at the castle, she huffed and snuffed and smelled only a reek of meat, not the least whiff of sulphur, nor of familiarity. She settled down on her hunkers with that dog's sigh that is only the expulsion of breath and does not mean either relief or resignation.

The Duke is sere as old paper; his dry skin rustles against the bedsheets as he throws them back to thrust out his thin legs scabbed with old scars where thorns scored his pelt. He lives in a gloomy mansion, all alone but for this child who has as little in common with the rest of us as he does. His bedroom is painted terracotta, rusted with a wash of pain, like the interior of an

Iberian butcher's shop, but for himself, nothing can hurt him since he ceased to cast an image in the mirror.

He sleeps in an antlered bed of dull black wrought iron until the moon, the governess of transformations and overseer of somnambulists, pokes an imperative finger through the narrow window and strikes his face: then his eyes start open.

At night, those huge, inconsolable, rapacious eyes of his are eaten up by swollen, gleaming pupil. His eyes see only appetite. These eyes open to devour the world in which he sees, nowhere, a reflection of himself; he passed through the mirror and now, henceforward, lives as if upon the other side of things.

Spilt, glistering milk of moonlight on the frost-crisped grass; on such a night, in moony, metamorphic weather, they say you might easily find him, if you had been foolish enough to venture out late, scuttling along by the churchyard wall with half a juicy torso slung across his back. The white light scours the fields and scours them again until everything gleams and he will leave paw-prints in the hoar-frost when he runs howling round the graves at night in his lupine fiestas.

By the red early hour of midwinter sunset, all the doors are barred for miles. The cows low fretfully in the byre when he goes by, the whimpering dogs sink their noses in their paws. He carries on his frail shoulders a weird burden of fear; he is cast in the role of the corpse-eater, the body-snatcher who invades the last privacies of the dead. He is white as leprosy, with scrabbling fingernails, and nothing deters him. If you stuff a corpse with garlic, why, he only slavers at the treat: cadavre provençale. He will use the holy cross as a scratching post and crouch above the font to thirstily lap up holy water.

She sleeps in the soft, warm ashes of the hearth; beds are traps, she will not stay in one. She can perform the few, small tasks to which the nuns trained her, she sweeps up the hairs, vertebrae and phalanges that litter his room into a dustpan, she makes up his bed at sunset, when he leaves it and the grey beasts outside howl, as if they know his transformation is their parody. Unkind to their prey, to their own they are tender; had the Duke been a wolf, they would have angrily expelled him from the pack, he would have had to lollop along miles behind them, creeping in submission on his belly up to the kill only after they had eaten and were sleeping, to gnaw the well-chewed bones and chew the hide. Yet, suckled as she was by wolves on the high uplands where her mother bore and left her, only his kitchen maid, who is not wolf or woman, knows no better than to do his chores for him.

She grew up with wild beasts. If you could transport her, in her filth, rags and feral disorder, to the Eden of our first beginnings where Eve and grunting Adam squat on a daisy bank, picking the lice from one another's pelts, then she might prove to be the wise child who leads them all and her silence and her howling a language as authentic as any language of nature. In a world of talking beasts and flowers, she would be the bud of flesh in the kind lion's mouth: but how can the bitten apple flesh out its scar again?

Mutilation is her lot; though, now and then, she will emit an involuntary rustle of sound, as if the unused cords in her throat were a wind-harp that moved with the random impulses of the air, her whisper, more obscure than the voices of the dumb.

Familiar desecrations in the village graveyard. The coffin had been ripped open with the abandon with which a child unwraps a gift on Christmas morning and, of its contents, not a trace could be found but for a rag of the bridal veil in which the corpse had been wrapped that was caught, fluttering, in the brambles at the churchyard gate so they knew which way he had taken it, towards his gloomy castle.

In the lapse of time, the trance of being of that exiled place, this girl grew amongst things she could neither name nor perceive. How did she think, how did she feel, this perennial stranger with her furred thoughts and her primal sentience that existed in a flux of shifting impressions; there are no words to describe the way she negotiated the abyss between her dreams, those wakings strange as her sleepings. The wolves had tended her because they knew she was an imperfect wolf; we secluded her in animal privacy out of fear of her imperfection because it showed us what we might have been, and so time passed, although she scarcely knew it. Then she began to bleed.

Her first blood bewildered her. She did not know what it meant and the first stirrings of surmise that ever she felt were directed towards its possible cause. The moon had been shining into the kitchen when she woke to feel the trickle between her thighs and it seemed to her that a wolf who, perhaps, was fond of her, as wolves were, and who lived, perhaps, in the moon? must have nibbled her cunt while she was sleeping, had subjected her to a series of affectionate nips too gentle to wake her yet sharp enough to break the skin. The shape of this theory was blurred yet, out of it, there took root a kind of wild reasoning, as it might have from a seed dropped in her brain off the foot of a flying bird.

The flow continued for a few days, which seemed to her an endless time. She had, as yet, no direct notion of past, or of future, or of duration, only of a dimensionless, immediate moment. At night, she prowled the empty house looking for rags to sop the blood up; she had learned a little elementary hygiene in the convent, enough to know how to bury her excrement and cleanse herself of her natural juices, although the nuns had not the means to inform her how it should be, it was not fastidiousness but shame that made her do so.

She found towels, sheets and pillowcases in closets that had not been opened since the Duke came shrieking into the world with all his teeth, to bite his mother's nipple off and weep. She found once-worn ball dresses in cobwebbed wardrobes, and, heaped in the corners of his bloody chamber, shrouds, nightdresses and burial clothes that had wrapped items on the Duke's menus. She tore strips of the most absorbent fabrics to clumsily diaper herself. In the course of these prowlings, she bumped against that mirror over whose surface the Duke passed like a wind on ice.

First, she tried to nuzzle her reflection; then, nosing it industriously, she soon realized it gave out no smell. She bruised her muzzle on the cold glass and broke her claws trying to tussle with this stranger. She saw, with irritation, then amusement, how it mimicked every gesture of hers when she raised her forepaw to scratch herself or dragged her bum along the dusty carpet to rid herself of a slight discomfort in her hindquarters. She rubbed her head against her reflected face, to show that she felt friendly towards it, and felt a cool, solid, immovable surface between herself and she – some kind, possibly, of invisible cage? In spite of this barrier, she was lonely enough to ask this creature to try to play with her, baring her teeth and grinning; at once she received a reciprocal invitation. She rejoiced; she began to whirl round on herself, yapping exultantly, but, when she retreated from the mirror, she halted in the midst of her ecstasy, puzzled, to see how her new friend grew less in size.

The moonlight spilled into the Duke's motionless bedroom from behind a cloud and she saw how pale this wolf, not-wolf who played with her was. The moon and mirrors have this much in common: you cannot see behind them. Moonlit and white, Wolf-Alice looked at herself in the mirror and wondered whether there she saw the beast who came to bite her in the night. Then her sensitive ears pricked at the sound of a step in the hall; trotting at once back to her kitchen, she encountered the Duke with the leg of a man over his shoulder. Her toenails clicked against the stairs as she padded incuriously past, she, the serene, inviolable one in her absolute and verminous innocence.

Soon the flow ceased. She forgot it. The moon vanished; but, little by little, reappeared. When it again visited her kitchen at full strength, Wolf-Alice was surprised into bleeding again and so it went on, with a punctuality that transformed her vague grip on time. She learned to expect these bleedings, to prepare her rags against them, and afterwards, neatly to bury the dirtied things. Sequence asserted itself with custom and then she understood the circumambulatory principle of the clock perfectly, even if all clocks were banished from the den where she and the Duke inhabited their separate solitudes, so that you might say she discovered the very action of time by means of this returning cycle.

When she curled up among the cinders, the colour, texture and warmth of them brought her foster mother's belly out of the past and printed it on her flesh; her first conscious memory, painful as the first time the nuns combed her hair. She howled a little, in a firmer, deepening trajectory, to obtain the inscrutable consolation of the wolves' response, for now the world around her was assuming form. She perceived an essential difference between herself and her surroundings that you might say she could not put her *finger* on – only, the trees and grass of the meadows outside no longer seemed the emanation of her questing nose and erect ears, and yet sufficient to itself, but a kind of backdrop for her, that waited for her arrivals to give it meaning. She saw herself upon it and her eyes, with their sombre clarity, took on a veiled, introspective look.

She would spend hours examining the new skin that had been born, it seemed to her, of her bleeding. She would lick her soft upholstery with her long tongue and groom her hair with her fingernails. She examined her new breasts with curiosity; the white growths reminded her of nothing so much as the night-sprung puffballs she had found, sometimes, on evening rambles in the woods, a natural if disconcerting apparition, but then, to her astonishment, she found a little diadem of fresh hairs tufting between her thighs. She showed it to her mirror littermate, who reassured her by showing her she shared it.

The damned Duke haunts the graveyard; he believes himself to be both less and more than a man, as if his obscene difference were a sign of grace. During the day, he sleeps. His mirror faithfully reflects his bed but never the meagre shape within the disordered covers.

Sometimes, on those white nights when she was left alone in the house, she dragged out his grandmother's ball dresses and rolled on suave velvet and abrasive lace because to do so delighted her adolescent skin. Her intimate in the mirror wound the old clothes round herself, wrinkling its nose in delight at the ancient yet still potent scents of musk and civet that woke up in the sleeves and bodices. This habitual, at last boring, fidelity to her every movement finally woke her up to the regretful possibility that her companion was, in fact, no more than a particularly ingenious variety of the shadow she cast on sunlit grass. Had not she and the rest of the litter tussled and romped with their shadows long ago? She poked her agile nose around the back of the mirror; she found only dust, a spider stuck in his web, a heap of rags. A little moisture leaked from the corners of her eyes, yet her relation with the mirror was now far more intimate since she knew she saw herself within it.

She pawed and tumbled the dress the Duke had tucked away behind the mirror for a while. The dust was soon shaken out of it; she experimentally inserted her front legs in the sleeves. Although the dress was torn and crumpled, it was so white and of such a sinuous texture that she thought, before she put it on, she must thoroughly wash off her coat of ashes in the water from the pump in the yard, which she knew how to manipulate with her cunning forepaw. In the mirror, she saw how this white dress made her shine.

Although she could not run so fast on two legs in petticoats, she trotted out in her new dress to investigate the odorous October hedgerows, like a débutante from the castle, delighted with herself but still, now and then, singing to the wolves with a kind of wistful triumph, because now she knew how to wear clothes and so had put on the visible sign of her difference from them.

Her footprints on damp earth are beautiful and menacing as those Man Friday left.

The young husband of the dead bride spent a long time planning his revenge. He filled the church with an arsenal of bells, books and candles; a battery of silver bullets; they brought a ten-gallon tub of holy water in a wagon from the city, where it had been blessed by the Archbishop himself, to drown the Duke, if the bullets bounced off him. They gathered in the church to chant a litany and wait for the one who would visit with the first deaths of winter.

She goes out at night more often now; the landscape assembles itself about her, she informs it with her presence. She is its significance.

It seemed to her the congregation in the church was ineffectually attempting to imitate the wolves' chorus. She lent them the assistance of her own, educated voice for a while, rocking contemplatively on her haunches by the graveyard gate; then her nostrils twitched to catch the rank stench of the dead that told her her co-habitor was at hand; raising her head, who did her new, keen eyes spy but the lord of cobweb castle intent on performing his cannibal rituals?

And if her nostrils flare suspiciously at the choking reek of incense and his do not, that is because she is far more sentient than he. She will, therefore, run, run! when she hears the crack of bullets, because they killed her foster mother; so, with the selfsame lilting lope, drenched with holy water, will he run, too, until the young widower fires the silver bullet that bites his shoulder and drags off half his fictive pelt, so that he must rise up like any common forked biped and limp distressfully on as best he may.

When they saw the white bride leap out of the tombstones and scamper off towards the castle with the werewolf stumbling after, the peasants thought the Duke's dearest victim had come back to take matters into her own hands. They ran screaming from the presence of a ghostly vengeance on him.

Poor, wounded thing . . . locked half and half between such

strange states, an aborted transformation, an incomplete mystery, now he lies writhing on his black bed in the room like a Mycenaean tomb, howls like a wolf with his foot in a trap or a woman in labour, and bleeds.

First, she was fearful when she heard the sound of pain, in case it hurt her, as it had done before. She prowled round the bed, growling, snuffing at his wound that does not smell like her wound. Then, she was pitiful as her gaunt grey mother; she leapt upon his bed to lick, without hesitation, without disgust, with a quick, tender gravity, the blood and dirt from his cheeks and forehead.

The lucidity of the moonlight lit the mirror propped against the red wall; the rational glass, the master of the visible, impartially recorded the crooning girl.

As she continued her ministrations, this glass, with infinite slowness, yielded to the reflexive strength of its own material construction. Little by little, there appeared within it, like the image on photographic paper that emerges, first, a formless web of tracery, the prey caught in its own fishing net, then in firmer yet still shadowed outline until at last as vivid as real life itself, as if brought into being by her soft, moist, gentle tongue, finally, the face of the Duke.

WISE CHILDREN

Brush up your Shakespeare.
COLE PORTER

It's a wise child that knows its own father.
OLD SAW

How many times Shakespeare draws fathers and daughters, never mothers and daughters.
ELLEN TERRY

ONE

Q. WHY IS LONDON like Budapest?

A. Because it is two cities divided by a river.

Good morning! Let me introduce myself. My name is Dora Chance. Welcome to the wrong side of the tracks.

Put it another way. If you're from the States, think of Manhattan. Then think of Brooklyn. See what I mean? Or, for a Parisian, it might be a question of *rive gauche, rive droite*. With London, it's the North and South divide. Me and Nora, that's my sister, we've always lived on the left-hand side, the side the tourist rarely sees, the *bastard* side of Old Father Thames.

Once upon a time, you could make a crude distinction, thus: the rich lived amidst pleasant verdure in the North speedily whisked to exclusive shopping by abundant public transport while the poor eked out miserable existences in the South in circumstances of urban deprivation condemned to wait for hours at windswept bus-stops while sounds of marital violence, breaking glass and drunken song echoed around and it was cold and dark and smelled of fish and chips. But you can't trust things to stay the same. There's been a diaspora of the affluent, they jumped into their diesel Saabs and dispersed throughout the city. You'd never believe the price of a house round here, these days. And what does the robin do then, poor thing?

Bugger the robin! What would have become of *us*, if Grandma hadn't left us this house? 49 Bard Road, Brixton, London, South West Two. Bless this house. If it wasn't for this house, Nora and I would be on the streets by now, hauling our worldlies up and down in plastic bags, sucking on the bottle for comfort like babes unweaned, bursting into songs of joy when finally admitted to the night shelter and therefore chucked out again immediately for disturbing the peace, to gasp and freeze and finally snuff it disregarded on the street and blow away like rags. That's a thought for a girl's seventy-fifth birthday, what?

Yes! Seventy-five. Happy birthday to me. Born in this house, indeed, this very attic, just seventy-five years ago, today. I made my bow five minutes ahead of Nora who is, at this very moment, downstairs, getting breakfast. My dearest sister. Happy birthday to us.

This is *my* room. We don't share. We've always respected one another's privacy. Identical, well and good; Siamese, no. Everything slightly soiled, I'm sorry to say. Can't be doing with wash, wash, wash, polish, polish, polish, these days, when time is so precious, but take a good look at the signed photos stuck in the dressing-table mirror – Ivor; Noel; Fred and Adèle; Jack; Ginger; Fred and Ginger; Anna, Jessie, Sonnie, Binnie. All friends and colleagues, once upon a time. See the newest one, a tall girl, slender, black curls, enormous eyes, no drawers, 'your very own Tiffany' and lots of XXXXXs. Isn't she lovely? Our beloved godchild. We tried to put her off show business but she wasn't having any. 'What's good enough for you two is good enough for me.' 'Show business', right enough; a prettier girl than little Tiff you never saw but she's showed her all.

What did we do? Got it in one. We used to be song and dance girls. We can still lift a leg higher than your average dog, if called for.

Hello, hello . . . here comes one of the pussy cats, out of the wardrobe, stretching and yawning. She can smell the bacon. There's another, white, with marmalade patches, sleeping on my pillow. Dozens more roam freely. The house smells of cat, a bit, but more of geriatric chorine – cold cream, face powder, dress preservers, old fags, stale tea.

'Come and have a cuddle, Pussy.'

You've got to have something to cuddle. Does Pussy want its breakfast, then? Give us a minute, Puss, let's have a look out of the window.

Cold, bright, windy, spring weather, just like the day that we were born, when the Zeppelins were falling. Lovely blue sky, a birthday present in itself. I knew a boy, once, with eyes that colour, years ago. Bare as a rose, not a hair on him; he was too young for body hair. And sky-blue eyes.

You can see for miles, out of this window. You can see right across the river. There's Westminster Abbey, see? Flying the St George's cross, today. St Paul's, the single breast. Big Ben, winking its golden eye. Not much else familiar, these days. This is about the time that comes in every century when they reach out for all that they can grab of dear old London, and pull it down. Then they build it up again, like London Bridge in the nursery rhyme, goodbye, hello, but it's never the same. Even the railway stations, changed out of recognition, turned into souks. Waterloo. Victoria. Nowhere you can get a decent cup of tea, all they give you is Harvey Wallbangers, filthy cappuccino. Stocking shops and knicker outlets everywhere you look. I said to Nora: 'Remember *Brief Encounter*, how I cried buckets? Nowhere for them to meet on a station, nowadays, except in a bloody knicker shop. Their hands would have to shyly touch under cover of a pair of Union Jack boxer shorts.'

'Come off it, you sentimental sod,' said Nora. 'The only brief encounter *you* had during the war was a fling with a Yank behind the public convenience on Liverpool Street Station.'

'I was only doing my bit for the war effort,' I replied sedately, but she wasn't listening, she started to giggle.

''ere, Dor', smashing name for a lingerie shop – Brief Encounter.' She doubled up.

Sometimes I think, if I look hard enough, I can see back into the past. There goes the wind, again. Crash. Over goes the dust-bin, all the trash spills out . . . empty cat-food cans, cornflakes packets, laddered tights, tea leaves . . . I am at present working on my memoirs and researching family history – see the word processor, the filing cabinet, the card indexes, right hand, left hand, right side, left side, all the dirt on everybody. What a wind! Whooping and banging all along the street, the kind of wind that blows everything topsy-turvy.

Seventy-five, today, and a topsy-turvy day of wind and sun-shine. The kind of wind that gets into the blood and drives you wild. Wild!

And I give a little shiver because suddenly I know, I know it in my ancient water, that something will happen today. Something exciting. Something nice, something nasty, I don't give a mon-key's. Just as long as something happens to remind us we're still in the land of the living.

We boast the only castrato grandfather clock in London.

The plaque on the dial of our grandfather in the front hall says it was made in Inverness in 1846 and, as far as I know, it is a unique example of an authentic Highland-style grandfather clock and as such was exhibited at the Great Exhibition of 1851. Its Highlandness consists of a full set of antlers, eight points, on top of it. Sometimes we use the antlers as a hat rack, if either of us happens to go out wearing a hat, which doesn't happen often, but now and then, when it rains. This clock has got a lot of sentimental value for Nora and me. It came to us from our father. His only gift and even then it came by accident. Great, tall, butch, horny mahogany thing, but it gives out the hours in a funny little falsetto ping and always the wrong hour, always out by one. We never got round to fixing it. To tell the truth, it makes us laugh, always has. It was all right until Grandma fixed it. All she did was tap it and the weights dropped off. She always had that effect on gentlemen.

But, as I passed by our grandfather clock this windy birthday morning, cats scampering in front of me maddened by the smell of bacon, it struck. And struck. And struck. And this time got it right, straight on the nosey – eight o'clock!

'Nor'! Nor'! Something's up! Granddad in the hall got the right time, for once!'

'Something else is up, too,' Nora says in a gratified voice and slings me a thick, white envelope with a crest on the back. 'Our invites have arrived at last.'

She starts to pour out tea, while Wheelchair fizzes and stutters when I pull out that stiff, white card we thought would never come.

The Misses Dora and Leonora Chance
are invited
to a celebration to mark the one hundredth birthday
of
Sir Melchior Hazard
'One Man in his Time Plays Many Parts.'

Wheelchair fizzed, sputtered and boiled right over; she screeched fit to bust but Nora consoled her:

'Hold hard, ducky, we're never going to leave you behind! Yes, Cinders, you *shall* go to the ball, even if you aren't mentioned by name on the invite. Let's have *all* the skeletons out of the closet, today, of all days! God knows, we deserve a spot of bubbly after all these years.'

I squinted at the RSVP, to that posh house in Regent's Park and Lady Hazard, the third and present spouse. Whereas our poor old Wheelchair, here, was his first, which accounts for her spleen, as ex, at failing to feature personally on the invitation. And the Misses Leonora and Dora, that is, yours truly, are, of course, Sir Melchior Hazard's daughters, though not, ahem, by any of his wives. We are his *natural* daughters, as they say, as if only unmarried couples do it the way that nature intended. His never-by-him officially recognized daughters, with whom, by a bizarre coincidence, he shares a birthday.

'They've not given us much time to reply,' I complained. 'It's only tonight, isn't it?'

'Something makes you think they don't want us to go?' Nora's lost a couple of back molars, you can't help but notice when she laughs. I've kept all mine. Otherwise, like as two peas, as ever was. Years ago, the only way you could tell us apart was by our perfume. She used Shalimar, me, Mitsouko.

All the same, identical we may be, but symmetrical – never. For the body itself isn't symmetrical. One of your feet is bound to be bigger than the other, one ear will leak more wax. Nora is fluxy; me, constipated. She was always free with her money, squandered it on the fellers, poor thing, whereas I tried to put a bit by. Her menstrual flow was copious to a fault; mine, meagre. She said: 'Yes!' to life and I said, 'Maybe . . .' But we're both in the same boat, now. Stuck with each other. Two batty old hags, buy us a drink and we'll sing you a song. Even manage a knees-up, on occasion, such as New Year's Eve or a publican's grandbaby.

What a joy it is to dance and sing!

We're stuck in the period at which we peaked, of course. All women do. We'd feel mutilated if you made us wipe off our Joan Crawford mouths and we always do our hair up in great big Victory rolls when we go out. We've still got lots of it, thank God, iron grey though it may be and tucked away in scarves, turban-style, this very moment, to hide the curlers. We always make an effort. We paint an inch thick. We put on our faces before we come down to breakfast, the Max Factor Pan-Stik, the false eyelashes with the three coats of mascara, everything. We used to polish our eyelids with Vaseline, when we were girls, but we gave up on that during the war and now use just a simple mushroom shadow for day plus a hint of tobacco brown, to deepen the tone, and a charcoal eyeliner. Our fingernails match our toenails match our lipstick match our rouge. Revlon, Fire and Ice. The habit of applying warpaint outlasts the battle; haven't had a man for yonks but still we slap it on. Nobody could say the Chance girls were going gently into that good night.

We'd got our best kimonos on, because it was our birthday. Real silk, mine mauve with a plum-blossom design on the back, Nora's crimson with a chrysanthemum. Our beloved Uncle Perry, that is, the late, and by his nieces grievously lamented, Peregrine Hazard, sent us back our kimonos from Nagasaki, years ago, before Pearl Harbor, when he was on one of his trips. Underneath, camiknickers with a French lace trim, lilac satin for me, crushed rose crepe for her. Tasty, eh? Course, we were wearing camiknickers before they *came back*.

Our hipbones stick out more than they used to; we look quite gaunt in our undies, these days, but she's the only one who sees me in the altogether, and me her, and we pass muster with our clothes on. Our cheekbones stick out more than they used to, too, but they're the very best cheekbones, I'd have you know – these cheekbones are descended from some of the most profitable calcium deposits in the world. Like all those who spend much time before the public eye, our father has always been dependent on his bone structure. God bless the Hazard calcium; it's kept osteoporosis at bay. Long and lean we always were and long and lean we are now, thank God. Some superannuated hoofers put on the avoirdupois like nobody's business.

'What shall we wear tonight?' asked Nora, stubbing her fag out in her saucer, pouring herself another cup. She's a regular teapot. Wheelchair moaned a little.

'Don't fret, dear,' Nora soothed. 'You can wear your Normal Hartnell and the pearls, all right? We'll do you up something lovely.'

That calmed it down, poor old stick. Known to us as Wheelchair, known to the world, once upon a time, as Lady Atalanta Hazard. A Lady in her own right, she'd have you know, a perfect lady, unlike our father's next two wives. She married Melchior Hazard when he was just a matinée idol, and divorced him long before that knighthood they gave him for 'services to the theatre'. Née Lady Atalanta Lynde, 'the most beautiful woman of her time', born with a silver spoon, etc. etc. etc. but now an antique divorcee in reduced circumstances, to whit, the basement front of 49 Bard Road.

All in good time I shall reveal to you how it has come to pass that we inherited, in her dotage and, come to that, in ours, the first wife of our illegitimate father. Suffice to say that nobody else would have her. Least of all her own two daughters. Bloody cows. 'The lovely Hazard girls', they used to call them. Huh. Lovely is as lovely does; if they looked like what they behave like, they'd frighten little children.

We've been storing Wheelchair in the basement for well-nigh thirty years. We've got quite attached to her. Earlier on, Nora used to take her out shopping, give her some fresh air and that, until she nearly starts a riot, she says to the bloke at the salad stall: 'Have you got anything in the shape of a cucumber, my good fellow?' After that, we had to keep her home for her own sake.

Sometimes she goes on a bit, on and on, on and on and bloody on, in fact, worrying away at how Melchior took the best years of her life then deserted her for a Hollywood harlot – his Number Two bride – and how the 'lovely Hazard girls' did her out of all her money and how she fell downstairs and can never walk again and on and on and on and on until you want to throw a blanket over her, like you do to shut up a parrot. But there's not a scrap of harm in her and, besides, we owe her one from way back.

I had a go at the teapot, too, but too late, got half a cup of sodden leaves, went out to the scullery to put the kettle on, again. Here we sit, in our negligées, in the breakfast room in the leather armchairs by the Readicole electric fire. Sometimes we sit there all day, drink tea, chew the fat. Wheelchair plays solitaire, does tapestry. The cats come and go.

At six we switch to gin.

Sometimes when we've had our supper we plug Wheelchair into the TV – she loves the commercials, she watches out for the ones with Melchior in them, then she heckles the screen – we go and don some bits and bobs of former finery such as, for example, those matching silver-fox trench coats Howard Hughes gave us, and we sally forth to the local, where we are occasionally invited to perform one of the numbers that brought us fame, once upon a time. And sometimes we perform uninvited.

'Anything else in the mail?'

Nora shoved across the bundle. The electricity bill, again; Neighbourhood Watch, again; next door complaining about the cats, again; some kid in New Jersey wanting to interview us for his Ph.D., Film Studies, bloody *Midsummer Night's Dream*, again. At our age, you feel you've seen it all before. I note that little Tiff, our darling love, our chick, our cherished one, our goddaughter, is too preoccupied with her Big Affair at present to drop us birthday greetings. Youth, youth.

Then the doorbell rang and made me jump. The gas man? Never the gas man, he never leans on the bell with all his weight like that, he just gives a reticent little tinkle ever since he got Nora in her altogether except for her nail polish, she'd jumped straight out of the bath, she'd thought he was a telegram. No. This was a fierce, long ring. Then another. And another. We started up, we stiffened. Then he on the doorstep hammers with his fists and shouts:

'Aunties!'

Our father's youngest son, young Tristram Hazard. Why does he call us 'aunties' when we are, in fact, his half-sisters, even if on the wrong side of the blanket? You will find out in due course. And has he come to wish us 'Happy birthday'? If so, why the panic? He shouted so, I was all of a flutter. I fumbled with the lock, the bolts, the chain – like Fort Knox, round here. You can't be too careful, these days. We had a mass breakout from Brixton Nick last year, they came over the garden wall like formation dancers.

Young Tristram fell into my arms as if legless when I got the door open. Unshaven, mad-eyed and all his red hair was coming out of his funny little pigtail and blowing about in the wind that was blowing all the garbage in at the front gate. He looked deranged. And he'd put on a lot of weight since I last saw him, too. He hung on to me, panting for breath.

'Tiffany . . .' (pant, heave, pant) '. . . is Tiffany here?'

'Do pull yourself together, Tristram, you've made a big, wet patch on my silk,' I said sharply.

'Didn't you catch last night's programme?'

'You wouldn't catch me dead watching your poxy programme.'

But Wheelchair catches it from time to time, cackling away in her genteel fashion, rejoicing even in her approaching senility at how low the house of Hazard has sunk in this its last generation – or, as she sometimes wittily puts it, cackling harder than ever, 'the final degeneration of the House of Hazard'. And we did watch the first five minutes, once, we felt we ought to take in our little Tiff's television debut.

Tiffany is the 'hostess', whatever that means. She smiles a lot, she shows her tits. What a waste. She'd have made a lovely dancer, if only she'd stuck with it. We watched her first five minutes. Five minutes was enough, I can tell you; then we adjourned to the boozer, muttering. His programme goes out live. That's its speciality.

'They'd get better ratings if he was dead,' said Nora. 'The only posthumous presenter on TV. What a coup.'

Tristram wiped his eyes with the back of his hand and then I saw he had been crying.

'Tiffany's missing,' he said.

That took the smile off my face, I can tell you. Nora yelled up from the kitchen. 'What's biting young Lochinvar?' He *was* in a state, blubbering and babbling, Scotch on his breath to knock you over. When we got him settled in an armchair, he thrust a cassette into my hand.

'Have a look,' he says. 'I can't explain. Watch it, see what happened.'

Then he spotted the photo of little Tiff in the silver frame that we keep on the breakfast-room mantelpiece and the waterworks started up again. I felt quite sorry for the poor kid. 'Kid', I say. He's all of thirty-five; he'll be pushing forty in no time. All the same, his stock in trade is boyish charm. God knows what he'll do when he loses that. But we were all a-tremble, all anxiety; what the fuck was going on? So Nora bunged his cassette in the VCR sharpish.

We got the VCR to catch up with those Busby Berkeley musicals they put out Saturday afternoons. We tape them, watch them over and over, freeze-frame our favourite bits. It drives Wheelchair mad. And Fred and Ginger, of course. Good old Fred. Nostalgia, the vice of the aged. We watch so many old movies our memories come in monochrome.

A burst of buzz and static shocked Wheelchair out of the trance she falls into when she's nicely greased with bacon after breakfast. 'What's happening? What's *he* doing here?' She fixed

Tristram with a suspicious eye, for he was no kin of hers, while the picture settled down on a flight of neon steps in a burst of canned applause as he came bounding down with his red hair slicked back, his top-of-the-milk-coloured rumpled linen Giorgio Armani whistle and flute, Tristram Hazard, weak but charming, game-show presenter and television personality, last gasp of the imperial Hazard dynasty that bestrode the British theatre like a colossus for a century and a half. Tristram, youngest son of the great Melchior Hazard, 'prince of players'; grandson of those tragic giants of the Victorian stage, Ranulph and Estella 'A star danced' Hazard. Lo, how the mighty have fallen.

'Hi, there! I'm Tristram!'

The camera closes in as he sings out, 'Hi, there, lolly lovers! I'm Tristram Hazard and I've come to bring you . . .' Now he throws back his head, showing off his throat, he's got a real, old-fashioned, full-bodied, Ivory Novello-type throat, he throws his head back and cries out in the voice of an ecstatic: 'LASHINGS OF LOLLY! LASHINGS OF LOLLY!'

The show begins.

Freeze-frame.

Let us pause awhile in the unfolding story of Tristram and Tiffany so that I can fill you in on the background. High time! you must be saying. Just who is this Melchior Hazard and his clan, his wives, his children, his hangers-on? It is in order to provide some of the answers to those questions that I, Dora Chance, in the course of assembling notes towards my own autobiography, have inadvertently become the chronicler of all the Hazards, although I should think that my career as such will go as publicly unacknowledged by the rest of the dynasty as my biological career has done for not only are Nora and I, as I have already told you, by-blows, but our father was a pillar of the legit. theatre and we girls are illegitimate in every way – not only born out of wedlock, but we went on the halls, didn't we!

Romantic illegitimacy, always a seller. It ought to copper-bottom the sales of my memoirs. But, to tell the truth, there was sod all romantic about *our* illegitimacy. At best, it was a farce, at worst, a tragedy, and a chronic inconvenience the rest of the time. But the urge has come upon me before I drop to seek out an answer to the question that always teased me, as if the answer were hidden, somewhere, behind a curtain: whence came we? Whither goeth we?

I know the answer to the second question, of course. Bound for oblivion, nor leave a wrack behind. Never spawned, neither of us, although Nora wanted to, everso, and towards the end of her menstrual life greeted each flow with tears. Me, no. I was pleased as Punch each time I saw it and even more so when it stopped, short, never to go again, like grandfather's clock in the old song though not at all like *our* grandfather clock, which remains in fine if high-pitched fettle, thank you very much.

But, as to the question of origins and past history, let me plunge deep into the archaeology of my desk, casting aside the photo of Ruby Keeler ('To Nora and Dora, four fabulous feet, from your Ruby').

Here it is. A fraying envelope stuffed with antique picture postcards. We've put together quite a collection over the years, bought, begged, borrowed, some sepia-toned, some tinted to show off her red, red hair. Our paternal grandmother, the one fixed point in our fathers' genealogy. Indeed, the one fixed point in our entire genealogy; our maternal side founders in a wilderness of unknowability and our other grandmother, Grandma, Grandma Chance, the grandma who fixed the grandfather clock, the grandma whose name we carry, she was no blood relation at all, to make confusion worse confounded. Grandma raised us, not out of duty, or due to history, but because of pure love, it was a genuine family romance, she fell in love with us the moment she clapped her eyes on us.

But we never met our *real* grandmother and only know her as you see her here, captured in the eternal youth of the publicity photo. 'A star danced and she was born,' they said. She was called Estella. Here she is as Juliet, as Portia, as Beatrice. See that 'Come hither!' smile. As Lady Macbeth, she manages to summon up a stern frown, quite the Miss Whiplash, but you can see a wicked little twinkle if you look hard.

She wasn't your Edwardian drayhorse type, she was little and skinny, with enormous eyes. She was a will-o'-the-wisp, all air and fire, and she could break your heart with one single sob but her son, our Uncle Perry, said she used to get the giggles, sometimes, in the middle of some big scene, the casket scene, the sleep-walking scene, she'd double up, everybody else would have to cover for her. Her hair was always coming undone, too, tumbling down her back, spraying out hairpins in all directions, her stockings at half-mast, her petticoat would come adrift in the middle of the street, her drawers start drooping. She was a marvel and she was a mess.

Here she is in drag as, famously, Hamlet. Black tights. Tremendous legs. Wasted on a classical actress. We've got the legs from her. She's emoting with the dagger: 'To be or not to be . . .' The obituary in *The New York Times* – careful with it, the paper's starting to crumble – says how she 'owed much to her New York Horatio, a superbly athletic young American with an exceptional gift of gravitas'.

Watch out for him, he'll pop up again. Cassius Booth. Yes. One of *those* Booths. His parents had a nerve, to call him Cassius.

The obituary hints at our paternal grandmother's enthusiasm for ahem indoor sports in the most tactful way. 'Generous, gallant, reckless; a woman who gave her all to life . . .' But she didn't so much give it away as throw it away, poor thing. She came to a sticky end, all right. This is her as Desdemona, in a white nightie with her spray of willow, just about to go into her number: 'A poor soul sat sighing by a sycamore tree . . .' This one is a real collector's item because –

No. Wait. I'll tell you all about it in my own good time.

Some time in or around the year 1870 (her date of birth, like that of so many actresses, a movable feast) our paternal grandmother was born in a trunk and trod the boards from toddlerhood as fairy, phantom, goblin, eventually, an old stager of eight (give or take a year or two) making her London debut as Mamillius in *The Winter's Tale* at the Theatre Royal, Haymarket, in, it says here, a 'somewhat pedantic' production by the younger Kean (Charles), and a costume copied from a Greek vase, rolling a hoop, a bit of business copied off another Greek vase. Lewis Carroll saw her, sent her an inscribed copy of *Alice*, invited her to tea and got her to slip her frock off after the crumpets, whereupon he snapped her in the altogether but she drew the line at imitating the action depicted upon certain other Greek vases, or so she always maintained. Here's the evidence of the encounter. See? He called it *Sprite*. I bought it at an auction at Christie's. Cost an arm and a leg. Couldn't resist. Not many people can boast a photo of their grandmother posing for kiddiporn. I sold one of poor old Irish's letters to pay for it.

Irish? Who's he?

You'll find out, soon enough. Suffice to say, if it hadn't been for poor old Irish and his philanthropic passion for the education of chorus girls, I'd not be sitting here, now, writing this. He taught me one end of a pen from the other. He gave me the confidence to use a word like 'philanthropic'. In return, I broke his heart. Fair exchange is no robbery.

When she played Mamillius, she doubled up as Columbine in the Harlequinade. Here's the programme. 'Little Estella'. She could do it all – make you laugh, make you cry, dance for you, sing you a song, but she was a fool for love.

It was a hard life. I will tell you what her life was like: greasepaint, gaslight, horseshit, coal smoke, railways – change at Crewe on Sundays. She was a child star but she grew up. She worked the provincial circuits, Juliet, Rosalind, Viola, Portia, Manchester, Birmingham, Liverpool, Nottingham, a big fish in a small pond; Hermia, Bianca, Iras in London, small fish in a big pond, until, in 1888, back she came to the Haymarket, her big chance, Cordelia to the Lear of Ranulph Hazard.

Ranulph, one of the great, roaring, actor-managers such as they don't make any more. I've read how, during his Macbeth, Queen Victoria gripped the curtains of the royal box until her knuckles whitened. Regicide, no fun for a reigning monarch. On his night, he'd scare you witless in the banquet scene even if his wife, caught by a fit of giggles, had her back to the audience, her shoulders shaking. (Peregrine said she'd told him she thought the Macbeths ought to sack the cook.) Ranulph Hazard's Richard III, 'the very incarnation of human evil', wrote GBS, not one to go overboard about a ham.

Don't let's sell Ranulph Hazard short. He was *good* on his night, although the punter never knew for sure when that night might be. Because the old man might come reeling on and slur out the words from another play altogether than that billed; or else he might be mopish, hungoverish, out of sorts and you couldn't hear a word beyond the first-row stalls, whatever he might be saying; or then again he might be too sober by half and sunk in some deep vale of despond when he'd just walk through it. There was always that element of chance with Ranulph, he was volatility in person, you'd diagnose a manic depressive, these days, and stick him on lithium.

But, on his night, a marvel.

And Shakespeare was a kind of god for him. It was as good as idolatry. He thought the whole of human life was there.

So it was on one of his marvellous nights, he met a shooting star. What an ecstasy the two of them provoked! Rivers of tears. Tempests of applause. One famous bit of business has got into all the theatre books – when poor old Lear makes it up with his daughter at last, Ranulph always used to put his fingers to his cheek, then look at his fingertips in wonder, touch his mouth then say in a trembly, geriatrically uncertain way: 'Be your tears wet?' That brought out the hankies, all right. They said her smile in answer, 'tremulous, through tears, as April sunshine', almost, but not quite, capped it. So he and Estella fell in love. How could they resist? An old man and a prodigal daughter, the stuff that dreams are made of.

Here's a funny thing. That was just how Tristram's mother, Lady Hazard III, collared Melchior – by playing Cordelia to his Lear.

Old Ranulph was a good thirty years older than Estella, or more, or even much more – *his* date of birth is as variable as hers. All the same, they tied the knot *toot sweet* (as that other grandma, Grandma Chance, used to say) in St Paul's, Covent Garden, the actors' church, with half the profession crossing their fingers for them and the other half staying away on principle due to Ranulph owing them money or having adulterized them. She wore her red hair hanging down her back, a wreath of lilies of the valley, she was nineteen or thereabouts. Lamb to the slaughter, one might have said, seeing his grey hairs, his shaking hand, his dubious finances – he was a drunk, a bankrupt, a gambler, he'd fretted and philandered and beaten and betrayed three wives into early graves, already. But no sacrificial lamb nor shrinking violet she. She was a wild thing, even if she was always true to him in her fashion. I don't have anything of her in me, not at all. I am the sentimental one. But Nora, sometimes.

There's a recording of Ranulph, made on a wax cylinder, I went to that place off Kensington High Street, they played it for me. Crackle, hiss, and then his voice: 'Tomorrow and tomorrow and tomorrow . . .' A shudder ran through me, not because of sentiment, but because of the voice itself. It wasn't what I expected, it was ugly, almost – harsh, grating, the words sounded as if they'd been wrenched out of him. And there I was, in tears, too, like the snufflers in the Haymarket all those years ago, but not just because of what he said and who he was but because of the way he said it, that sounded so alien to me, so strange in my ears, because of his flattened 'a's, and his consonants, that were cut, like glass. Only a hundred years ago . . . My own grandfather. Yet it was a voice from before the Flood, from another kind of life entirely, so antique-sounding that it scarcely seems possible his granddaughters now sit in silk camiknickers in the basement of a house in Brixton, drinking tea and watching on television his great-grandson address an invisible audience out of a plastic box, in that between-two-worlds, neither Brit nor Yank, twang of the game-show host:

'Say it again for me! LASHINGS OF LOLLY!'

Lo, how the mighty have fallen. An S-M game show? How low can you get?

So Ranulph and Estella were married and first of all he loved her madly and vice versa and then Barnum, P. T. Barnum, Barnum of Barnum and Bailey, *that* Barnum, struck by her legs in *As You Like It*, made her an offer. *Hamlet* in a tent in Central Park. A tent because, he prophesied, no theatre on Broadway would be big enough to hold the crowds.

She must have eyed her old man sideways, wondering how he took it; he'd been the most melancholy Dane of his generation, hadn't he, but that had been a generation or two before, Hamlet is nothing if not a *juve* role. Ranulph, though, was all agog to give to America the tongue that Shakespeare spake. So they crossed the Atlantic and Ranulph did them proud as Hamlet's father, while suave young Cassius Booth stepped into the limelight beside her as Hamlet's best friend.

Hamlet under canvas, a smash. It ran and ran and would have run ad infinitum except the twins announced that they were on the way and a female Hamlet is one thing but a pregnant prince is quite another. So twin boys, our fathers, were born in the USA. Melchior and Peregrine. What names, eh? What delusions of grandeur went into the naming of them? If you shorten them to 'Mel' and 'Perry', they've got a democratically twentieth-century and transatlantic ring to them but Old Ranulph, rattling old nineteenth-century romantic that he was, never did that, although Estella, with a wink, often.

Note how I call them both 'our fathers', as if we had the two and, in a sense, so we did. Melchior it was who did the biologically necessary, it's true, but Peregrine *passed* as our father – that is, he was the one who publicly acknowledged us when Melchior would not. I should tell you, now, that Melchior's entire family, Wheelchair apart, always maintained this fiction, too, which is why Saskia told Tristram we were his aunts and not his sisters. But Peregrine was so much beloved by us and behaved so much more fatherly to us, not to mention paying most of the bills, that I know I need to claim him as something more than uncle.

Speaking of illegitimacy, there was more than a hint of romantic, nay, melodramatic illegitimacy in the Hazard family long before Nora and myself took our first bows. Because Ranulph Hazard, during all his lengthy marital and extramarital career, had produced no issue, as yet, until his wife's transvestite Hamlet met her Horatio's exceptional gift of gravitas, not to mention his athleticism. Tongues wagged. Did Melchior lend an ear? Who can tell, at this distance in time. All the same, he loved his boys. He cast them as princes in the tower as soon as they could toddle.

One thing you must know about Ranulph. He was half mad and thought he had a Call. Now he saw the entire world as his mission field and out of all of us it has turned out that Gareth Hazard, SJ, has stayed most faithful to the family tradition of proselytizing zeal, for now the old man was seized with the most imperative desire, to spread and go on spreading the Word overseas. Willy-nilly, off must go his wife and children, too, to take Shakespeare where Shakespeare had never been before.

In those days, there was so much pink on the map of the world that English was spoken everywhere. No language problem. Off to the ends of the Empire they went, rolling to the rhythms of the sea as they crossed, crisscrossed the oceans. I see it in my mind's eye as if it were a movie – the ocean liner slipping her moorings, gliding away from the quay, the siren blaring, the crowd throwing flowers, the red-haired woman on the deck, smiling, waving, smiling.

Our Uncle Peregrine inherited her scarlet hair. So did our half-sisters, Saskia and Imogen. Tristram, too. Not us, worse luck. The red hair only went to the legit. side. As for me and

Nora, first of all, we were mouse. Then we dyed it. When we stopped dyeing (black), we found out that we had, all unbeknownst to ourselves, gone grey.

Our Uncle Peregrine was his mother's boy.

We were hurrying down the street, he told me, on tour in Australia. It was in Sydney, down by the Circular Quay. We were on our way to some ladies' lunch club – she did guest appearances, it helped with the finances, Ranulph was chronically short of a bob. We were late, of course, because she hadn't been able to find a clean frock but after much rummaging came up with one with only a couple of little wine stains and smear of marmalade so she pinned a bunch of frangipani over the worst of it and got her hair up, somehow. Melchior stayed behind with Father, to watch him running through Julius Caesar. We came to an organ-grinder, we stopped to admire the monkey. She gave the organ-grinder sixpence and he played 'Daisy, Daisy'. She took my hand and we danced, right there, on the pavement. Her hairpins scattered everywhere. My celluloid collar burst in two. The monkey clapped its paws together. Everybody stared. 'Come on!' she said to the world in general. 'Join in!' Then everybody started dancing, they all took hold of the hand of the next perfect stranger. 'I'm half crazy, all for the love of you.' She looked upon what she had accomplished and was glad. We missed soup, we missed fish, we arrived at the table at the same time as the chicken. Her hair was down her back, she'd lost her flowers, one slipper with a broken heel, her small son collarless, tieless, and I'd got the monkey on my shoulder – she'd swapped her gold watch for it. She did them Portia's speech, 'The quality of mercy ...' She made them happy. There was mango ice-cream for dessert, our favourite. We had three bowlfuls each. In Melbourne, they named a sundae after her, 'Ice-cream Estella', mango ice-cream topped with passionfruit purée. If ever we get to Melbourne, together, Floradora, I'll treat you to an 'Ice-cream Estella'.

Always the lucky one, our Peregrine, even in his memories, which were full of laughter and dancing; he always remembered the good times.

Peregrine Hazard, adventurer, magician, seducer, explorer, scriptwriter, rich man, poor man – but never either beggarman or thief. At our age, Nora and I have got more friends among the dead than with the living. We often go visiting in cemeteries to trim the grass growing over the friends of our youth but we don't even know where your grave might be, dear Perry, to go and lay a flower on it. You spent your childhood on the road, here today, gone tomorrow; you grew up a restless man. You loved change. And fornication. And trouble. And, funnily enough, towards the end, you loved butterflies. Peregrine Hazard, lost among the butterflies, lost in the jungle, vanished away as neatly and completely as if you had become the object of one of those conjuring tricks you were so fond of.

If an ice-cream sundae was named after Estella in Melbourne, then an entire dried-out township in New South Wales was renamed Hazard, after she and Ranulph put on al fresco *Coriolanus*. A street in Hobart, Tasmania. And they toured India, not once, but several times – crossing, crisscrossing the subcontinent. The gleaming rails sliding beneath the churning wheels, the puffing smokestack, the leaves falling off the calendar and blowing away in the wind . . . A maharajah gave the boys a baby elephant but they couldn't take it with them on the train. He fell in love with Estella, and promised her her weight in rubies if she would stay behind and recite him every night Viola's 'willow cabin' speech. What did she do? we asked. She made him happy, said Peregrine. She had a gift for that. She made him happy, then she left him. She had a gift for leaving, too.

The red-haired woman, smiling, waving to the disappearing shore. She left the maharajah; she left innumerable other lights o' passing love in towns and cities and theatres and railway stations all over the world. But Melchior she did not leave.

A theatre, long since demolished, named the Hazard, in Shanghai. Then Hong Kong. Then Singapore. Everything a little threadbare, now, a little shabby. The ocean, again. North America, again – Montreal. Toronto. Crossing, crisscrossing the prairies. Hazard, Alberta, flat as a plateful of snow. Hazard, North Dakota – no township too small to receive them, nor to reciprocate the honour by rechristening itself. The touring was turning into a kind of madness. In Arkansas, the Hazards' patched and ravaged tent went up in the spaces vacated by the travelling evangelicals: Ranulph, lean, haggard, bearded, more and more resembled John the Baptist had John the Baptist reached old age.

They arrived at last in the south-west and pitched their tent in arid scrub in a town called Gun Barrel, Texas, renamed

Hazard, after the Hazards played *Macbeth* there with a hired band of campesinos as the Scottish army, holding spiked ears of prickly pear above their heads to mimic Birnam Wood. Of all these wild, strange and various places, Hazard, Texas, was the one that Perry remembered best; he went back there, later, a grizzled old-timer or two wept in his beer to recall how Estella made him happy, they made her son an honorary sheriff.

Props and costumes were lost or stolen or fell to pieces and then were begged or improvised or patched and darned. Ranulph drank and gambled and declaimed; he was going to pieces, too. He shouted at America but it would no longer listen to him. One night, in a bar at Tucson, Arizona, he gambled away his crown from *Lear* and Estella put together a new one for him out of a bit of cardboard. She dabbed on some gold paint. 'Here you are.'

Why did she stay with him? Perish the thought, perhaps she truly loved him; perhaps all those people she made happy were just so many sideshows. But she'd lost the knack of making Melchior happy.

Then, one day, deep in the Midwest, as they were setting up in a townlet where they had hopes of a decent-sized audience since all there was to do in the evenings, otherwise, was to watch the corn grow, Ranulph received a cable from New York. While the Hazards roamed themselves to rags for the greater glory of Shakespeare, Cassius Booth, Estella's old Horatio, stayed in one place and prospered. Now he was an actor-manager himself, with his very own theatre on the Great White Way. And was he a man to forget old friends? Not he! Estella looked enigmatic and she smiled, said Perry. She was still a girl, remember. No more than thirty. Or, at most, thirty-five. While Old Ranulph was pushing seventy and staked his final gamble on it, on one last triumphant prayer meeting. He'd show 'em all! He'd flare up one last incandescent time on Broadway in a sort of Shakespearian funeral pyre. But the play he picked on was, alas, *Othello*.

Thirty or thirty-five, whatever she was, she doesn't look more than a schoolgirl in the picture on the postcard, in her nightie, with her hair down her back. 'Sing willow, willow, willow.' Cassius Booth played Iago. There is no handkerchief in this story. All the same, her husband killed them both, first her, then him. They'd slipped out together during the first-night party. Old acquaintances. Perhaps, by then, Old Ranulph couldn't tell the difference between Shakespeare and living. Next morning, the notices were magnificent but the murder itself had to wait for the noon editions because the chambermaid didn't find the bodies on the bed in Estella's hotel room until she brought up late breakfast. Three bodies. He shot them both and then he shot himself.

Exeunt omnes. She'd always had a gift for exits.

But life goes on.

The two little boys were stranded in New York, poor tragic waifs, and there they almost expired themselves, or so Perry said, because they were so stuffed with candy, hot dogs and pie à la mode by the lovely ladies with low-slung bosoms and feathered hats who went about their business in the hotel lobby. There was no money left as such, only an actor's inheritance of unpaid bills, paste jewellery, flash attitudes, but the Plaza extended them credit and so they learned to live beyond their means.

Now, although these two were twins, they were *not* alike as two peas. Melchior, at ten, was dark and brooding, registering already the beginnings of the profile which would dominate Shaftesbury Avenue. That profile was to Melchior what Clark Gable's ears were to him. Dark eyes, lashes of the kind they say are 'wasted on a boy' and a physique that turned out to be ready-made for leaping and fencing and climbing up to balconies and all the things a Shakespearian actor needs to do. I know that all these things, not forgetting his 'splendid gift of gravitas', all together point the finger at Cassius Booth as his father, but don't forget that poor old Ranulph had been a matinée idol, too, in his day, even if in his day women wore crinolines, and there remains a gigantic question mark over the question of their paternity, although whoever it was who contributed the actual jism, no child need ever have been ashamed of either contender and, as for me, the grandchild, I like to think *both* of them had a hand in it, if you follow me.

But Peregrine was a holy terror and couldn't keep a straight face, just like his mother. As young Macduff, he'd entered with a piss-pot on his head and given an audience of sheepshearers outside Perth their best moment of the evening. Melchior never let him on the stage again. Even as little scraps, Melchior was all for art and Peregrine was out for fun. Don't think that, just because they were brothers, they liked one another. Far from it. Chalk and cheese.

They lived on room service and the kindness of strangers until the boat docked from Leith and off it came their comeuppance – Miss Euphemia Hazard, dour as hell, Presbyterian to the backbone, their aunt. Warden of a workhouse near Pitlochry and sworn enemy of the stage and all who trod it, who never shed a tear for brother or for sister-in-law because she thought their violent ends were the Lord's revenge, a kind of wild justice. She grabbed Melchior by the scruff, stuffed him shrieking into a trunk marked 'Not wanted on voyage', and reached out for Peregrine but he gave a shrug and a wriggle and left his old tweed jacket in her hand while he himself was gone, whoosh! out of the window, down the fire escape, a shirtsleeved, carrot-topped ten-year-old hurtling helter-skelter down the pavement, sending a hot-dog stand flying, a bootblack sprawling and . . . he vanished.

Vanished clean away into America and though, later on, he told a wondrous tale of all his doings and hoboings as a boy, as to what *really* befell him, I do not have a notion except that it can have been no cakewalk and, when he first found us, he was as rich as Croesus.

So Peregrine ran for it, lickety-split, hell for leather, but Melchior was trapped.

Now, Melchior had adored his father, worshipped him, even, and took away from the grand catastrophe of his parents' lives only one little souvenir – the pasteboard crown that Ranulph wore for Lear, the one Estella made. God knows how Melchior smuggled this relic past his aunt.

It was in his blood, wasn't it? Every night, during the dour years of rain and porridge, as he lay in his freezing bed under the one plaid rug his aunt permitted him, he'd recite to himself word for word his father's greatest roles. Macbeth. Hamlet. (Although never Othello, of course.) Aunt Effie's Highland clock – you've seen it for yourself, the antlered grandfather now resident at 49 Bard Road – struck twelve, then one, then two. He would so move himself with these solitary renditions he would cry himself to sleep. His aunt forbade Melchior point-blank to so much as think of the stage, although she recognized how he had sufficient talent in that direction – that is, rhetoric, etc. – to urge him to give the ministry a go and, when she became insistent, then he took matters into his own hands.

He wrapped the pasteboard crown up in a change of shirt and

underthings, tied all in a handkerchief and said goodbye to Pitlochry for ever. I can see him now, setting out to seek his fortune like Dick Whittington in panto. Miss Effie's clock sang out five times as he shut the workhouse door behind him. It would have been bitter cold, no stars, still pitch-dark. A cart went past with a load of kale; he got a lift a mile or two. The sun would have been coming up, by then. No friends, no kin except a lost brother half a world away whom he'd never got on with. Mad with pride and ambition and nothing in the world except his dark eyes and gift of gravitas and a toy crown with the gold paint peeling off.

And so he finally found his way to London, and, in due course, down on his uppers, nay, down on the uppers of his uppers, he arrived at this very house, which was, in those days, a boarding house that catered for theatricals, though not, I should say, theatricals of the well-heeled variety.

Brixton, before the lights went out over Europe, hub of a wheel of theatres, music halls, Empires, Royalties, what have you. You could tram it all over from Brixton. The streets of tall, narrow houses were stuffed to the brim with stand-up comics; adagio dancers; soubrettes; conjurers; fiddlers; speciality acts with dogs, doves, goats, you name it; dancing dwarves; tenors, sopranos, baritones and basses, both solo artistes and doubled up in any of the permutations of the above as duets, trios etc. And also those who wrung a passion to tatters for a living and therefore considered themselves a cut above.

In those days, our mother emptied the slops, filled the washstand jugs, raked out the grates, built up the fires, brought up the cans of hot water, scrubbed the back of the occasional gentleman and herself occasionally –

or perhaps only the one time.

Chance by name, Chance by nature. We were not planned.

Melchior slept here. This attic, the cheapest room in the house, cheaper still because he never paid. I picture him in front of a square of mirror, trying on that shabby crown, emoting, listening to the sycamores at the end of the garden thrashing about in the wind and pretending the sound they made was applause. Desperate, ravenous, on the make, tramping round the agents day after day after day, back to the boiled cabbage at Bard Road and the hard, narrow bed. I wonder if he lent his mouth here, his arsehole there, to see if that would do the trick. I suppose my mother must have felt sorry for him. I can imagine her stripping off in the cold room, turning towards the starving boy. How did she do it? Shyly? Nervously? Lewdly?

Then everything fades to black. I can't bear to think any further. It hurts too much. You always like to think a bit of love, or at least a little pleasure, went into your making but I do not know, I cannot guess, if the dark-eyed stranger who put his hand up the skirt of the penniless orphan was cynical, or tender, or desperate, or carried away by the moment. Had she done it before, did she know what she was doing? Was she scared? Or full of desire? Or half raped? He was good-looking enough, God knows. Women went mad for him. Perhaps she was the first woman who went mad for him. Did she think about him when she made his bed up in the mornings? Had she pressed her cheek against the pillow and wished the pillow were his cheek?

'She was only a slip of a thing but she was bold as brass,' Grandma used to say.

I'd like to think it went like this: She closed the door behind her, locked it. There he was on the bed, brushing up his Shakespeare. He looked up, hastily laying aside his well-thumbed copy of the *Collected Works*. She started pulling off her chemise. 'Now I've got you where I want you!' she said. What else could a gentleman do but succumb?

Nine months later, her heart gave out when we were born. Apart from that, I don't know anything about her. We don't even know what she looked like, there isn't a picture. She was called Kitty, like a little stray cat. Fatherless, motherless. Perhaps Mrs Chance's house was even a haven to her, in spite of the stairs – she must have run up and down the stairs twenty times a day, thirty times a day. And the grates to be leaded, the front steps to be scoured.

Not that Mrs Chance was what the French call *exigeante*. She didn't run the fanciest boarding house in Brixton, it barely managed to cling on to respectability by the skin of its teeth, and you could have said the same of her. There were Boston ferns, in green glazed pots, on stands, and Turkey rugs, but the whole place never looked *plausible*. It looked like the stage set of a theatrical boarding house, as if Grandma had done it up to suit a role she'd chosen on purpose. She was a mystery, was Mrs Chance.

Melchior Hazard slept here, but not for long. His theatre-doorstep vigils, his audition ordeals paid off. He and his cardboard crown were gone by the time our mother missed her first period. She vomited every morning, quietly, so that Mrs Chance would not hear. The war began, that August, but I don't think our mother cared. Mrs Chance never heard the vomiting but she heard the tears.

We came bursting out on a Monday morning, on a day of sunshine and high wind when the Zeppelins were falling. First one wee, bawling girl; then the other, while Mrs Chance did all the necessary. She'd called the doctor but he never got there. Our mother took a look, too weak to hold us, she'd been in labour since the day before yesterday, but Mrs Chance always told us she took a good look and managed a smile.

Why should she have smiled? She was just seventeen years old, no man, no home. There was a war on. All the same, Mrs Chance always told us that she smiled and Mrs Chance was sometimes stingy with the truth but never lied. 'Why shouldn't she smile? She hadn't got a mum or dad. A baby is the next best thing.'

The sky was blue, that morning, said Mrs Chance, and there was a wind that made the washing on the clotheslines dance. Monday, washday. What a sight! All over Brixton, long black stockings stepping out with gents' longjohns, striped shirts doing the Lambeth Walk with flannel nighties, French knickers doing the cancan with the frilly petticoats, pillowslips, sheets, towels, hankies all a-flutter, like flags and banners, everything in motion. The bombs stopped and the little kids came out to play again. The sun shone, the kids were singing. When Grandma Chance had had a couple, she sometimes sang the song they sang when we were born:

> The moon shines bright on Charlie Chaplin
> And his shoes are crackin'
> For want of blackin'
> And his little baggy trousers they need mendin'
> Before they send him
> To the Dardanelles.

Poor old Charlie, pushing up the daisies, now. Old Charlie. Hung like a horse.

So there was dancing and singing all along Bard Road and Mrs

Chance picked us up, one on each arm, and took us to the window so the first thing we saw with our swimming baby eyes was sunshine and dancing. Then a seagull swooped up, past the window, up and away. She told us about the seagull so often that although I cannot really remember it, being just hatched out, all the same, I do believe I saw that seagull fly up into the sky.

There was a little sigh behind us and she was gone.

The doctor got there ten minutes after, he wrote out the death certificate. That was that. So Mrs Chance adopted us but never let us call her 'mother', out of respect for the dead. We always called her 'Grandma', and 'Chance' became our handle.

But I don't think for one moment that 'Chance' was her own name, either. All that I know about her is: she'd arrived at 49 Bard Road on New Year's Day, 1900, with a banker's draft for the first year's rent and the air of a woman making a new start in a new place, a new century and, or so the evidence points, a new name. If she decided to call herself 'Mrs', it was part and parcel of that shaky swipe after respectability I've mentioned, because I never caught one whiff of husband and, to tell the truth, she never lost a rakish air.

She wasn't tall, about five foot two, five two and a half, but solid-built like an armoured car. She always put on so much Rachel powder she puffed out a fine cloud if you patted her. She rouged big, round spots in the middle of her cheeks. She used so much eyeblack that kiddies on Electric Avenue used to give her a chorus of 'Two Lovely Black Eyes' as she passed by. For all the thirty years we knew her, thanks to peroxide, she was canary-coloured blonde. She always pencilled in a big, black beauty spot below the left-hand corner of her mouth.

For outdoors, she wore black and she never went out without one of those square oilcloth carrier bags in which she kept her fat leather purse, a clean handkerchief in an envelope she'd marked in pencil 'clean hankercheif', a couple of safety pins, in case, as she said, her drawers fell down, and often an empty or two on its way back to the off-licence. There'd be a little black toque on her head, with a spotted veil. And I always remember her grey lisle stockings, that she secured below each knee with two lengths of knotted elastic.

Indoors, providing the boarders weren't around, she never wore a stitch, as often as not. She was a convert to naturism. She thought it was good for us kiddies, to get the air and sunlight on our skins, as well, so we saved a lot of wear and tear on clothes and often gambolled naked in the backyard, to the astonishment of the neighbours, who were a proper lot. Brixton's changed, a good deal. These days, you could stage a three-point orgy in the garden and nobody would bat an eye except that bloke with the earring next door might pipe up, 'Got enough condoms?'

She didn't so much talk as elocute. She rhymed 'sky' with 'bay', and made 'mountaynes' out of 'molehills', except sometimes she forgot herself, the air turned blue. We'd been out in the market, once, stocking up on rabbit food – she'd a passion for salads, it went with all that naturism. During her strictest periods, she'd make us a meal of a cabbage, raw in summer, boiled in winter. There we were, picking over the greens, when some prim voice behind us, rudely referring to Grandma, opined: '. . . no better than she oughter be . . .'

Grandma swung round, dukes up: 'What the fuck d'you mean?'

We never found out who set her up in Bard Road and she never volunteered the information of her own accord. She'd invented herself, she was a one-off and she kept her mystery intact until the end, although she left us everything, we owe her everything and the older we grow, the more like her we become. Triumph of nature over nurture, ducky. Only goes to show.

To this day I swear, sometimes, late at night, I hear a soft thump, thump, her bare feet on the stairs, coming down to make sure the gas is off in the kitchen, the front door is locked, us girls are safe home. And there's a smell of crushed mint that lingers in the breakfast room, sometimes, because her favourite tipple was crème de menthe frappé, with a sprig of mint, in season, but she'd drink whatever she could lay her hands on the rest of the time. And that boiled cabbage of hers. There's an aroma in the area we can't get rid of, no matter what we try. At first we thought it was the drains. We never touch cabbage, ourselves, not now we're grown up. I couldn't look a cabbage in the eye after what Grandma did to them. Boiled them to perdition. The abattoir is kinder to a cow.

She took to children like a duck to water, enough to make you wonder why she'd not had any of her own. I asked her about that, once, years later; she said she'd never, not until she picked us up and cuddled us that very first morning, known what men were *for*. 'I'd often wondered,' she said. 'When I saw you two, the penny dropped.'

You must remember that there was a war on, when we were born. If we made her happy, then we didn't add much to the collective sum of happiness in the whole of South London. First of all, the neighbours' sons went marching off, sent to their deaths, God help them. Then the husbands, the brothers, the cousins, until, in the end, all the men went except the ones with one foot in the grave and those still in the cradle, so there was a female city, red-eyed, dressed in black, outside the door, and Grandma said it then, she said it again in 1939: 'Every twenty years, it's bound to happen. It's to do with generations. The old men get so they can't stand the competition and they kill off all the young men they can lay their hands on. They daren't be seen to do it themselves, that would give the game away, the mothers wouldn't stand for it, so all the men all over the world get together and make a deal: you kill off our boys and we'll kill off yours. So that's that. Soon done. Then the old men can sleep easy in their beds, again.'

When the bombardments began, Grandma would go outside and shake her fist at the old men in the sky. She knew they hated women and children worst of all. She'd come back in and cuddle us. She lullabyed us, she fed us. She was our air-raid shelter; she was our entertainment; she was our breast.

The boarders dwindled off. Too much babyshit in the bathroom. Naked babies crawling in the hall. Nobody made the beds, nobody made the porridge – the help all found good jobs in the armaments factories, didn't they, much to Grandma's disgust. They would depart while she harangued them. What did Grandma do for money? The odd, and I mean 'odd', lady vocalist might rent a room for an hour, to practise her scales, or a not too-fussy adagio dancer want to put her feet up for twenty minutes, ahem, ahem. Visitors used the front door, up the front steps; we went down the area steps to the door in the basement.

When we were just babbling our first 'g'anma', that clock turned up. The stag-topped grandfather. Shipped to us direct from Pitlochry, from the estate of Miss Euphemia Hazard, deceased, with a note to say that 49 Bard Road was the last known address of her nephew, Melchior, so they sent it here. She left it to him in her will. Everything else went to the poor.

Grandma cursed and swore when she read that. She couldn't bear to think that clock was all we'd get. She moved hell and high water to seek our father out. She left no stone unturned lest, as she told us later, she found him lurking underneath. Then, all of a sudden, it was the Armistice, and there he was, in the West End, playing Romeo, no less! so Grandma put on her toque and went to a matinée. Some acrobatic dancer who'd put up in the first-floor back while she was resting kept an eye on us while Grandma was gone, she taught us back-flips, we were having a whale of a time until Grandma came back with a face like the wrath of God. 'You look like you need a cuppa,' said the acrobatic dancer so they adjourned and we went on back-flipping until we fancied a bit of bread and dripping, which is when, tripping into the breakfast room, we overheard our grandma. 'He flatly denies it and there's sod all I can do.' Neither Nora nor I could make head or tail of that, but both of them picked us up and hugged us. 'Poor little things!' And we got double rations, two slices each, and a bit of raspberry jam on it, too.

That acrobatic dancer upped and married a peer, in the end. It's a funny old world.

So life went on, as usual, until, one fine day that self-same year, just a few weeks later, came a knocking at the door.

Knock, knock; who's there? And off I stumped to answer it.

Knock, knock.

The knocker got a shock.

A naked child greeted the stranger. Not a scrap on but for the big, blue bow in my brown hair, and a black eyepatch. There was a big scimitar of silver paper in my hand and another child perched on the stairs, the spitting image, not so much a twin, more of an optical illusion, like as two peas except that *her* ribbon was green and she wore a red flag with the skull and crossbones on it knotted round her shoulders as a cloak. Both of us little girls stared at the newcomer with cold, round eyes: what have we here?

What an unwelcome! Such an unwelcome that he couldn't help but laugh.

Ooh, wasn't he a handsome young man, in those days. If I find myself describing him in the language of the pulp romance, then you must forgive me – there was always that quality about Perry, especially when he was glorious in his twenties, broad of shoulder, heavy of thigh, with his unruly thatch of burnished copper hair, the lavish spattering of freckles across his nose, laughing green eyes flecked with gold. He wore a scratched, weathered flying jacket with the shoulder flash of the US Flying Corps and his left arm was in a sling. It was our Uncle Peregrine from America but we didn't know him from Adam.

When he saw that he was hurting our feelings he smothered his laughter but there was still a delighted little quiver playing around his lips as he dropped down to his knees so that we were all three more equal in height to inspect his new-found nieces more thoroughly. He rummaged in his pocket and produced, not candy, nor pennies, but a pristine white handkerchief which he shook out and displayed to the girls: am I hiding anything?

We shook our heads. No. We could see that, like ourselves, he hid nothing.

He knotted the handkerchief and showed it to us again. A simple knot: nothing but a knot.

We inched closer to him, fascinated.

Ceremoniously he unknotted his handkerchief and, lo and behold! a white dove flew out, flew twice round the hall, then perched on top of the antlers on the grandfather clock, went: 'Voo, croo!' and, to the immense annoyance of our grandma, who just then ascended the basement staircase to find out what was going on, crapped on the carpet. Grandma had got her knickers on, thank God. Then we all went into the kitchen and drank tea and we little lady pirates sat on Peregrine Hazard's knee and ransacked his pockets in search of more doves, finding none, but a Fuller's walnut cake, instead, which Grandma accepted with wary politeness. Fuller's walnut cake has gone the way of all flesh, worse luck, I wouldn't mind a slice of Fuller's walnut cake right now. It turned out we were all very partial to Fuller's walnut cake so we had some slices of that and things eased up a bit, although Peregrine was thoroughly upset and embarrassed by the mission he'd undertaken out of a sense of duty to the brother he'd only just met again.

And not even so much out of a sense of duty to Melchior as to the dead ones, the grandparents.

Now, how had it come to pass that Peregrine Hazard, with a

dove in his pocket, popped up in Brixton that glorious afternoon to make us all happy? Remember, you last saw him haring down the Great White Way out of the clutches of his Aunt Effie into –

Into what? That's a poser.

Over the years, Peregrine offered us a Chinese banquet of options as to what happened to him next. He gave us all his histories, we could choose which ones we wanted – but they kept on changing, so. That was the trouble. Did he really meet up with Ambrose Bierce in a flophouse in El Paso and go off with him to fight in Mexico? (In confirmation of this, in *sole* confirmation, I'm bound to say, one personalized dedication in a copy of *The Devil's Dictionary*.) Was it true he'd posed as Ben Traven? I knew for a fact he'd worked in circuses. Unless it was on the halls. Or else he'd perfected his stage magic, his juggling and conjuring tricks, to entertain his fellow prospectors during the long winter evenings in Alaska. Above all, how did he grow so rich?

'That's easy,' he said and his face split in a big grin. 'I struck gold in Alaska.'

But he was a *very* good juggler. You couldn't deny him that. He told me once that W. C. Fields taught him how to juggle, but I'm not sure I believe that.

Grandma was pleased to see that such a handsome young man had got out of the clutches of the old men with only a flesh wound to show for it, i.e. shrapnel in the upper arm; it gave her hope for the continuance of the human race, she said. The more he and Grandma chewed the fat, the more they saw eye to eye until at last, all embarrassment, he told her the reason for his visit . . . it turned out that he'd volunteered to bear Grandma the glad tidings of Melchior's impending marriage.

Yes! Melchior was engaged to be married and wanted to pay us all off in case we made trouble at some future date.

'He's changed his tune,' said Grandma. 'I bearded the bastard in his den after a matinée of *Romeo* the other day; he was at a disadvantage, he'd only got his tights and some mascara on but he still denied paternity.'

'Between you and me,' confided Peregrine, 'I do believe he's afraid you'll show up at the wedding with the girls in tow.'

They roared. We kiddies didn't understand one word, of course, but we looked from one to the other and started laughing because they were laughing. 'Poor little innocents,' said Grandma. The pirates' father was joining high society – a grand wedding in St John's Smith Square, with twelve bridesmaids, and dukes present, and the bride in white by Worth, which is when we first heard the name, Lady Atalanta Lynde.

'The bride is loaded, ladies,' Perry assured us.

'Well,' said Mrs Chance, 'let him unload some of his ill-gotten gains on us.' Seeing Perry's dubious look: 'If you haven't got a ticket, you can't win, me old duck. Remember the Russian proverb: "Hope for the best, expect the worst".'

That was her motto. Ours, too.

But after all that, it was Peregrine himself who did the gentlemanly thing. That is, *his* name was on the cheques that now started to arrive the first of every month at Bard Road. When Grandma quizzed him, he went pink under his freckles and said, Melchior and he decided to give out that it was Peregrine who'd done the dirty deed, if anybody asked, and, begging her pardon, would she ever forgive him? but he'd used her name in vain. That is, Mrs Chance, our adoptive grandma and guardian, had gone down in the account books as our mother to keep the accountants happy. 'They've as good as married us!' she said. She laughed so much she fell off her chair.

But we little girls paid no attention; we crouched over Perry's latest gift, a phonograph, as, with the most exquisite care, Nora set down the needle on the wondrous black Bakelite pancake our Uncle Perry had told us would sing for us, if we wound up the handle. Hiss. Whirr. Then, thin, faint and as astonishing as if it were another of his tricks, out of the big horn came music – a trumpet, a trombone, a banjo, drums. A song, our song, a song that made us a promise our father never kept, though others did: 'I can't give you anything but love, baby.'

At the first bars, we couldn't help it, it was as if a voice told us to do it, we were impelled, we got up and danced. 'Dance,' I say, but we didn't know how – we jumped about in time and clapped our hands. Perry watched us for a bit, smiling, then said: 'Come on, girls, I'll show you the real thing.' He gave the gramophone another wind.

I can't give you anything but love, baby,
That's the only thing I've plenty of, baby . . .

Grandma calmed down a bit, he held his hand out. She'd still got the rudiments, stout though she was; the way she danced was the only clue to her past she ever gave. Then we were all dancing, right there, in the breakfast room, and, as for us, we haven't stopped dancing, yet, have we, Nora? We'll go on dancing till we drop.

Dream awhile, scheme awhile . . .

What a joy it is to dance and sing!

Perry gave us a lot more than love, in those days. He added another digit to his monthly cheque to pay for dancing lessons. He was a dutiful father. He doubled as sugar daddy, too. Every other Sunday, he arrived with parcels from Hamleys and Harrods and Selfridges, he'd pull red ribbons out of our ears and flags from his nostrils, he'd sit us on his knee and feed us Fuller's walnut cake and then he'd wind up the gramophone and we'd dance. After that, he and Grandma would have a couple of drinks and a few laughs; they were like conspirators.

But, pilgrim by name, pilgrim by nature, came the day the wanderlust seized him by the throat again. He must be up and off, he must be up and doing. He dropped off a crate of crème de menthe for Grandma, tap shoes for me and Nora. Then he was gone and left no forwarding address although the postcards came every month or so and every Christmas we'd get a hamper full of rotten fruit or a box of straw and shards that had been fine china when he packed it from places we could never find on the map. He never knew what would travel and what wouldn't.

But one last little gift arrived on its own two legs and announced itself, not with a knock on the front door but a humble little scrabble down the area, where the family went. When Grandma went to open up, there she was, a wee scrap of humanity thin as a lathe, busted shoes, no stockings, just a shawl around her shoulders and a man's cap on her head. She'd have been fourteen, then. She thrust forth a scrap of paper and there was our address, in Perry's hand.

'He said you'd give us a job,' she said. 'Help look after the kids, or something. He said you'd give us a roof.'

'I wasn't planning on running a hostel for fallen women,' said

Grandma in a huff. It was pissing down with rain, Our Cyn was soaked.

'I haven't fallen yet,' said Our Cyn. 'But I *might*.'

Once she got her feet under the table, she never took them out again. One of the fixtures and fittings. She was a breath of fresh air. If Grandma lingered too long down the local and forgot to grate the evening carrots, Cyn would do us a couple of lamb chops, a bit of liver and bacon. Forbidden fruit! Delish. Her kids were in and out all the time after she married that cabby, the second generation to call our grandma 'Grandma'. It was Cyn's eldest, Mavis, who got off with a GI which resulted in our Brenda, whom we took care of when she had *her* bit of trouble and brought home our precious little Tiffany, the first Black in the family.

'Family', I say. Grandma invented this family. She put it together out of whatever came to hand – a stray pair of orphaned babes, a ragamuffin in a flat cap. She created it by sheer force of personality. I only wish she'd lived to see our little Tiffany. There is a persistent history of absent fathers in our family, although Tiffany *did* get a daddy of her own, in the end, because Brenda married this ex-boxer, after all that. Light-heavyweight. Strict Baptist. They live round the corner, Acre Lane. Brenda's a pillar of the community, now, you'd never think her first fellow was here today and gone tomorrow.

Tiffany. So pretty! I never saw such a pretty baby. 'Born for the stage,' I said to Nora. We took her on, ballet and tap, from the age of three. We used to run a little school, in those days, the Brixton Academy of Dance. In the ground-floor front. Our Bren would bang away at the piano; she played the harmonium in church, too. We'd roll back the carpet. It's quite a lovely room, the ground-floor front – big, with a bay. We'd done it up in a Thames green Regency-stripe wallpaper. We put in a big mirror. The little girls laboured with sweat moustaches on their upper lips. One, two, three. The cats kept out in the garden, well away. One, two, three. Not good enough for Tiffany, though, not when she got to nine, ten, eleven. She wanted to do disco and funk, that kind of thing. Greek to us, of course. After our time.

She moved out into a flat with some other girls. After that, she blossomed out. She'd still come back to see her old aunties whenever she got a moment, wearing black leather and red eye-shadow and hairpieces down to her bum and God knows what. Her dad wouldn't let her into the house done up like that, he's a lay preacher, so she'd stop off at our place from the club where she was working, wash off her make-up, slip on flatties and a nice frock she kept in the spare room.

Correction: *one* of the spare rooms. This house is nothing but spare rooms, these days. Wheelchair lives in the front basement, so that she can roll her appliance in and out of the breakfast room and get to the downstairs lavvy on her own. Nor' and I take up an attic apiece. The rest is old clothes, dust, newspapers stacked in piles tied up with string, cuttings, old photographs.

The rest is silence.

So Tiffany dropped in one fine day and who did she find taking tea with her aunties but a handsome young man she'd never seen before and who came as a bit of a shock to Nora and me, too, because he was the first Hazard child who'd ever come to visit us.

And no sooner did poor little Tiff set eyes on him than she fell.

Tristram. His twin brother is called Gareth. Bloody silly Celtic names. The other one, that Gareth, is a Jesuit, he converted in his teens. Then he went off to be a missionary, or so his Old Nanny told us. His Old Nanny drops round from time to time, friend of the family, it's a complicated connection – she used to be Wheelchair's Old Nanny, back in the Dark Ages, before the Flood. Then she was Wheelchair's daughter's Old Nanny. Then Tristram and Gareth's Old Nanny. She is, you might say, the Hazard family's generic Old Nanny. Indestructible old girl. We rely on her for gossip, to tell the truth. Old Nanny told us how Gareth went off to the jungle, it must have been ten years ago. He's probably been barbecued long ago, or had his head shrunk by the Jivaro.

Gareth and Tristram, the priest and the game-show presenter. Not so different, really, I suppose. Both of them in show business. Both, in their different ways, carrying on the great tradition of the Hazard family – the willing suspension of disbelief. Both of them promise you a free gift if you play the game.

Tristram and Gareth, the offspring of our father's third wife. Let me recapitulate. Number One: Lady Atalanta Hazard, née Lynde (a.k.a. 'Wheelchair'). Number Two: Miss Delia Delaney, of Hollywood, USA (a.k.a. Daisy Duck). Number Three: the girl who, once upon a time, played Cordelia to our father's Lear; marrying your Cordelia, evidently something of a Hazard family tradition. She was just twenty-one years old, in those days, and fresh out of RADA, where she had been, oh! the betrayals of youth! Melchior's own daughter, Saskia's, best friend. As for Melchior, he was old enough to draw his pension, already, and freshly knighted, for his 'services to the theatre', so at least he made a lady of her but she and Saskia never spoke again from that day to this, although Old Nanny, she's an indefatigable gossip, told us Saskia turned up at the boys' christening like the wicked fairy in *Sleeping Beauty*, balefully eyeing the plump little bundled twins, perhaps already laying out her wicked plans for the future.

Numero Tre, however, had her own plans for the future. She was a forward-looking woman. She looked ahead and she saw – television! In those days, all everybody else saw was a little grey rectangle the size of a cornflakes packet, with vague forms flickering across it, like Trafalgar Square in a peasouper. Who would have thought that little box of shadows would put us all out of business, singers, dancers, acrobats, Shakespearians, the lot? But Melchior's third wife planned for the late twentieth century. She put the entire family on camera. They prospered.

Or perhaps it was a case of, needs must. Melchior was starting to muff his lines, trip over his sword, muddle up his business so you could hardly tell his Brutus from his Antony; old age was creeping up behind him and now he started to cash in on his own fame. He deeply mined the rich new seam that opened up before him – old buffers in pipe tobacco, vintage port and miniature cigar commercials. You started to associate his face – and though I take the piss out of him from time to time, all the same I have to thank him for bequeathing me the good old Hazard bones that improve like fine wine with age – with the music of Elgar.

His clever young wife gave up her own career to devote herself to her two wonderful sons but she often found time to pop up on the box, too, touting pan-scrubbers, washing-up liquid, toilet paper . . . 'The Royal Family of the theatre gives its seal of approval.' Her *pièce de résistance* was a turn in a long yellow frock with a ruff, standing on a rampart, gazing sternly at a half-pound pack on a dish before her: 'To butter or not to butter . . .' My

Lady Margarine. She also did celebrity guest appearances and bazaar openings at negotiable fees. She reached middle-age quicker than any woman I ever knew.

Not that I *knew* her, exactly, but we read the papers, we kept in touch. After all, the Hazards belonged to everyone. They were a national treasure.

In the fullness of time, the older stepchildren took to television, too. Saskia, my half-sister and *bête noire*, started that cookery series; now she's the TV chef *par excellence*. Imogen, the other one, developed a unique line as a goldfish. I kid you not. It was a series for the kiddies, set in an aquarium, about this carp called Goldie. It's run for twenty years, now, carp live a long time. Sometimes I don't understand the English.

Apart from catching the odd glimpse if we mistuned the set, we never saw hair nor hide of any of the Hazards, except in the papers. Ever since his doomed production of *A Midsummer Night's Dream*, Melchior's one and only stab at the movies, he steered clear of us because he only had us in the film for mascots and look what a débâcle that turned out to be! We've sat at the same table with him only the one time since World War II, and that encounter ended in tears, too. As for My Lady Margarine, she never fancied breaking bread with her husband's by-blows, especially since those by-blows were old enough to be mother to *her*. But we read in the papers how the boys went to Bedales, from whence Tristram was expelled for tippling and fornication, although Gareth, not.

What a rustling of the tabloids when Tristram was expelled! Wheelchair cackled with glee. Little Tris, busted for pot in '68, in a satin vest and velvet knickers. Titian ringlets. He danced naked on the stage in *Hair*. In '76, he crashed his first Lotus Elan whilst under the influence, wearing (ever the snappy dresser) his hair in spikes and tartan bondage trousers. Ooh, he was a naughty boy and how his mother worried. Never off the gossip pages, always in the papers, sex and drugs and rock-and-roll.

Gareth, no.

It must have been My Lady Margarine got Tristram the job on the telly. She must have been at her wits' end. Unless it was that Saskia, the conniving bitch. The first time he came to see us, a couple of years ago, it was before his first major investment in gents' natty suiting, he was still at the jeans-with-necktie stage, just an assistant producer, and he wanted us, or so he said, for a chat show.

'Gawd,' said Nora. Though it was not yet the time we usually dressed, she'd slipped on a frock because he'd come on business, and had muzzed up her hair a bit. She looked quite debauched. 'We're as old as the hills and still you want us to show a bit of leg!'

'I'm proud of my aunts,' said Tristram. 'When Saskia told me the legendary Chance sisters were my very own aunts, I was over the moon.'

'Aunts', see? That Saskia! We raised our eyebrows at each other but we held our peace. He's got charm, I must say. A slippery kind of charm. I could tell Nora was almost taken with the idea, she was tapping her front teeth with her fingernail in the way she has. We could have done with a bob or two, at that juncture, too. But the very thought of us two aged ladies performing a geriatric Charleston for the delight of the viewers made me nauseous and if Saskia had anything to do with it, I smelled a rat.

Then Tiffany came in. She's got her own key, she can come and go. No knock. The door opened. There she was.

What an entrance! She looked like a proper harlot, poor little thing, in her fishnets and her leather mini. Bren and Leroy always overprotected her. Nothing was too good for her. First kid in the school to have a personal stereo. 'You just wait until she kicks over the traces!' we always said. Only a virgin would have worn a skirt like that. Never a sweeter or more innocent girl than our Tiffany, even though she didn't know enough not to flash her tits all over the papers. 'Six feet two of lithe, coffee-coloured loveliness,' said the caption on page three. She never dared tell her father but he won't have the *Sun* in the house on principle, fortunately. The sweetest girl in London, but naïve.

Tristram knocked over his chair as he got up when she came in. He was all of a dither and no wonder. Wheelchair was widely touted as 'the most beautiful woman in England' in her day but she never held a candle to our Tiffany, she says so herself.

The chat show never came off because he was offered the game show the week after on the other channel, so he took that. And he took Tiffany, too. He took her home to his flat, in a warehouse in Bermondsey, above a wine bar, and he bought her a beaded gown, and there she was, every week, with her five-year-old's smile, offering the entire viewing public a peek down her cleavage while she sang out: 'Yessir! Lashings of Lolly!' with a ringing conviction that could only have been born out of true love.

Because she fell for him, head over heels. Her dad fumed and cursed when she went home to pick up her spare underwear; she came round to our place, she wept. Brenda nipped round on the q.t., gave her a big hug. 'I love him, Mum.' 'Aunty Dora, I love him.' 'I love him, Aunty Nora.'

The three of us looked at each other sadly. We'd well nigh two centuries' experience of love, between us, and the omens were not good. She sat knuckling her eyes, getting mascara everywhere. She'd got it bad and Tristram wasn't worth the paper she wiped her bum with. So we prepared ourselves for heartbreak, but the organ was proving a touch more resilient than we'd feared. No sign of shipwreck, yet.

Mind you, we hardly ever saw her, these days. She'd swanned down in a cab at Christmas with a bottle of gin tied up in red ribbon, printed a lipstick heart on our cheeks, left a big package for her mum and buggered off out again to some soirée or other. She was always good to her mother, mind, though Bren had to keep all the prezzies at our house so Leroy wouldn't lay eyes on the wages of sin. Easter, she brought us some daffs.

But Nora and I know what hoops the kept woman has to jump to work her passage and our little Tiff had looked very haggard and wan last time we saw her and kept excusing herself to go to the bathroom, too.

Press the button for 'Play'.

'Lashings of Lolly!' cried Tristram Hazard, live from London in a special birthday tribute to his famous father. If, God help you, you've seen the rotten show before, you'll know this is the moment when Tristram introduces the lovely Tiffany. She shimmers forward in her beaded gown, smiling like a good child on its birthday, and she adds her sweet little husky voice to his: 'Yessir! Lashings of Lolly!'

But where is the lovely Tiffany tonight? Nowhere to be seen, although Tristram gives an expectant look towards the neon staircase down which she usually descends. No bloody Tiffany, and we're going out live, too!

Still, consummate pro that he is, he doesn't miss a beat.

'And I'd like you to give a very special "Lashings of Lolly" hi, there! to a truly grand old gentleman, to – Mr British Theatre, himself.' His voice dropped a tone; he adopted a plummy smile and made a half-bow, half-curtsey, a sort of unisex obeisance. 'My father . . . Sir Melchior Hazard.'

Radiant, he swung round, open-armed: 'Hi, there, Dad!'

Roars of applause as My Lady Margarine, the face that launched a thousand pot-scourers, assisted the old man to the microphone. We felt the queasiest mixture of emotions – at seeing him in flesh and blood, after so long, in the first place; at seeing him make a fool of himself like this, in the second place; and in the third place, seeing him so silver-haired and shaky, too. But Wheelchair wasn't so complicated. She perked right up, and said:

'Well, well, well! He's awfully well preserved, I must say! He looks quite *pickled*!'

If you haven't seen Tristram's bastard show, it goes like this: there in the studio, which is all done up with neon palm trees for the occasion, there's this big wheel, like a roulette wheel, or a blackjack wheel, only bigger, all over lightbulbs, with a neon arrow in the middle. This is how you play the game: you say a number and Tiffany gives the wheel a twirl. Round and round goes the bloody great wheel, pardon me, vicar, and if it stops when the arrow points to the number you've chosen, they give you half a grand. That's the first round.

Second round: double your money, triple it, quadruple it or lose it altogether, depending upon where the arrow comes to rest. Simplicity itself. It's all about greed. The camera lingers on the faces in the audience, their eyes are popping out, they're drooling and slobbering. Money! Money for nothing! A win on Tristram Hazard's Lashings of Lolly, almost as good as a Civil List pension. Tristram starts up this slow chant as the wheel goes round; they all begin to clap their hands. 'LASHINGS OF LOLLY!'

Every time I catch a glimpse, I think I've gone mad.

Now Tristram says to his father: 'Are you ready to play Lotsa Birthday Lolly, Dad?'

The old man gives a blink and looks round, as if he's just woken up, doesn't know where he is, startled by the lights. He might be just about to cry. God knows why he's humiliating himself. Is it for his boy's sake, to help out with Tristram's pathetic career? Or just to give his ancient face another airing before the grave? Or . . . is he down on his luck at last, does he need the money?

Funny. I never thought of that.

Our father gathers himself together and gives us, in full measure, that wonderful old smile that goes right to the back row of the gallery, goes down to the depths of the vitals.

Our father smiles and says: 'I'm ready.'

But where is Tiffany, in her purple sequin boob tube?

Tiffany is not.

Remember, all this is going out live, isn't it, so Tris is in a nasty spot. You can see the panic in his eyes.

And then a change comes over the invisible audience, the only evidence of whose existence we've had so far the odd cough and titter, some patters of applause. But now there is an audible shiver. They can see something that we can't, and it bewilders them. An uneasy silence falls. And then is broken.

I never knew our Tiff could sing. Sweet and true. La, la, la. And still you couldn't see her, only hear her song, her wordless song that didn't seem to have an end nor a beginning, that created the silence in which you heard it, so that an awed hush spread like ripples in a pond around that unearthly singing.

Tristram turns his head towards the sound; there is a close-up, in which we see he looks aghast.

Why didn't they kill the transmission then and there? It turns out that one of the cameramen was sweet on Tiffany, thought Tristram, the legover champion of the commercial channels, treated the poor kid like shit. Which Tristram did. But, what have you, he's a feller and I doubt this chivalrous cameraman would have done any better by her, over a period of time. Anyway, this cameraman wouldn't let them pull the plug and he it was who now swung his lens round on to Tiffany herself as she stood at the top of the flight of neon steps.

She was a spectacle to move the hardest heart, I must say. She didn't have her make-up on, she hadn't done her hair and she wore a pair of grey satin French knickers with real lace inserts, purple stilettos and one of those American footballer's shirts with numbers on it – it was purple, too, but with a giant size 69 in red. Tristram put it in her stocking for a joke, last Christmas. Shows what he thought of her, really.

There was a bit of wallflower stuck in her hair, over her ear, and her hands were full of flowers, daffs, bluebells, narcissi, she must have picked them out of the front gardens and the window boxes and the public parks that she'd passed by on her way to the studio during that long walk from Bermondsey.

She wobbled something chronic on those purple shoes, she'd turned the heels right over on the way and now she kicked them off. One, two. She scored a palpable hit with the second one, though I don't think she'd intended to, it got Tristram on the shin. (The real Tristram, sitting here beside his aunties in the flesh, let out a short, sharp cry in unison with himself on the screen, which made the cat on his lap leap up and hump off.)

When Tristram cried out, that attracted her attention and her big, brown eyes fixed on him with some kind of recognition, though only in the vaguest way, as if she were remembering a dream, not a very pleasant dream, but not a nightmare. A sad dream, not a bad dream.

The audience hadn't the faintest what was going on and shuffled and tittered a bit, half trying to convince itself that this distraught girl was just another part of the action and would do something funny, shortly; or else take off her football shirt and give them all a treat. But she just went on singing. La, la, la.

Then, slowly, slowly, keeping her eyes fixed on Tristram – he kept quite still, as if she'd mesmerized him – she started down the staircase.

If Nora and I had a pound for every staircase we'd descended in our lives as showgirls, we'd be rolling in it.

But Tiffany never came down that staircase like a star, poor kid. She wobbled so much on each step I was sure she'd fall and I leaned forward to the screen so that I could reach out and catch her if she tumbled, I was so caught up in it. Nora was crying her eyes out already and even old Wheelchair was sniffing away, reaching up her sleeve for her hankie. But, though my eyes were misting over, too, I saw the hang of our Tiff's shirt, remembered how she'd spent her last visit with us in the toilet, and put two and two together.

'You've put her in the club, Tristram!' I couldn't hold it back, I came right out with it.

Nora turned the tap off sharpish, stopped crying in a flash and pressed the Standby button so the screen froze on our lovely Tiff in mid-teeter.

'What's that? A little baby?'

'I'm not ready to be a father,' said Tristram. 'I can't take the responsibility. I'm not mature enough.'

'No man ever is,' announced Wheelchair, in her grande dame voice.

We all three glowered at him. He cowered.

'Aunties,' he said. 'Forgive me.'

'It's not for us to do the forgiving,' said Nora. 'It's up to that sweet, innocent child and how you make amends to her if she can ever see it in her heart to forgive you. And you'd better make your bloody amends pronto before her father finds out you wouldn't do the right thing or your days of close-ups are numbered. Not to mention your days of breathing. Now let's see what foul thing you did next.'

With that, she smartly pushed the Play button and shut him up.

I can't say if Tiffany *knew* it was Tristram down there at the bottom of the staircase or if she didn't know him at all; whether he seemed familiar from some scarcely remembered time before her heart broke, or if his face seemed to her a new face that reminded her, just a little bit, of somebody else's face. Somebody dead and gone. But down the stairs she came towards him, without a smile, flowers in her hair, half-naked on her poor, bare, shaky feet.

Such pretty feet she always had, long, but perfectly formed, and pretty little piggies, nicely gradated, not like those long, root-like toes some people have. Her bare, pretty feet tracked blood behind her; she'd rubbed her heels raw on her purple stilettos. Fancy walking all the way from Bermondsey in those heels!

Tristram looked as though he was propping old Melchior up, now, unless it was Melchior holding up his son; each clutched the other like drowning men at spars. Tristram's career in pieces! His old man's birthday tribute ruined! The flower-like child he'd violated turning up to shame him, mad as a hatter in front of an audience of millions! Was there no end to his troubles?

She reached up behind her ear, fished out the bit of wallflower and offered it to Tristram. He, not knowing what to do with it, sniffed at it. That made her smile. He tried to give it back to her but she wasn't having any.

'Wallflower,' she said. 'You know what they say about wallflowers – many are called but few are chosen.'

All this while, there's the uneasy shuffling of the studio audience and every now and then some minion would dash across the set on a frenzied bid to stop the whole business in its tracks. But on it all went, and on, and on, and on.

'Here,' she says. 'Cop hold.'

Now she thrusts her battered little spring posy at Tristram, retaining for herself the one daffodil, which she holds to her mouth as if it were the mouthpiece of one of those sit-up-and-beg telephones we used to have, years ago. Hello, hello? Then she holds it to her ear. Nobody at home. And offers that flower to Tristram, too, with such a sad smile – a smile that changes when she looks at it again and notes that it is not, in fact, a telephone at all, to a pale giggle.

'Daffy dill, daffy dilly,' she said. And once more broke into song, but one with words, this time.

> Oh, my little sister, Lily, is a whore in Piccadilly,
> And my mother is another in the Strand –

I thought: That's it! They'll fade her now, for sure! But still and still and still they didn't, not even when, now she'd got rid of her flowers, she cried out suddenly:

'Off with it! You only lent it to me! Nothing was mine, not ever!'

And stripped off her Number 69 shirt, threw it to the floor and trampled on it. It was a shock to see her breasts under the cruel lights – long, heavy breasts, with big dark nipples, real breasts, not like the ones she'd shown off like borrowed finery to the glamour lenses. This was flesh, you could see that it would bleed, you could see how it fed babies.

Then Melchior did something wonderful. Who'd have thought the old man had it in him? Suddenly, Melchior is in shot, holding out a blond mink stole which he must have plucked off the very shoulders of his wife. He put his hand on her bare shoulder and said, 'Pretty, pretty lady.'

Perhaps it was his tone of voice attracted her attention, that of a man selling old-fashioned rich black treacle toffee. When she turned towards him, he draped the stole round her shoulders, he covered her up.

Then My Lady Margarine stepped in, too. They'd been keeping her on the sidelines, the while, so that she could come in at the end and take charge of the cheque lest her better half did something senile with it. She's in good nick, I must say; lots of exercise does it, and the odd nip and tuck helps. Her cheeks give the game away; they've got that tight, full, shiny chipmunk look that spells out: facelift. You can always tell. Nevertheless, good nick. She was a brunette at her wedding, but had gone blonde with age, evidently, and now sported a pale gold chignon. She's crying, too, possibly for the loss of her mink stole but, be fair, more likely as a tribute to the moment. If My Lady Margarine gave up the stage for the sake of her family thirty-five years ago, she must have always regretted it in a tiny corner of her heart for when Fate offered her another chance out of the blue she grabbed it with both hands.

'Oh, my dear,' she said to Tiffany. 'We wanted him to marry you so much. I begged him, I implored him.'

That brought Tristram out of his daze with a start, as if this was the first *he'd* heard of it. But Tiffany didn't register, didn't seem to hear. She was still shivering, in spite of the mink, but when she stroked her cheek against the fur, that made her smile, so lovely, so touching, she smiled that good child's birthday smile and it was as if the touch of the fur gave her some of the strength of the animal, she came back together, again. She seemed to grow stronger before our very eyes; she didn't come back to herself, exactly, but to somebody else who was in perfect control. She called out to an unseen presence off the set in a big, ringing voice: 'Hey! Somebody call me a cab, right? A cab! Right away!'

Then she turned towards the camera, as she did every week. The cameraman who was in love with her zoomed in as she tossed one end of the mink stole over her shoulder in a devil-may-care way, as if anything could happen, now, and she gave the viewers the full force of her big smile, the professional one that offered a view of her hundred-octane teeth as far back as the emerging wisdoms. She raised her hand. She waved.

'Goodnight, everybody!' Signing off, as she always did: 'Sleep tight, don't let the bedbugs bite! Goodnight!'

Then, in mid-wave, this new, strong, defiant person with Tiffany's face covered her mouth with her hand as if she were going to be sick, her face crumpled, she bolted off the set in the mink stole and the silk knickers and there they were, the Hazards, all three, left gaping like loons.

Tristram came to himself first, although his hands were still full of flowers. But he remembered the camera was watching him and even managed to scrape up a smile.

'And goodnight, too, from me, Tristram Hazard, and my very special hundredth birthday guest, Sir Melchior Hazard – '

The good old goodbye formula. It reassured the studio audience. One or two of them started to clap, as if by doing that they could change what they had seen into what they ought to have seen.

' – and his Lady – '

More applause.

' – my very own extra special Dad and Mum – '

Applause doubled, trebled.

' – and come and watch the lucky people win Lotsa Lolly! again, next week!'

Roars. Applause. Up came the credits over the three of them bravely waving farewells to the invisible punters. Nora rose up with some ceremony and killed the tape. The set crackled. Then there was silence.

'I thought Tiff might be here,' said Tristram after a bit, snuffling and wiping his eyes with the back of his hand. 'We've looked everywhere else.'

'Why didn't you come here first of all, then?'

'God, such a terrible night . . . The police. The casualty wards. We searched the night shelters.'

'Who are this "we"?' enquired Nora sharply.

'Finally, well, I just passed out,' said Tristram. 'I couldn't cope any more. She took me back to her place.'

'Who,' I asked, more sharply still, 'is this "she"?'

As if we didn't know. He was too scared to say out loud or else he wanted to keep it from Wheelchair. Then, again, he'd never shown any consideration for her sensibilities in the past; why did he want to start now? But Nora leaned forward and, with her long, lean fingertips, delicately plucked from his lapel one single hair, as red as his own hair but very, very much longer. She held it high, she let it dangle, proof positive that last night of all nights he'd spent with –

And that is the single, most unmentionable secret in this entire family's bulging closetful of skeletons, that ever since he was little, Tristram and Saskia, although she is his half-sister and old enough to be his mother, in fact, his mother's best friend, once upon a time . . . I thought our Tiff had weaned him off the nipple, but here was the evidence to prove the contrary.

'Like a dog,' said Nora, sneering at the hair, 'returning to its own vomit.'

'Oh, God!' said Tristram. 'Try to be a little understanding. Tiffany had vanished clean away, I was half mad with fear – '

The area door slammed, such a bang the back windows shuddered. Came heavy footsteps down the passage. We harkened. Brenda always let herself in.

'I suppose,' said Nora with heavy irony, for she knew swift retribution was at hand, 'it never occurred to you to ask at her mother's, did it?'

The kitchen door burst open. You could tell by the look on her face that she had seen his Porsche outside. She'd been a real slip of a thing, when she was a girl, but she'd put on a lot of weight after the kids, now she could give Leroy a pound or two, and strong as a horse, with it. She still had her rollers in, her carpet slippers on, but she was past grief, white with rage.

At least Tristram was spared the task of telling Brenda, the police had done that already. Leroy tried Tristram in his absence and found grounds for a verdict of justifiable homicide. When Bren told him that: 'If her Dad gets his hands on you . . .' she aimed a big whack at him and I thought I'd slip outside and put the kettle on, leave them to get on with it.

All of a sudden, I felt my age. If the youngest goes before you . . .

There's a photo of Evelyn Laye on the wall above the tea caddy. 'To twenty twinkling toes, with loads of love.' I thought of Tiffany, 'this little piggy goes to market'. And her feet, leaving blood behind them as she came down the staircase. She'd have made a cracking dancer, if she'd put her mind to it.

Then my heart felt as if a hand had squeezed it because I'd thought of our darling Tiffany in the past tense, hadn't I?

Little Tiff.

Nora came out into the scullery and slipped her arm through mine. We watched the kettle bounce and hiss on the gas and listened to the sounds of fracas coming from the breakfast room. Smash! There goes a plate. The cats trampled themselves underfoot as they streaked out of the cat door. 'Not good enough, was she!' Muffled cry of pain from Tristram. 'Treat her like dirt, did you! Well, see where it gets you!' Then the telephone rang. I looked at Nora. She shut her eyes. We knew that ring meant bad news.

We took the tea in. Wheelchair was dealing with the telephone because the others hadn't noticed it, in the heat of battle – Tristram, black eye, bloody nose, ripped jacket, torn shirt and it looked as if she'd tried to throttle him with his necktie but that was the worst of the damage, he was still conscious. The breakfast things had been trashed in the course of the tussle, bacon fat everywhere, but Brenda was spent, her hands hung limp, she was whimpering. 'In her knickers, on the telly, in front of all those people, singing dirty songs. Her dad was watching everything. I can't ever forgive you. Never.' Wheelchair put the telephone down. One look at her face told us the worst.

'That was the police, dear,' she said to Brenda. You've got to hand it to the old girl, she's got the manner pat, cool but not cold, sympathetic without slobbering. 'Do sit down. I'm afraid it's bad news.'

Brenda did not sit down, as if she thought that if she did, she'd never summon the heart to get up again; she hung on to the chair like grim death, making little noises in the back of her throat.

'They found the body of a young girl in the river, this morning.'

There was a whoosh of rubber tyres as Wheelchair made a compassionate swoop upon Brenda, put her arms around as much of her lower torso as she could grapple. Ever the lady social worker.

'Poor darling, prepare yourself. It's something very terrible.'

In the war, in the mornings after air raids, you saw people look like Brenda looked, just then.

'She hasn't got a face left, Brenda. Evidently a police launch, the propellers – '

I remember that thin, high scream from the war, too.

Then she pulled herself together and had a cup of hot, sweet tea, which you give them for shock although she didn't seem to notice drinking it and she and Tristram went off to the morgue in his Porsche. No point in rowing with him, now, was there? All he could say was: 'I'm most frightfully sorry.' He kept saying it over and over again. I'd have clocked him one for that, alone, if I'd been Brenda, but I don't think the poor girl could so much as see him, now, couldn't hear him, could think of nothing but our Tiff in the cold store drowned dead with the baby inside her drowned dead, too.

Wheelchair made her excuses and wheeled off into the basement front and after a while her gramophone started up, she's got her own in there, there'd be bloodshed if we had to share. She'd put on a bit of funeral music, classical stuff, lugubrious, a big, brown, lugubrious voice: 'What is life for me without thee?'

She's overdoing it a bit, I thought. She didn't know Tiff *that* well. And I wish she could have picked a less affecting song.

> What is life for me without thee?
> What is left if thou art gone?

Nora lifted off the lid of the teapot and poured in a tot of rum. 'That'll set us up.'

'D'you think we ought to ring up Saskia and tell her where her boyfriend's gone?'

'We haven't spoken to Saskia for forty years, don't see why we should start now. Let her stew in her own juice. It's all her bloody fault, anyway. If she hadn't got her claws into Tristram . . .'

The singer on Wheelchair's gramophone reprised the query, what would be left; then she sang: 'Eurydice . . .' The saddest sound. 'Eurydice!'

Nora made a dismissing gesture and fell silent. We left the clearing away till after dinner, we put our feet up. Grey skies. Still that big wind, banging away outside. To think, this morning, I thought that wind would blow us an adventure, it wouldn't matter what. Now look what it had blown us! Rain came in gusts over the garden, buffeting the forsythia. Forsythia, the exact colour of peroxide blond. Whenever I see forsythia, I think of Grandma.

'He's left his cassette behind,' said Nora. 'Worth a bit, I should think.'

But she didn't sound too keen. Our blackmailing days are long gone.

'Do you think they'll cancel the party?'

'Oh, no,' said Nora. 'I mean, she wasn't really family, was she? Only in the family way.'

We put more rum in the tea. After all, it *was* our birthday.

'What about us? Are we still going to the party?'

'Life must go on,' said Nora, all of a sudden full of life. 'I wouldn't miss it for a hundred million pounds.'

TWO

ONE, TWO, THREE, hop! See me dance the polka.

Once upon a time, there was an old woman in splitting black satin pounding away at an upright piano in a room over a haberdasher's shop in Clapham High Street and her daughter in a pink tutu and wrinkled tights slapped at your ankles with a cane if you didn't pick up your feet high enough. Once a week, every Saturday morning, Grandma Chance would wash us, brush us and do up our hair in sausage curls. We had long, brown stockings strung up to our liberty bodices by suspenders. Grandma Chance would take firm hold of one hand of each of us, then – ho! for the dancing class; off we'd trot to catch the tram.

We always took the tram from Brixton to Clapham High Street. The stately progress of the tram, occupying by right of bulk and majesty the centre of the road, not veering to the left nor right upon its way but sometimes swaying every now and then with a sickening lurch, like Grandma, coming home from the pub.

One, two, three, hop.

Big mirrors blooming like plums with dust along the walls. I can see us now, in our vests and knickers and our little pink dancing slippers, dipping a curtsey to our reflections. Grandma sat by the door with her bag in her lap, squinting at us between the spots on her veil. She looked grieving, as if she was scared we might sprain ourselves, but this was because she was sucking on a Fox's glacier mint. Everything smelled of sweat and gas fire. The old woman thumped the piano and Miss Worthington in her droopy tutu showed us how to *fouetté*, poor thing, sixty if she was a day.

One, two, three, hop! See us cover the ground.

We did our exercises at the barre. Nora's bum in her navy-blue bloomers jiggled away in front of me like two hard-boiled eggs in a handkerchief. We'd turn around, then she could feast her eyes on mine. Outside, a tram went by with a whirr and a click, knocking out sparks from the overhead cables.

To tell the truth, we lived for that dancing class. We thought that was what the week was for, for Saturday mornings.

Then we were seven.

There was a cake with seven candles in the larder iced up to the eyebrows, its stunning pink and white beauty marred only by one little fingerprint – Nora, unable to resist. It sat in state in the larder, awaiting our return from our birthday treat, our first matinée. Our Cyn waved us off. We had our best coats on, green tweed, quite hairy, with velvet collars so the tweed didn't scratch our necks, and little hats to match. Grandma dressed us like princesses. We always had glacé kid gloves, for best.

Grandma lashed out, she got us seats in the stalls. It was almost too much for me and Nora. We were mute with ecstasy. The plaster cherubs lifting aloft gilt swags and crystal candelabra on the walls; the red plush; the floral and pastel silks of the afternoon frocks of the ladies in the stalls, from whom mingled odours of talc and scent and toilet soap arose; and the wonderful curtain that hung between us and pleasure, the curtain that, in a delicious agony of anticipation, we knew would soon rise and then and then . . . what wonderful secrets would be revealed to us, then?

'You just wait and see,' said Grandma.

The lights went down, the bottom of the curtain glowed. I loved it and have always loved it best of all, the moment when the lights go down, the curtain glows, you know that something wonderful is going to happen. It doesn't matter if what happens next spoils everything; the anticipation itself is always pure.

To travel hopefully is better than to arrive, as Uncle Perry used to say. I always preferred foreplay, too.

Well. Not *always*.

When the lights went down and the curtain glowed that first time of all, Nora and I gave one another a look. Our little hearts went pit-a-pat.

Up went the curtain; there were Fred and Adèle, evicted, out on the street with all their bits and pieces. She set out the chairs, she straightened the sofa, she hung a sign on the lamppost: 'Bless this house'. We thought that we would die of pleasure. We clung on to one another's hands like grim death, we thought we might wake up and find out we had been dreaming. Nora liked Adèle best; she liked it when she dressed up like a Mexican widow and did her Spanish dance, but it was old Fred for me, then and for ever, with his funny little nutcracker face and the Eton crop that looked painted on, it shone so, and not a hair ever moved. Who'd have thought we'd be on 'Hi, Fred,' 'Hi, girls' terms when we grew up?

God knows what sixth sense made Grandma pick out *Lady Be Good* for our seventh birthday treat. 'I was looking for a nayce musical comedy,' she said, 'but nothing with that Jessie Matthews in it.' She thought Jessie Matthews was common although *I* always found her a perfect lady. But *Lady Be Good* showed us the way. It was the Damascus road for us. We spent hours, at home, afterwards, in the ground-floor front, rolling back the rug, getting the numbers off pat. That finale, she in her Tyrolean costume, him like a sailor doll. We took it in turns to be the lady.

'You've got stars in your eyes, girls,' said Grandma in the interval.

Then tea on a tray arrived, no expense spared. Hotel silver service, cucumber sandwiches. Grandma rolled her veil up over her nose and slipped an iced fancy in between her magenta lips. Even in those days, we always felt defiant of the world when we went out with Grandma, we knew she looked a bit of a funniosity. Just as we were brushing off the crumbs came something of a commotion in the dress circle. Grandma was handing the tray back to the waitress when she froze, the way a dog does when it sees a rabbit. The girl caught hold of the tea-things just in time; Grandma rose up and raised her hand, she pointed.

If you'd drawn a line straight from the end of her finger up into the dress circle, it would have landed on the nose of a man, a very handsome young man, a tall, dark, young man with big, dark eyes, well turned out, red rose in his buttonhole, black hair just a touch long therefore bespeaking an artistic profession. He was escorting a fair-haired lady with a sheep's profile in a chic afternoon frock of lavender wool and they'd evidently freshly arrived, come to kill the hour before cocktails at the smartest show in town, no doubt; they cut a bit of a swathe as they 'excuse me'd' their way along the row. Glances, stares, even the odd 'ooh' and 'aah'. They were young and glamorous. Everybody there knew who they were but us. The lights were going down, the band was tuning up. Grandma still stood there, quivering.

'That man is . . . your father!'

Her revelation didn't have the force it might have had for us because, at that age, we still weren't sure just what it was that fathers did. Since we didn't know how to put one and one together to make two, we didn't know we were different, either. You'd think, wouldn't you, the neighbours would have nudged and winked a bit but Grandma kept her lip buttoned and maintained the outward appearance of propriety, at least in the hours before opening time, although if the milkman or the postie ever peeked in through the net curtains in the middle of the morning, they might have spotted her doing the dusting in her altogether and *then* there would have been talk.

So when Grandma announced so dramatically, that's your father! we dutifully took a look because she told us to but then the curtain glowed, the overture began.

'I say, do sit down, madame,' said a bloke in the row behind so she subsided mutinously. But it ruined the second half for her. She kept craning round, she was muttering the filthiest things under her breath but we had been transported to a different world, we were oblivious. For us, Fred and Adèle were everything.

There was such a press of people, at the end, and it took so long to get our coats, and we were in such a dream because of the dance and song that we missed them. We got out on to the pavement as our father and his missus sailed off in a cab leaving Grandma waving her umbrella uselessly after them.

'Damn,' said Grandma. 'Damn, damn, damn.'

Her face told you that she meant it.

Now that the spell of the show was broken, we had time to ponder her words.

'Grandma,' said Nora. 'Tell us some more about fathers.'

On top of the tram, on the way home, she told us the lot. She was a naturist, she was a vegetarian, she was a pacifist; when it came to sex education, what do you expect? But we found it hard to believe, neither what she said about the prong and how it could change its shape, etc., but also what she said the prong came in handy for. We thought she made it up to tease us. To think that we girls were in the world because a man we'd never met did *that* to a girl we didn't remember, once upon a time! What we knew for certain was, our grandma loved us and we had the best uncle in the world. Although Our Cyn, the worldly one, thought that Perry was our father.

But something took root in us that afternoon, some kind of curiosity. At first it was a niggling thing. We'd spot his picture in the paper and exclaim. When we went up West to buy new dancing shoes at Freed's, we'd make a detour round Shaftesbury Avenue, to look at the photographs wherever he was playing. Over the years, the curiosity turned into a yearning, a longing. I tucked a postcard of him in ermine as Richard II into a secret place at the back of the drawer where I kept my underwear, and, it was the one thing Nora kept from me, she only told me this afternoon, she did the same with one of him as young Prince Hal on the q.t. You could say, I suppose, that we *had a crush* on Melchior Hazard, like lots of girls. You could say he was our first romance, and bittersweet it turned out to be, in the end.

Anyway, that was the first time we ever saw our father. And the first time we saw Fred Astaire. And the first time we spent a penny – that is, used a public convenience. The one at Piccadilly Circus, with white tiles and a little old lady in a white pinny to take your penny off you and put it in the lock so you wouldn't soil your hands. A child remembers these things. It was a red-letter day all round and its wonders were by no means over. When we got home, the cake had moved out of the larder on to the kitchen table, its candles were blazing and, in our absence, a packing case that took up half the kitchen had arrived. Our Cyn pointed to the label: 'For my two lovely girls.'

'He hasn't forgotten,' she said, pleased for our sakes and also pleased for the sake of fatherhood – that Perry might be errant but did his duty, all the same. Little did she know.

In that packing case there was a toy theatre. It was a lovely one, a marvel, an antique – he'd got hold of it in Venice. In the middle of the gilt proscenium arch there they were, side by side, the comic mask, the tragic mask, one mouth turned up at the ends, the other down, the presiding geniuses – just like life. The *commedia*, that's life, isn't it?

Backdrops of trees and flowers and fountains, a moony night, blue clouds, a carnival, a bedroom, a feast, and little men and women on metal rods, Harlequin, Columbine, Pantaloon, all the old-timers. It was a plaything for princesses and we unpacked it out of its woodshavings with a kind of solemn delight; we hadn't known until that very moment it was exactly what we wanted.

We treasured that toy theatre. We played with it as if we were in church, always on Sunday afternoons, never any other time; we washed our hands, after dinner we put our best frocks on. I cried my eyes out when we were forced to part with it. It went to Sotheby's when Brenda had her bit of trouble. You wouldn't believe what we got for it. It kept young Tiffany in disposables until she learned to piss in a pot.

Grandma lit the candles on our cake.

'Make a wish and blow,' she said. You can guess what wish it was these stagestruck children made.

We closed our eyes and there we were, under the painted moon on the other side of the curtain, where the painted clouds will never move and everything is two-dimensional. Nora looked at me and I at Nora; frills, sequins, fishnet tights, high heels and feathers in our hair. We smiled. We raised our right legs, thus . . . ready for the orchestra.

Let's face the music and –

Of course, we didn't know, then, how the Hazards would always upstage us. Tragedy, eternally more class than comedy. How could mere song-and-dance girls aspire so high? We were destined, from birth, to be the lovely ephemera of the theatre, we'd rise and shine like birthday candles, then blow out. But, that birthday tea-time sixty-eight years ago, we blew out all our birthday candles with one breath and, yes, indeed! life gave us our birthday wish, in due course, because the Lucky Chances faced the music and they danced for well-nigh half a century, although we would always be on the left-hand line, hoofers, thrushes, the light relief, as you might say; bring on the bears!

Or, bares. Our careers went down the toilet along with the profession itself. We ended up showing a leg at the fag end of vaudeville in all those touring revues with titles such as *Nudes, Ahoy! Here Come the Nine O'clock Nudes! Nudes of the World!* and so on, backing up Archie Rice and other comics of that ilk. The showgirls would stand there, topless, living statues, and we would do our number in and out the nipples in our tasselled bras. I saw more nipples in those last five years of touring after World War II than in all my life till then and I was brought up by a naturist, don't you forget.

We had a raddled middle age, all right, but I swear to you we were respectable, in youth. There was nothing so stuffy as the lives of small-time theatricals, in those days, and South London was a ghetto of chorus girls and boys and what not. In the semis, behind the dusty privet hedges, they rested between engagements, sitting on a piece of the leatherette suite in the sitting room where the fumed oak sideboard contained a single bottle of sweet sherry and half a dozen dusty glasses stood on a tarnished silver tray inscribed 'To a great little trouper from the Merry Martins, Frinton-on-Sea, 1919', or something like that, beneath framed photographs of girls with big thighs in tights and men in crepe hair signed with Xs galore and framed colour reproductions on the walls of scenes depicting red-nosed monks eating big meals of venison and boar.

We begged and pleaded until Grandma stood us extra classes and after that we were the teacher's pets, while Grandma and Miss Worthington and her old mother, who played piano, often enjoyed a port and lemon or two under the picture of 'Simon the Cellarer' in the back parlour behind the dance studio, as Miss Worthington chose to call it. Grandma with her little finger hoist aloft, on her best behaviour, all smiles, spitting out her famous vowels like cherrystones; she'd give a big belch in the street, afterwards, glare around, say: 'Who let that out?'

So it went on, year in, year out. The mirror in Miss Worthington's front room showed two times two Chance girls, us and our reflections, doing high kicks like trick photography in flesh and blood. Bang, crash, wallop went Miss W.'s old mum on the piano, and smack! smack! smack! Miss W.'s cane on our legs but she knew her stuff, I'll give her that. Grandma made pencil marks on the door of the breakfast room at home. Three foot, three and a half foot, four foot, four foot six, five foot, five foot two. Miss Worthington said:

'They're casting.'

'What?'

'Those girls could bring you in a bob or two, Mrs Chance,' said Miss Worthington in her superannuated pink tutu, leaning on her cane, eyeing us in our vests and knickers, five foot two, glossy brown ringlets Grandma did up each night in rags, like as two water drops. Miss Worthington, who used to be a pro herself until her arches fell.

'Only,' she added, because she kept up with the times, 'you'll have to do something about those sausage curls.'

So we were bobbed, sitting in the barber shop, swathed to our necks in hot towels, enduring the dreadful grinding crunch of the scissors, watching the mouse-brown locks fall round us to the ground; we knew that we were shedding our childhoods with those ringlets and we were pleased as punch. When we were cleaning out Grandma's stuff, after she copped it, there was an envelope in her bottom drawer, two curls: 'Dora's', tied with a blue ribbon, 'Nora's', green.

It was a panto, wasn't it? To cut a long story short, we made our first professional appearance on any stage as birds – little brown birds, sparrows, probably, one, two, three, hop, in the forest scene in *Babes in the Wood* at the Shepherd's Bush Empire, Grandma escorting us there and back with a half-bottle of gin in her handbag just in case.

In case of what? In case the pubs run dry, ducky, she said.

Identical birds. They gave us our own speciality number because we were identical. We were the ones who covered up the 'babes' with leaves, what's more. By ourselves, neither of us was nothing much but put us together, people blinked. Which is Dora? Which is Nora? In those days, we even smelled the same. Phul Nana. We didn't know any better. We used to nick it from Bon Marché.

That first night, of all the first nights of all our years in show business, the dressing room crammed with chorus kiddies, our insides turned to water, our make-up wouldn't stay on, nothing went right. My stocking laddered, her beak came off. All the same, we did our dance, we scattered leaves, we fluttered off, they ate us up. Roars, applause. Come the finale, we pelted the front row with crackers. They went mad. We'd done what we were born to do and, what was more, we'd do it again tomorrow.

Grandma had brought Our Cyn, of course, but, sharing our little triumph, bearing a hatbox full of Fortnum's chocs and bronzed under his freckles by hotter suns than ours . . . our prodigal uncle made his way between the frilly chorus with arms held wide: 'My clever ones!'

Our cup was full to overflowing; he had come home in time to witness our début.

We loved it all, showing off, fancy dress, Leichner's No. 7.

We'd take great gulps of the stale air as soon as we got inside the theatre to set us up for the night. Give me that incomparable old fug of oranges, Jeyes Fluid, humanity, gas . . . I'd rather dab it behind my ears than Mitsouko, even. That moment when the band in the pit tuned up . . . We were *wet* for it, I tell you! Such a rush of blood to our vitals when we started to dance!

We loved it so much we could scarcely believe it when they gave us our pay packets but Grandma banked the cash, said, the sooner we started earning, the better, although Perry's cheque came regular as clockwork and now he had come home again, his presents fell like rain. But Grandma said, *you never can tell.* Hope for the best, expect the worst, she said.

Impossible to comprehend as it might seem at that time to his bedazzled nieces, our Uncle Perry *did* possess a fault. One single fault. It was his boredom threshold. Our little Tiff at three years old had more capacity for continuous effort than Perry. For him, life had to be a continuous succession of small treats or else he couldn't see the point.

One August bank holiday, we would have just turned thirteen, he roared up in a cab. Big hugs. He pinched our cheeks. 'You look peaky, girlies! Can't have that.' He piled us all in the back of the cab, Nora, me, Grandma, not forgetting Our Cyn ('Oh, Mr Hazard!') along with a ruddy great hamper from Jackson's, Piccadilly. 'Dr Brighton is indicated, my man!' First the cabby gaped; then he beamed. 'You're on, guv'nor.' And off we went.

There was a linen tablecloth to spread out on the beach over the shingle and Perry and the cabby, bosom chums, by now, toddled off arm in arm to pick up some bubbly while we put out the ham and chicken and cut up the loaf and opened the can of foie gras, nothing but the best when Uncle Perry stood the treat. All the punters stared, I can tell you – three skinny girls and a fat lady in a spotted veil, Perry with his shock of bright red hair and his stevedore's shoulders and his big, fat smile, and the cabby in the leather jacket. Grandma filled the glasses, gave her toast: 'Champagne to all here, *real* pain to the other bastards.' Perry picked hard-boiled eggs out of our noses and gave us our coffee piping hot poured from the neb of the cabby's cap.

When we'd all done eating, Perry took hold of the two

corners of one end of the cloth and – whoosh! the fine china, the knives and forks (good, heavy silverware, nothing mean), the bones, the crusts, the empties, vanished clean away. He said he'd sent them back to the shop. How did he do it? Search me. Our Uncle Perry knew a trick or two. Bloody marvellous conjurer. Should have set up professionally. Half the beach broke into spontaneous applause and, much encouraged, Perry said: anybody got a saw? If so, he'd saw Grandma in half. Not on your life, she said, God knows what might come out. She'd tucked up her skirts, shown off her big, red bloomers, had her little paddle. She took a crème de menthe frappé, to settle her digestion, she belched, she nodded off. Our Cyn and the cabby were deep in conversation so the rest of us set off for a walk along the pier.

Perry was the size of a polar bear, bless him, in his vanilla tussore suit and the straw boater with the red and black ribbon and white shirt with a red stripe, stiff collar, red tie. He was huge but dapper. The citric brisk smell of his cologne. Later on, during the war, dragging myself up from my slumbers in the blackout, I got a big whiff of it, Trumper's Essence of Lime. I thought: I must have had it off with Peregrine!!! Dread and delight coursed through my veins; I thought, what have I done . . . But when I switched the light on, it turned out to be not Perry at all, but that Free Pole.

Peregrine in his ice-cream suit with a girl on either arm, neither of us anything special on our own – skinny things with mouse-brown bobs – but, put us together, we turned heads. Past the donkey rides and the hokey-pokey man and all the minarets, turrets and trellises of Brighton Pavilion, which always reminds me of our Grandma, somehow, although she tended towards the subfusc, she was like the Brighton Pavilion in blackout. Highly unlikely the Pavilion looked, too, that afternoon. Such a lovely day. The shiny, frilly waves; cackling of the seagulls; laughter of little children; plashing of water. And he'd let us have a glass of bubbly, each, at lunch. Everything conspired to make us happy.

I've been happy before and I've been happy after, but, swinging along the front at Brighton with Nora and our Uncle Perry, not a care in the world, it was the first time I was old enough and wise enough and knew my way about my own feelings well enough, to put it into words: 'Goodness! I'm happy!' When I think of happiness, I always think of Brighton, and of that

August bank holiday when I was thirteen, because we did the heights and depths, that day. How frail a thing your happiness can be! We went from the ridiculous to the sublime, and broke our hearts, as well.

'Why are they called Pierrots?' asked Nora outside the Pier Pavilion.

'Because they do their stuff on piers.'

I love the artificial dark of the matinée, the same, exciting dark you get when you draw the curtains after lunch to go to bed. The sea was swishing back and forth beneath the Pier Pavilion and it was moist and warm, inside, and full of holiday scents of Evening in Paris and Ashes of Violets mixed with dry fish, that is, fried, from outside, and wet fish, that is, dead, from down below, and hot tin, from the roof, and armpits. Nobody there to take a ticket; the first half of the show was nearly over so we sneaked in at the back.

The Pierrots were standing around in their white frills, looking spare, and there was a comic up on stage halfway through his act. He'd got on a pair of plus-fours, huge things, big as a couple of hot-air balloons, in the kind of pink Grandma called 'fraizy crazy' (crushed strawberry, to you; work it out for yourself) – shiny pink satin plus-fours tucked into mauve golfing socks with pink clocks plus a pair of pink suede brogues with big, mauve, flapping tongues hanging out. He'd got a golf club in his hand, to go with his outfit, and he made lewd gestures with it; mothers covered their children's eyes.

I'd never heard of him in those days, though he made a big name for himself later on, but when he started out, you'd have thought it was going to be a name you couldn't print in a family newspaper. He called himself . . . he called himself . . . I'll remember it in a minute. He had a catch phrase, 'Nothing queer about our George.' He popped up again in Hollywood, in *The Dream*, with us, what a surprise; he played, of course he would, what else, Bottom.

Gorgeous George. He billed himself as Gorgeous George.

'. . . and this boy's thoughts turned lightly to' – big poke in the air with the golf club – 'so he says to his dad, "I want to get married to the girl next door, Dad."

'"Ho, hum," says his dad. "I've got news for you, son. When I was your age, I used to get me leg over – "'

Roars, shrieks, hoots; but all so much titillation without any substance, I tell you, because he gave them a shocked look, pursed his lips together, shook his golf club in reproof.

'*Filthy* minds, some of you have,' he grieved in parenthesis. Renewed hoots and shrieks.

'What I was about to say before I was so rudely interrupted . . .'

That was his other catch phrase.

'. . . was, I used to get me leg over – '

Mothers covered their children's ears.

' – I used to get me leg over the garden wall – '

He made a fierce lunge in the air with his golf club and looked around, working his eyebrows as if to defy misinterpretation.

'. . . and, cut a long story short, you can't marry the girl next door, son, on account of she's your sister.'

The air turned blue. Mothers forced reluctant children outside, bribing with ice-cream.

'So this boy buys a bike' – he straddled his golf club, mimicked pedalling, renewed roaring – 'and pedals off. *Pedals*, I said, Missus; what d'you think I said? He pedals off to Hove.'

Wonderful diction. Grandma herself couldn't have done more with that long 'O'.

'He comes back, he says to his father: "I've met this nayce girl from Hove, Dad." "Hove?" says Dad. "Sorry to say, son, I frequently hove to in Hove when I was your age and – "'

He halted, working his eyebrows, manipulating his golf club. Say no more. They laughed until they cried.

'This poor boy, he buys himself a day return, he goes up to Victoria, he meets a girl under the clock. *Clock*, I said, Missus. But his father says: "We had trains in my young day, son . . ."'

Appreciative gurgles.

'The boy goes into the kitchen for a cup of tea. Big sigh. His mum says: "You've got a face as long as a – "'

Eyebrows. Golf club. Roars.

'What I was going to say, before I was so rudely interrupted, was . . . as long as a fiddle!'

They pounded the floorboards with their feet.

'"Looks like I'll never get married, Mum." "Why's that, son?" He told her all about it, she says: "You just go ahead and marry who you like, son – "'

Split-second timing. That pause. Perfect.

''*E*'s not your father!'

They stamped and pounded so you would have thought the floor was going to give way. Perry gazed on, amazed. 'Well, God bless the bloody British,' he said. 'I never thought they had it in them.'

When the audience quieted down, they put a pink filter on the spot so Gorgeous George flushed all over. He put on a lugubrious look and sucked in his cheeks. It was time for his tenor number. The lady accompanist, one of Mrs Worthington's ilk, gave the piano a good thump. George clasped his hands together on his club, adopted a reverential air, and, would you believe it, there, in his pink suit in the pink spot, on the end of Brighton Pier, on August bank bloody holiday, he gave out with 'Rose of England'.

Rose of England, breathing England's air,
Flower of majesty beyond compare . . .

The Pierrots, all turned pink themselves, formed groups reminiscent of posies and nosegays and sank to their knees for the throbbing finale. You couldn't get away with that sort of thing, these days, not unless it was what they call 'camp'. Then George held up his hand to quell the applause and, stepping forward, announced in a voice heavy with emotion:

'Ladies and gentlemen, boys and girls . . . long live the King!'

The lady accompanist struck up 'Land of Hope and Glory' in spite of a couple of bum notes in the bass and George shouldered his golf club as if it were a rifle and commenced to march round and round the stage in military fashion, the mauve tongues of his suede brogues lolling voluptuously half a beat behind him.

Left, right, halt.

He salutes the audience under the spot, which is now bright white again, the limelight falling on his shoulders like dandruff. The lady accompanist simulates a drumroll, to the best of her ability. Off comes his satin cap.

Nora and I looked at one another, puzzled. What on earth was going on?

Another drumroll.

Off comes his rose-pink jacket.

Odder and odder.

And it turned out that George himself, in himself, in his skin, is the prime spectacle on offer, this afternoon.

For George was not a comic at all but an enormous statement.

If I hadn't seen it with my own two eyes, I'd never have believed it. Displayed across his torso there was, if you took the top of his head as the North Pole and the soles of his feet as the South, a complete map of the entire world.

He flexed his muscles and that funny little three-cornered island with appendages on the right bicep sprang out, the Irish Free State giving a little quiver. The lady accompanist hit the first few notes of 'God Save the King' and half the punters, from sheer force of habit, began to struggle to their feet, scattering shed gloves and chocolate papers, but soon sank down again and let him get on with it when the next thing he did was, take off his plus-fours.

Nora and I were only girls, never seen a man without his trousers on although Grandma had drawn us pictures, and, I must say, we were quite keenly curious so we craned forward eagerly but it turned out he stripped off only to reveal a gee-string of very respectable dimensions, more of a gee-gee string, would have kept a horse decent, and it was made out of the Union Jack. Amply though the garment concealed his privates, now you could see the Cape of Good Hope situated in his navel and observe the Falkland Islands disappear down the crack of his bum when he did his grand patriotic ninety-degree rotation, to the reawakened applause that never quite died down during the entire display but sometimes rose in greater peaks than at other times.

We gazed enraptured on the flexing pecs. 'Rule, Britannia' accompanied his final turn, which revealed how most of his global tattoo was filled in a brilliant pink, although the limelight turned it into morbid, raspberry colour that looked bad for his health.

Then George made a few passes with his golf club, and simulated bayonet practice with it in his patriotic bathers for a bit, with a few more imitation drumrolls and stern cheers from the crowd. And some had tears in their eyes, I swear, and shouted: 'Good old George! Hurrah for George!' But we girls were bemused: what kind of a show was this? Hadn't Grandma told us that wars were a way to get the young men out of the picture, leave all the women for the ugly old codgers who wouldn't have got any, otherwise? So we knew what wars were for and, to tell the truth, from George's joke, it looked as though he thought that that was what fathers always wanted, too.

And as regards the pink bits on his bum and belly, we knew already in our bones that those of us in the left-hand line were left out of the picture; we were the offspring of the bastard king of England, if you like, and we weren't going to inherit any of the gravy, so the hell with it.

After his bayonet practice, Gorgeous George donned his golfing jacket once again, made a reassuringly obscene gesture with that golf club and retired backwards, kissing his hands to the hallooing crowd and murmuring: 'God bless you!' We were all three sweating like pigs, so we beat it, sharpish, before anyone noticed we hadn't paid. The fishermen were out in force on the pier – somebody pulled up a mackerel that shone like a new tin can. Or perhaps it *was* a tin can. I misremember. It was sixty-odd years ago, you know. They used to fancy those patriotic tableaux, in those days. We didn't know what to make of it, really. We were just girls, we'd never seen a man's bare bum before, though one another's, often.

Perry ran a finger round his collar to wipe away the sweat. He looked quite dazed.

'I'll never understand the British,' he opined, and so say all of us, ducky.

'Now,' he said to us girls after having ingested several lungfuls of fresh air, 'you show us what *you* can do, my little chorines.'

Sunshine and glitter off the sea and a little breeze and laughter all around us. People being happy. As I remember it, a band struck up out of nowhere. Lovely little band. Nothing elaborate, just three or four pieces, with a drummer. God knows how they got there, unless they'd come down from London on a cheap day excursion, to busk. Or maybe they were booked into the Grand Hotel or something like that, as cabaret. But I certainly seem to remember four Black gentlemen in suits and straw hats, trumpet, trombone, clarinet, percussion. Or perhaps it was Perry on his harmonica, all the time, who provided the music, so that we could dance for him. We danced the Black Bottom for him; we loved the Black Bottom, he'd given us a record, the one about

Ma Rainey's Big Black Bottom. We danced the dance but didn't sing the song, that would have been presumptuous.

Instead, we had a think, we held a consultation, we picked out a song in honour of Gorgeous George's joke, we gave them, 'Is You Is or Is You Ain't My Baby', and Perry went purple in the face, wanting to laugh and trying to blow at the same time. Then he stowed his harmonica, doffed his boater, took it round the crowd. I can't remember what happened to the band. They faded away. Would you believe it, a quid? In those days, a quid *was* a quid. A quid less a tanner, all in small change. He counted it out and handed it over.

'Buy us a cup of tea, you can afford it,' he said. We went into town to look for a Fuller's Tea Room because he fancied a bit of walnut cake, too, and that is how we came to find ourselves outside the Theatre Royal.

'Shit,' said Perry but he said it in American, like this: 'Shee-it.'

Melchior Hazard and Company
in
Macbeth
His acclaimed production.
'Sheer Genius.'
The Times.

We clustered, we stared, we were overcome, we sought the protection of his bulk, we hid our faces as if shy of the photographs.

'You do know,' Perry told us, 'that you ain't my babies, worse luck. I am not now nor ever have been your father. No. And you *do* know, don't you, that *he* – '

– gesture towards the photographs –

'is.'

We nodded. We knew that Melchior Hazard was our father and now we also knew exactly what it was a father did, and how, and where, and who he'd done it to, and what had happened after that. We knew it all. And here he was, treading the boards like billy-oh, in Shakespeare, and weren't we fresh from singing in the streets? We'd never felt quite so illegitimate in all our lives as we did that day we were thirteen, looking at the glossy photos of Father togged up in a kilt.

And one of my suspenders had come undone, my left stocking at half-mast.

Perry drew out his watch, consulted it.

'Birnam Wood,' he said, 'is just now creeping up on Dunsinane.'

I had an inkling of what he might be at and I was frightened.

'Let's get back to Grandma Chance,' I said in a strangled voice.

But, more than anything else in the world, I longed and longed to push through the glass doors and feast my eyes on the sight of my father, my gloriously handsome father, my gifted, sensationally applauded genius of a father, and I knew, without speech, without even so much as glancing at her, that Nora, too, wanted it more than anything. I reached out for Nora's hand. It was hot and sticky, still a child's hand, although I suppose we looked like quite young ladies, already, being tall for our ages and we had on the yellow dresses Perry picked out for us in Paris, from Chanel, and the bows on our heads, more coquette than finishing school, to tell the truth. Nymphettes, I suppose they'd call us now. Jail-bait.

Nora and I clutched each other's hands.

'Grandma will be wondering where we are,' said Nora. 'She'll worry.'

But she never budged and her voice broke on 'worry', she wailed. Perry looked from one to the other of us forlorn little creatures, tears standing in our eyes, love locked out.

'Dammit,' he said. 'Come with me.'

And grabbed our arms and raced us to the stage door, where a bank note changed hands. Whisked up a draughty backstairs, another bank note went to the dresser who let us into our father's empty dressing room, put his finger on his lips to tell us to keep our mouths shut, and left us. Perry parked us on the sofa and we gazed with moonstruck adoration at the very towel our father had dried his hands on, the razor he'd shaved with, the greasepaint he'd put on his beloved face – all these things had far more intimate relations with him than we did and seemed almost holy, in our eyes. His mirror, that had the joy and honour of reflecting him.

I badly wanted to reach out and pinch a stick of his No. 7, to remember him by, but I didn't dare.

There was a photo, head and shoulders, of a sheep in a tiara; we eyed it askance. We knew full well who *she* was; hadn't we seen her on his arm at the first matinée, when we fell in love with him? (Little did we know then that we'd share our twilight years with her, poor old thing.)

But don't think we ransacked the room. Just to sit there and breathe in air he had breathed out was more, much more than we'd ever hoped for. Now we knew for certain that Perry was better than a conjurer, was a genuine magician who could divine our most secret desire of all, the one we'd never confided even to one another because we hadn't needed to, because I knew she knew and she knew *I* knew.

God, we were humble. We'd sneaked off, now and then, now we knew what was what, paid our sixpences, sat in the gods and watched him strut and fret his hour upon the stage, happy with just the sight of him. But as soon as we were in his very dressing room, where we'd never even dared to hope we might one day find ourselves, we grew ambitious. Perhaps, discovering us here so unexpectedly, his lovely girls, lost before birth and now rediscovered on the springtime verge of blossoming (as Irish would have put it), he might let us touch his hand, even allow us to kiss his cheek . . . and we might be permitted, just the once, to say the word we'd never used in all our lives: 'Father.'

Father!

The very thought made our skins prickle.

Perry, meanwhile, was gazing absently out of the open window at the roof and chimneys and brick backs; a seagull landed on a chimneystack and mewed. There was a gust of military brass brought on the wind from the seafront bandstand: 'Colonel Bogey'. He drummed his fingertips on the window ledge. If I hadn't been so stunned and glorified by the prospect at last of meeting him, I might have noted that, for once, our Perry was suffering second thoughts and, if I'd done that, I might have worried more about our welcome. But I was too overwhelmed to make much of it, at the time. It was warm and close in the dressing room, our armpits moistened. All of a sudden I wanted to pee.

Enormous volumes of applause surged through the old building and, when it faded away, then, more quickly than we thought could have been possible, so that we had no time at all to prepare ourselves, as if he'd flown from the stage to the dressing room on wires, there he was.

He was tall, dark and handsome. God, he was handsome, in those days. And smashing legs, which a man must have for Shakespeare, especially the Scottish play; you need a good calf to get away with a kilt. I do believe we get the legs from him, as well as the cheekbones.

I *did* piss myself when I saw him, in fact, but only a little bit, hardly enough to stain the sofa.

Such eyes! Melchior's eyes, warm and dark and sexy as the inside of a London cab in wartime. His eyes.

But those very eyes, those knicker-shifting, unfasten-your-brassiere-from-the-back-of-the-gallery eyes, were the bitterest disappointment of my life till then. No. Of all my life, before and since. No disappointment ever after measured up to it. Because those eyes of his looked at us but did not *see* us, even as we sat there, glowing because we couldn't help it; our helpless mouths started to smile.

To see him fail to see me wiped that smile right off my face, I can tell you, and off Nora's, too. Our father's eyes skidded right over us, never touched us, didn't make contact. They came to rest on Perry.

'Peregrine!' he cried. His voice still sends a shiver down my spine to this day. Up he pops on the telly, tamping down his pipe. 'Rich, dark, fruity . . .' You can say that, again.

He held out his hands in greeting to Perry, to Perry only.

'Peregrine . . . how nice of you to come and visit me.' And then, and only then, we got our little crumb of attention although it shot us down like the same bullet through both hearts.

'And you've brought your lovely daughters, too!'

I have a memory, although I know it cannot be a true one, that Peregrine swept us up into his arms. That when our father denied us, Peregrine spread his arms as wide as wings and gathered up the orphan girls, pressed us so close we crushed against his waistcoat, bruising our cheeks on his braces' buttons. Or perhaps he slipped us one in each pocket of his jacket. Or crushed us far inside his shirt, against his soft, warm belly, to be sustained by the thumping comfort of his heart. And then, hup! he did a back-flip out of the window with us, saving us. But I know I am imagining the back-flip and the flight.

But, truly, what he did was, he held out his arms to us and we scampered to harbour, whimpering.

'It's a wise child that knows its own father,' hissed Peregrine, like the gypsy's warning. 'But wiser yet the father who knows his own child.'

He slammed the door behind us. Us. Unkissed, unwelcome, worse than unacknowledged. Our washers were leaking, I can tell you. How we blubbered. Cried so much we couldn't see where we were going but all at once there we were, back on the beach, transferred from Perry to Ma Chance's voluminous arms and she dried our eyes, sent Our Cyn for a jug of hot tea from a café, so we had some of that, to give us strength, and a cream bun or two that Perry extricated from Grandma's cleavage along with a big puff of talc, to bring back a smile to our lips, which we managed palely, so as not to disappoint him, and we had something to nibble on, to take our minds off, but not much appetite, I can tell you.

It turned out that Our Cyn and the cabby had got along so well together on their day out they'd decided to make a go of it so it was kisses and handshakes all round and Cyn sat in the front with him while Nora and I leaned on Perry's shoulders as we drove back to London through the yellowish, greenish light of a Sussex evening, sweet summer coming in through the windows and the low murmur of the voices of Perry and Grandma talking softly so as not to disturb us as we trembled on the brink of sleep, for it had truly been an exhausting day, but we didn't nod off altogether until Norbury so they had to carry us up to our little beds in the back attic which, at that time, in our white girlhood, we shared.

Cyn and the cabby wanted to go up West, to celebrate, so they dropped Perry off at Eaton Square. Eaton Square? That's what Cyn told us. What could he be doing in Eaton Square, on the spur of the moment, the naughty boy? They left him on the front steps of a most elegant dwelling, he was straightening his tie and dusting off his jacket. He tipped his boater at them as they drove off, flashed them his great, big, cheeky grin.

Love him as I did, I must confess he had a wicked streak.

Although our half-sisters, old Wheelchair's girls, resembled sheep with bright red fleece when grown, they were bald as any other baby when they were born, the dead spit of one another, not far away from Bard Road as the crow flies but the crow is a bit of a prole as far as the bird world goes and most other birds would think those girls were born in a different country, with Sheraton furniture, Persian rugs, constant hot water, and staff, and christened Saskia and Imogen in long lace clothes at St John's Smith Square, shortly thereafter to be photographed with Mamma, the 'loveliest lady in London', by Cecil Beaton, and have their picture published in the *Sketch*, caption: 'Darling buds of May'. For it was in May that they were born, the same day as the first of Our Cyn's five.

We started the very same day those two were born, as it happens. Funny coincidence. I went to have a wee and there was the evidence, all over my underwear. I hotfooted it to Nora and she took a look on her own account. Same thing with her. Grandma got us some cotton wool. Although we are asymmetrical, in many ways, we always, funnily enough, came on in unison every time since that first time, barring accidents; came on in unison until we stopped, short, never to go again, the tap turned off just twenty-five years ago.

I always think there was a sort of mean connection between their birth and our puberty. Typical dirty trick that Saskia might pull on us, that we should turn into women just at the very moment when they turn into babies. Always a different generation. That's the rub. We've never been equals. They've always had that final edge on us. So rich. So well-connected. So legitimate.

Sod all that.

So young.

'Darling buds of May.' Grandma Chance did sums upon her fingers and assumed an inscrutable expression but the proud parents looked pleased as punch with the new arrivals although Perry seemed strangely sad, these days, when Saskia and Imogen took the air in a high-wheeled baby carriage pushed by a ribboned nanny while Dora and Nora pounded away on splintering boards the length and breadth. Glasgow Empire. Prince's, Edinburgh. Royalty, Perth. Freeze off a girl's bum, the winters up there. Somebody threw a grouse on stage, once, as a gesture of appreciation. Not even a pair. That was in Aberdeen. Tight as arseholes, in Aberdeen.

We pounded the boards like nobody's business because, by that time, Perry had lost all his moolah in the Wall Street crash, every red cent, and couldn't keep up his contributions any more, so it was just as well we girls could earn our living because after that we had to.

When he came to say goodbye, it was by tram. Lo, how the mighty have fallen. No cab softly ticking away on the kerb, this time. No chocolates from Charbonnel & Walker. And he'd weaned us off Phul Nana ('Phew!') only to find he couldn't afford to give us the French stuff any more. Not that we cared. We only thought how much we'd miss him. We sat on the arms of his chair, one on each side, and watched him eat his buttered crumpets, too down at heart to eat anything ourselves.

He'd work his passage home, he said. Home, to that part of the torso of Gorgeous George that was *not* tinted pink. He'd work his Atlantic passage on the liner doing tricks in the ballroom after dinner.

'What will you do once you get there?' asked Grandma Chance, shoving another pan of crumpets under the grill because he was eating as if he might not eat again until he reached Los Angeles.

'Go into the movies,' said Peregrine.

Dora and Nora. Two girls pounding the boards. At Christmas, we did a panto. One year we did *Jack and the Beanstalk* at Kennington. Would you believe a live theatre in Kennington, once upon a time? Alive and kicking. Beans, in green tights; our speciality number was Mexican jumping beans, in red tights. Two pounds a week each. It went a long way, in those days. Those were the days of pounds, shillings and pence. Two pounds was forty silver shillings; forty shillings was four hundred and eighty of those big, brown, cartwheel pennies that made your hands smell, and every one of those pennies had a hole ready and waiting for it to patch in the threadbare economy of 49 Bard Road. Being at Kennington was a saving on digs. We lived at home, we came home on the night tram, every bone in our body aching in concert and our feet burning, we girls half asleep, half awake, propping against one another, rain slashing the window, soaking our coats as we ran from the stop for home. If we caught cold, disaster! Even identical Mexican jumping beans were expendable so we jumped away with low fevers and septic throats and influenza and the curse, jump, jump, jump, carrying on smiling, smilin' thru', show those teeth, kick those legs, tote that barge, lift that bale.

We could even get home for tea after the matinée, Wednesdays and Saturdays, and that saved the money we'd have spent on a poached egg at a Lyons teashop so we'd put aside those four pennies to save up for silk stockings. Stockings were always a problem. The hours we spent, darning the bloody things.

Then, one afternoon, such a fuss and flutter backstage; what's going on? What a shock we got. A sheep in a couture afternoon frock in a box, with a nanny in ribbons and two little russet ewe lambs. Our humble little company had been honoured by a visit from theatrical royalty.

'I won't go on,' said Nora, always impetuous. She threw her sombrero on the floor and jumped on it. 'What humiliation!'

But the first Lady Hazard was a proper lady, not like the present incumbent, and I didn't think, even then, that she'd set out for Kennington with the gross intention of letting her baby daughters relish the spectacle of her husband's by-blows performing high kicks. I've asked her about it since, of course, and she said that *he* was away on tour, again, and she was banging about all by herself in that great, big house at her wits' end how to pass a wet Saturday afternoon and her Old Nanny, the very same Old Nanny who'd looked after her when *she* was a baby and now was looking after *her* little babies, Old Nanny wanted to take the little girls to the panto in Kennington because her, Old Nanny's, that is, her sister lived round the corner. (And as it turned out that sister was an aunt by marriage of Our Cyn's new husband, so a bond was forged and after Old Nanny's sister moved to Worthing, Old Nanny used to drop in and visit Grandma.) Old Nanny thought she might pop in to see her sister after the panto and the Lady Atalanta, on the spur of the moment, said: 'Hang on, I'll get my hat and come, too.'

The show went on, of course, and so did we. What? Lose a day's pay? Lose the job, too, like as not, and then back to the dreary round of agents' waiting rooms. Anything but that.

She says, as soon as she set eyes on us, she *knew,* and then she checked the programme and was certain, because Perry told her all about us after they got together. She sent us flowers, after, anonymously, but easy to guess where they came from – forget-me-nots. I thought that was quite touching but Nora thought, bad taste. And once she asked us to tea, as well, but Nora said: 'Not on your life.'

Our half-sisters responded to the show in ways already characteristic of their future personalities. Saskia set up a howl like a banshee the moment she saw the beans come on, as if she knew us at first sight and was all agog to steal our thunder, while Imogen fell asleep and left her mouth open through the entire proceedings, in preparation for her career as a fish. But the Lady A. watched us, or so she told me, years on, with tears in her eyes and guilt in her bosom. She may have slipped up the once, but, all the same, she truly loved our father. She *must* have loved him, her with her handle and her bank account and her father in the House of Lords, to marry a man with nothing to offer but the best legs in the British Isles.

She'd had no news from Perry, either.

Then the panto season was over and we were on the road again. Fifteen years old, now. Five foot, six inches. Little brown bobs, though Nora often talked wistfully about going blonde. She felt the future lay with blondes. Should we? Shouldn't we? One thing was certain – she couldn't do it unilaterally. On our own, you wouldn't look at us twice. But, put us together . . .

We were hardened old troupers, by now. We had our printed cards: 'Dora and Leonora, 49 Bard Road, London S.W.2'. You always had to travel on a Sunday, when the trains went slow out of respect for the Sabbath and sometimes stopped dead in the middle of a field as if taken short. We feared not bedbugs, nor cockroaches; fleas could not daunt our spirits. We learned to despise the 'Wood' family, that is, the empty seats. We lived off the Scotch eggs the landladies put out for late supper, after the show. Grandma went spare when she heard about the Scotch eggs. 'It's only sausage meat,' I said. 'They wrap some sausage meat round the hard-boiled egg. You know what they make sausage meat out of, sawdust and the bits of old elastic.' Grandma wasn't having any. 'Cannibals!' she said.

But now we knew the world didn't end when Grandma disapproved. Greatly daring, knowing what she'd say, egged on by the other girls, we finally invested in some little bits of rabbit fur to snuggle into when the wind blew chill. 'Dead bunny,' said Grandma when she saw. As we grew up, cracks appeared between us. She loved us but she often disapproved.

We were just slips of girls but we soon knew our way around. We had our little handbags with the little gilt powder compacts and the puffs; when in doubt, we powdered our noses, to give us time to think up repartee. A rat once ate my powder puff in the dressing room at the Nottingham Theatre Royal. We kept our make-up in the standard two-tier tin – rouge, Leichner, that solid mascara you sliced off into a tiny tin frying pan and melted over a candle. Then you put it on with a matchstick, quick, quick, quick, before it got hard.

Grandma kept the programmes, every show we ever were in, right from that first *Babes in the Wood* up to the ones from ENSA. She made up big scrapbooks. After she went, there they were, stored away in a trunk in the loft – the whole of our lives. We felt bad when we saw those scrapbooks, we remembered how we'd teased her, we'd brought home sausage rolls and crocodile handbags, but she'd kept on snipping out the cuttings, pasting them in. Piles of scrapbooks, the cuttings turned by time to the colour of the freckles on the back of an old lady's hand. Her hand. My hand, as it is now. When you touch the old newsprint, it turns into brown dust, like the dust of bones.

The last scrapbook stops short in 1944, leaving us marooned for ever just turning thirty, on the cusp, caught up in one last pose, would you believe, done up as bulldogs. *Bulldog Breed*. For some bloody silly charity matinée, drumming-up cash to replace lost lovers, lost sons, boys dead on the Burma Road, the irreplaceable. Why did we do it, Nora? 'We had to do something,' she said. 'Anyway, we entertained the troops.'

And so we did.

I can see Grandma now, sitting at the kitchen table, sticking the picture in the book, the tip of her tongue between her teeth, breathing hard, all concentration. She picks up her pen, dips in the ink, writes underneath, in her round, careful hand: 'Duke of York's Theatre, May 20, 1944'.

Then she reached for the stout and found the bottle empty. Oh, Grandma! Talk about the 'fatal glass of beer'! If you'd been able to curb your thirst that night, you'd have lived to see VE-day. She pulled herself up by the back of a chair, humming a tune, humming, maybe: 'There'll be bluebirds over The white cliffs of Dover . . .' or: 'I'll get lit up when the lights go up in London.' She arranged her little toque with the black-dotted veil on top of her head in the fly-blown square of mirror over the sink. She touched up her beauty spot with eyeblack, stowed away the empties in that eternal lino-cloth bag. The siren blared but she wasn't going to let Hitler inconvenience her drinking habits, was she?

She was taken out by a flying bomb on her way to the off-licence.

When we got home after the all-clear, we found the scrapbook where she left it, beside the scissors and the pot of Gloy. And the empty glass, with the lacy remnants of the foam gone hard inside it.

And that was how we lost Grandma.

It was Grandma and Guinness caused us to become brunettes. One night, when we were resting between engagements, we were all sitting round this very kitchen table, our one and only kitchen table, having a few drinks.

'If not blonde,' said Nora, 'why don't we henna it? Copper-nobs. Gingernuts. Let's face it, Dora, we need a little something extra to make us stand out.'

'Not red,' I said, 'because of Saskia and Imogen.'

Grandma took a good look at us, at our big, grey eyes and our good, strong Hazard bones that would come in handy, later on, but weren't much use to fifteen-year-olds because we never had the ingénue look. Hard as nails, they said. That's the Chance girls.

Grandma was partaking of the bottled stout she never knew would later prove her downfall.

'Not red,' said Grandma, eyeing her glass. 'Black.'

The dye came in a bottle labelled 'Spanish Ebony'. The bathroom was as cold as hell. Still is. We stood there, shivering in our camisoles, eyeing the dye as if there were a genie in the bottle and we were scared to let it out. This was a big step for us, remember. We were about to change our entire personality.

'In for a penny, in for a pound,' said Nora, at last, and plunged her head into the washbasin, and I anointed her, poured on the colour, rubbed it in, thick, black stuff, it gave me mourning fingernails for weeks. When she straightened up, big drips ran down her forehead, got in her eyes, stung them, she wept. The splashes got everywhere, the towels looked like bath night at the Minstrel Show and we had to cut ourselves fringes when our hair dried out because of the five o'clock shadow on our foreheads that never washed off. So she was crying off the whole idea before it came to my turn but if one of us dyed, so did the other, no choice, that was that. Then we slipped on our kimonos, cleaned up the bathroom as best we could – but we never got the marks off the towels – put each other's hair in pins to fix the kiss curls and went down to have a cuppa with Grandma looking so downhearted she made us lace it with a spot of the brandy she'd just opened on account of the cold snap.

'Very unseasonal weather for July,' she said, topping up.

But when it dried out and we'd given it a good brush, we didn't know ourselves. Half a yard of black satin that turned into our cheeks like commas. It was the turning point. We called ourselves 'The Lucky Chances' after that. After that, we were a featured turn. After that, we were sixteen and we were legal.

Nora was always free with it and threw her heart away as if it were a used bus ticket. Either she was head over heels in love or else she was broken-hearted. She had it off first with the pantomime goose, when we were Mother Goose's goslings that year in Newcastle upon Tyne. The goose was old enough to be her father and Grandma would have plucked him, stuck an apple up his bum and roasted him if she'd found out and so would the goose's wife, who happened to be principal boy. So finding a place to, as Irish might have put it, consummate their passion (although Irish abhorred a split infinitive) was something of a problem for them because it was before the days we could boast a dressing room to ourselves and his wife was eversuch a hairy woman, always a fresh growth between her eyebrows, under her arms, on her legs, to pluck or shave so she was always holed up in the one she shared with the goose, depilating herself.

The goose had Nora up against the wall in the alley outside the stage door one foggy night, couldn't see your hand in front of your face, happily for them. You don't get fogs like that, these days. It was after the cast Christmas party. I looked round the Green Room but they'd gone.

Don't be sad for her. Don't run away with the idea that it was a squalid, furtive, miserable thing, to make love for the first time on a cold night in a back alley with a married man with strong drink on his breath. He was the one she wanted, warts and all, she *would* have him, by hook or by crook. She had a passion to know about Life, all its dirty corners, and this is how she started, in at the deep end, for better or worse, while I stood shivering on the edge like the poor cat in the adage.

When she saw her man was gone, the plume-hatted goose-wife slapped her thigh. There was a jealous madness in that woman. I took the bull by the horns and started off the masquerade – I answered to the name of Nora and kept out of the same place as myself until Nora came back to the party, ripped stockings, smelling of dead fish, smiling like the cat that got the cream, and pregnant.

But we never found out she was pregnant until she lost it in Nottingham, the Royalty, when she haemorrhaged during a *fouetté*, we were a pair of spinning tops. Nothing like real blood in the middle of the song-and-dance act. It was long past panto-time, the goose gone off to Glasgow to do a *Chu Chin Chow*, he never wrote. Nora cried her eyes out but not because she'd lost the goose. She blazed and then she cooled; she'd always blaze, she'd always cool. No. She wept the loss of the baby.

Oh, my poor Nora! She was a martyr to fertility. After that miscarriage, I took steps, got her to get herself fitted up with the full equipment, but Nora never bothered with the diaphragm, not when she got carried away. A sort of grand carelessness possessed her each time she fell in love. She opened up, she melted down at the first touch, the first kiss; each time she fell in love, she fell in love for the first time, no matter how many times she fell in love and, when she fell in love, a Dutch cap was the last thing on her mind. I was in charge of the chequebook, too. She didn't trust herself with that, either.

After the miscarriage, she went round with a face like a month of Sundays for all of three weeks, then, whoops! head over heels, again, this time with the man who played the drums in the pit band and *he* was old enough to be her grandfather. She was particularly attracted to older men, in those days. Even if her diaphragm always stayed in its little box, the drummer took good care, always pulled out in time, and that went on for half a year, on and off, depending on the touring, although sometimes, when she stripped off, she'd be black and blue. 'Love-taps,' she said. I thought, preserve me from the passion of a percussionist.

The more I saw of love, the less I liked the look of it. I might well have reached the age of consent but that didn't mean I *had* to consent to it, whether I wanted to or not. Until that fateful engagement in Croydon, when I fell. Such was the effect of our new haircuts and our new, bubbling, brunette personalities that we now had second billing and a number in white satin pyjamas sitting side by side on a crescent moon. And, bliss! a dressing room of our very own. Nibbles from London managements. And we always liked Croydon, although it was a dump, just a dormitory town, just outside London, but we could get the late tram home and save on digs. I told you, Brixton used to be everso convenient for public transport.

I felt as if I'd met him somewhere else before, although I never had. I didn't think of love or passion when I thought of him; I only thought about the down on his delicious cheek.

As if it were yesterday. The show was called *Over to You*. Nora was ready for a change. She ditched the aged drummer and took up with a wee scrap of a lad pale as a lily, blond as a chick. He didn't know what hit him. Nora used to give her all. Because we shared the dressing room, I used to have to sit on the stairs outside and listen to them through the wall going at it like hammer and tongs on the horsehair sofa where we were supposed to put our feet up between shows. He muttered broken phrases, sometimes sobbed. Something about him touched my heart. Nora said, he was young enough to be grateful but it wasn't that.

I sat on the stairs outside and listened to them and my mind began to change, until I came to a decision: by hook or by crook, I said to myself, come what may, the day that I am seventeen, I'll do it on that horsehair sofa.

Do *what* on the horsehair sofa?

What do you think?

It was late April but still chilly. Little cold winds whipped round the wings and the bare backstage corners. We turned up our gas fire and plucked our eyebrows. There was a bunch of flowers for our birthday and a cake with candles ready for the party after the show.

'Nora . . .'

'Yes?'

'Give me your fella for a birthday present.'

She put down her tweezers and gave me a look.

'Get your own fella,' she said.

They'd sent us early lilac. The scent of white lilac always brings it back. Seventeen hurts.

'He's the only one I want, Nora.'

I'll only do it once, I said. He's really stuck on you, Nora, he's crazy about you and he's never given me a second look. But won't he be able to tell the difference? I don't know, we won't know until we try; but why should he notice any difference? Same eyes, same mouth, same hair. If it was only the once and if I keep my mouth shut . . . he is as innocent as asparagus, his heart as pure as Epps' cocoa, poor lamb. Why should he guess?

'Nora, I want him so.'

'Oh, *Dora*,' she said, for then she knew that only he would do.

She put on my Mitsouko and I put on her Shalimar. She had a new dress, floral chiffon, peonies, rhodies, dusty pink and misty blue and mauve, long skirts were back, I looked romantic. We took big breaths and blew out the candles on the cake; our wish at seven had come true and ever since I was a true believer in birthday-candle magic so you can guess what it was I wished for at seventeen. I smelled the unfamiliar perfume on my skin and felt voluptuous. As soon as they started to call me Nora, I found that I could kiss the boys and hug the principals with gay abandon because all that came quite naturally to her. To me, no. I was ever the introspective one.

As for Nora/Dora, she kept herself to herself until she'd had a couple and then she forgot to behave herself and carried on in her usual fashion but by the time she started dancing on the table most of the party was plastered so nobody noticed she was behaving out of character and that's how Dora got off with the pianist, to my considerable embarrassment in subsequent months.

There was a scratchy gramophone going full tilt. I laid claim to my birthday present as soon as he came shyly through the door. His face was still shining with cold cream. I took his hand. 'Let's dance,' I said.

'Nothing for me but to love you, just the way you look tonight . . .' sang the voice on the gramophone.

I know I wanted him more than anything, that his sweet face and his silken floss of flaxen hair moved me like nothing else had done in the masculine line before, but, all the same, I scarcely knew what it was I wanted, when all is said and done, in spite of Grandma's comprehensive sex education and all I'd seen during my life in the chorus and, more than all that, I'd seen my sister cry for love, and nearly bleed to death for love, and I'd listened while the one she loved made her shout out loud, when I was full of envy and desire. I thought I knew the lot, didn't I?

And yet I didn't know a thing.

Lilac; and a wind blowing in through the window they'd opened to let the fug out; and the smoke of the candles that I'd just blown out, still lingering in the room, catching at the throat; and the first kiss. I nearly fainted when we kissed, I was scared witless, I thought he'd recognize the ruse at once and suddenly I didn't want to go through with it. I wanted to go home to Grandma, to go back to yesterday's things we'd lost already – back to Mrs Worthington's piano, to our shorn sausage curls, to pick up our discarded liberty bodices and encase ourselves again in them. But he was just my own age, just seventeen, a child, too; nothing to be afraid of. And for the purpose of the act, I wasn't Dora, any more, was I? Now I was Nora, who was afraid of nothing provided it was a man.

So I kissed him back and we slipped off.

He went to have a wash in the basin, first, while I stripped off and lay on the sofa watching him, the back of his neck bent humbly as he attended to himself. The water purled. Just the lights round the mirror were burning. A cab stopped outside and panted like a dog; there was a chink of coins: 'Ta, guv'nor.' These sounds might have come from another world.

He was too young for body hair. His tender flesh was all rosy in the light behind him. He smiled as he came towards me. It stuck out like a chapel hat peg. What did? What do you think? I couldn't keep my eyes off it. I'd never seen a naked man before although Grandma had drawn us pictures. There was a little clear drop of moisture trembling on the tip, it came to me to lick it off. He gave a gasp. His nipples were quite stiff, too. He was shivering a bit, not that it was cold, we'd left the gas fire on.

He never said: 'Nora, there's something different about you, something more enchanting, tonight.' I never wanted him to, either. I'd have been ashamed. I'll never know if he could tell the difference. If he did, he was too much of a gent to say. Skin like suede. Eyes the blue of the paper bags they used to sell you sugar in, years ago. I never bled or hurt; a decade and a half of *fouettés*, jetés and high kicks had done in the membrane without leaving a trace. He used a French letter, don't ever believe them if they tell you it takes away the romance. He sighed, his eyes rolled back so you could see the whites. Eyelashes a foot long.

Some things you can't describe.

Afterwards, I pretended to be asleep, I didn't dare talk. He spread my dressing gown on top of me, to keep the draughts off, and kissed my cheek. After a bit, he got up and put his clothes on, singing softly under his breath snatches of the song we'd danced to. 'That laugh that wrinkles your nose, touches my foolish heart . . .' I watched him secretly between my lashes. He gave me another kiss and a big smile he thought I couldn't see and went to catch the late trolley home to his mum and dad in Camberwell. Off he went, smelling of Shalimar and sex, and I lay on the sofa, and breathed in the smells of him and me that were really the smells of him and Nora and I kept a little sentimental tryst with silence and the night and the full moon over Croydon and he never would have done it if he'd known I wasn't Nora. He was the faithful type.

Did we betray the innocence of the boy with our deception? Of course we did. Does it matter? Let the one without sin cast the first stone. He really thought I was the one he loved so he was not deceived. And I got the birthday present that I wanted and then I gave him back to Nora and if Nora's heart had been less easily distracted, they would have gone on together, and on . . . until they stopped.

As it was, they went on together until they stopped, anyway. So that was that.

The lilac started to rot the morning after, went brown at the edges, reeked of bad breath. Irish, who taught me about metaphor, would have made a meal, if you follow me, out of that lilac.

After a decent interval, I got up, too, got dressed, again, dabbed on a bit more scent and went back to the party. By now, most of the guests had faded away, Dora included – she'd roared off in the piano player's little red sports car back to his flat in Chelsea. But that same record was still turning on the gramophone and chorus boys too tired to go home were swaying in each other's arms and there was a lingering sense in the air that something exciting had been happening while I'd been away. Then I saw what that exciting something was; he was fixing himself a Scotch and soda at the drinks tray, the man we'd last seen in a kilt, in the act of repudiating us. But now he was romantically garbed in evening dress, with a black evening cape with a scarlet lining over it. And he was, oh, wonders! smiling! At me!

It transpired the taxi I had heard draw up delivered me – our father.

God knows why Melchior felt the time had come to give us girls a call but I do think the Lady A., who soon emerged out of the shadows in a white Molyneux frock, had a hand in it, which is one of the reasons why we're prepared to put up with the old bag now, in her dotage.

I'll say this for the old man, he always had a sense of style. He took my hand.

'Strange how potent cheap music is,' he said.

The Lady A. smiled kindly on us and went so far as to wind up the gramophone. My heart went pit-a-pat. 'I will feel a glow . . .' You'd have thought they only had the one record, the song that might have been written exclusively for that night. '. . . just thinking of you, and the way you look tonight.' I'd never so much as shaken his hand before that night of nights. He didn't dance badly, for a Shakespearian. It was all too much for me, suddenly. I couldn't help it, I burst out crying.

'Don't cry, little girl,' my father said. 'Happy birthday. And I've got you a very special birthday present.'

Although he did not live in heaven, our father was in constant communication with the angels. And that is how we came to star, alongside his very self, in that soon-to-be-famous West End revue entitled *What You Will*.

The music stopped, the lights were going out, the boys departing. The party was over. He dropped a kiss on top of my head, a light little kiss, a butterfly kiss, but a kiss, all the same. I thought: I'll never wash my hair again. Then they were gone.

I lashed out, took a cab home, but I was in such a state I stopped it at Leigham Court Road, got out and walked the rest of the way. I needed air. It was getting light by the time I got back to Brixton, the sky was the colour of a gas jet. I had on a new pair of shoes I was very fond of, I thought they were the peak of chic – red morocco. High heels, ankle straps. Cost a fortune. My high heels went clip, clip, clip on the pavement and I never felt more grown-up in all my life ever after than I did that early morning, watching my shadow teeter-totter home in front of me in those sexy shoes. Because, during the night that now was over, I had made love to a boy for the first time; and my father had kissed me, for the first time; I'd heard my name would be up in lights on Shaftesbury Avenue, for the first time, and I was choked up inside with the pleasure and the terror of the world.

Grandma was still up when I got home, sucking at one last crème de menthe frappé in her kimono. When she saw my face with all the glory in it, she put the kettle on the stove for tea and gave me a hug.

'Whoever he is,' she said, 'he's not worth it.'

Why was Grandma still up?

Why was she dealing the *coup de grâce* to a freshly opened bottle of liqueur?

The answer to these questions sprawled at immense and magnificent ease in Grandma's best armchair, fast asleep and snoring. God, he'd put on weight! Busting out of his waistcoat, and his bookie's suit of ginger plaid, and his fingers a-glitter with big, fat, diamond rings, and his shoes black and white like spotted dogs – correspondent's shoes.

My uncle had come home again.

We dressed up, we made up and then we spent the hour before curtain-up on the West End premiere of *What? You Will?* dashing for the lavatory to throw up. First I thought I'd fallen for it, a bittersweet emotion – I *was* in a state, but my friend, Mr Piano Man, made a speedy diagnosis – nerves, so we all had a brandy and felt better. All London and his dog packed out the house. We'd done a roaring try-out in Manchester, we'd been a smash, but all the same Mr Piano Man now confessed to a touch of nausea himself, because there was more to him than met the eye as one might have guessed by his style, his smart motor, his apartment, etc. etc. He'd done all the music, hadn't he? Every note. It was make or break for him, that night, but after another brandy we started to feel fine.

He went out a piano player and came back a star, *What! You Will?* his first big hit. After that he did a string of musicals, all smashes in their time, every one forgotten now. Not a soul remembers. He always thought of me as 'Dora' and, this was the confusing thing, I *was* 'Dora', but not the Dora he'd fallen for, although he didn't notice any difference, either, and always sent me lilac, lots and lots of lilac, the sentimental thing. I'd got nothing whatever against him; he gave me lovely hot dinners, we had some good times, but when he gave me a kiss for luck that night, I turned the other cheek, I didn't like the way his breath smelled and Nora, ever worldly wise, said: 'That means you're going off him.' I lived in fear he would propose.

'Break a leg,' he said.

He joined up, first thing. Missing in action in 1942. I used to go and see his mother, sometimes, in Golders Green. There was his photo on the piano, and the music for the song I sang, he made a fuss, he got his way – Dora's very own number. 'O Mistress Mine'. You can't say fairer than that. The piano was open, there was the music, nobody to play it. I used to take his mother the occasional black-market egg.

Melchior came in at the last moment and gave us his blessing, with a look that said he knew we knew but he wasn't going to ask for our forgiveness because wasn't he just about to give us our big chance? With the bald wig on, he looked uncannily like; he was personating, who else – the 'Will', in *What! You Will!* in person. Shakespeare.

I must tell you that our father had become a truly great man of the theatre, by this time. Now he was fortyish – although he didn't look it, with all that velvet glamour – and peaking. At the apex. 'Our greatest living Shakespearian'. Luck had a lot to do with it, not to mention the Lady A.'s private fortune financed his Shylock and his Richard III and his Macbeth in Brighton that gave us girls so much grief. (He'd always steered clear of Hamlet, though, and now he was too old; perhaps he was nervous the critics might think he wasn't half the man his mother had been.)

Yet still he yearned for new fields to conquer. Wheelchair swears that ever since she told him how she'd seen his left-hand daughters do the splits, he'd nourished a yen to try out song and dance. I used to think that he and Perry were chalk and cheese – never take them for brothers, let alone twins. But nowadays I'm not so sure. Ambition, the curse and glory of the Hazards, who'll risk everything they've got and a little bit more on a throw of the dice.

For, if Melchior Hazard starred as the eponymous William Shakespeare, then who had written it, conceived it, planned it, put it all together?

Why, Peregrine Hazard.

So they were a team at last.

What You Will! Dazzling new revue!

They were a team at last and they were a triumph.

We were eighteen years old, hair like patent leather, legs up to our ears. We sported bellhop costumes for our *Hamlet* skit; should, we pondered in unison and song, the package be delivered to, I kid you not, '2b or not 2b'. We performed a syncopated Highland fling in tasselled sporrans after, as weird sisters, we burst out of a giant haggis in a number based on the banquet scene; in abbreviated togas, led the chorus during the 'Roman Scandals' number; I sang my solo 'O Mistress Mine' in fifteenth-century drag to a mutely mutinous Nora on a balcony – she got the last laugh when she poured a bucket of water over me, and I didn't have much of a voice, anyway, but Mr Piano Man was besotted; we did a Morris dance with bells upon our ankles, then sang 'It was a lover and his lass' in harmony and parts ('Hey nonny bloody no'); and went through a spirited version of the Egyptian sand dance on the deck of a large gilded barge that glided slowly from one side of the stage to the other in the spectacular conclusion of the first part of the show.

Our frocks were sumptuous. No short-cuts, no half measures – real silk, real satin, real feathers, sequins by the truckload. There's a lot of conspicuous consumption in show business. Even the backdrops were awesome. There was a mural copied from the British Museum for the *Cleopatra* number, a bit of a John Martin behind *Macbeth*. The actual finale featured the Lady A. as Good Queen Bess. She didn't have much to do but stand around which was just as well because she wasn't the song-and-dance type but she stood magnificently, in a red wig and a frock copied off a miniature in the V and A with a farthingale the size of the Albert Hall and half a ton of imitation pearls round her neck. Nice touch, her two little girls debuted in doublet and hose as pages.

Saskia and Imogen would have been, ooh, sixish, sevenish, by then and, God, we cordially hated one another, especially me and Saskia. She was only a wee scrap with big eyes and carrot curls but she'd stick her foot out and trip me up, she snagged my tights on nails, she was a little terror and if he'd featured her in Alexandria, I'd have dumped her off the barge and let her drown.

Either the markets had recovered, by this time, or a good deal of fiddling went on while Rome was burning because we had charge accounts opened for us at Harrods by gents who kept it from their wives. All day long, vans delivered to Bard Road the proceeds of our shopping – silk underwear, cashmere jumpers, silk stockings in quantity, we couldn't get enough stockings. We never even thought of darning our stockings, now, once we'd holed them, we passed them on to the girls in the chorus and treated ourselves to more.

Grandma ate the contents of the ribboned baskets of exotic fruits delivered daily, but the flowers set the cat among the pigeons.

Grandma read it in a book. I swear, to this day, she only did it to annoy us but, from this book, she took into her head the notion flowers suffered pain. How, when you cut a flower, it emits a fearful scream of anguish – happily, audible only to other flowers, but Grandma claimed her ears were sensitive enough to catch the echo; has a fearful spasm; a crisis, then goes into rigor mortis. After that, she'd cross the road if she saw a florist's shop, so as not to ravage her sensibilities or injure her eardrums. What with dodging butcher's shops, too, and furrier's, going out with Grandma was all ducking and weaving, like a short walk through no-man's-land.

But boys on bikes delivered flowers hourly. Roses, carnations, tuberoses, lilies, orchids, mixed bunches, flowers I'd never known existed, flowers that looked as though they were rotting, flowers that looked rude. Grandma would greet the delivery boy with a long face and moan and keen over our floral tributes.

'Wires through their hearts, poor things . . . criminal!'

She'd take them out to the back yard and stick them in the compost, wailing glumly the while. Then there was the jewellery. Which we concealed from her, in case it entered her unaccountable head to make us give it back. Sometimes we thought, in our youthful, heedless vanity, that the old bag was jealous of us.

Stars on our door, stars in our eyes, stars exploding in the bits of our brains where the common sense should have been.

Our Uncle Peregrine was rich, again, and always laughing. It made a noise in his belly like barrels rolling around a cellar. Melchior went so far as to offer him a walk-on as Falstaff but Perry turned it down. He was happier in the wings. He liked to pull the strings and see the puppets move, he said; you might think, if you heard him say that, he was a cold-hearted bugger but cold-hearted, never! He was the heart and soul of mirth.

He and Grandma would sit hugely wedged in the breakfast-room armchairs, gossiping away for hours, breaking into fruity chuckles, the bottle of crème de menthe, the bucket of ice beside them – nothing but the best for Grandma Chance, these days. When it was growing light, outside, they'd hear our key in the lock, they'd hush up as best they could, one last hiccup of merriment, then the old lady would rise up and put on the kettle. 'Condescended to come home at last, have you, you celestial bodies.' If one of us came home alone, she'd roll her eyes and intone hollowly: 'Ooh la fucking la!' She'd check our handbags to make sure we had our Dutch caps with us. 'Give the girls a break,' said Perry. 'They're only young once. I bet you raised hell yourself, when you were their age.' But references to that forbidden country, her past, were taboo.

Then tenor, Nora's boyfriend, went off somewhere up North, lost touch, and Nora fell, again – blazed, cooled; fell again, blazed, cooled; and again – I lost count of how many times she fell in love, that year. Meanwhile, my friend offered me a fur coat. He liked me very much.

'Not a fur, Mr Piano Man, thank you very much,' I said. 'Whatever would Grandma say?' But he wouldn't take no for an answer and a van delivered a big box next morning. In the box, among the tissue paper, a grey squirrel jacket, fingertip length, frail and lovely, 'like her own virtue', as poor old Irish would have put it a year or so hence in another country, but Irish could never afford to give me furs, he taught me to eschew the double negative, instead.

Once that jacket arrived I hadn't the heart to give it back although Grandma cut up something terrible. I've got it still, it's in the big wardrobe in Grandma's room that we don't use any more, wrapped up in a white sheet, there's a ghost of antique Mitsouko clinging to the hairs, mothballs in one pocket, in the other the dehydrated skeleton of a gardenia left where I stuffed it after a Certain Distinguished Person took it out of his button-hole and slipped it down my cleavage, such as it was, not that Nora and I were ever over-endowed in the bosom department, but, if I'd had a cleavage, that is what his nose would have come up to, he was only a little chap.

Grandma was apoplectic when I got home. The juxtaposition of flora and fauna on my person was too much for her. 'You wouldn't cut off a baby's head and stick it on your best friend's flayed corpse for decoration, would you?' 'I never met a squirrel socially,' I said. I cheeked her. I brazened it out. Perry guffawed but Grandma blew down her nose, huff huff huff, and when she found out who it was that gave me the gardenia, her fury knew no bounds. She had a real down on the Royal Family.

You know the song about the girl who 'danced with a man who danced with a girl who danced with the Prince of Wales'? I was the original girl. Nora, too. He couldn't tell the difference any more than anybody else could.

He dearly loved to tango. He'd have tangoed all night, if he could. He'd tango on remorselessly for a good half-hour at a time, it was a real test of your stamina. The band had to go on playing as long as he could keep it up, since he was royalty, but a tango normally lasts just the four minutes so it was as much of an ordeal as anything, especially if you'd done two shows and a matinée already. We preferred to do it in the afternoons, at the Ritz, tango teas, after they brought in dancing in the restaurant. I once picked up a flea at the Ritz in the Marie Antoinette Suite but that was later on, during the war, when I was entertaining the Free French.

Now we frequented fashionable nightclubs, smart restaurants and flash hotels. Perry took us all to the Savoy Grill on our birthday, that year, not forgetting Grandma, although she hated going into town, these days, we'd had to push and prod her into her corset and bribe her with gin into the taxi. She'd overdone the rouge, perhaps because she'd overdone the gin, and she looked rakish as hell, sneering at the waiters on two fronts – she despised them for being servile but was the first to take umbrage if they spoke out of turn. And there we were, us girls, done up to the nines, little navy suits, gloves to match, red hats with big brims down over one eye, nice shoes, nice handbags, trying to look as if she didn't belong to us, and Peregrine, at ease, as ever, enjoying every minute, the bastard.

The waiter hovered: 'For the first course may I suggest oysters, caviar, smoked salmon . . .' 'That sounds quayte nayce, thanks very much,' she said so she had all three, washing them festively down with crème de menthe, lifting her pinky like a dog lifts its leg as she raised her glass. 'Bottoms up, ducky!' she said to Peregrine. 'Just say the word, babes!' he replied, clinking. He led her on. We could have dropped through the floor.

She kept her clothes on more and more. I noticed that. She came into the bathroom, once, she never dreamed of knocking, she hadn't got a stitch on. Me neither, I was just drying off after my bath. There we both were, captured in the mirror, me young and slim and trim and tender, she vast, sagging, wrinkled, quivering. I couldn't help but giggle. I shouldn't have. I could have slapped myself, afterwards. But I couldn't take that giggle back.

'That's all very well, Dora,' she said, 'but one fine day, you'll wake up and find you're old and ugly, just like me.'

Then she cackled. I'd never even thought that, years back, she might have been pretty. She cackled and she cackled. All the same, she went to get a dressing gown before she came back to have her wee and there was a coolness between us, after that, lasted for months.

I see it, now, as a defeat that we, her beloved grandchildren, inflicted upon her out of heedlessness and vanity and youth. A nudist might be able to grow old gracefully in the company of other ageing nudists, but she had the misfortune to live with two teenage sexpots, didn't she, who weren't about to honour their Grandma's naturism when it offended their aesthetics and, worse still, might put off any of the young men who came to pick us up and drop us off if they caught sight of it. Nevertheless, we should have spared her feelings more.

All that spring, all that summer, the telephone rang for the Lucky Chances and Grandma took our messages in a wheezing, grumbling, ungracious manner, occasionally announcing our abode as: 'Battersea Dogs' Home'.

She was our grandma and we loved her but, at times, during our year of grace, not much.

I can see, now, that we were à la mode, that year, because we were something piquant, something new; there's a kind of style you can only acquire on the wrong side of the tracks and our grace was a scrawny, alley-cat grace, even if we thought that we were really something. We never saw what other people saw. I would look at Nora, faithful as my looking glass, and see a suave sophisticate with geranium lips and that *faux*-naïve Dutch doll hairdo which had become our trademark. Yet when I flick back through Grandma's scrapbooks, the pictures I see are of a couple of street urchins decked up like Christmas trees in all kinds of risky, frisky, flighty, unbecoming gladrags that they wear as if it were a joke.

We looked as if we had dressed up as grown-ups to go out on the town and, such was the force of our innocence, the champagne they poured out for us would turn to ginger pop the moment it touched our pretty little, silly little lips.

Fate continued to deal kindly with Melchior. Not only had our greatest living Shakespearian triumphed in musical comedy, he was rolling in money. The revue was a licence to print it. He lived in considerable style. Besides the big house in Eaton Square (to which I couldn't help but note we'd never been invited except the once, and then unilaterally by the Lady A., for nursery bloody tea, to which we hadn't gone), there was a major estate in Sussex that had been in the Lady A.'s family since Guillaume Brede de Lynde knocked out some Saxon yokel the year after the Battle of Hastings, and the big house that went with it, plus the Home Farm, assorted hovels for the plebs and a village or two. He'd used his new wealth to do a lot of work on Lynde Court, done it out as befitted the country residence of the Royal Family of the British Theatre – that is, palatially.

But his heredity was too strong for him. He couldn't help it, but that manor house always retained a look of here today, gone tomorrow; he was a player to his marrow so he lived in a permanent stage set. He wanted a house that looked as if each leather armchair in the library had been there at least a half a century, where a misty patina of age softened the reflections in the mirror so they would be kind to the crow's-feet as they gently settled round his eyes, poor old thing, but the Mayfair peeress he'd got in to do it up for him incorporated into the interior just that little bit extra you need for the stage, as if in tribute to his profession. So the aged leather was cracked and fissured a little bit more than was absolutely necessary; the mirrors were distressed so much as to look quite marbled; and the walls turned out the colours of very rare roast beef and gravy, too Garrick Club for words.

'He has given himself,' said Peregrine, looking at the picture papers, 'marginally too august a setting.' Grandma went off in shrieks.

Now I am old, I think I know why Grandma didn't like us at eighteen – we felt no irony; how easily we were impressed!

In this 'marginally too august a setting' Melchior gave the performance of his life as Lord of the Manor, even if the Lady A., though ever at his side, always showed faint signs of embarrassment and little Saskia plus, when she hadn't nodded off, little Imogen gave spirited impersonations of imps of Satan for, amongst the suits of armour, the dead fish in glass cases, the antique weapons crossed upon the panelling, there was always a place to hide and then jump out of with ear-splitting screeches, something priceless to caress with sticky fingers, a stuffed fox to look for maggots in at dinner-time, and guests, so many guests, to torture at leisure during the extended rural incarceration of the English country-house weekend. Holly in the beds, frogs in the bathtubs. On one memorable occasion, or so I was told, frogspawn in the porridge.

Not that *we* were ever invited down there for the weekend.

So I have to admit, although through gritted teeth, we were thrilled – although we were suspicious – when, that first, triumphant Christmas of the run of *What You Will*, we were bidden, though more in the manner of a royal command than an invitation, to attend the Lynde Court Twelfth Night Costume Ball.

We would drive down, after the show, and join in the fun as if by right and it turned out we didn't even need to worry, 'What to wear?' since we were told to keep on our 'weird sister' sporrans and be prepared to burst out of a bloody great Hogmanay haggis at a given signal clutching lumps of coal and first-foot them with a brisk jig. Melchior's social secretary assured us we would find the stone-flagged floor of the Great Hall admirably suited to this purpose.

'If they want us to sing for our supper,' said Nora, 'they can stuff it.'

'Don't you realize who'll be there?' said my friend, the famous composer, tingling all over. 'Half Hollywood will be there!'

Don't misunderstand me, his breath didn't smell bad; nevertheless, the smell of his breath so repulsed me by now that whenever I paid off an instalment on my squirrel jacket I had to turn my back, to which he, having been to public school, was nothing loath.

Perry laughed and slapped his belly.

'Hurray for Hollywood! Who d'ya think invited these guys? This could be your big break, girls!'

We understood at last that Melchior's party was the cover for a gigantic audition and it behooved us to polish up our tap-shoes until we snugged ourselves in rugs and piled into my soi-disant or now virtually ex-lover's sports car after the show, clutching a greasy paper package of bacon sandwiches we'd picked up from the cabbies' coffee-stall the other side of Battersea Bridge to sustain us en route, because it was a two-hour drive through a raging blizzard and I was starving, again, when we arrived.

The snow had finished falling, there was a muffled hush. Everything gleamed because of the icy moon, up high, and not even later on, in Hollywood, at MGM, whose slogan was, 'More stars than there are in Heaven', never did I see so many. The ancient lawns wore thick pelts of snow, the rose trees loaded with it. A terrace, with statues in capes and hats of snow; a choked fountain. Lynde Court was built in the eclectic style, that is, a little bit of this and that, but all of it ancient, turrets and pediments snow-capped, swagged cornices and fairy-tale lattices caked and frosted. I never saw a house look lovelier. It took my breath away.

All relocated to Memory Lane, now, of course, lock, stock and barrel.

To greet us on the steps, a consort of lutes, in costume, plucking away at some ancient air. Oh, very tasteful, very sweet. Their breath smoked, their noses glowed; the only discordant note, the horn-rimmed spectacles. We'd been to some smart parties since we got the star on our door but never one as smart as this. We clutched hands, we were intimidated, we hung back.

But then we saw our Uncle Perry, who'd gone down earlier with the hosts, bursting genially out of his white tie and tails, blazing away in the middle of the snow like a hot stove, caught in the act of withdrawing a rabbit from a bass viol. And even though the rabbit instantly turned into our little cousin, Saskia, whom he kissed and cuddled with an enthusiasm that filled us with a jealous rage, the sight of him gave us enough heart to jump out of the motor and run towards him.

As soon as she saw us coming, Saskia wriggled out of his arms, pouting, shaking herself like a wet dog, and legged it. Perry was downcast; he could turn her into a rabbit at will but he could never make her love him. He cheered up when he saw us, picked us up one after the other and swung us off our feet up in the air, as he used to do to us when we were Saskia's age but she, evidently, never let him do it to her. I could see her at a distance, glowering malevolently at us.

We made our entrance into the Great Hall in style, on either arm of Perry's. All around there was a rustle and a whisper: 'Here come the Lucky Chances. Of course, they're really Peregrine's daughters, you know.' They all believed it. Only the immediately affected parties knew it wasn't so.

The Lady A., in full Gloriana wig and frock, and Melchior, as – you've guessed! – received their motley guests, all garbed consistently with the Shakespearian motif. A kiss and a handshake, respectively. We were not excluded; we got our kiss and our handshake like everybody else and then we got a glass of bubbly and trooped off into the Great Hall, where my beau, done up in cap and bells, was already installed at a white grand piano tinkling away at a selection of songs from the show while glossy women propped their cleavages on the Bechstein lid.

There was a log fire in a hearth that took up half one wall and a sky like Bristol glass outside the leaded windows and stuffed swan on the buffet, I kid you not. The waiter carved for me, I gagged. Nora, I noticed, was already deep in vivacious conversation with a little, bald, fat man who'd come in boots and riding breeches, I couldn't think as what, who, as he talked, sketched wide circles in the air with his cigar.

'I couldn't fancy swan,' I said to the waiter. 'Too many feathers. Have you got anything else a girl could nibble?'

He raised his face from the carving knife. Those eyes. My heart went pit-a-pat.

'Fancy meeting you,' I said, I stammered, so full of joy I could have wept.

'Times are hard,' he said. 'Too many tenors, not sufficient songs.'

So he was doubling as a waiter. We could not stop looking at each other. Behind my back, my sister's voice was raised in song and, glory be, she'd borrowed mine: 'In delay, there lies no plenty, So come kiss me . . .'

'Nora,' he said to me.

'. . . sweet and twenty.'

We leaned towards each other across the carcass of the violated swan. There was a great press of people. We hid behind the feathers, we kissed, and kissed, and kissed, until by unspoken but mutual consent we ducked under the tablecloth, dropped down on all fours and ran along the whole length of the buffet, under the table. The big, white tablecloth hung down on either side, it was like bolting down a hospital corridor. I put that midnight date with the haggis out of my mind; I'd got other fish to fry. When we came out the other end, Nora was dancing with the bald, fat man; he must have put his cigar down, somewhere, to leave his mouth free so he could nuzzle her neck while the hand that did not stroke her bare back was beating a tattoo on her bum.

My boy and I held hands. We ran up the black oak staircase, everything in monochrome, moonlight, shadow, snow, past carved wreaths of bay and piles of fruit and big-bosomed women with garlands on their heads, until we found what we were looking for, the master bedroom – instantly recognizable by my father's fetish, the cardboard crown once worn by Old Ranulph in *Lear*, under a glass case on the mantelpiece.

There was a log fire glowing away here, too, and the bedcover turned back, and a little draught came down the chimney gently agitating the stumpwork curtains on the fourposter so that Samson and Delilah, Judith and Holofernes, all the needlework men and women moved a little as we lay down as if those old lovers were greeting these ones who now were hastening to renew their acquaintance with one another.

I offed the false eyelashes, snitched a handful of the Lady A.'s cotton wool to wipe off my make-up. Tonight, this night of all nights, I wanted to look like myself, whoever that was.

'I dye my hair,' I said.

'I know,' he said.

To die for love runs in the family. My grandmother did it; so did my mother. And that night was the one time in all my life I thought that such a thing might be worth while. He took his time and I took mine. In the time we'd been apart, a little crown of golden hairs had sprung up around his nipples but not so that you'd notice, unless you were looking hard.

'Nora,' he said, as we lay wet and panting. 'Nora . . . you've changed your perfume.'

I only had to speak, to say: 'Not Nora, my darling, but Dora, who loves you only.' And there would have been one more happy housewife behind some garden fence in Slough or Cheam, and a bellyful of kids. Those words that would have changed everything were on the tip of my tongue, would you believe; but there they stayed, because, at that very moment, my lover crinkled up his nose.

'Can you smell burning?'

I pointed to the cosy logs. He shook his head.

'Not that . . .'

Came a big red scream from down below:

'FIRE!'

After that, pandemonium. Shouting, cries, screams. A crashing of smashing plates from overturned tables; clattering footsteps; and all the lutes went out of tune in unison when dropped in haste. And, yes; now I could hear the roar of the flames.

We were up and running for the door *toot sweet*, I can tell you, but the old oak felt warm and when we got it open a huge hot wind tossed us backwards, we saw the stairwell was alight already. The gargoyles on the beam ends sparked, glowed and blackened; there was a crash below as a ceiling gave way and in the middle of all the rest of the noise I could tell it fell on the grand piano because of one last jangled chord before it expired with a noise like an angel falling off its harp.

A long tongue of flame licked up the stairs, in through the bedroom door; up went the bed curtains behind us – flaming so soon after we got off the mattress that you might have thought the bed caught fire due to what we had got up to on it. I was stuck staring at my little sporran, tossed up and spinning round in the fierce winds that came with the fire, and then the fire snapped it up like a frog snaps a gnat. He gave me a big shove.

'Quick.'

I snapped out of it sharpish and we made it to the window before the tapestries went up, which they did with a whoosh whilst we hand-over-handed it down the ivy, bringing down a deluge of snow with us. Only when we stood once more upon the lawn, chilled to the marrow, singed at the edges, half frozen cod, half barbecued spareribs, did I recall that the fire had got not only my 'weird sister' outfit but also his waiter's monkey suit, so we both were 'naked as nature intended', to quote the title of another of the dubious vehicles of the Chance sisters' declining years. I buried my blushes in his bosom. He stroked my hair. 'Nora,' he said tenderly. 'Nora . . .'

So very tenderly the truth was on the tip of my tongue, again, but then, while Lynde Court blazed and the survivors of the party mopped and mowed upon the terrace, wringing their hands and making noise, and the clanging of the fireman's bell announced the arrival of the engines, even in the midst of all this turmoil I felt the stirring of, ahem, his manhood and couldn't resist. So we bundled off into the shrubbery and did it again on an uncomfortable carpet of twigs and dried earth under the cover of the rhododendrons which our enthusiasm whipped into a storm so they pelted down snow and more snow on us while all around, backwards and forwards, there passed a swift parade of running feet, churning the fall to slush. As far as ambience was concerned, it was from the sublime to the ridiculous, but needs must, it was urgent.

Surprise, surprise, we were quick about it, this time.

And, to my everlasting shame, it was only after he rolled off me and I sat up did I stop to think: 'Oh, my God – *my sister*!'

Believe me, even then, when so much in love, I never, not for one moment, thought, if . . . she's burned to a crisp . . . then . . . he's mine for ever.

Not even for one second.

To tell the truth, I love her best and always have.

It was a proper raree show, out on the Great Lawn. All the former revellers were black with soot and the Lady A., in a scorched wig and a skeleton petticoat of black sticks and smoke, clutched one scrap to her bosom tight enough to choke her, although that scrap, being Imogen, was unconcerned, and slept, while the Lady A. wept and wailed and kept on calling for the other one, who'd made herself scarce, although I, for one, wouldn't have put it past that Saskia to have torched the family seat out of some small pique such as not enough cream on her strawberries or having been sent to bed before the cabaret.

But of Nora I could see no trace and my heart sank.

Nor of Uncle Perry, neither, although, until his plane crashed in Amazonia and, weeks lengthening into months, then years, we were finally forced to acknowledge that he, too, owed a debt to mortality, Nor' and I both privately thought he was indestructible.

Then I spotted Saskia. She, oblivious of her distracted mother, was tucked away under a rosebush, pigging it. She'd dragged out with her the entire carcass of the swan from the Great Hall. Its feathers were so blackened by the soot it looked more like an upstart crow but *that* didn't put the little greedyguts off as she crouched, legs akimbo, disarticulating one by one its limbs and chewing off the meat with every appearance of enjoyment. Of course, later on, she made a career out of piggery. She'd half-inched a bowl of salad, too, but unaccountably left behind the haggis, no doubt upon discovering that it was hollow.

So there was Saskia. But Nora, not.

They say, if you get your leg cut off, you don't notice it, at first, until you try to put your weight on it. Then you fall down. It was like that with me and Nora. The young man was flat on his back under the rhodies, panting heavily, lost to the world, and well might he sing out, 'O, Mistress Mine, where are you roving?' when he came to, for I took off in frantic search.

The fire had unleashed a kind of madness. A babble of agitated chorines cross-dressed in ruched knicks and hose had commandeered a crate of bubbly on their way out and now, pop! with a fusillade of small explosions, opened the bottles and hurled the contents into the fire, whinnying helplessly under the strain of their fruitless endeavours, while a row of chorus boys, in jester's garb, lacking champagne, unfastened their flies and added their own liquid contributions to the great arcs of solid water directed by the stout fellows of the East Sussex Fire Brigade into the heart of the blaze, where enormous rainbows formed in the air above the jets.

The tenor and me weren't the only ones who'd succumbed to nature, either. Nothing whets the appetite like a disaster. Out of the corner of my eye, I spotted Coriolanus stoutly buggering Banquo's ghost under the pergola in the snowy rose-garden whilst, beside the snow-caked sundial, a gentleman who'd come as Cleopatra was orally pleasuring another dressed as Toby Belch. Not only that. I spied with my little eye an egg-shaped depression in a snowdrift on the parterre surmounted by the lead soubrette who was grinding away for dear life in the woman-on-top position and it turned out the moaning recipient of her favours was who else but my now definitively ex-lover, his cap was gone, but his bells were all tinkling, and he made her a star in her own right in his next production. Good for her. She said she saw him coming and tripped him up. Irish girl, from Derry. Staunch Republican, in those days. She's a Dame of the British Empire, now.

So there was an orgiastic aspect to this night of disaster and all around the blazing mansion, lit by the red and flickering flames, milled the lamenting revellers in togas, kilts, tights, breeches, hooped skirts, winding sheets, mini-crinolines, like guests at a masquerade who've all gone suddenly to hell. It was a keen and icy night and the stars were sharp as needles.

I ran like one possessed from group to group of thwarted party-goers, searching for my lost limb, the best part of me, whom I'd so thoughtlessly forgotten – forgotten! – in the heat of passion. Then and there, although my nipples were still bruised with kisses, I thought, well, that's it for passion, because, without Nora, life wasn't worth living.

That's sisters for you.

I was crying so much I could hardly see straight so I blundered right into Melchior, still in his hose and doublet, but black with soot all over, and gave myself a big bruise on the hip because he was pushing, pulling, grunting, heaving at a big carved chair with arms that ended up in lions' heads. He'd salvaged it from the blaze, somehow or other, and now he was dragging it into a commanding position in the very middle of the lawn, a place that offered a front-stalls view of the fiery finale of the house he'd planned to be so famous in. 'Give us a hand,' he said.

When we'd got the armchair where he wanted it, down he plumped.

'Champagne!' he called and, marvellous to relate, a waiter popped up like a conjuring trick with a silver ice-bucket on a sterling salver. I wiped off my face with the back of my hand.

'Dora?' he said. 'Or is it Nora? Come and take a glass of wine with the prince in exile, dear child.'

I stepped closer. He cracked me an enchanting smile. Not the sign of a tear. I gaped. Never seen such sang-froid as Melchior's before.

'I must say, you're taking it very well, sir,' I said. (We always called him 'sir' to his face.)

'Can't a man enjoy a glass of wine at his own fireside?'

The waiter poured one for me, so I took it. We clinked.

'You've lost your eyebrows,' he remarked.

'Worse than that,' I said, and sobbed. 'I've lost my sister.'

'I've lost,' he said, 'my crown.'

From the way he said it, I knew the loss of a natural daughter weighed less heavy on his heart than the loss of the old Hazard heirloom I'd just seen in his bedroom. For a weak moment, there, my unreconstructed daughter's heart wished I could have saved it for him but, though my front was toasty warm due to the flames of Lynde Court, my backside was bitter cold and so were my spirits.

'My crown, my foolish crown, my paper crown of a king of shreds and patches,' he lamented. 'The crown my father wore as Lear – to have survived so many deaths, so much heartbreak, so many travels ... and now, gone up in smoke! Oh, my dear girl, we mummers are such simple folk ... superstitious as little children. The fire was welcome to take everything, the frills and furbelows, the toys and gewgaws, the oil paintings, the cloisonné, the Elizabethan oak ... but, oh, my crown! That cardboard crown, with the gold paint peeling off. Do you know, can you guess, my dear, how much it meant to me? More than wealth, or fame, or women, or children ...'

I'd better believe that, what he said about children. I was amazed to see him so much moved, and on account of what? A flimsy bit of make-believe. A nothing.

'What shall I do without my crown? Othello's occupation gone!'

He began to cry. The tears ran down his sooty cheeks like chalk down a blackboard but, and this was the funny thing, although my own tear ducts remained untickled, my palms itched and prickled like anything and I knew the only way to ease the irritation was to clap them together. Just as I was about to give the old fraud a big hand, couldn't help it, the waiter, who was hovering by, as struck with this performance as I was, caught hold of my arm, spilling my champagne.

'Look!'

A miracle.

Out of the heart of the blaze, through the very portals of flame that now upheld what had been the lintel of the front door of Ye Old Lynde Court, came, vaguely at first and yet his outlines growing every instant more distinct, an enormous figure.

The currents of the heat distorted his shape and size; he looked as big as the burning house, or bigger, and flames lapped and licked around him until it looked as if he were wearing fire. Something was shining; for one dreadful minute, I thought that he was dead and it was his haloed ghost approaching but, as he left the fire behind him, I saw what it was he'd got on his head.

In his arms, a girl.

'Oh!' went I; and, 'Ah!' went Melchior.

Who else could that girl be but Nora? And what else could that shining something be but a battered old crown of gilded cardboard, cocked at a rakish angle, unsinged, unmarked by fire, sootless, as Peregrine was himself and as was Peregrine's burden.

We tried to run to meet them but found we could not, found we bounced back upon an invisible barrier of air so hot it made the hairs upon my forearms sizzle. Peregrine walked firmly towards us, leaving black footprints behind him on the lawn. He walked out of the fire, smiling at Melchior, offering up to Melchior his safe, sleeping child.

That tenor had found something to cover up his nakedness, a cashmere coat, property, it turned out, of the Hollywood producer whose cigar, abandoned on the edge of the dining table while he danced with Nora, had fallen to the floor, there to smoulder away unnoticed on the stone flags until the hem of the white tablecloth began to smoulder, too.

And, after the hem of the white tablecloth had smouldered for a while, an adventurous little blue flame licked up the side of that white linen cloth, to see what was on top of the table and, if that first little flame, satisfied with what it found, fell back, unnoticed, then the second little flame crept up a wee bit further, unnoticed, too.

Why didn't a waiter see and stamp out the conflagration while it was in its infancy?

Because the waiter at whose station the fire had chosen to begin wasn't a *serious* waiter, no pro, just a body hired for the big do, and he, as it happened, quit his post precipitately to slip upstairs with a female guest at the urgent promptings of his –

But we did not know all this until much later.

There they all were, gathering on the lawn behind us, all the guests, every one, in their rags of finery blackened as if plunged into mourning, and the Lady A. and our little cousins, whom even I could pity, now, poor homeless creatures, Saskia still sucking on a charred wing of swan, the arsonist producer, my ex-lover buttoning his fly, all the chorus, every principal, the musicians, the waiters, the cooks, the scullery-maids. Even the firemen abandoned their pumps and came to see.

All watched as Perry brought out my sister safe.

Everything held its breath.

She stirred. Her eyelids shivered.

Before I could move a muscle, my boyfriend, *her* boyfriend, shoved past me and scooped her up right out of Perry's arms; he was laughing and crying all at once, hugging her and showering her face with kisses.

Now she opened her eyes, all right, but she didn't smile to see him, nor did she kiss him back.

'Where's Dora?' she said. Her first words.

'Oh, you brave little girl!' said that innocent young man. 'So you went back to look for Dora! You risked your life!'

Nora looked round a touch wildly, I thought. Then – discretion is the better part – she fainted. Melchior had no eyes for her at all. He was fairly dancing with distress.

'Give me that crown!' he rasped, having suddenly transformed himself into Richard III. 'Give me the crown, you bastard!'

Peregrine threw his brother a marvelling look; then he laughed out loud.

'Now, God, stand up for bastards!' he crowed.

He seemed to grow, to put it out in all directions – bigger, taller, wider. Huge. When he whipped off that crown and shook it like a tambourine, to tease, the famous Hazard crown, shabby as a prop in nursery charades, it was as far out of reach as if Perry had been a grown-up and Melchior a little kid, although Melchior was a tall man, ordinarily.

'If you want it,' said Peregrine, quaking with the joke, 'jump for it!'

But now the focus of attention abruptly shifted to the Hollywood producer, only begetter of this inferno, who had found himself another cigar, although it was tasteless of him in the extreme, I thought, to light up again so soon after his last smoke burned down his host's stately home. Nevertheless, his jaws were clamped around another fat cigar like a babe's around a bottle as he announced through clenched teeth:

'Ladies and gentlemen, out of these ashes . . .'

The whites of their eyes looked huge and livid in their blackened faces under the moonlight as all turned to look at him.

'. . . a work of genius will arise!

'There's an up-side to everything, ladies and gentlemen. I'm gonna take all of you fabulously talented people, yes, all of you! to Hollywood, USA. Yessir! Under the direction of this great genius of the English stage – '

But Melchior's mind was only on his heirloom.

'My crown!'

'Jump!' hissed Peregrine and Melchior, disconsolate, essayed a little hop that got him nowhere near.

' – your great genius, Melchior Hazard. Script by that other great genius in the family, my friend . . . Peregrine Hazard – '

' – my crown!'

'Jump!'

' – with additional dialogue by William Shakespeare!'

He puffed out a triumphant plume of smoke and the stunned throng managed a baffled patter of applause. Peregrine, evidently caught by surprise, doubled up in a raucous guffaw when he caught those last words, reeling with astonished pleasure.

'My God!' he said. 'A dream come true!'

And then he just lost interest in the crown, he didn't want to tease old Melchior any more. When Melchior wailed: 'My crown!' again, Perry tossed it to him negligently. He didn't care one way or other about the crown. It was a toy, he was playing a game, Melchior was a fool to take the game so seriously, a fool to clasp the thing as if it were alive, and kiss it. A fool. When I saw how, since babyhood, they'd hated one another's guts, it gave me a goose-walking-on-my-grave feeling.

Or perhaps it was just the cold finally getting to me. I was turning blue with it. Perry doffed his tux and covered me up, this soot- and tear-besmirched nude, his niece, as the snow began to drift down again and the company adjourned to make the long drive home.

'Time to go, Dora,' he said, and gave me a cuddle. 'Time to take poor Nora home.'

Nora, apparently insensible in our boyfriend's arms, opened one eye in order to tip me a wink. Perry told him, 'I can give you a lift as far as Clapham Common, you can catch the night tram from there.' So he came a bit of the way with us but Perry wouldn't let him come in and I never saw him again.

THREE

WE SAW IT again just the other week, hadn't seen it for years. Haven't been to the pictures for years, in fact, what with one thing and another, not least of which the fact the local fleapit only shows stuff in the original Serbo-Croat with subtitles, a touch tough on yours truly's peepers. My eyes are dim, I cannot see, I have not brought my specs with me; nor do I intend to, ducky. All I have left to sustain me is my vanity. It was showing at three o'clock on a Sunday afternoon, miles away, in Notting Hill. We had to take two buses, change at the Scotch Shop.

God! Times have changed. More people on the screen than in the auditorium, and fleapit's the word, a flea bit me on the inner upper thigh, a particularly sensitive area well-nigh impossible to scratch in public without getting run in. It came on to rain while we were inside and dripped on Nora until we were forced to either raise an umbrella or to move our seats. As we got up, we spotted a bloke in the next row down on his knees at trough in his boyfriend's fly. It was the only thing about the entire expedition that cheered me up, in fact, to think that *somebody* was having a bit of fun in all the damp, draughty emptiness, with the smell of mice, old tobacco, Jeyes Fluid, damp plush, because fun was the last thing *I* was having, sitting there in my used body, watching it when it was new.

Nora nudged me in the ribs one time. 'Gawd!' she said. 'We were a pretty girl!'

Enough to make you weep.

Thin though the audience was, there was a little patter of applause when it was all over, although I nervously suspected irony, and a boy came running down the street, afterwards: 'Can you really be the Chance sisters?' It made our day. We signed his *City Limits*, then he leaned forward and asked us, confidentially, if it was true that *her* real name was Daisy Duck. When he got that close, I could see the little pearly drops of come – is that how you spell it? – on his moustache. They mesmerized me. I said, yes, it *was* true, then – couldn't help it, could have bitten my tongue out, after – I said, had he noticed what a funny shape her mouth was? That it got that way because she'd sucked off every producer in Hollywood, so after he trotted away Nora swore I'd hurt his feelings and *his* mouth looked perfectly normal, to her, but he hadn't seemed at all put out, anyway.

Nora was squinting away at a leaflet she'd picked up on her way out of the cinema. *A Midsummer Night's Dream*, dir. Melchior Hazard, Hollywood, USA. 'Dora,' she said, 'why do they call it a "masterpiece of kitsch"?'

We went to look for somewhere to have a cup of tea, but no more Joe Lyonses, gone the way of all flesh. Do you remember the Lyons teashops? Thick, curly white plaster on the shopfronts, like walking into a wedding cake, and the name in gold: J. Lyons. Poached eggs on toast keeping snug in little tin pigeon holes as you shuffled down the counter. The moist and fruity Bath buns with crumbs of rock candy glistening on the top, and a little pat of butter lined up alongside. The girl would pour hot water, whoosh! in a steaming column into a fat white pot and there you were, your good, hot cup of tea, with the leaves left in the bottom of the cup, afterwards, to tell your fortune with.

I haven't had a cup of tea with leaves in it for years. For decades. I wonder what the fortune-tellers do, these days. Palms?

Fancy getting nostalgic for a Joe Lyons. We only ever used them for a spot of lunch when times were hard, when we were tramping the rounds, agents, stage doors, etc. Then we'd expend a tanner each on something with chips, a banger, some beans.

You only miss an institution like a Joe Lyons teashop when it's gone.

But we couldn't find a place to get a cup of tea at all, nowhere on the Hill, after all that, so we had a gin, instead, to fortify us, in that great, draughty barn of a place down the Portobello. Outside, it was raining still, and the dark coming on. I sometimes wonder why we go on living.

In those days, four farthings made a penny and Britain was entirely surrounded by water; in these days, there is no such thing as a penny any more and it is as if this foggy old three-cornered island were dangling from a cloud – now we're in the air. You feel that you could pucker up and *blow* away the miles between

49 Bard Road and that apartment in New York where I could be tomorrow morning, if the apartment still existed, if Peregrine still existed, if the past weren't deeper than the sea, more difficult to cross.

The only time I ever flew was in a harness at the end of a steel cable, on the set of *The Dream*, in Hollywood, USA. Hollywood was a long haul from London, in those days; it took weeks, transatlantic, transcontinental. First leg, we went by water, Nor' and I, and so arrived in Manhattan, the gateway to our father's dream, early in the morning and stood at the rail, gawping.

Never seen anything like it. What we'd seen at the pictures had been a pale shadow. All the high towers, in long rows, shifting and parting in front of us as we came into port. Everything seemed to rise up before us out of the sea like a lost city coming up for air. Our hearts began to pound. We thought that anything might happen.

We leaned on the rail and gawped, like mere trippers, although we were smart as paint and I can prove it, I've got the cutting here. There we are, see? On the front page of the *New York Post*, in our best suits – Schiaparelli, I kid you not – charcoal wool, fox wrap collar and cuffs, buttons, typical Schiap touch, in the shape of crochets and quavers, soft little high-crowned hats pulled down over our left eyes. Look hot, stay cool, we'd instructed one another; we'd got the stance to match the suits off pat, you stuck your hipbone forward, let your shoulders droop, put all your weight on the one leg.

Look at the headline: 'New York welcomes Shakespeare treasure.' Sub-head: 'Twins bear precious gift.' See that thing in Nora's arms, that looks like a decapitated doll? You'll never believe it. It was a pot, a sort of jar, about the size of the ones they use for ashes in the crematoria, and it was hollow inside and in the shape of a bust of, that's right, William Shakespeare; our father had had it specially made, in Stoke-on-Trent, and the bald patch lifted off, that was the lid.

And what did this bizarre vessel contain?

Earth.

We travelled with a box of earth, like Dracula, and never let it out of sight. Earth from Stratford-upon-Avon, dug out of the grounds of that big theatre by some reverential sidekick and then entrusted to Nora and myself, a sacred mission, to bear the precious dust to the New World so that Melchior could sprinkle it on the set of *The Dream* on the first day of the shoot.

He and the Lady A. and the twins had all gone ahead long before, of course, to do the 'pre-production'. It took an age to set it up. The bald man – we soon learned to call him Genghis Khan, as everybody else did – had made his announcement on the night of the fire in the heat of the moment and there'd been a long haul after that until 'a wood near Athens' started to go up on the lot near Culver City. But now, oh, thrilling thought! Hollywood was only a three-day train ride away and we trembled on the brink of stardom, or so we might have thought that New York morning. I never saw so many cameras. Snap, snap, flash. We docked. Snap, flash, snap. We even featured in the *Pathé News*. That was when we took the earth through Customs. But we'd had Grandma's motto drummed into us since babyhood: 'Hope for the best, expect the worst.' We were prepared.

Then: 'Girls!'

Perry, the welcome committee, crushed us to his bosom, the old bear hug, blushing and giggling like a little kid.

'Like it?' he asked us, gesturing round the grand horizon as if he'd bought it us for a present. 'Like it?' he said, gesturing around the glove-leather inside of the long, white car that took us home. 'Like it?' he asked us, gesturing around our destination.

It was *outrageous*. Done up like a Spanish chapel in gilded leather panelling with a genuine El Greco nativity under a neon strip that swung back to reveal a wet bar. He popped champagne. Big wrought-iron chairs scattered here and there, enough to give you piles just to look at them. That was the living room. Then you went up a spiral staircase and, in a room with half the wall a window, where you could see all Central Park and the lacy, steely chorus line of skyscrapers across the other side, there was a round bed a good six feet across with polar bear skins heaped upon it, and a round mirror in the ceiling over it.

'Who's the lucky girl?' I asked him as we peeked, wondering, into her lavish closet. He put his finger on his lips: 'Top secret!' Then the white telephone interrupted us, it rang. Perry picked up the receiver but did not speak; listened, looked grieved; replaced it with a sigh.

'Poor cow,' he said, but did not tell us whom he meant.

A big Persian cat, white to match the telephone, jumped off

the bed and came up for a bit of attention, shoving its head against our charcoal skirts, covering us with hairs. Where did Puss do its wee-wee? We were on the fifteenth floor. That was a problem. But a positive *embarras de richesse* as regards toilet facilities for humans – one bathroom for the lady, whoever she might be, done out in pink marble and chrome; one for him, more austere, in black tile, with, smart touch, black towels. Nora put down her glass, stripped off, had a shower. I fancied a lie-down, stretched out on the bearskin rug. Perry took the weight off his feet, too.

'Come on, old man. Tell all.'

You'd never have thought that Perry was past forty. I don't know what infernal deal the Hazard brothers made with time, but he'd not aged so you'd notice. Old Uncle Carrot-Top. His hair was still that bright, offensive, bad-boy red, and still stuck up in spikes. The trowelful of freckles flung over his nose never faded and he was bigger than ever, the size of a warehouse. As for his suit, it was a chocolate brown in colour, with a broad, white stripe; his shoes were dappled white and chocolate. He looked every inch a pimp, but one who'd risen to the top of his profession.

'All this belongs,' he said, 'including me,' he added, 'to . . .'

At that, as if on cue, in she swept; why shouldn't she make an entrance? It was her own house, her very own New York pied-à-terre, after all! She wasn't one whit abashed to find a naked chorine in the shower, nor a clothed one prone upon her mattress dallying, to all appearances, with her inamorato, but cracked us all her famous grin, kicked off her shoes.

'When does the orgy begin?' she enquired.

Delia Delaney. Even the name has a period ring; stars are called Finkelbaum or Hackenbush or Brown, these days. She was a raucous one, née Daisy Duck, on Hester Street, youngest of seven, her father a fish peddler, not a pot to piss in. She was but twenty-five years old that New York morning long ago, just the age of the big sister we never had, and fresh back from her hair-dresser, who'd touched up the roots of her pubics, she kept them bleached, then trimmed them into a heart shape. She didn't miss a trick, did Daisy.

From babyhood she sang at weddings, talent shows, Daisy Duck a.k.a. 'Little Dolly Daydream', another period handle. In the movies in New York from 1918, rescued by dogs from burning houses, softening the hearts of crusty misanthropes, etc. In Hollywood from 1921 she dropped the 'Little Dolly'. She became a Mack Sennett bathing belle; then she danced on tables, she rode in rumbleseats, she was 'flaming youth' personified. She was custom-built for the pictures – teeny tiny, one inch less than five foot, and a perfectly enormous head. Her face went right from one side of the screen to the other. Gloria Swanson was like that, as well. Joan Crawford, too. You need the big face, for the close-ups.

Subduing her naturally nasal tones – she hailed from the Bronx – with sound she triumphed, the classic thirties blonde, tough, sweet, lewd, funny, fast, tender. I've got a lot of time for Daisy Duck. She used to lend us all her couture frocks.

She used to punch and pummel old Perry as if he were a giant teddy bear, she fancied older men, her father having been caught in the crossfire in a shoot-out in Fulton Fish Market through no fault of his own in the early days of Prohibition, and her fancy did her no harm at all in Hollywood, I can tell you, where she had, I kid you not, left lipstick on every pair of underpants further up the hierarchy than assistant director on her way to the top.

In she came, in her barathea suit, white, to match the cat that matched the telephone. She thought the world of that cat, it went everywhere with her. After she'd slipped off her mink, we all had some more champagne. Then, brr brr! brr brr! The telephone rang again.

'For you,' said Peregrine. 'I did it, last time.'

She picked up the receiver, put it to her ear – and then she shouted 'DROP DEAD!' down the telephone, you could have heard her clear through to Yonkers. She gave a mighty tug and ripped the cable off the wall, then tossed the entire contraption straight, with a tinkle of broken glass, through the bedroom window, mouthpiece and receiver going up in separate arcs high into the sky to land, who knows where but I trust softly, on the grass in Central Park.

'That's the way to deal with nuisance calls,' she said to Perry.

She'd got real style, she could put on a show. When she was peckish, she'd shout: 'Fishy!' and snap her fingers and up would pop a slavey out of nowhere with a peeled shrimp on a toothpick. She spelled Duck with an umlaut, thus: Dück. No relation to

'Donald Duck and Henry Hen, Were two rather unusual men', said Perry.

Transvestite poultry?

'You'd better believe it,' said Daisy. 'That's Hollywood.'

He loved us both but I was the one he talked to. Just one of those things. I was the one he took out in the white car that last morning in New York. He drew up at the kerb, by a hole in the ground, a construction site.

'That's New York,' he said. 'See it come down, see it go up.'

'What used it to be, Uncle Perry?'

'It was the site . . . the site . . .' He couldn't go on. The tears were running down his cheeks and so I knew he'd brought me on a pilgrimage, the site of the old Plaza, and Desdemona, Desdemona dead.

We left for California on the Twentieth Century Ltd. Now we were part of Daisy's entourage, it was long-stemmed roses all the way. When her white car deposited us all at Grand Central, cops in hats like threepenny bits held back the crowds, who cried and shrieked, thrust flowers at her, papers, pencils: 'Delia! Delia!' and fought and clawed to get at her. She was only a little thing, but she sailed through as to the manner born, smiling, waving, blowing kisses, she couldn't get enough of it, but we were scared stiff, huddling under Perry's greatcoat, hiding from all the hungry eyes and mouths come to gobble you up, like the wolf in *Red Riding Hood*. Daisy was the dish of the day, and we'd have been snapped up, too, like side salads, if we hadn't dashed down the red carpet to the private car sharpish, Daisy's cat racing before us, ears flattened by its own speed.

Even while the train steamed out of the station, the fans still sprinted down the track alongside, 'Delia! Delia!' until forced to fall back as the train plunged into the tunnel, left forlorn, bereft, starving for her.

That was when I got my first taste of fame. It scared me stiff.

Do you want your name card on the door? If you do, you want to party. Daisy always wanted to party. Her berth – well, not really a berth, more of a suite. Done out in white, which was her colour, except her mink, and that was blue. Ubiquitous wet bar; I never met a dry bar. Next door, a three-quarter bed.

Lewdly, she opined she'd have to sleep on *top* of Perry, and it was true he took up all of that bed himself – he seemed to grow before our eyes, swell up, expand inside the train that speeded us all across the continent towards our fortunes in a great state of alcoholic euphoria and erotic disturbance, that is to say, of booze and sexy fun.

Needless to say, Nora was soon in love again. There was a young kid on his way to Hollywood to seek his fortune, too, but not in front of the cameras, in front of a hot stove – off to join his uncle in a catering business, or so he said. Very musical kid; never parted with his violin case, came to Daisy's party clutching it, but wouldn't give us a tune, he said a string was broken. He was from what they call Little Italy, below Houston Street, but his father hailed, originally, from Palermo. Eyes drawn in with charcoal, hair like pitch. I'll say this for Nora, she liked a change.

> Tony, Tony, macaroni,
> Show us all your big baloney.

Pardon me, vicar.

Tony was a nice boy but he never moved me. We changed trains at Chicago. Onwards! To the Dearborn Station! To the Super-Chief!

Nora's Tony wasn't, as you might say, in our class, he travelled third, so Nora would tippy-toe down the train and climb up to his upper berth, behind the green baize curtains; they did it for hours in there, she said, like snakes. Once he'd got it in her, they never moved, they let the train do all the work. CHOO-choo-choo-choo, CHOO-choo-choo-choo. The engine would get up steam, the pistons go faster, faster, faster until: WHEEEEEEEEEeeeeeeeeee . . . So Nora never partied, after she met Tony, but I was nothing loath. That white cat sat on the pillow and purred. When I'd a moment, I'd exercise my mind with the problem: where did it do its wee-wee on the Super-Chief?

Daisy put away the gin like nobody's business, pissed as a newt half the time and never wore panties. She said they were bad for the health. Perry had not lost his magic touch and used to saw her in half whenever a few guests gathered together. And amongst those guests was always one man who struck my eye, although he was no chicken, wore glasses, pepper and salt hair.

His suit was rumpled, sometimes stained. His tie was loose and sometimes off. If he had a certain air of distinction, down on his luck was written all over him. He always smelled of liquor. Yet of all the gaudy company that partied with Daisy Duck, a.k.a. Delia Delaney, as the Super-Chief rolled down through New Mexico and Arizona, he was the one whom Perry picked out most for conversation, and I would watch them from the corner of my eye even when some assistant producer, or stunt man, or second lead had his leg wedged in my thigh, talk about dancing being sexual intercourse standing upright. I could tell you a tale. But shabby old horn-rims was no dancing man; he'd gulp that Mother's Ruin, gesticulate, pass out, but something drew me.

'Dora, my dear,' said Perry, who hadn't missed my roving eye, 'I want you to meet my dear friend, *mon semblable, mon frère*, my collaborator, just he and I, and William Shakespeare, working on the script. Irish, meet Floradora.'

I had it in my handbag, you never know when you might need it. Nora was off with her Tony, so I had our room to myself. He wanted to go out into the corridor while I fixed myself up, but I said, 'Don't go; either you can avert your eyes or take a look – I'm not shy.' But *he* was shy, Irish by name, Irish by nature; he looked out of the window at the moon on the mountains while I fixed myself up.

Night, silence, desert, rock, moonlight.

'God, you're lovely,' he said, when he turned to look. I knew he'd say that. They all say that. I'd known in advance I wouldn't be able to return the compliment, alas.

My first old man. No, I do him an injustice. He wasn't really old, not old like I am now; he was only just past forty, neck and neck with my wicked uncle who, at that very moment, was giving Daisy what she always said was the best time she ever had. But Irish had an old soul, you might say. He was a man with a great future behind him, already. He was a burned-out case. I knew I must be very gentle.

See, the row of books. Over there. Take a look at the dedications: 'Light of my life', 'Joy in the morning', 'My last chance'. My half-brother/nephew, young Tris, was very impressed with those dedications, he wanted me to do a programme, one time; I said 'No.' No suck old bones. Sometimes a graduate student writes; I burn the letter. Poor old Irish. I gave him all a girl can give – a little pleasure, a little pain, a carillon of laughter, a kerchief full of tears. And, as for him, well, it was he who gave me the ability to compose such a sentence as that last one. Don't knock it. That's lyricism.

You'll find me in his famous *Hollywood* stories. The last flame of a burned-out case, but oh, it had a glorious light! I never rate more than a footnote in the biographies; they get my date of birth wrong, they mix me up with Nora, that sort of thing. And I'm bound to say my best friend wouldn't recognize me in the far-from-loving portrait he'd penned after I'd gone. I'm the treacherous, lecherous chorus girl with her bright red lipstick that *bleeds* over everything, and her bright red fingernails and her scarlet heart, sexy, rapacious, deceitful. Vulgar as hell. The grating Cockney accent. The opportunism. The chronic insensitivity to a poet's heart. And you couldn't trust her behind a closed door, either. Such turned out to be the eternity the poet promised me, the bastard.

But all this disillusion lay before him, and indeed, before me, that night in the Super-Chief with moonlight outside on the bare mountains into which the train began to climb. I straightened up and faced him. He was so shy he hadn't even got his jacket off, although it was quite dark inside and the only sounds the chuff and click and rattle of the train and, drifting on the wind, the laughter out of Daisy's everlasting party. I started to undo his tie. 'Irish' to his friends and of descent, although American to the core. Ross 'Irish' O'Flaherty, a.k.a. the Chekhov of Southern California.

Of course, I remember his name. How could I not? You never forget the difficult customers.

Welcome to the Land of Make-Believe! To where the moon shone on Charlie Chaplin every moonlight night. Welcome to Dreamland.

We'd only ever seen a palm tree before at Bournemouth, it came as a shock. So big, so hairy. And the sunshine. 'Like a benediction,' said Irish. He was so pleased I'd got it up for him that even the weather seemed intentional. But I wouldn't move in with him, not on your life, I'd got too much residual sense for that, although, I must say, I was very struck – struck with his faded but still potent charm; his vulnerability, under his surface assurance; his soft, light baritone with its gracious East Coast modulations; his wasted talent, of which even the morbid scripts he now churned out at so many dollars the yard retained some wizened gleam. And he did wonders for my grammar, not to mention my grasp of metaphor, as witness the style of this memoir. But cohabitation, no. Nora and I put up at the Forest of Arden.

The legendary Forest of Arden, the residential motel of the stars, with its Olde English motif. What could have been more appropriate, in the circumstances? All the little bungalows, half-timbered, thatched – replicas of Anne Hathaway's cottage – each one nestled under clematis, set in wee herbaceous gardens, tended with loving care by Japanese gardeners, and there were Warwickshire apple trees, imported oaks, you name it. Perry set up there, in a bungalow, too, when he wasn't nine-to-fiving it with Irish at the studio, busy on the script in the office they shared. But Daisy came and went because she'd got her own home, hadn't she? Indeed, she'd got her own thirty-bedroom mansion, besides a tremendous many domestic duties. She was a married woman, after all.

But the Forest of Arden was a lovely, flimsy, fantastic place, where you could live in grand, two-dimensional style among the hissing lawns – those incessant sprinklers! – and there was a pool, shaped like an acorn leaf, of bright turquoise, planted with shocking pink flamingos, everso *As You Like It* even if out of period, and we would lie for hours on canvas loungers, exposing our pale, unaccustomed torsos to what Irish, in one of his *Hollywood* stories, calls the 'ardent yet somehow insincere sunlight'.

Note it's already ceased to be a blessing.

And how can sunlight be insincere, Irish?

He gave me a pitying look and went on reading *The House of Mirth*. God forgive me, I'd been vulgar again. He'd already noted, with some distress, how vulgar I could be from time to time. All the same, that sunlight's insincerity perplexed me. Did he mean, the sunshine didn't really mean it? And, if so, what did *that* mean? Or, is it that if it saw somebody better than me to shine on, it would switch off me and shine on them, instead? And yet it shone on everyone, whether they had a contract or not. The most democratic thing I'd ever seen, that California sunshine.

And, tell the truth, it changed me. It changed me for good and all. All manner of things conspired to change me, during those months in California, though from what to what I scarcely know, except, if you offered me a tango with the Prince of Wales today, I'd tell you where to stuff it.

Irish was banned from the Forest of Arden because he'd set fire to a thatched roof during the welcome party when he first arrived from New York as fresh talent, years ago, before the hair on his chest turned grey and he started stowing a shaker of martinis in the briefcase he took to the studio every morning. All the same, we'd smuggle him in past the desk clerk whenever we could, trussed up in Perry's cashmere overcoat and a fedora, disguised as a big-name director, and then he'd lay down some speakeasy-style boogie-woogie on Perry's white piano, Irish was a man of parts even if some of them didn't work too well. They'd have a sing-song. 'When Irish Eyes are Smiling', obviously. 'Down by the Sally Gardens'. And that old song about the man who resurrects. They loved that song, they roared out the choruses:

> Whack fol de dah, dance to your partner,
> Welt the flure, yer trotters shake,
> Wasn't it the truth I told you,
> Lots of fun at Finnegan's Wake.

Irish would flop down flat on his back at the last verse and Perry would scatter a few drops of liquor on him.

> Bedad he revives, see how he rises,
> And Timothy rising from the bed

Irish, suiting the action to the words –

> Says, 'Whirl your liquor round like blazes,
> Thunder and lightning, do ye think I'm dead?'

What larks.

Apart from that, I used to cab it to his place, out in the sticks. You climbed steps to a cabin. There was a little, narrow bed, a chair, a table. All clean and neat, the way men on their own keep things. Clean, neat, a little drear – not a flower in a cup, nor a postcard on the mantel, nothing like that. Only his pencils in a jam jar, a pile of yellow legal pads and a cardboard carton where he stashed his empties. I stretched him out upon that narrow bed and pleasured him, poor old thing, and he was grateful, at the time.

Apart from a few small necessities, his monastically austere cabin was furnished with books. After his day at the studio he'd drive home, unwind over a few drinks, then leaf through his own back numbers – a bestseller at twenty-two years old, a second novel that didn't live up to the promise at twenty-five, a stinker at twenty-eight, and then the one at thirty-two that didn't sell, which is the one they remember him by. That, and the *Hollywood Elegies*, which were yet to come and would be inspired by yours truly – this painted harlot over here, still indecently hale and hearty if by the world forgot on her seventy-fifth birthday while he's dead and gone and immortal.

After he'd thoroughly depressed himself with contemplation of his wasted genius, he'd turn to higher things and finger Shelley, say, until both glass and book slipped from his fingers and he slept.

When did it first enter his head to educate me? Because he didn't have sufficient cash to buy a mink. Therefore he gave me Culture.

I balked at Proust.

His sweet, befuddled head; that faded golden hair; the large, light eyes with the long lashes; the short, straight nose like the nose of Daisy's Persian cat; the soft, weak mouth indicative of that guilty sensuality so characteristic, I've found, of the North American temperament – that is, they like it, all right, but, all the same, they think it's going to give them hairy palms.

Attracted as he was to my conspicuous unrefinement, all the same Irish thought it would only make sleeping with me all right in the end if we could read Henry James, together, afterwards, and I was nothing loath because there'd been precious little time for book-learning in my short life as I'd been earning a living from age twelve and sometimes Irish, when he remembered that, would forgive me everything.

Don't misunderstand me. He was a lovely man in many ways. But he kept on insisting on forgiving me when there was nothing to forgive.

Meanwhile, Nora was eating pasta and making love with the magnificent simplicity I always envied. She was learning how to make cannoli, too, and cannelloni – and she was still all ablaze with love, no sign of cooling, yet, helping out at Tony's uncle's business every spare moment, in fact, apart from whatever else they did together. Sometimes she even sported a domestic air on her return to the Forest of Arden, a smudge of flour on her frock, a trace of tomato paste on her cheek. She was preoccupied with love and so was I, labouring with my lover over his erections, which were difficult to procure and arduous to maintain, not that I ever grumbled, I didn't want to hurt his feelings, and, after all that was done with, we'd send out for a hamburger and attack his well-used library. We did it alphabetically, we started out at A.

He was so smitten by my youth and beauty he started to dry out, poor old thing, so he put away soda, soda, soda by the crateful and belched in an operatic manner, arias of wind. After we'd done a couple of hours on the author of the night, we'd relax with a soda. He'd read me a sonnet: 'Shall I compare thee to a summer's day . . .'

Then up would come the thunder.

The wood near Athens covered an entire stage and was so thickly art-directed it came up all black in the rushes, couldn't see a thing, so they sprayed it in parts with silver paint to lighten it up. The concept of this wood was scaled to the size of fairy folk, so all was twice as large as life. Larger. Daisies big as your head and white as spooks, foxgloves as tall as the tower of Pisa that chimed like bells if shook. Gnarled, fissured tree-trunks; sprays of enormous leaves – oak, ash, thorn, like parasols, or glider planes, or awnings. Bindweed in streamers and conkers, deposited at intervals in heaps on the ground. Yes, conkers. All spikes. And rolling around at random underfoot, or stuck on buds, or hanging in mid-air as if they'd just rolled off a wild rose or out of a cowslip, imitation dewdrops, that is, big *faux* pearls, suspended on threads. And clockwork birds, as well – thrushes, finches, sparrows, larks – that lifted up their wings and lowered their heads and sang out soprano, mezzo, contralto, joining in the fairy songs.

Because no wind blew of its own accord in this wood, they'd got in a wind machine. I'd have let old Irish loose after a 7-Up to do the job myself, but nobody asked for my advice. When the artificial wind stirred the leaves and flowers, they were stiff enough to clank.

What I missed most was illusion. That wood near Athens was too, too solid for me. Peregrine, who specialized in magic tricks, loved it just because it was so concrete. 'You always pull a *live* rabbit out of a hat,' he said. But there wasn't the merest whiff about of the kind of magic that comes when the theatre darkens, the bottom of the curtain glows, the punters settle down, you take a deep breath . . . none of the person-to-person magic we put together with spit and glue and willpower. This wood, this entire dream, in fact, was custom-made and hand-built, it left nothing to the imagination.

> You spotted snakes with double tongue,
> Thorny hedgehogs, be not seen –

And there they were, waiting in cages, snakes and hedgehogs, not to mention newts, worms, spiders, black beetles and snails, with snake handlers and hedgehog handlers ad lib at hand to keep them happy, waiting for their cue to scatter this way and that across the set as soon as the fairy chorus started up.

It was all too literal for me.

It took me donkey's till I saw the point but saw the point I did, eventually, though not until the other day, when we were watching *The Dream* again in Notting Hill, that time, couple of batty old tarts with their eyes glued on their own ghosts. *Then* I understood the thing I'd never grasped back in those days, when I was young, before I lived in history. When I was young, I'd wanted to be ephemeral, I'd wanted the moment, to live in just the glorious moment, the rush of blood, the applause. Pluck the day. Eat the peach. Tomorrow never comes. But, oh yes, tomorrow *does* come all right, and when it comes it lasts a bloody long time, I can tell you. But if you've put your past on celluloid, it keeps. You've stored it away, like jam, for winter. That kid came up and asked for our autographs. It made our day. I could have wished we'd done more pictures.

Genghis Khan spared no expense. Even the wee folk were real; the studio scoured the country for dwarfs. Soon, true or not, wild tales began to circulate – how one poor chap fell into the toilet and splashed around for half an hour before someone dashed in for a piss and fished him out of the bowl; another one got offered a highchair in the Brown Derby when he went out for a hamburger; and one of the girls in the wardrobe, as she tried on my Peaseblossom costume – pink bra, knicks and fright wig, ever so artistic – told me, giggling and winking, that this one she was measuring up looked to her to be about nine or ten years old, so she did her Mickey Mouse impression to put him at his ease, tempted him with bubble gum, slipped off his jacket for him. Goodness! He was shy. Then his shirt. 'No! No!' he cried in his little piping voice, but she insisted until off came his pants.

'Lo and behold, this is a full-grown, thirty-year-old *man* we have here!'

She was so tickled by the memory she stuck a pin in my left buttock. In my guided tour of the literary alphabet, Irish had just introduced me to the letter B for Burns.

'A man's a man, for a' that,' I suggested and the wardrobe lady blushed and said that some men had more of 'a' that' than others did and, on the whole, the boy-fairies cut something of a swathe among the ladies, except for Puck, who made them run a mile.

Puck looked like a little man but wasn't; he was an aged child. Puck was all fingers, goose you as soon as look at you, unmentionable habits. You might find that Puck in your laundry basket, when you least expected it, curled up inhaling your soiled lingerie. Out at dinner, no matter how chic the venue, if a questing hand reached up from under the tablecloth, you knew it was Puck's night out, too, and he was rummaging round the room at knee level, seeking what he could find. He'd started out years ago as a Hollywood toddler and still ploughed a rich furrow of cute kids, although now well-nigh geriatric, and we were stuck with Puck for box-office reasons, although he drilled holes in the walls of the ladies' toilets and liked to take a peep and I don't know what else. He was the spy on the set, too; would report back to Genghis Khan on the empties in poor Irish's wastepaper basket, the used condoms in the back lot. He had a vile temper, he bit a policeman in the leg, one time, on account of an alleged traffic violation.

Old ladies loved him. He had the most fan mail of any of us, requests for photographs on cards with hearts and flowers on, plus gifts of sailor suits and teddy bears and Kiddicars and offers of adoption because he had the high tenor of an angel. I never heard anything like it. I can hear him now:

'Philomel with melody . . .'

Enough to melt your heart.

Now, if our father was to take the part of Oberon, I'll give you three guesses as to who will play Titania.

Give up?

Why, Daisy Duck, of course.

For was she not the wife of Genghis Khan!?!

And it turns out the whole 'magnificent, foolish, heroically vulgar enterprise' – as Irish called it – was intended just to show her off, to, as they say, 'showcase' her glamour, her talent, her star quality, her – pardon me while I emit a titter – *sheer class*.

Dear old Daisy. She was a trouper and a half all right; she'd got guts, legs, leather lungs, tits out to here, chutzpah, sass, star quality. But class – no.

So it went on. Pre-production they called it. Then the phone rang. The white telephone in Anne Hathaway's Cottage. Nora and I were standing on our heads, at the time; all that pasta was taking its toll on Nora's bum while the sodas up at Irish's place were blowing me up something shocking, so we were doing a few exercises. I picked up the receiver with my foot and toppled over when I heard that voice. It always set me a-flutter. I never got used to it, I never will. If I turn on the telly and get an earful of that magisterial baritone ecstasizing over no matter what, from after-dinner mint to toilet roll, I grow alert and wistful as the dog on the record label: His Master's Voice.

Is it as bad as that, Dora?

You've only got the one father.

Melchior's feet were firmly underneath the Hollywood table. He'd rented a lovely hacienda-style home up in the hills, there installed the Lady A., who appeared transfixed in a permanent state of gracious amusement at the antics surrounding her, and, before you could say 'Jack Robinson', he was lording it over what they called 'the English Colony'.

The English Colony was a rum lot. The men all wore monocles, the women all wore tiaras, and they turned up in costume dramas as Gladstone and Disraeli, Queen Victoria and Florence Nightingale, etc. As a group, they kept themselves to themselves, away from the hoi polloi, held tea parties on Saturday afternoons when everybody else was having group sex, played cricket on Sundays, drank pink gin at sundown and talked as if their upper lips wore plaster casts. Old Nanny, the very one whose sister lived in Kennington, small world, wearing a uniform and veil, could occasionally be seen in the Hazards' big yard, supervising a brace of russet-haired moppets in braids and cotton frocks, our bloody cousins, who, it turned out, would tumble through *The Dream* as supernumerary fairies. It was Family Time all round.

But had our father called us up to welcome us to Hollywood? To tell us no dream of his would have been complete without us? Did he, hell. All he wanted was, his little bit of earth.

The Shakespeare casket was the last thing we'd been thinking of in the heady weeks since we lit down in the Forest of Arden. I couldn't think who'd had it last. I wondered if we'd left it on the train? We turned that cottage inside out, went through all our trunks . . . We were in a cold sweat until we stumbled on it at last, by accident, in a little cubbyhole off the master-bedroom, which I think was meant to be a dressing room, or the place where the missus could stow away the master if the master came home plastered. We'd never ventured into this little cranny before, it was quite dark, the curtains always drawn against the sunshine, but *there* was the Shakespeare casket, safe and sound, sitting on the minuscule dresser as if in a little shrine, because somebody had set it up and flanked the pot with candles and lit them. There was a stick of incense on the go too. What a rich sense of ritual, of occasion, in that room. We were astonished.

Who'd gone to all that bother? We found out later it was the Mexican cleaning lady. Catholic. Ever so Catholic. She thought there must be a holy relic in the casket, because it was packed with such care, and she treated it accordingly. We hardly liked to disturb the casket, but we thought we ought to check the earth was still intact so we opened it up. Whew! No wonder she'd lit up incense. She must have thought the relic was starting to rot. As soon as we lifted the lid, a rank aroma wafted from the pot and filled the little improvised chapel with an unmistakable smell.

And that was how we found out where Daisy's Persian cat did wee-wee whilst on the Super-Chief.

We tipped Pussy's night-soil out the window but whatever were we to do now that the sacred earth, thoroughly desecrated, was gone for good? Easy. We filled the casket up again with soil from the Forest of Arden, from the facsimile Elizabethan knot garden itself; we thought that would make it more authentic. So there was the sacred earth, as good as new; and Melchior's plan was, the first day of the shoot, to sprinkle it all over the wood near Athens, as a consecration of the grounds, a dedication of the actors and a photo-opportunity of the first water.

I remember that day, the day *The Dream* began, as if it were yesterday. We all arrived in costume – we were a motley crew and no mistake. None of your soppy fairies with butterfly wings and floral wreaths. No, sir. As Peaseblossom and Mustardseed, our bras and knicks had leaves appliquéd at the stress points, there were little lights in our shaggy wigs, and when we saw how the rest had fared in the wardrobe, we thought we'd got off lightly, I must say, because some had antlers sprouting out of their foreheads and fur patches covering up the rude bits; others were done up as flying beetles, in stiff, shiny bodices split up at the back; and one or two with boughs, not arms, plus a lavish use of leather and feathers all round.

Furthermore, remember that not fairies alone inhabited the wood near Athens. A giant mouse, saddled and bridled, trotted past. A bunny, in a wedding wreath and veil. Some dragonflies, in masks. Several enormous frogs. Dwarfs, giants, children, all mixed up together. Suddenly I had a sinking feeling; I knew it in my bones. This film is going to lose a fortune.

Genghis Khan had dug deep into his pocket for this opening spectacle. There was a hundred-piece orchestra of ancient instruments *in situ*, he'd brought them down from Berkeley and dressed them up in tights and ruffs. One wore a yarmulke. Lutes are a bugger to tune, one reason why they went out, so the wood near Athens twanged and pinged with discords as they tried to get them all in tune.

Puck somersaulted past and goosed me. Irish blew a kiss. Drunk as a skunk and clutching his briefcase to his bosom, soon he would be drunker. He'd fallen off the wagon because I'd missed a date. He didn't own me, you know. He'd got a nerve. I'd only started taking German lessons, hadn't I? One lunchtime when Nora was having a quick linguine and cunnilingus *chez* Tony, I'd taken the book of the day to share with my hot dog in the commissary. This runty little German chap with cropped hair and smelly feet, baggy blue suit, no tie, some kind of script consultant somewhere, he took one look at the title of my book. 'Schopenhauer!' he sneered. His conversation was brusque and surprising. He always looked on the black side. He was a tonic in Hollywood. He kept my feet on the ground.

Irish blew me an ironic kiss. Peregrine had an arm round Irish's shoulders, not only to express affection but to help keep him upright. The Lady A. was there, in a Lanvin frock and pearls, her role in *this* production was only that of the director's wife, but her daughters were there in costume. Melchior had given his little Saskia a cameo. The Indian prince.

> For Oberon is passing fell and wrath
> Because that she as her attendant hath
> A lovely boy, stol'n from an Indian king.

That Indian prince, in gold lamé pyjamas and matching turban with purple feather fastened with an amethyst pin. Pure jail-bait. Imogen was just another fairy, with the one line: 'And I.' But the assistant director, the besotted Peregrine, twisted the wardrobe's arm until off came the owl mask and feather camisole of the original design and on went a tiny pink tutu, so Imogen stuck out like a sore thumb.

There was a newsreel team, energizing a wisecrack out of Daisy Duck in her fairy queen frock, tulle and spangles, look! no panty-line, while Genghis Khan, in his usual jodhpurs accessorized with whip, straddled a canvas chair and gloated upon the fairyland that he had built. Journalists, photographers, secretaries, sycophants, script girls, continuity girls, and set dressers milled and stirred around him, activity, according to Irish's acid-tipped pen, irresistibly reminiscent of the movements of maggots upon rotting meat.

But there was one figure in all this mêlée who didn't quite belong, who drew attention to itself by being so inconspicuous, so that it caught my eye – huddled in raincoat, dark glasses, headscarf, as if wardrobe had equipped her with a 'disguise' outfit from a B-feature. Everywhere that Daisy went, this sad little shadow would go, slipping after her, dissolving into the crowd if ever Daisy looked in her direction. That was odd. What was going on?

Then the ancient musicians gathered themselves together at last at the behest of the conductor: what power on earth had got

Stokowski into tights? Amid a welter of twangs, all embarked upon a mass rendition of, possibly, a galliard, although it sounded as if the lute section might have been making a stab at a pavane. When it ground to a halt, Melchior stepped out from among the trees in a burst of flashbulbs to address us, bearing aloft, on a crimson velvet cushion with gold fringe that I knew for a fact, because wardrobe told me, came off the set of *Elizabeth and Essex*, the Shakespeare pot that held, and you know I kid you not, veritable soil, rich with association, from the Forest of Arden.

Melchior smiled upon us, I had to put a hand out and steady myself on Nora's arm just the same time she put her hand out for *my* arm. He smiled and then he said: 'Friends,' in his voice like Hershey's Syrup, and although the old enchantment instantly overcame me, I quivered with anxiety: would he now continue, 'Romans, countrymen', so tense with the significance of the moment that he cued himself into the other speech? But he did not get the chance to get it wrong.

'Friends!'

Genghis Khan dragged his eyes off Daisy, took one look at Melchior and leapt up as if shot.

'Cut!'

Melchior clutched the casket and gaped.

'Take five minutes break, you guys,' said Genghis.

The lutenists left off anxiously trying to tune up on the q.t., the photographers stopped snapping. There was a babble of surprise. Peregrine and Irish rocked together, overcome with mirth. The Lady A. exhibited puzzle and affront, but not half so much as her husband did, who dropped his dignity pronto, and snapped at Genghis: 'What is the meaning of . . .'

'Get 'em off!' roared Genghis. Daisy, I saw, was stuffing her hankie in her mouth or else she would have burst out laughing, too.

'What?'

I thought his costume was a masterpiece, myself. It was balletic, really; there was a high, spiky crown of what might have been fishbones. And a long, black wig, down his back. And a fur bolero over his chest, which was bare. And a necklace of what looked like babies' skulls. And snakeskin tights.

How well he filled those tights!

'Get 'em off!'

Because the way that Melchior filled those tights was the snag; Genghis hadn't gone to all this expense so that his wife would be upstaged by her co-star's package, and he explained, in loud and rasping tones, that, before the show went on again, Melchior must retire to his dressing room and don an extra heavy-duty athletic supporter. Or even two.

'Get it?'

Otherwise, one felt, Genghis would tear off the offending parts with his bare teeth. And now all present were too scared to laugh. Even Irish sobered up, although Daisy wasn't the only one red in the face and chewing on a hankie, I can tell you. It took a moment or two for her husband's predicament to sink into the Lady A.'s gentility and then she took a daughter by each hand and swept off with some dignity. I admired her for that. It was suddenly so quiet on the stage you could hear little Saskia's voice trailing behind them: 'Mummy, what had Daddy done? Mummy? Why are we going away? Mummy, why is everybody angry with Daddy?'

First Melchior went bright red. Then he went stark white. His dark eyes glowed like hot coals. He clutched his casket of sacred soil and glared at Genghis, mute with fury. If he'd had any class, I mean, *real* class, he'd have turned upon his heel and stalked off then and there. But that's unfair. Think what was at stake. The entire production was at stake. His Hollywood future – that is, his chance to take North America back for England, Shakespeare and St George. That is, to make his father's old dream everybody's dream. And his chance to make an awful lot of money, too. Don't let's forget the money.

But, for the moment, it was a Mexican standoff. Genghis glared. Melchior glared. They went on glaring at each other under the fascinated attention of the fairies and the fools and the scriptwriters until Peregrine it was who broke the tension, and he broke it with a trick. Although his belly was still agitating with suppressed merriment, he kept his presence of mind, picked his way over the electric cables, among the lights and cameras, knelt down in front of his brother, then and there, with Genghis and the rest of us looking on.

'I know what's causing the trouble,' said Peregrine.

With one swift pass of his hand he removed, from the problematic portion of Melchior's costume, a scarlet macaw.

He rose up, bowed to every quarter of the compass, every section of the audience, presenting the macaw upon his finger to us all as it flexed its wings and turned its head inquisitively from side to side. Something about its sharp little beady eyes reminded me of Grandma.

'I think you'll find everything perfectly acceptable, now,' said Peregrine to Genghis, who was lost for words.

But the macaw wasn't lost for words. It cocked its head to one side and announced in stentorian tones: 'It ain't no sin!'

It hopped off Peregrine's finger, took to the air and landed on Daisy's shoulder, which gave the poor girl a chance to laugh, which was just as well as she was just about to choke.

'It ain't no sin!' said the macaw again, dancing from foot to foot and winking. 'It ain't no sin!'

And then, thank God, reprieve. First Genghis Khan chuckled reluctantly, then he let rip a coarse guffaw. The cameras clicked, the cameras whirred, the cameras flashed and the show was on the road again. Thank God for that macaw. It saved the situation. It was trained up for a Mae West promotion, apparently. It was an escape.

In the midst of all this, I saw that one of the gorillas from studio security had got hold of Daisy's raincoated shadow, clamped one of its great, hairy paws over her mouth to stop her noise, was escorting her outside in the most unceremonious way, in a fireman's lift, but he also looked quite bored about it, as if he'd done the same to her before. What on earth was going on? But now a heavy silence suddenly fell; all eyes were turned towards Melchior, as he held aloft the Shakespeare pot as if it were the Holy Grail.

'Friends, we are gathered here together in remembrance of a sacred name – the name of Shakespeare.'

Irish, I noticed, was raising a brown paper bag to his lips in a spontaneous toast to Peregrine. The macaw had taken off again and was flapping about somewhere under the roof. Peregrine got hold of the brown paper bag and drank a toast to the macaw.

'I bear here, in this quaintly shaped casket – a casket in the image of, for me, the greatest of all our English heroes – only a little bit of earth. Nothing more. Earth. And yet it is especially precious to me because it is English earth, perhaps some of the most English earth of all, precious above rubies, above the love of women. For it is earth from William Shakespeare's own home town, far away, yes! Sleepy old Stratford-upon-Avon, earth gathered up and borne hither as tenderly as if it were a baby by two lovely young Englishwomen, nymphs, roses, almost as precious to me as my own daughters ... my nieces. Peaseblossom! Mustardseed!'

He called us and we knew what we must do, although he'd betrayed us once again, and this time, in public. Even so, we flitted up to him and knelt one on each side, coiling round his knee, Nora in yellow, I in pink, both of us near tears. Almost as precious as his own daughters, indeed!

'Dora ... Leonora ...'

He got us wrong, of course. He didn't even know us well enough to smell the difference, but he was well away, now it was family time. He waved his arm towards Peregrine, exiled among the writers.

'And my brother, my own brother ... welcome! Welcome to our great enterprise, in which you've played so noble a part! And welcome, welcome, to all of you come together here, so many, many folk, to engage with us in the great task at hand, to ransack all the treasuries of this great industry of yours to create a glorious, an everlasting monument to the genius of that poet whose name will be reverenced as long as English is spoken, the man who knew the truth about us all and spoke those universal truths in every phrase ... who left the English language just a little bit more glorious than he found it, and let some of that glory rub off on us old Englishmen too, as they set sail around the globe, bearing with them on that mission the tongue that Shakespeare spoke!'

When he said that, as it came rolling out, you could almost see the tongue, on a red satin cushion, under glass.

Melchior now swung on his heel and made a sort of obeisance; his voice switched to a mellifluous croon.

'Let us hail the vision of this great man ...'

Genghis Khan, thwacking the crop against his thigh, stood up and took a bow, sneaking a peak at Melchior's crotch to make sure all was still in order.

'This great man, who first came to me in London and said, "Let us give the world the splendour of your art, and, what is more, let us dedicate that splendour to Shakespeare!"'

Everybody clapped, having no option, except Irish, who had got his paper bag back and formed a permanent attachment to it.

'And let us hail the Queen of Fairyland herself – Titania!'

Daisy Duck parked her bum on the arm of her chair, gave the cameras a friendly wave, plus a glimpse of cleavage, and climbed up to the dais next to Melchior. Puck had managed to keep his hands to himself for ten whole minutes, but now he goosed a passing vole, who squealed. The macaw, high on a strut, abruptly extruded a greenish, semi-liquid substance that gathered sufficient impetus as it sped downwards to announce its arrival on terra firma with a lingering SPLAT!

'Now, we poor players, let us all take hands.'

He clasped Daisy Duck's hands very firmly and gave her the full force of his lovely smile, hot and brown as Bovril, and she fluttered. Tough as old boots, yet she visibly fluttered. There was a universal satisfied stir and contented rustle in the studio. It was as if he'd put them under a spell, that voice, such glamour. Everybody reached out to catch hold of everybody else as if it were New Year's Eve, time to sing 'Auld Lang Syne'. Fairy clutched Amazon, Amazon clutched Athenian, rude mechanical clutched lover, Nora and I clutched one another but not before that Puck copped hold of my spare hand.

> Give me your hands, if we be friends,
> And Robin shall restore amends.

Melchior raised his face to the bright lights on this concluding piece of nonsense, with his lips a little bit ajar in that selfsame knicker-shifting smile that must have been the downfall of my poor mother. Daisy looked at him as if the heavens had opened and she'd glimpsed inside. Smitten. The thunderbolt had struck. Cameras whirred, clicked, flashed. But Puck cried out with rage, dropped my hand like a hot brick and commenced to pummel with his little fists in the disputed region of Melchior's athletic supporter, yelping the while: 'That's my line, you bastard!'

Out of the corner of my eye, I saw Irish lean over and throw up.

Genghis Khan struck down Puck's hands with one cut of his crop and hissed: 'Ever heard of the face on the cutting-room floor?' That shut Puck up. He fell back. Then Melchior raised aloft the casket of earth in the hand that was not holding on to Daisy Duck.

> Every fairy takes his gait,
> And each several chamber bless,
> Through this palace, with sweet peace . . .
> In the blessed name of . . . SHAKESPEARE!

He looked deep into Daisy's eyes and she looked deep back. Then he let go of her, dipped his hand in the pot, scattered the earth from the Forest of Arden around him on the floor in a lovely, stately gesture and raised two fingers in benediction. What a splendid pontiff he would have made, given half the chance. Then the ancient instruments started up again and I saw Daisy furtively wipe away a tear because it had all been so very lovely and, furthermore, while Peregrine assisted Irish from the scene as the best boy tipped sand from a fire-bucket over Irish's deposit, little Miss Sharp Eyes here was privileged to witness a positive disturbance in Melchior Hazard's perhaps not wholly well-functioning jockstrap that boded ill for marital bliss all round.

Genghis Khan's office was full of orchids, he grew them himself. He liked the carnivores best and often fed them flies while some little actress quaked on the couch on the other side of his desk, where he kept a photograph of Daisy in a silver frame displayed conspicuously to show the poor things to what dizzy heights Genghis Khan could take a girl if she was nice to him. The very sight of Daisy made them drop their drawers. It was all a dream come true for Genghis. Crude power. He was the Master/Madam of a very peculiar brothel, where all the girls for sale were shadows; he bought and sold them, but the cash involved was just as real as the cash he used to pocket long ago, in Brooklyn, when he had all his hair and the Brooklyn wife he'd left for Daisy and had started out in life as a trolley-car conductor. They used to thank him at the garage when he brought his vehicle back at night. I mean to say, he could have sold it for scrap, couldn't he? How could a boy of such vision resist Hollywood? So out he came and made his dreams come true. Literally. That was how he made his living, making dreams come true.

He carried on like a bloody dictator in that studio. The studio covered about the same area as, say, Monaco, and employed about the same population, and had a barber shop of its own, a dentist, a hospital, a canteen, a police department, as well as the actors and the directors, assistant directors, assistants to the assistants, second unit directors, art directors, costume designers, needlewomen, cameramen, assistant cameramen, key grips, best boys, gaffers, carpenters, scene painters, make-up girls, hairdressers, pimps, astrologers, whores, fortune-tellers, abortionists, writers, assistant writers, writers of additional dialogue, and common fellows, and all day long they bustled about the dusty streets of the lot, although at night it was a ghost town, only the nightwatchman, a few dogs, an abandoned newspaper blowing down a cardboard street.

There was a lawn, where you could eat your sandwiches, and a big lilypond with carp in it. Daisy's Persian cat came to the studio with her and used to sit and stare for hours into the lilypond. Sometimes it would slip its paw up to the elbow in the water, but the fish twitched and swam away, she never caught anything. Perhaps her shadow on the bottom of the pool warned them off.

Daisy loved that cat. She went out with a net one afternoon, after she'd had a couple with Peregrine for old times' sake, caught a carp, tossed it, all alive-oh, to Pussy. 'There!'

She told me: on the wedding night, between the satin sheets, he said, whatever you want, Daisy. Anything. And she said, a million bucks. In cash. He blenched, chewed a cigar ragged, but he was daft with love, he made a few phone calls, kicked ass. She sat up in bed in her negligée. First of all the hotel manager came in, ushering the chairman of the bank, in monkey suit and white gloves, as if it wasn't three o'clock in the morning, and he was followed by a copper with holsters. Enter a little messenger boy in bum-freezer and pillbox, carrying a carpet bag; another little messenger boy, likewise; lastly, a third to match. Concluding the procession, another policeman.

At a sign from the chairman of the bank, the boys all set down their bags on the wall-to-wall and bowed. Their eyes were bugging at the sight of Daisy Duck in her nightie, I can tell you, they sneaked peeks from the corners of their eyes until the chairman snapped his fingers and they scampered out. One of the coppers asked for an autograph. Genghis Khan, rendered solemn by the presence of so much money, shook the hand of the chairman.

As soon as they were alone again, Daisy opened up the carpet bags and there it was. Her million. In hundreds, fifties, twenties. Nothing, to her regret, smaller than a ten, so that she was somewhat disappointed by the sheer volume of paper that she emptied out on the bed, but it was new, and fresh and crisp as spinach.

If there'd been a burner in the room she might have cooked it up and ate it, but no burner, nor oil nor lemon for a salad, so she *rolled* in it, like a dog in shit. Ripped off her satin nightie to feel the touch of greenbacks on her skin, scooped up handfuls and poured them over herself, shrieking with glee, and kicked her heels up to the ceiling until Genghis, unable to hold back, ripped off his jodhpurs and consummated that morning's marriage *toot sweet*, leaving the greenbacks somewhat stained.

Stained or not, back to the bank they went, next day. Daisy never forgave him for that. She'd wanted to stuff a mattress. She'd never forgiven him and now she was wreaking her revenge.

She'd been an old man's folly, as far as he was concerned. He'd cast off that old, grey-haired, loyal Brooklyn wife for Daisy, the one who'd stuck with him through thick and thin since trolley-car days and was now mad with love, poor thing. She was the phantom caller on Daisy's telephone, it turned out. Yes; the cast-off Brooklyn wife kept calling Daisy up, she wouldn't speak, there would be heavy breathing and a tear-stained silence. She'd called her up in New York, those times; no wonder Perry said, 'Poor cow.' And, Daisy said, she called up all the time in Hollywood, in spite of vile abuse. 'And,' said Daisy, 'she follows me around.' So *that* was the solution to the mystery of Daisy's rain-coated shadow whom I'd seen expelled from the studio, that time! I felt quite sorry for her, but Daisy didn't spare her a second thought. She was the wife in residence, and she was going to make Genghis pay.

In spite of all that, Daisy was neither more nor less pretty, more nor less smart than any other one of the hundred, nay, thousand girls who lay back on the couch and thought of stardom while he shoved it in. But she was the one who got the wedding-band because she didn't care.

And now, she didn't care who knew she didn't care. Before our father could say, 'Ill met by moonlight', she had him up against a pasteboard tree, in the wood near Athens, under a giant daisy, in the lunch break and all the lights went out, they fused them. She thought that that macaw had got it right: 'It ain't no sin.' She was in love, she was like a force of nature, but Genghis Khan was blind and deaf. Blind, deaf and dumb. He thought that he who paid the piper played the tune. An orchid never bit him back before.

And now began a dreary time. Early to bed, up before dawn and out along the mean streets as the forlorn lights were extinguished one by one to join our fellow-workers on the production line. But we ourselves weren't so much part of the process as pieces of the product. They laid us back in chrome recliners and sprayed us with paint, as if we were a motor chassis. We watched the mirror as if the faces it reflected were those of two other women. Greenish in colour; spangles on the cheekbones. Arms and hands, greenish. The green looked weird on monochrome. We had on artificial fingernails that looked like bark. Genghis Khan was staking his all on Art.

We had been cast adrift from what we knew and how to do it. We felt we had been dislocated. Or, as if we, too, had surrendered to the dream but did not know for sure who dreamed us.

We had a lot of dancing to do. A woman came out from the east, specially. Black hair scraped back, scrawny throat, leotards. None of your one, two, three kicks, for her. Angular movements, she said. She stuck out her bum and did peculiar things with her fingers. No tap-shoes, no character shoes, no point shoes; we danced barefoot. Very arty. She told us, if we smiled, she'd kill us.

I'll say this for Daisy, I didn't recognize her in the dailies. I wouldn't say she looked every inch the fairy queen; she looked as if, given half a chance, she'd drop her frock and twirl her tassels but Irish cut her lines down until she scarcely said a word, just stood in the wood and shimmered, and that big head took a lovely photo, I must say, even if it made cows' eyes at Oberon all the time. The Lady A. kept off the set, she knew which way the wind was blowing. All the same, she toddled over for a photocall occasionally, pictured picking up her daughters from the lot, plastered all over the papers, next day. Nothing a republic loves better than a Lord, unless it is a Lady.

Peregrine hovered round those girls all the time. He was foolish fond. Saskia would curl up on his knee and he'd fetch a little something for her out of her ear or her nostril. A pearl. A flower. The ends of her mouth went down to see the rose, she was a mercenary bitch even in those days. Skin like milk and amber eyes. Peregrine watched her wistfully as she danced off towards Melchior as soon as she saw him coming, leaving behind his own little gift without a second thought, as often as not.

When Genghis Khan saw the rushes of the fairy dance, he put Art on hold. Out went the lady in leotards, in came a little henna'd man who used mascara with discretion. One, two, three, kick! We joined up; we went down on our hunkers and kicked like cossacks; leaned over backwards and plucked daisies with our teeth; somersaulted over one another; the splits. We'd been here before, we could have done it in our sleep. Bucks, wings, struts, stumps, shuffles, coffee-grinders. If Melchior hadn't been so besotted with the wife of Genghis Khan, he wouldn't have let him get away with the production numbers but Genghis Khan thought he was hedging his bets. Kaleidoscope effects; fifty identical twins, twenty-five of each. One, two, three, kick! Then we stood on one leg. He wanted a cascade, a water ballet, he drenched us. Water, water, everywhere! Did he think it was the bloody *Tempest*?

The foxgloves trembled, the King and Queen of the Fairies were up to their usual tricks. And, to complete my pleasure, Irish was waiting in the dressing room eager to berate me. He berated me, then wept. I'd have a pound of schlap on, my wig kept flashing on and off, all I wanted was a good wash, a sit-down, a cup of tea. He clutched my knees, he cried so much he soaked my tights, but I never promised him anything.

I was his flawed chorine. Like a glass he didn't know was cracked until it fell apart when he poured his passion in it. But what's a girl to do? It was a real treat when he read me *Daisy Miller* out loud. But we'd reached the point in our relationship when, in a straight choice between him and Henry James, I'd have taken Henry James any day even if Henry James were dead and not much of a one for the girls when living, either. The more I said, 'It was lovely, Irish, but it's over,' the keener he became. I said, 'I'm very busy with my German lessons, Irish,' and he called me his beloved harlot.

I never went to his place, any more. On Sunday, I slept in at the Forest of Arden, got up late, lay in the blue, unnatural air beside the blue unnatural pool. Nora was never there on weekends any more. She was busy making ravioli. I felt that we were drifting apart.

I wasn't the only lonely one. Daisy's cat slept on the canvas chair marked 'Delia Delaney', it never stirred a muscle, it lay quite flat and sometimes, when Genghis Khan came on to the set, he'd pick up that cat and cuddle it in a way that told me Daisy wasn't available in the cuddling department any more. He'd gaze at her cooing at the King of the Fairies and he'd massage that white cat's back until you thought he'd snap its spine. Don't think Daisy was oblivious; she knew full well he went through hell. That was the way she kept her chaps in line.

By the time we got our make-up off, it would be dark outside and there was a wind, sometimes, that smelled of the desert and the valley would be full of lights like diamanté in a black box, and a soft, deep dew was falling. As we were driven home to our thatched cottage, our steak and baked potato, our turned-down bed and early night, I felt we were marooned in Wonderland and victims of a plot.

I know full well who plotted it. Not Melchior. Not Peregrine. Not even Genghis Khan. My German teacher was keen to ascribe everything to a cash nexus but I didn't need him to tell me what was going on.

The love of Mammon lay behind it all.

We worked like slaves. Take after take after take. The same routine, the same song, the same line – over and over and over. We were both product *and* process, simultaneously, and it very near broke us. And what did all our hard work add up to? Just another Saturday night at the pictures! Your one shilling and ninepenn'orth. Your helping of dark. What an equation. Our sweated labour = your bit of fun.

'Like tarts,' said Nora, with prim distaste.

I thought: as soon as all this is finished, we'll go straight back to Brixton. We'll softly and silently steal away, although we'd had plenty of offers, don't think otherwise. We could have stayed out there, cut ourselves a nice little niche out there, hit the high spots. But I was pining away for home – for the whirr and rattle of the trams, the lights of Electric Avenue glowing like bad fish through a good old London fog, longing for rain and weather and bacon sandwiches, for the healthy chill of 49 Bard Road on a frosty morning, for the smell of home, the damp, the cabbage, the tea, the gin.

'Cockney to the core,' said Perry fondly. I felt I was in exile. I knew just what my German teacher felt. I thought that Nora felt it, too. I thought she, too, was pining away for home. But when I said to her: 'I'm counting the days until the wrap, aren't you?' she said, 'It all depends on Tony.'

I saw which way the wind was blowing; she nourished aspirations towards the shoes and rice, the white lace and the orange blossoms. All of a sudden, even though I'd got thoroughly pissed off with her when she cramped our style in London, I started to miss Grandma, and not the way you miss a toothache when you lose a tooth, either.

Then Perry buggered off. He reached his boredom threshold and was gone. He didn't forget his salary cheque; he left a note on the white piano in his suite: 'Find me poste restante in Hazard, Texas; I've saved enough to buy a ranch.' I looked it up in the gazetteer. It was in the panhandle. When our grandparents played it late last century, it was a one-horse town but, from what the gazetteer had to say, it seemed the horse had died. Bit of a change from Hollywood! That's why he went, of course.

So, no Peregrine no more.

Then something started to go wrong with time. We were all spellbound, now. The shooting schedule started out at eight weeks. Then it stretched to twelve. Then to twenty and then on ad infinitum. The director didn't have his mind on the job, for one thing. He and Titania got on with, ahem, making the beast with two backs whenever the company knocked off for a ham and Swiss on rye with mayo. And nothing would satisfy Mascara, he was an obsessional, he was a perfectionist. And that 'wood near Athens' was a deathtrap. A couple of bunnies were concussed by swinging dewdrops; a gnome missed his footing on a toadstool and fractured a fibula; we backed into one of the spiky conkers by mistake, laddered our tights, punctured our posteriors and Nora's went septic, off work for ten days on her front and *hors de combat* in the Forest of Arden, swearing and cursing and leafing through *Brides* magazine.

The next Sunday morning, Nora on her belly, me on my back

enjoying to the full my weekly lie-in, high drama strikes. Daisy herself comes knocking at the door.

'I'm pregnint!'

Was she going to pass it off as Genghis's? Once we'd rubbed the sleep from our eyes and drunk our orange juice, we earnestly advised this course. Daisy accepted juice, herself, but poured into her goblet a slug from the silver flask she always carried with her. She was still in her nightie (café au lait chiffon) and hadn't combed her hair but she'd brought us a breakfast of lox and bagels in spite of her fluster, she was a dear, really. She stopped in the middle of splitting her bagel. Her jaw dropped. What? Put one over on Genghis? What kind of a girl did we think she was?

Such moral horror as suffused her features! You never saw anything like it. We were quite surprised and felt shoddy, by comparison, as if we lived in an ethical twilight, a cockroach world of compromise, lies, emotional sleight of hand. And so we did, I suppose. We called it 'Life'. But Daisy wanted something better. So did Irish, come to think of it. It's the American tragedy in a nutshell. They look around the world and think: 'There must be something better!' But there isn't. Sorry, chum. This is it. What you see is what you get. Only the here and now.

'He really wants children, you know,' Nora suggested delicately.

How did she know this herself? Easy. He'd offered her one. There was a memo from his desk, delivered to the set: Miss Leonora Chance, please call. She thought she ought to go, although she had a twinge of unease on account of Tony, who was jealous as Othello. We weren't wanted on the set that day so I was busy with my studies (W. for Wedekind).

He only made her wait for half an hour, in itself a wonder. He had a sliding time-scale for appointments. Actors cooled their heels from seven hours to five days, depending on their box-office. Agents, a week to three. Writers, six weeks minimum. Irish once waited five months in the outer office.

But Genghis Khan's very own navy-blue-suited secretary sat Nora on a leather sofa, even offered her some coffee before she retired behind her mahogany desk to be evasive on the telephone. Over her head was a big Grünewald crucifixion, the kind where the Christ has gangrene. No matter where you sat in that outer office, the eyes of that agonized Christ would follow you around.

Nora took her coffee black and patted her handbag; she hadn't forgotten to bring with her the wee, pearl-handled handgun Tony gave her on her birthday, just in case.

She knew, because Daisy told her so, that all the time she sat and waited, Genghis would keep an eye on her through a special spyhole he'd had drilled in one of those Grünewald eyes.

Then she was buzzed in; she was admitted to the holy of holies, the orchid arbour. He was leaning over a glass case. Although he wore white gloves he did not wear a shirt. He was giving a close inspection to something that looked like a rotting pudenda and didn't answer her cheery, 'What'cher, Mr Khan?' but dropped a scrap of raw meat into the orifice, which gnashed its snappers in appreciation. There was a plate of steak tartare on his desk beside the photograph of Daisy which Nora could not help but note stood upside down. He stripped off his bloody gloves and tossed them in the wastepaper basket. He gave Nora his full attention.

'I'm not going down on my knees to you,' he said. 'Not to an actress. Why, actresses go down on their knees to me!' He gave a caw of mirth. Perhaps he thought this quip would break the ice. Nora, sat on a leather chair with a dental look about it, crossed and recrossed her legs and fingered the outlines of her little gun. 'Out with it,' she said. He was quite taken aback to find the chorus girl so forward, so earthy; 'out with it' is *not* a US idiom. She hastily translated: 'Say what you've got to say and get it over with.'

'My mother's name was Leonora,' he said. 'I've chosen you to bear my child.' He must have been fond of his mother, the sentimental old thing. He pressed a button on his desk and Nora's chair collapsed. She was everso surprised. The back fell down, the seat shot out, it turned into a chaise longue and she went sprawling, legs in the air. While she had been fingering her bag, she must have accidentally slipped the safety catch because the gun went off – her bag was ruined – and blew a hole in the orchidarium. The secretary came beating on the door: 'Everything all right, Mr Khan?'

Nora always had respect for Genghis after that because he took one look at the gun, one look at her, switched on his intercom and told the secretary everything was fine.

'I'd feel everso much more comfortable if you'd put your shirt back on, Mr Khan,' she said, so he did and then something inside him broke, he grovelled, he said his heart was broken and he wanted his revenge on Melchior, etc. etc. etc. Then he said: 'Well, if you won't, how about your sister?' Then he said, could she put in a good word for him with Daisy, anyway?

But Genghis Khan was yesterday's papers as far as Daisy was concerned. She vowed she'd marry Melchior if it was the last thing she did. We tried to stop her but she leapt into her white roadster again as soon as she'd gobbled up her bagel and roared off in the direction of Hacienda Hazard.

'She's everso overwrought,' said Nora. 'Do you think we ought to go, too, Dora, to make sure she's all right?'

I reached to ring a cab.

'Oh, yes,' I said. 'Oh, bloody yes. Try and keep me away!'

By chance, the English Colony had foregathered in its entirety at the Hazard place that sunny forenoon in order to consume the contents of a box of kippers that had arrived, like us, on the Super-Chief, and, brunch done, to play a game of cricket on the extensive lawn so there they all were, in the Santa Fe-style dining hall, picking away at bones and spreading the Cooper's Oxford on their toast, the men with their monocles, the women in gloves, while the Lady A. presided behind a silver teapot.

Enter Daisy.

She overshot the drive and screeched to a halt on the cricket pitch, demolishing a wicket. Then in she burst through the French windows, spilling out of her nightie in all directions, hair like knitting the kittens had got at. Besides, you wouldn't recognize her without her make-up, she was a plain little thing, under all that.

It was the Lady A. that I felt sorry for. I could even find it in my heart, at that moment, to feel sorry for Imogen and Saskia. The girls clung to their mother's skirts (she was wearing a lovely mid-calf pink floral crepe de Chine with fichu plus a wide-brimmed straw with an old rose ribbon), too scared to cry, too overwhelmed by the horror of it, the madwoman in her underwear, the screams, the tears, the recriminations. Meanwhile, the English Colony, ever unflappable, took their final bites of kipper and laid their knives and forks together on their plates.

'Such kippers, Attie! Delish. Quite like home.'

'Lovely party, Attie. Must run!'

'Darling Attie, 'byee. Don't forget, our place next week. Roast beef!'

They made their excuses and left; you'd never have thought Daisy was raving all the while, improvising innumerable variations on the theme of: 'It's your baby, I swear it! Your baby! This baby's got a right to a father!'

Nora and I held hands, at that, and could not bear to look at Melchior. The Lady A., too British or too embarrassed to bring up the rights of her own babies, gave the girls a little hug and said:

'Now, you just run upstairs, and see what Nanny's doing.'

They wore white organdie. Saskia had a pink sash, Imogen a blue one. They wore their hair in braids. At their age, we were keeping our Grandma.

'Be off with you, like good chicks,' said Melchior, undergoing stress.

'Scoot!' said Daisy, with menace.

The Lady A. felt the side of the teapot. Evidently the temperature was no longer satisfactory. She rang a handbell.

'I'm sure we'd all feel better for a cup of tea.'

That stopped Daisy in her tracks. She rolled her eyes.

'I can't *believe* this!'

And sat down suddenly on the chintz settee with a big, hissing sigh, as though expending all the air inside her. She was deflated. The Lady A. held out her arms to my sister and me.

'Nora . . . Dora . . . How lovely to see you!' She smelled of Arpège. And that's another reason why we took the old trout in, because she gave us a hug and kissed us each on the cheek as if we were family. Then she let Daisy Duck take away her husband. She didn't even put up a fight. She smiled bravely and let him go. By the time the shadows lay along the lawn everything was settled. A swift, Mexican divorce for both parties, to be fitted in while the second unit dealt with Hermia, Helena, Lysander and Demetrius, and then Oberon and Titania could make it legal. They call it 'serial monogamy'. Daisy gave us a lift back to the Forest of Arden; she was planning her new wedding already. She wanted us to be bridesmaids but we said, bad taste.

So that was that.

I do believe that Melchior thought he knew what he was doing when he offed with the old, onned with the new in such spectacular fashion; I think he thought that he was marrying, not into Hollywood but Hollywood itself, taking over the entire factory, thus acquiring control of the major public dreaming facility in the whole world. Shakespeare's revenge for the War of Independence. Once Melchior was in charge of this fabulous machine, he would bestride the globe.

And now I come to think of it, his father passed on in America, didn't he? Did that have something to do with his ambition, which now reached its peak? He was drunk with glory. He left *The Dream* largely to its own devices, to Mascara's inventions, to Genghis's interventions. He was certain it could come to no harm, that he could do no wrong.

But some sixth sense told me we'd passed that fine line that divides the socko from the flopperoo some time before; now the production headed faster and faster towards disaster.

But what about Genghis?

'You can deal with Genghis,' I said. 'He wants to make a mother of you, after all.'

'Oh, no, I can't deal with Genghis. Tony would kill me. *You* deal with Genghis. He'll never tell the difference?'

'What about poor old Irish?'

'I thought you weren't seeing Irish any more. Oh, go on, Dora; you can do it. My opinion is, that Genghis Khan will ring us up and propose to whichever one of us answers the telephone in' – and here she consulted her watch – 'about fifteen minutes' time, as soon as Daisy gets home and tells him he's been relegated to second division.'

And so it turned out. I didn't want to do it but Nora was inexorable. That's how I knew she was in love.

We decided to announce all three engagements – Daisy to Melchior, myself to Genghis, Nora to Tony – at the end-of-shoot party on the 'wood near Athens' set. I sent a telegram to Grandma: 'I'm going to marry the most powerful man in Hollywood when his divorce comes through.' I had brushed up my Shakespeare; I recognized for what it was the game that Nora and I had played out once before as romance. And now we'd perform the 'substitute bride' bit, as in *Measure for Measure* and *All's Well That Ends Well*, as farce. I didn't want to do it. I broke down in the post office when we went to send the telegram. But Nora wouldn't let me off the hook. I'd never known her quite this way before. She said that when the shoot was over, she was going to take instruction. 'They're a very devout family, Dora.'

She sent a telegram to Grandma, too. 'I'm going to marry the most wonderful man in the world as soon as I've converted.'

He telephoned her every night when we came in from work; he chattered away impenetrably in Sicilian and she never understood one word but she would stand there blushing while he was talking to her. She would look pliant and voluptuous. She clutched the receiver as tenderly as if it were his prick but *that* she kept her hands off. The plan was, a white wedding. I was at a loss for words.

The studio publicity went to town on me and Genghis. Hedda Hopper hinted coyly at romance. Rumours were dropped of secret dates and private suppers. All the US asked: 'Will this great man of the cinema propose to little Miss Nobody from Nowhere, England?' Louella Parsons ran a piece about the first Mrs Khan, the poor old Brooklyn wife: 'I knew it would never last with Delia but I thought that he would come back to his senses in the end and come home to me.' Louella ran a piece about me: 'I'm planning on a beige and ecru trousseau.' She ran a picture of me, except that it was Nora's picture, by mistake. *Photoplay* ran a spread. Hedda Hopper scooped; she ran an interview with Genghis: 'My English rose: this time it's for keeps, says Mr Hollywood.'

Genghis and I were a hot number on paper. In the flesh, no. Now I was a fiancée, he put me on a pedestal. No nooky until the ring was on my finger, he declared, and I wasn't going to argue with that. I'd gone on to automatic, I felt I didn't have a will of my own. I did what Nora wanted because I loved her best.

The telephone began to ring for me, too, every night. It was a phantom caller. Just heavy breathing and sometimes a sob, sometimes as if she'd started saying something and then choked it back, not knowing what to say. I had inherited the Brooklyn wife. I saw that raincoat whisking round the lot; I felt unseen eyes upon me.

I waited for a sign from Grandma, a letter, a telegram. Nothing doing. I waited in vain but still I waited because I knew what she'd say. 'Come off it, gel. It just won't do. Come home.' But now I was so mixed up in it all, I couldn't get out by myself. I told my German teacher everything. 'Go ahead and marry him,' he advised me. 'Marry him and ruin them. That's the way to do it. What I say is, fuck the bourgeoisie.' It was a dizzying prospect. Did I have the temperament for a Delilah?

If ever I ran into Irish on the lot, he'd turn away.

And God alone knows where Peregrine had got to.

Daisy's beloved cat now took to sleeping on my chair. That cat knew in its bones how Genghis's wife was a better bet for an ongoing cat-food supply than Melchior's wife. Not that it would have taken a cat of more than average intelligence to foresee the cash *The Dream* would lose.

We wrapped up with the rude mechanicals. They were another catastrophe, more mechanical than rude, worse luck – like robots. Lifeless. There's a kind of reverence the custard-pie brigade can't keep out of its voice when it plays Shakespeare and it scuppered the entire proceedings in that department, although Melchior had personally imported the rudest man in England to play Bottom.

Yes! Gorgeous George.

George had gone from strength to strength since Nora and I first caught his act, that time, on Brighton Pier. 'Clown Number One to the British Empire'. He'd started a riot at the Royal Variety Show when he held up a couple of spuds and said: 'King Edwards.' That was just before the abdication. Peregrine had a theory and convinced his brother of it, as follows: all the comic roles in Shakespeare were originally intended for stand-up comedians. Melchior swallowed it whole. First of all, Melchior wanted George to get his clothes off, somehow, as a little reminder, according to Melchior, of the essential *Englishness* of Shakespeare, but Peregrine had managed to persuade his brother that Bottom was supposed to be a citizen of Athens, Greece, and hence unlikely to sport a map of the British Isles on his pecs, let alone Africa on his abdomen. They let him keep his famous plus-fours, too; at least, those plus-fours were famous in the UK, and, or so Melchior thought, in his folly and delusion, soon to be famous in the USA, to boot.

So there was George, in golfing garb, plus brogues, all pink and purple, he should have been in Technicolor; you burst out laughing just to look but when he opened his mouth, he took the smile right off your face. He was like a fine wine if only in the one respect, he didn't travel. The moment he stepped off his native soil, he stopped being funny. In California, he was not bawdy, he was lewd. Genghis Khan caught the rushes and kicked up hell; not Genghis Khan's idea of a class act, no, indeed! So Bottom's part was cut to pieces, until he had almost as little to do as Daisy and, these days, he wore a baffled look as if, when nobody laughed, he didn't know what to do with himself.

Gorgeous George's stab at global fame was dying on its feet. Melchior, at his wits' end, adopted the following stratagem: fairies, all around, peeking through the leaves to watch, the idea being, if the audience sees the fairies laughing, then it might even bring itself to raise a titter, too. But it was hard going, I can tell you.

'Thisbe,' said Bottom, 'the flower of odious savouries sweet –'

'Savours! Savours!' bellowed Melchior through his megaphone. He cut a dashing figure in his snakeskin tights; he'd dressed ready for the party afterwards and, in former days, George would have been quick with the repartee, I can tell you, but now poor old George was shillyshallying with nerves. I thought, the poor sod's on the skids, he should never have come to Hollywood.

'Thisbe, the flower of odours savours sweet –'

He must have thought, to hell with it! Because, suddenly, a flicker of authentic George illuminated his now cadaverous features. His eyebrows worked and he gave his bum a wiggle to ram home the idea of 'Bottom'. He sang out his line in grand style and he gave that 'odours' the full force of all his genius for innuendo. I blushed. Perry had another theory: that a truly great comedian could make a laundry list sound filthy. George touched greatness at this moment.

' – odours savours sweet – '

'Cut!' cried Melchior, white with rage.

The wretched business wasn't in the can until past seven but could we then adjourn to hot baths and stiff drinks? Could we, hell. The doors burst open and in came a torchlit procession, those bloody lutenists, again, in costume as ever was; plus the entire English faculty of UCLA in their graduation robes; and a hundred-voice boys' choir drafted in for the occasion, piping up in trebles: 'The Boar's Head in Hand Bear I.'

So they all came in, plus an Elizabethan feast borne by blue-chinned men in shirts slashed to the waist and knee breeches; it turned out Tony's uncle catered it and not quite seasonal, also, overdoing the garlic and marinara sauce. The fairies stumped over en masse to the bar and started on the serious drinking. Nanny came for Saskia and Imogen because the Lady A. thought it would be in the worst possible taste for the girls to attend their father's engagement party and Imogen went quietly but Saskia cried and clung to her father's leg until Daisy lost her temper and snapped: 'Beat it, kid!' At which Saskia's eyes spat fire but what could she do? She was only twelve and had no rights.

Then Irish came in on a bender, white of face and red of eye and upright only with the greatest difficulty, to press into my hands his poisoned gift, the page proofs of *Hollywood Elegies*, inscribed to his 'gilded fly', and signed with his full name, thank God. I sold it at Sotheby's last winter when we were a touch pressed as to how to pay the electricity bill.

'If I'm a fly,' I said to him, 'what does that make you? Flypaper?'

Then, big-hearted me, I introduced him to the Helena. She'd come out from an East Coast stock company, she was a Bryn Mawr graduate, English major, low mileage, only one careful boyfriend. I wanted nothing but happiness for poor old Irish. I was really very fond of him. But what he wanted for himself was, an infinitely renewable virgin – one he could do every night who'd be untouched again by morning. My German teacher said it was inherently a metaphysical desire and I agree with him. *His* needs were much simpler and we parted friends.

Journalists in hats came in. Harlots, actresses and wives in satin frocks came in. The English Colony in its entirety in gloves and pearls came in. An entire swing band plus leader in d.j. and baton came in, to battle it out musically with the massed pluckers; Genghis confided he'd had it up to *here* with lutes. Tony came in in a nice black suit and black fedora and Nora ran to his side, blushing and giggling. An Italian tenor came in with a mandolin and sang 'Come Back to Sorrento' in high counterpoint to the swing band playing 'Satin Doll' and the consort of lutes still having a valiant go at 'Fine Knacks for Ladies', while Gorgeous George, having stayed himself with a flagon, was trying out a chorus of 'Rose of England' in a defiant and self-conscious manner.

In those days, with Irish's hideous example ever before me,

I was quite abstemious but when Genghis Khan took from his jodhpur pocket a little box and showed me the ring inside, I thought: If I don't get drunk tonight, I'll kill myself.

It wasn't a diamond as big as the Ritz, only the size of the Algonquin. It sat on my hand like a knuckleduster as we took the floor to foxtrot amidst an explosion of flashbulbs. My chin skidded the top of his head, he trod on my feet – he wasn't looking where he was going, he was gazing helplessly at Daisy in her Titania gown, wrapped round Melchior like skin round sausage. I tried to laugh but it was wry. I felt sad.

Sad. Nothing more than sad. Let's not call it a tragedy; a broken heart is never a tragedy. Only untimely death is a tragedy. And war, which, before we knew it, would be upon us; replace the comic mask with the one whose mouth turns down and close the theatre, because I refuse point-blank to play in tragedy.

So tragedy it wasn't. But I couldn't help thinking of that blond tenor and the last time I'd swapped beds with Nora, which made me sentimental. And I do believe old Genghis thought *his* heart was breaking, he lurched, he stumbled, I led, I steered him, picking my way with care among the towering foxgloves, the swollen daisies, the vicious conkers on the silver gravel floor. Genghis patted my behind but I knew his heart was not in it; he gazed at Daisy and burned with vengeance.

Hope for the best, expect the worst, as Grandma used to say. I hoped that Genghis Khan would think he'd had enough revenge by marrying Daisy's lover's daughter; I did hope so, I was always partial to Daisy. But what I thought he'd really do was, smash them.

High above the heads of the convivial throng I saw the crown of spikes that showed me where my father was. Hither and thither, the perfect host, graciousness personified. I caught a glimpse of Irish as Helena helped him from the scene. Little did he know that she would play herself in the movie based on his final years; I forget who it was played me. Some painted harlot. Poor old Irish didn't have long left. Keeled over at *The Dream* premiere, outside Grauman's Chinese. Dicky ticker. Nora and I had gone home, by then. 'Don't worry,' they said, carting him out of the way of the stars, 'it's only a writer.' Then *Hollywood Elegies* came out, but what's the point of a posthumous Pulitzer? Ross O'Flaherty, RIP.

I saw my German tutor, who'd gate-crashed, looking starved, as usual. He'd got some front-office type by the arm and was haranguing him. Puck passed by and goosed me. The noise, the smoke, the smell of garlic, the blaring lights were beginning to discompose me. Not to mention the liquor. Nora waltzed by with Tony, clinging close; her eyes were closed, a dreamy smile upon her lips. I'm going to throw up, I thought. Influence of Irish. Never thrown up at a party before.

I sat in the cool, white bathroom for a while, listening to the gently plashing gurgling water in the cistern, which soothed me. I looked at myself in the mirror and saw my eyes were bright as if I were on drugs, bright as the diamond for which, to tell the truth, I'd sold myself. My heart went thump, thump, and I felt shuddery. A cluster of retching pixies broke in upon my troubled solitude but I wasn't fit to go back to the party and face Genghis's damp hands, my father's empty triumph, my sister's mindless bliss, Irish's contempt and the cynicism of my German tutor, which he called common sense, and though I knew in my heart he, out of all of them, knew about life, I was only a girl and did not want to believe him. I never listened to the news, in those days.

I *was* feeling sorry for myself, I can tell you, so I picked about a bit in those dense, artificial woods, and the music and the voices filtered, altered, through the weird shadows and everything started to go strange. I knocked my knee on a dewdrop and as I rubbed the bruise, the foliage parted.

I thought I'd gone mad.

I saw my double. I saw myself, me, in my Peaseblossom costume, large as life, like looking in a mirror.

First off, I thought it was Nora, up to something, but it put its finger to its lips, to shush me, and I got a whiff of Mitsouko and then I saw it was a replica. A hand-made, custom-built replica, a wonder of the plastic surgeon's art.

The trouble she'd gone to! She'd had her nose bobbed, her tits pruned, her bum elevated, she'd starved and grieved away her middle-age spread. She'd had her back molars out, giving the illusion of cheekbones. Her face was lifted up so far her ears had ended up on top of her head but, happily, the wig hid them. And after all that she looked very lifelike, I must say, if not, when I looked more closely, not *all* that much like me, more like a blurred photocopy or an artist's impression, and, poor cow, you could still see the bruises under the Max Factor Pan Stik, however thickly she applied it, and the scars round where the ears should be. Ooh, it must have hurt! It was a good job for her we were about the same height, Daisy was a real shortarse.

Before me stood the exed Mrs Khan, who loved her man so much she was prepared to turn herself into a rough copy of his beloved for his sake.

'How much do you want?' she said. I'd heard that voice so often, breathing brokenheartedly down the telephone. I was quite moved to hear it speak.

'How much do I want for what?'

'My husband back again.' Her lip quivered, her eyelids fluttered. Fancy taking so much trouble over a man. My sentimental heart went right out to the old bag. Would you believe it, she really loved him.

Then came a great noise, drowning out the party sounds – Genghis, on the megaphone, and he was paging me.

'Dora! DORA!!'

All the lutes began to play at once and, oh, my God! they played the Wedding March. If her face could have crumpled, it would have, but it was too tightly stretched.

'I thought it was an engagement party,' she wailed. 'Not a wedding party!'

'So did I!' I said. I panicked. I didn't think twice, I offed that diamond bruiser as if it were a burning coal. 'Here. Shove it on your finger. *You* go and marry him. Go on. You've done it before, haven't you? But I should get a veil on, sharpish, if I were you.'

I don't think she believed it, at first. She kept on turning the ring round and round in her hands, which were wrinkled and freckled on the backs, they can't do a thing with hands, cosmetically, but there was no time to find her some gloves, let's hope he doesn't look until too late. She stared at me in the strangest way; I couldn't make it out, at first, but, then, she couldn't call her face her own, could she, and after a bit I realized she was giving me a smile.

'DORA!!!'

All around us, crystal dewdrops shook and tinkled, such was the decibellage of his cry. She gave me a quick little peck on the cheek. Then she showed a clean pair of heels, never saw a woman move so fast, not a thank-you or a backward glance – off, before I changed my mind. And that was the nearest I ever got to wedded bliss, thank you very much.

I thought I'd better slip into something inconspicuous, for the nonce, as it wouldn't do to have *three* Chance sisters walking round, under the circumstances, so I was making for the exit when I tripped over Bottom, right over, fell flat on my face.

Bottom was dead to the world, feeling no pain, forgetful at last of the miseries and humiliations of the last few months, and wouldn't be needing his ass's head. I got off his plus-fours, too, and his jacket, and so I inadvertently exposed the British Empire, all that pink on his torso, not to mention the lesser breeds without the law. I didn't want our nation's shame out in the open for all to see so I rolled him under an imitation bush, picked off a handful of imitation leaves and covered him up. It felt like the end of something, when I did that, but there was no time to ponder as to the end of what.

I've done many a quick change, in the wings, in panto, in revue, but never one as quick as this. And so it came to pass that it was as Bottom the Weaver, in plus-fours and an ass's head, that I went to my own wedding. I was beginning to see the funny side. It isn't every day you see yourself get married.

It was a strange night, that night, and stranger still because I always misremember. It never seems the same, twice, each time that I remember it. I distort. Remember, though I was on my feet and compos mentis, I was still half tight, if not more so; everything seemed disembodied, distant, peculiar. The tin roof over our heads seemed to have cracked open and disappeared, somehow, because there was real, black sky above us, although the crescent moon was made of painted plywood and swung backwards and forwards with Puck perched on it, looking perky. The swing band was pizzicatoing away and Puck was vocalizing with them, in that high soprano that made you think you'd died and gone to heaven:

> 'It's only a paper moon, sailing over a cardboard sea.
> But it wouldn't be make-believe, if you'd believe in me . . .'

A brisk wind made the stiff twigs rattle yet I doubt that wind came from a machine because it blew all the sweet wet dewiness of the California night through the set.

And I no longer remember that set *as* a set but as a real wood, dangerous, uncomfortable, with real, steel spines on the conkers and thorns on the bushes, but looking as if it were unreal and painted, and the bewildering moonlight spilled like milk in this wood, as if Hollywood were the name of the enchanted forest where you lose yourself and find yourself, again; the wood that changes you; the wood where you go mad; the wood where the shadows live longer than you do.

These days, half a century and more later, I might think I did not live but dreamed that night, if it wasn't for the photos, see? This one of Bottom, being hugged by –

There I go again! Can't keep a story going in a straight line, can I? Drunk in charge of a narrative.

Where was I?

There I was, one of the crowd, among the fairies, goblins, spirits, mice, rabbits, badgers, etc. etc. etc. crowding around the brides, who all three seemed somewhat taken aback, even put out, by the spontaneous nature of the unexpected marriage ceremony and were babbling agitatedly to one another whilst minions scurried hither and thither, pushing aside the undergrowth to create more of a chapel-like atmosphere and bringing in stands of calla lilies, baby's breath and satin bows. Some girls from wardrobe sprinted in with wedding veils and orange blossom wreaths so there was a bit of trying on of those while the three grooms consorted together in a male huddle, clearing their throats, pulling on ciggies and looking anxious.

Then came a diversion. A little old lady that I'd never seen before popped up out of nowhere, maybe up through a trap in the floor, as if in a thunderclap. Tony looked quite post-operative with shock. She'd got on a long black overcoat and a big black veil and she flung her arms round Tony's neck and burst into floods of tears and Italian exclamations and so did he. The old lady came out of the clinch long enough to look daggers at Nora and then she and Tony were at it again, so that Nora blushed and cowered behind her veil. Then Tony's Mamma – for it was she, freshly arrived from Little Italy on the train – disengaged and commenced haranguing him. Daisy, meanwhile, was taking a surreptitious swig from a silver flask while the substitute Dora had cannily covered herself up with the thickest veil and now perched upon a dewdrop, biding her time.

Then the lutes began to play, of all things, 'Home on the Range'.

Clip-clop, clip-clop, clip-clop.

Picking its way delicately among the detritus on the floor now entered the scene the biggest white horse I ever saw and, on top of it, the biggest cowpoke, in the biggest goddamned white hat and a chequered shirt with a silver star on the lapel. Genghis Khan hugged himself, he was so pleased to see the cowboy, but Melchior looked quite green. Tony's Mamma was now upbraiding him so fiercely he did not even give the cowboy a glance, but everybody else laughed, cheered and clapped so I brayed, too, and stamped my hooves.

Genghis Khan looked proud and shy. This impromptu cowboy wedding was his brilliant idea, it seemed. Clip-clop, went the horse, and stopped. The cowboy twanged out in a broad drawl that halted just this side of self-parody:

'Which of you goshdarned sinners is the best man?'

Puck leapt gracefully off his half-moon, assisted by a wire, and, dangling three feet in the air above us, squeaked: 'I am!'

'Got the goshdarned rings, sonny?'

A monstrous suspicion awoke within me. I knew that voice. I knew that bulk.

Puck displayed a handful of gold.

'Let's get the ball rolling!'

Everything was hurting my eyes, the glitter, the bright, white light, but I knew who it was, all right, on that white horse. It was –

'Let it be known to all present,' sang out the cowboy, 'that by the powers invested in me as sheriff of the county of Hazard, Texas, I now pronounce you men – and wives.'

Tony's Mamma let out a shrill scream of outrage. Too late. Three rings slipped on to three fingers. Three women pushed back three veils. I couldn't help it, I started crying. I made a lovely bride. I looked quite radiant. I wept buckets, inside that ass's head.

Then Tony's Mamma, gibbering with fury, heaved up a vat of marinara sauce and – emptied it all over Nora.

Blood on the bridal veil! All those tomatoes, it looked like a massacre. Mamma fell backwards, clutching her heart. A coronary? Tony cried out and flung himself down beside her. Then – bang! bang! bang! Machine-gun fire? No, only a barrage of champagne corks from the buffet timed to blast off in unison as soon as the knot was tied but we only found *that* out afterwards, it was panic stations, at the time. All present flung themselves down on their bellies. The white horse took fright and reared up. The cowboy's hat fell off. Red hair. I'd known it was Peregrine from the very first moment but Melchior's jaw dropped and Daisy creased up. Then, pandemonium.

The iris closes.

Everything went blank.

I knew I should have gone to comfort Nora but I couldn't take any more, I was punch-drunk. I clawed my way out through the nightmare party into the cool, dark outdoors and blundered straight into, was almost winded by –

'I say, steady on,' she said.

My nostrils filled with the aroma I loved best in all the world, surpassing all others – that consummate blend of gin, cabbage, stale undergarments, mothballs.

'Grandma!'

Flash! A passing paparazzo took a picture of an old lady who looked like St Pancras Station, monumental, grimy, full of Gothic detail, startled in the arms of a half-man, half-donkey.

'Who the fuck are you?' she said.

She seemed to fill up all the space available, so there wasn't any room left in the whole of southern California for insecurity. She had her oilcloth carrier with her, evidently her only luggage. Daisy's white cat, who had been sleeping peacefully on a bank of wild thyme the while, now made its appearance like a cork from a bottle out of that madhouse behind us. It stopped short when it saw Grandma. It rubbed its head against her knee and started to purr. She bent down and picked it up.

'I feel the need of something to cuddle,' she said.

She'd flown, as it turned out, the intrepid old cow. She'd pawned the grandfather clock and flown. Not all the way, of course, only from New York, but it got her here in half the time. As soon as she'd got our telegrams, she'd gone to Thomas Cook's in Piccadilly. 'Get me to Hollywood *toot sweet*.'

We took the white cat to Brixton with us, in the end. It didn't have any time for Daisy any more. It never showed much sign of either sex while it lived with Daisy but it turned out she never got pregnant because Daisy would lock her in a wardrobe when she came on heat and as soon as that cat arrived at Bard Road, it turned into a breeding machine. The founding mother of the Chance cat dynasty. We had her all through the blitz. Six kittens twice a year, regular, until the cat flu took her off in '51. She was our only souvenir of Hollywood unless you count our silver-fox trenches, about which the less said the better, and a few signatures in a few books.

So we went home with Grandma, sadder and wiser girls. Tony's Mamma prevailed, of course. What? Her son marry a born-again virgin? Not good enough for Little Italy! Nora was so angry she never shed a tear but broke his jaw when he came round to take back the engagement ring and went on packing. Meanwhile, Genghis Khan and the imitation Dora lived happily ever after, once he'd got over the shock, and if you believe that, you'll believe anything, but I do know, for a fact, he never got together with Daisy again and though he tried to ruin her career, she didn't give a damn. It finished Melchior in the movies, though. Kaput. The end.

Furthermore, it turned out, after all that, that Daisy *wasn't* pregnant, just a touch of dysmenorrhoea and a twinge of indigestion. She came on with a vengeance in the middle of the wedding night and by the end of the honeymoon they were fighting like terriers so Daisy went to Mexico again and Melchior came home to London, wifeless, childless, jobless, hopeless, quenched. Then war was declared in the nick of time; he joined up pronto and turned into a war hero. The Fleet Air Arm. No, really. Who'd have thought it?

But Hollywood was a closed book to him, thereafter.

Daisy still sends us a card at Christmas. Not a shred of malice in her. Turn on the telly, you'll see her. She's worn well. She never had the looks to lose and so she never lost them. Still blonde, still with that same rude joke of a mouth. She does the matriarchs in soaps, these days. She gives good décolleté, for an octogenarian.

Still on the go. I was always fond of Daisy.

FOUR

'LET OTHER PENS dwell on guilt and misery.' A., for Austen, Jane. *Mansfield Park*. I do not wish to talk about the war. Suffice to say it was no carnival, not the hostilities. No carnival.

Yes, indeed; I have my memories, but I prefer to keep them to myself, thank you very much. Though there are some things I never can forget. The cock that used to crow, early in the morning, in Bond Street. And I saw a zebra, once, he was galloping down Camden High Street, one night, about midnight, in the blackout – the moon was up, his stripes fluoresced. I was in some garret with a Free Norwegian. And the purple flowers that would pop up on the bomb-sites almost before the ruins stopped smoking, as if to say, life goes on, even if you don't.

We kept a patriotic pig in the back garden, fed him with swill – potato peelings, tea leaves. Grandma loved that pig and wouldn't listen to one word about the slaughterhouse, of course, but it ended up the funeral baked meats after Grandma copped it. She'd have created something shocking if she'd known we'd feasted off her beloved porker, nicely roasted, as soon as we'd cremated her, but what else could we have done for the funeral tea? People had come for miles, we couldn't give them grated cabbage. Old Nanny brought up a bushel of apples for the sauce from the Lady A., who'd retreated to the sticks in a state of disarray. No flowers, by request; we stuck to Grandma's principles on that score, at least.

Cyn and her kids were there but not the cabby, he was in North Africa and there he stayed, poor chap, under the desert in a box. Cyn never got over it, she faded away, after that, until the Asian flu took her off in '49. Ex-tenants by the score – geriatric adagio dancers, antique sopranos. Neighbours. The man who ran the salad stall in Brixton market. Publicans galore. Half the cast of *What? You Will?* came, plus the composer's mother, in her new black coat. I half thought that blond tenor might have heard about it on the grapevine and turned up but no such luck.

We missed Peregrine something shocking but he was off being heroic in the Secret Service. God knows what it was but they gave him a medal for it. God knows *where* he was, either; we put a notice in *The Times* and there was a knock at the door, a jeep, an army driver, a dozen crates of crème de menthe, a barrel of Guinness, so the mourners all went home with grease on their chins and strong drink on their breath and that was how Peregrine paid his respects to Grandma.

Once we'd burned the bones – because that pig met its fate strictly on the q.t., it was a hanging matter, to slaughter your own meat in wartime – Nora and I sat down right here, in the breakfast room, in these very leather armchairs, and listened to the silence in that long, narrow house where we would live alone, in future, and had a good cry, just the two of us, for this was childhood's end with a vengeance and we were truly on our own, now, good and proper.

We hadn't just lost Grandma, either. She was the only witness of the day our mother died when we were born, and she took with her the last living memory of that ghost without a face. All our childhood went with her into oblivion, so we were bereft both of her in person and of a good deal of ourselves, too, and when we remembered how we'd mocked her nakedness in her old age we were ashamed.

Now we were on the high road to our third decade, though, looking back from my present great pinnacle and eminence of years, I can scarcely credit it, that, once upon a time, we thought our lives would end when we reached thirty; at the time it felt like the end of the road, all right, even if there hadn't been a war on, and we were never the same again after the war was over, either.

After the war was over, it was always chilly. Our fingers were pale blue for years. Before the war, we were young, and then we were in sunny California; during the war, adrenalin kept you going and there was always some fella or other around to warm you up. But afterwards, there was a weariness, and the blood was a touch thinner, and people said it was the Age of Austerity – yet I do believe that chilliness we felt was more to do with Grandma being gone than with the economic policies of Stafford Cripps or the cold winters of the late forties and all that.

Without Grandma in it, minding the fires, leaving the lights on for us at nights, up in the morning putting on the kettle, banging the big brass gong to tell us she'd scrambled the dried eggs already, and they were congealing on the plate, the house was nothing but a barn and we rattled around uncomfortably, piles of dirty dishes in the sink, the steps filthy, baked beans fossilizing at their leisure in the bottoms of pans on the cold stove, etc. etc. etc.

We let the house go. We'd come back to sleep, that was all. Sometimes we'd burn ourselves a slice of toast. The heart went out of this house when Grandma died. The draughts raced through the hall and the rugs rose up and shimmied, we never changed the sheets so they were grey and stained and full of crumbs. Times were a touch hard for hoofers, too, although we put a brave face on it.

Then began those dreary days of touring shows, smaller and smaller theatres, fewer and fewer punters, the showgirls wearing less and less, the days of our decline. The nadir, a nude show-cum-pantomime in Bolton, *Goldilocks and the Three Bares*. 'Take off your trousers, call it *Goldibollocks*,' said Nora to the a.s.m., but he wouldn't. Those nude shows! Music hall's last gasp. There was a law that said, a girl could show her all provided she didn't move, not twitch a muscle, stir an inch – just stand there, starkers, letting herself be looked at. That's what the halls had sunk to, after the war. No more costumes by Oliver Messel, sets by Cecil Beaton. We always kept our gee-strings and our panties on, mind. Never stripped. We'd still sing, we'd still dance. But we felt our art was swirling down the plughole and those were the days when high culture was booming, our father cutting a swathe with the senior citizen roles in Shakespeare – Timon, Caesar, John of Gaunt – but he still didn't want anything to do with us, as ever was.

It is a characteristic of human beings, one I've often noticed, that if they don't have a family of their own, they will invent one. Now we often found ourselves slipping down to Sussex to visit the Lady A. Lynde Court was just a pile of blackened bricks, and they'd sold up the Eaton Square place when they divorced so after the Lady A. came home from California she turfed the tenant out of the Lynde Court Home Farm and moved in with the Aga and the exposed beams. She always kept a full-length portrait of Melchior in her sitting room. That portrait took up most of one wall and cast gloom in spite of the gilt frame because there he was, as Richard III, Tricky Dicky, all in black with an evil glint in his eye. She fixed up a light over it, which she kept on all the time, and always a little bunch of flowers in a glass jar on a footstool in front of it – wild daffs in March, wallflowers, daisies, according to season, always fresh. Even when the snow lay on the ground, out she'd go, scouring the Downs for celandines, early violets, snowdrops, headscarf and wellington boots, always a little dog yapping behind her.

That bitter winter of '46, me and Nora couldn't stand it, to think of her rooting about among the snowdrifts, so we took her a big bunch of hothouse carnations. Cost more than a supper at the Savoy Grill. Bloody Saskia was there, fresh and frisky. Imogen, too. Doing their stint at the Royal Academy of Dramatic Art, were Saskia and Imogen, and Saskia'd brought her best friend with her, some prinking minx in black velvet slacks and ballet slippers. Saskia laughed like anything when she saw those carnations.

'How apt!' she said. ' ". . . which some call nature's bastards." *Winter's Tale*, Act IV, Scene iii.'

Little did she know it was a case of the pot calling the kettle black. Her mother was mortified and tried to cover up.

'My little Saskia's playing Perdita this term. Isn't it lovely?'

But if that was the kind of thing they taught her girls at Radi-bloody-da, then Nora and I didn't want to know. Such cheap gibes! We rose above.

The girls might be away at RADA but there was Old Nanny to keep her company and a woman in from the village to do the heavy work and I was always tickled when concerned weekend guests asked her: 'How do you survive out here all on your own, Attie?' You could hardly move for help, you even tripped over a little old man crouched above the herbaceous border on your way to the outside lavvy. But the Lady A. would give a little smile and say, she'd got used to solitude, and make some reference to the garden. She was always out there in a big hat telling the gardener what to do. There were articles in magazines. She was famous for her clematis. In the evenings she'd sit stitching away at her embroidery hoop with Melchior glowering on the wall and listen to records on her gramophone the same way she does now, in the front basement of 49 Bard Road. Then Old Nanny used to come to tuck her up in bed at ten, with Horlicks.

Her girls would go and visit their father, sometimes, and come back with new wristwatches and gold crucifixes once owned by Sarah Bernhardt and The Duse and copies of the *Complete Works* signed by Ellen Terry but never so much as a Christmas card arrived for her from Melchior, as though it had been *her* fault they split up.

As the Lady A. grew older, so she looked more and more British. Her features became more transparent, her expression ever more modestly valiant. She started to wear cardigans. She'd begun to look sad even before the war broke out; sadness became her, like pastel shades. She developed a reputation for sadness in spite of, or perhaps because of, her indomitable smile, real Mrs Miniver smile.

That farmhouse was lovely. Mellow brick, lichened tile, nestling in a Down, the vista rimmed with English Channel. There was a little walled orchard with lambs in it. I always think of that orchard in early spring, primroses among the roots of the apple trees, first buds, blue smoke rising from the chimney and Nor' and me getting out of the village taxi, red morocco heels, mud.

I've never been so cold in all my life as in that farmhouse. Cold and scared. Not even in air-raid shelters. At night, we'd huddle up in our cold bed with our silver-fox trenches spread out on top of the quilts for extra warmth, bruising our toes on the stone hot-water bottles Old Nanny had tucked in for our comfort, watching the moonlight through the lattice, listening to night-birds hoot and shrieks of mice and voles when owls pounced. Things were killing one another all around. We were stiff with cold and frozen with terror. Give me Railton Road at half past Saturday midnight, any time.

To tell the truth, picturesque and evocative as that farmhouse was, we only went down there because we were fond of her.

She'd put us up in the one bed, in always the same whitewashed room, Old Nanny used it as a sewing room – iron bedstead, pitch-pine washstand and a dressmaker's dummy which cast a headless shadow that gave me the willies. I'll draw a veil over the bathroom, with the iron tub that formed an informal vivarium for every spider in Sussex. We never ventured into the darling buds' room but the Lady A.'s was a shrine to Guess Who, all the photographs of him, plus one, just one, of Perry, snapped drawing Saskia out of a top hat. There was a steep staircase of narrow steps of polished oak – the Lady A. wouldn't have carpeting, she said she loved the living wood – down which Nora and I would pick and slither, fully aware that Saskia and Imogen, if they were home, were laughing at our shoes.

A big Chinese bowl full of pot-pourri on a worm-eaten oak chest in the hall gave out a sad, pungent smell of old ladies and heartbreak. There were watercolours everywhere perpetrated by Lyndes of long ago in Venice, the Alps, the lakes; faded chintz; old rugs worn to a web. Everywhere a threadbare, expensive shabbiness that had a class to which we knew we never could aspire. Not the Lucky Chances. We were doomed to either flash or squalor.

The food was nothing much. We lived in hopes she'd get the East Sussex black market organized but Old Nanny always asked us to be sure to bring our coupons and served up cottage pie, shepherd's pie, nothing ever looked like whatever it was made of although the plates were Chelsea and the knives and forks were silver, knobbed, blackened, engraved with the Lynde seal, a pelican pecking at its breast. Rotten food. All the same, we were still nervous as to which ancestral fork to use.

And always bloody freezing, not just in bed. We'd sit at table in our fur coats in spite of the satirical gaze of Saskia and Imogen in their ballerina-length dirndls, turtlenecks and inherited upper-class capacity to withstand extremes of temperature. No love lost, and they could scarcely abide to see we'd got our feet under the table, at last, not now that they'd been abandoned, too. So when the Lady A. said, could we possibly come down for Saskia and Imogen's twenty-first, Nora said satirically: 'Go on!'

'No, truly, my dears,' said the Lady A. 'I want you both to be there.' Then she twinkled, just a little, but it was a rare sight these days and I was glad to see it. 'It'll be a real family affair!'

A nod is as good as a wink. We'd not seen hair nor hide of Perry since VJ Day, except a postcard from Rio de Janeiro showing a macaw, but I knew the Lady A. still kept a soft spot for him after all these years and I'd even hoped that she and Perry might make a go of it, one fine day. I taxed her with it, once, when we were having Lapsang in the orchard. It was May and the apple blossom was out but, all the same, I kept my coat on.

'Don't you ever miss Perry?' I asked her tactfully.

She had the grace to twinkle right up at the very thought of him but she twinkled dismissively.

'One doesn't *marry* a man like that, my dear,' she said. Faded blue eyes, broken veins, a straw hat tied under her chin with a silk paisley scarf. The dowager sheep. But she knew a thing or two about Perry. Here today and gone tomorrow, not so much a man, more of a travelling carnival. I warmed my fingers on her china cup, since I had no option – it didn't have a handle, although it *did* have a big crack down the side – and wondered if my own mother had thought the same thing about Melchior, that he was splendid over the short haul but would never go the distance.

My feeling was, neither of the brothers were built to be good husbands. But I didn't say a word. A lot was left unsaid at the Lady A.'s. I've never known such profound silences as those Lynde silences especially when her daughters were there, silences in which the unspoken hung like fog that got into your lungs and choked you.

'God knows why we keep on going down there, anyway,' said Nora. 'We could stay up here on a Sunday, have a bath, do our hair.'

She hadn't the slightest desire to grace the darling buds' twenty-first, not she. Perry can come to us, she said. She was adamant. 'No! No! And no!' Then our Uncle Perry called us up and said he'd drive us down, we could be back to Brixton that same night.

'But not birthday presents,' said Nora. 'Not for those vipers. I draw the line at birthday presents.'

Because we were going down exclusively for the Lady A.'s sake, weren't we? We took *her* a bottle of Scotch. So there was Peregrine, blowing the horn outside in Bard Road in a bloody great Bentley convertible ready to take us to Lynde Court Home Farm for the worst Sunday lunch of our lives.

'Sorry I'm late,' he said. 'I slipped in a quick visit to a friend in Gunter Grove.' Big wink, the reprobate. But it was only twenty minutes.

Perry was bigger than ever and brown as a berry from the Brazilian sun and you'd never have believed, from the cut of his jib, that he'd turned sixty, nor that his twin brother was just at the time rehearsing *Lear*. Not one grey hair in all that russet mop, nor yet a crow's-foot among the freckles, and as full of bounce and bonhomie as when he first knocked on the front door. Of course, his fortunes had turned, again, since he struck oil.

Yes. Oil. That bit of semi-arid scrub he'd bought out of sentiment with his money from *The Dream*, his ranch in Hazard, Texas. Oil. He was filthy rich again and the back of the Bentley was stacked with cans and packages and bottles, most with labels from Rio, Paris and New York, I was glad to see, because, back here in Brixton, it was still half a rasher of bacon a week, a little pat of butter, that was your lot, that was rationing.

He sat and beeped the horn and there was a general rustle of net curtains all along Bard Road as the old biddies sneaked a peek at our escort.

He gave us the biggest hugs and kisses but he wasn't his usual self, I could tell. It was my turn to sit in front and he was all of a twitter, nervous, joyful, on edge, abstracted, all at once. He jumped red lights; the speedometer touched ninety, once, and when he braked to miss a fox, Nora, in the back with a box of Belgian chox, shot forward, got her nose stuck in a violet cream. Sometimes he broke into snatches of song; sometimes he did not hear a question and needed his arm tugged. After a few miles, Nora and I maintained a sympathetic silence. 'Hope for the best, expect the worst.' I knew in my water there'd be tears before bedtime so I crossed my fingers and so did Nora because we didn't want the old devil's feelings hurt, nor those of the Lady A., either, this day of all days, but I couldn't see how else the day might end.

Of course, we'd always known deep down inside he was their father. We tried to pretend otherwise. I was jealous as hell of it, but there you are. Biology is biology. You can't fool a sperm. I'm not sure that Melchior ever knew. If 'his' daughters were redheads, then so had his own mother been and, besides, who'd have thought it of the Lady A., Caesar's wife in person? Perhaps those girls themselves smelled a rat and were unhappy; you might put all the bad behaviour down to that, if you felt so inclined, though you wouldn't have felt half so magnanimous if you'd met them.

Streatham, Norbury, Thornton Heath, Croydon. Nora had eaten all her chocolates by Redhill and said she was lonely in the back so she climbed over the seat and inserted herself between us. He'd brought the sunshine with him, we put the hood down and sang: 'Please direct your feet To the sunny sunny sunny side of the street.' He perked up. We were still girls, only just past thirty; we cut a dash, the three of us. Little did we know it was to be our last ride together.

He started to open up a bit by the time we got to Three Bridges and told us about Brazil. That was his new enthusiasm, the jungle and its denizens. He was going to give a lecture at the Royal Society, wasn't he, about the butterflies he'd discovered in the jungle and after he'd given this lecture he was going to go right back and look for more.

'I'm going,' he announced grandly, 'to devote the rest of my life to lepidoptera.'

We raised our brows at one another. Another fad. Like conjuring. Like movies. Like oil. Like espionage. How soon would he reach his boredom threshold in the jungle? We didn't know, we never could have guessed, that he would reach oblivion first.

Saskia, it turned out, was doing the honours in the kitchen. She'd just, that winter, made her first appearance on any stage in one of her father's productions, a witch in *Macbeth*, typecasting, along with her velvet-slacked best friend, but she'd shown more interest in the contents of her cauldron than her name in lights and so it came to pass that her best friend, the RADA Gold Medal winner, was picked out to play as Melchior's Cordelia, while Saskia tinkered with the pans.

She's ended up as television's top cook, of course. Every time I switch on the set there she is, eviscerating something, skinning something else, having a go at some harmless piece of meat with her little chopper.

Old Nanny had been banished from the kitchen and Saskia was catering her own lunch party, trying out a roast duck and green peas, and the Lady A., not of the class or generation that cooked, itself, was nevertheless doing her fumbling, incompetent best to help, because it was the girls' birthday, and Old Nanny was sitting in the orchard in a deck-chair with her feet up and a copy of *Tatler* and *that* was Old Nanny's treat, before she stirred her stumps to serve up. Even Imogen had roused herself and was out in the garden laying the table because they'd decided to eat outside since it was such a lovely day and Imogen was weighing the napkins down with pebbles so they wouldn't blow away. There was a bunch of pinks in a glass jar in the middle of the starched white cloth under an arbour of old-fashioned roses and the lilacs were out, the Lady Attie's famous white lilacs, that featured in *Country Life*, once.

As we drew up, I saw a Roller, parked already, and was overcome with that indigestible mix of emotions I always felt each time that he came near me – joy, terror, heartsick, lovesick. The white lilacs didn't help. That perfume. I felt as if someone had taken hold of my heart and squeezed it.

There was a grey wing over each ear; our father had aged more evidently than his brother, but very graciously. We were all a little frigid with one another, at first, although the Lady A. was twinkling away valiantly, but Perry popped a cork and we drank a toast: 'To the girls!' before we sat down and I joined in, much as I disliked them, and so did Nora, because, however randomly we'd been assembled, we were all family, and they were the only family we had. After the second bottle, things began to thaw, a bit.

Soup. Old Nanny was now pressed back into service and bore a steaming tureen out of the kitchen, more proud of Saskia's handiwork than she'd ever been of her own, so we had some of that, to start with, a nettle soup Saskia had discovered in an old book, or so she said. An old, Elizabethan soup. Perhaps Shakespeare had eaten just such a soup! When she said that, she gave her 'father' a special smile, she and Imogen worshipped the ground, etc. etc. etc. Shakespeare may well have eaten that filthy soup but I doubt he'd kept it down. I forced in a spoon or two out of politeness and it was very, very bitter, but the men, foolish fond, drank it all and Perry asked for seconds.

Then the duck came in, swimming in blood. I gagged, had a spot more champagne, to fortify myself, picked out, for my share, the merest sliver of blackened skin – that duck was certainly well-cooked on the outside – but the peas, when I helped myself, bounced off the server and Saskia gave me a dirty look, as if she'd known I'd show my true colours at some point during her elegant repast so, to spite her, I scooped the peas up and ate them with my pudding spoon. But the men finished off that duck between them, engaging in a battle as to who could eat most and praise her best although I was racked with hunger and heartburn until it occurred to me: 'Has she done it on purpose?' A poison meat! Her face gave nothing away, calm and oval as a cake of soap.

She'd done her hair up in a huge, soft chignon. If only we'd inherited that red, red hair. We were still brunettes, at that time, but permed by then, of course. Poodle-cuts. She'd got on a twin-set of heather-coloured wool and pearls but Imogen, always the fey one, had 'dressed up to match the Downs around us', she simpered, in an eighteenth-century shepherdess's dress, complete with crook with a blue bow on it. Happily, I saw no sign about her person of her pet white rat, although it said in the William Hickey column she never went anywhere without it.

'Delicious, darling,' said the Lady A. 'Clever Saskia!' But she ate like a bird, herself.

It was a peculiar meal. The ugly food, the flies, and little stinging creatures and ants crawling up your leg – all the discomfort of eating in the garden – and the precarious peace among the Hazard clan all gave the occasion a special flavour, sweet and sour, like Chinese pork. After we'd toyed with a disgusting syllabub, came a cake, ordered from Harrods, thank God, with twenty-one candles. They blew, we clapped. Perry brushed his eyes with his hands and I saw that he was on the verge of tears.

I never thought what it might be to be a father until that moment, when I saw Perry almost cry. Yet, truly, I think he loved Nora and myself as much as he loved Saskia and Imogen, if not more. But not, you understand, in the *same way.* We were not flesh of his flesh.

But then, again, a person *isn't* flesh of its father's flesh, is it? One little sperm out of millions swims up the cervix and it is so very, very easy to forget how it has happened. And Melchior, whose flesh we were, or, rather, whose emission sparked off our being, felt for us only occasional pity and now and then a vague affection that seemed to puzzle him as to the cause. But he was head over heels in love with Saskia and Imogen, too, and when they blew out their birthday candles, I saw his eyes were moist, as well.

I wished we'd come by train and got a taxi from the station, as per usual. Then we could have buzzed off, pronto. As it was, we'd have to stay until Perry was good and ready to depart, which might be hours.

Then the Lady A. rapped her glass with her knife and said that Peregrine wanted to give a little speech. He got up on his feet, his face an April study of joy and sadness, as Irish might have put it, and he said:

'My lovely girls, all four of you' – his eyes crinkled round the edges as he raised his glass in our direction, but Saskia looked daggers – 'I can't tell you how much it means to this old sinner to be among you all on the day you two precious copperknobs finally reach your majorities, key of the door, licence to marry . . . but don't rush off and marry too quickly, dearest ones, and leave us all lonely.'

They smirked.

'It was tough, I can tell you, to think of a present fine enough for you two on this day of days. I cast around in my mind for a long time, I furrowed this old brow. Not baubles, or bangles, or beads, but something that would last, something as beautiful as you both that would go on for ever. So . . . here you are, with all my love.'

His eyes were swimming, now, as he took from each jacket pocket a wrapped box just diamond bracelet size. They smirked in pleasurable anticipation.

'Look what's inside, my darlings!'

He watched expectantly as they tore off the wrappings. The boxes were of metal, it turned out, with little holes drilled in the top. Curiouser and curiouser. Imogen got hers open first, peered in, then gave a little scream and dropped it. Saskia looked at hers and said: 'Good God!'

Inside each box was a little nest of leaves and, inside the nest, a caterpillar.

'Named after you,' said Peregrine. 'Saskia Hazard. Imogen Hazard. Two of the most beautiful butterflies in all the rainforest. You'll go down in all the textbooks. As long as people love butterflies, your names will be on their lips, you'll have a kind of beautiful eternity. They are rare species, just like you both.'

Saskia and Imogen stared blankly at their boxes. No doubt they'd hoped for a little oil well each.

'Is that all?' said Imogen. She poked the caterpillar with her fork. It did not stir. 'I think mine's dead,' she said.

Saskia snapped her box shut and dropped it on the table.

'Thanks a lot,' she said, with heavy irony.

Peregrine's face crumpled. All at once he looked his age. More. He looked a hundred. He looked a hundred and ten. And he deflated. Instantly, within his suit, as if somebody had stuck a pin in him and let the energy out. Perhaps Melchior was fond of him, after all, in his way; anyway, he hurried up to smooth things over. He got up, too, and raised his glass.

'To your birthdays, my darling buds of May!' We all knocked back another glass and then he said: 'I, too, have prepared a very special present for my best beloved daughters . . . a new – '

Such timing. All eyes were upon him.

' – stepmother!'

Then, oh! was I glad I'd come, all right! What a picture! Their jaws flew open, their eyes popped out. Imogen let out a wail. Saskia rose up and seized the cake knife. Her chignon unravelled. Red snakes of hair flew out around her head while hairpins rattled down like hail.

'What's this?'

Melchior stood his ground.

'I'm going to marry my Cordelia,' he said, tenderly. His tongue caressed the 'I' and rolled it round.

'Your Cordelia,' repeated Saskia flatly. Her rage departed her, replaced by amazement. She let the cake knife drop. 'Your Cordelia!'

'Your Cordelia!' echoed Imogen, a beat behind. 'But your Cordelia is – '

' – is my best friend!' wailed Saskia.

And so she was. The RADA Gold Medallist, plucked from obscurity to play against Melchior's Lear and now to marry him, in spite of the horrid shadow that a superstitious person might have seen cast over them by the union of Ranulph Hazard and Estella Ranelagh, which also kicked off with such a May/December union and ended in tears both before, after and during bedtime. At least Melchior hadn't tucked Cordelia into the boot and brought her along to show her off at this psychologically inappropriate moment but he must have realized what a bombshell his news would be. Even the Lady A. looked green around the gills but Perry lightened up wonderfully and clapped his brother on the shoulder.

'No fool like an old fool!' he bellowed.

'Why,' gritted Saskia between her teeth, 'that scheming little bitch, I'll – '

'Oh, Saskia, Saskia,' said the Lady A. 'Don't stand in the way of your father's last chance of happiness – '

Saskia picked up the birthday cake on its plate and pitched it against an apple tree. It shattered. Crumbs and candles scattered everywhere. Then she started to break the pots, throwing the dessert plates on the ground and stamping on them. Imogen, giggling in a febrile manner, laid about her smashing glasses with her ribboned crook, sparing nothing. When he saw his caterpillars reduced to pulp, Perry gave a piteous whimper. The Lady A., apprehending carnage among her heritage tableware, started to wring her hands and ululate while Saskia's wails approached hysteria, whereupon Melchior smartly smacked her cheek, the way they do in the movies.

'Stop that, young lady!'

She shut up at once, put her hand to her cheek, stared at him incredulously with her blue Lynde eyes. Then, tears. He took her in his arms, murmuring, 'Hush, hush, darling.' She shook him off and flounced into the house, slamming the door behind her, followed a minute or two later by Imogen, except that Imogen had to open the door her sister had just slammed before she could slam it herself. The rest of us were left staring at one another across the broken crockery and I never felt more spare in all my life and neither did Nora. We got up in unison.

'I'm going to call a bloody taxi,' I said. 'I've had enough of this.'

'Don't go before you've had coffee,' said the Lady A. heroically but Perry was pushing back his wicker chair so peremptorily it fell over, briefly trapping beneath it a small, yapping dog, probably a Yorkshire terrier.

'I'm off, too,' he announced. 'Back to the jungle. Now. This minute. I'll look forward to the company of crocodiles, after the bosom of my family.'

We found the bottle of Scotch we'd planned to give the Lady A. rolling around forgotten in the back of the car so we drew up on a verge and passed it round. Perry looked like the picture of Dorian Gray, I'm sorry to say, a ghastly sight. The sky closed in, the sun disappeared and all was cold and grey as we went home.

'And yet I love them,' he said. 'God, I love them. That's my punishment, isn't it? My crime is my punishment.'

He wouldn't come in with us. He sat in the car and watched us climb the steps with a face a mile long. We turned and blew him kisses and waved goodbye but he didn't budge. Finally we were so chilled we went inside and closed the door. I had a premonition: 'We won't see him again.' His hair was still bright, foxy red. It was twilight, the lamps just coming on. There he sat, in that grand car that was about to bear him off on his last journey.

We peered out between the curtains and watched him draw away, at last, into the dusk. He went back to his rooms in the Albany and packed a bag. He cancelled his lecture at the Royal Society; he left for Southampton that very night, he was good as his word. After the Lady A.'s accident, we tried the police. We even tried Interpol. They couldn't find him, he was travelling incognito, he'd erased himself.

That was that.

If he babbled of green fields in Cuzco or Iquitos, we never heard.

Our footsteps echoed in the hall of 49 Bard Road with an inconsolable sound. 'Empty,' the echoes said. 'Empty.'

'They should have made a go of it,' Nora said. 'In spite of everything.'

'She told me once, "One doesn't marry a man like that!"'

'I didn't mean him and the Lady A. I meant him and Grandma.'

Nora had the forethought to bring the Scotch in with her and though never my favourite tipple, any port in a storm. We put on the electric fire in the front room and had a couple and got the gramophone going and after we'd rolled the rug back we dug out all the golden oldies, the old favourites, Jessie, Binnie, 'I'll See You Again', even though we never thought we never would see him again, and the scratched and faded ones, songs about the harbour lights and parting, dolefully prophetic, did we but know it, and the 'baby songs' such as 'Is You Is or Is You Ain't', and finally we found at the bottom of the stack the very first one of all, the one he brought us all those years ago when we first found out what joy it was to sing and dance, 'I Can't Give You Anything but Love'.

We were singing and dancing and loud music playing and both of us a touch tiddly when the phone rang and it was the Lady A.'s Old Nanny and so it came to pass, in the fullness of time, that the Lady A. moved into the front basement minus the use of her legs, because what Nanny had to tell us was, the Lady A. had taken a tumble down those very shiny and uncarpeted stairs we'd warned her about so often, come cracking on her bum to land on the stone flags in the hall and so jarred, snagged or dislocated her spine that she'd never walk again, but we didn't know that, then, only that the Lady A. had gone arse over tip and Old Nanny didn't know which way to turn.

'Have you called the ambulance?'

She'd had the presence of mind to do that, at least.

'What about Saskia and Imogen?'

She burst into such a harangue I couldn't make out one word and had to hold the receiver some distance from my ear, the noise was causing me such distress. But when I finally got the gist, I scarcely could believe it, because it turned out they'd buggered off.

It seemed that Melchior had left them shortly after we did, under a cloud, and the Lady A. had taken to her bed, emotionally prostrate. Old Nanny, doing the washing-up, crouched over a sinkful of dishes, heard raised voices in the room above and then a godalmighty crash, bang, wallop! and she went flying out of the kitchen with the drying-up cloth in her hand to find the Lady A. moaning in her Viyella nightie all of a heap at the stairfoot.

Then the girls came flying down the stairs, both of them clutching kit-bags, carriers, pillowslips, bulging with this and that, and pushed Old Nanny brusquely aside, off into the night they went. They hiked down to the village in their little flatties and knocked up the baker who, out of a brute feudal loyalty to the Lynde clan and their kin, drove them to the station in the bread van, unaware of the terrible accident that had just occurred back at Lynde Court Home Farm.

Did she fall or was she pushed? That was the question. But not a word, not a whisper upon the subject ever wormed its way through the Lady A.'s stiff upper lip. If ever we raised it, even if everso tactfully, she would look teddibly, teddibly British and, quietly but firmly, change the subject. But I *do* know those dreadful girls had just made her sign the Home Farm over to them both, plus all that remained of her last bit of capital, before she took her tumble. We couldn't help but be aware of that because now she hadn't got a penny to bless herself, and nowhere to go, either.

Peregrine was gone. I called my father but it turned out he was overnighting at his fiancée's basement flat in Gunter Grove, so no joy there, either. The Lady A. lay flat on her back in Lewes General Hospital with one tear trickling out of the corner of her left eye, enough to break your heart.

And that was how we came to inherit the Lady A., though she's no trouble, really, even if she used to thump on the ceiling with the head of her silver-knobbed cane: 'Stop that racket immediately!' during the one, two, three, hop! days of the Brixton Academy of Dance.

She used to babysit our little Tiff, too, when she was a toddler. She used to sing her a lullaby, about horses, all the pretty little horses. 'Sing', I say; more of a tuneless hum, but Tiff went to sleep, anyway. She taught her how to cross-stitch, though I can't say it's a talent Tiff's ever used.

And the unrighteous prospered.

I always thought Saskia's fame was to do, mostly, with the back of her neck. She had a lovely nape, on which that knot of scarlet hair sat like a Rhode Island red on a clutch and her nape was on display in all she did, intimate, exposed and sexy as she bent over the stove to poke around with a spoon suggestively in a pot or stick a prong into a drumstick with quite sadistic glee. I never saw anything so rude as her TV shows, not even Gorgeous George at the Royal Variety Performance.

We watched her jug a hare, once, on television, years ago, when she was just getting into her stride. She cut the thing up with slow, voluptuous strokes. 'Make sure your blade is up to it!' she husked, running her finger up and down the edge, although the spectacle of Saskia with a cleaver couldn't help but remind me and Nora of how she'd run amok with the cake knife on her twenty-first. Next, she lovingly prepared a bath for the hare, she minced up shallots, garlic, onions, added a bouquet garni and a pint of claret and sat the poor dismembered beast in that for a day and a half. Then she condescended to sauté the parts briskly in a hot pan over a high flame until they singed. Then it all went into the oven for the best part of another day. She sealed the lid of the pot with a flour-and-water paste. 'Don't be a naughty thing and peek!' she warned with a teasing wink. Time to decant at last! The hare had been half-rotted, then cremated, then consumed. If there is a god and she is of the rabbit family, then Saskia will be in deep doodoo on Judgment Day. 'Delicious,' she moaned, dipping her finger in the juice and sucking. She licked her lips, letting her pink tongue-tip linger. 'Mmmm . . .'

As we watched this genuinely disgusting transmission, the ghost of Grandma manifested itself in a sharp blast of cabbage. When we saw what Saskia did to that hare, we knew that we did wrong by eating meat.

Why do we go on doing it, then? I'll tell you straight. We're scared that, if we eat too much salad, one fine day, we'll find we've turned into Grandma.

Saskia jugged a hare for Tristram, once, that cooked his goose. She was living in a bijou houselet in Chelsea, in those days, penning the occasional article for *Harper's Bazaar.* ('Eel . . . oh, curvaceous, curvilinear, cursive denizen of the deep!' and etc. etc. etc.) She must have thought long and hard as to how to revenge herself upon the third Lady Hazard for taking away her father and finally she wrote to little Tristram, then only a lad, at Bedales, hinting at Hazard mysteries to which only she, Saskia, held the key. God knows what she wrote or promised, who can tell; or whether he came ringing her doorbell on his half-term holiday out of prurience or duty, but she had his bondage trousers off before you could say *crème renversée*, although she was old enough to be his mother.

In fact, exactly the same age as his mother and now she felt she'd evened scores and she and My Lady Margarine made friends, again, and once even did a ketchup commercial together but Saskia never forgave a grudge and, when we ran into one another, which we did now and again, at the stocking counter in Peter Jones' store, once, another time waiting for a taxi in Sloane Square, I could tell from the look in her Lynde-blue eye that when she saw me she still thought of only one thing: 'Cascara evacuant'.

She was revenged upon her father's wife, and on her father, too. The twins never forgave him for cutting off their allowances. Old Nanny told us how he'd given the girls this glad news after we left, that afternoon of their twenty-first. Cool as you please, he'd told them he couldn't afford to support two families and now the girls were old enough to earn their keep, he'd see they got nice jobs. As they sat gaping, he assured them they weren't losing a friend but gaining a mother and then it came on to rain so he hopped in his Roller and was off while they were still stunned with shock, before they had a chance to berate him. And that was the root cause, according to Old Nanny, of the dreadful quarrel over funds that transformed the whilom Lady A. into our Wheelchair and left her homeless, penniless, reliant on the left-hand line.

Old Nanny told us everything, of course. She went on telling us everything even after she moved in with Melchior to raise little Tristram and little Gareth. What else could she do, poor old cow, she was stuck. The Lady A. hadn't the cash to keep her, now, and what would *we* have done with an Old Nanny clicking her tongue against her teeth when she saw the gin bottles in the wastepaper basket and the condoms in the toilet?

Though, alas, the little rubber swimmers sadly declined in numbers during the sixties and dropped off altogether in the subsequent decade, which was nothing to do with the Pill, everything to do with lack of opportunity.

Old Nanny often picked up the 137 bus in Camden Town and popped over the river and when she told us the news about Saskia and Tristram, the Lady A. dropped her embroidery frame with a shocked squeak. He was a babe, just seventeen, in those days, while Saskia had pushed forty aside some time before and was now steering towards her climacteric. Yet it wasn't the May and December aspect of their union that affected us so much, we were quite French about that; it was that we all knew Saskia. Old Nanny had reservations of her own, however.

'Prohibited degrees,' said Old Nanny. She was drinking a cup of tea. I noticed how she always drank her tea from the wrong side of the cup, in our house. Admittedly, Nora was a careless washer-up, especially after sundown, but Old Nanny never went to the lavatory in our house, either, not even when you could tell she was busting for a wee. I wondered, are we letting standards slip?

'Prohibited degrees.'

'Cheer up, Nana. Remember, Melchior's not her – '

But Wheelchair put her finger to her lips because Old Nanny wasn't supposed to know. (Although she *did* know, of course; she it was who personally confirmed our worst suspicions, years ago. But Wheelchair never knew she knew and thought she ought to keep it from the servants.)

'But, then,' said Nora, 'perhaps Perry – '

Why hadn't we thought of it before? The wicked old man! 'Just been visiting a friend in Gunter Grove', indeed! But how had he met My Lady Margarine and why had they done it? Was Peregrine bent on perpetrating the Hazard tradition of disputed paternity even unto the bitter end? But none of us had any means of checking out the theory, since Peregrine was gone, and only Old Nanny on speaking terms with the third Lady H., and she wasn't intimate, so we could only speculate, thus: that Tristram was red as fire, in the mould of Peregrine and of poor, passionate, murdered Estella, while gaunt and hollow-eyed Gareth had raven hair and Bovril eyes – the boys, in fact, the duplicates of Peregrine and Melchior themselves; in person, at least, though not in personality. So who had been the master of ceremonies was anybody's guess.

Not that we'd ever met Gareth. He was a mystery. He converted when he was seventeen, found God the same time Tristram discovered sex, and departed to a seminary shortly after. Never a word from that department, not a letter nor a Christmas card, for the actor and the priest might have a good deal in common but the Jesuit and the chorus girl, outside lewd jest, not.

Perhaps that Saskia put something in young Tristram's food, some love potion she'd got out of the same old book in which she found that emetic Shakespearian nettle soup we'd had on her birthday. Back he went to her, back and back and back. It remained a deadly secret outside the family, of course. He boasted a wide variety of official girlfriends, of whom our little Tiffany had the highest profile, headlines in the *News of the World*, and, do you know, I think he really loved her.

Love. What is love? What do I mean by love? For a while he wanted her nearby. But it turned out she was not sufficient to break him of the Saskia habit, even if Saskia was sixty if she was a day. His sexuagenarian mistress. Saskia, the sexy sexuagenarian.

'Come off it, Dor', you wouldn't have said no to a chap when you were sixty, if you'd had any offers,' reproved Nora. She thought I was jealous.

Perhaps I am.

Saskia.

But Wheelchair grieved about it, too, and all the more because her daughters had now maintained their radical indifference to her for well-nigh forty years and she thought she'd snuff it without another sight of them, so we knew we'd have to take her with us when the invitation to our father's birthday party came at last, even if she wasn't on the official list, and this is just what we are about to do, as soon as we've got ourselves suitably tarted up.

'What shall we wear tonight?' said Nora.

No problem for Wheelchair. She'd got a lovely Norman Hartnell gown left over from the forties we could still fork her into, she ate like a sparrow, she never put on a milligram. White satin bodice, tulle skirt, which we would fluff up so as to conceal her carriage. Pearls. Her daughters robbed her blind, stuffing pillowslips with bibelots, but they'd refrained from snatching the pearls off her neck. We gave her a bath with her favourite Floris's Tuberoses poured in. What a business that bath was! Nora took one arm, I took the other, we lowered her. Nora scrubbed her back with a flannel. Then we wrapped her up in a big, soft towel and Nora did her hair.

'You're very good to me,' said Wheelchair with a suspicious quiver.

'Pipe down, you old bag,' said Nora. You've got to be firm with her, or else she cries. We dusted her with talc, tucked her in a rug and left her in the kitchen with the fire on and a fresh pot of tea, watching *Brief Encounter* on afternoon television. We had to wait for the water to heat up again until we could have our own baths. I picked up a scent bottle and inhaled nostalgia.

'Tell you what,' I said to Nora. 'You put on some Shalimar, tonight; I'll use Mitsouko.'

'Quite like old times,' she said with a glint.

'Don't let's exaggerate.'

Because here was a couple of scraggy hags about to ease into frocks that first saw light about the year our Tiff was born, for we had bought no evening wear since then, having no need for it in middle age; and it was our little Tiff who'd brought us our lovely scent, for old times' sake, bless her little heart, got it for us from the duty-free when Tristram took her to Tuscany for a week.

That was an ill-fated trip. Although he *must* have loved her, for a little while, at least, because she was the first girl he was ever brave enough to take to visit Saskia.

Saskia's villa was perched on a hill between Florence and Siena, among the fields of Chianti, pine trees up the drive, you know the kind of thing. You may even have seen it featuring in her bloody programme. She wrote it off against her taxes because she'd done a series there, *In Bocca Toscana*. I caught it once, repeated in the afternoons, I was housebound with a stinking cold, there was Saskia, caressing a ham. 'Lucky the porkers of Parma!' she intoned. 'They dine every day on curds and whey, like so many little Miss Muffets, and posthumously achieve porcine apotheosis – prosciutto!'

I questioned Tiff closely when they got back and she rabbited on about ripe figs and fresh basil for a while before she admitted she'd been incapacitated with the runs for the greater part of their stay, confined to bed in the spacious room with the tiled floor and view of vineyards, her only entertainment a stack of Saskia's videos, which she'd been forced to watch endlessly, not being of a reading temperament, but which had given her so much confidence, although she'd never even boiled an egg before, that she proposed fixing for us, then and there, a spaghetti *carbonara*, only we said, no way.

These gastric disorders sounded to me as though Saskia had slipped a little something extra into the *trippa fiorentina*, but, all the same, Saskia had been sufficiently polite to this unexpected wee scrap as to arouse my suspicions, because she was a snob and a half, ordinarily. But Tiffany suspected nothing and was over the moon. 'His family has started to accept me! See how his aunt has taken me to her bosom!'

Bosom of flint. Tiff didn't know, how could she, that a history existed already between Tristram and that woman and I must admit she was good-looking, still, had always been good-looking, with that pale skin and red hair, even if she always had to paint in her eyebrows and eyelashes. Half the drama went out of her appearance once she'd had a good wash. But little Tiff looked best of all with no make-up on, with her hair just hanging down her back and –

– and there I go, again, thinking of little Tiff when it behooves the Chance girls to put on their brightest smiles, check out their wardrobes for their smartest gowns, and celebrate their father's centenary.

* * *

I thought, there must be something upstairs we can wear because we've never thrown a stitch away but stowed the old schmutter in Grandma's room, the big first-floor front with the bay window, the best room in the house, although neither of us had the heart to take it over and move in after she went, so all her old stuff was still there, too.

It was perishing cold in Grandma's bedroom and gloaming, only the one forty-watt bulb, but I didn't want to open the curtains, as if the light might scare away the smell of mothballs, boiled cabbage and gin hanging in the air, by which we liked to think she made her posthumous presence felt. Her photos were still lined up on the mantelpiece. Peregrine in pride of place, in the middle, in his conjuring suit, with a dove perched on every plane surface, like a statue in a public square, and a smile you could warm your hands on, even though it was a photograph and he was dead. Lots of pix of us, stark naked in babyhood in the backyard with, if you looked carefully, a neighbour at once outraged and prurient peering through the fence. As baby sparrows in our very first panto, when we were half-pints. In black tights and blonde bobbed wigs from *What! You Will!* Even a still of Peaseblossom and Mustardseed, all moonlit in the wood, and a lovely snap from the Forest of Arden, partying it around the pool, with Peregrine. In sailors' hats, as forces' sweethearts. Always the two of us, together, forever young on Grandma's mantelpiece.

She never liked that portrait Cecil Beaton did for *Vogue*, she always kept it in the dressing-table drawer. He'd done us up as painted dolls, rouged spots on our cheeks and terrible artificial grins, sitting on the floor in frills with our legs at angles, as if they were made of wood. Rich men's playthings. Very subtle. His Nanny used to hold the flash, you know.

Our Cyn was on the mantelpiece, on her wedding day; Our Cyn with one, two, three, in arms and various stages of toddlerhood; I was glad Grandma went before the Asian flu took Cynthia in '49, she never wanted to outlive any of us.

And there was her enormous bed she never shared, to my knowledge, all the time we knew her except, towards the end, with the occasional cat. Her bed, stripped, the naked pillows huddled like a corpse. We felt we ought to hush and tiptoe.

As we opened up the wardrobe, we saw ourselves swimming in the mirrored door as if in a pool of dust and, for a split second, in soft focus, we truly looked like girls, again. And going through those cast-offs was a trip down Memory Lane and a half, I can tell you. First, there was the lingerie – silk, satin, lace, eau de nil, blush rose, flesh, black and red ribbons, straight up and down things from the twenties, slithering things from the thirties, curvy things from the forties, waspies, merry widows, uplift bras. At the very bottom of the pile, I seized on something navy blue – the bloomers from our dancing class! From Miss Worthington's dancing class! To think that Grandma had kept our old bloomers!

Then there were the frocks. Some things we'd put away in plastic bags: bias-cut silk jersey, beaded sheaths that weighed a ton. Others we'd covered up with sheets, the big net skirts, the taffeta crinolines, halter necks, strapless, backless, etc. etc. etc., all heaped high on Grandma's bed.

'Half a century of evening wear,' said Nora. 'A history of the world in party frocks.'

'We ought to donate it to the V and A,' I said.

'Why should somebody pay good money to look at my old clothes?'

'They used to pay to see you without them.'

'They ought put *us* into a museum.'

'We ought to turn this house into a museum.'

'Museum of dust.'

Nora rummaged among the rags and gave a soft little chuckle. She held up a foamy white georgette number with crystal beads.

'The Super-Chief!' she said. 'Remember?'

'"She wore something sheer and white and deceptively virginal, that emitted a hard glitter when she moved, a subtle, ambiguous cobweb softness veined with a secret of ice. 'Got a light?' Half trusting, half insolent, a hoarse voice, older than that pale face with its purple heart of lipstick, flourishing its rasp of gutter like a flag, with pride."' I for Irish, Ross 'Irish' O'Flaherty. *Hollywood Elegies*. The very frock! He never knew I'd borrowed it from Daisy.

'Why don't you sell it to that library in Texas? I read in the paper they bought a crate of his empties.'

But I'd spotted an ambivalent memento of hers, to tease her with.

'Here, Nora . . . I never knew you kept this.'

'Gimme!'

She snatched it out of my hands, the veil they'd brought out of wardrobe on *The Dream* set for her to marry Tony in.

'The bastard,' she said. 'I hope he's six feet deep in concrete.'

She stuffed the veil out of sight under her air-raid warden's siren suit and something chiffon slithered to the floor.

'Dora? Remember this?'

She held it up. Floral print, big splashy roses, rhodies, peonies, muted tones, dusky pinks, soft mauves, lavender. I pressed it to my face, it was as soft as dust. First kiss, first love, eyes as blue as sugar paper and skin like cream.

'I pray you, love, remember.'

He never came back from the Burma Road. Some comic told me, backstage, *Nude Frolics* '52, in Sheffield.

'Here, Dora, nothing to cry about.'

'Do *you* remember his name?'

She asked me, whose name, with her eyebrows.

'You gave me a present the day we were seventeen, remember? Today's our anniversary, fifty-eight years ago today. It was my first time, remember?'

She tried and tried but she could only remember her own first time and the goose and the miscarriage and then the corners of her mouth turned down.

'Sometimes,' she said, 'I feel a little lonely in the world. Don't you ever feel a little lonely, too, Dora? No father, no mother, no chick nor darling child. Don't you even want something to cuddle?'

No darling child. Which was the nub of it, as far as she was concerned, as well I knew, but no use crying over spilled milk, although that be not the appropriate metaphor in this instance. Too late to do anything about it, now.

'I must admit, sometimes, it gets everso lonely, especially when you're stuck up in your room tapping away at that bloody word processor lost in the past while I'm shut up in the basement with old age.'

'Don't talk like that about poor Wheelchair.'

'I don't mean Wheelchair and well you know it. I mean *our* old age, the fourth guest at the table.'

'Look on the bright side,' I counselled her. 'I've got you and you've got me and we've both got Wheelchair and you could call her our geriatric little girl, seeing as we bathe her, feed her, change her nappies, even. Our father might have reneged on the job but we *did* have a right old sugar daddy in our Uncle Perry and well you know it. We never knew our mother but Grandma filled the gap and you can say that again.'

The bulb flickered on, off, on again as if to signify Grandma's assent.

'All the same,' she said, 'I wish . . .'

She crumpled up that old chiffon and cradled it to her bosom.

'If little Tiff had come to us,' she said, rocking the chiffon baby in her arms, 'I'd – '

I knuckled out my swimming eyes. No more tears, today.

Then a funny thing happened. Something leapt off the shelf where the hats were. No, not leapt; 'propelled itself', is better because it came whizzing out like a flying saucer, slicing across the room as if about to knock our heads off, so we ducked. It knocked against the opposite wall, bounced down to the ground, fluttered and was still.

It was her hat, her little toque, with the spotted veil, that had spun out like a discus. And as we nervously inspected it, there came an avalanche of gloves – all her gloves, all slithery leather thumbs and fingers, whirling around as if inhabited by hands, pelting us, assaulting us, smacking our faces, so that we clutched hands for protection and retreated like scared kids as more and more of Grandma's bits and pieces – oilcloth carriers, corsets, bloomers like sails, stockings hissing like snakes – cascaded out of the wardrobe on top of us. We backed off until our calves hit the side of the bed with a shock of cold metal and then the wardrobe door closed of its own accord upon its own emptiness with a ghastly creak, leaving us looking at our scared faces looking back out of the dust.

'Grandma's trying to tell us something,' said Nora in an awed voice.

Creak, creak went the door.

'She's telling us Memory Lane is a dead end,' I said. I could hear her voice clear as a bell: 'Come off it, girls! Pluck the day! You ain't dead, yet! You've got a party to go to! Expect the worst, hope for the best!'

We threw caution to the winds and raided the jam jar where we keep the seventy-plus emergency fund, that is, cash for wreaths for sudden funerals and taxis to hospices, etc. etc. etc.

The shops were still open, we threw on our silver-fox trenches, we dashed off to the market. Down Electric Avenue, past the vegetable stalls. 'Here, gel, fancy a widow's comfort?' he says, thrusting forth an aubergine. 'Is that the best you can do?' I riposted.

All of a sudden, I was feeling chipper. Then I spotted them. 'Here, Nor', here come the Animal Rights.' We drew ourselves up to our full height; we've learned to be defensive about our trenches.

'It'd look better on a fox, auntie,' said the young man, knees poking through his trousers, shaven nape, why does he make us run the gauntlet every time?

'It wouldn't look better on *this* fox,' said Nora, on her high horse. 'Which was humanely trapped in the Arctic Circle by the age-old methods of an ecologically sound Inuit hunter circa 1935, young man, before either you or your blessed mother, even, was yet pissing on the floor, which trapper has probably succumbed to alcohol and despair due to having his traditional source of livelihood taken away from him and, anyway, these foxes would be long dead, by now, besides, and rotted, if we weren't wearing their lovingly preserved pelts.'

'I'm glad you're feeling guilty, girls,' said the young man.

He slipped us the usual tract. 'I like to sink my teeth into a nice juicy sausage, too!' Nora confided lasciviously. He covered up his privates *toot sweet*.

'I sometimes think Grandma was born before her time,' I said to Nora.

'At least he doesn't picket flower stalls,' she said.

You can buy anything you want in Brixton market. We got stockings with little silver stars all over, 'more stars than there are in Heaven', recollected Nora. I shoved over a twenty for the stockings and spotted Old Bill on the back. That gave me a start, to see how Shakespeare, to whom our family owed so much, had turned into actual currency, not just on any old bank note but on a high denomination one, to boot. Though not as high as Florence Nightingale, which gives me satisfaction as a woman.

Lovely, shiny stockings and a couple of little short tight skirts in shiny silver stuff to match, that clung on like surgical bandage, and showed off our legs. Legs, the last thing to go. We were modelling stockings as late as the late sixties, I'd have you know; Bear Brand. They had to cut us off mid-thigh, of course, so the wrinkles wouldn't show. For women of our age, our legs still aren't half bad. Nora toyed with a spaghetti-string boob tube in lynx-print Lycra; I thought, maybe something with feathers . . . Kids gathered round, tittering; the man at the red mullet stall shook his head, sadly. They thought the Chance sisters had gone over the top, at last. There was a sale of gold stilettos, so we treated ourselves to those. We came back with an armful of junk, earrings, beads, everything you can think of, cheap and cheerful, we haven't laughed so much in years, and the water was hot enough for us to share a bath, by then. After that, we slipped on our towelling robes, we creamed off our morning faces, we started off from scratch.

Foundation. Dark in the hollows of the cheeks and at the temples, blended into a lighter tone everywhere else. Rouge, except they call it 'blusher', nowadays. Two kinds of blusher, one to highlight the Hazard bones, another to give us rosy cheeks. Nora likes to put the faintest dab on the end of her nose, why I can't fathom, old habits die hard. Three kinds of eyeshadow – dark blue, light blue blended together on the eyelids with the little finger, then a frosting overall of silver. Then we put on our two coats of mascara. Today, for lipstick, Rubies in the Snow by Revlon.

It took an age but we did it; we painted the faces that we always used to have on to the faces we have now. From a distance of thirty feet with the light behind us, we looked, at first glance, just like the girl who danced with the Prince of Wales when nightingales sang in Berkeley Square on a foggy day in London Town. The deceptions of memory. That girl was smooth as an egg and the lipstick never ran down little cracks and fissures round her mouth because, in those days, there were none.

'It's every woman's tragedy,' said Nora, as we contemplated our painted masterpieces, 'that, after a certain age, she looks like a female impersonator.'

Mind you, we've known some lovely female impersonators, in our time.

'What's every man's tragedy, then?' I wanted to know.

'That *he* doesn't, Oscar,' she said. She still has the capacity to surprise me. Fancy her knowing about Oscar Wilde. I did her nails, she did mine. After some debate – should we match them to our lips? – we fixed on silver, to match them to our legs. She did my hair, I did hers. Silver, too, worse luck. We disappeared behind a cloud of scent and re-emerged, transformed, looking just like what, for all those years, the bloody Hazards always thought we were, painted harlots, and over the hill, at that.

'Oh, I say!' Wheelchair murmured, tapping her lips with a tissue to set the Lancôme Bois de Rose. 'Don't you think you've gone a little far?'

In her white ballgown and pearls, she looked quite lovely, not so much Miss Havisham, more the Ghost of Christmas Past.

'Got to keep up with the times, darling,' said Nora.

'Not me,' said Wheelchair. 'I live mostly in the past, these days. I find it's better.'

Her eyes swivelled reverently round to that portrait of Melchior she'd insisted on bringing with her when she came, although we'd had to cut it down to fit it in and she no longer kept flowers in front of it because we refused point-blank to fetch her any and she couldn't go out and get them herself.

So she was still eating her heart out for Melchior, after all these years, was she? Don't think she was a hypocrite, to have loved him all those abused, neglected decades, when she hadn't been averse to a fling in her youth herself and brought home a brace of bonny babes whose biological origins owed more to A. N. Other's DNA. If you think she was a hypocrite, then you know sod all about women. No. She loved old Melchior, all right, and, poor cow, she still loved her wicked daughters, too, for there they were, on her bedside table, beside the phials of pills and the half-bottle of Malvern water, in a rosewood frame, the darling buds of bloody May as ever was, looking as if butter wouldn't melt in their mouths.

Rain came and settled at the window. April showers. The twenty-third of April. Yes! The destination of Melchior had been prepared for him since birth; he was doomed to wear the paste-board crown. Hadn't he first seen light of day on Shakespeare's birthday?

So had we two, of course. But all the little children in Bard Road were singing a hymn to Charlie Chaplin the day that we were born and Grandma took us to the window to look at the shirts and bloomers dancing on the washing-lines all over

Lambeth. That made a difference, you know. We were doomed to sing and dance.

Then we did Wheelchair's nails, just a manicure and buff, she's never said but I know she thinks varnish is vulgar. We gave her a squirt of Arpège. The phone never rang. Each time I looked at it, it didn't ring. And Brenda never came round again, either.

FIVE

HE CROSSED OVER the river to the other side. The river lies between Brixton and glamour like a sword. I wonder why they call it Old *Father* Thames.

In Regent's Park, the bushes crouched like bears and the stands of daffs and tulips wore a pale and ghostly look as they swayed in our birthday wind, which was getting fresh, again, moist after the rain, and warmish. In the street outside the Hazard home, what a bustle! A retinue of vans, blaring lights on stands, power cables to trip you up and a muster of personnel – bald men in specs and parkas conversing in huddles, girls in jeans hither and thithering with clipboards, plus fans, the idle and the curious, rubbernecking in quantity.

The Hazard residence was very handsome. Once or twice, we'd sauntered past it casually, just to have a little look . . . love locked out, ducky. Stuccoed, pillared and porticoed, with a bay thrust out front and a flight of stone steps to the door up which we'd often dreamed one day we might ascend and now would do so to the manner born, although we'd have to commission some staunch retainer to deal with Wheelchair.

But Wheelchair balked at the sight of the TV crews. There she was, in the back of the cab – we'd booked a hack, we'd never have got her into a minicab – she wept and wailed. What? Transmitted all over the country on the nine o'clock news carted about like laundry? What a public humiliation! Behold, the sad decline of the most beautiful woman of her time! She set up a lament but, luckily, Nora had slipped a big white chiffon square into her gold-mesh evening bag, in case the poor old thing's shoulders got chilly towards the end of the evening, so she dropped it over Wheelchair's head. Instant hush. I hailed a passing minion, who was all done up in hose and doublet.

'Just carry this lady up the stairs, will you, and we'll follow with the appliance.'

'Pleasure,' he said, smiling and coaxing Wheelchair the way

they do the very old, the same way they do kiddies. She was so light he hoisted her up easily in his arms in her white gown and her veil and she looked like a nun, or a ghost, or a very ancient bride until, out from under that veil, she gave him a flash of her Lynde-blue eyes and he blushed, he straightened his back, he bore her off with surprise and pride amidst a whirr of TV cameras, a staccato barrage of flashbulbs and a mutter: 'Who's that? Who's she?' because, when her eyes flashed, her beautiful old bones stuck out, suddenly, she turned back into the Lady A. of long ago and they all gaped.

Nora struggled with the wheelchair, trying to fold it up, while I paid off the cabby.

All round us, scenes of the kind poor Irish loved to hate were taking place. Swish cars drew up to disgorge tuxedos and long frocks from interiors that lit up at the moment of exit so each couple made a brief but striking cameo appearance. The crowd went wild. Though all the guests so far looked old crocks like us I'm bound to say there was not one body I recalled from days gone by, no doubt because they were all legitimate.

And then I felt a tugging at my sleeve, some old cove in rags, begging. As soon as I set eyes on him, he struck a chord, although I couldn't place him, not at first.

At my age, memory becomes exquisitively selective. Yes; I remember, with a hallucinatory sensitivity, sense impressions. A hand on my breast, even if I cannot recall precisely whose hand. The taste of a bacon sandwich back in the days when bacon in the pan buzzed like a bee in a lavender bush. The sensation of sunlight on the tender nape the day we'd had our hair cut for the first time. But it takes an effort to dredge up anything else, I can tell you. I couldn't for the life of me remember the brand name of Irish's favourite tipple, when I tried, the other day, even though he chucked a bottle of it at me when we parted in lieu of farewell. A full bottle, to boot. It smashed against the wall and trickled down. 'Oh, look,' I said, 'it's left a map of Ireland.' He couldn't see the joke. 'He must have loved you very much, to toss a whole bottle,' said Nora, when I told her.

But what was the brand? If you get little details like that right, people will believe anything.

Old Bushmills? Perhaps it was Old Bushmills. Poor old Irish. Gone to the great distillery in the sky these many years.

I've got a perfectly serviceable memory in some respects but not in others and there I was, racking my brains, when he rasped out: 'Spare us half a bar for a cup of tea, lady.'

He stretched out his hand and I glimpsed, between the edges of his unspeakable shirt, off which the buttons had all fallen, below the stained lapels of his ex-army greatcoat, the outlines of Europe and Africa. The penny dropped. Before me stood all that was left of Gorgeous George.

Lo, how the mighty are fallen. Though I saw which way things were going back then, in *The Dream*. It was a wonder he'd hung on for another half-century. When I came to think about it, he must have been as old as Melchior, himself; as old as Perry, if Perry'd lived.

I found I had reminded myself of untimely death and the festive mood that I was striving bravely to achieve evaporated.

But why, in that case, had we put on our gladrags and come out into the night when our hearts were freshly broken? Good question. For our old man's sake, I suppose. To celebrate the author of our being, even if he had relegated us to the 'remaindered' pile.

I may never have known my father in the sense of an intimate acquaintance, but I knew who he was. I was a wise child, wasn't I?

I was stuck staring at Gorgeous George but he didn't recognize me.

'Give us a bob, then,' he said, having relinquished some hope but not all. His voice had been destroyed by time and liquor. The harsh light of the yellow streetlamps took all the pink out of his continents. I'd got a twenty in my hand, ready to pay the cabby. Shakespeare, on the note, said: 'Have a heart.'

'Take that,' I said and pressed his literary culture into the hand of he who once personated Bottom the Weaver. 'Take it for the sake of *The Dream*. You can have it on the one condition, that you spend it all on drink.'

He grabbed hold of the currency, all right, but gave me an old-fashioned look.

'Surely you'd never think that of an old soldier,' he reproached.

'On your way,' I said. 'Don't you know it's Shakespeare's birthday? Cry God for England, Harry and St George. Go off and drink a health to bastards.'

He looked askance at that, as if he misunderstood my turn of phrase, but he wasn't about to make an issue of it, not when the price of an insult was a cool twenty quid, so he toddled off, clutching his loot, scarcely able to believe his luck, no doubt.

'You shouldn't have encouraged him,' reproved the taxi-driver.

'I used to know him, once upon a time,' I said and settled up, slipping him another Shakespeare to compensate for my generosity to the undeserving poor. I can take a hint.

'Come *on*,' said Nora, dancing on the spot.

Up the steps we marched in unison, exhibiting our antique but not quite catastrophic legs with wild abandon; with one accord, we stripped off our silver-fox trenches and trailed them behind us, and all the flashes went off at once. I felt quite revived.

Fame and beauty milled in the entrance hall below as little ladies in period cleavage took the coats and wraps. Lutenists in costume, always a feature of our father's parties, massed on the upstairs landing and ancient music floated from above. There was, bliss! another staircase that went up in florid curves, like Mae West.

'Where's Wheelchair? What did that chap do with her?'

'Search me.'

We gave up on Wheelchair, surrendered our furs and, hand in hand, did another Hollywood ascension up the staircase although I suffered the customary nasty shock when I spotted us both in the big gilt mirror at the top – two funny old girls, paint an inch thick, clothes sixty years too young, stars on their stockings and little wee skirts skimming their buttocks. Parodies. Nora caught sight of us at the same time as I did and she stopped short, too.

'Oooer, Dor',' she said. 'We've gone and overdone it.'

We couldn't help it, we had to laugh at the spectacle we'd made of ourselves and, fortified by sisterly affection, strutted our stuff boldly into the ballroom. We could still show them a thing or two, even if they couldn't stand the sight.

That house boasted a ballroom and that ballroom was a sight to see. The bay stuck out right over the park and there were long windows at the other end. Red marble columns with gold tops held up the ceiling, which was plastered with acanthus wreaths, pineapples, harps, palm fronds, bunches of grapes and lurking cherubs. There was a ten-gallon wedding cake in the shape of a chandelier hanging by a chain, winking, blinking and sending out rainbows and it was lit with real candles. There were real candles everywhere else, too, in sconces, in branches, in single spies, in battalions, filling the air with the smell of hot wax, warming us all up, flattering complexions which were, one and all, aged, except for those of the waiters, all in doublet and hose, who circulated amongst the throng with fizzing flutes of bubbly on silver salvers, reflected upside down like a conjuring trick in the parquet underfoot.

And my heart stood still, I was seventeen, again, I was a virgin powdering my nose with beating heart, for there was lilac, lilac, everywhere. In bowls, in jars, in cornucopias. White lilac, the evening's floral theme. I was all misty because of the smell of lilac as we processed in the long line towards where our father was receiving, in an alcove, seated on a sort of throne.

He wasn't wearing either monkey suit or tails, unlike most of his guests, but had on a rather majestic and heavily embroidered purple caftan. I thought, colostomy; but that caftan made a lovely contrast with his longish, pewter-coloured hair, still thick and heavy. There were rings on his fingers, like a king, or pope, and a big gold medallion round his neck. He looked regal, but festive. My heart gave a thump and the beat started to speed up.

We waited patiently in line to wish him 'Happy birthday', standing between a theatrical knight and a TV presenter who babbled inanities at one another across us, which pissed us off, but we decided to tolerate the invisibility of old ladies – note that, even dressed up like fourpenny ham-bones, our age and gender still rendered us invisible – because it was a special occasion, although as a general rule, we debate invisibility hotly. I snatched at the champagne a couple of times as it waltzed past, I was bloody nervous, I can tell you.

I looked round for Wheelchair but I couldn't see her anywhere and would have started to worry about her if I hadn't started to worry about myself, specifically, to worry about my bladder capacity because the theatrical knight kissed Melchior's hand once, then twice, then yet again for the cameras because first something went wrong, then something else and life was like a loop of tape repeating itself and I wished I hadn't had that second glass of bubbly when I remembered how I'd pissed myself from nerves the first time I met him. But Nora remained calm, although the lutenists were playing tunes to break your heart, 'Semper Dowland, semper dolens', 'Lachrymae'.

The third Lady Hazard, wearing a Vivienne Westwood somewhat too witty for her years, stood watchful guard beside her husband, her hand, weighed down by diamonds, protectively upon his shoulder but her eyes roving all round the thronged room, where the odours of expensive scent and aftershave vied with the lilac and the candle-wax and the smell of delicious cooking began to waft upstairs, too. A doublet and hose tottered past beneath a groaning tray of chicken-legs; I was starving, we'd skipped lunch, but we couldn't kneel down and ask our father's blessing flourishing a drumstick, could we? My Lady Margarine wore a smile so fixed it strained the stitches of her nip and tuck but you could tell she wasn't happy.

Of course! She was looking out for Tristram.

Of whom no sign.

I wondered if the mysterious Father Gareth Hazard SJ were going to turn up and, if so, if he would do so in his canonicals. I suffered from a powerful curiosity about Father Gareth; I'd never set eyes on him and would have given a lot to do so in my capacity as unofficial chronicler of the Hazard family because, given the history of fathers in our family, it seemed only right and proper we should have finally turned up a celibate one – a non-combatant, as it were.

The cameramen were everywhere, like flies. You never knew when you'd find one poking his proboscis in your drink. I gleaned from a waiter the info that the entire party, from first hello to last hiccup, was being taped for posterity; our father was bent on making an exhibition of himself until the bitter end.

'Peaseblossom !' he exclaimed. 'And Mustardseed!'

He put an arm round each of us while My Lady Margarine smiled on remorselessly, she didn't pause to change her smile between clients and her thoughts were unquestionably elsewhere or she'd have asked us who the fuck we were, we miniskirted senior citizens on our teetering heels. She no longer knew us from Adam although we remembered *her*, all right, on Sundays at the Lynde Court Home Farm in a patchwork dirndl giggling sycophantically at some barbed jibe of Saskia's. But Melchior gave us each as big a hug as he could manage, sitting down. Then he closed his eyes and inhaled deeply.

'Now, my darlings, you must refresh my memory . . . which of you is it who uses Shalimar and which Mitsouko?'

That smile! And, dammit, we fell in love with him, again, just as we'd done that August bank holiday all those years ago, when he first broke our hearts when he was scared and young and foolish. We saw that he was none of these things, now. We fell head over heels. We didn't need any words. Words would have been no good. His smile. Nora was chucking down buckets and he stretched out his old, veined, freckled hand and touched her cheek hesitantly, tremulously, so as to break your heart.

'You shouldn't cry,' he said. 'Not at our birthday party.'

That did it. Now I was at it too.

'Dad,' said Nora, and I said, 'Dad.' He gave us another hug. 'My lovely girls.' I don't know what changed him. Perhaps . . . perhaps, when he saw poor little Tiff distracted on the game show, he thought of Pretty Kitty for the first time in decades. Perhaps. He kept his profile at an angle so the cameras wouldn't shoot his double chin, he couldn't help it, it was in his blood. Just because he repented in public with half England watching didn't mean it wasn't genuine. He gave us another hug, and another, making up for all the hugs we never got. One fine night filled with white lilac when I was seventeen, he'd asked me to dance and now, by rights, he ought to close the circle, take the floor with Nora, but that TV presenter behind us was pushing and shoving to make his presence felt so we said: 'See you later, Dad,' and pushed off.

We got ourselves another drink and hid behind a pillar to compose ourselves. We were grinning away like Cheshire cats, we couldn't help it. Not that he'd said anything. Not that anything had changed. But we'd had a bit of love.

The chicken passed by, she lifted a thigh off. 'I could eat a horse.' She bit into the flesh. 'Delish.' She was recovering her equanimity. A spike of herb trapped between her front teeth; she hooked it out with her fingernail and looked at it.

'Rosemary,' she said. '*At Table in Tuscany*, BBC 1, Friday evenings, eight thirty. That Saskia's doing the catering.'

She dropped the thigh half-eaten in an ashtray.

'Your mascara's run something awful,' I said. I was dying for a pee, too, so we went off to the ladies' toilet and there we found the Lady A., turned back into Wheelchair as if by some bad spell and tucked away behind the bidet, still veiled, quivering, with Old Nanny done up to look like Juliet's Nurse soothing her with gentle murmurs. They'd stationed Old Nanny in the toilet, evidently, so that she could deal with drunks.

'I couldn't face him,' said the Lady A. 'Not after what I did to him. I loved him but I betrayed him.'

'You need a stiffener,' said Nora. Old Nanny pursed her lips at first but she knocked a quick one back herself once Nora got the gin out of her gilt-mesh bag and we got Wheelchair into the ballroom at last, between us, although she quivered well-nigh to the point of shaking to pieces whenever the crowds parted and she caught sight of Melchior, so we parked her behind a Canova nude, where she had another snifter and settled down to see what on earth would happen next.

What happened next was, Daisy Duck.

There was a fanfare of baroque trumpets. No kidding. I hadn't heard a baroque trumpet in the flesh since the wrap party for *The Dream*. There was a general hushing and muttering and the crowd pressed back but the Lady A. became unwontedly animated and craned forward, would have had her veil off for a better view but I stayed her hand – I had an inkling the time wasn't right, yet, for her to show herself. She grumbled and mumbled but covered up again and settled down to watch the royal entrance happily enough, even if as through a mist.

And royal entrance it was. Tootle, tootle, tootle, too! went the trumpets. Then the lutenists, unaccustomed to the tuning and with a good many bum notes, had a go at 'Hello, Dolly!' and in she came, to a round of cheers. People stood on chairs. She looked a million dollars, I must admit, even if in well-used notes. Tiny as ever, five foot nothing in her heels, but a stunning advertisement for hormone replacement therapy, I must say, not a line on that skin but, then, sharkskin doesn't wrinkle, does it, don't be a bitch, Dora. She was brown and glossy, like a Sunday roast, plump brown shoulders, bright brown hair with a few grey strands – she was smart enough not to try to look as though she were thirty-five, she'd settle happily for forty. Teeth like a Bechstein grand, I blinked in the glare of her smile. In the slinky wake of her white satin sheath staggered a tiny figure almost invisible under the weight of her bouquet, a hundred red roses. I thought it must be Daisy's gigolo, he came in like a tacked-on afterthought, but he wasn't my idea of a gigolo – tiny little man, ill-fitting peroxide hair, one of those grey silk Italian suits that glow in the dark, face like an old child. I hoped for her sake he'd got hidden talents.

Good old Daisy. I could tell at a glance she was tight as a tick.

She got to the middle of the floor and then she stopped. She raised her arms above her head in an extrovert gesture and turned her nonstop, whiter-than-white smile to all four corners before she blasted Melchior with it. 'Hello, Dolly!' stopped at last, thank God. Roars of applause.

Melchior managed to stagger to his feet, wobbled off the podium and hugged her, making it up in public with her after all those years just as he'd done with us but they spent more time negotiating their profiles to advantage than we had done and Daisy won because, even if half seas over, she was compos mentis.

Because it grieves me but I must admit it – I fear our father's softening of the heart was not unconnected to the softening of his brain. Old Nanny told us he'd never been the same since, one day, he was in the Tube on the way to the Garrick Club and some old codger grasped him by the hand and cried out, so all the carriage heard: 'Good God, weren't you Melchior Hazard, once?' He started to mope, after that, to suffer from uncertainty, refused to go out, even hid away that precious old cardboard crown of his and swore he was too old to wear it any more. He was getting a touch dottled. But there you are; no silver lining without a cloud.

Dear old Daisy. She caught sight of us during the camera call, abandoned him in mid-embrace. The media people hallooed after her: what's she doing, kissing those two bedizened bag ladies? We'd been younger than her, once upon a time, but she was wearing well, and worth a bob or two, of course.

The gigolo trailed unhappily a few steps, then unhappily back, carting his roses, at a loss, until Melchior was kind, beckoned him over, relieved him of the roses and, in a spontaneous improvisation, gave them to My Lady Margarine, who looked shocked, and thrust them at that TV presenter, who was still hanging around, who got rid of them to some deliquescent thesp in a Jean-Paul Gaultier cat suit, and then that bunch of roses started to play pass-the-parcel all round the ballroom until a serving wench retrieved it and took it to the Ladies', where Old Nanny, ever resourceful, stuck it down a toilet bowl for the duration of the party, since there was no other receptacle ample enough to receive it.

Daisy shrieked with joy when she caught sight of Wheelchair in her shroud but no time to catch up because the press now left us in a body and cantered to the door as Margarine pointed like a terrier and began to shake and whimper: here came the prodigal son at last!

How could anyone have thought that Tristram might find it in his heart to skip his father's centenary, even if that very day he'd lost his lover and his child? Wasn't it heart-warming? Heart-warming, my foot. The only decent thing young Tristram could have done was hara-kiri, in my opinion. But the show must go on, must it not?

Tristram looked wrecked. In a d.j., all right, but greenish in the face, as if he'd been throwing up all day, and very tottery on his feet, held up by an aunt on either side. We hadn't spoken to the darling buds since the fateful twenty-first birthday party, only the occasional sighting in a department store. The Lady A. moaned and clutched the arms of her chair. 'Calm down!' we hissed. She sucked in a mouthful of her veil and gagged herself. Daisy produced a silver hip flask from her handbag and offered her a pull; chewing chiffon, the Lady A. shook her head. I was glad to see that time had healed the wounds between these two.

But time does not necessarily heal everything. I felt that old, familiar shudder of distress when I saw Saskia, with her hair redder than ever, done up in a French pleat, looking quite lissom in a putty-coloured sliver of something by Jean Muir. As for Imogen, she'd gone right over the top. She'd got a fishbowl on her head with a fish in it. I kid you not. A live fish. The flashes popped and flared like Guy Fawkes' Night and Imogen turned this way and that, nodding, bowing and smiling and acknowledging the attention, the goldfish slopping around at considerable danger to itself. I furiously pondered the significance of the fish, then it clicked: *Goldie the Goldfish* – her kiddies' programme. She had come to the party as a commercial for herself. She had on a bronze shift sequined in scales and she greeted her father in a manner appropriate to her heroine, she opened and shut her mouth a lot, and it was just as well she'd come along in costume and mimed her birthday greeting to him as a goldfish because it lightened up the mood.

As it was, after the girls – 'girls', I call them; they wouldn't see sixty, again; show us your bus pass, ladies – gave the old man their birthday kisses, one on each cheek, he wept, again, and they retreated, leaving Tristram behind. That was the moment the paparazzi had been waiting for, when he tumbled forward on his knees, his face in Melchior's lap. His shoulders shook. Over the plangent lutes, I heard the sound of sobbing. The cameramen surged round to get a closer view.

His mother crouched down and cuddled him, Melchior cradled his head. Old Melchior did something pathetic, he tried to wave the cameras away, tried to get them to leave them alone so they could endure the moment without the world, his wife and dog looking on, but it was too late in their lives for that. Smile in public, cry in public, live in public, die in public. There was a raw emotion on their faces that you don't see on actors'. Tonight, they were in the newsreel. The worst thing, to see your children suffer.

But when I remembered Brenda's face, that morning, I knew there was an even worse thing and then I cheerfully could have slaughtered Tristram Hazard.

Still the bloody show went on.

Saskia, who was well in control of the situation being, unique amongst mammals, a cold-blooded cow, telegraphed a signal with her eyebrows and the baroque trumpets rang out again. A host of little boys from the Italia Conte School in mini-ruffs and slashed knickers ran round snuffing out the scones with their fingers, releasing dozens of puffs of acrid smoke.

In came the cake.

I should have realized that Saskia would bake the cake. It was her masterpiece. It was enormous. It was a model of the Globe Theatre, I tell no lie. It was spherical, in tiers, roofed with chocolate frosting ridged to simulate tiles. It was big enough to ring a hundred candles all around the roof and they were blazing away as a dozen little pageboys bore in this edifice at shoulder-height, on a sort of litter, amidst roars of applause in which Daisy enthusiastically joined, after parking her bag and hip flask with the gigolo, but the Lady A. was sobbing very quietly and discreetly to herself under her veil and *we* didn't feel like applauding ourselves, not at all, at all.

A pageboy handed Saskia a sword, the kind they fence with.

Nora and I sharply ingested breath, recalling another birthday, another cake, a sudden act of shocking violence – but, in what was obviously a well-rehearsed routine, she offered it by the hilt to Melchior, who, well done, old stager! gently thrust Tristram to one side with his foot and rose tottering to his feet.

The only light, that fluttering of birthday candles on the cake, casting weird shadows, making the old man look haggard.

There was a hush; there was a drumroll.

My Lady Margarine, who was distractedly patting Tristram's hand, belatedly remembered her cue.

'A happy hundredth birthday, darling!' You could tell, from the power of her smile, *that* cake wasn't made with butter. Another fine trouper.

Our father lifted up the sword. I felt for him, you could see it was an effort. He lifted up the sword and –

– and –

I would like to be able to say that at this thrilling point, drumroll, celebration, flames, sudden hush, the big cake blew up or cracked open and out popped –

– but, if I did, I would be lying.

What happened was this: drumroll, flames, hush, uplifted cake knife but, before it could descend, came a tremendous knocking at the front door. TREMENDOUS. Such a knocking that the birthday candles dipped and swayed and dropped wax on the chocolate tiles; the boughs of lilac tossed, scattering nodes of bloom; the very parquet underneath us seemed to tremble, about to rise up.

A thrill ran through the room. Something unscripted is about to happen.

They let the wind in when they opened the door. The same amazing wind that whipped up the leaves and Dora Chance's weary corpuscles this morning came roaring and galloping up the stairs into the ballroom, blowing up skirts, so women squealed, buffeting the candle-flames almost to extinction then whipping them back to life, again, whirling the Lady A.'s veil this way and that way, threatening to blow it away altogether, but she trapped it in her mouth. Laughter like sweet thunder blew on the wind in front of him and every head turned to see whom it might be, arriving late, in such a genial tempest.

Who else could it have been?

Remember the old song he used to sing with Irish, 'In Dublin town lived Michael Finnegan . . .' and the corpse jumps up at the wake, a resurrection. And the last line went like this:

'Thunder and lightning!' sang our Peregrine. 'Did yez think I was dead?'

The size of a warehouse, bigger, the size of a tower block, in what looked like the very same scratched, weathered flying jacket he'd worn when we first laid eyes on him when we were still pissing on the floor, splitting a grin, hair as red as paprika – not one speck of grey, evidently untouched one jot by age.

He could have telephoned from the airport, couldn't he, to say he would be here. No doubt they even have telephones in Brazil, in this day and age. But if he'd called ahead, it would have spoiled our wonderment. It was just like Peregrine, to upstage his own brother.

Then, again, it was our Uncle Perry's hundredth birthday, too.

I knew in my water today would be the kind of day things happen.

In on the wind that came with Perry blew dozens and dozens of butterflies, red ones, yellow ones, brown and amber ones, some most mysteriously violet and black, tiny little green ones, huge flapping marbled blue and khaki ones, swirling around the room, settling on women's bare shoulders, men's bald spots. Nora and I got a couple each in our hair.

Melchior dropped the sword and sat down again, abruptly, white as a sheet, and the cameras held their fire, for once, as if Peregrine had not only upstaged his brother but also plausibility. The uncut cake on its dozen legs hovered in front of Melchior uncertain what to do and there was a buzz of questions because of course nobody was left who knew who Perry was, but she and me and him and them, and perhaps Melchior even thought he'd seen a ghost.

But such a material ghost. Ever heavy-footed. The chandelier shook, the lilac shed. The cake veered off to one side at Peregrine's approach. He was wreathed in butterflies. Very, very gently, he detached a splendid, crimson one with an ethereal wingspan about six inches, offered the pulsing handful to Melchior.

'All our daughters,' he said. 'I've named a butterfly for each one. And I've named *this* one after you, you miserable old sod.'

The unmistakable language of male affection. Was it: absence made the heart grow fonder? Or shall we put it down to ambivalence, perhaps? But I was glad to see them fond. Melchior looked at the butterflies, so lovely, so improbable, and then he looked up at his brother, and then he smiled. And then the butterfly curator from the zoo came in with a big net, caught up all the beauties and took them somewhere warm and snug for Peregrine had their welfare at heart. All was uproar and commotion but we pressed forward for our kisses.

'Floradora! You haven't changed one bit!'

I was about to say him nay, draw his attention to the crow's-feet, the grey hairs and turkey wobblers but I saw by the look in his eye that he meant what he said, that he really, truly loved us and so he saw no difference; he saw the girls we always would be under the scrawny, wizened carapace that time had forced on us for, although promiscuous, he was also faithful, and, where he loved, he never altered, nor saw any alteration. And then I wondered, was I built the same way, too? Did I see the soul of the one I loved when I saw Perry, not his body? And was his fleshly envelope, perhaps, in reality in much the same sorry shape as those of his nieces outside the magic circle of my desire?

But when I registered I'd used those words, 'my desire', I stopped thinking in that direction *toot sweet*. I'd properly shocked myself and I had to knock off another glass of champagne to cool myself while Nora came in for her share of hugs and kisses and then Daisy Duck, and all the rest, because not since the Change had yours truly felt such a sudden rush of blood in that department, down there.

Saskia was standoffish and turned the cold shoulder. Imogen tried to slip away but was impeded by her headgear so he grabbed hold of her and gave her such a hug the goldfish slopped out of the bowl and she went down on her knees in a puddle to pick it up again, it was slippery as soap and gave them a fine chase all over the dancefloor while the camera crews and the photographers and the reporters didn't know where to turn next, so much grief, joy, resentment and pursuit was going on, while the multitude babbled and got in the way until suddenly Peregrine caught sight of a certain heavily veiled figure tucked away behind a pillar and stopped short with the gasping goldfish in his hand.

'It isn't . . .' he said.

'Put it back in!' urged Imogen, kneeling at his feet. Perry absently dropped the fish back in the bowl and a hush spread in ever-increasing circles over the crowd until there was perfect silence. All eyes were focused on the invisible Lady A. Her fingers clenched and unclenched on the arms of the wheelchair. She pushed herself backwards, as if she were trying to roll offstage back into the wings, where nobody could see her, but she banged against the wall because there was nowhere to go except here.

Melchior, sensing something was up, craned forward, leaning heavily on Margarine, so he got a good view when Perry plucked off the veil. Then came a bewildered pause. Melchior sank back on his throne, again, with a puzzled look, quite grey with exhaustion, although things were only just livening up. I don't think he'd got the foggiest who the lady in the wheelchair was. You could hear Margarine going: 'Who's that? Who's that?' But Saskia and Imogen backed off aghast, as well they might.

Perry said softly, 'Hi, there, bright eyes.'

The Lady A. said, 'Why! It's Peregrine!' and twinkled.

He wheeled her round to face the crowd.

'Ladies and gentlemen,' he said, 'the Lady Atalanta Hazard. The most beautiful woman of her time.'

Suddenly she looked her old self again, but, due to her white curls, even more like a sheep, to my way of thinking, but it would seem that sheep are irresistible; everybody gasped. Perry led the applause that followed. She scrabbled at her veil, as if half-inclined to cover up again, but I could tell she was pleased. Melchior gave a jump.

'Attie!'

So now all three Lady Hazards were together in one room and I wondered if our mother's ghost was somewhere here, too, floating in the smoky air above the cake, which was waving about, a bit, because its arms were getting tired.

'I've brought you something special, in my trunk,' said Peregrine to Melchior. 'Give us a little light on the subject, if you please.' The little pages dashed up and down relighting everything until the room was brilliant.

Perry must have tipped the baroque trumpets because they let loose another fanfare as half a dozen stocky wee brown men in penis sheaths and feathers, friends of Perry's from Brazil, evidently, heaved in a cabin trunk covered with labels of hotels that had long since ceased trading, shipping lines long since defunct, railways long since torn up. They hauled it into the middle of the ballroom, set it down on the parquet. Peregrine spat on his hands and rubbed, strode boldly forth and first of all I thought: He's going to do a conjuring trick, because he put on his conjuring manner that I hadn't seen for years: 'Ladies and gentlemen, I have nothing up my sleeve.' He was a sprightly walker. A hundred? Never!

'He's made a pact,' said Nora in a whisper.

He addressed Melchior. He gave as low a bow as his paunch permitted.

'Melchior, my dear brother,' he said, 'I give you . . . the future of the Hazard family.'

He lifted up the lid of the trunk.

'If,' he added, 'she'll have you.'

We had an intuition who it was.

Out of that trunk stepped our little Tiff, as fresh as paint, not a tad the worse for wear except her eyes were no longer those of a dove, stabbed or whole, and she looked sound in mind and body almost to a fault. She'd changed her clothes; she'd got on a pair of overalls and those big boots, Doc Marten's, but she looked lovelier than ever, enough to make you blink. Our Tiff as ever was, our heart's delight.

We were all tears and laughter. We skidded across that skating rink of a floor on our ridiculous heels and held her as if we'd never let her go while the baroque trumpets went on and on until I thought: perhaps we've died and gone to heaven. But the first paroxysm subsided and there we still were.

I'll say this for Tristram's reflexes, he was down on his knees in front of her in a flash, laughing and crying at the same time or doing a fair simulacrum thereof.

'I love you, Tiffany,' he said. 'Forgive me.'

She stared down at him as if sunk deep in thought, which I was glad to see in itself – she'd never been one for reflection, before. She wiped her nose with the back of her hand, she'd picked up a dreadful cold, somewhere, though not at the bottom of the river, as it turned out.

'Fat chance,' she announced at last.

Tristram was stunned. He sat back on his heels.

'But, Tiffany, I'll marry you!'

'Not on your life, you bastard,' she said, right out in front of all those people. God, I was proud of her at that moment! 'Not after what you did to me in public. I wouldn't marry you if you were the last man in the world. Marry your auntie, instead.'

A palpable hit. Saskia turned white and dropped her glass. Poor old Melchior was at sea, couldn't make head nor tail of *this* bit of cut and thrust, of course, but he was pierced to the heart by the riveting sight of his son's rejection.

'Oh, my dear,' he murmured in that thick, rich, vintage port voice. 'Take pity on him; have pity on your own unborn child.'

I felt quite sorry for Melchior, having his grandchild given and taken away before it was so much as born. He looked so pitiful, and, after all, it *was* his birthday, that Tiff might have wavered but Tristram spoiled it all. He waxed histrionic.

'My baby! Think of my baby!' He tore his hair, he gnashed his teeth.

'Pull yourself together and be a man, or try to,' said Tiffany sharply. 'You've not got what it takes to be a father. There's more to fathering than fucking, you know.'

We each squeezed the hand we held, she squeezed back. I thought, we'll teach the baby tap and ballet, when the time comes. Then came another banging on the door.

'That'll be my mum and dad,' she announced confidently. All the help was in the ballroom, now, transfixed by all this real-life drama, nobody to let in the new arrivals, but a splintering crash indicated that the locked front door posed no problems to a ranked light-heavyweight. Tiff let off her parting shot.

'Not that your old man and mother aren't perfectly welcome to take a peek at the baby when it's born but don't you come sniffing around until you've dried off behind the ears, Tristram.'

He was too stunned to get up off his knees as Bren and Leroy stepped round him to embrace their daughter in a fusillade of flashes. The lutes started up again, Lord Somebody or Other's Puff, I think Perry slipped them a couple of quid. Quite like old times, lights, music, action. There was a patter of applause as Tiff and Bren and Leroy departed for their cab and were followed by no photographers after Leroy sent one of them downstairs on his ear.

Perry said he found our little Tiff by chance, wandering in the street the previous night, on his way from the airport; his taxi nearly ran her over.

'So I took her back with me to the Travellers' Club – '

'Oh, Peregrine!' I cried, struck by an awful thought. 'You never!'

'I most certainly did not,' he huffed. 'What a suggestion! There was a damsel in distress, if ever I saw one.'

Tristram was crying on Saskia's shoulder. I could tell by the look in his mother's eye she'd no love lost for Saskia, either, even if they *had* been best friends at Ro-de-o-do back in the year dot. And here was bloody Saskia now, elbowing her out of her big scene with her own son. Margarine blazed away with thwarted mother love and snatched up a lump of cake, that had sunk down to the ground out of sheer weariness, pulled off a candle that had burned down to a stump, and pressed the cake into her son's hand.

'Eat something, my dear,' she said. 'Just a mouthful, to give you strength.'

There was a piercing screech and crumbs everywhere because Saskia dashed the cake from Tristram's lips and collapsed in a fit in the arms of her sister, who promptly commenced her celebrated goldfish imitation again, her lips opened, her lips closed, oh! oh! oh! but no sound came out. Perry, ever quick off the mark, seized Imogen's goldfish bowl and dashed the water over Saskia, shocking her out of her fit and into you never saw such a shimmy as she shook that goldfish out of her vee-neck.

Yes, she confessed; she *had* slipped something into the cake she'd baked with her own hands for her father's birthday, though whether it would have made him rather ill or very ill or finished him off altogether I never found out because now such a hullabaloo broke out, lights, cameras, the wailing of that poor old man, the recriminations of his wife, the exclamations of his son, and everybody else putting their vocal tuppence ha'p'orth in as well. Even Perry looked grave and as if he were to blame, stricken with compunction, possibly for the first time in a century. He and the Lady A. drew close together, the guilty parties, when Saskia wailed to Melchior:

'You never loved us!'

It was high time that Saskia got wise. Remember Gorgeous

George on Brighton Pier long ago, and the punch line of his joke? I couldn't resist, I came out with it:

'Don't worry, darlin', '*e*'s not your father!'

What if Horatio had whispered that to Hamlet in Act I, Scene i? And think what a difference it might have made to Cordelia. On the other hand, those last comedies would darken considerably in tone, don't you think, if Marina and, especially, Perdita weren't really the daughters of . . .

Comedy is tragedy that happens to *other* people.

Brighton Pier broke up with mirth when Gorgeous George said, ''*e*'s not your father'; when I said the same thing in the Hazard residence, you could have heard a pin drop. Then I wished I'd held my peace and let the world wag on its old, unconscious way, for after that split second of silent, suspended time while they all took it in, if all had been hullabaloo before now it was pandemonium as Saskia sprang at Peregrine and pummelled him with her fists while the Lady A., quick as her wheels allowed, interposed her body, crying out piteously, while Imogen, now aquarium-less, thank God, trotted after the Lady A. begging for full details of the entire scenario and giggling in a hysterically retarded manner but Nora and Daisy Duck, having evidently copiously refreshed themselves from Daisy's hip flask, were clinging to one another for dear life and, I'm sorry to say, laughing fit to bust a gut.

Melchior flashed a 'how could you' œillade at the Lady A., who reared up in her chair – 'bright eyes', indeed! more like Medusa. She got it all off her chest in one go. What a performance. Those who could secure one perched on the little gilt chairs that stood around, the rest roosted on the floor at risk to gowns and trousers and all turned into the perfect audience, quiet as mice, rustling at tense moments, indrawing breath at startling disclosures and sometimes rippling with discreet mirth, while the waiters lolled against the walls, more disengaged, professionals themselves, keeping a critical eye upon the show rather than being carried away by it.

'And wasn't it the Hazard blood?' she cried, full-throated, clarion-like. We'd never heard her sound like that before. 'The Hazard blood! The precious, unique Hazard blood that blinds parents to their children and turns daughter against mother!'

Melchior coughed, spluttered and writhed upon his throne;

she'd been bottling up his embarrassment for years and now, pop! bubble, bubble, bubble, or more like hubble, bubble, toil and trouble, out it came all over the floor. Perry got Saskia in a half-nelson and she hushed up, staring at the Lady A. with saucer eyes; she'd never thought her mother had so much passion in her, and neither had I.

'You left me at home hugging the empty womb you couldn't fill, Melchior!'

Spasm of shock.

'You couldn't fill *my* womb, Melchior, although you'd been so profligate of your seed before me, seduced and abandoned an innocent girl, left her to die, alone, and then, to compound the betrayal, you abandoned her daughters – '

– she gestured towards us and Nora swiftly assumed a po-face as a fresh gasp ran through the crowd and all eyes turned towards us, as with the crowd at Wimbledon. I wondered, ought we to take a bow?

'– oh, yes! the daughters you never acknowledged, as though you thought the Hazard blood lost all its virtue once it was mixed with that of a chambermaid – '

He made a furious gesture of denial. She snapped:

'Oh, yes you did!'

Touch of the pantomime; would be riposte: 'Oh, no I didn't!' No such luck. She was unstoppable.

'It was your blood, the Hazard blood, that went to make the "darling buds of May", the girls you loved so dearly even when they robbed their mother of her home and money – '

Gasps; muffled exclamations; all eyes now swivelled towards Saskia and Imogen, who flinched and quailed.

'Your blood, the Hazard blood, runs in their veins but the "darling buds" never sprang from the *seed* of Melchior Hazard!'

'Ooh!' and 'Aah!' said everybody. Myself, I'd been wondering how the Lady A. would verbalize the technical aspect of her adultery, given the refinement of her vocabulary. Having made the distinction between 'blood' and the actual procreative juice, what would she call the latter? 'Jism'? 'Come'? (Or do you spell it 'cum', I'm never sure.) Sperm and semen seemed altogether too technical for her rhetorical mode. I was glad she'd settled on the tasteful compromise of 'seed', although it occurred to me, not for the first time, that a serious language problem existed between the two branches of the Hazard family.

Don't misunderstand me. We've got very fond of her. She's always been welcome to the basement front, we'd never deny her a crust and I know she can't help it – I truly think she'd change if only she could. But, always, the high tone, even today, when she was letting rip and all those decades of understatement were going up in smoke. The nub of what she was saying now was, she'd had a tumble with her brother-in-law, once upon a time, and, as a result, there were two more girls in the world. Sorry, pardon, Melchior. But she couldn't just *say* that, could she? She had to make a meal of it. Some of the things she said were news to me, of course, and made a lot of things make sense, but she was going on about it all as if it were a matter of life and death. And how could we Chances believe that? We knew that nothing is a matter of life and death except life and death.

'Not your seed, Melchior, but those girls were cast in your mould, all the same! They robbed me and turned me out of my own home and spurned the love I felt for them just as you did yourself, Melchior!'

She burst into tears. There was a flutter of sympathetic handkerchiefs. Peregrine's cheeks were streaming, too, and the darling buds clung on to one another, pictures of shame and grief. When the Lady A. had composed herself, she mopped her face with Nora's crumpled veil, blew her nose on it and continued, as if refreshed:

'You left me lonely, Melchior, while you pursued that restless, thirsty quest for fame, while you engaged in that titanic contest with your dead father – '

Titanic conquest? First I've heard of it, I sniffed. But how could I have heard of it, on reflection? Our father and I had never been on what you could call speaking terms.

' – I was left lonely, with my empty womb. And then – '

But she couldn't finish the sentence, perfect lady that she was. She raised her eyes imploringly to Peregrine and in one bound he was beside her, his arms around her shoulders and her daughters, weeping, scampered over, too, and crouched at her feet in attitudes of contrition. Peregrine looked Melchior right between the eyes.

'They're mine, Melchior, little monsters that they are. Forgive me, Melchior. Forgive us all.'

There was a patter of applause that petered out as soon as people realized that everything was real. Frail, lovely Lady A., her forces spent, exhaustedly accepted a pull at Daisy's flask while the videotape recorded every move for posterity. Daisy was impressed and wondered aloud who held the mini-series rights.

Meanwhile, Saskia and Imogen each seized hold of a piece of the Lady A.'s skirt, kissed it and begged her to forgive and forget, etc. etc. etc. Poor old Perry was left right out in the cold during the ensuing emotional reconciliation and I drew away a little, sunk in my own thoughts, as follows: how a mother is always a mother, since a mother is a biological fact, whilst a father is a movable feast. But Melchior, head buried in his hands, looked the picture of misery and Margarine beat the air with her hands, at a loss as to what to do to cheer him up.

Daisy and Nora had got their heads together. Then Daisy nudged her gigolo back to life – he looked as if he'd gone off into a trance, temporarily. There was some discussion with the lutes and then they struck up all together as such a voice! the voice of an angel soared up and tickled the chandelier – a boy soprano, such purity, such vigour. A voice I'd heard before, in Hollywood but this time it was not raised to warn us against spotted snakes.

'Oh,' he sang, 'my beloved father . . .'

No gigolo accompanied Daisy but he who'd once stood best man to her and Melchior. Bewigged, befuddled, still his vocal cords could move a heart of stone. She'd met him again when he presented her with her 'lifetime contribution on the cinema' Academy Award. He was filthy rich, and gaga, and when she told him to, he sang. 'My very best marriage,' she said. From Daisy Duck to Daisy Puck.

'I love thee, yes, I love thee . . .'

Nora signed me with her eyes. It was time for me and she to go public about our paternity. Our skirts had ridden right up our crotches, we pulled them down, we patted our hair, our heels went click, click, click on the carpet, that sexy sound, but we looked like wizened children got up in our mum's clothes for a dare and our hearts were brimming over. We pressed our cheeks against his hands. This was too much for Melchior. He melted for all to see.

'Oh, my beloved father – '

The crystals rang with the last notes of Puck's glorious aria. Not a dry eye in the house as Melchior raised his head and gave his girls a watery, tremulous smile.

'I am the one deserves to weep,' he said, and kissed us.

I could have sworn that then the curtain came down, the lights went up and there was a standing ovation but, as Nora pointed out later, there was no curtain, the lights were on already, and it would have been discourteous of that audience to applaud. So I imagined all that. But, anyway, after this inexpressibly moving reconciliation, came a short intermission. Everybody got up and stretched and vivaciously discussed the action so far while the waiters cleared the cake away. Nobody blew out the candles on this birthday, they went out of their own accord, but all our wishes had come true and we just sat there, beaming.

When the lutes settled down again after their excursion into Puccini, it was nostalgia-time. I pricked up my ears; forgotten melodies drifting up from Memory Lane . . . selections from – what else – *What? You Will!?!* We hummed along and when they came to 'O Mistress Mine', they did it as a foxtrot and Nora gave Melchior a nudge.

'Here, old man,' she said. 'What about a dance? Give us the pleasure.'

She gave him a hand, got him on to the dancefloor. On the night of my seventeenth birthday long ago he danced with me. Tonight, on our father's grand centenary, he took the floor with the other half of the apple and the band played music from the days when men wore hats. Not a dry eye in the house. Again. He was a touch unsteady on his pins, inclined to wobble, but she knew how to lead, and they were wreathed in smiles of foolish fondness for that which had been lost was found and so on.

But Perry was in a right old state, left out of each and every reunion. He materialized beside me, disconsolate. 'They still don't want to know me,' he said. 'And I can't blame them. God, Dora, I've been a cad.'

I was feeling quite sentimental, watching Dad and Nora.

'You were always good to us, darling,' I reminded him. 'Nora always thought you should have married Grandma.'

'What?!?'

'Made a real family for us.'

He chewed on that in stunned silence until he guffawed.

Once Nora had set the ball rolling, other couples took the floor. Margarine led out Tristram, who was still shaky on his feet but starting to get a bit of colour back. Daisy scooped up her Puck and took him through the motions, for which I was thankful, as he seemed quite out of it unless he was singing. The Lady A. was too preoccupied with her daughters and they with her to pay the dancing much attention but soon everybody else was doing it and Perry stuck out a paw:

'How about it, Dora?'

'I don't fancy a foxtrot, Perry,' I said. 'But I wouldn't say no to a –'

It slipped out before I thought twice. I'm not proud of it, I'm not ashamed of it although I thought, there'll be hell to pay with Nora tomorrow morning; even though he *was* my uncle on my father's side; and don't think I didn't know he got some salve to his battered old male ego out of it, apart from anything else, but I didn't do it just to cheer him up, oh, no. Nor, I swear, was I trying to get even with Saskia. No. It was the tune, the moonlight and the scent of lilac that did it. I hadn't felt like this for twenty years. Nobody noticed when we slipped away because they were all dancing.

The day's exciting wind, having done its bit to liven up the evening, had died down to a little whisper from the direction of the park, full of damp earth and springtime, that blew the white linen curtains ballooning backwards into the front bedroom. It was quite chilly, I shivered. Peregrine went to close the window, then stopped. 'Hark at the lions!' In the distance, in the zoo, over the waving treetops, the lions were roaring their hearts out.

It was a stark white room with operating-theatre walls and a white leather disc on the end of a metal spike for an armchair, bare boards, and an enigmatic bed like something therapeutic with a steel frame. Margarine got some earringed, crewcut decorator in to do it. There were a few spare coats from the party spread on the bed, they spoiled the whole effect – you couldn't afford to have a slipper out of place. I'd clipped the piece about that room out of *World of Interiors* to go into my Hazard dossier and, oddly enough, although it was a masterpiece of pared-down understatement, the room still had just the same self-conscious look as that other long-combusted bedroom at Lynde Court had done – it was a room designed to be looked at, like Melchior's whole life had been, but now all the dirty secrets hidden in the cupboards had come out at last, had come to fuck in his bed, in fact. We didn't even bother to shove off the coats.

Even in old age, it was easy to see why Peregrine had always had such success with women.

'How long has it been, Dora?'

'Too long, me old cock!' I responded heartily, though, rack my brains as I might, I couldn't for the life of me remember sleeping with him before and I shocked myself, to have forgotten that – if I *had* forgotten, that is, and if he wasn't making a general rather than a particular enquiry, but it wasn't the time nor place to ask him to elucidate, was it? All the same, to have forgotten so much else, so many other names, yes, all water under the bridge – but to have forgotten whether ever I slept with my beloved Perry . . . and then I thought, perhaps he can't remember, either. But, even so.

But don't think I thought these thoughts in a reasoned sequence and a coherent manner. Far from it.

You never forget the first time. I'll never forget the last time, either.

At least, I'm pretty sure this is going to be the last time, but you never know what may turn up.

He cracked his old back and soughed and wheezed. 'Whoa there, old sport! You don't want to peg it on your birthday!'

'Don't care if I do,' he says, red in the face, all of a sweat. 'Not bad for a centenarian, eh?'

I put my arms around him, although they didn't meet, and said: 'I love you more than ever I loved any young kid, short pants, mother doesn't know he's out.'

Not bad for a centenarian.

Not bad at all.

Not bad.

Not –

Nora told me afterwards how the agitations of the steel bed began to make the chandelier downstairs directly beneath it, shiver, so that the music of the lutes, now plucking away at a selection of show tunes for the delight of the dancing guests, was almost imperceptibly augmented by the tinkle, tinkle, tinkle of all the little lustres as the tiers of glass began to sway from side to side, slopping hot wax on the dancers below, first slowly, then with a more and more determined rhythm until they shook like Josephine Baker's bottom –

'What a clatter!' said Nora. 'Like cymbals, darling. Don't you think I didn't guess what you were up to?'

There was just one ecstatic moment, she opined, when she thought the grand bouncing on the bed upstairs – remember, Perry was a *big man* – would bring down that chandelier and all its candles, smash, bang, clatter, and the swagged ceiling, too; bring the house down, fuck the house down, come ('cum'?) all over the posh frocks and the monkey jackets and the poisoned cake and the lovers, mothers, sisters, shatter the lenses that turned our lives into peepshows, scatter little candle-flames like an epiphany on every head, cover over all the family, the friends, the camera crews, with plaster dust and come and fire.

But such was not to be. There are limits to the power of laughter and though I may hint at them from time to time, I do not propose to step over them.

Perry and I had no idea what was going on below, of course. Not bad for a centenarian at all, at all.

But do not think I went to bed with the ribald ancient who'd arrived with my darling godchild in a box an hour before. Oh, no. I lay in the arms of that russet-mopped young flyer in the weathered leather jacket who'd knocked at the door of 49 Bard Road, and saved us all from gloom the day the war to end all wars ended, just twenty years before the next one started. And wars are facts we cannot fuck away, Perry; nor laugh away, either.

Do you hear me, Perry?

No.

He was himself, when young; and also, while we were making love, he turned into, of all people, that blue-eyed boy who'd never known my proper name. Then who else but Irish passed briefly through the bed; fancy meeting you. There was a whiff of Trumper's Essence of Lime but not Perry, this time, instead, that Free Pole the night I caught a flea in the Ritz. And then a visit from Mr Piano Man, only he'd used a powerful mouthwash, thank goodness. Don't think I'd gone wandering off down Memory Lane in the midst of it all; but Peregrine wasn't only the one dear man, tonight, but a kaleidoscope of faces, gestures, caresses. He was not the love of my life but all the loves of my life at once, the curtain call of my career as lover.

And who was I?

I saw myself reflected in those bracken-coloured eyes of his. I was a lanky girl with a green bow in her mouse-brown hair, blinking away the first, worst disappointment of her life in the sun on Brighton Prom.

When I was just thirteen years old, Perry! You dirty beast!

Evidently, back downstairs in the ballroom, the chandelier, after a last, terrifyingly violent paroxysm, commenced to decelerate until one final chink and tinkle and then it was as morose and static as it ever was, the candles settled down again and everybody had another glass of bubbly.

'And what were *you* doing, Nora?'

'Sitting on our dad's knee, like a good daughter ought to on her old man's birthday, Dora.'

What would have happened if we *had* brought the house down? Wrecked the whole lot, roof blown off, floor caved in, all the people blown out of the blown-out windows . . . sent it all sky high, destroyed all the terms of every contract, set all the old books on fire, wiped the slate clean. As if, when the young king meets up again with Jack Falstaff in *Henry IV, Part Two*, he doesn't send him packing but digs him in the ribs, says: 'Have I got a job for you!'

While we were doing it, everything seemed possible, I must say. But that is the illusion of the act. Now I remember how everything seemed possible when I was doing it, but as soon as I stopped, not, as if fucking itself were the origin of illusion.

'Life's a carnival,' he said. He was an illusionist, remember.

'The carnival's got to stop, some time, Perry,' I said. 'You listen to the news, that'll take the smile off your face.'

'News? What news?'

I saw he was incorrigible but I gave him a big kiss all the same. When he got his breath back, he wiped us both off with a silk scarf he reached for and picked up where it had fallen on the floor, Gucci or Pucci or something like that. It was Saskia's, must have dropped out of her pocket. I discovered I was lying on her mink. She hadn't trusted her fur coat to the promiscuous crush of the downstairs cloakroom, had she, she must have thought the help might nick it, but look at the horrid stains it had acquired upstairs! When I saw what I had done to Saskia's coat, my cup of happiness ran over.

Then I was seized with panic, and a crippling doubt.

''Ere, Perry . . . you're not, by any chance, my father, are you?'

He was quite taken aback, for a moment. Then he laughed until he choked so I had to beat him on the back. He laughed and shook his head and laughed and coughed and sputtered.

'Dora, Dora, I've got *some* standards! I never set eyes on either you or your Grandma until the Armistice, I promise!'

'I thought I'd ask,' I said, 'seeing as how you're everybody else's.'

He reached out for his trousers.

'I'm not your father, Dora. I spent seventy-odd years regretting it, my precious, but mighty glad I am of it, this minute.' Always the *mot juste*, our Perry. He stood up. He commenced to dress.

'But . . . has it ever occurred to you that your mother might not be your mother?'

I was putting on my tights. There was a ladder running from a star. I stood stock-still with one leg stuck up in the air.

'What?'

'Did you ever see your mother's grave, Dora?'

'What are you trying to get at, Perry?'

'I'm not sure,' he said slowly. 'I've got no concrete evidence. But sometimes I used to wonder about your Grandma.'

'Grandma?'

'Her last fling,' suggested Perry. 'Pinning old Melchior down on the mattress and – '

'You've got a very filthy mind, I must say, Perry.' I tucked my tits away neatly into my lynx-print top. 'Possible but not probable. Grandma was fifty if she was a day when we came along and she'd have been proud as a peacock, she'd never have made up some cock and bull story about a chambermaid to explain us away, why should she?'

'Just a thought,' he said. 'She never talked about your mother. I asked her, a couple of times, but she clammed up. She liked to keep her secrets. I asked her, once, where she came from herself and she said, "Out of a bottle, like a bloody genie, dearie."'

'Come off it, Perry. "Father" is a hypothesis but "mother" is a fact. Grandma never buried her, she didn't believe in people's bodies lying around cluttering up the place once the owners were through with them. She had our mum cremated and put the ashes in the garden. We put Grandma's there, too. It's everso good for the roses.'

'Mother is as mother does,' said Perry. 'She loved you just as much as if – '

'Don't start me off, again. Talk about April showers.' I dabbed my eyes carefully on account of the three shades of eyeshadow. He put his flying jacket on. We looked each other up and down. We couldn't stop smiling. I'd known in my bones today would be a red-letter day.

'Come on back downstairs,' he said. 'I've got a little present for you and Nora. Would I forget your birthdays?'

'Just a sec – '

For then I knew what I must do.

Not that I believe in telepathy but Perry caught on at once and we turned that room over together. Not that there was much to turn, since it was so minimal, but then we found that Margarine tucked away all the evidence of Melchior in a slip of a room next door, with a little narrow bed, a brown fug of theatrical prints and a faint aroma hinting at incontinence. The *Interiors* photographer never got wind of its existence.

When I saw that picture on the wall, first off, I thought it was the man himself, because it was of an old man in purple who looked just like. But then I saw how thick and brown the varnish was, how grandiose and nineteenth-century the brushwork. And *this* man wore a crown. It was older by far than Melchior and there was the legend on the frame: 'Ranulph Hazard, "Never, never, never, never, never . . ."'

Here was the source of all that regal, tragic fancy dress – the purple robe, the rings, the pendant. On his hundredth birthday, a man may indulge in any whim he chooses; Melchior had donned the costume of his father. The slandered, the abused, the cuckolded Ranulph. Ranulph, wife-murderer, friend-murderer, self-murderer, 'a little more than kin and less than kind'. You can say that again. The son put on the lost father's clothes and when I saw what he had done I could have cried because I'd never taken into consideration that he'd got problems of his own where family was concerned. His childhood, which stopped short at ten years old, never to go again, like grandfather's clock (only not like *our* grandfather's clock, which is still in very fair fettle, thank you very much). No love, no nothing. And, tonight of all nights, he'd chosen to become his own father, hadn't he, as if the child had not been the father of the man, in his case, but, during his whole long life, the man had waited to become the father of himself.

When, later on, we finally got ourselves home after the wonderful events of the night, I confided some of these thoughts to Nora. She knitted her brows.

'If the child is father of the man,' she asked, 'then who is the mother of the woman?'

Speaking of which, has it ever occurred to you to spare a passing thought as to the character of the deceased *Mrs* Lear? Didn't it ever occur to you that Cordelia might have taken after her mother while the other girls . . .

Melchior had dressed up as his father but had left off that crown. Peregrine climbed up on a stool and rooted round on the highest shelves of Melchior's closet and first he found a box of stiff collars, and then a box of spats, and then a box that once contained a topper. And there it was, inside. Melchior must have come home and hidden it away with all his other posthumous clothing the day the man on the Underground thought he was dead.

It was battered and tattered and the gilt was peeling off but Perry made a few magic passes over it and it came up lovely.

'I made him jump for it, once,' he said. 'You can give it to him for nothing, today.'

Downstairs it was only family. Not one media person left, nor guests, just dirty glasses fallen on their sides, crumpled serviettes, chicken-bones, wilting lilac, candles keeling over. The lutenists were gone, the waiters gone, the serving wenches and the pages were gone, Perry's Brazilian friends adjourned to their rooms in the Travellers' Club, but Old Nanny had emerged from the ladies' toilet to take her rightful place amongst us and they were all sitting round convivially picking away at a big platter of left-over chicken. When I saw the chicken, I felt peckish, but there was a little ceremony I must perform before I could eat it.

I picked a cushion off one of the gilt chairs and shook it. Broken glass fell out. They were all ignoring us with elaborate politeness, except for Nora, who winked, so nobody was looking when I plumped up that cushion and set that old crown nicely out upon it. Where were the baroque trumpeters now that I needed a fanfare? But when I said:

'Father, look what I've found!'

and processed towards him bearing aloft my cushion, Perry began to imitate a drumroll to perfection: 'Rub-a-dub-a-dub-a-dub.' Nora, sitting on his knee, looked sentimental. Daisy smacked away the wandering hand her aged husband had, from force of habit, placed in her bosom and adopted a reverential air. Everybody sat with drumsticks suspended halfway to their mouths as Perry brought the imaginary drumroll to a magnificent conclusion and said, in a round, rich, mahogany-coloured voice well-suited to the occasion:

'Prince of players! Reclaim your crown!'

I stood up on tiptoe. I placed the crown on his long, grey hair. Sometimes you know it's sentimental and sometimes you just don't care. I was a touch long in the tooth for Cordelia but there you are.

'My princesses,' he said. 'My two dancing princesses.' No, he did. Really! If only our mother could have been there to see. But – which mother? Pretty Kitty? Grandma? That's a problem. I don't know what Pretty Kitty might have said, but Grandma would have managed something acid. The Lady A. looked pleased. My Lady Margarine looked pissed off. The darling buds looked chastened.

Yet Nora and I were well content. We'd finally wormed our way into the heart of the family we'd always wanted to be part of. They'd asked us on the stage and let us join in, legit. at last. There was a house we all had in common and it was called, the past, even though we'd lived in different rooms. Then Perry, wearing his conjuring smile, said:

'Look in my pocket, Nora.'

Her lipstick was all over the place because she'd been at the chicken, her hair was coming down, she looked ribald. I daresay I did, too.

'In your pocket, eh?' she said, richly. She had a feel. Then her face changed. I'd never seen her look like that before, not in all the years we've been together. She looked as if she were about to fall in love, was teetering on the brink – but more so. As if about to fall in love terminally, once and for all, as if she'd met the perfect stranger.

'Oh, Perry!' She expelled a sigh and pulled it out.

Brown as a quail, round as an egg, sleepy as a pear. I'll never know how he got it in his pocket.

'Look in the other one, Dora.'

One each. They were twins, of course, three months old, by the look of them.

'*Oooh*, Perry!' said Nora. 'Just what I always wanted.'

'Gareth's,' said Peregrine to Melchior. So it turned out the Hazard dynasty wasn't at its last gasp at all but was bursting out in every direction and, to add to the hypothetical, disputed, absent father that was such a feature of our history, now you could add a holy father, too. Put it down to liberation theology.

Margarine grabbed hold of Perry: have you seen him? How is he? Who is the mother? Where is she?

But who she was or where they both were do not belong to the world of comedy. Perry told us, of course, because we were family, but I don't propose to tell *you*, not now, when the barren heath was bloomed, the fire that was almost out sprung back to life and Nora a mother at last at seventy-five years old and all laughter, forgiveness, generosity, reconciliation.

Yes.

Hard to swallow, huh?

Well, you might have known what you were about to let yourself in for when you let Dora Chance in her ratty old fur and poster paint, her orange (Persian Melon) toenails sticking out of her snakeskin peep-toes, reeking of liquor, accost you in the Coach and Horses and let her tell you a tale.

I've got a tale and a half to tell, all right!

But, truthfully, these glorious pauses do, sometimes, occur in the discordant but complementary narratives of our lives and if you choose to stop the story there, at such a pause, and refuse to take it any further, then you can call it a happy ending.

There was a full moon out over Regent's Park when we piled into Saskia's van, that she'd brought the food in; the inside still smelled of rosemary. Such was the power of Peregrine's personality that nobody, not even Margarine, the official grandmother, nor better yet, Old Nanny, dreamed for one moment of contesting Nora's possession of the newest Hazard twins who, as she found out when she changed their nappies, she let out a squawk – were boy and girl, a new thing in our family.

Not only that. Margarine went personally up to the attic to fetch us a double pram, the one that Tristram and Gareth had when they were babies, so our babies would ride home like royalty, and we planned to stop off at the all-night Boots in Piccadilly for formula and bottles.

Perry took Tristram to one side and asked him, did he want to go back to South America with him to help look for Gareth. Tristram took a big gulp and said, 'Yes.' So that's what's going to become of Tristram. Perhaps he will come back fit to be a father and take up his responsibilities; and perhaps not. Margarine and Melchior looked scared and proud; they loved him. I am not sure if this is a happy ending. I cross my fingers.

The chauffeur came and Daisy and he between them carried Puck down to Daisy's limo, he was well away, borne up and elsewhere on the lovely wind of his own voice.

While teeing off a game of golf
I may make a play for the caddy –

Off he went downstairs; when I went to open the window to let the fug out, they were loading him into the car and he was still singing:

'. . . but my heart belongs to daddy.'

'Oh, very apt,' said Nora, but I thought it was bad taste.

The Lady A. nodded off in her wheelchair while we were fixing up the pram business because she was getting very frail, poor old thing, and the evening had tired her out, no wonder, so Perry carried her up to the spare room in his arms, a very touching sight to see. Saskia said, did we need a lift and I was sufficiently overcome by the prevailing spirit of goodwill that I said, take us as far as the Elephant, we'll walk from there, because it's a lovely night and we could do with a walk, clear our heads.

Margarine was going round snuffing out the candles when we bade them our farewells and she kissed the babies and made as if about to kiss us, too, but thought better of it and backed off. The jury is still out on the question of her boys' paternity. But in my heart I think, not. Not her and Perry. No way. He must have known someone else in Gunter Grove. Melchior with his crown still on, though much askew by now, came to the window to wave and then we got into the back of the van along with several plastic vats of salad which Saskia had forgotten to serve up, so much had been going on.

Tristram was staying in his own old room for the night, to his mother's soft, glowing satisfaction, and Saskia had sufficient savvy to know when not to press him but I could tell by the look in her eyes that if we all stopped short at this point it wouldn't be a happy ending for her, no, sir! She hadn't finished with the boy, by any means, so I thought, the sooner he gets off to Amazonia, the better.

Yet, no matter how fragile or brief it might be, there was a truce that night between the Chance girls and the Hazard sisters. We never said one word about the past, the taunts, the farmhouse, the chicanery, the staircase. Imogen sat in the front, next to Saskia, with the fishbowl on her knee. She looked content enough but she was always a strange one. Now and then she did those goldfish movements with her mouth.

'What are you saying?' Saskia asked her.

'Goldie say: "Goodnight! God bless!"' she said. I felt nauseous. Truce! I reminded myself. Truce!

Nora pushed the pram. I carried the Boots' bag. Gawd, it was heavy. A heart-shaped glow appeared to surround our Nora in the night but you mustn't go away thinking I wasn't pleased about our babies, too.

But coming so late in our lives and so unexpectedly . . .

'What shall we do about the cats, Nora?'

'I thought we might clear out Grandma's old room for a nursery,' said Nora, ignoring my question. 'Get rid of all that junk. Get a bloke in to paint it all white, with maybe a Beatrix Potter frieze. What do you think?'

'We won't be able to go out in the evenings, Nora.'

'*You* can go out, dear,' she said magnanimously. 'I'll be perfectly content to stay at home with these little cherubs.'

She must have thought she heard a coo, because she bent down over the pram to peer under the hoods.

'Babies!' she said, and cackled with glee.

'No fun, going out without you,' I said.

'Come off it, Dora. Grow up.'

'It's all very well for you, Nora. You always wanted kids. Now you've got them.'

She cackled again.

'We're both of us mothers and both of us fathers,' she said. 'They'll be wise children, all right.'

She peered in at the babies, again; they slept on undisturbed. No sound but the whirring of the rubber wheels and a cat, somewhere, giving a mating call. I told Nora what was on my mind.

'Here, Nora . . .'

She cocked her head.

'Nora . . . don't you think our father looked two-dimensional, tonight?'

She gave me a look that said, tell me more.

'Too kind, too handsome, too repentant. After all those years without a word. Remember that terrible bank holiday when he pretended to our faces that he thought we were Perry's? And tonight, he had an imitation look, even when he was crying, especially when he was crying, like one of those great, big, papier-mâché heads they have in the Notting Hill parade, larger than life, but not lifelike.'

Nora sunk in thought for a hundred yards.

'D'you know, I sometimes wonder if we haven't been making him up all along,' she said. 'If he isn't just a collection of our hopes and dreams and wishful thinking in the afternoons. Something to set our lives by, like the old clock in the hall, which is real enough, in itself, but which we've got to wind up to make it go.'

'Oh, very profound. Very deep.'

'Think about it,' she said. 'We can tell these little darlings here whatever we like about their mum and dad if Perry doesn't find them but whatever we tell them, they'll make up their own romance out of it.'

But thinking of the twins put me in mind of something more pressing than family romances.

'Here, Nora . . . if we've got those twins to look out for, we can't afford to die for at least another twenty years.'

'Thank goodness we're a long-lived family.' She'd thought of that herself.

We went past the Oval; we were doomed to a century. Just when I'd been thinking it was high time for the final curtain. Which only goes to show, you never know in the morning what the night will bring and I'd had a little bonus of my own, hadn't I, but Nora never pried because twins we may be but we respect each other's secrets. So we turned into Bard Road, at last, when there came a wee stirring from the depths of the pram.

'What's up, small fry?'

They mewed and rustled.

'I say, Dora, let's give them a song. After all we're song-and-dance girls, aren't we?'

'We're dancing princesses,' said Nora. 'What an old fraud he is!'

'You wouldn't want him any different.'

'I used to want him dead.'

We put our handbags in the pram, for safety's sake. Then and there, we couldn't wait, we broke into harmony, we serenaded the new arrivals:

> 'We can't give you anything but love, babies,
> That's the only thing we've plenty of, babies – '

The window on the second-floor front window of 41 Bard Road went up, a head came out. Dreadlocks. That Rastafarian.

'You two, again,' he said.

'Have a heart!' we said. 'We've got something to celebrate, tonight!'

'Well, you just watch it, in case a squad car comes by,' he said. 'Drunk in charge of a baby carriage, at your age.'

We'd got so many songs to sing to our babies, all our old songs, that we didn't pay him any attention. 'Gee, we'd like to see you looking swell, babies!' and the Hazard theme song, 'Is You Is or Is You Ain't'. Then there were songs from the show that nobody else remembers. '2b or not 2b', 'Hey nonny bloody no', 'Mistress Mine', and Broadway tunes, and paper moons, and lilacs in the spring, again. We went on dancing and singing. 'Diamond bracelets Woolworths doesn't sell.' Besides, it was our birthday, wasn't it, we'd got to sing them the silly old song about Charlie Chaplin and his comedy boots all the little kids were singing and dancing in the street the day we were born. There was dancing and singing all along Bard Road that day and we'll go on singing and dancing until we drop in our tracks, won't we, kids.

What a joy it is to dance and sing!

DRAMATIS PERSONAE
(in order of appearance)

Dora Chance Nora Chance }	identical twins, illegitimate daughters of Melchior Hazard but officially known as the daughters of Peregrine Hazard
Tiffany	their goddaughter
(Sir) Melchior Hazard Peregrine Hazard }	fraternal twins, sons of the marriage of Estella and Ranulph Hazard q.v.
Lady Atalanta Hazard, née Lynde	first wife of Melchior Hazard, mother of Saskia and Imogen
Delia Delaney, née Daisy Duck	second wife of Melchior Hazard, previously second wife of 'Genghis Khan' q.v.
Saskia Hazard Imogen Hazard }	identical twins, legally daughters of Melchior Hazard, biologically daughters of Peregrine Hazard
Tristram Hazard Gareth Hazard }	fraternal twins, sons of Melchior Hazard's third marriage
'My Lady Margarine'	third wife of Melchior Hazard, mother of Tristram and Gareth
'Grandma' Chance	guardian of Nora and Dora Chance
Estella 'A Star Danced' Hazard	mother of Melchior and Peregrine Hazard
'Lewis Carroll'	a photographer of children
Ranulph Hazard	husband of Estella Hazard
Cassius Booth	boyfriend of Estella Hazard
'Pretty Kitty'	a foundling, mother of Nora and Dora Chance

'Our Cyn'	a foundling, mother of Mavis, grandmother of Brenda, great-grandmother of Tiffany
Miss Worthington	a dance teacher
Mrs Worthington	her mother, an accompanist
Gorgeous George	comedian and patriot
'Pantomime Goose'	Nora Chance's first boyfriend
Principal boy	wife of Pantomime Goose
Blond tenor with unmemorable name	Dora Chance's first boyfriend
'Mr Piano Man'	musician, composer, boyfriend of Dora Chance
'Genghis Khan'	a film producer
His first wife	a jealous woman
Tony	an Italian American, fiancé of Nora Chance
Ross 'Irish' O'Flaherty	American writer, boyfriend of Dora Chance
Unnamed radical German exile in Hollywood	boyfriend of Dora Chance
'Puck'	male soprano, third husband of Delia Delaney
Brenda	granddaughter of 'Our Cyn', mother of Tiffany
Leroy	her husband
	In no particular order of appearance: rough children, cats, chorus girls, chorus boys, nudes, spear-carriers, comics, fans, Free French, Free Poles, Free Norwegians, soldiers, sailors, airmen of all nations, media personalities, television crews, market traders, pupils of the Italia Conte School, Amazonian tribesmen, photographers, film buffs, the public, extras.

FIREWORKS

A SOUVENIR OF JAPAN

WHEN I WENT outside to see if he was coming home, some children dressed ready for bed in cotton nightgowns were playing with sparklers in the vacant lot on the corner. When the sparks fell down in beards of stars, the smiling children cooed softly. Their pleasure was very pure because it was so restrained. An old woman said: 'And so they pestered their father until he bought them fireworks.' In this language, fireworks are called *hannabi*, which means 'flower fire'. All through summer, every evening, you can see all kinds of fireworks, from the humblest to the most elaborate, and once we rode the train out of Shinjuku for an hour to watch one of the public displays which are held over rivers so that the dark water multiplies the reflections.

By the time we arrived at our destination, night had already fallen. We were in the suburbs. Many families were on their way to enjoy the fireworks. Their mothers had scrubbed and dressed up the smallest children to celebrate the treat. The little girls were especially immaculate in pink and white cotton kimonos tied with fluffy sashes like swatches of candy floss. Their hair had been most beautifully brushed, arranged in sleek, twin bunches and decorated with twists of gold and silver thread. These children were all on their best behaviour because they were staying up late and held their parents' hands with a charming propriety. We followed the family parties until we came to some fields by the river and saw, high in the air, fireworks already opening out like variegated parasols. They were visible from far away and as we took the path that led through the fields towards their source they seemed to occupy more and more of the sky.

Along the path were stalls where shirtless cooks with sweatbands round their heads roasted corncobs and cuttlefish over charcoal. We bought cuttlefish on skewers and ate them as we walked along. They had been basted with soy sauce and were very good. There were also stalls selling goldfish in plastic bags and others for big balloons with rabbit ears. It was like a fairground

– but such a well-ordered fair! Even the patrolling policemen carried coloured paper lanterns instead of torches. Everything was altogether quietly festive. Ice-cream sellers wandered among the crowd, ringing handbells. Their boxes of wares smoked with cold and they called out in plaintive voices, 'Icy, icy, icy cream!' When young lovers dispersed discreetly down the tracks in the sedge, the shadowy, indefatigable salesmen pursued them with bells, lamps and mournful cries.

By now, a great many people were walking towards the fireworks but their steps fell so softly and they chatted in such gentle voices there was no more noise than a warm, continual, murmurous humming, the cosy sound of shared happiness, and the night filled with a muted, bourgeois yet authentic magic. Above our heads, the fireworks hung dissolving earrings on the night. Soon we lay down in a stubbled field to watch the fireworks. But, as I expected, he very quickly grew restive.

'Are you happy?' he asked. 'Are you sure you're happy?' I was watching the fireworks and did not reply at first although I knew how bored he was and, if he was himself enjoying anything, it was only the idea of my pleasure – or, rather, the idea that he enjoyed my pleasure, since this would be a proof of love. I became guilty and suggested we return to the heart of the city. We fought a silent battle of self-abnegation and I won it, for I had the stronger character. Yet the last thing in the world that I wanted was to leave the scintillating river and the gentle crowd. But I knew his real desire was to return and so return we did, although I do not know if it was worth my small victory of selflessness to bear his remorse at cutting short my pleasure, even if to engineer this remorse had, at some subterranean level, been the whole object of the outing.

Nevertheless, as the slow train nosed back into the thickets of neon, his natural liveliness returned. He could not lose his old habit of walking through the streets with a sense of expectation, as if a fateful encounter might be just around the corner, for, the longer one stayed out, the longer something remarkable might happen and, even if nothing ever did, the chance of it appeased the sweet ache of his boredom for a little while. Besides, his duty by me was done. He had taken me out for the evening and now he wanted to be rid of me. Or so I saw it. The word for wife, *okusan*, means the person who occupies the inner room and rarely, if ever, comes out of it. Since I often appeared to be his wife, I was frequently subjected to this treatment, though I fought against it bitterly.

But I usually found myself waiting for him to come home knowing, with a certain resentment, that he would not; and that he would not even telephone me to tell me he would be late, either, for he was far too guilty to do so. I had nothing better to do than to watch the neighbourhood children light their sparklers and giggle; the old woman stood beside me and I knew she disapproved of me. The entire street politely disapproved of me. Perhaps they thought I was contributing to the delinquency of a juvenile for he was obviously younger than I. The old woman's back was bowed almost to a circle from carrying, when he was a baby, the father who now supervised the domestic fireworks in his evening undress of loose, white drawers, naked to the waist. Her face had the seamed reserve of the old in this country. It was a neighbourhood poignantly rich in old ladies.

At the corner shop, they put an old lady outside on an upturned beer crate each morning, to air. I think she must have been the household grandmother. She was so old she had lapsed almost entirely into a somnolent plant life. She was of neither more nor less significance to herself or to the world than the pot of morning glories which blossomed beside her and perhaps she had less significance than the flowers, which would fade before lunch was ready. They kept her very clean. They covered her pale cotton kimono with a spotless pinafore trimmed with coarse lace and she never dirtied it because she did not move. Now and then, a child came out to comb her hair. Her consciousness was quite beclouded by time and, when I passed by, her rheumy eyes settled upon me always with the same, vague, disinterested wonder, like that of an Eskimo watching a train. When she whispered, *Irrasyaimase*, the shopkeeper's word of welcome, in the ghostliest of whispers, like the rustle of a paper bag, I saw her teeth were rimmed with gold.

The children lit sparklers under a mouse-coloured sky and, due to the pollution in the atmosphere, the moon was mauve. The cicadas throbbed and shrieked in the backyards. When I think of this city, I shall always remember the cicadas who whirr relentlessly all through the summer nights, rising to a piercing crescendo in the subfusc dawn. I have heard cicadas even in the busiest streets, though they thrive best in the back alleys, where they ceaselessly emit that scarcely tolerable susurration which is like a shrill intensification of extreme heat.

A year before, on such a throbbing, voluptuous, platitudinous, subtropical night, we had been walking down one of these shady streets together, in and out of the shadows of the willow trees, looking for somewhere to make love. Morning glories climbed the lattices which screened the low, wooden houses, but the darkness hid the tender colours of these flowers, which the Japanese prize because they fade so quickly. He soon found a hotel, for the city is hospitable to lovers. We were shown into a room like a paper box. It contained nothing but a mattress spread on the floor. We lay down immediately and began to kiss one another. Then a maid soundlessly opened the sliding door and, stepping out of her slippers, crept in on stockinged feet, breathing apologies. She carried a tray which contained two cups of tea and a plate of candies. She put the tray down on the matted floor beside us and backed, bowing and apologizing, from the room whilst our uninterrupted kiss continued. He started to unfasten my shirt and then she came back again. This time, she carried an armful of towels. I was stripped stark naked when she returned for a third time to bring the receipt for his money. She was clearly a most respectable woman and, if she was embarrassed, she did not show it by a single word or gesture.

I learned his name was Taro. In a toy store, I saw one of those books for children with pictures which are cunningly made of paper cut-outs so that, when you turn the page, the picture springs up in the three stylized dimensions of a backdrop in Kabuki. It was the story of Momotaro, who was born from a peach. Before my eyes, the paper peach split open and there was the baby, where the stone should have been. He, too, had the inhuman sweetness of a child born from something other than a mother, a passive, cruel sweetness I did not immediately understand, for it was that of the repressed masochism which, in my country, is usually confined to women.

Sometimes he seemed to possess a curiously unearthly quality when he perched upon the mattress with his knees drawn up beneath his chin in the attitude of a pixie on a door-knocker. At these times, his face seemed somehow both too flat and too large for his elegant body which had such curious, androgynous grace with its svelte, elongated spine, wide shoulders and unusually well developed pectorals, almost like the breasts of a girl approaching puberty. There was a subtle lack of alignment between face and body and he seemed almost goblin, as if he might have borrowed another person's head, as Japanese goblins do, in order to perform some devious trick. These impressions of a weird visitor were fleeting yet haunting. Sometimes, it was possible for me to believe he had practised an enchantment upon me, as foxes in this country may, for, here, a fox can masquerade as human and at the best of times the high cheekbones gave to his face the aspect of a mask.

His hair was so heavy his neck drooped under its weight and was of a black so deep it turned purple in sunlight. His mouth also was purplish and his blunt, bee-stung lips those of Gauguin's Tahitians. The touch of his skin was as smooth as water as it flows through the fingers. His eyelids were retractable, like those of a cat, and sometimes disappeared completely. I should have liked to have had him embalmed and been able to keep him beside me in a glass coffin, so that I could watch him all the time and he would not have been able to get away from me.

As they say, Japan is a man's country. When I first came to Tokyo, cloth carps fluttered from poles in the gardens of the families fortunate enough to have borne boy children, for it was the time of the annual festival, Boys' Day. At least they do not disguise the situation. At least one knows where one is. Our polarity was publicly acknowledged and socially sanctioned. As an example of the use of the word *dewa*, which occasionally means, as far as I can gather, 'in', I once found in a textbook a sentence which, when translated, read: 'In a society where men dominate, they value women only as the object of men's passions.' If the only conjunction possible to us was that of the death-defying double-somersault of love, it is, perhaps, a better thing to be valued only as an object of passion than never to be valued at all. I had never been so absolutely the mysterious other. I had become a kind of phoenix, a fabulous beast; I was an outlandish jewel. He found me, I think, inexpressibly exotic. But I often felt like a female impersonator.

In the department store there was a rack of dresses labelled: 'For Young and Cute Girls Only'. When I looked at them, I felt as gross as Glumdalclitch. I wore men's sandals because they were the only kind that fitted me and, even so, I had to take the largest size. My pink cheeks, blue eyes and blatant yellow hair made of me, in the visual orchestration of this city in which all heads were dark, eyes brown and skin monotone, an instrument which played upon an alien scale. In a sober harmony of subtle plucked instruments and wistful flutes, I blared. I proclaimed myself like in a perpetual fanfare. He was so delicately put together that I thought his skeleton must have the airy elegance of a bird's and I was sometimes afraid that I might smash him. He told me that when he was in bed with me, he felt like a small boat upon a wide, stormy sea.

We pitched our tent in the most unlikely surroundings. We were living in a room furnished only by passion amongst homes of the most astounding respectability. The sounds around us were the swish of brooms upon *tatami* matting and the clatter of demotic Japanese. On all the windowledges, prim flowers bloomed in pots. Every morning, the washing came out on the balconies at seven. Early one morning, I saw a man washing the leaves of his tree. Quilts and mattresses went out to air at eight. The sunlight lay thick enough on these unpaved alleys to lay the dust and somebody always seemed to be practising Chopin in one or another of the flimsy houses, so lightly glued together from plywood it seemed they were sustained only by willpower. Once I was at home, however, it was as if I occupied the inner room and he did not expect me to go out of it, although it was I who paid the rent.

Yet, when he was away from me, he spent much of the time savouring the most annihilating remorse. But this remorse or regret was the stuff of life to him and out he would go again the next night, or, if I had been particularly angry, he would wait until the night after that. And, even if he fully intended to come back early and had promised me he would do so, circumstances always somehow denied him and once more he would contrive to miss the last train. He and his friends spent their nights in a desultory progression from coffee shop to bar to *pachinko* parlour to coffee shop, again, with the radiant aimlessness of the pure existential hero. They were connoisseurs of boredom. They savoured the various bouquets of the subtly differentiated boredoms which rose from the long, wasted hours at the dead end of night. When it was time for the first train in the morning, he would go back to the mysteriously deserted, Piranesi perspectives of the station, discoloured by dawn, exquisitely tortured by the notion – which probably contained within it a damped-down spark of hope – that, this time, he might have done something irreparable.

I speak as if he had no secrets from me. Well, then, you must realize that I was suffering from love and I knew him as intimately as I knew my own image in a mirror. In other words, I knew him only in relation to myself. Yet, on those terms, I knew him perfectly. At times, I thought I was inventing him as I went along, however, so you will have to take my word for it that we existed. But I do not want to paint our circumstantial portraits so that we both emerge with enough well-rounded, spuriously detailed actuality that you are forced to believe in us. I do not want to practise such sleight of hand. You must be content only with glimpses of our outlines, as if you had caught sight of our reflections in the looking-glass of somebody else's house as you passed by the window. His name was not Taro. I only called him Taro so that I could use the conceit of the peach boy, because it seemed appropriate.

Speaking of mirrors, the Japanese have a great respect for them and, in old-fashioned inns, one often finds them hooded with fabric covers when not in use. He said: 'Mirrors make a room uncosy.' I am sure there is more to it than that although they love to be cosy. One must love cosiness if one is to live so close together. But, as if in celebration of the thing they feared, they seemed to have made the entire city into a cold hall of mirrors which continually proliferated whole galleries of constantly changing appearances, all marvellous but none tangible. If they did not lock up the real looking-glasses, it would be hard to tell what was real and what was not. Even buildings one had taken for substantial had a trick of disappearing overnight. One morning, we woke to find the house next door reduced to nothing but a heap of sticks and a pile of newspapers neatly tied with string, left out for the garbage collector.

I would not say that he seemed to me to possess the same kind of insubstantiality although his departure usually seemed imminent, until I realized he was as erratic but as inevitable as the weather. If you plan to come and live in Japan, you must be sure you are stoical enough to endure the weather. No, it was not insubstantiality; it was a rhetoric valid only on its own terms. When I listened to his protestations, I was prepared to believe he believed in them, although I knew perfectly well they meant nothing. And that isn't fair. When he made them, he believed in them implicitly. Then, he was utterly consumed by conviction. But his dedication was primarily to the idea of himself in love. This idea seemed to him magnificent, even sublime. He was prepared to die for it, as one of Baudelaire's dandies might have been prepared to kill himself in order to preserve himself in the condition of a work of art, for he wanted to make this experience a masterpiece of experience which absolutely transcended the everyday. And this would annihilate the effects of the cruel drug, boredom, to which he was addicted although, perhaps, the element of boredom which is implicit in an affair so isolated from the real world was its principal appeal for him. But I had no means of knowing how far his conviction would take him. And I used to turn over in my mind from time to time the question: how far does a pretence of feeling, maintained with absolute conviction, become authentic?

This country has elevated hypocrisy to the level of the highest style. To look at a samurai, you would not know him for a murderer, or a geisha for a whore. The magnificence of such objects hardly pertains to the human. They live only in a world of icons and there they participate in rituals which transmute life itself to a series of grand gestures, as moving as they are absurd. It was as if they all thought, if we believe in something hard enough, it will come true and, lo and behold! they had done and it did. Our street was in essence a slum but, in appearance, it was a little enclave of harmonious quiet and, *mirabile dictu*, it was the appearance which was the reality, because they all behaved so well, kept everything so clean and lived with such rigorous civility. What terrible discipline it takes to live harmoniously. They had crushed all their vigour in order to live harmoniously and now they had the wistful beauty of flowers pressed dry in an enormous book.

But repression does not necessarily give birth only to severe beauties. In its programmed interstices, monstrous passions bloom. They torture trees to make them look more like the formal notion of a tree. They paint amazing pictures on their skins with awl and gouge, sponging away the blood as they go; a tattooed man is a walking masterpiece of remembered pain. They boast the most passionate puppets in the world who mimic love suicides in a stylized fashion, for here there is no such comfortable formula as 'happy ever after'. And, when I remembered the finale of the puppet tragedies, how the wooden lovers cut their throats together, I felt the beginnings of unease, as if the hieratic imagery of the country might overwhelm me, for his boredom had reached such a degree that he was insulated against everything except the irritation of anguish. If he valued me as an object of passion, he had reduced the word to its root, which derives from the Latin, *patior*, I suffer. He valued me as an instrument which would cause him pain.

So we lived under a disoriented moon which was as angry a purple as if the sky had bruised its eye, and, if we made certain genuine intersections, these only took place in darkness. His contagious conviction that our love was unique and desperate infected me with an anxious sickness; soon we would learn to treat one another with the circumspect tenderness of comrades who are amputees, for we were surrounded by the most moving images of evanescence, fireworks, morning glories, the old, children. But the most moving of these images were the intangible reflections of ourselves we saw in one another's eyes, reflections of nothing but appearances, in a city dedicated to seeming, and, try as we might to possess the essence of each other's otherness, we would inevitably fail.

THE EXECUTIONER'S BEAUTIFUL DAUGHTER

HERE, WE ARE high in the uplands.

A baleful almost-music, that of the tuneless cadences of an untutored orchestra repercussing in an ecstatic agony of echoes against the sounding boards of the mountains, lured us into the village square where we discover them twanging, plucking and abusing with horsehair bows a wide variety of crude stringed instruments. Our feet crunch upon dryly whispering shifting sawdust freshly scattered over impacted surfaces of years of sawdusts clotted, here and there, with blood shed so long ago it has, with age, acquired the colour and texture of rust . . . sad, ominous stains, a threat, a menace, memorials of pain.

There is no brightness in the air. Today the sun will not irradiate the heroes of the dark spectacle to which accident and disharmony combined to invite us. Here, where the air is choked all day with diffuse moisture tremulously, endlessly on the point of becoming rain, light falls as if filtered through muslin so at all hours a crepuscular gloaming prevails; the sky looks as though it is about to weep and so, gloomily illuminated through unshed tears, the *tableau vivant* before us is suffused with the sepia tints of an old photograph and nothing within it moves. The intent immobility of the spectators, wholly absorbed as they are in the performance of their hieratic ritual, is scarcely that of living things and this *tableau vivant* might be better termed a *nature morte* for the mirthless carnival is a celebration of a death. Their eyes, the whites of which are yellowish, are all fixed, as if attached by taut, invisible strings upon a wooden block lacquered black with the spilt dews of a millennia of victims.

And now the rustic bandsmen suspend their unmelodious music. This death must be concluded in the most dramatic silence. The wild mountain-dwellers are gathered together to watch a public execution; that is the only entertainment the country offers.

Time, suspended like the rain, begins again in silence, slowly.

A heavy stillness ordering all his movements, the executioner himself adopts beside the block an offensively heroic pose, as if to do the thing with dignity were the only motive of the doing. He brings one booted foot to rest on the grim and sacrificial altar which is, to him, the canvas on which he exercises his art and proudly in his hand he bears his instrument, his axe.

The executioner stands more than six and a half feet high and he is broad to suit; the warped stumps of villagers gaze up at him with awe and fear. He is dressed always in mourning and always wears a curious mask. This mask is made of supple, close-fitting leather dyed an absolute black and it conceals his hair and the upper part of his face entirely except for two narrow slits through which issue the twin regards of eyes as inexpressive as though they were part of the mask. This mask reveals only his blunt-lipped, dark-red mouth and the greyish flesh which surrounds it. Laid out in such an unnerving fashion, these portions of his meat in no way fulfil the expectations we derive from our common knowledge of faces. They have a quality of obscene rawness as if, in some fashion, the lower face had been flayed. He, the butcher, might be displaying himself, as if he were his own meat.

Through the years, the close-fitting substance of the mask has become so entirely assimilated to the actual structure of his face that the face itself now seems to possess a parti-coloured appearance, as if by nature dual; and this face no longer pertains to that which is human as if, when he first put on the mask, he blotted out his own, original face and so defaced himself for ever. Because the hood of office renders the executioner an object. He has become an object who punishes. He is an object of fear. He is the image of retribution.

Nobody remembers why the mask was first devised nor who devised it. Perhaps some tender-heart of antiquity adopted the concealing headgear in order to spare the one upon the block the sight of too human a face in the last moments of his agony; or else the origins of the article lie in a magical relation with the blackness of negation – if, that is, negation is black in colour. Yet the executioner dare not take off the mask in case, in a random looking-glass or, accidentally mirrored in a pool of standing water, he surprised his own authentic face. For then he would die of fright.

The victim kneels. He is thin, pale and graceful. He is twenty years old. The silent throng in the courtyard shudders in common anticipation; all their gnarled features twist in the same grin. No sound, almost no sound disturbs the moist air, only the ghost of a sound, a distant sobbing that might be the ululation of the wind amongst the scrubby pines. The victim kneels and lays his neck upon the block. Ponderously the executioner lifts his gleaming steel.

The axe falls. The flesh severs. The head rolls.

The cleft flesh spouts its fountains. The spectators shudder, groan and gasp. And now the string band starts to bow and saw again whilst a choir of stunted virgins, in the screeching wail that passes for singing in these regions, intones a barbaric requiem entitled: AWFUL WARNING OF THE SPECTACLE OF A DECAPITATION.

The executioner has beheaded his own son for committing the crime of incest upon the body of his sister, the executioner's beautiful daughter, on whose cheeks the only roses in these highlands grow.

Gretchen no longer sleeps soundly. After the day his decapitated head rolled in the bloody sawdust, her brother rode a bicycle interminably through her dreams even though the poor child crept out secretly, alone, to gather up the poignant, moist, bearded strawberry, his surviving relic, and take it home to bury beside her hen-coop before the dogs ate it. But no matter how hard she scrubbed her little white apron against the scouring stones in the river, she could not wash away the stains that haunted the weft and warp of the fabric like pinkish phantoms of very precious fruit. Every morning, when she goes out to collect ripe eggs for her father's breakfast, she waters with felt but ineffectual tears the disturbed earth where her brother's brains lie rotting, while the indifferent hens peck and cluck about her feet.

This country is situated at such a high altitude water never boils, no matter how deceptively it foams within the pan, so their boiled eggs are always raw. The executioner insists his breakfast omelette be prepared only from those eggs precisely on the point of blossoming into chicks and, prompt at eight, consumes with relish a yellow, feathered omelette subtly spiked with claw. Gretchen, his tender-hearted daughter, often jumps and starts to hear the thwarted cluck from a still gelid, scarcely calcified beak about to be choked with sizzling butter, but her father, whose word is law because he never doffs his leather mask, will eat no egg that does not contain within it a nascent bird. That is his taste. In this country, only the executioner may indulge his perversities.

High among the mountains, how wet and cold it is! Chill winds blow soft drifts of rain across these almost perpendicular peaks; the wolf-haunted forests of fir and pine that cloak the lower slopes are groves fit only for the satanic cavortings of a universal Sabbath and a haunting mist pervades the bleak, meagre villages rooted so far above quotidian skies a newcomer might not, at first, be able to breathe but only wheeze and choke in this thinnest of air. Newcomers, however, are less frequent apparitions than meteorites and thunderbolts; the villages breathe no welcome.

Even the walls of the rudely constructed houses exude suspicion. They are made from slabs of stone and do not have any windows to see out with. An inadequate orifice in the flat roof puffs out a few scant breaths of domestic smoke and penetration inside is effected only with the utmost difficulty through low, narrow doors, crevices in the granite, so each house presents to the eye as featureless a face as those of the Oriental demons whose anonymity was marred by no such commonplace a blemish as an eye, a nose or a mouth. Inside these ugly, unaccommodating hutches, man and domestic beast – goat, ox, pig, dog – stake equal squatting rights to the smoky and disordered hearths, although the dogs often grow rabid and rush frothing through the rutted streets like streams in spate.

The inhabitants are a thick-set, sullen brood whose chronic malevolence stems from a variety of both environmental and constitutional causes. All share a general and unprepossessing cast of countenance. Their faces have the limp, flat, boneless aspect of the Eskimo and their eyes are opaque fissures since no eyelid hoods them, only the slack skin of the Mongolian fold. Their reptilian regards possess an intensity which is in no way intimate and their smiles are so peculiarly vicious it is all for the best they smile rarely. Their teeth rot young.

The men in particular are monstrously hirsute about both head and body. Their hair, a monotonous and uniform purplish black, grizzles, in age, to the tint of defunct ashes. The womenfolk are built for durability rather than delight. Since all go always barefoot, the soles of their feet develop an intensifying consistency of horn from earliest childhood and the women, who perform all the tasks demanded by their primitive agriculture, sprout forearms the size and contour of vegetable marrows while their hands become pronouncedly scoop-shaped, until they resemble, in maturity, fat five-pronged forks.

All, without exception, are filthy and verminous. His shaggy head and rough garments are clogged with lice and quiver with fleas while his pubic areas throb and pulse with the blind convulsions of the crab. Impetigo, scabies and the itch are too prevalent among them to be remarked upon and their feet start early to decompose between the toes. They suffer from chronic afflictions of the anus due to their barbarous diet – thin porridge; sour beer; meat scarcely seared by the cool fires of the highlands; acidulated cheese of goat swallowed to the flatulent accompaniment of barley bread. Such comestibles cannot but contribute effectively to those disorders that have established the general air of malign unease which is their most immediately distinctive characteristic.

In this museum of diseases, the pastel beauty of Gretchen, the executioner's daughter, is all the more remarkable. Her flaxen plaits bob above her breasts as she goes to pluck, from their nests, the budding eggs.

Their days are shrouded troughs of glum manual toil and their nights wet, freezing, black, palpitating clefts gravid with the grossest cravings, nights dedicated solely to the imaginings of unspeakable desires tortuously conceived in mortified sensibilities habitually gnawed to suppuration by the black rats of superstition whilst the needle teeth of frost corrode their bodies.

They would, if they could, act out entire Wagnerian cycles of operatic evil and gleefully transform their villages into stages upon which the authentic monstrosities of Grand Guignol might be acted out in every unspeakable detail. No hideous parody of the delights of the flesh would be alien to them ... *did they but know how such things were, in fact, performed*.

They have an inexhaustible capacity for sin but are inexorably baulked by ignorance. They do not know what they desire. So their lusts exist in an undefined limbo, for ever *in potentia*.

They yearn passionately after the most deplorable depravity but possess not the concrete notion of so much as a simple fetish, their tormented flesh betrayed eternally by the poverty of their imaginations and the limitations of their vocabulary, for how may one transmit such things in a language composed only of brute grunts and squawks representing, for example, the state of the family pig in labour? And, since their vices are, in the literal sense of the word, unspeakable, their secret, furious desires remain ultimately mysterious even to themselves and are contained only in the realm of pure sensation, or feeling undefined as thought or action and hence unrestrained by definition. So their desires are infinite, although, in real terms, except in the form of a prickle of perturbation, these desires could hardly be said to exist.

Their lives are dominated by a folklore as picturesque as it is murderous. Rigid, hereditary castes of wizards, warlocks, shamans and practitioners of the occult proliferate amongst these benighted mountain-dwellers and the apex of esoteric power lies, it would seem, in the person of the king himself. But this appearance is deceptive. This nominal ruler is in reality the poorest beggar in all his ragged kingdom. Heir of the barbarous, he is stripped of everything but the idea of an omnipotence which is sufficiently expressed by immobility.

All day long, ever since his accession, he hangs by the right ankle from an iron ring set in the roof of a stone hut. A stout ribbon binds him to the ceiling and he is inadequately supported in a precarious but absolute position sanctioned by ritual and memory upon his left wrist, which is strapped in a similar fashion with ribbon to an iron ring cemented into the floor. He stays as still as if he had been dipped in a petrifying well and never speaks one single word because he has forgotten how.

They all believe implicitly they are damned. A folk-tale circulates among them, as follows: that the tribe was originally banished from a happier and more prosperous region to their present dreary habitation, a place fit only for continuous self-mortification, after they rendered themselves abhorrent to their former neighbours by the wholesale and enthusiastic practice of incest, son with father, father with daughter, etc. – every baroque variation possible upon the determinate quadrille of the nuclear family. In this country, incest is a capital crime; the punishment for incest is decapitation.

Daily their minds are terrified and enlightened by the continuous performances of apocalyptic dirges for fornicating siblings and only the executioner himself, because there is nobody to cut off his head, dare, in the immutable privacy of his leathern hood, upon his blood-bespattered block make love to his beautiful daughter.

Gretchen, the only flower of the mountains, tucks up her white apron and waltzing gingham skirts so they will not crease or soil but, even in the last extremity of the act, her father does not remove his mask for who would recognize him without it? The price he pays for his position is always to be locked in the solitary confinement of his power.

He perpetrates his inalienable right in the reeking courtyard upon the block where he struck off the head of his only son. That night, Gretchen discovered a snake in her sewing machine and, though she did not know what a bicycle was, upon a bicycle her brother wheeled and circled through her troubled dreams until the cock crowed and out she went for eggs.

THE LOVES OF LADY PURPLE

INSIDE THE PINK-STRIPED booth of the Asiatic Professor only the marvellous existed and there was no such thing as daylight.

The puppet master is always dusted with a little darkness. In direct relation to his skill he propagates the most bewildering enigmas for, the more lifelike his marionettes, the more godlike his manipulations and the more radical the symbiosis between inarticulate doll and articulating fingers. The puppeteer speculates in a no-man's-limbo between the real and that which, although we know very well it is not, nevertheless seems to be real. He is the intermediary between us, his audience, the living, and they, the dolls, the undead, who cannot live at all and yet who mimic the living in every detail since, though they cannot speak or weep, still they project those signals of signification we instantly recognize as language.

The master of marionettes vitalizes inert stuff with the dynamics of his self. The sticks dance, make love, pretend to speak and, finally, personate death; yet, so many Lazaruses out of their graves they spring again in time for the next performance and no worms drip from their noses nor dust clogs their eyes. All complete, they once again offer their brief imitations of men and women with an exquisite precision which is all the more disturbing because we know it to be false; and so this art, if viewed theologically, may, perhaps, be blasphemous.

Although he was only a poor travelling showman, the Asiatic Professor had become a consummate virtuoso of puppetry. He transported his collapsible theatre, the cast of his single drama and a variety of properties in a horse-drawn cart and, after he played his play in many beautiful cities which no longer exist, such as Shanghai, Constantinople and St Petersburg, he and his small entourage arrived at last in a country in Middle Europe where the mountains sprout jags as sharp and unnatural as those a child outlines with his crayon, a dark, superstitious Transylvania where they wreathed suicides with garlic, pierced them through the heart with stakes and buried them at crossroads while warlocks continually practised rites of immemorial beastliness in the forests.

He had only the two assistants, a deaf boy in his teens, his nephew, to whom he taught his craft, and a foundling dumb girl no more than seven or eight they had picked up on their travels. When the Professor spoke, nobody could understand him for he knew only his native tongue, which was an incomprehensible rattle of staccato k's and t's, so he did not speak at all in the ordinary course of things and, if they had taken separate paths to silence, all, in the end, signed a perfect pact with it. But, when the Professor and his nephew sat in the sun outside their booth in the mornings before performances, they held interminable dialogues in sign language punctuated by soft, wordless grunts and whistles so that the choreographed quiet of their discourse was like the mating dance of tropic birds. And this means of communication, so delicately distanced from humanity, was peculiarly apt for the Professor, who had rather the air of a visitant from another world where the mode of being was conducted in nuances rather than affirmatives. This was due partly to his extreme age, for he was very old although he carried his years lightly even if, these days, in this climate, he always felt a little chilly and so wrapped himself always in a moulting, woollen shawl; yet, more so, it was caused by his benign indifference to everything except the simulacra of the living he himself created.

Besides, however far the entourage travelled, not one of its members had ever comprehended to any degree the foreign. They were all natives of the fairground and, after all, all fairs are the same. Perhaps every single fair is no more than a dissociated fragment of one single, great, original fair which was inexplicably scattered long ago in a diaspora of the amazing. Whatever its location, a fair maintains its invariable, self-consistent atmosphere. Hieratic as knights in chess, the painted horses on the roundabouts describe perpetual circles as immutable as those of the planets and as immune to the drab world of here and now whose inmates come to gape at such extraordinariness, such freedom from actuality. The huckster's raucous invitations are made in a language beyond language, or, perhaps, in that ur-language of grunt and bark which lies behind all language. Everywhere, the same old women hawk glutinous candies which seem devised only to make flies drunk on sugar and, though the outward form of such excessive sweets may vary from place to place, their nature, never. A universal cast of two-headed dogs, dwarfs, alligator men, bearded ladies and giants in leopard-skin loin cloths reveal their singularities in the sideshows and, wherever they come from, they share the sullen glamour of deformity, an internationality which acknowledges no geographic boundaries. Here, the grotesque is the order of the day.

The Asiatic Professor picked up the crumbs that fell from this heaping table yet never seemed in the least at home there for his affinities did not lie with its harsh sounds and primary colouring although it was the only home he knew. He had the wistful charm of a Japanese flower which only blossoms when dropped in water for he, too, revealed his passions through a medium other than himself and this was his heroine, the puppet, Lady Purple.

She was the Queen of Night. There were glass rubies in her head for eyes and her ferocious teeth, carved out of mother o' pearl, were always on show for she had a permanent smile. Her face was as white as chalk because it was covered with the skin of supplest white leather which also clothed her torso, jointed limbs and complication of extremities. Her beautiful hands seemed more like weapons because her nails were so long, five inches of pointed tin enamelled scarlet, and she wore a wig of black hair arranged in a chignon more heavily elaborate than any human neck could have endured. This monumental *chevelure* was stuck through with many brilliant pins tipped with pieces of broken mirror so that, every time she moved, she cast a multitude of scintillating reflections which danced about the theatre like mice of light. Her clothes were all of deep, dark, slumbrous colours – profound pinks, crimson and the vibrating purple with which she was synonymous, a purple the colour of blood in a love suicide.

She must have been the masterpiece of a long-dead, anonymous artisan and yet she was nothing but a curious structure until the Professor touched her strings, for it was he who filled her with necromantic vigour. He transmitted to her an abundance of the life he himself seemed to possess so tenuously and, when she moved, she did not seem so much a cunningly simulated woman as a monstrous goddess, at once preposterous and magnificent, who transcended the notion she was dependent on his hands and appeared wholly real and yet entirely other. Her actions were not so much an imitation as a distillation and intensification of those of a born woman and so she could become the quintessence of eroticism, for no woman born would have dared to be so blatantly seductive.

The Professor allowed no one else to touch her. He himself looked after her costumes and jewellery. When the show was over, he placed his marionette in a specially constructed box and carried her back to the lodging house where he and his children shared a room, for she was too precious to be left in the flimsy theatre and, besides, he could not sleep unless she lay beside him.

The catchpenny title of the vehicle for this remarkable actress was: *The Notorious Amours of Lady Purple, the Shameless Oriental Venus*. Everything in the play was entirely exotic. The incantatory ritual of the drama instantly annihilated the rational and imposed upon the audience a magic alternative in which nothing was in the least familiar. The series of tableaux which illustrated her story were in themselves so filled with meaning that when the Professor chanted her narrative in his impenetrable native tongue, the compulsive strangeness of the spectacle was enhanced rather than diminished. As he crouched above the stage directing his heroine's movements, he recited a verbal recitative in a voice which clanged, rasped and swooped up and down in a weird duet with the stringed instrument from which the dumb girl struck peculiar intervals. But it was impossible to mistake him when the Professor spoke in the character of Lady Purple herself for then his voice modulated to a thick, lascivious murmur like fur soaked in honey which sent unwilling shudders of pleasure down the spines of the watchers. In the iconography of the melodrama, Lady Purple stood for passion and all her movements were calculations in an angular geometry of sexuality.

The Professor somehow always contrived to have a few handbills printed off in the language of the country where they played. These always gave the title of his play and then they used to read as follows:

> *Come and see all that remains of Lady Purple, the famous prostitute and wonder of the East!*
>
> A unique sensation. See how the unappeasable appetites of Lady Purple turned her at last into the very puppet you see

before you, pulled only by the strings of *lust*. Come and see the very doll, the only surviving relic of the shameless Oriental Venus herself.

The bewildering entertainment possessed almost a religious intensity for, since there can be no spontaneity in a puppet drama, it always tends towards the rapt intensity of ritual, and, at its conclusion, as the audience stumbled from the darkened booth, it had almost suspended disbelief and was more than half convinced, as the Professor assured them so eloquently, that the bizarre figure who had dominated the stage was indeed the petrification of a universal whore and had once been a woman in whom too much life had negated life itself, whose kisses had withered like acids and whose embrace blasted like lightning. But the Professor and his assistants immediately dismantled the scenery and put away the dolls who were, after all, only mundane wood and, next day, the play was played again.

This is the story of Lady Purple as performed by the Professor's puppets to the delirious *obbligato* of the dumb girl's samisen and the audible click of the limbs of the actors.

The Notorious Amours of Lady Purple
the Shameless Oriental Venus

When she was only a few days old, her mother wrapped her in a tattered blanket and abandoned her on the doorstep of a prosperous merchant and his barren wife. These respectable bourgeois were to become the siren's first dupes. They lavished upon her all the attentions which love and money could devise and yet they reared a flower which, although perfumed, was carnivorous. At the age of twelve, she seduced her foster father. Utterly besotted with her, he trusted to her the key of the safe where he kept all his money and she immediately robbed it of every farthing.

Packing his treasure in a laundry basket together with the clothes and jewellery he had already given her, she then stabbed her first lover and his wife, her foster mother, in their bellies with a knife used in the kitchen to slice fish. Then she set fire to their house to cover the traces of her guilt. She annihilated her own childhood in the blaze that destroyed her first home and, springing like a corrupt phoenix from the pyre of her crime, she rose again in the pleasure quarters, where she at once hired herself out to the madame of the most imposing brothel.

In the pleasure quarters, life passed entirely in artificial day for the bustling noon of those crowded alleys came at the time of drowsing midnight for those who lived outside that inverted, sinister, abominable world which functioned only to gratify the whims of the senses. Every rococo desire the mind of man might, in its perverse ingenuity, devise found ample gratification here, amongst the halls of mirrors, the flagellation parlours, the cabarets of nature-defying copulations and the ambiguous soirées held by men-women and female men. Flesh was the speciality of every house and it came piping hot, served up with all the garnishes imaginable. The Professor's puppets dryly and perfunctorily performed these tactical manoeuvres like toy soldiers in a mock battle of carnality.

Along the streets, the women for sale, the mannequins of desire, were displayed in wicker cages so that potential customers could saunter past inspecting them at leisure. These exalted prostitutes sat motionless as idols. Upon their real features had been painted symbolic abstractions of the various aspects of allure and the fantastic elaboration of their dress hinted it covered a different kind of skin. The cork heels of their shoes were so high they could not walk but only totter and the sashes round their waists were of brocade so stiff the movements of the arms were cramped and scant so they presented attitudes of physical unease which, though powerfully moving, derived partly, at least, from the deaf assistant's lack of manual dexterity, for his apprenticeship had not as yet reached even the journeyman stage. Therefore the gestures of these *hetaerae* were as stylized as if they had been clockwork. Yet, however fortuitously, all worked out so well it seemed each one was as absolutely circumscribed as a figure in rhetoric, reduced by the rigorous discipline of her vocation to the nameless essence of the idea of woman, a metaphysical abstraction of the female which could, on payment of a specific fee, be instantly translated into an oblivion either sweet or terrible, depending on the nature of her talents.

Lady Purple's talents verged on the unspeakable. Booted, in leather, she became a mistress of the whip before her fifteenth birthday. Subsequently, she graduated in the mysteries of the torture chamber, where she thoroughly researched all manner of ingenious mechanical devices. She utilized a baroque apparatus of funnel, humiliation, syringe, thumbscrew, contempt and spiritual anguish; to her lovers, such severe usage was both bread and wine and a kiss from her cruel mouth was the sacrament of suffering.

Soon she became successful enough to be able to maintain her own establishment. When she was at the height of her fame, her slightest fancy might cost a young man his patrimony and, as soon as she squeezed him dry of fortune, hope and dreams, for she was quite remorseless, she abandoned him; or else she might, perhaps, lock him up in her closet and force him to watch her while she took for nothing to her usually incredibly expensive bed a beggar encountered by chance on the street. She was no malleable, since frigid, substance upon which desires might be executed; she was not a true prostitute for she was the object on which men prostituted themselves. She, the sole perpetrator of desire, proliferated malign fantasies all around her and used her lovers as the canvas on which she executed boudoir masterpieces of destruction. Skins melted in the electricity she generated.

Soon, either to be rid of them or, simply, for pleasure, she took to murdering her lovers. From the leg of a politician she poisoned she cut out the thighbone and took it to a craftsman who made it into a flute for her. She persuaded succeeding lovers to play tunes for her on this instrument and, with the supplest and most serpentine grace, she danced for them to its unearthly music. At this point, the dumb girl put down her samisen and took up a bamboo pipe from which issued weird cadences and, though it was by no means the climax of the play, this dance was the apex of the Professor's performance for, as she stamped, wheeled and turned to the sound of her malign chamber music, Lady Purple became entirely the image of irresistible evil.

She visited men like a plague, both bane and terrible enlightenment, and she was as contagious as the plague. The final condition of all her lovers was this: they went clothed in rags held together with the discharge of their sores, and their eyes held an awful vacancy, as if their minds had been blown out like candles. A parade of ghastly spectres, they trundled across the stage, their passage implemented by medieval horrors for, here, an arm left its socket and whisked up out of sight into the flies and, there, a nose hung in the air after a gaunt shape that went tottering noseless forward.

So foreclosed Lady Purple's pyrotechnical career, which ended as if it had been indeed a firework display, in ashes, desolation and silence. She became more ghastly than those she had infected. Circe at last became a swine herself and, seared to the bone by her own flame, walked the pavements like a desiccated shadow. Disaster obliterated her. Cast out with stones and oaths by those who had once adulated her, she was reduced to scavenging on the seashore, where she plucked hair from the heads of the drowned to sell to wigmakers who catered to the needs of more fortunate since less diabolic courtesans.

Now her finery, her paste jewels and her enormous superimposition of black hair hung up in the green room and she wore a drab rag of coarse hemp for the final scene of her desperate decline, when, outrageous nymphomaniac, she practised extraordinary necrophilies on the bloated corpses the sea tossed contemptuously at her feet for her dry rapacity had become entirely mechanical and still she repeated her former actions though she herself was utterly other. She abrogated her humanity. She became nothing but wood and hair. She became a marionette herself, herself her own replica, the dead yet moving image of the shameless Oriental Venus.

The Professor was at last beginning to feel the effects of age and travel. Sometimes he complained in noisy silence to his nephew of pains, aches, stiffening muscles, tautening sinews, and shortness of breath. He began to limp a little and left to the boy all the rough work of mantling and dismantling. Yet the balletic mime of Lady Purple grew all the more remarkable with the passage of the years, as though his energy, channelled for so long into a single purpose, refined itself more and more in time and was finally reduced to a single, purified, concentrated essence which was transmitted entirely to the doll; and the Professor's mind attained a condition not unlike that of the swordsman trained in Zen, whose sword is his soul, so that neither sword nor swordsman has meaning without the presence of the other. Such swordsmen, armed, move towards their victims like automata, in a state of perfect emptiness, no longer aware of any distinction between self or weapon. Master and marionette had arrived at this condition.

Age could not touch Lady Purple for, since she had never aspired to mortality, she effortlessly transcended it and, though a man who was less aware of the expertise it needed to make her so much as raise her left hand might, now and then, have grieved to see how she defied ageing, the Professor had no fancies of that kind. Her miraculous inhumanity rendered their friendship entirely free from the anthropomorphic, even on the night of the Feast of All Hallows when, the mountain-dwellers murmured, the dead held masked balls in the graveyards while the devil played the fiddle for them.

The rough audience received their copeck's worth of sensation and filed out into a fairground which still roared like a playful tiger with life. The foundling girl put away her samisen and swept out the booth while the nephew set the stage afresh for next day's matinée. Then the Professor noticed Lady Purple had ripped a seam in the drab shroud she wore in the final act. Chattering to himself with displeasure, he undressed her as she swung idly, this way and that way, from her anchored strings and then he sat down on a wooden property stool on the stage and plied his needle like a good housewife. The task was more difficult than it seemed at first for the fabric was also torn and required an embroidery of darning so he told his assistants to go home together to the lodging house and let him finish his task alone.

A small oil-lamp hanging from a nail at the side of the stage cast an insufficient but tranquil light. The white puppet glimmered fitfully through the mists which crept into the theatre from the night outside through all the chinks and gaps in the tarpaulin and now began to fold their chiffon drapes around her as if to decorously conceal her or else to render her more translucently enticing. The mist softened her painted smile a little and her head dangled to one side. In the last act, she wore a loose, black wig, the locks of which hung down as far as her softly upholstered flanks, and the ends of her hair flickered with her random movements, creating upon the white blackboard of her back one of those fluctuating optical effects which make us question the veracity of our vision. As he often did when he was alone with her, the Professor chatted to her in his native language, rattling away an intimacy of nothings, of the weather, of his rheumatism, of the unpalatability and expense of the region's coarse, black bread, while the small winds took her as their partner in a scarcely perceptible *valse triste* and the mist grew minute by minute thicker, more pallid and more viscous.

The old man finished his mending. He rose and, with a click or two of his old bones, he went to put the forlorn garment neatly on its green-room hanger beside the glowing, winy purple gown splashed with rosy peonies, sashed with carmine, that she wore for her appalling dance. He was about to lay her, naked, in her coffin-shaped case and carry her back to their chilly bedroom when he paused. He was seized with the childish desire to see her again in all her finery once more that night. He took her dress off its hanger and carried it to where she drifted, at nobody's volition but that of the wind. As he put her clothes on her, he murmured to her as if she were a little girl for the vulnerable flaccidity of her arms and legs made a six-foot baby of her.

'There, there, my pretty; this arm here, that's right! Oops a daisy, easy does it . . .'

Then he tenderly took off her penitential wig and clucked his tongue to see how defencelessly bald she was beneath it. His arms cracked under the weight of her immense chignon and he had to stretch up on tiptoe to set it in place because, since she was as large as life, she was rather taller than he. But then the ritual of apparelling was over and she was complete again.

Now she was dressed and decorated, it seemed her dry wood had all at once put out an entire springtime of blossoms for the old man alone to enjoy. She could have acted as the model for the most beautiful of women, the image of that woman whom only a man's memory and imagination can devise, for the lamplight fell too mildly to sustain her air of arrogance and so gently it made her long nails look as harmless as ten fallen petals. The Professor had a curious habit; he always used to kiss his doll good night.

A child kisses its toy before she pretends it sleeps although, even though she is only a child, she knows its eyes are not constructed to close so it will always be a sleeping beauty no kiss will waken. One in the grip of savage loneliness might kiss the face he sees before him in the mirror for want of any other face to kiss. These are kisses of the same kind; they are the most poignant of caresses, for they are too humble and too despairing to wish or seek for any response.

Yet, in spite of the Professor's sad humility, his chapped and withered mouth opened on hot, wet, palpitating flesh.

The sleeping wood had wakened. Her pearl teeth crashed against his with the sound of cymbals and her warm, fragrant breath blew around him like an Italian gale. Across her suddenly moving face flashed a whole kaleidoscope of expression, as though she were running instantaneously through the entire repertory of human feeling, practising, in an endless moment of time, all the scales of emotion as if they were music. Crushing vines, her arms, curled about the Professor's delicate apparatus of bone and skin with the insistent pressure of an actuality by far more authentically living than that of his own, time-desiccated flesh. Her kiss emanated from the dark country where desire is objectified and lives. She gained entry into the world by a mysterious loophole in its metaphysics and, during her kiss, she sucked his breath from his lungs so that her own bosom heaved with it.

So, unaided, she began her next performance with an apparent improvisation which was, in reality, only a variation upon a theme. She sank her teeth into his throat and drained him. He did not have the time to make a sound. When he was empty, he slipped straight out of her embrace down to her feet with a dry rustle, as of a cast armful of dead leaves, and there he sprawled on the floorboards, as empty, useless and bereft of meaning as his own tumbled shawl.

She tugged impatiently at the strings which moored her and out they came in bunches from her head, her arms and her legs. She stripped them off her fingertips and stretched out her long, white hands, flexing and unflexing them again and again. For the first time for years, or, perhaps, for ever, she closed her blood-stained teeth thankfully, for her cheeks still ached from the smile her maker had carved into the stuff of her former face. She stamped her elegant feet to make the new blood flow more freely there.

Unfurling and unravelling itself, her hair leaped out of its confinements of combs, cords and lacquer to root itself back into her scalp like cut grass bounding out of the stack and back again into the ground. First, she shivered with pleasure to feel the cold, for she realized she was experiencing a physical sensation; then either she remembered or else she believed she remembered that the sensation of cold was not a pleasurable one so she knelt and, drawing off the old man's shawl, wrapped it carefully about herself. Her every motion was instinct with a wonderful, reptilian liquidity. The mist outside now seemed to rush like a tide into the booth and broke against her in white breakers so that she looked like a baroque figurehead, lone survivor of a shipwreck, thrown up on a shore by the tide.

But whether she was renewed or newly born, returning to life or becoming alive, awakening from a dream or coalescing into the form of a fantasy generated in her wooden skull by the mere repetition so many times of the same invariable actions, the brain beneath the reviving hair contained only the scantiest notion of the possibilities now open to it. All that had seeped into the wood was the notion that she might perform the forms of life not so much by the skill of another as by her own desire that she did so, and she did not possess enough equipment to comprehend the complex circularity of the logic which inspired her for she had only been a marionette. But, even if she could not perceive it, she could not escape the tautological paradox in which she was trapped; had the marionette all the time parodied the living or was she, now living, to parody her own performance as a marionette? Although she was now manifestly a woman, young and beautiful, the leprous whiteness of her face gave her the appearance of a corpse animated solely by demonic will.

Deliberately, she knocked the lamp down from its hook on the wall. A puddle of oil spread at once on the boards of the stage. A little flame leaped across the fuel and immediately began to eat the curtains. She went down the aisle between the benches to the little ticket booth. Already, the stage was an inferno and the corpse of the Professor tossed this way and that on an uneasy bed of fire. But she did not look behind her after she slipped out into the fairground although soon the theatre was burning like a paper lantern ignited by its own candle.

Now it was so late that the sideshows, gingerbread stalls and liquor booths were locked and shuttered and only the moon, half obscured by drifting cloud, gave out a meagre, dirty light, which sullied and deformed the flimsy pasteboard façades, so the place, deserted, with curds of vomit, the refuse of revelry, underfoot, looked utterly desolate.

She walked rapidly past the silent roundabouts, accompanied only by the fluctuating mists, towards the town, making her way like a homing pigeon, out of logical necessity, to the single brothel it contained.

THE SMILE OF WINTER

BECAUSE THERE ARE no seagulls here, the only sound is the resonance of the sea. This coastal region is quite flat, so that an excess of sky bears down with an intolerable weight, pressing the essence out of everything beneath it for it imposes such a burden on us that we have all been forced inward on ourselves in an introspective sombreness intensified by the perpetual abrasive clamour of the sea. When the sun goes down, it is very cold and then I easily start crying because the winter moon pierces my heart. The winter moon is surrounded by an extraordinary darkness, the logical antithesis of the supernal clarity of the day; in this darkness, the dogs in every household howl together at the sight of a star, as if the stars were unnatural things. But, from morning until evening, a hallucinatory light floods the shore and a cool, glittering sun transfigures everything so brilliantly that the beach looks like a desert and the ocean like a mirage.

But the beach is never deserted. Far from it. At times, there is even a silent crowd of people – women who come in groups to turn the fish they have laid out to dry on bamboo racks; Sunday trippers; solitary anglers, even. Sometimes trucks drive up and down the beach to and fro from the next headland and after school is over children come to improvise games of baseball with sticks and a dead crab delivered to them by the tide. The children wear peaked, yellow caps; their heads are perfectly round. Their faces are perfectly bland, the colour as well as the shape of brown eggs. They giggle when they see me because I am white and pink while they themselves are such a serviceable, unanimous beige. Besides all these visitors, the motorcyclists who come at night have left deep grooves behind them in the sand as if to say: 'I have been here.'

When the shadows of the evening lie so thickly on the beach it looks as though nobody has dusted it for years, the motorcyclists come out. That is their favourite time. They have marked out a course among the dunes with red wooden pegs and ride round it at amazing speeds. They come when they please. Sometimes they come in the early morning but, most often, by owl-light. They announce their presence with a fanfare of opened throttles. They grow their hair long and it flies out behind them like black flags, motorcyclists as beautiful as the outriders of death in the film *Orphée*. I wish they were not so beautiful; if they were not so beautiful and so inaccessible to me, then I should feel less lonely, although, after all, I came here in order to be lonely.

The beach is full of the garbage of the ocean. The waves leave torn, translucent furls of polythene wrapping too tough for even this sea's iron stomach; chipped jugs that once held rice wine; single sea-boots freighted with sand; broken beer bottles and, once, a brown dog stiff and dead washed up as far as the pine trees which, subtly warped by the weather, squat on their hunkers at the end of my garden, where the dry soil transforms itself to sand.

Already the pines are budding this year's cones. Each blunt, shaggy bough is tipped with a small, lightly furred growth just like the prick of a little puppy while the dry, brown cones of last year still cling to the rough stems though now these are so insecure a touch will bring them bounding down. But, all in all, the pines have a certain intransigence. They dig their roots into dry soil full of seashells and strain backwards in the wind that blows directly from Alaska. They are absolutely exposed to the weather and yet as indifferent as the weather. The indifference of this Decembral littoral suits my forlorn mood for I am a sad woman by nature, no doubt about that; how unhappy I should be in a happy world! This country has the most rigorous romanticism in the world and they think a woman who lives by herself should accentuate her melancholy with surroundings of sentimental dilapidation. I have read about all the abandoned lovers in their old books eating their hearts out like Mariana in so many moated granges; their gardens are overgrown with goosegrass and mugwort, their mud walls are falling to pieces and their carp pools scaled over with water-lily pads. Everything combines with the forlorn mood of the châtelaine to procure a moving image of poignant desolation. In this country you do not need to think, but only to look, and soon you think you understand everything.

The old houses in the village are each one dedicated to seclusion and court an individual sequestered sadness behind the weather-stained, unpainted wooden shutters they usually keep closed. It is a gloomy, aridly aesthetic architecture based on the principle of perpetual regression. The houses are heavily shingled and the roofs are the shapes and colours of waves frozen on a grey day. In the mornings, they dismantle the outer screens to let fresh air blow through and, as you walk past, you can see that all the inner walls are also sliding screens, though this time of stiff paper, and you can glimpse endlessly receding perspectives of interiors in brownish tones, as if everything had been heavily varnished some time ago; and, though these perspectives can be altered at will, the fresh rooms they make when they shift the screens about always look exactly the same as the old rooms. And all the matted interiors are the same, anyway.

Through the gaping palings of certain fences, I sometimes see a garden so harmoniously in tune with the time of year it looks forsaken. But sometimes all these fragile habitations of unpainted wood; and the still lives, or *natures mortes*, of rusting water pumps and withered chrysanthemums in backyards; and the discarded fishing boats pulled up on the sand and left to rot away – sometimes the whole village looks forsaken. This is, after all, the season of abandonment, of the suspension of vitality, a long cessation of vigour in which we must cultivate our stoicism. Everything has put on the desolate smile of winter. Outside my shabby front door, I have a canal, like Mariana in a moated grange; beyond the skulking pines at the back, there is only the ocean. The winter moon pierces my heart. I weep.

But when I went out on the beach this morning with the skin on my face starched with dried tears so I could feel my cheeks crackle in the wind, I found the sea had washed me up a nice present – two pieces of driftwood. One was a forked chunk like a pair of wooden trousers and the other was a larger, greyish, frayed root the shape of the paw of a ragged lion. I collect driftwood and set it up among the pine trees in picturesque attitudes on the edge of the beach and then I strike a picturesque attitude myself beside them as I watch the constantly agitated waves, for here we all strike picturesque attitudes and that is why we are so beautiful. Sometimes I imagine that one night the riders will stop at the end of my garden and I will hear the heels of their boots crunch on the friable carpet of last year's shed cones and then there will be a hesitant rattle of knuckles on the seaward-facing door and they will wait in ceremonious silence until I come, for their bodies are only images.

My pockets always contain a rasping sediment of sand because I fill them with shells when I go on to the beach. The vast majority of these shells are round, sculptural forms the colour of a brown egg, with warm, creamy insides. They have a classical simplicity. The scarcely perceptible indentations of their surfaces flow together to produce a texture as subtly matt as that of a petal which is as satisfying to touch as Japanese skin. But there are also pure white shells heavily ridged on the outside but within of a marmoreal smoothness and these come in hinged pairs.

There is still a third kind of shell, though I find these less often. They are curlicued, shaped like turbans and dappled with pink, of a substance so thin the ocean easily grinds away the outer husk to lay bare their spiralline cores. They are often decorated with baroque, infinitesimal swags of calcified parasites. They are the smallest of all the shells but by far the most intricate. When I picked up one of those shells, I found it contained the bright pink, dried, detached limb of a tiny sea creature like a dehydrated memory. Sometimes a litter of dropped fish lies among the shells. Each fish reflects the sky with the absolute purity of a Taoist mirror.

The fish have fallen off the racks on which they have been put out to dry. These bamboo racks spread with fish stand on trestles all along the beach as if a feast was laid for the entire prefecture but nobody had come to eat it. Close to the village, there are whole paddocks filled with bamboo racks. In one of these paddocks, a tethered goat crops grass. The fish are as shiny as fish of tin and the size of my little finger. Once dried, they are packed in plastic bags and sold to flavour soup.

The women lay them out. They come every day to turn them and, when the fish are ready, they pile up the racks and carry them to the packing sheds. There are great numbers of these raucously silent, and well-muscled, intimidating women.

The cruel wind burns port-wine whorls on their dour, inexpressive faces. All wear dark or drab-coloured trousers pinched in at the ankle and either short rubber boots or split-toed socks on their feet. A layer of jacket sweaters and a loose, padded, cotton jacket gives them a squat, top-heavy look, as if they would not fall over, only rock malevolently to and fro if you pushed them. Over their jackets, they wear short, immaculate aprons trimmed with coarse lace and they tie white baboushkas round their heads or sometimes wind a kind of wimple over the ears and round the throat. They are truculent and aggressive. They stare at me with open curiosity tinged with hostility. When they laugh, they display treasuries of gold teeth and their hands are as hard as those of eighteenth-century prize-fighters, who also used to pickle their fists in brine. They make me feel that either I or they are deficient in femininity and I suppose it must be I since most of them hump about an organic lump of baby on their backs, inside their coats. It seems that only women people the village because most of the men are out on the sea. Early in the morning, I go out to watch the winking and blinking of the fishing boats on the water, which, just before dawn, has turned a deep violet.

The moist and misty mornings after a storm obscure the horizon for then the ocean has turned into the sky and the wind and waves have realigned the contours of the dunes. The wet sand is as dark and more yieldingly solid than fudge and walking across a panful is a promenade in the Kingdom of Sweets. The waves leave behind them glinting striations of salt and forcibly mould the foreshore into the curvilinear abstractions of cliffs, bays, inlets, curvilinear tumuli like the sculpture of Arp. But the storms themselves are a raucous music and turn my house into an Aeolian xylophone. All night long, the wind bangs and rattles away at every wooden surface; the house is a sounding box and even on the quietest nights the paper windows let through the wind that rattles softly in the pines.

Sometimes the lights of the midnight riders scrawl brilliant hieroglyphs across the panes, especially on moonless nights, when I am alone in a landscape of extraordinary darkness, and I am a little frightened when I see their headlamps and hear their rasping engines for then they seem the spawn of the negated light and to have driven straight out of the sea, which is just as mysterious as the night, even, and also its perfect image, for the sea is an inversion of the known and occupies half, or more, of the world, just as night does; whilst different peoples also live in the countries of the night.

They all wear leather jackets bristling with buckles, and high-heeled boots. They cannot buy such gaudy apparel in the village because the village shops only sell useful things such as paraffin, quilts and things to eat. And all the colours in the village are subfusc and equivocal, those of wood tinted bleakly by the weather and of lifeless wintry vegetation. When I sometimes see an orange tree hung with gold balls like a magic trick, it does nothing but stress by contrast the prevailing static sobriety of everything, which combines to smile in chorus the desolate smile of winter. On rainy nights when there is a winter moon bright enough to pierce the heart, I often wake to find my face still wet with tears so that I know I have been crying.

When the sun is low in the west, the beams become individually visible and fall with a peculiar, lateral intensity across the beach, flushing out long shadows from the grains of sand and these beams seem to penetrate to the very hearts of the incoming waves which look, then, as if they were lit from within. Before they topple forward, they bulge outward in the swollen shapes and artfully flawed incandescence of Art Nouveau glass, as if the translucent bodies of the images they contain within them were trying to erupt, for the bodies of the creatures of the sea are images, I am convinced of that. At this time of day, the sea turns amazing colours – the brilliant, chemical green of the sea in nineteenth-century tinted postcards; or a blue far too cerulean for early evening; or sometimes it shines with such metallic brilliance I can hardly bear to look at it. Smiling my habitual winter smile, I stand at the end of my garden attended by a pack of green bears while I watch the constantly agitated white lace cuffs on the colourful sleeves of the Pacific.

Different peoples inhabit the countries of the ocean and some of their emanations undulate past me when I walk along the beach to the village on one of those rare, bleak, sullen days, spectral wraiths of sand blowing to various inscrutable meeting places on blind currents of the Alaskan wind. They twine around my ankles in serpentine caresses and they have eyes of sand but some of the other creatures have eyes of solid water and when the women move among trays of fish I think they, too, are sea creatures, spiny, ocean-bottom-growing flora and if a tidal wave consumed the village – as it could do tomorrow, for there are no hills or sea walls to protect us – there, under the surface, life would go on just as before, the sea goat still nibbling, the shops still doing a roaring trade in octopus and pickled turnips greens, the women going about their silent business because everything is as silent as if it were under the water, anyway, and the very air is as heavy as water and warps the light so that one sees as if one's eyes were made of water.

Do not think I do not realize what I am doing. I am making a composition using the following elements: the winter beach; the winter moon; the ocean; the women; the pine trees; the riders; the driftwood; the shells; the shapes of darkness and the shapes of water; and the refuse. These are all inimical to my loneliness because of their indifference to it. Out of these pieces of inimical indifference, I intend to represent the desolate smile of winter which, as you must have gathered, is the smile I wear.

PENETRATING TO THE HEART OF THE FOREST

THE WHOLE REGION was like an abandoned flower bowl, filled to overflowing with green, living things; and, protected on all sides by the ferocious barricades of the mountains, those lovely reaches of forest lay so far inland the inhabitants believed the name, Ocean, that of a man in another country, and would have taken an oar, had they ever seen one, to be a winnowing fan. They built neither roads nor towns; in every respect like Candide, especially that of past ill-fortune, all they did now was to cultivate their gardens.

They were the descendants of slaves who, many years before, ran away from plantations in distant plains, in pain and hardship crossed the arid neck of the continent, and endured an infinity of desert and tundra, before they clambered the rugged foothills to scale at last the heights themselves and so arrive in a region that offered them in plentiful fulfilment all their dreams of a promised land. Now, the groves that skirted those forests of pine in the central valley formed for them all of the world they wished to know and nothing in their self-contained quietude concerned them but the satisfaction of simple pleasures. Not a single exploring spirit had ever been curious enough to search to its source the great river that watered their plots, or to penetrate to the heart of the forest itself. They had grown far too contented in their lost fastness to care for anything but the joys of idleness.

They had brought with them as a relic of their former life only the French their former owners had branded on their tongues, though certain residual, birdlike flutings of forgotten African dialects put unexpected cadences in their speech and, with the years, they had fashioned an arboreal argot of their own to which a French grammar would have proved a very fallible guide. And they had also packed up in their ragged bandanas a little, dark, voodoo folklore. But such blood-stained ghosts could not survive in sunshine and fresh air and emigrated from the villages in a body, to live only the ambiguous life of horned rumours in the woods, becoming at last no more than shapes with indefinable outlines who lurked, perhaps, in the green deeps, until, at last, one of the shadows modulated imperceptibly into the actual shape of a tree.

Almost as if to justify to themselves their lack of a desire to explore, they finally seeded by word of mouth a mythic and malign tree within the forest, a tree the image of the Upas Tree of Java whose very shadow was murderous, a tree that exuded a virulent sweat of poison from its moist bark and whose fruits could have nourished with death an entire tribe. And the presence of this tree categorically forbade exploration – even though all knew, in their hearts, that such a tree did not exist. But, even so, they guessed it was safest to be a stay-at-home.

Since the woodlanders could not live without music, they made fiddles and guitars for themselves with great skill and ingenuity. They loved to eat well so they stirred themselves enough to plant vegetables, tend goats and chickens and blend these elements together in a rustic but voluptuous cookery. They dried, candied and preserved in honey some of the wonderful fruits they grew and exchanged this produce with the occasional traveller who came over the single, hazardous mountain pass, carrying bales of cotton fabrics and bundles of ribbons. With these, the women made long skirts and blouses for themselves and trousers for their menfolk, so all were dressed in red and yellow flowered cloth, purple and green chequered cloth, or cloth striped like a rainbow, and they plaited themselves hats from straw. They needed nothing more than a few flowers before they felt their graceful toilets were complete and a profusion of flowers grew all around them, so many flowers that the straw-thatched villages looked like inhabited gardens, for the soil was of amazing richness and the flora proliferated in such luxuriance that when Dubois, the botanist, came over the pass on his donkey, he looked down on that paradisial landscape and exclaimed: 'Dear God! It is as if Adam had opened Eden to the public!'

Dubois was seeking a destination whose whereabouts he did not know, though he was quite sure it existed. He had visited most of the out-of-the-way parts of the world to peer through the thick lenses of his round spectacles at every kind of plant. He gave his name to an orchid in Dahomey, to a lily in Indo-China and to a dark-eyed Portuguese girl in a Brazilian town of such awesome respectability that even its taxis wore antimacassars. But, because he loved the frail wife whose grave eyes already warned him she would live briefly, he rooted there, a plant himself in alien soil, and, out of gratitude, she gave him two children at one birth before she died.

He found his only consolation in a return to the flowering wilderness he had deserted for her sake. He was approaching middle age, a raw-boned, bespectacled man who habitually stooped out of a bashful awareness of his immense height, hirsute and gentle as a herbivorous lion. The vicissitudes of a life in which his reticence had cheated him of the fruits of his scholarship, together with the forlorn conclusion of his marriage, had left him with a yearning for solitude and a desire to rear his children in a place where ambition, self-seeking and guile were strangers, so that they would grow up with the strength and innocence of young trees.

But such a place was hard to find.

His wanderings took him to regions ever more remote from civilization but he was never seized with a conviction of homecoming until that morning, as the sun irradiated the mists and his donkey picked its way down a rough path so overgrown with dew-drenched grass and mosses it had become no more than the subtlest intimation of a direction.

It took him circuitously down to a village sunk in a thicket of honeysuckle that filled with languorous sweetness the rarefied air of the uplands. On the dawning light hung, trembling, the notes of a pastoral aubade somebody was picking out on a guitar. As Dubois passed the house, a plump, dark-skinned woman with a crimson handkerchief round her head threw open a pair of shutters and leaned out to pick a spray of morning glory. As she tucked it behind her ear, she saw the stranger and smiled like another sunrise, greeting him with a few melodious phrases of his native language she had somehow mixed with burned cream and sunshine. She offered him a little breakfast which she was certain he must need since he had travelled so far and, while she spoke, the yellow-painted door burst open and a chattering tide of children swept out to surround the donkey, turning up to Dubois faces like sunflowers.

Six weeks after his arrival among the Creoles, Dubois left again for the house of his parents-in-law. There, he packed his library, notebooks and records of researches; his most precious collections of specimens and his equipment; as much clothing as he felt would last him the rest of his life, and a crate containing objects of sentimental value. This case and his children were the only concessions he made to the past. And, once he had installed all those things safely in a wooden farmhouse the villagers had interrupted their inactivity long enough to make ready for him, he closed the doors of his heart to everything but the margins of the forest, which were to him a remarkable book it would take all the years that remained to him to learn to read.

The birds and beasts showed no fear of him. Painted magpies perched reflectively on his shoulders as he pored over the drawings he made among the trees, while fox cubs rolled in play around his feet and even learned to nose in his capacious pockets for cookies. As his children grew older, he seemed to them more an emanation of their surroundings than an actual father, and from him they unknowingly imbibed a certain radiant inhumanity which sprang from a benign indifference towards by far the greater part of mankind – towards all those who were not beautiful, gentle and, by nature, kind.

'Here, we have all become *homo silvester*, men of the woods,' he would say. 'And that is by far superior to the precocious and destructive species, *homo sapiens* – knowing man. Knowing man, indeed; what more than nature does man need to know?'

Other carefree children were their playfellows and their toys were birds, butterflies and flowers. Their father spared them enough of his time to teach them to read, to write and to draw. Then he gave them the run of his library and left them alone, to grow as they pleased. So they thrived on a diet of simple food, warm weather, perpetual holidays and haphazard learning. They were fearless since there was nothing to be afraid of and they always spoke the truth because there was no need to lie. No hand or voice was ever raised in anger against them and so they did not know what anger was; when they came across the word in books, they thought it must mean the mild fretfulness they felt when it rained two days together, which did not happen often. They quite forgot the dull town where they had been born. The green world took them for its own and they were fitting children of their foster mother, for they were strong, lithe and supple, browned by the sun to the very colour of the villagers whose liquid *patois* they spoke. They resembled one another so closely each could have used the other as a mirror and almost seemed to be different aspects of the same person for all their gestures, turns of phrase and manner of speech were exactly similar. Had they known how, they would have been proud, because their intimacy was so perfect it could have bred that sense of loneliness which is the source of pride and, as they read more and more of their father's books, their companionship deepened since they had nobody but one another with whom to discuss the discoveries they made in common. From morning to evening, they were never apart, and at night they slept together in a plain, narrow bed on a floor of beaten earth while the window held the friendly nightlight of a soft, southern moon above them in a narrow frame. But often they slept under the moon itself, for they came and went as they pleased and spent most of their time out of doors, exploring the forests until they had gone further and seen more than ever their father had.

At last, these explorations took them into the untrodden, virginal reaches of the deep interior. Here, they walked hand in hand beneath the vaulted architraves of pines in a hushed interior like that of a sentient cathedral. The topmost branches twined so thickly that only a subdued viridian dazzle of light could filter through and the children felt against their ears a palpable fur of intense silence. Those who felt less kinship with the place might have been uneasy, as if abandoned among serene, voiceless, giant forms that cared nothing for man. But, if the children sometimes lost their way, they never lost themselves for they took the sun by day and the stars by the otherwise trackless night for their compass and could discern clues in the labyrinth that those who trusted the forest less would not have recognized, for they knew the forest too well to know of any harm it might do them.

Long ago, in their room at home, they began work on a map of the forest. This was by no means the map an authentic cartographer would have made. They marked hills with webs of feathers of the birds they found there, clearings with an integument of pressed flowers and especially magnificent trees with delicate, brightly coloured drawings on whose watercolour boughs they stuck garlands of real leaves so that the map became a tapestry made out of the substance of the forest itself. At first, in the centre of the map, they put their own thatched cottage and

Madeline drew in the garden the shaggy figure of their father, whose leonine mane was as white, now, as the puff ball of a dandelion, bending with a green watering can over his pots of plants, tranquil, beloved and oblivious. But as they grew older, they grew discontented with their work for they found out their home did not lie at the heart of the forest but only somewhere in its green suburbs. They were seized with the desire to pierce more and yet more deeply into the unfrequented places and now their expeditions lasted for a week or longer. Though he was always glad to see them return, their father had often forgotten they had been away. At last, nothing but the discovery of the central node of the unvisited valley, the navel of the forest, would satisfy them. It grew to be almost an obsession with them. They spoke of the adventure only to one another and did not share it with the other companions who, as they grew older, grew less and less necessary to their absolute intimacy, since, lately, for reasons beyond their comprehension, this intimacy had been subtly invaded by tensions which exacerbated their nerves yet exerted on them both an intoxicating glamour.

Besides, when they spoke of the heart of the forest to their other friends, a veil of darkness came over the woodlanders' eyes and, half-laughing, half-whispering, they would hint at the wicked tree that grew there as though, even if they did not believe in it, it was a metaphor for something unfamiliar they preferred to ignore, as one might say: 'Let sleeping dogs lie. Aren't we happy as we are?' When they saw this laughing apathy, this incuriosity blended with a tinge of fear, Emile and Madeline could not help but feel a faint contempt, for their world, though beautiful, seemed to them, in a sense, incomplete – as though it lacked the knowledge of some mystery they might find, might they not? in the forest, on their own.

In their father's books they found references to the Antiar or Antshar of the Indo-Malay archipelago, the Antiaris Toxicaria whose milky juice contains a most potent poison, like the quintessence of belladonna. But their reason told them that not even the most intrepid migratory bird could have brought the sticky seeds on its feet to cast them down here in these land-locked valleys far from Java. They did not believe the wicked tree could exist in this hemisphere; and yet they were curious. But they were not afraid.

One August morning, when both were thirteen years old, they put bread and cheese in their knapsacks and started out on a journey so early the homesteads were sleeping and even the morning glories were still in bud. The settlements were just as their father had seen them first, prelapsarian villages where any Fall was inconceivable; his children, bred in those quiet places, saw them with eyes pure of nostalgia for lost innocence and thought of them only with that faint, warm claustrophobia which the word, 'home', signifies. At noon, they ate lunch with a family whose cottage lay at the edges of the uninhabited places and when they bade their hosts goodbye, they knew, with a certain anticipatory relish, they would not see anyone else but one another for a long time.

At first, they followed the wide river which led them directly into the ramparts of the great pines and, though days and nights soon merged together in a sonorous quiet where trees grew so close together that birds had no room to sing or fly, they kept a careful tally of the passing time for they knew that, five days away from home, along the leisurely course of the water, the pines thinned out.

The bramble-covered river banks, studded, at this season, with flat, pink discs of blossom, grew so narrow that the water tumbled fast enough to ring out various carillons while grey squirrels swung from branch to low branch of trees which, released from the strait confines of the forest, now grew in shapes of a feminine slightness and grace. Rabbits twitched moist, velvet noses and laid their ears along their backs but did not run away when they saw the barefoot children go by and Emile pointed out to Madeline how a wise toad, squatting meditatively among the kingcups, must have a jewel in his head because bright beams darted out through his eyes, as though a cold fire burned inside his head. They had read of this phenomenon in old books but never seen it before.

They had never seen anything in this place before. It was so beautiful they were a little awe-struck.

Then Madeline stretched out her hand to pick a water lily unbudding on the surface of the river but she jumped back with a cry and gazed down at her finger with a mixture of pain, affront and astonishment. Her bright blood dripped down on to the grass.

'Emile!' she said. 'It bit me!'

They had never encountered the slightest hostility in the forest before. Their eyes met in wonder and surmise while the birds chanted recitatives to the accompaniment of the river.

'This is a strange place,' said Emile hesitantly. 'Perhaps we should not pick any flowers in this part of the forest. Perhaps we have found some kind of carnivorous water lily.'

He washed the tiny wound, bound it with his handkerchief and kissed her cheek, to comfort her, but she would not be comforted and irritably flung a pebble in the direction of the flower. When the pebble struck the lily, it unfurled its close circle of petals with an audible snap and, bewildered, they glimpsed inside them a set of white, perfect fangs. Then the waxen petals closed swiftly over the teeth again, concealing them entirely, and the water lily again looked perfectly white and innocent.

'See! It *is* a carnivorous water lily!' said Emile. 'Father *will* be excited when we tell him.'

But Madeline, her eyes still fixed on the predator as if it fascinated her, slowly shook her head. She had grown very serious.

'No,' she said. 'We must not talk of the things we find in the heart of the forest. They are all secrets. If they were not secrets, we would have heard of them before.'

Her words fell with a strange weight, as heavy as her own gravity, as if she might have received some mysterious communication from the perfidious mouth that wounded her. At once, listening to her, Emile thought of the legendary tree; and then he realized that, for the first time in his life, he did not understand her, for, of course, they had heard of the tree. Looking at her in a new puzzlement, he sensed the ultimate difference of a femininity he had never before known any need or desire to acknowledge and this difference might give her the key to some order of knowledge to which he might not yet aspire, himself, for all at once she seemed far older than he. She raised her eyes and fixed on him a long, solemn regard which chained him in a conspiracy of secrecy, so that, henceforth, they would share only with one another the treacherous marvels round them. At last, he nodded.

'Very well, then,' he said. 'We won't tell father.'

Though they knew he never listened when they spoke to him, never before had they consciously concealed anything from him.

Night was approaching. They walked a little further, until they found pillows of moss laid ready for their heads beneath the branches of a flowering tree. They drank clear water, ate the last of the food they had brought with them and then slept in one another's arms as if they were the perfect children of the place, although they slept less peacefully than usual for both were visited by unaccustomed nightmares of knives and snakes and suppurating roses. But though each stirred and murmured, the dreams were so strangely inconsequential, nothing but fleeting sequences of detached, malign images, that the children forgot them as they slept and woke only with an irritable residue of nightmare, the dregs of unremembered dreaming, knowing only they had slept badly.

In the morning, they stripped and bathed in the river. Emile saw that time was subtly altering the contours of both their bodies and he found he could no longer ignore his sister's nakedness, as he had done since babyhood, while, from the way she suddenly averted her own eyes after, in her usual playful fashion, she splashed him with water, she, too, experienced the same extraordinary confusion. So they fell silent and hastily dressed themselves. And yet the confusion was pleasurable and made their blood sting. He examined her finger and found the marks of the lily's teeth were gone; the wound had healed over completely. Yet he still shuddered with an unfamiliar thrill of dread when he remembered the fanged flower.

'We have no food left,' he said. 'We should turn back at noon.'

'Oh, no!' said Madeline with a mysterious purposefulness that might have been rooted, had he known it, only in a newborn wish to make him do as she wanted, against his own wishes. 'No! I'm sure we shall find something to eat. After all, this is the season for wild strawberries.'

He, too, knew the lore of the forest. At no time of the year could they not find food – berries, roots, salads, mushrooms, and so on. So he saw she knew he had only used a pale excuse to cover his increasing agitation at finding himself alone with her so far from home. And now he had used up his excuse, there was nothing for it but to go on. She walked with a certain irresolute triumph, as though she were aware she had won an initial victory which, though insignificant in itself, might herald more major battles in the future, although they did not even know the formula for a quarrel, yet.

And already this new awareness of one another's shapes and outlines had made them less twinned, less indistinguishable from one another. So they fell once more to their erudite botanizing, in order to pretend that all was as it had always been, before the forest showed its teeth; and now the meandering path of the river led them into such magical places that they found more than enough to talk about for, by the time the shadows vanished at noon, they had come into a landscape that seemed to have undergone an alchemical change, a vegetable transmutation, for it contained nothing that was not marvellous.

Ferns uncurled as they watched, revealing fronded fringes containing innumerable, tiny, shining eyes glittering like brilliants where the ranks of seeds should have been. A vine was covered with slumbrous, purple flowers that, as they passed, sang out in a rich contralto with all the voluptuous wildness of flamenco – and then fell silent. There were trees that bore, instead of foliage, brown, speckled plumage of birds. And when they had grown very hungry, they found a better food than even Madeline had guessed they might, for they came to a clump of low trees with trunks scaled like trout, growing at the water's edge. These trees put out shell-shaped fruit and, when they broke these open and ate them, they tasted oysters. After they consumed their fishy luncheon, they walked on a little and discovered a tree knobbed with white, red-tipped whorls that looked so much like breasts they put their mouths to the nipples and sucked a sweet, refreshing milk.

'See?' said Madeline, and this time her triumph was unconcealed. 'I told you we should find something to nourish us!'

When the shadows of the evening fell like a thick dust of powdered gold on the enchanted forest and they were beginning to feel weary, they came to a small valley which contained a pool that seemed to have no outlet or inlet and so must be fed by an invisible spring. The valley was filled with the most delightful, citronesque fragrance as sharply refreshing as a celestial eau-de-cologne and they saw the source of the perfume at once.

'Well!' exclaimed Emile. 'This certainly isn't the fabled Upas Tree! It must be some kind of incense tree, such as the incense trees of Upper India where, after all, one finds a similar climate, or so I've read.'

The tree was a little larger than a common apple tree but far more graceful in shape. The springing boughs hung out a festival of brilliant streamers, long, aromatic sprays of green, starlike flowers tipped with the red anthers of the stamens, cascading over clusters of leaves so deep a green and of such a glossy texture the dusk turned to discs of black glass those that the sunset did not turn to fire. These leaves hid secret bunches of fruit, mysterious spheres of visible gold streaked with green, as if all the unripe suns in the world were sleeping on the tree until a multiple, universal dawning should wake them all in splendour. As they stood hand in hand gazing at the beautiful tree, a small wind parted the leaves so they would see the fruit more clearly and, in the rind, set squarely in the middle of each faintly flushed cheek, was a curious formation – a round set of serrated indentations exactly resembling the marks of a bite made by the teeth of a hungry man. As if the sight stimulated her own appetite, Madeline laughed and said: 'Goodness, Emile, the forest has even given us dessert!'

She sprang towards the exquisite, odoriferous tree which, at that moment, suffused in a failing yet hallucinatory light the tone and intensity of liquefied amber, seemed to her brother a perfect equivalent of his sister's amazing beauty, a beauty he had never seen before that filled him, now, with ecstasy. The dark pool reflected her darkly, like an antique mirror. She raised her hand to part the leaves in search of a ripe fruit but the greenish skin seemed to warm and glow under her fingers so the first one she touched came as easily off the stem as if it had been brought to perfection by her touch. It seemed to be some kind of apple or pear. It was so juicy the juice ran down her chin and she extended a long, crimson, newly sensual tongue to lick her lips, laughing.

'It tastes so good!' she said. 'Here! Eat!'

She came back to him, splashing through the margins of the pool, holding the fruit out towards him on her palm. She was like a beautiful statue which has just come to life. Her enormous eyes were lit like nocturnal flowers that had been waiting only for this especial night to open and, in their vertiginous depths, reveal to her brother in inexpressible entirety the hitherto unguessed at, unknowable, inexpressible vistas of love.

He took the apple; ate; and, after that, they kissed.

FLESH AND THE MIRROR

IT WAS MIDNIGHT – I chose my times and set my scenes with the precision of the born artiste. Hadn't I gone eight thousand miles to find a climate with enough anguish and hysteria in it to satisfy me? I had arrived back in Yokohama that evening from a visit to England and nobody met me, although I expected him. So I took the train to Tokyo, half an hour's journey. First, I was angry; but the poignancy of my own situation overcame me and then I was sad. To return to the one you love and find him absent! My heart used to jump like Pavlov's dogs at the prospect of such a treat; I positively salivated at the suggestion of unpleasure, I was sure that *that* was real life. I'm told I always look lonely when I'm alone; that is because, when I was an intolerable adolescent, I learned to sit with my coat-collar turned up in a lonely way, so that people would talk to me. And I can't drop the habit even now, though, now, it's only a habit, and, I realize, a predatory habit.

It was midnight and I was crying bitterly as I walked under the artificial cherry blossom with which they decorate the lamp standards from April to September. They do that so the pleasure quarters will have the look of a continuous carnival, no matter what ripples of agitation disturb the never-ceasing, endlessly circulating, quiet, gentle, melancholy crowds who throng the wet web of alleys under a false ceiling of umbrellas. All looked as desolate as Mardi Gras. I was searching among a multitude of unknown faces for the face of the one I loved while the warm, thick, heavy rain of summer greased the dark surfaces of the streets until, after a while, they began to gleam like sleek fur of seals just risen from the bottom of the sea.

The crowds lapped round me like waves full of eyes until I felt that I was walking through an ocean whose speechless and gesticulating inhabitants, like those with whom medieval philosophers peopled the countries of the deep, were methodical inversions or mirror images of the dwellers on dry land. And

I moved through these expressionist perspectives in my black dress as though I was the creator of all and of myself, too, in a black dress, in love, crying, walking through the city in the third person singular, my own heroine, as though the world stretched out from my eye like spokes from a sensitized hub that galvanized all to life when I looked at it.

I think I know, now, what I was trying to do. I was trying to subdue the city by turning it into a projection of my own growing pains. What solipsistic arrogance! The city, the largest city in the world, the city designed to suit not one of my European expectations, this city presents the foreigner with a mode of life that seems to him to have the enigmatic transparency, the indecipherable clarity, of dream. And it is a dream he could, himself, never have dreamed. The stranger, the foreigner, thinks he is in control; but he has been precipitated into somebody else's dream.

You never know what will happen in Tokyo. Anything can happen.

I had been attracted to the city first because I suspected it contained enormous histrionic resources. I was always rummaging in the dressing-up box of the heart for suitable appearances to adopt in the city. That was the way I maintained my defences for, at that time, I always used to suffer a great deal if I let myself get too close to reality since the definitive world of the everyday with its hard edges and harsh light did not have enough resonance to echo the demands I made upon experience. It was as if I never experienced experience *as* experience. Living never lived up to the expectations I had of it – the Bovary syndrome. I was always imagining other things that could have been happening, instead, and so I always felt cheated, always dissatisfied.

Always dissatisfied, even if, like a perfect heroine, I wandered, weeping, on a forlorn quest for a lost lover through the aromatic labyrinth of alleys. And wasn't I in Asia? Asia! But, even though I lived there, it always seemed far away from me. It was as if there were glass between me and the world. But I could see myself perfectly well on the other side of the glass. There I was, walking up and down, eating meals, having conversations, in love, indifferent, and so on. But all the time I was pulling the strings of my own puppet; it was this puppet who was moving about on the other side of the glass. And I eyed the most marvellous adventures with the bored eye of the agent with the cigar watching another audition. I tapped out the ash and asked of events: 'What else can you do?'

So I attempted to rebuild the city according to the blueprint in my imagination as a backdrop to the plays in my puppet theatre, but it sternly refused to be so rebuilt; I was only imagining it had been so rebuilt. On the night I came back to it, however hard I looked for the one I loved, she could not find him anywhere and the city delivered her into the hands of a perfect stranger who fell into step beside her and asked why she was crying. She went with him to an unambiguous hotel with mirror on the ceiling and lascivious black lace draped round a palpably illicit bed. His eyes were shaped like sequins. All night long, a thin, pale, sickle moon with a single star pendant at its nether tip floated upon the rain that pitter-pattered against the windows and there was a clockwork whirring of cicadas. From time to time, the windbell dangling from the eaves let out an exquisitely mournful tinkle.

None of the lyrical eroticism of this sweet, sad, moon night of summer rain had been within my expectations; I had half expected he would strangle me. My sensibility wilted under the burden of response. My sensibility foundered under the assault on my senses.

My imagination had been pre-empted.

The room was a box of oiled paper full of the echoes of the rain. After the light was out, as we lay together, I could still see the single shape of our embrace in the mirror above me, a marvellously unexpected conjunction cast at random by the enigmatic kaleidoscope of the city. Our pelts were stippled with the fretted shadows of the lace curtains as if our skins were a mysterious uniform provided by the management in order to render all those who made love in that hotel anonymous. The mirror annihilated time, place and person; at the consecration of this house, the mirror had been dedicated to the reflection of chance embraces. Therefore it treated flesh in an exemplary fashion, with charity and indifference.

The mirror distilled the essence of all the encounters of strangers whose perceptions of one another existed only in the medium of the chance embrace, the accidental. During the durationless time we spent making love, we were not ourselves, whoever that might have been, but in some sense the ghosts of ourselves. But the selves we were not, the selves of our own habitual perceptions of ourselves, had a far more insubstantial substance than the reflections we were. The magic mirror presented me with a hitherto unconsidered notion of myself as I. Without any intention of mine, I had been defined by the action reflected in the mirror. I beset me. I was the subject of the sentence written on the mirror. I was not watching it. There was nothing whatsoever beyond the surface of the glass. Nothing kept me from the fact, the act; I had been precipitated into knowledge of the real conditions of living.

Mirrors are ambiguous things. The bureaucracy of the mirror issues me with a passport to the world; it shows me my appearance. But what use is a passport to an armchair traveller? Women and mirrors are in complicity with one another to evade the action I/she performs that she/I cannot watch, the action with which I break out of the mirror, with which I assume my appearance. But *this* mirror refused to conspire with me; it was like the first mirror I'd ever seen. It reflected the embrace beneath it without the least guile. All it showed was inevitable. But I myself could never have dreamed it.

I saw the flesh and the mirror but I could not come to terms with the sight. My immediate response to it was, to feel I'd acted out of character. The fancy-dress disguise I'd put on to suit the city had betrayed me to a room and a bed and a modification of myself that had no business at all in my life, not in the life I had watched myself performing.

Therefore I evaded the mirror. I scrambled out of its arms and sat on the edge of the bed and lit a fresh cigarette from the butt of the old one. The rain beat down. My demonstration of perturbation was perfect in every detail, just like the movies. I applauded it. I was gratified the mirror had not seduced me into behaving in a way I would have felt inappropriate – that is, shrugging and sleeping, as though my infidelity was not of the least importance. I now shook with the disturbing presentiment that he with his sequin eyes who'd been kind to me was an ironic substitute for the other one, the one I loved, as if the arbitrary carnival of the streets had gratuitously offered me this young man to find out if I *could* act out of character and then projected our intersection upon the mirror, as an objective lesson in the nature of things.

Therefore I dressed rapidly and ran away as soon as it was light outside, that mysterious, colourless light of dawn when the hooded crows flap out of the temple groves to perch on the telegraph poles, cawing a baleful dawn chorus to the echoing boulevards empty, now, of all the pleasure-seekers. The rain had stopped. It was an overcast morning so hot that I broke out into a sweat at the slightest movement. The bewildering electrographics of the city at night were all switched off. All the perspectives were pale, gritty grey, the air was full of dust. I never knew such a banal morning.

The morning before the night before, the morning before this oppressive morning, I woke up in the cabin of a boat. All the previous day, as we rounded the coast in bright weather, I dreamed of the reunion before me, a lovers' meeting refreshed by the three months I'd been gone, returning home due to a death in the family. I will come back as soon as I can – I'll write. Will you meet me at the pier? Of course, of course he will. But he was not at the pier; where was he?

So I went at once to the city and began my desolate tour of the pleasure quarters, looking for him in all the bars he used. He was nowhere to be found. I did not know his address, of course; he moved from rented room to rented room with the agility of the feckless and we had corresponded through accommodation addresses, coffee shops, poste restante, etc. Besides, there had been a displacement of mail reminiscent of the excesses of the nineteenth-century novel, such as it is difficult to believe and could only have been caused by a desperate emotional necessity to cause as much confusion as possible. Both of us prided ourselves on our passionate sensibilities, of course. That was *one* thing we had in common! So, although I thought I was the most romantic spectacle imaginable as I wandered weeping down the alleys, I was in reality at risk – I had fallen through one of the holes life leaves in it; these peculiar holes are the entrances to the counters at which you pay the price of the way you live.

Random chance operates in relation to these existential lacunae; one tumbles down them when, for the time being, due to hunger, despair, sleeplessness, hallucination or those accidental-on-purpose misreadings of train timetables and airline schedules that produce margins of empty time, one is lost. One is at the mercy of events. That is why I like to be a foreigner; I only travel for the insecurity. But I did not know that, then.

I found my self-imposed fate, my beloved, quite early that morning but we quarrelled immediately. We quarrelled the day away assiduously and, when I tried to pull the strings of my self and so take control of the situation, I was astonished to find the situation I wanted was disaster, shipwreck. I saw his face as though it were in ruins, although it was the sight in the world I knew best and, the first time I saw it, had not seemed to me a face I did not know. It had seemed, in some way, to correspond to my idea of my own face. It had seemed a face long known and well remembered, a face that had always been imminent in my consciousness as an idea that now found its first visual expression.

So I suppose I do not know how he really looked and, in fact, I suppose I shall never know, now, for he was plainly an object created in the mode of fantasy. His image was already present somewhere in my head and I was seeking to discover it in actuality, looking at every face I met in case it was the right face – that is, the face which corresponded to my notion of the unseen face of the one I should love, a face created parthenogenetically by the rage to love which consumed me. So his self, and, by his self, I mean the thing he was to himself, was quite unknown to me. I created him solely in relation to myself, like a work of romantic art, an object corresponding to the ghost inside me. When I'd first loved him, I wanted to take him apart, as a child dismembers a clockwork toy, to comprehend the inscrutable mechanics of its interior. I wanted to see him far more naked than he was with his clothes off. It was easy enough to strip him bare and then I picked up my scalpel and set to work. But, since I was so absolutely in charge of the dissection, I only discovered what I was able to recognize already, from past experience, inside him. If ever I found anything new to me, I steadfastly ignored it. I was so absorbed in this work it never occurred to me to wonder if it hurt him.

In order to create the loved object in this way and to issue it with its certificate of authentication, as beloved, I had also to labour at the idea of myself in love. I watched myself closely for all the signs and, precisely upon cue, here they were! Longing, desire, self-abnegation, etc. I was racked by all the symptoms. Even so, in spite of this fugue of feeling, I had felt nothing but pleasure when the young man who picked me up inserted his sex inside me in the blue-movie bedroom. I only grew guilty later, when I realized I had not felt in the least guilty at the time. And was I in character when I felt guilty or in character when I did not? I was perplexed. I no longer understood the logic of my own performance. My script had been scrambled behind my back. The cameraman was drunk. The director had a *crise de nerfs* and been taken away to a sanatorium. And my co-star had picked himself up off the operating table and painfully cobbled himself together again according to his own design! All this had taken place while I was looking at the mirror.

Imagine my affront.

We quarrelled until night fell and, still quarrelling, found our way to another hotel but this hotel, and this night, was in every respect a parody of the previous night. (That's more like it! Squalor and humiliation! Ah!) Here, there were no lace drapes nor windbells nor moonlight nor any moist whisper of lugubriously seductive rain; this place was bleak, mean and cheerless and the sheets on the mattress they threw down on the floor for us were blotched with dirt although, at first, we did not notice that because it was necessary to pretend the urgent passion we always used to feel in one another's presence even if we felt it no longer, as if to act out the feeling with sufficient intensity would re-create it by sleight of hand, although our skins (which knew us better than we knew ourselves) told us the period of reciprocation was over. It was a mean room and the windows overlooked a parking lot with a freeway beyond it, so that the paper walls shuddered with the reverberations of the infernal clamour of the traffic. There was a sluggish electric fan with dead flies caught in the spokes and a single strip of neon overhead lit us and everything up with a scarcely tolerable, quite remorseless light. A slatternly woman in a filthy apron brought us glasses of thin, cold, brown tea made from barley and then she shut the door on us. I would not let him kiss me between the thighs because I was afraid he would taste the traces of last night's adventure, a little touch of paranoia in *that* delusion.

I don't know how much guilt had to do with the choice of this décor. But I felt it was perfectly appropriate.

The air was thicker than tea that's stewed on the hob all day and cockroaches were running over the ceiling, I remember.

I cried all the first part of the night, I cried until I was exhausted but he turned on his side and slept – he saw through that ruse, though I did not since I did not know that I was lying. But I could not sleep because of the rattling of the walls and the noise of traffic. We had turned off the glaring lamp; when I saw a shaft of light fall across his face, I thought: 'Surely it's too early for the dawn.' But it was another person silently sliding open the unlocked door; in this disreputable hotel, anything can happen. I screamed and the intruder vanished. Wakened by a scream, my lover thought I'd gone mad and instantly trapped me in a stranglehold, in case I murdered him.

We were both old enough to have known better, too.

When I turned on the lamp to see what time it was, I noticed, to my surprise, that his features were blurring, like the underwriting on a palimpsest. It wasn't long before we parted. Only a few days. You can't keep *that* pace up for long.

Then the city vanished; it ceased, almost immediately, to be a magic and appalling place. I woke up one morning and found it had become home. Though I still turn up my coat collar in a lonely way and am always looking at myself in mirrors, they're only habits and give no clue at all to my character, whatever that is.

The most difficult performance in the world is acting naturally, isn't it? Everything else is artful.

MASTER

AFTER HE DISCOVERED that his vocation was to kill animals, the pursuit of it took him far away from temperate weather until, in time, the insatiable suns of Africa eroded the pupils of his eyes, bleached his hair and tanned his skin until he no longer looked the thing he had been but its systematic negative; he became the white hunter, victim of an exile which is the imitation of death, a willed bereavement. He would emit a ravished gasp when he saw the final spasm of his prey. He did not kill for money but for love.

He had first exercised a propensity for savagery in the acrid lavatories of a minor English public school where he used to press the heads of the new boys into the ceramic bowl and then pull the flush upon them to drown their gurgling protests. After puberty, he turned his indefinable but exacerbated rage upon the pale, flinching bodies of young women whose flesh he lacerated with teeth, fingernails and sometimes his leather belt in the beds of cheap hotels near London's great rail termini (King's Cross, Victoria, Euston . . .). But these pastel-coloured excesses, all the cool, rainy country of his birth could offer him, never satisfied him; his ferocity would attain the colouring of the fauves only when he took it to the torrid zones and there refined it until it could be distinguished from that of the beasts he slaughtered only by the element of self-consciousness it retained, for, if little of him now pertained to the human, the eyes of his self still watched him so that he was able to applaud his own depredations.

Although he decimated herds of giraffe and gazelle as they grazed in the savannahs until they learned to snuff their annihilation upon the wind as he approached, and dispatched heraldically plated hippopotami as they lolled up to their armpits in ooze, his rifle's particular argument lay with the silken indifference of the great cats, and, finally, he developed a speciality in the extermination of the printed beasts, leopards and lynxes, who carry ideograms of death in the clotted language pressed in brown ink upon their pelts by the fingertips of mute gods who do not acknowledge any divinity in humanity.

When he had sufficiently ravaged the cats of Africa, a country older by far than we are yet to whose innocence he had always felt superior, he decided to explore the nether regions of the New World, intending to kill the painted beast, the jaguar, and so arrived in the middle of a metaphor for desolation, the place where time runs back on itself, the moist, abandoned cleft of the world whose fructifying river is herself a savage woman, the Amazon. A green, irrevocable silence closed upon him in that serene kingdom of giant vegetables. Dismayed, he clung to the bottle as if it were a teat.

He travelled by jeep through an invariable terrain of architectonic vegetation where no wind lifted the fronds of palms as ponderous as if they had been sculpted out of viridian gravity at the beginning of time and then abandoned, whose trunks were so heavy they did not seem to rise into the air but, instead, drew the oppressive sky down upon the forest like a coverlid of burnished metal. These tree trunks bore an outcrop of plants, orchids, poisonous, iridescent blossoms and creepers the thickness of an arm with flowering mouths that stuck out viscous tongues to trap the flies that nourished them. Bright birds of unknown shapes infrequently darted past him and sometimes monkeys, chattering like the third form, leaped from branch to branch that did not move beneath them. But no motion nor sound did more than ripple the surface of the profound, inhuman introspection of the place so that, here, to kill became the only means that remained to him to confirm he himself was still alive, for he was not prone to introspection and had never found any consolation in nature. Slaughter was his only proclivity and his unique skill.

He came upon the Indians who lived among the lugubrious trees. They represented such a diversity of ethnic types they were like a living museum of man organized on a principle of regression for, the further inland he went, the more primitive they became, as if to demonstrate that evolution could be inverted. Some of the brown men had no other habitation than the sky and, like the flowers, ate insects; they would paint their bodies with the juice of leaves and berries and ornament their heads with diadems of feathers or the claws of eagles. Placid and decorative, the men and women would come softly twittering round his jeep, a mild curiosity illuminating the inward-turning, amber suns of their eyes, and he did not recognize that they were men although they distilled demented alcohol in stills of their own devising and he drank it, in order to people the inside of his head with familiar frenzy among so much that was strange.

His half-breed guide would often take one of the brown girls who guilelessly offered him her bare, pointed breasts and her veiled, limpid smile and, then and there, infect her with the clap to which he was a chronic martyr in the bushes at the rim of the clearing. Afterwards, licking his chops with remembered appetite, he would say to the hunter: 'Brown meat, brown meat.' In drunkenness one night, troubled by the prickings of a carnality that often visited him at the end of his day's work, the hunter bartered, for the spare tyre of his jeep, a pubescent girl as virgin as the forest that had borne her.

She wore a vestigial slip of red cotton twisted between her thighs and her long, sinuous back was upholstered in cut velvet, for it was whorled and ridged with the tribal markings incised on her when her menses began – raised designs like the contour map of an unknown place. The women of her tribe dipped their hairs in liquid mud and then wound their locks into long curls around sticks and let them dry in the sun until each one possessed a hairdo of rigid ringlets the consistency of baked, unglazed pottery, so she looked as if her head was surrounded by one of those spiked haloes allotted to famous sinners in Sunday-school picture books. Her eyes held the gentleness and the despair of those about to be dispossessed; she had the immovable smile of a cat, which is forced by physiology to smile whether it wants to or not.

The beliefs of her tribe had taught her to regard herself as a sentient abstraction, an intermediary between the ghosts and the fauna, so she looked at her purchaser's fever-shaking, skeletal person with scarcely curiosity, for he was to her no more yet no less surprising than any other gaunt manifestation of the forest. If she did not perceive him as a man, either, that was because her cosmogony admitted no essential difference between herself and the beasts and the spirits, it was so sophisticated. Her tribe never killed; they only ate roots. He taught her to eat the meat he roasted over his camp fire and, at first, she did not like it much but dutifully consumed it as though he were ordering her to partake of a sacrament for, when she saw how casually he killed the jaguar, she soon realized he was death itself. Then she began to look at him with wonder for she recognized immediately how death had glorified itself to become the principle of his life. But when he looked at her, he saw only a piece of curious flesh he had not paid much for.

He thrust his virility into her surprise and, once her wound had healed, used her to share his sleeping bag and carry his pelts. He told her her name would be Friday, which was the day he bought her; he taught her to say 'master' and then let her know that was to be his name. Her eyelids fluttered for, though she could move her lips and tongue and so reproduce the sounds he made, she did not understand them. And, daily, he slaughtered the jaguar. He sent away the guide for, now he had bought the girl, he did not need him; so the ambiguous couple went on together, while the girl's father made sandals from the rubber tyre to shoe his family's feet and they walked a little way into the twentieth century in them, but not far.

Among her tribe circulated the following picturesque folk-tale. The jaguar invited the anteater to a juggling contest in which they would use their eyes to play with, so they drew their eyes out of the sockets. When they had finished, the anteater threw his eyes up into the air and back they fell – plop! in place in his head; but when the jaguar imitated him, his eyes caught in the topmost branches of a tree and he could not reach them. So he became blind. Then the anteater asked the macaw to make new eyes out of water for the jaguar and, with these eyes, the jaguar found that it could see in the dark. So all turned out well for the jaguar; and she, too, the girl who did not know her own name, could see in the dark. As they moved always more deeply into the forest, away from the little settlements, nightly he extorted his pleasure from her flesh and she would gaze over her shoulder at shapes of phantoms in the thickly susurrating undergrowth, phantoms – it seemed to her – of beasts he had slaughtered that day, for she had been born into the clan of the jaguar and, when his leather belt cut her shoulder, the magic water of which her eyes were made would piteously leak.

He could not reconcile himself to the rain forest, which oppressed and devastated him. He began to shake with malaria. He killed continually, stripped the pelts and left the corpses behind him for the vultures and the flies.

Then they came to a place where there were no more roads.

His heart leaped with ecstatic fear and longing when he saw how nothing but beasts inhabited the interior. He wanted to destroy them all, so that he would feel less lonely, and, in order to penetrate this absence with his annihilating presence, he left the jeep behind at a forgotten township where a green track ended and an ancient whisky priest sat all day in the ruins of a forsaken church brewing fire-water from wild bananas and keening the stations of the cross. Master loaded his brown mistress with his guns and the sleeping bag and the gourds filled with liquid fever. They left a wake of corpses behind them for the plants and the vultures to eat.

At night, after she lit the fire, he would first abuse her with the butt of his rifle about the shoulders and, after that, with his sex; then drink from a gourd and sleep. When she had wiped the tears from her face with the back of her hand, she was herself again, and, after they had been together a few weeks, she seized the opportunity of solitude to examine his guns, the instruments of his passion and, perhaps, learn a little of Master's magic.

She squinted her eye to peer down the long barrel; she caressed the metal trigger, and, pointing the barrel carefully away from her as she had seen Master do, she softly squeezed it in imitation of his gestures to see if she, too, could provoke the same shattering exhalation. But, to her disappointment, she provoked nothing. She clicked her tongue against her teeth in irritation. Exploring further, however, she discovered the secret of the safety catch.

Ghosts came out of the jungle and sat at her feet, cocking their heads on one side to watch her. She greeted them with a friendly wave of her hand. The fire began to fail but she could see clearly through the sights of the rifle since her eyes were made of water and, raising it to her shoulder as she had seen Master do, she took aim at the disc of moon stuck to the sky beyond the ceiling of boughs above her, for she wanted to shoot the moon down since it was a bird in her scheme of things and, since he had taught her to eat meat, now she thought she must be death's apprentice.

He woke from sleep in a paroxysm of fear and saw her, dimly illuminated by the dying fire, naked but for the rag that covered her sex, with the rifle in her hand; it seemed to him her clay-covered head was about to turn into a nest of birds of prey. She laughed delightedly at the corpse of the sleeping bird her bullet had knocked down from the tree and the moonlight glimmered on her curiously pointed teeth. She believed the bird she shot down had been the moon and now, in the night sky, she saw only the ghost of the moon. Though they were lost, hopelessly lost, in the trackless forest, she knew quite well where she was; she was always at home in the ghost town.

Next day, he oversaw the beginnings of her career as a markswoman and watched her tumble down from the boughs of the forest representatives of all the furred and feathered beings it contained. She always gave the same delighted laugh to see them fall for she had never thought it would be so easy to populate her fireside with fresh ghosts. But she could not bring herself to kill the jaguar, since the jaguar was the emblem of her clan; with forceful gestures of her head and hands, she refused. But, after she learned to shoot, soon she became a better hunter than he although there was no method to her killing and they went banging away together indiscriminately through the dim, green undergrowth.

The descent of the banana spirit in the gourd marked the passage of time and they left a gross trail of carnage behind them. The spectacle of her massacres moved him and he mounted her in a frenzy, forcing apart her genital lips so roughly the crimson skin on the inside bruised and festered while the bites on her throat and shoulders oozed diseased pearls of pus that brought the blowflies buzzing about her in a cloud. Her screams were a universal language; even the monkeys understood she suffered when Master took his pleasure, yet he did not. As she grew more like him, so she began to resent him.

While he slept, she flexed her fingers in the darkness that concealed nothing from her and, without surprise, she discovered her fingernails were growing long, curved, hard and sharp. Now she could tear his back when he inflicted himself upon her and leave red runnels in his skin; yelping with delight, he only used her the more severely and, twisting her head with its pottery appendages this way and that in pained perplexity, she gouged the empty air with her claws.

They came to a spring of water and she plunged into it in order to wash herself but she sprang out again immediately because the touch of water aroused such an unpleasant sensation on her pelt.

When she impatiently tossed her head to shake away the water-drops, her clay ringlets melted altogether and trickled down her shoulders. She could no longer tolerate cooked meat but must tear it raw between her fingers off the bone before Master saw. She could no longer twist her scarlet tongue around the two syllables of his name, 'mas-tuh'; when she tried to speak, only a diffuse and rumbling purr shivered the muscles of her throat and she dug neat holes in the earth to bury her excrement, she had become so fastidious since she grew whiskers.

Madness and fever consumed him. When he killed the jaguar, he abandoned them in the forest with the stippled pelts still on them. To possess the clawed she was in itself a kind of slaughter, and, tracking behind her, his eyes dazed with strangeness and liquor, he would watch the way the intermittent dentellation of the sun through the leaves mottled the ridged tribal markings down her back until it seemed the blotched areas of pigmentation were subtly mimicking the beasts who mimicked the patterns of the sun through the leaves and, if she had not walked upright on two legs, he would have shot her. As it was, he thrust her down into the undergrowth, amongst the orchids, and drove his other weapon into her soft, moist hole whilst he tore her throat with his teeth and she wept, until, one day, she found she was not able to cry any more.

The day the liquor ended, he was alone with fever. He reeled, screaming and shaking, in the clearing where she had abandoned his sleeping bag; she crouched among the lianas and crooned in a voice like soft thunder. Though it was daylight, the ghosts of innumerable jaguar crowded round to see what she would do. Their invisible nostrils twitched with the prescience of blood. The shoulder to which she raised the rifle now had the texture of plush.

His prey had shot the hunter, but now she could no longer hold the gun. Her brown and amber dappled sides rippled like water as she trotted across the clearing to worry the clothing of the corpse with her teeth. But soon she grew bored and bounded away.

Then only the flies crawling on his body were alive and he was far from home.

REFLECTIONS

I WAS WALKING in a wood one late spring day of skimming cloud and shower-tarnished sunshine, the sky a lucid if intermittent blue – cool, bright, tremulous weather. A coloratura blackbird perched on a bough curded with greenish may-blossom let fall a flawed chain of audible pearl; I was alone in the spring-enchanted wood. I slashed the taller grasses with my stick and now and then surprised some woodland creature, rat or rabbit, that fled away from me through long grass where little daisies and spindly branches of buttercups were secreted among gleaming stems still moist at the roots from last night's rain that had washed and refreshed the entire wood, had dowered it with the poignant transparency, the unique, inconsolable quality of rainy countries, as if all was glimpsed through tears.

The crisp air was perfumed with wet grass and fresh earth. The year was swinging on the numinous hinges of the solstice but I was ingenuous and sensed no imminence in the magic silence of the rustling wood.

Then I heard a young girl singing. Her voice performed a trajectory of sound far more ornate than that of the blackbird, who ceased at once to sing when he heard it for he could not compete with the richly crimson sinuosity of a voice that pierced the senses of the listener like an arrow in a dream. She sang; and her words thrilled through me, for they seemed filled with a meaning that had no relation to meaning as I understood it.

'Under the leaves,' she sang, 'and the leaves of life – ' Then, in mid-flight, the song ceased and left me dazzled. My attention abstracted from my surroundings, all at once my foot turned on an object hidden in the grass and I tumbled to the ground. Though I fell on the soft, wet grass, I was shaken and winded. I forgot that luring music. Cursing my obstacle, I searched among the pale, earth-stained rootlets to find it and my fingers closed on, of all things, a shell. A shell so far from the sea! When I tried to grasp it in order to pick it up and examine it the better, I found the act unexpectedly difficult and my determination to lift it quickened although, at the same time, I felt a shiver of fear for it was so very, very heavy and its contours so chill that a shock like cold electricity darted up my arm from the shell, into my heart. I was seized with the most intense disquiet; I was mystified by the shell.

I thought it must be a shell from a tropic ocean, since it was far larger and more elaborately whorled than the shells I'd found on the shores of the Atlantic. There was some indefinable strangeness in its shape I could not immediately define. It glimmered through the grass like a cone of trapped moonlight although it was so very cold and so heavy it seemed to me it might contain all the distilled heaviness of gravity itself within it. I grew very much afraid of the shell; I think I sobbed. Yet I was so determined to wrench it from the ground that I clenched my muscles and gritted my teeth and tugged and heaved. Up it came, at last, and I rolled over backwards when it freed itself. But now I held the prize in my hands, and I was, for the moment, satisfied.

When I looked at the shell more closely, I saw the nature of the teasing difference that had struck me when I first set eyes on it. The whorls of the shell went the wrong way. The spirals were reversed. It looked like the mirror image of a shell, and so it should not have been able to exist outside a mirror; in this world, it could not exist outside a mirror. But, all the same, I held it.

The shell was the size of my cupped hands and cold and heavy as death.

In spite of its fabulous weight, I decided to carry it through the wood for I thought I would take it to the little museum in the nearby town where they would inspect it and test it and tell me what it might be and how it could have arrived where I found it. But as I staggered along with it in my arms, it exerted such a pull downwards on me that, several times, I nearly fell to my knees, as if the shell were determined to drag me, not down to the earth but into the earth itself. And then, to complete my confusion, I heard that witching voice again.

'Under the leaves – '

But, this time, when a gasp stopped the song, the voice changed at once to the imperative.

'Sic 'im!' she urged. 'Sic 'im!'

Before I had a chance to do more than glance in the direction of the voice, a bullet whirred over my head and buried itself in the trunk of an elm tree, releasing from their nests in the upward branches a whirring hurricane of crows. An enormous black dog bounded towards me from the undergrowth so suddenly I saw no more than his yawning scarlet maw and lolling tongue before I went down on my face beneath him. The fright nearly bereft me of my senses. The dog slavered wetly over me and, the next thing I knew, a hand seized my shoulder and roughly turned me over.

She had called the dog away and now it sat on its haunches, panting, watching me with a quick, red eye. It was black as coal, some kind of lurcher, with balls the size of grapefruit. Both the dog and the girl glanced at me without charity. She wore blue jeans and boots, a wide, vindictively buckled leather belt and a green sweater. Her tangled brown hair hung about her shoulders in a calculated disorder that was not wild. Her dark eyebrows were perfectly straight and gave her stern face a gravity as awful as that of the shell I held in my hand. Her blue eyes, the kind the Irish say have been put in with a sooty finger, held no comfort nor concern for me for they were the eyes that justice would have if she were not blind. She carried a sporting rifle slung across her shoulder and I knew at once this rifle had fired the shot. She might have been the gamekeeper's daughter but, no, she was too proud; she was a savage and severe wood-ranger.

Why I do not know, but every impulse told me to conceal my shell and I hugged it close to me, as if my life depended on keeping it, although it was so heavy and began to throb with a wild palpitation so that it seemed the shell had disordered my own heart, or else had become my own disordered heart. But my brusque captress poked at my hands with the barrel of her rifle so roughly my bruised fingers let the shell fall. She bent forward so that her necromantic hair brushed my face and picked up the shell with amazing ease.

She examined it for a moment and then, without a word or sign to me, tossed it to her lurcher, who seized it in his mouth ready to carry it for her. The dog began to wag his tail. The rhythmic swishing of his tail upon the grass was now the only sound in the clearing. Even the trees had ceased to murmur, as though a holy terror hushed them.

She gestured me to my feet and, when I was upright, she thrust the mouth of the gun in the small of my back and marched me through the wood at gunpoint, striding along behind me while the dog padded beside her with the shell in his mouth. All this took place in unadulterated silence, but for the raucous panting of the dog. The cabbage white butterflies flickered upon the still air as if nothing whatsoever were out of the ordinary, while delicious-looking apricot and violet coloured clouds continued to chase one another across the sun according to the indifferent logic of the upper heavens, for the clouds were moved by a fierce wind that blew so high above the wood everything around me was as tranquil as water trapped in a lock, and mocked the inward perturbation that shook me.

Soon we reached an overgrown path that took us to a gate set in a garden wall where there was an old-fashioned bell-pull and, dangling above it, a bell stained with moss and rust. The girl with the rifle rang this bell before she opened the gate as if to warn whoever was at home that visitors were arriving. The gate led into a graceful and dilapidated walled garden full of the herbaceous splendours of early summer, hollyhocks, wallflowers, roses. There was a mossed sundial and a little stone statue of a nude youth stretching his arms up out of a cuirass of ivy. But, though the bees hummed among the flower bells, the grass was as long as it had been in the wood and just as full of buttercups and daisies. Dandelions expired in airy seed heads in the flowerbeds; ragged robin and ground elder conspired to oust the perennials from the borders and a bright sadness of neglect touched everything as though with dust, just as it did the ancient brick house, almost covered with creepers, that slept within the garden, an ancient, tumbledown place with a look of oracular blindness in windows that were stopped up with vines and flowers. The roof was lichened quite over, so that it seemed upholstered in sleek, green fur. Yet there was no peace in the dishevelled loveliness of the place; the very plants that grew there seemed tensed in a curious expectancy, as though the garden were a waiting room. There was a short, crumbling flight of steps that led to a weathered front door, ajar like the door of a witch's house.

Before the door, I involuntarily halted; a dreadful vertigo seized me, as if I stood on the edge of an abyss. My heart had been thumping far too hard and far too fast since I had picked up the shell and now it seemed about to burst from too much strain.

Faintness and terror of death swept over me; but the girl prodded me cruelly in the buttocks with her rifle so I was forcibly marched into a country-house hall with dark stained floorboards, a Persian carpet and a Jacobean oak chest with an antique bowl on it, all complete yet all as if untouched for years, for decades. A maze of dust danced in the beam of sunshine that disturbed the choked indoors air when we broke into it. Every corner was softened by cobwebs while the industrious spiders had wound filaments of geometric lace this way and that between the crumbling furniture. A sweet, rank smell of damp and decay filled the house; it was cold, inside, and dark. The door swung to behind us but did not close and we went up a staircase of worm-eaten oak, I first, she after and then the dog, whose claws clattered on the bare wood.

At first I thought the spiders had cast their nets on both sides of the stair but then I saw the workmanship that wound down the inner side of the staircase was not that of the spiders for, though it was the same colour, this web had a determinate pattern that resembled nothing so much as openwork knitting, the kind of featherlike, floating stuff from which they make courtesans' bed-jackets. This knitting was part of an interminable muffler that, as I watched it, crept, with vegetable slowness, little by little downstairs towards the hall. Yard upon yard of the muffler was coiled up in airy folds on the landing and there I could hear the clack, clack, clack of a pair of knitting needles ticking away monotonously near at hand. The muffler came out of a door that, like the front door, stood a little open; it edged through the gap like a tenuous serpent.

My captress motioned me aside with the muzzle of her rifle and knocked firmly on the door.

Inside the room, someone coughed dryly, then invited us: 'Come in.'

It was a soft, rustling, unemphatic, almost uninflected, faded, faintly perfumed voice, like very old lace handkerchiefs put away long ago in a drawer with potpourri and forgotten.

My captress thrust me through the door before her; when I was close to her, my nostrils quivered at the vicious odour of her skin. It was a large room, part drawing room, part bedroom, for the being who lived in it was crippled. She, he, it – whoever, whatever my host or hostess may have been – lay in an old-fashioned wicker Bath chair beside a cracked marble fireplace bossed with swags and cupids. Her white hands finished in fingers indecently long, white and translucent as candles on a cathedral altar; those tapering fingers were the source of the bewildering muffler, for they held two bone needles and never ceased to move.

The volatile stitchery they produced occupied all the carpetless area of the floor and, in places, was piled up as high as the crippled knees of its maker. There were yards and yards of it in the room, perhaps even miles and miles of it, and I stepped through and across it very carefully, nudging it out of the way with my toes, to arrive where the girl directed me with her gun, in the position of a suppliant before the Bath chair. The crippled being who lay in it had the most regal cast of chin and mouth imaginable and the proud, sad air of the king of a rainy country. One of her profiles was that of a beautiful woman, the other that of a beautiful man. It is a defect in our language there is no term of reference for these indeterminate and undefinable beings; but, although she acknowledged no gender, I will call her 'she' because she had put on a female garment, a loose negligee of spider-coloured lace, unless she, like the spiders, spun and wove her own thread and so had become clothed, for her shadowy hair was also the colour of the stuff she knitted and so evanescent in texture it seemed to move of its own accord on the air around her. Her eyelids and the cavernous sockets of her eyes were thickly stuck with silver sequins that glittered in the strange, subaqueous, drowned, drowning light that suffused the room, a light filtered through windows caked with grime and half covered by creeper, clairvoyant light reflected, with an enhanced strangeness, by the immense mirror in a chipped gilt frame hanging on the wall opposite the fireplace; it seemed the mirror, like the moon, was itself endowed with the light it gave back to us.

With a touching fidelity, the mirror duplicated the room and all it contained, the fireplace, the walls covered with a stained white paper stippled with fronds of greenery, every piece of neglected ormolu furniture. How pleased I was to see my experiences had not changed me! though my old tweed suit was stained with grass, my stick gone – left behind where I had dropped it in the wood. And so much dirt on my face. But I looked as if I were reflected in a forest pool rather than by silvered glass for the surface of the mirror looked like the surface of motionless water, or of mercury, as though it were a solid mass of liquid kept in place by some inversion of gravity that reminded me of the ghastly weight of the shell that now dropped at the androgyne's feet from the dog's mouth. She never stopped knitting for one moment as she nudged it with a beautiful toe painted with a rime of silver; woe gave her a purely female face.

'Only one little stitch! And I only dropped one little stitch!' she mourned. And she bowed her head over her work in an ecstasy of regret.

'At least it wasn't out long,' said the girl. Her voice had a clanging resonance; mercy was a minor key that would never modify its martial music. '*He* found it!'

She gestured towards me with her gun. The androgyne directed upon me a pair of vague, too large, stagnant eyes that did not shine.

'Do you know where this shell comes from?' she asked me with a grave courtesy.

I shook my head.

'It comes from the Sea of Fertility. Do you know where *that* is?'

'On the surface of the moon,' I answered. My voice sounded coarse and rough to me.

'Ah,' she said, 'the moon, the source of polarized light. Yes and no to your reply. It is an equivalence. The sea of fertility is a reversed system, since everything there is as dead as this shell.'

'He found it in the wood,' said the girl.

'Put it back where it belongs, Anna,' said the androgyne, who possessed a frail yet absolute air of authority. 'Before any harm is done.'

The girl bent and picked up the shell. She scrutinized the mirror and took aim at some spot within it that seemed to her a logical target for the shell. I saw her raise her arm to throw the shell into the mirror and I saw her mirrored arm raise the shell to throw it outside the mirror. Then she threw the duplicated shell. There was no sound in the room but the click of the knitting needles when she threw the shell into the mirror while her reflection threw the shell out of the mirror. The shell, when it met its own reflection, disappeared immediately.

The androgyne sighed with satisfaction.

'The name of my niece is Anna,' she said to me, 'because she can go both ways. As, indeed, I can myself, though I am not a simple palindrome.'

She gave me an enigmatic smile and moved her shoulders so that the lace negligee she wore fell back from her soft, pale breasts that were, each one, tipped by nipples of deep, dark pink, with the whorled crenellations of raspberries, and then she shifted her loins a little to display, savage and barbaric in their rude, red-purple repose, the phallic insignia of maleness.

'She can,' said Anna, 'go both ways, although she cannot move at all. So her power is an exact equivalent of her impotence, since both are absolute.'

But her aunt looked down at her soft weapon and said gently: 'Not, my darling, *absolutely* absolute. Potency, impotence *in potentia*, hence relative. Only the intermediary, since indeterminate.'

With that, she caressed her naked breasts with a stunted gesture of her forearms; she could not move her arms freely because she did not stop knitting. They looked at one another and laughed. Their laughter drove icicles of fear into my brain and I did not know which way to turn.

'You see, we must do away with you,' said the androgyne. 'You know too much.'

Panic broke over me like a wave. I plunged across the room towards the door, careless of Anna's gun in my attempted flight. But my feet were snared by the knitting and once again I plunged downwards but this time my fall half stunned me. I lay dazed while their renewed laughter darted cruelly about the room.

'Oh,' said Anna, 'but we shan't kill you. We shall send you through the mirror. We shall send you where the shell went, since that is where you belong, now.'

'But the shell vanished,' I said.

'No,' replied the androgyne. 'It did not vanish in reality. That shell had no business in this world. I dropped a stitch, this morning; only one little stitch . . . and that confounded shell slipped through the hole the dropped stitch made, because those shells are all so very, very heavy, you see. When it met its reflection, it returned to its proper place. It cannot come back, now; and neither will you, after we have sent you through the mirror.'

Her voice was so very gentle, yet she offered me a perpetual estrangement. I let out a cry. Anna turned to her aunt and placed her hand on her genitalia, so that the cock sprang up. It was of redoubtable size.

'Oh, auntie, don't scare him!' she said.

Then they tittered, the weird harpies, so that I was quite beside myself with fear and bewilderment.

'It is a system of equivalences,' said the androgyne. 'She carries the gun, you see; and I, too.'

She displayed her towering erection with the air of a demonstrator in a laboratory.

'In my intermediary and cohesive logic, the equivalences reside beyond symbolism. The gun and the phallus are similar in their connection with life – that is, one gives it; and the other takes it away, so that both, in essence, are similar in that the negation freshly states the affirmed proposition.'

I was more bewildered than ever.

'But do all the men in the mirror world have guns between their thighs?'

Anna exclaimed with irritation at my simplicity.

'That's no more likely than that I could impregnate you with this – ' she said, pointing her gun at me, 'here or in any other world.'

'Embrace yourself in the mirror,' said the androgyne, knitting, knitting, knitting away. 'You must go, now. Now!'

Anna maintained her menace; there was nothing for it but to do as they bid. I went to the mirror and examined myself in its depths. A faint ripple ran over its surface; but when I touched it with my fingers, the surface was just as smooth and hard as it should have been. I saw that my reflection was cut off at the thighs by the gilt frame and Anna said: 'Climb on a stool! Who'd want you truncated, here or there?'

She grinned in an appalling fashion and slipped back the safety catch on her rifle. So I pulled a little, cane-seated, gilt-backed chair to the mirror and clambered up. I gazed at myself in the mirror; there I was, complete from head to toe, and there they were, behind me, the androgyne weaving her ethereal coils and the armed young girl, who, now that she could kill me with one little flick of her finger, looked as beautiful as a Roman soldier plundering a North African city, with her unkind eyes and her perfume of murder.

'Kiss yourself,' commanded the androgyne in a swooning voice. 'Kiss yourself in the mirror, the symbolic matrix of this and that, hither and thither, outside and inside.'

Then I saw, even if I could no longer be astonished, that though she knitted in both the room and the mirror, there was, within the room, no ball of wool at all; her yarn emanated from inside the mirror and the ball of wool existed only in the medium of reflection. But I did not have time to wonder at this marvel for the rank stench of Anna's excitement filled the room and her hand trembled. Out of rage and desperation, I advanced my own lips to meet the familiar yet unknown lips that advanced towards mine in the silent world of the glass.

I thought these lips would be cold and lifeless; that I would touch them but they could not touch me. Yet, when the twinned lips met, they cleaved, for these mirrored lips of mine were warm and throbbed. This mouth was wet and contained a tongue, and teeth. It was too much for me. The profound sensuality of this unexpected caress crisped the roots of my sex and my eyes involuntarily closed whilst my arms clasped my own tweed shoulders. The pleasure of the embrace was intense; I swooned beneath it.

When my eyes opened, I had become my own reflection. I had passed through the mirror and now I stood on a little, cane-seated, gilt-backed chair with my mouth pressed to an impervious surface of glass I had misted with my own breath and moistened with my own saliva.

Anna cried: 'Hurrah!' She dropped her rifle and clapped her hands while her aunt, continuing, all the time, to knit, gave me a peculiarly sultry smile.

'So,' she said. 'Welcome. This room is the half-way house between here and there, between this and that, because, you understand, I am so ambiguous. Stay in the field of force of the mirror for a while, until you are used to everything.'

The first thing that struck me was, the light was black. My eyes took a little time to grow accustomed to this absolute darkness for, though the delicate apparatus of cornea and aqueous humour and crystalline lens and vitreous body and optic nerve and retina had all been reversed when I gave birth to my mirror self through the mediation of the looking-glass, yet my sensibility remained as it had been. So at first, through the glass, I saw darkly and all was confusion but for their faces, which were irradiated by familiarity. But, when the inside of my head could process the information my topsy-turvy senses retrieved for me, then my other or anti-eyes apprehended a world of phosphorescent colour etched as with needles of variegated fire on a dimensionless opacity. The world was the same; yet absolutely altered. How can I describe it . . . almost as if this room was the colour negative of the other room. Unless – for how could I ever be certain which was the primary world and which the secondary – the other room, the other house, the other wood that I saw, transposed yet still peeping through the window in the other mirror – all that had been the colour negative of the room in which I now stood, where the exhalations of my breath were the same as the inhalations of my mirror anti-twin who turned away from me as I turned away from him, into the distorted, or else really real, world of the mirror room, which, since it existed in this mirror in this room beyond the mirror, reflected all of this room's ambiguities and was no longer the room I had left. That endless muffler or web wound round the room, still, but now it wound round contrariwise and Anna's aunt was knitting from left to right, instead of from right to left, with hands that, I realized, had they wished, could have pulled a right-hand glove over the left hand and vice versa, since she was truly ambidexterous.

But when I looked at Anna, I saw she was exactly the same as she had been on the other side of the mirror and knew her face for one of those rare faces that possess an absolute symmetry, each feature the exact equivalent of the other, so one of her profiles could serve as the template for both. Her skull was like a proposition in geometry. Irreducible as stone, finite as a syllogism, she was always indistinguishable from herself whichever way she went.

But the imperturbably knitting androgyne had turned its face contrariwise. One half of its face was always masculine and the other, no matter what, was feminine; yet these had been changed about, so that all the balances of the planes of the face and the lines of the brow were the opposite of what they had been before, although one half of the face was still feminine and the other masculine. Nevertheless, the quality of the difference made it seem that this altered yet similar face was the combination of the reflection of the female side of the face and the masculine side of the face that *did not appear* in the face I had seen beyond the mirror; the effect was as of the reflection of a reflection, like an example of perpetual regression, the perfect, self-sufficient nirvana of the hermaphrodite. She was Tiresias, capable of prophetic projection, whichever side of the mirror she chose to offer herself to my sight upon; and she went on knitting and knitting and knitting, with an infernal suburban complacency.

When I turned from the mirror, Anna was holding out her right or left hand towards me but, although I felt sure I was walking towards her and lifted up my legs and set them down again with the utmost determination, Anna receded further and further away from me. Niece and aunt emitted a titter and I guessed that, in order to come to Anna, I must go away from her. Therefore I stepped sturdily backwards and, in less than a second, her hard, thin, sunburned hand grasped mine.

The touch of her hand filled me with a wild loneliness.

With her other hand, she opened the door. I was terribly afraid of that door, for the room that contained the mirror was all that I knew, and therefore my only safety, in this unknown world that Anna, who now smiled inscrutably at me, negotiated as skilfully as if she herself, the solstice in person, went on curious hinges between this place and that place unlike her aunt, who, since she was crippled, could not move unless her condition of permanent stasis meant she was moving too fast for me to see, with a speed the inertia of the eye registered as immobility.

But, when the door creaked open on everyday, iron hinges that had never been oiled in this world or any other world, I saw only the staircase up which Anna had led me, down which she would now lead me, and the muffler that still curled down to the hall. The air was dank, just as it had been. Only, all the alignments of the stairwell had been subtly altered and the light was composed of a reversed spectrum.

The webs of the spiders presented structures of white fire so minutely altered from those I had passed on my way upstairs that only memory made me apprehend how their geometrical engineering had all been executed backwards. So we passed under the spectral arch they had prepared for us and out into the open air that did not refresh my bewildered brain, for it was as solid as water, dense and compact, of an impermeable substance that transmitted neither sound nor odour. To move through this liquid silence demanded the utmost exertion of physical energy and intellectual concentration, for gravity, beyond the mirror, was not a property of the ground but of the atmosphere. Then Anna, who understood the physical laws of this world, exerted a negative pressure upon me by some willed absence of impulse and to my amazement I now moved as if propelled sharply from behind along the path to the gate, past flowers that distilled inexpressible colours from the black sky above us, colours whose names only exist in an inverted language you could never understand if I were to speak it. But the colours were virtually independent of the forms of the plants. Haloes of incandescence, they had arbitrarily settled about spread umbrellas of petals as thin yet as hard as the shoulder blade of a rabbit, for the flesh of the flowers was calcified and lifeless; no plant was sentient in this coral garden. All had suffered a dead sea-change.

And the black sky possessed no dimension of distance, nor gave none; it did not arch above us but looked as if it were pasted behind the flat outlines of the half-ruinous house that now lay behind us, a shipwreck bearing a marvellous freight, the female man or virile woman clicking away at her needles in a visible silence. A visible silence, yes; for the dense fluidity of the atmosphere did not transmit sound to me as sound, but, instead, as irregular kinetic abstractions etched upon its interior, so that, once in the new wood, a sinister, mineral, realm of undiminishable darkness, to listen to the blackbird was to watch a moving point inside a block of deliquescent glass. I saw these sounds because my eyes took in a different light than the light that shone on my breast when my heart beat on the other side of it, although the wood through whose now lateral gravity Anna negotiated me was the same wood in which I had been walking when I first heard her sing. And I cannot tell you, since there is no language in this world to do so, how strange the antithetical wood and sweet June day were, for both had become the systematic negation of its others.

Anna, in some reversed fashion, must still have been menacing me with her gun, since it was her impulse that moved me; on we went, just as we had come – but Anna, now, went before me, with the muzzle of her gun pressed in the belly of nothingness, and the dog, her familiar, this time in the van. And this dog was white as snow and its balls were gone; on this side of the mirror, all dogs were bitches and vice versa.

I saw wild garlic and ground elder and the buttercups and daisies in the fossilized undergrowth now rendered in vivacious yet unnamable colours, as immobile arabesques without depth. But the sweetness of the wild roses rang in my ears like a peal of windbells for the vibrations of the perfumes echoed on my eardrums like the pulse of my own blood since, though they had become a kind of sound, they could not carry in the same way that sound did. I could not, for the life of me, make up my mind which world was which for I understood this world was coexistent in time and space with the other wood – was, as it were, the polarization of that other wood, although it was in no way similar to the reflection the other wood, or this wood, might have made in a mirror.

The more my eyes grew accustomed to the dark, the less in common did the petrified flora seem to have with anything I knew. I perceived all had been starkly invaded with, yes, shells, enormous shells, giant and uninhabited shells, so we might have been walking in the ruins of a marine city; the cool, pale colouring of those huge shells now glowed with a ghostly otherness and they were piled and heaped upon one another to parody the landscape of the woodland, unless the trees parodied them; all were whorled the wrong way round, all had that deathly weight, the supernatural resonance of the shell which seduced me and Anna told me in a soundless language I understood immediately that the transfigured wood, fertile now, only of metamorphoses, was – for how could it be anything else – the Sea of Fertility. The odour of her violence deafened me.

Then, once again, she began to sing; I saw the mute, dark, fire burning like Valhalla in *Götterdämmerung*. She sang a funeral pyre, the swan's song, death itself, and, with a brusque motion of her gun, she forced me forward on my knees while the dog stood over me as she tore open my clothes. The serenade smouldered all around us and I was so much at the mercy of the weight of the air, which pressed down on me like a coffin lid, and of the viscosity of the atmosphere, that I could do nothing to defend myself, even if I had known how, and soon she had me, poor, forked thing, stretched out upon a bank of shells with my trousers round my knees. She smiled but I could not tell what the smile meant; on this side of the mirror, a smile was no clue whatsoever to intention or to feeling and I did not think she meant to do me a good deed as she unbuckled her uncouth leather belt and stepped out of her jeans.

Parting the air with the knives of her arms, she precipitated herself upon me like a quoit on a peg. I screamed; the notes of my scream rose up on the air like ping-pong balls on a jet of water at a funfair. She raped me; perhaps her gun, in this system, gave her the power to do so.

I shouted and swore but the shell grotto in which she ravished me did not reverberate and I only emitted gobs of light. Her rape, her violation of me, caused me atrocious physical and mental pain. My being leaked away from me under the visitation of her aggressive flesh. My self grew less in agony under the piston thrust of her slender loins, as if she were a hammer and were forging me into some other substance than flesh and spirit. I knew the dreadful pleasure of abandonment; she had lit my funeral pyre and now would kill me. I felt such outrage I beat in the air behind my head with my helpless fists as she pumped away indefatigably at my sex, and to my surprise, I saw her face cloud and bruises appear on it, although my hands were nowhere near her. She was a brave girl; she only fucked the harder, for she was intransigent and now resembled the Seljuk Turks sacking Constantinople. I knew there was no hope for me if I did not act immediately.

Her gun lay propped against the shells beside us. I reached the other way and seized it. I shot at the black sky while she straddled me. The bullet pierced a neat, round, empty hole in the flat vault of the heavens but no light, no sound, leaked through; I had made a hole without quality but Anna let out a ripping shriek that sent a jagged scar across the surface of the wood. She tumbled backwards and twitched a little. The dog growled at me, a terrible sight, and leaped at my throat but I quickly shot her, also, in this negative way and, now free, there remained only the problem of the return to the mirror, the return to the right-hand side of the world. But I kept tight hold of the gun, by grasping it loosely, because of the guardian of the mirror.

To return to the house, I struck out from the shell grotto where Anna lay, in the opposite direction from the one we had come from. I must have fallen into a mirror elision of reflected time, or else I stumbled upon a physical law I could not have guessed at, for the wood dissolved, as if the blood that leaked from Anna's wound was a solvent for its petrified substance, and now

I found myself back at the crumbling gate before her juices were dry on my cock. I paused to do up my flies before I made my way to the door; I used my arms like scissors to snip through the thickness of the atmosphere, for it grew, moment by moment, less liquid and more impalpable. I did not ring the bell, so great was my outrage, so vivid my sense of having been the plaything of these mythic and monstrous beings.

The knitting curled down the stairs, just as I expected, and, in another moment, I saw, on a staccato stave, the sound of the needles.

She, he, it, Tiresias, though she knitted on remorselessly, was keening over a whole dropped row of stitches, trying to repair the damage as best she could. Her keening filled the room with a Walpurgisnacht of crazy shapes and, when she saw I was alone, she flung back her head and howled. In that decompression chamber between here and there, I heard a voice as clear as crystal describe a wordless song of accusation.

'Oh, my Anna, what have you done with my Anna – ?'

'I shot her,' I cried. 'With her own weapon.'

'A rape! She's raped!' screamed the androgyne as I dragged the gilt chair to the mirror and clambered up on it. In the silvered depths before me, I saw the new face of a murderer I had put on behind the mirror.

The androgyne, still knitting, kicked with her bare heels upon the floor to drive her Bath chair over the wreathing muffler towards me, in order to attack me. The Bath chair cannoned into the chair on which I stood and she rose up in it as far as she could and began to beat me with her tender fists. But, because she did not stop knitting, she offered no resistance when I brought my ham-hand crashing down on her working face. I broke her nose; bright blood sprang out. I turned to the mirror as she screamed and dropped her knitting.

She dropped her knitting as I crashed through the glass
    through the glass, glass splintered round me driving unmercifully into my face
        through the glass, glass splintered
            through the glass –
                half through.

Then the glass gathered itself together like a skilful whore and expelled me. The glass rejected me; it sealed itself again into nothing but mysterious, reflective opacity. It became a mirror and it was impregnable.

Balked, I stumbled back. In Tiresias' bed-sitting room, there was the most profound silence, and nothing moved; the flow of time might have stopped. Tiresias held her empty hands to her face that was now irretrievably changed; each one snapped clean in two, her knitting needles lay on the floor. Then she sobbed and flung out her arms in a wild, helpless gesture. Blood and tears splashed down on her robe, but in a baleful, hopeless way she began to laugh, although time must have started again and now moved with such destructive speed that, before my eyes, that ageless being withered – a quick frost touched her. Wrinkles sprang out on her pale forehead while her hair fell from her head in great armfuls and her negligee turned brown and crumbled away, to reveal all the flesh that sagged from the bone as I watched it. She was the ruins of time. She grasped her throat and choked. Perhaps she was dying. The muffler was blowing away like dead leaves in a wind that sprang up from nowhere and raced through the room, although the windows stayed shut tight. But Tiresias spoke to me; she spoke to me once again.

'The umbilical cord is cut,' she said. 'The thread is broken. Did you not realize who I was? That I was the synthesis in person? For I could go any way the world goes and so I was knitting the thesis and the antithesis together, this world and that world. Over the leaves and under the leaves. Cohesion gone. Ah!'

Down she tumbled, the bald old crone, upon a pile of wisps of unravelled grey wool as the ormolu furniture split apart and the paper unfurled from the wall. But I was arrogant; I was undefeated. Had I not killed her? Proud as a man, I once again advanced to meet my image in the mirror. Full of self-confidence, I held out my hands to embrace my self, my anti-self, my self not-self, my assassin, my death, the world's death.

ELEGY FOR A FREELANCE

I REMEMBER YOU as clearly as if you'd died yesterday, though I don't remember you often – usually I'm far too busy. But I told the commissar about you, once. I asked him if I'd done the right thing; would he have done the same? But he said, if I wanted absolution, that he was the last person to ask for it, and, besides, everything is changed, now, and we are not the same.

I remember that I was living high up in an attic, in a house in a square. Most of the windows in the other houses round the square were boarded up and planks were nailed across the doors but they were not uninhabited. Although all these houses were waiting to be pulled down, they contained a handful of small, scarcely licit households whose members crept in and out through secret entries, lived by candlelight, slept upon the filthy mattresses the dossers who lived there before them had used and ate stews made from vegetables picked out of the greengrocers' garbage cans and butchers' bones begged for dogs that did not exist.

But our landlord – it was legal to own private property, to rent it out, in those days – refused to sell his house to the speculators who wanted to pull the entire terrace down. He'd spent the Blitz in his house; it was his foxhole. He pulled the carious walls up snug around his ears and felt himself enveloped in a safety that, although it was fictive, he believed in completely. He rented his rooms out at old-fashioned rents because he did not know that times had changed; how could he? He never left home. He was confined to a chair and almost blind. His room was his world, his house the unknown universe he knew of but never ventured into. Everything else was unknowable. He did not even know that the boys who lived in the basement filled milk bottles with petrol in their back room and made explosions.

A girl lived with them in the basement. She was fifteen. Her face was pale, mild and plump and always seemed a little surprised that she found herself stumbling under the weight of a pregnancy that had stunned her. She hardly ever spoke and moved with the heaviness of somebody moving under water. You kept a rifle in our room and loved to sit and scan the square and the street below us from the open window.

A young man and a girl came to do yoga in the square every morning. They adopted the tree position. A child on the swings swung more and more idly; he twisted round to watch them. They always had the same audience, the children in the playground and the apprentice sniper. They unfurled their right legs from the hip and reefed them in at the knee in order to place the soles of their bare right feet against the inner sides of their upper left thighs. They joined their hands together as if in prayer and then raised their joined hands above their heads. In order to keep their balance, they fixed their eyes on the worn grass in front of them with the utmost concentration. They maintained this position for an entire minute – I watched the hand on my watch move – and then they returned their right feet to the ground as they lowered their hands and arms and now raised their left legs in order to repeat the exercise. When it was over, they decorously stood on their heads. They were rapt with devotion.

X watched them through the sights of his rifle while they went through the entire repertory of movements. I was scared out of my wits when he slipped back the safety catch and did not dare say anything. I knew the couple below by sight. They squatted in a house on the other side of the square. They were harmless as the pigeons who lived on the roof. When they had finished, they went away again. X replaced the safety catch and laughed. I was very frightened of him in his feral moods but he told me an authentic assassin ought to be as indifferent as the weather and, when he scanned the square, all he was doing was practising indifference.

I went into his world when I fell in love with him and felt only a sense of privilege in its isolation. We had purposely exiled ourselves from the course of everyday events and were proud to live in parentheses. I went out for a little air at night, sometimes, when the streets were flooded with the ghastly yellow light that bleaches the blood that runs out of road accidents so that it doesn't look real. I used to walk through the streets for miles and I would clap my hands with childlike pleasure, I would enthusiastically applaud the detonating termini.

It hardly seemed possible the city could survive that summer.

The sky opened like the clockwork Easter eggs the Tsars gave one another. The night would part, like two halves of a dark shell, and spill explosions. Because I lived in a house full of amateur terrorists, I felt I myself lit the fuses and caused these displays of pyrotechnics. Then I would feel almost omnipotent, just as X did, when he sat with his rifle above the square at the window of my room.

I was living high up in an attic. I hung over the summer in my attic as though it were the gondola of a balloon. London lay below me with her legs wide open; she was a whore sufficiently accommodating to find room for us in her embraces, even though she cost so much to love.

She is so old she ought to be superannuated, you said, the old cow. She paints so thickly over the stratified residue of yesterday and the day before yesterday and the day before the day before's cosmetics you can hardly make out the wens and blemishes under all the layers of paint, graffiti and old posters – voluptuous, oppressive, corrupt, self-regarding London marinating in the syrup of her own decay like *baba au rhum*, while the property speculators burrow away at her guts with the vile diligence of gonococci.

A feverish, hysterical glamour played over this wasting city like summer lightning. While I watched it, the city changed shape. Towers of steel and glass thrust their way through the soft, soiled velvet rind of the rotting fruit. Nobody lived in those towers; how could anybody live there – like the architecture of the Third Reich, they looked as if they were intended to be most beautiful in ruins. Amongst this architecture of desolation, haunting the rat-infested rubble, mendicants and proselytizers rang bells and rattled tambourines as they offered to the passer-by a bewildering variety of salvations. Those in saffron robes who had shaved their heads invoked the gods of the Indian subcontinent though our neighbours told us we ought to trust in Jesus. But *our* salvation would be gelignite; the basement of the house in which I lived had become a little arsenal. Any wise child can get a hand grenade together; it was the time of the Children's Crusade.

It was a strange, suspended time. The city had never looked more beautiful but I did not know, then, that it seemed to me beautiful only because it was doomed and I was the innocent slave of bourgeois aesthetics, that always sees an elegiac charm in decay. I remember velvet nights spiked with menace and the beautiful showers of sparks when an amateur incendiarist ignited a police station. My house was always full of the shimmering sound of the trees in the square moving in the wind, so that it seemed the sea was rushing through the corridors, the rooms.

I was living on the fourth floor although I had such vertigo that the sight of any abyss, however insignificant, excited in me, almost intolerably, the desire to plunge. I was quite helpless before the attraction of gravity. I was overwhelmed. I became powerless. Therefore to live on the fourth floor meant that every day began with a small triumph of will over instinct. I wanted to jump; but I must not jump. Pallor, shallow breathing, a prickle of cold sweat – I exhibited all the symptoms of panic, as I did when I met X. *That* was like finding myself on the edge of an abyss but the vertigo that I felt then came from a sense of recognition. This abyss was that of my own emptiness; I plunged instantly, for my innocence was so perfect that I saw in this submission the height of sophistication.

It was as lovely a summer as those that precede wars. The West Indian lady who ran the neighbourhood launderette always wore a small felt hat with a veil, as if she were determined to keep up appearances even in the most extreme circumstances. She pushed the dirt around the floor with a sodden mop and, when her tasks were finished, she would sit on a chair and read her well-thumbed Bible aloud to herself in that ineffable, querulous lilt, like the voice of a reproachful bird. Sometimes she would exclaim over the things she found in the book; when I looked over her shoulder, once, while she was crying: HOSANNA! I saw she was reading the Apocalypse.

The squatters consecrated the house next door. All night long, while we fixed up our explosive devices in the basement, they chanted: BABY JESUS, BABY JESUS, BABY JESUS.

I would not have believed Lenin was right when he said there was no place for orgy in the revolution, even if I had read Lenin. What we were about in bed seemed to be activity that could in itself overturn the world. X's lycanthropic eyes glowed in the dark like fuses. I found most pleasure of all in the delicious dread that seized me when he clung too close. I wanted to be the Madonna of the Barricades; I would have shot anybody you told me to but only if they did not get hurt. I felt I needed to understand nothing beyond my own sensations. I felt, as primitives do, that ceremonials such as the ones we made could revivify dead earth. Your kisses along my arms were like tracer bullets. I am lost. I flow. Your flesh defines me. I become your creation. I am your fleshly reflection.

('Libido and false consciousness characterized sexual relations during the last crisis of Capital,' says the commissar.)

A man constructs his own fate out of his sense of the world. You engaged in conspiracies because you believed the humblest objects were engaged in a conspiracy against you. Your conviction was contagious; it impressed me. 'Even the strawberries smell of blood, this summer,' you remarked with anticipatory relish. I found you more and more often at the window, practising indifference.

You described the state of permanent revolution to me. It sounded like a series of beautiful explosions. Volcano after volcano would erupt under their own internal stresses in an endless reduplication of ecstasy. When the bed creaked beneath us, it sounded like the *Liebestod* from *Tristan and Isolde* performed with vehemence by a military band. The grand design of glorious convulsions you depicted was so beautiful I wept; but we would begin, you said, in small ways, we would begin with a single shooting. You made assassination sound as enticing as pornography. A, B and C were suspicious of me since you abandoned the basement for my bed. Now we were all gripped in the same obsession, they treated me more politely. *Folie à deux*, *à trois*, *à quatre*. We were living on the crater of a volcano and felt the earth move beneath us. What stirring times! What seismographic times!

('The bourgeoisie turned politics into an aspect of romanticism,' says the commissar. 'If it was only an art form, how could it threaten them?')

The city unravelled like knitting as the transport workers' strikes imposed vast distances between its various sections but we never went beyond walking distance of our house so the strikes did not affect us.

Our house was tall and narrow. Worn steps led down to the area. Our landlord lived in the front room on the ground floor. He crouched in front of his television set making what sense he could out of the random flickering that was all his eyes registered, poor old thing, with his stick and his cats. He had a sink and a gas ring and a little cupboard where he kept his cats' fish. He boiled up their dinners twice a week and stored their food in a plastic washing-up bowl when it was cooked. The house stank of stale fish; we had to burn incense all the time to cancel out the smell. He spread his table with clean newspapers and set out the fish for his cats in separate saucers. They all jumped up to eat. There was a soup plate full of water which, although it was refreshed each day, always managed to drown a fly or two by lunchtime, and a saucer of milk that had turned into junket by the six o'clock news. His three-legged chairs were balanced on piles of old newspapers and upholstered with cast-off garments. Cats of all colours sat upon the sideboard amongst the empty brown ale bottles, the open cans of condensed milk, the stopped clock, the yellowing circulars, the football coupons, the curded milk bottles, the plaster Alsatian dog with one ear chipped. There he sat, a king in his kingdom, thumping upon the floor when the conspirators in the basement went *bang!* by accident.

Once a week, in turn, we visited him to pay our rents for we were determined to be scrupulous and, if you must have a landlord at all, it's best if he's purblind. It was like paying tribute to a holy statue. Age had drawn his yellow, freckled skin so tight across his skull his head shone like polished bone and his eyes had faded to the innocent blue of baby ribbon – wandering, rheumy eyes, gummed at the corners. His bony fingers clutched the handle of his stick with a certain balked ferocity.

He was afraid of us, I suppose, and so he pretended to be fierce. In the pub, they said he kept roll upon roll of banknotes stored in Old Holborn tins tucked away here and there amongst the clutter. He ingested his rents like a sponge but he suspected nothing although the cats did and threshed their tails when we went into his room. Sometimes they spat. The ginger one once scratched you.

A middle-aged transvestite lived on the first floor but he was too immersed in his aberration to pay us much attention. He ventured out for little walks around the square in the dusk that tenderly veiled his eccentricity, tottering on his five-inch heels, spiking the ground before him in the manner of a climber with the point of his long, furled umbrella. He wore a black gaberdine two-piece with a pencil skirt for these expeditions and slung a fox-fur round his neck. The mask hung over his left shoulder and kept a good lookout behind with its little, beady eyes. Above him, a slack-witted unmarried mother pigged it with her brood. She did the old man's shopping for him, when she remembered, but he only wanted the fish, twice a week, a can or two of beans and the occasional bottle of brown ale.

A perpetual twilight dominated that house, with its characteristic odours of stale cooking, phantom bacon, lavatories and the cats who pissed in the hall. The bulbs on the stairways were always blown. It was an old, dark house; it was a cave. We saw visions on the walls. It was a slum. It was a citadel. That was the time of the freelance assassins; our cell was self-sufficient and took no orders nor cognizance of any other cell in the cancerous growth of the deathwardly inclining city. You had the plausibility of a Nechaev; to plot a murder became your sole preoccupation.

You arbitrarily selected a member of the cabinet. We consulted the I Ching, we threw the coins. The oracle seemed to be propitious, although, as always, its tone was guarded. We drew lots. Inexorably, the marked card found you. In the full consciousness of a young man about to become an assassin, you made love to me like the storming of the Bastille. But then I found you'd somewhere encountered an obstacle to indifference for now you were crying, though, when I asked why you were crying, you hit me.

Our neighbours were chanting so loudly they might have been chanting in the same room and I had no curtains at the window so the glaring, yellow light balefully illuminated your unhappy face, but I was too much under your spell to guess why you were crying. Hadn't everything been decided? Tomorrow we would go and murder the politician. I would ring the doorbell and then you would fire the gun. I could not understand why you were crying, you had so successfully impressed me with the model simplicity of the plan, so that I was sure we were in the right. I went to sleep again, sulking because I had been hit. The monotonous, droning chant – BABY JESUS, BABY JESUS, BABY JESUS – lulled me to sleep.

What an awakening! – there was so much blood on your shirt. You spilled the banknotes over me. They were in tight little blue rolls that bounced off my body, unfurling as they fell to the floor. Such a lot of money! I blinked in the violet dawn, astounded at the extravagance of your hysteria. You sobbed and babbled and hurled the furniture to the ground, smashed cups, overturned the wastepaper basket. I made you tea and slyly stoked up the mug with sleeping pills. I choked it down you and got you into the bed I had vacated for I could never lie in the same bed with you, now. I stayed with you until I was certain you were sleeping and locked the door behind you.

A, B and C had finished the night's work and were frying eggs and bread on their gas ring. A's girl lay on the mattress under her belly which was the size and shape of a dirigible, round enough, big enough to rise up into the air and carry her away with it from this vale of tears, over the rainbow, to a happy land far, far away. I told them what you had said to me, that you killed him for practice. We had intended to be such philosophic assassins! But what were your existential credentials when you murdered the landlord? Was it the dress rehearsal for an assassination or the audition of an assassin?

The old man lay on the floor in his rank pyjamas. His debilitated, senescent tool dangled out of his yellowed fly. The cats milled about him, mewing ravenously. There was blood on their whiskers and on their inquisitive paws. X had smashed in the old man's skull and he'd tumbled off the bed in his death agony. In spite of his age and weakness, he had put up a struggle; we could see the signs of it all over the room. The bedclothes were disordered and his little night-table had been knocked over. The chamber-pot it contained had fallen out on its side, spilling its contents on the floor. Then X must have gone through every cupboard and drawer in the room to find the fabled tobacco tins of money. We looked at the evidence in silence though all the time the neighbours went on wailing very loudly. We could hear them downstairs, even here, on the ground floor. The cats pressed against us, yowling, and I thought I had better feed the cats because I did not want them to practise necrophagy upon the landlord. I opened the food cupboard and took out their fish. I spread the table and laid out their meal as if nothing had happened. They all jumped up and tucked in, purring as they swallowed their dinners.

We had not let A's girl into the room because of her condition. Now, from behind the lace curtain, we saw her, with her shawl flung carelessly round her shoulders, pursuing her burden as it stumbled away down the street. A said: 'She's broken – she's gone for the police.' I rushed out of the house and ran after her. I soon caught up with her; she was too fat to run fast. She wept. She said how much she always disliked X; that he had cold eyes. Then she fainted. A came and helped me carry her back to the basement. Shortly after that, she went into labour. The neighbours continued to chant: BABY JESUS, BABY JESUS, BABY JESUS. While I held A's girl's frightened, hot, sticky hand and A heated water, B and C took some rope, went to my attic and tied X up. They said he was too surprised to struggle when they woke him. He must have felt it was the revolt of the toys.

Then a police car drew up outside and we shrank into ourselves, we were so scared. Poor Susie moaned and tore at the mattress on which she lay. But the police had come for our neighbours. The transvestite had complained about the noise and we watched from the area steps as the police took an axe to the boards that were nailed over the front door and entered it. A little while later, they came out again, half leading, half carrying the dazed and shaking occupants, who were all as white as sheets, tranced, emaciated, their eyes staring as still they mumbled their orisons, too limp and listless to protest.

I sterilized my nail scissors in the gas jet and A held his wailing son in his arms after I cut the cord. But, however pleased A was to be a father, he insisted on a fair trial for X. Perhaps, even then, B and C didn't quite trust me; I'd been a rich girl. But X confessed everything to us all quite freely.

We tried him in the attic. We left Susie downstairs nursing her baby. We untied X's legs and let him sit down on a chair but we did not untie his arms. He confessed as follows; he seemed agonizingly torn between humiliation and self-justification.

'I wasn't sure, I wasn't sure of myself. I kept thinking, what if I blow it? If I'd blown the whole thing, hadn't been able to pull the trigger, had just stood there in the doorway staring vacantly at him. What if I can't kill when I want to kill and am in the right to kill? What if I were paralysed? What if I'd spent so long looking at people through the sights of a rifle and holding back from shooting that I could never shoot? Fear I'd be weak shook me.

'What good did the landlord do to anyone? Sitting in his room, sucking in his rents. Nobody loves him. He's significant to nobody. He's hardly alive at all, he can't talk, hardly, he's almost blind, squatting like a toad on all that money.

'I was in a frenzy, I prayed. Yes, I did. The fear I'd fail threw me into a frenzy. I prayed and the answer came. I left her sleeping and took the gun and went to his room. He didn't wake up when I went in but the cats all woke and stretched themselves and jumped off the chairs and the sideboard and the bed and came towards me, mewing; it was a tide of fur with eyes and mouths in it. He woke up when he heard the cats and began to mew, too. "Who's there, pussies, what's the matter, pussies?" I had nothing against him when I went into the room – nothing. It was only an exercise in self-control.

'But I began to hate him when I saw how helpless he was. When I saw how easy it would be to kill him, nothing to it, then I began to hate him. I raised the rifle and looked at him through the sights. The sights changed the way I saw him. Through the sights of the rifle, now I saw he was not human, not even an old wreck of humanity. He was only an object to be extinguished. He asked some menacing person he could not see if that person had come for his money. When I realized that person was I, I thought that I might just as well take his money, while I was here, since he offered it to me. But I said nothing and my hands were shaking. He told me not to kill him. That was how he reminded me I *could* kill him, if I wanted to. Up till then, I had not wanted to but when he called me his murderer, I became so. He sealed his own fate. It was his own fault, what happened.

'Next door they were chanting away like mad things. He rolled about on his filthy bed clutching his head with his hands as if his hands would protect it. His pyjamas burst open and the old flesh spilled on the sheets. I felt nauseated to see his old flesh. My fingers tightened on the trigger. The cats screamed and pressed against my legs. The ginger one scratched me. They reared up on their hind legs and snarled, I could have sworn they were attacking me. How disgusting the old bedbug was, now he was at my mercy! But just as I was about to shoot, I thought: what a noise the gun will make. It will be much louder than the chanting, even. The noise will wake Sister Boy. Sister Boy will wake and throw his negligee round his shoulders and come and see what is the matter. The woman upstairs will wake, or her kids will wake. They'll all come down, even the four-year-old, wiping the sleep out of its eyes. I thought of a holocaust – mow them all down. But I was too self-restrained.

'I lowered the gun. He was fumbling in his little night-table, where he keeps his pisspot. The night-table rocked, he was fumbling so. Out jumped the pisspot and crashed on the ground. All the cats puffed out their fur, stuck up their backs and hissed and shrank away from me, because the crash of the pisspot startled them, but he was rummaging for his savings in the night-table and found one little tin. He shook the banknotes all over the floor, they were rolled up in the tin like curling papers, they fell in the spilled piss and the cats pounced on them and began to pat them this way and that way with their paws. He scooped up some banknotes in his fists and shoved them towards me. He said: "Take it, it's all I've got." But I knew he had lots of other old tobacco tins full of money, doesn't everybody say so? When he tried to buy me off so cheaply, I lost all mercy and bludgeoned him about the head with the butt of the rifle until he stopped moving.'

He looked at us as though he was certain we understood everything perfectly. I closed my eyes; I had the sensation of falling. Yet, when I opened my eyes, the abyss remained; I stood only upon its brink. Now my eyes were open, perception, lucidity became my new profession. At the conclusion of his story, X began to cry like a child, as though he were to be pitied, and then I felt most afraid of him, in case I began to pity him. While we watched him snivelling, we grew older. He cried like a baby and we became his parents. We must decide what would be best for him. Now I was his mother, they his father and we saw our common responsibility as his cause in the random nature of his effect.

'It must be worst for you,' A said to me, because I'd been the lover of this person; but the same terror gripped us all, for our complicity with him was over once he had acted only for himself and by himself and now we could stand apart from him and, in judging him, judge ourselves.

I will try and describe you better. I am glad you died before the barricades went up. We served our time and took our punishment upon them but I would not have liked to have you beside me with a machine-gun because you were your own hero, always your own hero, and would not have taken orders easily. But you might have made an exceptional Kamikaze pilot, had you not been so scared of dying. You made us believe you were our leader; so, while you were ordering us about, how could we become a confederacy? We were in the deepest complicity with you; we admired your paranoia. While we admired it, we believed it formed an explanation of events in itself. But I was always a little afraid of you because you clung to me far too tightly and made me come with the barbarous dexterity of a huntsman eviscerating a stag.

After we heard X's confession, we gave him some water to drink and tied up his arms again before we gagged him, in case he tried to cry to Sister Boy or the unmarried mother below for help. Then we went down to the basement to discuss what we should do with him. A's girl was suckling her baby. She seemed obscurely but entirely content with her own miracle. She was angry we had locked her into the basement and said she would never leave A because he was the father of her child but I thought she said that due to the emotion generated in the generation of the baby and we should still be wary of her. A cooked her some brown rice and vegetables and added a couple of eggs, because she needed nourishment. After a great deal of discussion, B took some food to X also, but X dashed the dish to the floor. He was petulant, now, B told us; he thought we were behaving irrationally.

He had quite recovered his old self-confidence, it seemed, but we no longer retained confidence in him. We reached our decision in unison, although C – what memories of old movies! – at first wanted to lock X alone in my attic with a revolver and let him take his own way out. But our consensus convinced C that X would not have done so, had we given him the chance.

B took a coil of stout rope from the cupboard under the sink. We waited until dark; we listened desultorily to the radio and heard the army had been called in to break the car-workers' strike but we were all stricken with such dreadful gravity at the unexpected turn of events in our cell that the news did not move us. Our private situation seemed to us far more significant.

X was in a foul state since we had not untied him all day so now he rolled in his own excrement and stank. He was in a filthy temper and cursed us but, when he saw the rope, first he laughed to try to bluff his way out of the noose; and then he blubbered –

there is no other word for his collapse in tears and pleadings. He seemed astonished we were capable of acting without him. A held the revolver. It wasn't far to Hampstead Heath.

We forced X along with his arms bound and the muzzle of the revolver in his back. We did not meet many others on the streets; those whom we did pass by edged away from us, they must have thought we were all drunk, and the Heath itself was empty apart from a distant bonfire that marked, probably, the camp of some homeless family. By now the moon was up; we soon found a suitable tree.

When X realized there was no hope for him, he relapsed into silence but, when I slipped the noose round his neck, he asked me if I loved him. I was surprised at that – it seemed to me so far from the point; but I replied, yes, I *had* loved him and I tested the running knot. B and C pulled the rope. Up, he went, like a flag. There was a russet-coloured moon of ominous size too low above the whispering bushes; he danced exuberantly for five minutes beneath it after the click when his neck broke. His bowels opened. What a mess!

When it hung limp, we cut his body down and threw it in the undergrowth. A vomited and B wept a little, but C and I covered it with leaves, like the robins in *Babes in the Wood*. I retained such a ferocious calm that C said to me, you are turning into a tiger lady when I always thought you were such a pussycat. I think that justice had been done, although we ourselves had been the perpetrators of both crime and punishment and we did not dig a hole to bury X because we wanted to leave a loophole in which the everyday circumstances of justice might catch up with us. We were beginning to behave with a certain dignity. Our illogic began to approach a kind of harsh virtue, although we looked at one another with veiled, estranged eyes; who were we, what were we becoming?

Was it possible we could have done what we had done; how could it have been possible we had planned what we had intended?

A's girl and the child slept quite peacefully in the basement where we made ourselves tea that did not taste any different from the tea we had drunk before we hanged him.

Now B revealed an intransigent morality. He wanted us to go to the police, make a clean breast of all and take our punishment, since we had done nothing of which we ourselves were ashamed. But A had his baby son to think of and wanted to take Susie and his child to a Welsh mountain where he had friends on a commune, there to recuperate from these excesses in the clean air. Apropos of nothing, he declared he'd never be able to look at meat again and would walk on the other side of the road when he passed a butcher's shop. He sat on the mattress by the sleeping girl and looked, every moment, more and more like an ordinary husband and father. But C and I did not know what to do, now, nor what to think. We felt nothing but a lapse of feeling, a dulled heaviness, a despair.

The pure, cool light of early September touched the contents of the room with fastidious fingers; we looked at the day with mild surprise, that it should be as bright as any other day, brighter, in fact, than most. Then I felt a drop like a heavy raindrop fall on the back of my hand but it was not a raindrop, for the sun was shining, nor a drip from a leaking cistern, because the landlord's room was directly over our heads. This was a red drop. Horror! It was blood; and, looking up, I saw the stain on the ceiling where the old man's blood was leaking through. Soon he would begin to smell.

We began to argue. Should we dig a hole in the backyard and bury the old man in it, pack our few things and leave the house under false names for secret destinations, as A wanted to do; or should we throw ourselves upon the law, as B thought was right? Instinct and will, again; I was poised on the window ledge of a fourth floor of a building I had never suspected existed and I did not know which was will and which was instinct that told me to jump, to run. While we were discussing these things, we heard a low rumble in the distance. We thought it was thunder but, when A turned on the radio to find out what time it was, only martial music was playing and the newsflash informed us the coup had taken place; the army was in power, as if this was not home but a banana republic. They were encountering some resistance in the north but were rapidly crushing it. All the time we had been plotting, the generals had been plotting and we had known nothing. Nothing!

The thunder grew louder; it was gun and mortar fire. The sky soon filled with helicopters. The Civil War began. History began.

ACKNOWLEDGMENTS

The Bloody Chamber and Other Stories

Some of the stories in this collection originally appeared in somewhat different form in the following publications: 'The Courtship of Mr Lyon', British *Vogue*; 'The Erl-King' and 'The Company of Wolves', *Bananas*; 'The Lady of the House of Love', *The Iowa Review*; 'The Werewolf', *South-West Arts Review*; 'Wolf-Alice', *Stand*; all are reprinted here with the permission of the editors. 'The Snow Child' was broadcast on the BBC Radio 4 programme *Not Now, I'm Listening*. 'Puss-in-Boots' appeared in an anthology, *The Straw and the Gold*, edited by Emma Tennant (Pierrot Books, 1979).

Wise Children

Extracts from 'It's only a Paper Moon' by Arlen/Harburg/Rose, 'My Heart Belongs to Daddy' by Cole Porter and 'The Way You Look Tonight' by Kern/Fields, copyright © Warner Chappell Music Ltd, are reproduced by permission of Warner Chappell Ltd, and Polygram Music. The lines from 'I Can't Give You Anything But Love' by Jimmy McHugh and Dorothy Fields, copyright © 1928 Mills Music Inc., USA, are reproduced by permission of Lawrence Wright Music Co. Ltd London WC2H 0EA.

TITLES IN EVERYMAN'S LIBRARY

CHINUA ACHEBE
The African Trilogy
Things Fall Apart

AESCHYLUS
The Oresteia

ISABEL ALLENDE
The House of the Spirits

MARTIN AMIS
London Fields

THE ARABIAN NIGHTS

ISAAC ASIMOV
Foundation
Foundation and Empire
Second Foundation
(in 1 vol.)

MARGARET ATWOOD
The Handmaid's Tale

JOHN JAMES AUDUBON
The Audubon Reader

AUGUSTINE
The Confessions

JANE AUSTEN
Emma
Mansfield Park
Northanger Abbey
Persuasion
Pride and Prejudice
Sanditon and Other Stories
Sense and Sensibility

JAMES BALDWIN
Giovanni's Room
Go Tell It on the Mountain

HONORÉ DE BALZAC
Cousin Bette
Eugénie Grandet
Old Goriot

MIKLOS BANFFY
The Transylvanian Trilogy
(in 2 vols)

JOHN BANVILLE
The Book of Evidence
The Sea (in 1 vol.)

JULIAN BARNES
Flaubert's Parrot
A History of the World in
10½ Chapters (in 1 vol.)

GIORGIO BASSANI
The Garden of the Finzi-Continis

SIMONE DE BEAUVOIR
The Second Sex

SAMUEL BECKETT
Molloy, Malone Dies,
The Unnamable

SAUL BELLOW
The Adventures of Augie March

HECTOR BERLIOZ
The Memoirs of Hector Berlioz

THE BIBLE
(King James Version)
The Old Testament
The New Testament

WILLIAM BLAKE
Poems and Prophecies

GIOVANNI BOCCACCIO
Decameron

JORGE LUIS BORGES
Ficciones

JAMES BOSWELL
The Life of Samuel Johnson
The Journal of a Tour to
the Hebrides

RAY BRADBURY
The Stories of Ray Bradbury

JEAN ANTHELME
BRILLAT-SAVARIN
The Physiology of Taste

ANNE BRONTË
Agnes Grey and The Tenant of
Wildfell Hall

CHARLOTTE BRONTË
Jane Eyre
Villette
Shirley and The Professor

EMILY BRONTË
Wuthering Heights

MIKHAIL BULGAKOV
The Master and Margarita

EDMUND BURKE
Reflections on the Revolution in
France and Other Writings

SAMUEL BUTLER
The Way of all Flesh

A. S. BYATT
Possession

JAMES M. CAIN
The Postman Always Rings Twice
Double Indemnity
Mildred Pierce
Selected Stories
(in 1 vol. US only)

ITALO CALVINO
If on a winter's night a traveler

ALBERT CAMUS
The Outsider (UK)
The Stranger (US)
The Plague, The Fall,
Exile and the Kingdom,
and Selected Essays (in 1 vol.)

ANGELA CARTER
The Bloody Chamber
Wise Children
Fireworks
(in 1 vol.)

GIACOMO CASANOVA
History of My Life

WILLA CATHER
Death Comes for the
Archbishop (US only)
My Ántonia
O Pioneers!

BENVENUTO CELLINI
The Autobiography of
Benvenuto Cellini

MIGUEL DE CERVANTES
Don Quixote

RAYMOND CHANDLER
The novels (in 2 vols)
Collected Stories

GEOFFREY CHAUCER
Canterbury Tales

ANTON CHEKHOV
The Complete Short Novels
My Life and Other Stories
The Steppe and Other Stories

G. K. CHESTERTON
The Everyman Chesterton

KATE CHOPIN
The Awakening

CARL VON CLAUSEWITZ
On War

S. T. COLERIDGE
Poems

WILKIE COLLINS
The Moonstone
The Woman in White

CONFUCIUS
The Analects

JOSEPH CONRAD
Heart of Darkness
Lord Jim
Nostromo
The Secret Agent
Typhoon and Other Stories
Under Western Eyes
Victory

JULIO CORTÁZAR
Hopscotch
Blow-Up and Other Stories
We Love Glenda So Much and
Other Tales
(in 1 vol.)

THOMAS CRANMER
The Book of Common Prayer
(UK only)

ROALD DAHL
Collected Stories

DANTE ALIGHIERI
The Divine Comedy

CHARLES DARWIN
The Origin of Species
The Voyage of the Beagle
(in 1 vol.)

DANIEL DEFOE
Moll Flanders
Robinson Crusoe

CHARLES DICKENS
Barnaby Rudge
Bleak House
A Christmas Carol and
Other Christmas Books
David Copperfield
Dombey and Son
Great Expectations
Hard Times
Little Dorrit
Martin Chuzzlewit
The Mystery of Edwin Drood

(CHARLES DICKENS cont.)
Nicholas Nickleby
The Old Curiosity Shop
Oliver Twist
Our Mutual Friend
The Pickwick Papers
A Tale of Two Cities

DENIS DIDEROT
Memoirs of a Nun

JOAN DIDION
We Tell Ourselves Stories in Order to Live (US only)

JOHN DONNE
The Complete English Poems

FYODOR DOSTOEVSKY
The Adolescent
The Brothers Karamazov
Crime and Punishment
Demons
The Double and The Gambler
The Idiot
Notes from Underground

ARTHUR CONAN DOYLE
The Hound of the Baskervilles
Study in Scarlet
The Sign of Four
(in 1 vol.)

W. E. B. DU BOIS
The Souls of Black Folk
(US only)

ALEXANDRE DUMAS
The Count of Monte Cristo
The Three Musketeers

DAPHNE DU MAURIER
Rebecca

MARGUERITE DURAS
The Lover
Wartime Notebooks
Practicalities
(in 1 vol.)

UMBERTO ECO
The Name of the Rose

GEORGE ELIOT
Adam Bede
Daniel Deronda
Middlemarch
The Mill on the Floss
Silas Marner

JOHN EVELYN
The Diary of John Evelyn
(UK only)

J. G. FARRELL
The Siege of Krishnapur
and Troubles

WILLIAM FAULKNER
The Sound and the Fury
(UK only)

HENRY FIELDING
Joseph Andrews and Shamela
(UK only)
Tom Jones

F. SCOTT FITZGERALD
The Great Gatsby
This Side of Paradise
(UK only)

PENELOPE FITZGERALD
The Bookshop
The Gate of Angels
The Blue Flower (in 1 vol.)
Offshore
Human Voices
The Beginning of Spring
(in 1 vol.)

GUSTAVE FLAUBERT
Madame Bovary

FORD MADOX FORD
The Good Soldier
Parade's End

RICHARD FORD
The Bascombe Novels

E. M. FORSTER
Howards End
A Passage to India
A Room with a View,
Where Angels Fear to Tread
(in 1 vol., US only)

ANNE FRANK
The Diary of a Young Girl
(US only)

BENJAMIN FRANKLIN
The Autobiography
and Other Writings

GEORGE MACDONALD FRASER
Flashman
Flash for Freedom!
Flashman in the Great Game
(in 1 vol.)

MAVIS GALLANT
The Collected Stories

ELIZABETH GASKELL
Mary Barton

EDWARD GIBBON
The Decline and Fall of the Roman Empire
Vols 1 to 3: The Western Empire
Vols 4 to 6: The Eastern Empire

KAHLIL GIBRAN
The Collected Works

J. W. VON GOETHE
Selected Works

NIKOLAI GOGOL
The Collected Tales
Dead Souls

IVAN GONCHAROV
Oblomov

GÜNTER GRASS
The Tin Drum

ROBERT GRAVES
Goodbye to All That

GRAHAM GREENE
Brighton Rock
The Human Factor

DASHIELL HAMMETT
The Maltese Falcon
The Thin Man
Red Harvest
(in 1 vol.)
The Dain Curse,
The Glass Key,
and Selected Stories

THOMAS HARDY
Far From the Madding Crowd
Jude the Obscure
The Mayor of Casterbridge
The Return of the Native
Tess of the d'Urbervilles
The Woodlanders

JAROSLAV HAŠEK
The Good Soldier Švejk

NATHANIEL HAWTHORNE
The Scarlet Letter

JOSEPH HELLER
Catch-22

ERNEST HEMINGWAY
A Farewell to Arms
The Collected Stories
(UK only)

GEORGE HERBERT
The Complete English Works

HERODOTUS
The Histories

MICHAEL HERR
Dispatches (US only)

PATRICIA HIGHSMITH
The Talented Mr. Ripley
Ripley Under Ground
Ripley's Game
(in 1 vol.)

HINDU SCRIPTURES
(tr. R. C. Zaehner)

JAMES HOGG
Confessions of a Justified Sinner

HOMER
The Iliad
The Odyssey

VICTOR HUGO
The Hunchback of Notre-Dame
Les Misérables

ALDOUS HUXLEY
Brave New World

KAZUO ISHIGURO
The Remains of the Day

HENRY JAMES
The Ambassadors
The Awkward Age
The Bostonians
The Golden Bowl
The Portrait of a Lady
The Princess Casamassima
Washington Square
The Wings of the Dove
Collected Stories (in 2 vols)

SAMUEL JOHNSON
A Journey to the Western Islands of Scotland

JAMES JOYCE
Dubliners
A Portrait of the Artist as a Young Man
Ulysses

FRANZ KAFKA
Collected Stories
The Castle
The Trial

JOHN KEATS
The Poems

SØREN KIERKEGAARD
Fear and Trembling and The Book on Adler

MAXINE HONG KINGSTON
The Woman Warrior and China Men
(US only)

RUDYARD KIPLING
Collected Stories
Kim

THE KORAN
(tr. Marmaduke Pickthall)

GIUSEPPE TOMASI DI LAMPEDUSA
The Leopard

WILLIAM LANGLAND
Piers Plowman
with (anon.) Sir Gawain and the Green Knight, Pearl, Sir Orfeo
(UK only)

LAO-TZU
Tao Te Ching

D. H. LAWRENCE
Collected Stories
The Rainbow
Sons and Lovers
Women in Love

MIKHAIL LERMONTOV
A Hero of Our Time

DORIS LESSING
Stories

PRIMO LEVI
If This is a Man and The Truce
(UK only)
The Periodic Table

THE MABINOGION

NICCOLÒ MACHIAVELLI
The Prince

NAGUIB MAHFOUZ
The Cairo Trilogy
Three Novels of Ancient Egypt

THOMAS MANN
Buddenbrooks
Collected Stories (UK only)
Death in Venice and Other Stories
(US only)
Doctor Faustus
Joseph and His Brothers
The Magic Mountain

KATHERINE MANSFIELD
The Garden Party and Other Stories

ALESSANDRO MANZONI
The Betrothed

MARCUS AURELIUS
Meditations

GABRIEL GARCÍA MÁRQUEZ
The General in His Labyrinth
Love in the Time of Cholera
One Hundred Years of Solitude

ANDREW MARVELL
The Complete Poems

W. SOMERSET MAUGHAM
Collected Stories
Of Human Bondage
The Skeptical Romancer (US only)

CORMAC McCARTHY
The Border Trilogy

IAN McEWAN
Atonement

HERMAN MELVILLE
The Complete Shorter Fiction
Moby-Dick

JOHN STUART MILL
On Liberty and Utilitarianism

JOHN MILTON
The Complete English Poems

YUKIO MISHIMA
The Temple of the Golden Pavilion

MARY WORTLEY MONTAGU
Letters

MICHEL DE MONTAIGNE
The Complete Works

THOMAS MORE
Utopia

TONI MORRISON
Beloved
Song of Solomon

JOHN MUIR
Selected Writings

ALICE MUNRO
Carried Away: A Selection of Stories

MURASAKI SHIKIBU
The Tale of Genji

IRIS MURDOCH
The Sea, The Sea
A Severed Head
(in 1 vol.)

VLADIMIR NABOKOV
Lolita
Pale Fire
Pnin
Speak, Memory

V. S. NAIPAUL
Collected Short Fiction (US only)
A House for Mr Biswas

R. K. NARAYAN
Swami and Friends
The Bachelor of Arts
The Dark Room
The English Teacher
(in 1 vol.)
Mr Sampath – The Printer of Malgudi
The Financial Expert
Waiting for the Mahatma
(in 1 vol.)

IRÈNE NÉMIROVSKY
David Golder
The Ball
Snow in Autumn
The Courilof Affair
(in 1 vol.)

FLANN O'BRIEN
The Complete Novels

FRANK O'CONNOR
The Best of Frank O'Connor

MICHAEL ONDAATJE
The English Patient

GEORGE ORWELL
Animal Farm
Nineteen Eighty-Four
Essays
Burmese Days, Keep the Aspidistra Flying, Coming Up for Air
(in 1 vol.)

OVID
The Metamorphoses

THOMAS PAINE
Rights of Man
and Common Sense

ORHAN PAMUK
My Name is Red
Snow

BORIS PASTERNAK
Doctor Zhivago

SYLVIA PLATH
The Bell Jar (US only)

PLATO
The Republic
Symposium and Phaedrus

EDGAR ALLAN POE
The Complete Stories

MARCO POLO
The Travels of Marco Polo

MARCEL PROUST
In Search of Lost Time
(in 4 vols, UK only)

PHILIP PULLMAN
His Dark Materials

ALEXANDER PUSHKIN
The Collected Stories

FRANÇOIS RABELAIS
Gargantua and Pantagruel

JOSEPH ROTH
The Radetzky March

JEAN-JACQUES ROUSSEAU
Confessions
The Social Contract and the Discourses

SALMAN RUSHDIE
Midnight's Children

JOHN RUSKIN
Praeterita and Dilecta

PAUL SCOTT
The Raj Quartet (in 2 vols)

WALTER SCOTT
Rob Roy

WILLIAM SHAKESPEARE
Comedies Vols 1 and 2
Histories Vols 1 and 2
Romances
Sonnets and Narrative Poems
Tragedies Vols 1 and 2

MARY SHELLEY
Frankenstein

ADAM SMITH
The Wealth of Nations

ALEXANDER SOLZHENITSYN
One Day in the Life of
Ivan Denisovich

SOPHOCLES
The Theban Plays

MURIEL SPARK
The Prime of Miss Jean Brodie,
The Girls of Slender Means, The
Driver's Seat, The Only Problem
(in 1 vol.)

CHRISTINA STEAD
The Man Who Loved Children

JOHN STEINBECK
The Grapes of Wrath

STENDHAL
The Charterhouse of Parma
Scarlet and Black

LAURENCE STERNE
Tristram Shandy

ROBERT LOUIS STEVENSON
The Master of Ballantrae and
Weir of Hermiston
Dr Jekyll and Mr Hyde
and Other Stories

BRAM STOKER
Dracula

HARRIET BEECHER STOWE
Uncle Tom's Cabin

SUN TZU
The Art of War

ITALO SVEVO
Zeno's Conscience

GRAHAM SWIFT
Waterland

JONATHAN SWIFT
Gulliver's Travels

TACITUS
Annals and Histories

JUNICHIRŌ TANIZAKI
The Makioka Sisters

W. M. THACKERAY
Vanity Fair

HENRY DAVID THOREAU
Walden

ALEXIS DE TOCQUEVILLE
Democracy in America

LEO TOLSTOY
Collected Shorter Fiction (in 2 vols)
Anna Karenina
Childhood, Boyhood and Youth
The Cossacks
War and Peace

ANTHONY TROLLOPE
Barchester Towers
Can You Forgive Her?
Doctor Thorne
The Duke's Children
The Eustace Diamonds
Framley Parsonage
The Last Chronicle of Barset
Phineas Finn
The Small House at Allington
The Warden

IVAN TURGENEV
Fathers and Children
First Love and Other Stories
A Sportsman's Notebook

MARK TWAIN
Tom Sawyer
and Huckleberry Finn

JOHN UPDIKE
The Complete Henry Bech
Rabbit Angstrom

GIORGIO VASARI
Lives of the Painters, Sculptors and Architects (in 2 vols)

JULES VERNE
Journey to the Centre of the Earth
Twenty Thousand Leagues under the Sea
Round the World in Eighty Days

VIRGIL
The Aeneid

VOLTAIRE
Candide and Other Stories

HORACE WALPOLE
Selected Letters

EVELYN WAUGH
(US only)
Black Mischief, Scoop, The Loved One, The Ordeal of Gilbert Pinfold (in 1 vol.)
Brideshead Revisited
Decline and Fall
A Handful of Dust
The Sword of Honour Trilogy
Waugh Abroad: Collected Travel Writing
The Complete Short Stories

H. G. WELLS
The Time Machine, The Invisible Man, The War of the Worlds (in 1 vol., US only)

EDITH WHARTON
The Age of Innocence
The Custom of the Country
Ethan Frome, Summer, Bunner Sisters (in 1 vol.)
The House of Mirth
The Reef

PATRICK WHITE
Voss

OSCAR WILDE
Plays, Prose Writings and Poems

P. G. WODEHOUSE
The Best of Wodehouse

MARY WOLLSTONECRAFT
A Vindication of the Rights of Woman

VIRGINIA WOOLF
To the Lighthouse
Mrs Dalloway

WILLIAM WORDSWORTH
Selected Poems (UK only)

RICHARD YATES
Revolutionary Road
The Easter Parade
Eleven Kinds of Loneliness (in 1 vol.)

W. B. YEATS
The Poems (UK only)

ÉMILE ZOLA
Germinal

This book is set in BEMBO which was cut
by the punch-cutter Francesco Griffo
for the Venetian printer-publisher
Aldus Manutius in early 1495
and first used in a pamphlet
by a young scholar
named Pietro
Bembo.

E L